ALSO BY REBECCA CANTRELL

Trace of Smoke
Night of Long Knives
Game of Lies

A C
Broken

REBECCA CANTRELL

A City of Broken Glass

A TOM DOHERTY ASSOCIATES BOOK
NEW YORK

This is a work of fiction. All of the characters, organizations, and events portrayed in this novel are either products of the author's imagination or are used fictitiously.

A CITY OF BROKEN GLASS

A Forge Book
Published by Tom Doherty Associates, LLC
175 Fifth Avenue
New York, NY 10010

www.tor-forge.com

Forge® is a registered trademark of Tom Doherty Associates, LLC.

Library of Congress Cataloging-in-Publication Data

Cantrell, Rebecca.
    A city of broken glass / Rebecca Cantrell.—1st ed.
        p. cm.
    "A Tom Doherty Associates book."
    ISBN 978-0-7653-2734-5 (hardcover)
    ISBN 978-1-4299-4643-8 (e-book)
    1. Women journalists—Fiction. 2. World War, 1939–1945—Refugees—
Fiction. 3. Jewish refugees—Fiction. 4. Kristallnacht, 1938—Fiction.
5. Germany—History—1933–1945—Fiction. I. Title.
PS3603.A599C58 2012
813'.6—dc23

                                                                2012011652

First Edition: July 2012

Printed in the United States of America

0 9 8 7 6 5 4 3 2 1

*To my husband, my son,
and those whose lives were shattered in November 1938*

Acknowledgments

Thank you to all who labor in the background to help bring the Hannah Vogel books into the light, including my fantastic agents, Elizabeth Evans, Mary Alice Kier, and Anna Cottle; and the wonderful staff at Tor/Forge: my clever and particular editor, Kristin Sevick, and my perspicacious publicist, Alexis Saarela.

This novel required extensive research, and I was ably aided by Robert Coleman at the U.S. Holocaust Memorial Museum. This novel, and my other novels, have been much improved by the cracker-jack Kona Ink writing group of Karen Hollinger, Judith Heath, Kathryn Wadsworth, and David Deardorff. Thanks also to the writer directors, Mischa Livingstone and Richard Gorey, for bringing their unique perspectives to the work. Finally, I would like to thank Mr. Sutherland for being such a great teacher to my son. A great teacher makes a profound difference in the life of a child, and I'm glad that my son found your classroom.

But the biggest thanks of all go to those who make it all happen and make it all matter: my mother, my tireless and supportive Ironman husband, and the most wonderful son in the world.

A City of
Broken Glass

1

A herd of black and white Friesian cattle, a pair of mismatched draft horses, and a blacksmith's shop passed by the Fiat's windows. Nothing looked any different from any other Polish village. Yet today there were twelve thousand reasons why Zbąszyń was no longer a simple farming town. If only I could find them.

"Where do we go, Frau Zinsli?" Our driver, Fräulein Ivona, used the only name of mine she knew, my Swiss alias. My real name was Hannah Vogel, but in all of Poland, luckily, only my son Anton knew it.

"On." I pointed forward, although I had no idea where the refugees were housed.

Once I found them, I would talk to as many as possible, then the local doctor, the townspeople, and the mayor if I could. Getting quotes should not be a problem, as I warranted that many in Zbąszyń spoke German. Less than twenty years had passed since it was ceded from Germany to Poland in the Treaty of Versailles.

We approached a large brick stable with armed Polish soldiers clustered in front. They stood awkwardly, as if not certain why they were there, and kept stealing glances inside. Somehow, I did not think they guarded horses so closely.

I directed Fräulein Ivona to stop. She rolled the car to a halt next to a cluster of military vehicles. Clad in a tight white dress and jacket and high-heeled pumps, shoulder-length ash blond hair perfectly combed, and China red lips made up into a Cupid's bow, she stroked a languid hand over her hair, checking that every strand was in place before she turned off the engine.

"Anton," I said. "Wait in the car."

He gave me a look of utter disbelief before ordering his features. "All right."

I stopped, fingers on the door handle. He never gave in so readily. I studied him. He had no intention of staying put. The moment I was out of sight, he would follow. My thirteen-year-old daredevil would plunge straight into trouble and stoically bear the punishment later. As if reading my thoughts, he gave me a deceptively innocent smile. Freckles danced on the bridge of his nose.

I had to smile back.

I had brought him to Poland to enjoy time together while I researched a light feature piece about the Saint Martin's Day festival. Every November 11, Poznań held Europe's largest parade to celebrate the saint, known for his kindness to the poor. 1938's event promised to be grand.

The assignment should have been fun, but I viewed it as punishment. I had been banished to this backwater from Switzerland because my recent anti-Nazi articles had resulted in a series of threatening letters, and my editor at Zürich's *Neue Zürcher Zeitung* did not want to risk anything happening to me. If I had been a man, he would not have cared.

But I was not, so I had resigned myself to enduring my sentence quietly until I read the newspapers this morning and discovered that Germany had arrested more than twelve thousand Polish Jews and deported them across the border. I could not let that pass unnoticed, so I had headed to Zbąszyń to see the refugees myself. The paper had no one nearer. My editor would grumble, but he would also be grateful.

At least I hoped that he would.

Anton rubbed two fingers down the clean stick he had whittled. He pursed his lips as if about to whistle a jaunty tune to prove how innocent his intentions were.

"Fine." He was safer where I could see him. "Come with me. Stay close."

He clambered out eagerly. "Will there be riding?"

He loved to ride. In Switzerland, the stables were his second home. This would be like no stable he had ever seen. Suddenly cold, I turned up the collar on my wool coat. "I think not."

I pulled my Leica out of my satchel and snapped shots of the stable and soldiers. Their silver buttons and the silver braid on their dark uniform collars gleamed in the weak autumn sun.

I turned my attention to the stout brick building. Its tall doors measured more than twice the height of the men. Thick, too, with sturdy hinges and wrought iron bands fastened on the outside of the wood. They could safely contain horses. Or people.

Behind me, the Fiat's door slammed. I winced at the sound, and as one, all the Polish soldiers in front of the stable swiveled in our direction. So much for doing a quick walk around unnoticed. I wished that I had procured a car without a driver.

I hung my camera around my neck and hefted my satchel's leather strap higher on my shoulder. We walked to the stable and the soldiers guarding it. The soldiers admired Fräulein Ivona as she sashayed up.

Perhaps she would choose to use her assets to our advantage.

"*Dzień dobry!*" she said brightly.

The soldiers answered enthusiastically and tipped their queer uniform caps to her. The caps were round where they fit the head, but the top was square and the corners extended out an extra centimeter, like a combination soldier's cap and professor's mortarboard.

I looked through the half-open door behind them. The stable teemed with people. Most had a suitcase or small bundle, but I saw no food. A few souls peered out, looking as confused as the soldiers in front.

I itched to take notes.

The autumn breeze carried the smell of horse manure and the unpleasant odor of human waste. Presumably, no one had had time to set up toilet facilities for those packed inside.

Next to me, Fräulein Ivona wrinkled her nose. "We can't go in there. It's full of vermin."

"It is full of human beings," I reminded her.

"It's a stable." She shuddered. "It's also full of rats."

"There are worse things than rats," I said.

A young boy wearing a thick overcoat two sizes too big waved from inside the dark building. I put his age at around four. Anton waved back and took a step toward him.

When a soldier blocked Anton's way, he stumbled back in surprise. In Switzerland, stables did not have armed guards. Yesterday, in Poland, they had not, either.

Touching the shoulder of Anton's brown coat, now almost too small for him, I said, "Wait."

I handed the soldier on the right my press credential. He turned the document over with puzzlement. A small-town soldier, he had probably never seen anything like it. It sported an official-looking Swiss seal that I hoped might sway him into letting us pass.

"I am authorized to go inside," I told him.

Fräulein Ivona raised one perfectly shaped eyebrow skeptically. I had no such authorization, of course, as she well knew.

"I don't know," he said in German. He handed the credentials to the soldier next to him, and they discussed my case in Polish.

If I did not get in, the view into the stable might be all I had to write about. I snapped pictures of people on the other side of the open door. Because of the lighting, the quality would be poor, but it would be better than nothing. The soldiers shifted uneasily, but did not stop me.

When I had finished, I turned impatiently, as if late for a most important appointment. "Well?" I used my most officious tone. "Will you give way or must I speak to your superior?"

I hated using that tone, but it was often effective on soldiers, a hint that perhaps I had authority somewhere.

The soldier handed me my papers. "A quick visit."

A look of surprised respect flashed in Fräulein Ivona's eyes.

Anton walked toward the stable with his shoulders back as if he expected a fight. I quickened my steps to catch up. Together we stepped across the threshold.

Fräulein Ivona lagged behind, exchanging flirtatious words with the soldiers before following.

The long rows of horse stalls had not been cleaned. I suspected from the smell that the animals had been turned out only minutes before they herded in the refugees. Horses and manure smelled fresh compared to the odor of unwashed bodies and human waste.

Fräulein Ivona wrinkled her nose again, Anton clamped his jaws together, and I breathed through my mouth. I paused, waiting for my eyes to adjust to the gloom.

So many people. When I tried to do a quick head count, I realized that too many people crowded into the small space for me to do more than guess. A few stood, but most sat dejectedly on the dirty wooden floor, mud-spattered long coats drawn close against the cold. The women wore torn stockings and proper hats; the men fashionable woolen coats and fedoras. These were city people. They had not expected to exchange their urban apartments for a Polish barn.

"The guards say we may stay inside the stable for a moment only." Fräulein Ivona shifted in her white pumps. Mud smudged the once immaculate heels. "Your press credentials worried them."

I photographed as fast as I could, hoping that the dim light would be enough. Pictures would show what had happened more convincingly than any words I could muster. No one took notice of me as I clicked away. The tall ceiling absorbed sounds, and the refugees spoke in hushed tones.

Anton kept close and quiet. I wished that I had insisted he stay in the car so that he would not see what had happened to these people.

But he lived in this world, and he was not keen on any attempt to protect him from it.

Yet I never would have brought him here had I known it was this bad.

I stopped in front of a woman sitting on the dirt floor, back propped against the edge of a stall. She cradled a baby inside her long black coat. I knelt next to her in the dirty straw.

"My name is Adelheid Zinsli." I used my best fake Swiss accent. "Do you speak German?"

"Of course I do." She sounded nettled, her accent pure Berlin. "I was born in Kreuzberg. In spite of what my passport says, I've never even been to Poland." She looked around the filthy stable and hugged her baby close. "I can't say I like it much."

"I am a reporter for a Swiss newspaper. The *Neue Zürcher Zeitung*. I want to tell your story."

She looked at me suspiciously, then shrugged. "What more have I to lose?"

"What is your name?"

"Ada Warski. This is my daughter, Esther Warksi. I don't imagine you much care, but my husband, Uriah Warski, is in Dachau for the newfound crime of being a Jewish man in Germany."

I pulled out my notebook and fountain pen. Anton knelt next to me, so close that his pant leg touched my dress. I wanted to send him away somewhere safe, but where would that be? "How long have you and Esther been traveling?"

"Three days. They took us from our apartment at night and arrested us. They gave me only a few minutes to put together a bag for the baby and a few more to pack up a lifetime of possessions." Frau Warski's voice shook with outrage. I wrote as quickly as I could. I did not want to forget a single detail.

"They took us to a train station under guard. Neighbors I'd known all my life stood in the streets, yelling 'Jews to Palestine!' although we were only going to Poland. The candy man who used to give me sweets when I was a girl was there, too. Yelling." She stared at the muddy floor. I thought of Berlin, my own home, having come to this and clenched the smooth shaft of my pen more tightly. I would tell this to the world.

"After that," she went on, "they made us stand for hours in the station. Many of the old fainted. Some people were lying down by the stairs, but we were too packed together to see much."

She rocked the baby. Anton watched with wide eyes. When I put my free hand on his shoulder, he let it rest there.

Fräulein Ivona seemed to cave in on herself as if she tried to make herself as little as possible. She wanted nothing to do with this place. I wondered why she did not simply leave.

"Trains came, and they ordered us in at gunpoint. More trains came behind ours. I can't speak for the others, but our car had two SS men. They stood guard, to keep us from escaping. As if we would jump off and run back into Germany." Frau Warski spit on the floor.

Anton started in surprise. In Switzerland, women did not spit—but then again, they did not have as much cause as Frau Warski did. "We ended up at the station at Neu Bentschen. What day is today?"

"Sunday, about noon," I said quietly.

She stroked the baby's soft black curls. "Saturday, then. They searched us and took all our money. They let us keep only ten Reichsmarks. They said, 'That's all you brought into Germany, and that's all you can take out.' My father came into Germany with much more than that, as I imagine most of us did. But we did not argue."

She looked up at me. "What will I do now? Ten Reichsmarks is enough for only a few meals. Here there isn't even food to spend it on."

Anton shifted closer to me.

"Did they bring you here in lorries?" I asked.

She sniffed. "No. When they'd taken all they could, they told us we had to march to the border on foot. Two kilometers, they said. Some people, the very old, couldn't walk, so—" She broke off and hugged her baby close. Its blanket looked pitifully thin in the cold stable.

"So, they beat them. I held Esther in one arm and my suitcase in the other, and I ran as if the Devil were at my heels." She shuddered.

"It was raining and very cold. I put Esther in my coat, but I worried that she would get sick."

I swallowed, not daring to make a sound.

"When we got to the border, someone fired guns. I don't know if it was Poles or Germans, although I don't suppose it would have mattered much if you'd been hit by one. A Polish bullet kills as well as a German one."

I scratched away at my notes. I would tell her story, but I wondered if it would help her, or the others here.

She took a deep breath before continuing, calmer now. "The Poles were surprised to see us here. I gave my papers to a Polish officer, and at first I thought that he would send us back toward the SS. I hear that some were marched back and forth through the rain. But not me. They let me through. Maybe because of Esther. They sent us here. We walked all the way in the rain." She shook her glossy dark hair, cut into a bob like my blond one. "I thought that the Third Reich would come and go and things would go back to the way they were before. Now I know they won't. Not ever."

"When did you last eat?" I did not see how such a small town could provide for this many refugees. Zbąszyń had only about five thousand inhabitants.

"Bread this morning. Nothing for the first two days." She brushed her fingers through the baby's curly hair again. "I'm glad Esther is still nursing. It has been difficult for the very young and the old."

Anton fished in his coat pocket and brought out a chocolate bar. He handed it to her.

"Thank you," she said, surprised.

"It's all I have," he said with a note of apology.

Shamed, I reached into my satchel and handed her the bread and salami that Fräulein Ivona had brought for our lunch.

"How many of you are there?" I asked.

She nibbled a corner of the chocolate. "I don't know. Thousands, I think. I heard that they arrested twelve thousand people. Some died on the journey. I don't know how many. The Polish government let some into the rest of the country, but I've heard there are about seven thousand of us trapped in Zbąszyń."

Dirty white pumps shifted in my peripheral vision. I glanced up at Fräulein Ivona. She looked as if she might be sick on the floor, either from the smell or from the enormity of the situation.

"Thank you," I said. "Your story will be heard."

"It will make no difference," Frau Warski said bitterly. "Since Évian, we have known that no one cares."

I had no ready answer. Months ago, the world had held an international conference in Évian, France, with the charter of addressing the burgeoning Jewish refugee problem. The only outcome had been a near consensus that no country wanted to take them in. The conference went so badly that the Nazis had been able to use it in their anti-Semitic propaganda.

"Please!" screeched a voice from across the stable.

A short woman dressed all in black called again. I looked at her more closely and drew in a quick breath. I knew her, and she knew my real identity, the one I struggled so hard to hide.

The one that could get me killed.

2

As I hurried to the woman's side, I hoped that she would be discreet. Her name was Miriam Keller, and although she was married to my longtime friend Paul, she did not much like me. I did not see him as I stepped through the crowd of refugees, but that was unsurprising. Only Polish Jews had been targeted so far, and Paul was German.

Her face shone pale in the stable's gloom. Although it was cold, beads of sweat stood out on her forehead. Like the last time I saw her, two years ago, she was pregnant. She lay curled on her side on the floor. Her stomach humped through her coat. She looked ready to deliver again.

A woman with blond hair tied back in a dark blue kerchief pillowed Miriam's sweaty head in her lap. Miriam's belly heaved. She was in labor. The poor woman might deliver her child on the filthy stable floor.

"Hello, Miriam." I knelt and took her hand. Even through my glove, it felt cold. "It's Adelheid."

She jabbered weakly in Polish. I wiped her forehead with my green scarf, a gift from my late brother. With her free hand she clutched a gold locket that hung around her neck. I had once worn it myself, but I had returned it to Paul after I decided not to marry him. He had kept it, then given it to the woman who became his wife. Where was he?

"Fräulein Ivona!" I called.

She came over. Her dazed expression told me that she had become overwhelmed by people and suffering.

I put my hand on her arm and squeezed. "Can you please translate?"

Her frightened blue eyes met mine. "I—"

"You can do this. Soon we will be back in Poznań. They will not." I gestured around the stable with my free hand. "We must glean what information we can so that their plight can be publicized, their suffering alleviated."

"I don't speak Polish," she said. "Beyond a few words."

She had made no claims of being a translator when she presented herself at my hotel that morning, claiming only to be a driver hired by the newspaper. I had assumed that whoever hired her had thought to ask if she could also translate.

A flood of urgent words poured out of Miriam.

"Miriam," I said. "In German?"

The woman with Miriam spoke in broken German with an accent more French than Polish. "She left Ruth. In a case. No, a cupboard. By the door. Ruth is good girl. Very strong."

"Who is Ruth? What cupboard?"

The woman spoke to Miriam, and Miriam gasped out a few syllables.

"Yes?" I asked when Miriam stopped talking.

"In Berlin," the woman said. "In the apartment. She says you know where it is."

"I do," I said.

Miriam's eyes fluttered closed. The metallic odor of blood spilled into the air.

"Is there a doctor or a midwife here?" I asked the woman.

"No," she said. "I asked."

Miriam spoke again, and the woman translated. "She says Ruth is her daughter. She's two."

My heart sped up. Unless someone had rescued her, a two-year-old girl had been stuck in a cupboard for three days. The poor child might be dead already. I swallowed. "Ask her where Paul is."

"Paul?" Fräulein Ivona asked. "That's a Christian name."

"He had a Christian father," I said.

Her companion did not bother to translate. "Gone. Many days."

I thought of Miriam, dragged off alone and pregnant, locking her daughter in a cupboard. It was too horrible to contemplate. Yet it was clearly true. She clutched her companion and spoke urgently.

"Get Ruth. Promise."

Miriam's bloodshot eyes bored into mine. *"Proszę!"* she pleaded.

"Please," the woman translated.

"Tell her I cannot go back." Going to Berlin was out of the question. The Gestapo had a file on me. If they caught me, they would kill me. Anton, too. But I wavered for a moment, wondering how I could abandon the little girl.

"Why can't you go back?" Fräulein Ivona asked.

"For reasons of my own."

The woman holding Miriam's head begged me with her eyes. "Promise anyway."

I stared into Miriam's frightened dark eyes and opened my mouth to lie. "I promise." I did not have to go back to Berlin to find Ruth. I still had friends there who could bring her to safety.

Miriam's body relaxed, and she gave me a huge smile of relief. I was probably her first hope that her daughter might be saved.

What had happened to Paul? She seemed to expect no help from him. Was he dead, or in prison or a concentration camp? Or was he somehow alive and free?

The woman holding Miriam's hand bowed her head in a quick thank-you.

Fräulein Ivona turned away quickly.

Behind me I heard shouting, first in Polish, then German. "All members of the press must leave!"

I was the only member of the press in the stable. I started to stand, but Miriam grasped my hand.

"Stay," the woman translated. "Not safe here for her. For the baby."

"I will fetch a doctor," I said. "From town."

The woman gestured around. "She does not want the baby to be born in a stall. Like an animal."

"I will try," I said.

A hard hand settled on my shoulder. I looked into the face of a stolid Polish officer.

"This woman needs medical help." I shook off his hand and stood. "She is having a baby. Could you send her to the local doctor?"

He shrugged. "She has no valid passport, so she can't leave the stable. I can put her on a list for medical care, but it may be long in coming. What's her number?"

"I do not know her number. But she is right here." I pointed to Miriam. "She is a person, not a number. If she does not get medical care soon, she might die. And her baby with her. Will those numbers matter then?"

He shook his head.

I knelt next to Miriam again. "I need your number."

I hated to help them to reduce her and the others to numbers instead of names, like prisoners. But there was no other way Miriam might get medical care. "Did someone give you—?"

Miriam held up her hand. On the back, someone had written a number in black ink. I copied it into a page of my journal. "I will get you a doctor. Don't worry."

The woman next to her translated my words. Miriam's eyes widened in fear. She whispered a few words.

"Soon," she said. "She says come back soon."

I copied the number onto a second page and then tore it out and handed it to the soldier. "Her condition is serious," I told him. "The baby could come at any moment."

He took the number from me, then hooked his thumbs in his wide leather belt.

"She will have to wait," Fräulein Ivona said, "like the other Jews."

"People," I said, "like the other people."

Two more soldiers arrived.

I turned to the soldiers. "Please put her on your list for medical care. A mother and a baby might die right here in the stable. Surely, as Christians—"

The new soldiers seized me by the elbows and started dragging me out. I struggled to pull free. "I will not leave her."

"Don't," Fräulein Ivona said. "They will arrest you. You can do her no good in jail. And what becomes of your boy?"

Anton looked from me to the soldiers, ready to fight.

The soldier on my left said, "Listen to your sister."

I looked at him, surprised. Fräulein Ivona as my sister? We did look strikingly alike, slight and blond with Aryan blue eyes. She was around the same age my brother, Ernst, would have been, had he lived. She could have been my sister.

She rested her white gloved hand on my shoulder. "Do listen to your sister. You cannot win this, but you can lose."

I let the soldiers lead me outside. I would find a doctor in town and bring him here to argue for Miriam's release. Perhaps they would listen to him. At the very least, he could help to deliver the baby.

We returned to the hired Fiat. Fräulein Ivona had not given up her bread to the refugees. With a dramatic sigh, she broke it into three pieces and shared them around. I had no appetite, but I ate a few bites of my portion anyway, so that Anton would eat his.

Then we drove through the village. At the inn, they directed me to a doctor's office nearby. The doctor's wife, Mrs. Volonoski, listened to my entreaty, round face more grave with each word.

"Anka!" she called.

A young girl of no more than ten rushed in. Honey blond braids bounced against her shoulders. Mrs. Volonoski rapped out quick instructions in Polish, and Anka sprinted down the hall and out the front door.

Mrs. Volonoski led us to an empty waiting room full of solid Polish furniture, walls painted forest green above dark oak wainscoting. A fire crackled in the fireplace.

"Where are the other patients?" I asked.

"I sent them away," Mrs. Volonoski said. "He will not be back here today, not with so many refugees to treat. Probably without pay, too. You sit now."

We each took a straight-backed spindle chair. Mrs. Volonoski said something in Polish to Fräulein Ivona and disappeared. She returned a moment later with three cups of strong black tea.

A knock sounded at the door.

"All day!" She wiped her long fingers on her striped dress. "Excuse me."

She trotted down the hall to answer the door to a blond girl carrying a baby bundled up against the cold.

Anton wrapped himself in his coat and curled up in his chair. I wondered if he, too, revisited the morning's events. His eyes closed, and I hoped that he slept.

I wished that I had left him in Switzerland. He would not soon forget today. But I had expected only to write an easy feature. I had not known that Poland was too close to the Nazis now.

Fräulein Ivona looked at Anton, then to me. "Do you know the woman in the stable well?"

"I met her once before, but I do not know her well," I said.

"Then why did she expect you to help her?" Her carefully outlined lips made a moue of surprise.

"She had no alternative." I stared out the window at a pair of chickens scratching in the brown grass of the front yard. "And I will help her, if I can. A child's life is at stake."

"You can't save them." She drew out a silver lipstick tube. "There are too many."

"I can save this one," I said.

"I thought you said you could not go back to Berlin." She applied her lipstick in two sure strokes.

"I know people in Berlin," I said. "I have written stories from there." The articles had been published in the paper, so I had no reason to deny it.

"Then why not go back yourself? Are you wanted by the Gestapo? Is that why you cannot go back?" Her question held too much curiosity.

I forced out a laugh. "Nothing so complicated as that. The newspaper has paid me to be here. If I leave, I could lose my job."

"Good that you are not wanted," she said. "The Gestapo are most persistent."

"Are you familiar with the Gestapo, then?" I glanced through the window at the yard. Chickens pecked in a desultory way at the dust, searching without much hope.

"No more than anyone else," she said. "I have heard stories."

"I, too, have heard stories." I left it at that.

"The man I am seeing? I think he worked for the Gestapo once, although he's never said."

"I imagine he would not." And I had no intention of telling her anything either.

"He is a curious type." She drew off her white gloves and tucked them in her pocket. "He speaks little of his past, even when drunk. I think he has dark secrets he drinks to contain."

"Drinking seems a poor way to keep secrets." I sensed that she spoke from nervousness. After what we had seen, she probably did not trust herself to be alone with her thoughts. I sympathized and tried to concentrate on what she said, but my thoughts strayed back to Miriam. She was so young, not much older than Fräulein Ivona.

Where was Paul? The Paul I remembered would never have abandoned his pregnant wife and child. But he had changed since the Nazis came to power and robbed him of his citizenship, his livelihood, and his freedom. When last we met, we had fought. He had accused me of being in league with the Nazis and refused to help me to investigate the death of a close friend. I no longer knew what he was capable of. Tellingly, Miriam herself did not seem to expect him to return to rescue their daughter.

Was she still alive to be rescued? Did she still have a mother? I looked out the door and down the empty road. No sign of Anka.

Fräulein Ivona moved her chair close to the fire and picked up the heavy poker. The firelight shone on thick red scars that ran up the back of her hand.

Anton sat up. "How did you hurt your hand?"

An impertinent question. I opened my mouth to scold him, but she answered before I spoke.

"My father—" She shook her head. "A long story."

I gave Anton a quelling look, and, chastened, he sat back.

"Do you like your father?" she asked him.

Anton nodded uncertainly. It was a complicated question, as we did not know who his father was.

"Mine died a few years ago." She rubbed the scars on the back of her hand. "And I miss him every day."

"I am sorry to hear of such a loss for you." The words sounded stiff, but I meant them.

She stared into the flames for a long time before answering. "I failed him too often, because I was weak, like my mother. Like many mothers."

My mind strayed to Ruth, trapped in a dark cupboard, Miriam terrified in the stable, and all I had been through with Anton. Motherhood was not for the weak.

"Some mothers are strong." Anton glanced at me meaningfully.

"Thank you, Anton." I smiled at him.

"Some mothers get up to all sorts of mischief." She shot me a furtive glance before returning her gaze to the shifting flames.

What mischief had her mother gotten up to?

We all watched the fire. My thoughts returned to Miriam and her daughter. As soon as I brought Miriam a doctor, I would call Bella Fromm in Berlin. A Jewish aristocrat, she had strong connections within the diplomatic community and had opted to stay and help others safely out of Germany. If she had remained in Berlin, I could trust her to check the cupboard and help the little girl. She also had worked with Paul and had met Miriam. Things had become so much worse in Germany in the past months that perhaps she, too, had left. For her sake, I hoped so.

If Bella was gone, I could call a Jewish physician friend. She would look for Ruth if she could. If both had managed to flee, however, I could think of no one else to send. My contacts in Berlin had not fared well under the Nazis.

"It is our fathers who shape us." Fräulein Ivona poked a burning log so hard, it split. The log atop it rolled off the andiron and into the back of the fireplace.

Anton blurted, "Not always. Sometimes—"

Anka burst into the room. She jabbered breathlessly, in Polish. Her mother hurried in behind her.

"She says that her father is at the old flour mill. He is helping people there," Frau Volonoski said.

I stood. "Where?"

She gave me careful directions. It was not close.

"Thank you!" I sprinted to the car, Fräulein Ivona and Anton close behind. Chickens in the yard fled from us.

"I am no good at directions," Fräulein Ivona said.

"May I drive?" I hoped that she would allow me, as she was a slow driver. All in all, she had been a terrible hire. I wondered how she made a living at it, but I supposed that her male passengers might overlook a great deal.

She seemed relieved as she handed me the keys. "Please."

I pulled out onto the rutted road.

3

Fräulein Ivona stripped off her gloves and lit a cigarette. She watched the flame burn down almost to her fingers before she blew it out. Then she took a deep drag. "Why do you take the boy on these excursions instead of leaving him with his father?"

I wrestled the car around a pothole before answering. "I did not know this trip would have excursions of this nature. And I cannot leave him with his father, because he is dead."

"I am sorry to hear that. I just assumed when I saw the wedding band that your husband was still alive." She sucked in another drag from her cigarette. "It must be difficult for you, a woman alone."

"Anton and I manage just fine." I floored it down a straight stretch of road.

"So there is no man since the father? No man now?"

"No."

She cocked her head to the side and said teasingly, "I cannot believe such a thing. You are a beautiful woman. You must have toyed with the hearts of many men."

"Toyed? No."

She tapped ash off her cigarette onto the floor of the car. I resisted the urge to chastise her. It was her car, after all. "I think you have more experience with the hearts of men than you admit."

"Have I?" I acted surprised, but perhaps she was correct. I'd had six opportunities to marry, which seemed extravagant when I thought about it. I ran through my suitors in my head. First, Walter. While still in my teens we were engaged, but he died in the Great War. My life would have been different had he lived.

Second, Paul. A few years after the War, he had asked me to marry him. I had declined. I had realized that I did not want marriage, but I was unsuited for lighthearted casual relationships with men. For years I avoided them.

My third and fourth proposals came from the same man. In 1931, and again in 1934, a powerful Nazi officer named Ernst Röhm had tried to force me to marry him to provide cover for his homosexual activities and claim Anton as his own. The adventure had brought Anton into my life and had helped me to solve my brother's murder. And both times we had eluded Röhm. I shuddered to think what would have happened otherwise.

Then, I had lived in Switzerland with a banker named Boris Krause, the man I probably should have married. A kind, stable man—with him I had enjoyed the happiest, most peaceful time of my life. Eventually he, too, asked for my hand in marriage, but only if I settled down as a proper wife and mother and gave up spying for the British against the Nazis. I had been tempted, but I refused his offer, too. Ironically, my career as a courier came quickly to an end. By then he had moved on to someone else, and I thought I had as well.

My sixth and final chance came by an accidental marriage on paper to a former SS officer named Lars Lang. He had been my contact when I worked against the Nazis. Together we had smuggled many secret documents to the British. We had been listed as married on a set of false paperwork created to help us escape Germany. Still, the feelings we had for each other were not false. I had been willing to turn that piece of paper into a real marriage, but he vanished on a trip to Russia two years ago. I assumed that he was dead, but I still wore his ring.

Fräulein Ivona turned and blew out a lungful of smoke. I coughed.

"Apologies," she said without looking contrite. "So, you have no man?"

I suspected she wanted to talk about her own man. She had alluded to him several times on the way to Zbąszyń. I decided to humor her before she suffocated me in her smoke. "Have you?"

"I do." She flapped her hand in the air as if that would chase the smoke out of the car. "But I am not certain if he is a good man or a bad one. How does one tell?"

"It is rarely that simple," I said.

"But surely you know about men. You were married, after all."

"Being married did not help to understand men better."

Fräulein Ivona flicked her cigarette out the window. "Even if he has done bad things, I think mine is a good man. I think he might have been led astray at times. Anyone can be led astray, can't they?"

"Perhaps." I braked to avoid a gray goose waddling across the road. "Although I do believe that we are responsible for our own actions. And that someone who has been led astray once may be led astray again."

The goose honked angrily as I eased past it.

Fräulein Ivona drew another cigarette out of a metal case. This time, she offered me one. I shook my head. "In spite of that, he's a good man."

"Indeed?"

"He is kind, handsome . . ." Ivona ticked points off on her fingers. Lars used to do that. I swallowed. I had not expected that I would still miss him as much as I did. Two years was not as long as it seemed. She prattled on. "He is reliable. And he is a very excellent lover."

Women had not spoken so frankly about men in my day. "How fortunate for you."

She nodded and unfolded a fifth finger. "That counts double."

I laughed.

"But," she announced. "He is not really mine. He is married to someone else. And yesterday . . . yesterday I saw him look at another woman, and I knew that he loved her, not me."

I pitied her, with her good man who was married to someone else and starting up a third dalliance. "A complicated situation."

She talked as if I had not spoken. "Soon—" She made a sound like *ffft*. "—he will be on to the next girl."

"He will?" She would probably be better off if he did move on.

She lit the second cigarette before answering. Again, she watched the flame creep close to her fingers before blowing it out or speaking. "He never stays with a girl longer than a month. He told me at the beginning that we had only a month."

I looked over at her, finally curious. "He gave you a deadline? Why did you choose him?"

"Because he is such an excellent lover, of course." She raised her arched eyebrows as if surprised that I could ask such a foolish question. "He is kind, too. After my mother died, I wanted that."

I turned a quick left at the large gray boulder, as Frau Volonoski had directed. I wished for street signs and hoped that this was the correct boulder. "When did your mother die?"

"A little more than a month ago now. Her heart gave out." She stared at the Fiat's dusty red hood. "The nuns were very kind to us through the end."

"I am sorry to hear of your recent loss. My mother has been dead many years, but I still think of her." Although I did not miss her.

"She had been ill for a long time, so it was for the best." Ivona leaned away from me. "Perhaps I shall be the one he settles on."

"If he is married, it seems that he has already settled on someone else." I kept my voice as gentle as I could. The girl was not so tough as her words.

"If he truly loved her," she said. "He would be with her, not dallying with others."

I did not want to second-guess the motivations of her philandering lover, but he sounded like trouble.

A City of
Broken Glass

ALSO BY REBECCA CANTRELL

A Trace of Smoke
A Night of Long Knives
A Game of Lies

REBECCA CANTRELL

A City of
Broken Glass

A TOM DOHERTY ASSOCIATES BOOK
NEW YORK

This is a work of fiction. All of the characters, organizations, and events portrayed in this novel are either products of the author's imagination or are used fictitiously.

A CITY OF BROKEN GLASS

A Forge Book
Published by Tom Doherty Associates, LLC
175 Fifth Avenue
New York, NY 10010

www.tor-forge.com

Forge® is a registered trademark of Tom Doherty Associates, LLC.

Library of Congress Cataloging-in-Publication Data

Cantrell, Rebecca.
    A city of broken glass / Rebecca Cantrell.—1st ed.
        p. cm.
    "A Tom Doherty Associates book."
    ISBN 978-0-7653-2734-5 (hardcover)
    ISBN 978-1-4299-4643-8 (e-book)
    1. Women journalists—Fiction.   2. World War, 1939–1945—Refugees—
Fiction.   3. Jewish refugees—Fiction.   4. Kristallnacht, 1938—Fiction.
5. Germany—History—1933–1945—Fiction.   I. Title.
PS3603.A599C58 2012
813'.6—dc23

                                                        2012011652

First Edition: July 2012

Printed in the United States of America

0 9 8 7 6 5 4 3 2 1

To my husband, my son,
and those whose lives were shattered in November 1938

Acknowledgments

Thank you to all who labor in the background to help bring the Hannah Vogel books into the light, including my fantastic agents, Elizabeth Evans, Mary Alice Kier, and Anna Cottle; and the wonderful staff at Tor/Forge: my clever and particular editor, Kristin Sevick, and my perspicacious publicist, Alexis Saarela.

This novel required extensive research, and I was ably aided by Robert Coleman at the U.S. Holocaust Memorial Museum. This novel, and my other novels, have been much improved by the crackerjack Kona Ink writing group of Karen Hollinger, Judith Heath, Kathryn Wadsworth, and David Deardorff. Thanks also to the writer directors, Mischa Livingstone and Richard Gorey, for bringing their unique perspectives to the work. Finally, I would like to thank Mr. Sutherland for being such a great teacher to my son. A great teacher makes a profound difference in the life of a child, and I'm glad that my son found your classroom.

But the biggest thanks of all go to those who make it all happen and make it all matter: my mother, my tireless and supportive Ironman husband, and the most wonderful son in the world.

A City of
Broken Glass

"You really have no man in your life?" she asked, as if surprised that a woman could exist in such a state.

"No." Since Lars's disappearance, I'd had no interest in dating men, and at thirty-nine, I had passed the age where they were interested in dating me. I had managed most of my life without them. I now hoped only to stay safely away from emotional attachments, besides Anton.

She clucked her tongue. "Why not?"

"Broken heart," I said lightly, although it was true.

"I think my man is broken. More than just his heart, but that, too. Still, I think it can be fixed." She took a long drag of her cigarette. "Don't you?"

"People are not clocks," I said. "It is difficult enough to know what is in someone else's heart, let alone fix it. But, as I said before, I am no expert."

"Didn't you find happiness, at least once?"

She sounded so sad that I hurried to answer her. "I did. More than once."

In the distance, the chimney of the flour mill loomed against a forbidding gray sky. The building was much bigger than I had expected, at least four stories tall. Like the stable, it was made of brick.

"It looks like a castle!" Anton said from the backseat.

"It does at that," I said. "With those crenellations along the roof."

"One thing I do know," I returned to my conversation with Fräulein Ivona, "there is much more to life than men and romantic love. It is part of the whole, of course. But it is not everything. Children, friends, work. I build my life on those things, too."

"It sounds like you have quit trying!" she said. "Did the man who broke your heart drive you away from love?"

"A man did not break my heart." I thought back to watching Lars board the train to Russia, fearing even then that he might not return. "Life did. But remember, life holds more than just men. Much more."

She pursed her lips and shook her head, clearly disbelieving my words.

I braked to a hasty stop in front of the mill. A cloud of dust roiled around us as we hurried to the front door.

As at the stable, soldiers surrounded the building. These could not be bullied. I showed them my press credentials. I told them again and again about Miriam and the baby, but they remained stony-faced.

Finally, Anton took matters into his own hands and darted past the soldiers and into the flour mill. I lunged toward him, but soldiers caught my arms.

"Anton!" I rounded on the soldier. "Anton Zinsli is a Swiss citizen, and if he comes to harm, there will be severe consequences."

A soldier broke off from the group and went into the mill after him. The others still held me fast.

"If I let you go, miss, can you behave yourself, as a sane adult?" The oldest soldier asked. He was about my own age.

"I will." I had spoken with precious few sane adults all day. Perhaps I could serve as a role model.

An eternity later, Anton reappeared at the door, accompanied by the soldier and a tall dark-haired man carrying a black bag. He had fetched the doctor.

I put my hand on Anton's shoulder. "You should not have gone in there."

He looked levelly into my eyes. "However you punish me, it will be worth it if the woman on the stable floor lives."

I caught him in a rough hug. "We shall discuss this later. But think for a moment. What if you could not have come back out? Watch your step, or you will not be able to help yourself or others."

The doctor held out his hand. "I believe I have another patient?" he said in German. "Doktor Volonoski."

I shook his hand. He had a firm, relaxed grip. "Frau Adelheid Zinsli. Thank you for coming out."

I opened the Fiat's passenger door for him. Fräulein Ivona climbed into the backseat, leaving me in the front seat with the doctor. Anton rode on the running board, arm looped over my window.

I drove more cautiously back toward the stable, mindful that An-

ton would pitch into the road if I was not careful. "There is a woman about to give birth in the stable. Could you get her released to a hospital?"

"Depends," he said. "Was the labor progressing normally, or was she in distress?"

"She was in distress." I lied to convince him to move Miriam elsewhere. Even if she could deliver her baby safely in the stable, that did not mean she should have to. "She is about twenty-eight years old. It is her second child. She was in full labor."

"Have you expertise in these matters?" the doctor asked.

"I was a nurse," I said. "During the War."

He gave me a tired smile. "Wonderful. Can you assist?"

Help to deliver a baby? I had worked with wounded soldiers, not expectant mothers. But there was no one else, so I must. "Of course."

When we arrived, I left Anton in the car. "Do not leave," I said. "Fräulein Ivona, please stay with him. Keep Anton in sight every second."

"Acting as a nanny was not in the terms of my hire," she said primly.

I gave her a handful of tattered Polish zlotys. She counted them, folded them, and tucked them into her pocket before answering. "Very well."

The doctor and I strode to the stable door.

"How bad is it?" I asked him. "In the mill."

"Very bad," he said. "Old and young were dragged from their homes and made to stand for days on platforms and in trains with no food and little water. Running through the forest at the end was too much for many of them. And the Germans set dogs on some and beat others. I studied medicine in Dresden, and I cannot believe what has happened to the German people." He shook his head sadly. "I've been treating heart attacks and strokes, although there's little enough I can do without medication."

"How can I help?" I asked.

"Could you be my nurse? Just for this afternoon? I believe that

the Jewish council in Warsaw is sending doctors and food tomorrow."

"I can."

When we reached the soldiers, Doktor Volonoski started a weary-sounding speech. The young soldier's face remained impassive. He already acted tougher than he had that morning, getting used to his new role.

"Please," I said in Polish. *"Proszę."*

An older soldier with muddy knees came out of the stable. I turned to him, ready to start again. Bureaucratic rules would not be enough to keep us from Miriam.

He muttered a few words in an undertone to the young one. The young soldier's face softened when he spoke to the doctor, and they all took their hats off.

I knew what he would say before he spoke. "I am very sorry, miss. Your friend did not survive the labor."

My knees threatened to give way. "And the baby?"

He asked the soldier, and the soldier mumbled his answer to the ground, ashamed and sad. I understood his answer before the doctor translated it. "The baby was lost, too."

4

The older soldier pressed a set of cold keys and a heavy locket into my palm. "She said: For Ruth."

I dropped the keys into my pocket, certain that they belonged to Miriam's Berlin apartment. The locket rested in my palm, a design of leaves surrounding a sun etched in its surface. It shone gold in the watery sunlight. I had not held it for years. The last woman to wear it had died alone in a stable. I hung the thin chain around my neck.

"I want to see her." The reporter in me needed to verify it.

The soldier looked uneasy.

"Please," I said.

"I will go with her," the doctor said. "I will keep her out of trouble."

He would not be the first one who was wrong about that.

"Quick," the soldier answered.

Doktor Volonoski and I followed the soldier into the fetid barn. The soldier led us to a pregnant body stretched in a corner. Someone had removed Miriam's threadbare black coat and placed it over her face. I lifted it. Her eyes were closed, her unruly hair plastered to her forehead. Damp strands formed ringlets around her temples.

Her still, bluish face told me what I would find, but I took off my glove and dropped my fingers to her neck. Her oily skin felt icy. No pulse. She must have died soon after I left the stable.

"I do not understand," I told the doctor. "When I left she was fine."

"I thought you said that she was in distress." He looked reassuringly at the soldier, as if to vouch that I would not make a scene.

"In distress, yes, but not near death."

"I am sorry. But things can change quickly during a labor." He gestured around the filthy barn. "Especially in conditions like this."

I drew the coat over her face and opened the locket. It contained a picture of a two-year-old girl. She looked like neither Paul nor Miriam. A dark ribbon tied back her long blond hair. She glanced sideways at the photographer, eyes alight with mischief. She looked a little like me. Indeed, if things had worked out differently with Paul, perhaps she would have been mine.

The edge of the little girl's picture curled forward. I gently pried it out with my fingernail. Underneath was a picture of a blond man who looked very much like Ruth. Was it Miriam's brother? Or was it Ruth's father? If so, it might explain why Paul had not followed his wife into Poland.

I smoothed Ruth's picture on top of the man's. Then I closed the locket and clasped it between my palms. Let it keep its secrets, for now.

The doctor helped me to my feet.

"Thank you." I stared at Miriam's inert body. She had been so young, and the baby had never had a chance to live. Two more innocents claimed by the Nazis. I sighed.

The doctor's worried gray eyes looked into mine. "I feel sorrow for your loss."

I wiped the back of my hand across my eyes. "As do I."

I would find out more about her last minutes. I glanced around the stable, searching for the blond woman who had served as her translator. She was nowhere in sight.

"Excuse me," I said to the old woman sitting closest to Miriam's body. "Where is the woman who was with her?"

She, too, looked around the stable. "Gone."

"Where did she go?"

"Out." She pointed toward the half-open front door.

I had thought no refugees were allowed through there.

"You can stay here no longer." The soldier took my arm and began steering me toward the door, his grip just short of painful.

"Wait!" I called back to the old woman. "What's your name?"

She put her finger to her lips and turned away.

The soldier and Doktor Volonoski ushered me out of the stable. I would help Doktor Volonoski with the refugees in the mill today, but tomorrow I would come back here and find out what had happened to Miriam's translator.

Fräulein Ivona and Anton stood where I had left them. He had both eyes fixed on the door, waiting for me. She looked everywhere but at the stable. She clearly wanted to be far away. I did not blame her. No one else wanted to be here either.

"Is she all right?" Anton asked.

I wavered. I hated to leave him with this kind of news alone.

"I have to help the others, in the flour mill." I inclined my head toward the doctor.

Fräulein Ivona fussed with her fashionable jacket. She knew the answer, too. "Are you sure that you shouldn't get some lunch and come back?"

I shook my head. "No time for that. I can eat later."

She tilted her head to one side. "You care about them so, though they are strangers? And Jews?"

"They are human beings, some injured and sick. If I can help them, I must."

"So their pain is more important to you than your hunger?" It appeared as if this thought had not occurred to her before.

"I will survive, Fräulein Ivona." I put my hand on her arm. "They might not be so fortunate."

"Let me get you food before you go," she said.

"If you could have something ready for me later," I said, "that would be a tremendous help."

I dropped them at the sole hotel. I handed Anton my satchel. "Take good care of this for me."

He slung the strap across his body. "When will you be back?"

"When the doctor says we are finished."

"I will have her back for dinner, young man," Doktor Volonoski said.

I turned to Fräulein Ivona. "Please stay with him."

She tugged her wrinkled jacket into position. "Of course, Frau Zinsli."

"I do not want him left alone."

"How long, exactly?" Her china doll blue eyes narrowed.

"Until I return," I said. "And there will be a sizable bonus for you then."

She ran her hand over her sleek hair. "Very well."

I drove Doktor Volonoski back to the flour mill, where most of the wounded and ill had been brought. I set arms broken by truncheons, bandaged heads grazed by thrown rocks, and helped make those who had suffered strokes and heart attacks comfortable.

Doktor Volonoski found doctors and nurses among the refugees and put them to work, too. I soon supervised three nurses, glad that someone would remain with the refugees after we left.

Even with help, by the time we finished, we could barely stand. Despair weighed heavier than the work. It felt so in the Great War when I worked in triage, consigning some patients to death so that others might live. Here, who knew what awaited the living. I feared that their troubles had only begun.

The weak autumn sun had already dropped below the horizon by the time we finished. Frigid air stung my cheeks when we stepped outside. I thought of Frau Warski making a dinner of our sandwiches. The stable would be a cold place for her and baby Esther to spend tonight.

"I believe that my driver procured us rooms at the inn near your house." My breath formed clouds in the night air. "Could I offer you a lift home, Doktor Volonoski?"

"That would be most kind."

"It would be my privilege." He had worked hard and ceaselessly for hours without a trace of anti-Semitism. He might be more accustomed to working with the sick than I, but it had worn on him, too.

He opened my car door. I climbed in and pulled on my cold leather gloves.

He sat in the other side and closed his door with a soft thump. "You were very good in there. You should have stayed with nursing."

"I could not stand watching people die," I said.

He stared out across the hood at the darkened windows of the mill. "It's not as it was in the war. Usually, the patients don't die. If you're good at your job."

I mustered a smile. "You are good at your job."

"Thank you," he said. "I don't imagine you expected to spend your day like this either."

"I had this idea I would research croissants with poppy paste for an article on Saint Martin's Day."

We both sighed.

I started the car and turned on the headlights.

"I can be good at my job only when it is possible," he said. "I fear I have months of an impossible job ahead of me."

"How long do you think the refugees will be stranded in Zbąszyń?" I pulled away from the flour mill and drove down the rutted dirt track toward town.

He stared at the dashboard for a long time before speaking. "Poland does not want them. Germany does not want them. I think it might take months to sort out."

Months. Thousands of people living through the end of winter outside or in stables and a flour mill.

We drove in silence.

"It's there." He pointed to a modest wooden house surrounded

by a wall and an arched entryway that probably supported roses in summer. I had left that house hours before, but it felt like weeks.

"Thank you, Frau Zinsli," he said. "If your companion could not find rooms for you and your son, my wife can make up a room. You are in no condition to drive to Poznań tonight."

"Thank you, Doktor Volonoski," I said, touched. "If I do not have a warm bed waiting for me, my son and I shall knock on your door."

I drove the few houses to the inn and turned off the ignition, but I did not get out. I rested my forehead on the hard steering wheel, trying not to remember the day's events. Miriam. The baby. The wounded refugees. And Ruth. Cold cut through my coat. I shivered.

I raised my head and climbed out. Exhaustion dragged down my limbs, but I had to call in the refugees' story to my paper and also telephone Bella. Only then could I sleep.

I stumbled into the smoky inn, grateful for its warmth. I rubbed my eyes with the back of my wrist. At the front desk the thin clerk recognized me immediately.

"Your sister got you a room. She and the boy wait in the dining room." He gestured toward the left, then pulled his arm back to adjust its too-short sleeve.

"Thank you," I said. "Is there a telephone? I must make a few calls. Private ones."

He pointed to a wooden booth in the corner of the lobby. I stumbled over, suddenly light-headed. I realized that I had eaten only bites of bread since I left the hotel in Poznań.

The telephone was an old-fashioned wooden box hanging from the wall. I had not seen one like it in years. It took a few moments for the Polish operator to understand me. Eventually she did, and the exchange rang through to Bella's number. An unfamiliar male voice answered Bella's phone. "Fromm."

"Frau Fromm, please," I said.

"May I ask who is calling?" The twinge of Berlin accent gave me pause. Bella's servants tended to speak perfect High German.

"Frau Petra Weill." I used a variation on my pseudonym from my days as a reporter for the *Berliner Zeitung* before I had fled in 1931. Bella would recognize it, and there would be no record of that name that the Gestapo might trace, as Petra Weill was never a real person.

"Frau Fromm is engaged." The butler's deep voice was impassive. "Where may she reach you?"

I paused. I hated to give the name of my Polish hotel, but surely the Gestapo's reach did not extend all the way to Poland? And if it did, Petra Weill was not wanted by anyone. Even if the name was noted in my Gestapo files, it seemed unlikely that it would be linked to Bella or that someone would bother to look it up. Bella had literally hundreds of troublemaking friends. She and I had spent little time together where we might be observed. Still, there was a risk.

"Frau Weill?" His voice rumbled patiently.

I had to leave a message. If Ruth had not been rescued by Paul or by neighbors, she had been locked in a cupboard for three days. Every minute mattered. I told him the inn's name and telephone number and hung up. She would know that my message was urgent. We had not spoken in over two years. She knew I would not telephone unless I needed to.

Next, I called a Jewish physician friend in Berlin, Frau Doktor Spiegel, but she did not answer either. Perhaps she had fled Germany, or perhaps she simply attended a patient.

The reedy desk clerk seemed occupied paging through a thick green ledger, but his attention looked staged. I wondered if I was being paranoid. I was in Poland, after all, not Germany.

Finally, I called the newspaper in Switzerland. Lucien Marceau answered. Smart, fast, and liberal, he would not censor my words, but he would not be pleased that I was on the scene reporting this story. He fancied himself the top political correspondent at the *Neue Zürcher Zeitung* and had been cool toward me for the past month, ever since my first political piece came out.

I quickly explained the situation. I told him what I had learned of

the deportations, Ada and Esther Warski, and the wounded patients I had treated. I finished with Miriam, dying with her unborn child inside her in the icy stable.

"Good god," he said. "Come home."

"I intend to stay here a few more days to cover the story."

"Of course you do." Disapproval permeated his words.

"Tell Herr Knecht that he will have to wait for his Saint Martin's coverage."

"He will rail about it," he said. "But he will be happy that you have such a solid story. And perhaps a trifle worried about you. Perhaps he should assign someone more experienced."

By which he meant himself. "I am no fashion reporter. I shall be fine."

He snorted. "How could anyone doubt that you might have troubles going up against the Polish army?"

"It is not the entire army," I said. "Just a few soldiers."

"Oh, god," he groaned. "Herr Knecht will be unbearable if something happens to you."

"More so than usual? Impossible!"

"He sent you to Poland to write about saints and cakes, not refugees and Nazis," he snapped.

"He sent me here to find news," I retorted. "And I found some."

"The police called today about your last letter." His words dripped vile glee. He enjoyed the amount of trouble the letters had caused.

I groaned. Ever since a secretary at the paper had accidentally opened the first threatening letter to me a month before, Herr Knecht had turned into an overprotective mother bear. "He sent the letters to the police?"

"Of course he did." I pictured him shaking his finger at the telephone, as he would a naughty child. "The police recovered fingerprints. You are to stop by the station to give yours up for comparison."

That was a disaster. If the Swiss ever shared fingerprint cards with the Germans, they might discover that I was wanted for kidnapping Anton and, perhaps, in connection with the murder of four Gestapo

men in 1936. "I certainly shall not. He never sends the letters that the men receive to the police. Some of theirs are as bad as mine."

"They're not as bad as yours." He huffed with indignation. "Even if they were, you are not a man. Herr Knecht does not want responsibility for a woman being injured because of his paper. This brings me back to my original suggestion: Come home."

"Tell Herr Knecht—"

"I imagine you're tired," he said. "So I shall stop fighting Herr Knecht's battles for him and ring off."

He disconnected so quickly, I had no time to reply. Let him be angry. I did not have time to have it out with him anyway. My stomach rumbled, and my eyes ached. Tomorrow would be another long day.

I asked the clerk to be alert for messages for Petra Weill, explaining it as newspaper business, and asking to be notified immediately if a call came, to wake me even in the middle of the night. Hopefully Bella would call soon.

I visited the washroom off the lobby. Icy water sputtered from the tap. I scrubbed my hands again and again with their hard soap, trying to scrape the blood of strangers from under my nails. My dress looked fairly clean, but mud, blood, and who knew what else spattered my coat. At least the coat's black color made it look clean.

I dried my hands on the rough towel, then smoothed them across my face. The bulb's harsh glare showed my exhaustion. Dark circles stood out against my pale skin, a tracery of red capillaries filled the whites of my eyes, and my hair hung limp. My brother's voice echoed in my mind: *I hope you had a good time to earn a face like that!* I smiled at the memory and hung up the towel. As usual, I had not earned my face by having too much of a good time.

5

I trudged to the dining room. It held four dark wooden tables and a bar with a handful of stools, most occupied. At one table a group of men played cards and smoked foul-smelling Polish cigarettes. Two tables were empty. Anton and Fräulein Ivona occupied the fourth.

Anton leaped to his feet when he saw me. He still wore the satchel with the strap across his narrow chest. "I waited to have dinner with you."

I embraced him and held him a second longer than usual. He was almost as tall as I. I reminded myself to lecture him for entering the flour mill without my permission, but after dinner.

Fräulein Ivona stood. "I will have them prepare a meal for both of you."

"I appreciate it," I said. "I have had nothing since lunch."

"Which you did not eat." She flounced across the room to the bar, skirt and jacket rumpled, but still shapely enough to draw the men's eyes from their card game. She stopped at the bar and began an animated conversation with a tall handsome man seated there. Was he her lover? He was attractive enough to cause many women to forget their better judgment.

I chose a chair with a view of the front desk so I would be ready if the call came. What if Bella did not call? Berlin lay only three hours away, but I dared not chance a trip. Still, Ruth was alone. As a mother,

how could I leave a two-year-old child to die alone in a cupboard? As I had left her mother to die alone in a stable.

"Mother," Anton asked, and the tone of his voice told that it was a serious question. "Is Sweetie Pie dead?"

He never asked about his real mother. I was grateful for that, because she had been a drug-addicted prostitute. She abandoned him with me when my brother's death stopped him from delivering money for Anton's care. I tried to decide what to tell him and what to spare him. "Yes. She is."

"Are you certain?" He brushed his fingers through his tousled blond hair, and it stuck up crazily. I resisted the urge to stroke it back into place.

"I read the police report of her death, and also saw it verified by a different policeman." Lars had added it to the file he compiled on me. Thorough, he had researched Anton back to his birth.

I put a hand on his shoulder, but he shifted it off. "How did she die?"

She had been found dead in the public toilets at Wittenbergplatz subway station. I had to tell him the truth, but I would omit what details I could. "Of a drug overdose."

"Cocaine?"

He had been only six, but he knew. Shocked, I answered. "How do you remember that?"

"I wasn't a child," he said indignantly. "I remember a lot from those years."

He had been a child, indeed he still was one, but I did not contradict him. "I see."

"Will you rescue the little girl in the cupboard?" he asked. "As you rescued me?"

He, too, had spent time locked in a cupboard. That was where his mother put him while she transacted business with her clients, probably when he was as young as Ruth. I gazed into his serious blue eyes. "I will try. I called two friends in Berlin to see if they can find her."

"If they can't, what then?" He fidgeted with his latest carving, tapping what looked like large webbed feet.

"I hope they can. If not, I think there might be a Jewish orphanage I can call." Although how I could find them in Poland was an open question.

"If none of them will help her, will you go back to Berlin?" He leaned forward in the round wooden chair, clearly ready to leave right now.

I did not lie to him, but in this case I did not know the truth. "It would be complicated for me."

"Because of your trip during the Olympics?" He folded his arms.

How much did he know or guess of my actions there? More than I wanted him to. "Because of that, too."

"And because you took me away," he said.

"You are too smart for your own good."

He smiled, and I noticed how grown up his face had become. He had lost the softness of his early boyhood. His features were sharpening toward the face he would wear as a man. "So, why can't you go back?"

He never relented. He would make a fine journalist, or a prosecuting attorney.

"Because." I chose my words with care. "Near the end of my last Berlin trip, the Gestapo arrested me and a colleague. We managed to escape, but I might not be so lucky again."

I did not tell him that I had a clean passport, one that identified me as Hannah Schmidt. I had it made to escape Germany in 1936, but had not needed it. Since then I kept it sewn into the thin lining of my satchel. If I had not been with Anton, I would already have cut it out and risked a quick trip into Berlin to find Ruth myself.

One of the men won the card game, to a loud roar from the others. He smiled bashfully, clearly unused to winning. Anton smiled back at him before firing another question at me. "Do the Gestapo have a file on me?"

"Yes." I gave him a stern glance. "You could not get in and out safely, if that is what you are thinking."

His surprised expression told me he had been thinking exactly that. "But if they don't know who I am—"

"They know who you are," I said. As Anton Röhm, he was still a liability to the Nazi government. "And in any case, you cannot cross the border alone. You are only thirteen. They would never let you through." At least not without a sheaf of papers I had no intention of filling out.

He set his chin mutinously, a bad sign. Anton never stopped searching for wrongs to right.

Before I could marshal an argument, someone tapped my shoulder.

It would have to be a convincing argument. I turned to see who it was.

My breath caught in my throat.

It was Lars Lang.

His eyes looked dazed. Mine probably did, too. Anton's face swung from me to Lars.

I stared at Lars. Relief flooded me. He was alive. I wanted to throw myself in his arms. But doubt burnt away the relief. For two years I had mourned his death. Where had he been?

A new scar intersected his right eyebrow. His dark hair was longer than I had ever seen it, and a strand curled into his forehead. His face, always sharp featured, was thinner than I had ever seen it, almost gaunt. Seems he had not enjoyed the last two years much. Neither had I.

He clicked his heels and bowed, as he had so long ago in the police station at Alexanderplatz when we met for the first time. He stood erect, hands clasped behind him, like the military man he had once been. His posture reminded me of my father's. I went still inside.

"How do you do, Frau Zinsli?" I felt his wedding band when he shook my hand. Was it the one he put there on the day we pretended to marry, or from a more recent, and equally faithless, liaison?

I dropped his hand and sat straight in my chair, too shocked to speak.

He touched the back of the chair next to mine. "May I?"

I had many things I wished to say to him, to shout at him, but not in front of Anton. I stared, unable to think of a single appropriate word. Without waiting for my permission, he sat.

Would he try to explain his absence? How? I tried to imagine what could constitute an adequate explanation, but my mind came up with only one: He had lied to me in Berlin. He had never intended to rejoin me in Switzerland. It had been a trick to get me into his bed, and I had been completely taken in.

Anton gave me a worried look.

"Struck dumb?" Lars said. "I know how difficult that is to achieve."

I cleared my throat. "It is not every day I see a ghost."

"A ghost?"

I swallowed. "I thought you were dead."

"Did you?"

"Yes." I clenched my trembling hands in my lap. I would not let him see how upset I was. That, at least, I could spare myself.

Anton watched us as if we were the most entrancing film he had ever seen.

"Anton," I said. "Please wait for me at the bar. I will be along in a moment."

He hiked my satchel up on his shoulder and went. He knew better than to argue with that tone. He took a seat a few stools away from Fräulein Ivona's handsome man.

The bashful man at the other table paused in his game, probably sensing something amiss, but with a quick shrug he went back to his cards.

"What is your name these days?" I asked.

"Lars Lang," he said. "Same as ever."

So he was not using the false identity under which we were married. It was as if I never existed. "Do you still work for the SS?"

"Discharged," he said with a grimace. "Under a personal cloud but not, in case you are worried, a criminal one."

"How did you find me?"

"Your Swiss paper said that you would be going to Poznań to cover the festival."

Of course. A teaser for my upcoming story had appeared in the newspaper. Since he knew my pseudonym, finding me must not have been that difficult. My hotel in Poznań had probably directed him here. "Why did you find me? And why now?"

"I am glad to see that you are well." His tone was matter-of-fact as he dodged these two questions. "Are you glad to see me?"

"I thought you had betrayed me or died." The hours wasted mourning when I should have been angry instead. "I suppose, for your sake, I should be happy it was the former."

The smell of alcohol drifted across the table. I gauged his state—neither visibly drunk nor completely sober. Hopefully sober enough to avoid causing a scene. "I've missed you, Spatz."

His term of endearment cut. "Really?"

He pulled on the cuffs of his white shirt. "What brings you here?"

"The refugees," I said. "You?"

"It is the last stop on my delivery route before Berlin."

I looked into his dark eyes. I had much I wanted to discuss with him, but I was so angry that nothing came to mind. Then one thing did. Ruth. She might still be locked alone in a cupboard, and so far no one had returned my calls. "Could you run an errand for me in Berlin? Tonight?"

"For you," he said. "Anything."

I bit back a retort. Ruth had no time for my hurt feelings. I summarized the happenings in the stable and gave him Paul's address. I also told him that Miriam's death had made me uneasy, so he should be careful.

"I am always careful." His lips curved up into a hollow smile. "I can leave immediately, once we have solved the question of my fee."

The Lars I remembered had never been interested in money. But

then again, perhaps that man had never existed outside of my memory.

"What is your fee for saving a child's life, Herr Lang?" My tone rang colder than the air outside.

"I'm certain that you and your banker can come up with something commensurate with my exertions." He cocked his head to the side, clearly expecting me to name a figure.

"I am afraid my pockets are not so deep as you seem to think. A reporter's salary is meager, but as you know, I have a few objects of value I could sell, if you were willing to wait for your payment." I still had some of my brother's jewelry, although with so many selling their possessions and fleeing Germany, that was worth less every day.

He rocked back in his seat. "The banker won't pay?"

"Why would he?" I had ended my relationship with Boris more than two years ago, before I had taken up with Lars. Boris continued to be a presence in Anton's life, but he was no longer a presence in mine.

I read surprise in Lars's eyes, something I had rarely seen there.

Fräulein Ivona walked into the dining room carrying two plates. She smiled at the man at the bar and set a plate in front of Anton. Then she came to our table and placed a thick white plate in front of me, looking smug.

She turned to Lars. "I see that you found my employer."

Lars's mouth dropped open.

"Fräulein Ivona." My words came out high and strained. "What is the meaning of this?"

She sat across from me and folded her hands in her lap like a schoolgirl. "I believe that you are acquainted with Herr Lang?"

"What is the meaning of this?" I repeated. No other useful words came to mind.

"I followed you," she said to Lars. "To the train station in Poznań yesterday."

That was the day that Anton and I had arrived.

Lars rubbed his forehead. "Why?"

"Because, my darling," she said. "I wanted to see where you were going."

Darling? I thought back to her conversation earlier in the day. Lars was the excellent lover with the one-month deadline. I had been mourning him for two years while he was sleeping his way across Poland. I pressed my dry lips together and watched him squirm.

"I saw how you looked at her." Disdain toward me was clear in her tone. Fair enough. I did not like her much right now, either. "And I realized that my month had ended early."

"I told you the very first night that I was not free," Lars said calmly.

Fräulein Ivona directed her ice blue eyes to me. "You're not the first. And you won't be the last."

"I am not in the race at all," I said. "Luckily."

"I spent the day with you, trying to see what he could possibly desire in you," Fräulein Ivona sneered. "But I saw nothing."

Lars cleared his throat.

"Good-bye." She stood and kissed him hard on the mouth. I looked toward Anton. He had stopped pretending to eat his soup with his spoon halfway to his mouth.

She strolled to the bar, where the handsome man handed her a glass. I longed for a shot of something myself. But I had a few things to resolve with Lars first. "Are you certain that she knows nothing incriminating about me?"

"I do not believe so." Face impassive, he watched her wrap her arms around the man at the bar. "I've never spoken of you to her, so I imagine that all she knows is that she saw me watching you at the train station and then whatever she has learned since you've been dragging her around all day."

I forced down a flash of rage. "Where the hell have you been for the last two years?"

"I'm sorry, Spatz. Things became rather complicated for me in Russia." He brushed a lock of black hair, too long in the front, out of his eyes and shifted on his chair.

"Somehow—" I gestured toward the bar. "—you manage to amuse yourself."

"I doubt that you have been idle yourself."

I had, in fact, been completely idle, but I had no intention of telling him that. I gritted my teeth. "Are you certain she poses no risk to me, or to Anton?"

"Yes." A muscle twitched under his eye, as it always did when he was angry. Let him be.

I took a deep breath. "How did you meet her?"

"In a bar. Late. I was drunk and she was beautiful. A familiar refrain."

Two men in dark coats entered the lobby, but I paid them little attention.

"And there was nothing odd in her wanting to take up with you?" She was much younger than he and very attractive. Surely that had made him suspicious. Suspicious was his natural state.

He smiled mechanically. "She wasn't the first, Spatz. I'm quite competent in bars."

I tried to ignore that. Apparently, that was none of my concern.

Lars leaned forward and reached for my hands. I pushed my chair back with a screech.

He sat back. "She's no risk to you. I checked her out shortly after I started sleeping with her. She's not involved in the Party and has no connections that are in any way suspicious."

"She strikes me as a very vulnerable young woman, Lars. You should not be toying with her affections." I thought of her mother's recent death and the eerie way she stared at the flames. She was not entirely stable.

"So, you two are friends?" he asked. "You wouldn't like her if you knew her. She's the most anti-Semitic woman I know, and my circle of Nazi acquaintances is quite wide, as you know."

The men rang the bell for the clerk. I realized with a start that under their dark coats they wore Gestapo uniforms. Gestapo in Poland? I stood to fetch Anton from the bar. We had to leave.

But the Gestapo officers already crossed the dining room, making a beeline for my table. Anton was now safer if I left him there. I sank back into my seat.

"Spatz?" Lars asked. "Why are you jumping up and down like a jack-in-the-box?"

A hand closed cruelly over my shoulder. I looked up into the lumpish face of a Gestapo officer. Another stood next to him, practically quivering with excitement. My stomach clenched.

"I beg your pardon." I tried to pry his massive fingers off, but he would not let go. My shoulder resembled a child's in his huge paw.

"I believe that you are Hannah Vogel?" he asked in a gravelly voice.

I tried to think. I had crossed the Polish border as Adelheid Zinsli. I had registered at the hotel as Adelheid Zinsli. The only living people in Poland who knew my real identity were Anton and Lars. Anton, I trusted. I wanted to blame this on Fräulein Ivona, but did not see how she could have known, unless Lars had told her. Had Lars turned me in?

"I am afraid that you are mistaken," I said. "My name is Adelheid Zinsli. I am a reporter for the *Neue Zürcher Zeitung*."

He jerked me to my feet as easily as if I were made of straw. Physical resistance was impossible.

My eyes darted around the table, looking for weapons. Two teacups, two saucers, and two spoons. And a plate of sausage and kraut. A laughable arsenal.

His smaller companion moved to the side, flanking us, perhaps worried that I would snatch up a spoon. Lars stood, too, but he stumbled as he did. How drunk was he? Not that it mattered. Even sober, he could do little against two armed and alert Gestapo men.

"I am a Swiss citizen," I said.

Anton swiveled on his barstool and caught sight of me.

Gravel Voice stuck a hard metal object in my back, where no one could see. A gun. I winced. Lars's face tightened. I trusted that he knew of the gun, and I hoped he would do nothing to get me shot.

Although perhaps he would enjoy it. I had no idea what he might be capable of, I reminded myself.

I looked up into Gravel Voice's impassive ash gray eyes. He dug the gun farther into my ribs. He would have no problem shooting me. My avenues were closing down fast.

"Let's not make a scene, Fräulein," he said. I did not think he would care if I did make a scene. It would give him a chance to hurt me.

"Could you please fetch my coat?" I asked Lars. Both he and the Gestapo men looked confused. *Lars,* I pleaded silently. *Get Anton out of here.* I had to trust that Lars would do that. That I had not been wrong about everything with him. "I gave it to that boy at the bar."

"Certainly." Lars bowed, clicked his heels, and limped toward Anton. When had he developed a limp? Before I had time to think on that, my captor dragged me toward the dining room door. His partner followed.

Anton walked toward me. He would not let me be taken without a fight. My heart quickened. Lars had to stop him.

"Why are you arresting me?" I spoke quietly so as not to cause a scene. I needed to keep them calm, and to keep their attention focused on me, instead of on Anton.

Lars pinned Anton against the wall and dropped a hand over his mouth. I closed my eyes so that the Gestapo men would not see my relief. But would Lars take Anton safely back to Switzerland? Anton's chances had to be better with Lars than with the Gestapo. I straightened my back and talked up to Gravel Voice. "I am a Swiss citizen. And you have no authority in Poland."

"I make the authority I need." His gravelly voice sounded matter-of-fact. For him, today was another ordinary day. Only for me was it a unique disaster.

We quick-marched across the lobby, his fingers digging painfully into my upper arm. Surprised murmurs followed us to the door. My body screamed to fight, but I could not. If I did, Anton would try to

help, and even if he were not hurt, they would take him back to Germany, too. I had to prevent that, whatever the cost.

Gravel Voice's colleague opened the hotel door, and he shoved me through it into the night. Gooseflesh sprang up on my arms. The air felt only a few degrees above freezing, and my coat hung in my hotel room. If I lived to be thrown into their car, I had a cold ride ahead.

Gravel Voice yanked my hands in front of me and snapped on tight handcuffs.

"You are a traitor to Germany." Outrage covered the pockmarked face of Gravel Voice's friend. His words lisped out in white clouds. "You are wanted for murder. For consorting with traitors and Jews."

"That is nonsense," I blustered. "I am a reporter for a Swiss newspaper. A Swiss citizen. You cannot—"

Gravel Voice picked me up like a toy and dropped me into the trunk.

6

He threw a blanket over me and slammed the trunk lid before I could move. I thrashed under the blanket. The car juddered to life, then jounced into motion.

We shot forward, and I bounced painfully around the trunk. Hoping that we would reach a paved road soon, I shielded my face with my cuffed hands. Would they take me into the woods and shoot me, or did they intend to drive me back to Berlin and interrogate me? A quick murder in the woods seemed the better option for me.

We stopped. I kicked against the trunk lid and shouted, but to no avail. Seconds later we started again, the road considerably smoother now. The stop could not have been the border. Surely the Polish border guards would take longer than that to let us across. As minutes passed and we did not stop again, I realized that it must have been.

For the first time in two years, I was in Germany.

I felt carefully around with my cuffed hands for a way to open the trunk, but I was securely entombed in the darkness.

I wrapped myself in the scratchy blanket as best I could. I wanted to sleep. Best to face the Gestapo rested. Just a few minutes' sleep would help. My eyelids grew heavier.

Gas must be leaking in from the car's exhaust system. I fought to stay awake. Each blink lasted longer than the one before.

I woke shivering. My teeth chattered. My head ached, my heart pounded, and my breaths came quick and shallow. A nursing lecture came back to me, on hypothermia, and I mechanically checked off symptoms.

I felt sluggish. How close were we to Berlin? It was a three- to four-hour drive from Zbąszyń, but I had no sense of how long I had been out.

If only the border guards had heard me, I might have had a chance. In spite of dragging me out of the hotel, the Gestapo had no authority there. People might shelter me. The police might protect me. But we had crossed into Germany. Matters were much more complicated. Here I could rely on no one, especially not the police.

The car slowed, crunched over gravel, and rolled to a stop. Doors slammed. Voices rumbled outside. Liquid pattered against the ground. They must be relieving themselves.

I pounded the trunk lid with numb fists.

The lid opened into night.

I squinted at the shape above me and cleared my throat. "P-p-ardon." My teeth chattered together so hard, I thought they would crack. "P-p-please. B-b-bathroom."

Two things stood between me and freedom: the men who had taken me. I must escape them before we got to Berlin. If not, I would die.

Gravel Voice called forward. "The traitor is awake."

"Not trait-t-t-or." I forced out. "Mistaken."

In actual fact, I took pride in being a traitor to the Nazi regime, but this did not seem the best time to bring that to their attention.

"We should let you lie in your own filth," he sneered.

"Your t-t-trunk." I shivered so hard, I could barely sit upright. I did not know how I could stand, let alone overpower one or both of them. But I must. My sluggish brain tried to formulate a plan.

"I don't fancy cleaning it." The pockmarked driver came around. "Get her taken care of. It's more than an hour to Berlin."

I struggled to control my panic. An hour away. And I was in the

woods in Nazi Germany. Even if I got out of their car alive, no one would help me.

I took several deep breaths. My immediate options had not changed. I had to escape from two men. After that, I would do what I could to get the handcuffs off and get back to Poland. One step at a time.

"Your problem." Gravel Voice yanked me out and dropped me on the roadside. I skidded on gravel on my hands and knees. I imagined the stones must be sharp, but I felt nothing. I stood awkwardly, still shivering, and stamped my numb feet, trying to get blood flowing into them.

If I slipped away, they might not be able to find me in the dark.

Gravel Voice walked back to the front seat, shaking his head. The driver stayed by me. He was barely taller than I. I felt a surge of relief that the larger man had returned to the car.

The running motor's exhaust puffed out in a cloud of blue. The headlamps cut through mist to reveal empty road in front. We were alone.

"P-p-rivacy?" If I got away from the car, they might not find me if I ran.

"It's no ladies' club," he said. "Piss where I can see you."

I would have no chance to run. Whatever happened, I would have to do it alone and right here. I pointed to the ditch a few meters away. "There?"

He shoved me toward the ditch. When we reached it, we both stopped.

"Get on with it," he said.

I looked past his head. Gravel Voice's silhouette faced forward in the passenger seat, back bent as if he leaned to adjust the radio. The driver moved his head to follow my gaze, turning his back to me.

I dared not think about what I had to do. I had one chance to survive. I swung my handcuffs over his head and pulled the chain that held my cuffs together taut across his warm throat. He scrabbled at it with both hands. I kicked the backs of his knees. He fell, landing

hard against my chest. I collapsed onto the ground with his weight atop me. My head struck a rock. The world swam in and out of focus. I struggled to retain consciousness.

He forced his fingers under the handcuffs. He twisted to the side. I yanked as hard as I could. With a crunch, his trachea collapsed under the metal encircling my wrists. He groaned. Even if he escaped, he would not be able to breathe properly.

His fingers tore at the metal. I forced my knees up behind his shoulders and yanked harder. His shoes kicked against sodden leaves in the ditch. I hoped that the radio would distract Gravel Voice a few more precious seconds.

The driver kicked convulsively. His head smashed my arm against the rock. I heard a crack as the bone broke. Hot pain shot up from my wrist. I bit my lips and did not let go. Soon, he went limp.

His chest stilled. I shifted my fingertips to the side of his bruised neck and felt for his pulse. None. I remembered checking Miriam's cold neck hours before and shuddered.

Grimacing, I lifted the handcuffs over his head and felt for the holster on his hip. If I had a gun, I could force Gravel Voice out and drive away. No one else need die. My fingers slid to the bottom of the holster. They ran along cold leather. Empty.

What options were left? Fight, flee, hide.

A gunshot cracked. Gravel Voice.

He was armed. I was not. That eliminated fight.

I rolled sideways into the shelter of the wet ditch. Cuffed hands in front of my face, I belly-crawled toward a stand of trees faintly visible in the murk. A second shot broke the muffled stillness, then silence.

I crawled past an oak and pushed myself into a standing position, hiding behind the trunk. I shook so that I could hardly stand. Any advantage I received from adrenaline had ended where I left the driver on the ground. I had killed him. My mind sheered away from that thought and tried to focus on the tree, the car, and Gravel Voice. I could regret my decisions, if I lived. Right now, I did not have that luxury.

I peered between gray trunks. He would have trouble finding me if I stayed still, but even if I eluded him, I could well freeze to death. Warmth trickled down the nape of my neck. Blood from where I had bashed my head, but I had no time to worry about it.

The engine of the Gestapo car still ran; its headlamps flooded the empty road with light. The driver lay on gravel next to the car, neck twisted into an unnatural angle. The car looked empty, but the dark made it hard to be certain. Where was Gravel Voice?

A twig cracked next to me. I bolted.

I told myself it was blind panic, and I should stop, but my legs had their own mission. A figure crashed painfully into me. We fell toward the ground together. At the last instant, he twisted and took the force of the fall on his own body. An odd thing for a Gestapo officer. Instinctive kindness? Or perhaps he wished to spare me for something worse later. We rolled when we hit the ground, and he pinned me under him.

My handcuffed hands were smashed between our bodies. I had nothing to fight with. I thrashed under him, trying to free my hands. My arm reminded me that it was hurt and badly. I groaned.

"Easy, Spatz!"

Lars. I stopped struggling, suddenly conscious of his familiar weight atop my body. I wriggled out from under him and struggled to a sitting position.

"Anton?" I asked.

"Safe in the lorry." He brushed wet leaves off my back.

"The other Gestapo man?" I asked.

"Dead," he said. "Both of them."

The gunshots I had heard were Lars killing Gravel Voice. Lars had come after me. But why?

He ran his bare hands along my arms. "You are frozen."

"You neglected to fetch my coat." I shook in earnest.

"How inconsiderate of me." I heard the familiar smile in his voice. "Would you attack me if I offered you mine?"

"I am f-f-fine." I hated that I could not speak.

A warm coat settled around my shoulders. Years before, he had given me his coat, back when I thought it meant something. I reached up to push it off.

"Don't interpret this as an amorous advance, but I fear that you are in no shape to walk to the road yet." He wrapped his arms around me.

My mind tried to argue about the wisdom of getting close to him, but my body only noticed how warm he felt. He smelled the same as he used to. I closed my eyes and tried not to think about the last time I had been in his arms, when I had wanted never to leave them.

"My god, Spatz!" he said. "You are cold clear through."

He pulled me closer and rubbed his hands up and down my back under the coat. I tried to push away from him. I would rather freeze to death than owe him.

"Damn it," he said. Long ago, he had always apologized for swearing in front of me. It seemed quaint now. "Why must you fight everything?"

He was correct, as usual. My pride would not get me out of this forest and back to Anton. I stopped struggling and relaxed against him. The shaking subsided to shivers. I tried to think about something other than the feel of his arms around me, his chest pressed close against mine. I reminded myself that he had not come to Zürich. He had not contacted me to explain why. I had been in mourning for two years for a man who was still very much alive.

Slowly, even the shivering stopped. I felt warm, relaxed, almost drugged. Now, I thought, is when trouble starts. I stayed put.

"Better?" His voice sounded soft, as it used to.

I nodded, not trusting myself to speak.

"Anyone else would have welcomed help," he said. "Instead of freezing to death."

"I am not anyone else," I whispered. A ridiculous point to make.

"No," he said. "You're not."

His lips found mine, and the last two years melted away. My heart beat so hard that I suspected he must feel it, too.

I thought of Fräulein Ivona and drew my head back. "No." I pushed away, gasping when my arm moved. Cuffed hands awkward in front of me, I struggled to my feet. "Thank you for keeping Anton out of danger," I said. "And for coming for me."

"It's become a habit," he said from his position on the ground.

"Not all the time," I said, bitterness strong in my words.

"Quite." He stood next to me. "Let's get back to the car. We have much to do."

"Where is your lorry?" I asked.

"Behind the car. You can't see it, but it's there."

I strained my eyes, but I could not see the lorry. I stumbled and slammed against a tree trunk. After that, I kept my eyes on the ground as we walked to the road. I did not want to fall down in front of Lars.

When we were within range of the car's headlamps, he stopped. A waltz now played from the car's radio. How curious that I had not noticed it until now.

He lifted my cuffed hands and winced when he examined my wrists. Blood coated my hands and ran halfway to my elbows. Metal must have sliced my skin during my struggle with the Gestapo driver. It looked dramatic, but was not so serious as the broken arm.

"I hope I did not stain your shirt." A dark smear ran along the front of his white shirt.

"I have a woman who washes them."

"You seem to have a woman for everything."

He released my hands and pulled on a pair of leather gloves. He stepped over the driver on the ground. I stared down at the body. A swollen tongue protruded between his teeth, and his sightless eyes stared at the stars. I had done that.

Revulsion climbed my throat. I turned from the body and vomited. The world darkened around me, but I was still awake and crouching by the roadside. Lars must have shut off the headlamps.

I wiped my mouth on my sleeve and sank back on my haunches. Lars appeared in front of me and with a quick movement unlocked

my handcuffs. Years of experience as a policeman. When he took the cuff off my right wrist, I smothered a yelp.

I gasped when I tried to rotate my swollen wrist.

"Broken?" he asked gently.

"I am no doctor." It was broken. As soon as I had a moment away from him, I intended to splint it. "We will have to see. But first, I think we must get away from this car."

"We need to move it off the road. I know a place nearby where it might never be found. If you can drive one of the automobiles, I'd like to bring the Gestapo car there. Can you drive?" He gestured to my swollen wrist.

"Of course." I pulled my injured arm up under the coat.

His face relaxed in relief. "Good. Once the sun rises, anyone who comes by will see it here otherwise. Would you prefer to drive the lorry?" He pointed back down the road to a barely visible rectangular shape. "Or this one?"

I looked at the dead man in the passenger's seat and realized that Lars had saved my life. I looked again at the dead man on the ground. The bodies would be traveling in the car. "I prefer the lorry."

He heaved the former driver into the backseat. He knelt and smoothed the gravel and leaves by the side of the road. I slid my hand inside Gravel Voice's still warm jacket and withdrew my Adelheid Zinsli passport from his pocket. As I suspected, he had retrieved it from the hotel manager before he arrested me.

"Follow me," Lars said. "I'll turn in about two kilometers, then drive along a dirt road. When I stop and turn off my headlamps, stop and turn off yours. I will keep driving and dispose of the car. In about fifteen minutes, I should be back at the lorry. If it takes longer, leave without me. Poland is a few hours away. Do you understand?"

"I am not deaf, despite everything." I slipped his coat from my shoulders.

"Keep it," he said. "You'll need it."

"As will you," I pointed out.

"The fewer foreign objects we bring into the Gestapo's car, the better."

He argued because he wanted me to keep the coat, but he was also correct. I let him help me put my arms into the sleeves, gentle with the broken one.

He walked me back to the lorry, both of us holding our hands in the air. "That's the signal," he said. "So Anton won't shoot us."

"Anton has a gun?" I asked.

Before he could answer, Anton sprinted across the road. He threw his arms around me and held on tight, for the moment not worried whether thirteen-year-old boys still hugged their mothers. Blinking back tears, I kissed him on the forehead.

"I thought you were gone," Anton said.

"It is much harder to get rid of me," I said, "than most people think."

Next to me, Lars chuckled.

When we arrived at the lorry, Lars helped me inside. I let him. For all my brave façade, I was exhausted. My wrist ached, my head throbbed, I had started shivering again, and I wanted nothing more than to curl up in a ball and sleep the clock around.

Lars leaned across me to pick up a pistol off the seat, probably not trusting me with it. With a practiced gesture, he stuck it in his belt.

"We'll drop the car off and go straight back to Zbąszyń," he said. "I have a compartment you can hide in while we cross the border. I promise to get you and Anton out safely."

What exactly were his promises worth? I took a deep breath. "Thank you."

"Getting you out of the Gestapo's hands is in my own best interest."

"How fortunate for me that saving your own skin will help me to save mine." I cradled my broken arm against my chest.

"Are you certain you can drive?" he asked.

"Have I ever given you cause to doubt me?" My voice shook at

the end of the sentence. I bit my tongue. Even if I was tired and in pain, I would not lose control in front of him.

He slammed the door and stomped back toward the car, limp more pronounced now that he was upset.

I fit the key into the ignition left-handed and started the lorry. I turned on the headlights awkwardly. Ahead of me, Lars started the Gestapo car.

"Anton," I said. "You must help me to shift the gears."

"I will," he said. "I've practiced on Boris's Mercedes. I could drive this by myself."

"Perhaps if both my arms were broken," I told him. "But not yet."

He smiled. I felt better.

I explained how and when to move the shift lever. If Anton could not manage it, I would have to shift with my left hand while he steered. He concentrated ferociously as I spoke, tip of his tongue sticking out the corner of his mouth, as it had since he was five.

We managed to shift into first. I pulled onto the road and followed Lars's taillights, closer than I would have liked, because I could not see far through the fog. Second gear went fairly well, too. I rested my broken arm on my chest and steered left-handed.

"He was amazing!" Anton said. "I tried to get to you when they first took you, but he grabbed me and promised we would take them on the road."

"He has promised many things." Such as his promise to return from Russia.

Anton shook his head, his hand resting on the gear shift. "He

was furious that they had you. I could tell. I knew that he would get you back."

"I see." Steering the heavy vehicle took more strength than I had expected. I hoped Lars had chosen a straight road. I gritted my teeth and turned the wheel. When did he ever choose the straight road?

"Then another car was ahead of us at the border, so we got farther behind. Plus we had to stop so I could hide to get across the border. He has a special compartment. He's very clever."

"Indeed," I said. A compartment? For smuggling people, or something else? Lars had certainly been busy the past two years.

"He planned to shoot out your tires," Anton said. "Soon, but your car stopped so he stopped, too."

"How thoughtful of him." On either side of the road, bare trees loomed out of the gloom and quickly vanished again. I was weaving more than I should, and Lars must see it, too. I concentrated on ignoring the pain in my arm and keeping the lorry steady.

"He pulled us over and jumped out practically before the lorry stopped moving. He can be very fast when he tries."

"Can he?" My head throbbed. The back of my throat burned. I would not vomit. I would not. I yanked the wheel straight. I could not drive the car one-handed much longer.

"I saw a flash of light from his gun, but he was too far away, and it was too dark for me to see much else."

I thought about strangling the driver, the dead face of Gravel Voice, and Lars kissing me in the woods. "That is just as well."

Almost exactly two kilometers from where the Gestapo men had died, we turned onto a rutted gravel road. Each bump worsened the pain in my head. When we hit a deep pothole, my broken bones grated against each other. I cursed.

"You said a curse word!"

"I may say quite a few before we stop." I risked a glance at him. Instead of looking shocked, he looked pleased.

When Lars turned off his headlamps, I stopped the lorry so suddenly, it stalled. My head throbbed, and I vomited bile out the side

window. Not good. How bad was my head injury? I extinguished our headlamps, too. Darkness rushed in around us.

I opened the door and looked down. My seat seemed farther from the ground than it had when I got into the lorry. The sound of Lars's engine receded. I climbed out, careful to avoid my mess.

Anton scooted to the edge of the seat and jumped to the ground. He landed next to me, missing the vomit. I leaned against the cold metal door, uncertain if I could stand much longer. I had not expected my head and arm to hurt this much.

"I can track him," he said. "Report on his movements."

"I have other uses for your woodcraft." I gestured with my good arm. "I need a flat stick to splint my arm. About this long. Two if you can find them."

I slipped down and sat on the running board. I had to stay conscious until Lars came back or fifteen minutes elapsed, and I had to drive to Poland without him, as agreed. But how would I get us across the border? Our passports had not been stamped. I closed my eyes.

"Mother!" Anton sounded frightened. I hauled my eyelids open. My ears protested against the volume of his voice. I ran off another checklist in my head. Symptoms of head injury: pain, nausea, sensitivity to light and noises, strong desire to sleep.

He shook my good arm.

"Awake," I said. "Hand me the stick."

With clumsy hands, I positioned the broad stick across my legs, then rested the back of my arm on top of it. "The perfect size. Thank you."

"The brave knows his woodcraft," he said. "I could light it on fire for you, if you'd like."

I forced a smile to keep him from worrying. "Just this is fine."

"If I don't light it, you'll miss my circus act." He crouched in front of me. Despite his light tone, I could see how upset he was. Me, too.

He handed me the second stick and I aligned it along my arm from palm toward elbow.

"Need something to tie this," I said.

He unlaced his shoes and proudly held up the laces.

"Smart young man." I was glad that he had taken first aid at school.

I ducked my head to tie the splint on with my left hand and my teeth. Hot pain shot up my arm. I jerked backwards and smashed my injured head into the lorry, but my arm stayed straight.

"Do you need help?" he asked.

"No." I spoke around the shoelace. "I have splinted quite a few arms in my life, including today. I can manage."

I tugged the knot snug. My stomach clenched against the pain. Cold sweat broke out on my forehead. Once I tied the splint and rested my arm against my chest, the pain changed to a steady, sickening ache. The ulna was not set, but at least it was stabilized.

I leaned against the lorry. Held at bay while setting my arm, my headache pounded back to life.

He examined my left wrist. "You're bleeding, too!"

"Cuts from the handcuffs," I said. "Nothing serious."

"You were handcuffed?" His clear young voice rang with outrage.

"Yes. I—" I fell to my knees and retched.

"How many times has she vomited?" Lars asked from behind me. Anton jumped. So neither of us had noticed his approach.

"Twice, sir," Anton said. "Once before she splinted her arm and just now."

Three times, but he had not seen the first one by the Gestapo car. I thought to chastise them for speaking about me as if I were not there, but decided to save my strength to crawl away from my mess one-handed.

"You splinted your own arm?" Lars knelt next to me. "I could have helped you."

I pushed hair off my forehead with my good hand, sweating in the cold air.

He brushed his fingertips across the nape of my neck. "What happened to the back of your head?"

"Hit a rock," I said. "Behind the Gestapo car."

"You might have mentioned it sooner."

My head spun. The ground rushed toward my face. I could not get my arms up in time.

Lars scooped me up. Pain stabbed in my arm. My stomach lurched again.

"Get the door, Anton," Lars said.

I fought going to sleep. Lars bundled me into a blanket, and I felt more bumping. Then, nothing.

Pain grated in my arm. I moaned and tried to wrench it away, but someone held it fast. I struggled to open my eyes. I lay on something soft in a brightly lit room. A man I did not know held my arm.

Lars stood on my other side. He cradled my head in one hand; with the other he stroked hair off my forehead. "Easy." He soothed. "He's set your arm. The worst is over."

Wetness slapped against my wrist. A plaster cast. My arm would heal. My head I was not so certain of. My heart I did not even want to think about.

I tried to push pain aside and figure out where I was. This was no time for weakness. I tried to speak.

"Don't move," Lars said. "Everything will be fine."

"Anton." I forced out the word.

"Here." The voice came from somewhere on my left. I turned my head but could not see him. My eyes watered in the glare. I closed them.

I had seen that I lay in a bedroom, on a bed. A man I did not know applied plaster to my arm. My head ached, and I wanted only to sleep again. I fought it.

"Switzerland," I said. "To Boris."

"Don't worry about that," Lars said.

"Promise." Every word took a hundred years to say.

"I promise," he said softly. "I will take him home for you, if it comes to that. Which it will not."

"Thank you," I said, and I was gone again.

*   *   *

I awoke to darkness. Where was I?

My head hurt worse than it ever had. My cheek rested against a stale pillowcase that smelled of Khasana perfume. When I lifted my aching right arm, it felt heavy and hard. What had happened to it?

Someone else lowered my arm back down to my side. "Shh," said a voice. "Sleep."

I turned my head to the voice. It belonged to Lars Lang. I lay in a bed with him. It must be a dream. I struggled to wake up.

"Lars?" My voice sounded thick.

"I'm here," he said. "You had nightmares, and I didn't want you to injure yourself thrashing around."

I touched his face with my heavy hand. I felt stubble on his cheek. It seemed real.

"Am I dead?" I asked.

He tightened his arms around me. "No."

"But you are dead." I wriggled out of his grasp. "I remember."

"No, Spatz." Worry tinged his words.

"Where is the little girl?" I remembered a little girl was in danger. I pushed myself into a sitting position. A mistake. My stomach heaved, and I vomited on the duvet.

"Fetch a basin," he called. "Her name is Ruth. She's fine."

I wiped my mouth on a clean corner of the duvet. I shook. My stomach twitched again. I looked around the room. Empty except for the bed and shadows that must have been nightstands. A heavy curtain covered the window, so I could not tell if it was night or day. Artificial light fell through the doorway. "I am sorry about the blanket."

Lars folded the duvet one-handed, his other arm tight around my shoulder. "It can be washed."

Anton stood suddenly next to the bed and handed Lars a white ceramic bowl. Anton wore a nightshirt too large for him. It must be the middle of the night. Lars took the basin with his free hand.

"Anton!" I said in shock. "You should not be here."

"Why not?" He rubbed his eyes with his fist.

"Because, then I have failed at everything." I tried to move toward him, but Lars eased me back against the mattress. Gray shapes swirled above my head.

My head throbbed. Later, a man came to shine a bright light into my eyes and speak in a rumbling voice that I could not understand. I slept.

My eyes opened. The sun was up, but half-drawn curtains dimmed the light. A stranger in a white coat sat on a chair next to me. I looked around. A bedroom, sparely furnished with a double bed, a wardrobe, a muted rug, and two nightstands, plus the chair upon which the stranger sat.

I cleared my throat. My head ached, but it was manageable.

"Ah, good," said the stranger. "You are awake." He held a glass of water to my lips. "I am a doctor."

He had not given his name. Neither should I.

8

A figure appeared in the doorway. I turned toward it. "Mother?" Anton said.

"Anton!" Relief flooded through me. Wherever I was, Anton was safe.

He came and sat on the edge of the bed. He took my hand in his warm one. "How are you?" He spoke with the Berlin accent he had used as a young child, not the Swiss one he used now.

"My head hurts." I used the same accent as he. "But I think I shall be fine."

Guardedly, I turned my head. I feared moving quickly, as if my head might come loose. The man in the chair was tall and spare, dressed in a well-tailored dark suit under his doctor's coat. He had an old-fashioned long mustache and a pink indentation on his nose where he must usually set his pince-nez. Near his shoes sat a black leather doctor's bag. "What do you think, Doktor Anonymous?"

"You remembered my name," he said in a delighted tone. "That's very promising."

"Where am I?" I asked.

Anton opened his mouth to answer, but the doctor shook his head. "Where do you think you are?"

"In a room, in a house." I struggled to recall. Switzerland? We

usually lived in Switzerland, but I remembered a vacation. A vacation with a promise of a white horse and fragrant pastry with almond paste and poppy seed. Poland. But Anton's accent led me to think we were no longer there. "Berlin?"

"Yes, Mother," Anton said. "We're in Berlin."

My head spun. Berlin was the most dangerous place in the world for us. "I see."

"Do you know how you came to be here?" The doctor settled his pince-nez on his nose.

I had no idea. But should I admit it?

"I think that's enough questions," someone spoke from the doorway.

I looked over at it. Lars? That made no sense. He was dead. Relief surged through me, then confusion. Why had he not come back from Russia? I closed my eyes. Anton squeezed my hand.

I had taken Anton on a holiday to Poland to cover Saint Martin's Day. Remembering that detail made me feel better. Fragments of my trip to Zbąszyń came back to me.

"Ruth." I opened my eyes. I did not know how I had gotten here or how Lars had become involved, but I knew why I was here. I had to find that little girl.

"Later, Spatz," Lars said. "Once you are finished with the doctor."

I stared at him. "Where have you been?"

"Later," he insisted. I sensed that he had a good reason for wanting my silence, that he did not trust the doctor. I kept my questions to myself. His quiet awareness of others was something I had once loved about him. It had saved our lives many times.

The doctor looked from Lars to me. "How do you feel?"

I described my headache and, to get rid of the doctor, lied when I answered no to questions about nausea, pain, and vision disturbances.

The doctor turned to Lars. "Physically, she is much improved. I would like to ask questions to ascertain how much of her memory is gone—"

Lars shook his head once.

The doctor polished his pince-nez on the edge of his white coat. "So," he said peevishly. "The questions you should ask are things about what she last remembers. If she has lost more than twenty-four hours before the incident and loses time again now, I would be concerned."

"What should we do?" Lars asked.

"Rest," he said. "And quiet. Nothing stressful."

I stifled a laugh. Anton and I were in Nazi Germany, and I was not to feel any stress about it.

"Can she be moved?" Lars asked.

He made me sound like a piece of furniture.

"I would advise against it," the doctor said. "I believe she lied to me about the state of her injuries."

Lars's lips curved into a smile. "Indeed?"

I did not see how a protestation of innocence would help my case, so I stayed silent while Lars saw the doctor out.

I pushed myself to a sitting position even though my head warned me that it was a mistake. "Anton, how long have I been here?"

Lars came back into the room, and Anton looked toward him before answering. I pushed down my irritation. He owed no loyalty to Lars. Did he?

"It's November fifth." Lars walked to the heavy curtains and pulled them open. Midday sun jumped into the room. "We arrived late last night."

"What happened?" I asked Anton.

"You slept, mostly." A closed look dropped over Anton's eyes. I recognized that look from my own face in the mirror. I would get no further information from him. But why not?

Lars sat on the bed and took my good hand. When I yanked it back, both he and Anton looked startled. What did they know that I had forgotten?

"Ruth," I said. "Please tell me."

"I went to Paul's apartment," Lars said. "No one was there so I let myself in."

The former police *kommissar* was skilled with lockpicks. "Did you have a key, Herr Kommissar?"

He gave me a conspiratorial look. Anton wrinkled his brow in annoyance. He did not like it that his mother had a life he knew nothing about.

"Once inside," Lars continued, "I checked all the cupboards, including the one by the door. I saw evidence that a small child had been in it, but no child."

I let out my breath. My head hurt so that I had trouble thinking. "Where is she?"

"I don't know. I couldn't do much more than look."

"Why not?" I sounded more irritated than I should have.

"Because, Spatz," he said gently. "You were hurt. No one knew if you would live or die. My place was here."

"Was it that bad?" I read the answer from his eyes. For the first time I realized how terrible he looked. He looked as if he had not slept, his clothes hung on him as if he had lost weight, and he had missed a patch shaving. I longed to reach over and trace the new scar in his eyebrow. And if he had not abandoned me for two years without a word, if I had not spent months grieving his death, I would have.

I turned to Anton. He, too, looked pale, but not so bad as Lars. Either he had more faith in my ability to recover than Lars did, or Lars had hidden the extent of my injury from him. Perhaps both. "How are you?"

"I am much better than either of you," Anton said. "Except I've been shut up in here since last night. So I cleaned Lars's guns and practiced on the flute."

I wondered how many guns he had, but all I said was, "The flute?"

"Lars has a flute." Anton pulled a long wooden instrument out from behind his back. "I learned a new song."

He started playing "O Tannenbaum." I stared at him, astonished. He did a creditable job. However, the sound burrowed into the pit

of my stomach. I struggled not to clap my hands over my ears. Another sign of a concussion: sensitivity to sounds.

"Nicely done," I managed when he finished.

"Your mother needs rest," Lars said. "This is the longest she's been awake yet."

Anton returned the flute to a long velvet sack and sat quietly.

Lars did not let me rest. He quizzed me on what I remembered: Gestapo men taking me from the hotel and disjointed images from a car's trunk. I thought I remembered waking up in Lars's arms.

"Anton," I said. "Could you please give us a moment of privacy?"

He grimaced but walked out twirling his flute sack.

As soon as he closed the door, I turned to Lars. "Were you in this bed with me?"

He suddenly became very interested in the floor. "I did not mean to presume, but the doctor said to tie you down, and I didn't have the heart."

"Next time," I said, "listen to the doctor."

"As you wish." He sounded hurt. Well, perhaps he should have come back two years ago.

"Please tell me what happened after I got out of the trunk."

He quickly filled me in on my abduction. How I managed to free myself by murdering a man. How could I have done such a thing? And how could I have forgotten it afterwards? Shame and horror filled me. I had taken away a life. Indirectly, I had taken two. My head ached. Tears pricked my eyelids.

He put his hand over mine. "They would have killed you."

"Does that make me better than they?" The man's family was slowly beginning to realize he would never come home. I had ensured that he would not. Worse still, I did not remember his death. I drew my hand back.

Lars talked, but I barely heard the words. Death surrounded me every time I came near Germany, and now I had dealt it out myself. I shivered.

He gently eased me from a sitting position to lying back down. I lifted the covers up to my chin. "So, after all that, when we got here I put you in that bed, and there you have mostly stayed since," he finished.

Mostly? He concealed something from me. "Did I wake at all?"

"You did, from time to time." He gave me a half smile. "You had a great deal to say."

I winced. I hated to think what I might have spilled. Once again, he knew more than I wanted him to. Only this time the fault was mine. "I wish to make sure that Ruth is with her father. Then, Anton and I return to Switzerland."

"How?" He crossed his legs. "Your Hannah Vogel and Adelheid Zinsli identities are compromised. And Anton has no papers."

I still had my Hannah Schmidt papers, but I did not tell him so. My old colleague, Herr Silbert the forger, could produce papers for Anton for the proper price. I only hoped that he still lived in Berlin and had not been arrested, and that I had enough money. "We cannot stay in Berlin with no papers either."

"I have a clean identity." He leaned closer and began to speak more quickly. "Lars Schmidt. I can use it to drive you and Anton across any border but Zbąszyń. I have a false gas tank in the lorry that I've used for smuggling. I'll put you both in it."

"Thank you." I hated to owe him more, but I would pay whatever price he asked to get myself and Anton out of Germany. "You have done much already."

"I am your husband," he said. "It's my duty."

I glanced quickly at the door to make certain that Anton had not heard. "Please do not jest about that, Lars. I am grateful for what you have done for us, but we both know that your actions clearly indicate you have no interest in assuming that role. I would prefer that you not confuse Anton." *As you once confused me,* I wanted to add.

"You were easier to deal with when you were raving," he said.

"That is because I could not remember."

"On the contrary. You remembered a great deal."

My head throbbed. "I—"

"Rest. You are in no condition to fight with me." He smiled wryly. "And I'm in no condition to fight with you, either."

"Then let me get dressed. We can fight in Switzerland," I said.

He grinned. "I agree."

I hauled my legs over the side of the bed and waited for the world to stop sloshing. My head injury was not going to make any of this easier.

"May I help you?" he asked.

"I can manage."

Lars raised a skeptical eyebrow, but he knew better than to object, as he must recall the hospital beds I had climbed out of over his objections. He handed me a dress. "I had it cleaned and mended."

"Thank you." I took it. I wore an unfamiliar slip. I tried not to think who had undressed me. It had to have been Lars. I closed my eyes and swallowed.

To my surprise, I felt better standing up. I dragged myself to the bathroom with my dress clenched in my good hand. Where had Lars been for the last two years, and what was he doing now? Could I trust him? He had risked his life to save mine and Anton's. That worked in his favor.

I raised my hand to my head. My dress. I shook out the sage green linen. I must have worn it when I was abducted, but I did not remember doing so. I turned it over in my hands, hoping it would spark memories. It did not.

While bathing, I recalled Fräulein Ivona's words in Doktor Volonoski's office. She claimed to be one in a string of Lars's lovers. My stomach clenched. *Think about it later*, I told myself. *First, get out of Germany*. Someone had rescued Ruth—probably Paul, or the mystery man from the locket. Even if Miriam's death was suspicious, there was little I could do about it. I had to get myself and Anton out of Germany as soon as I could.

I bathed and brushed my teeth before I chanced a glance in the mirror. I looked better than I had expected. My skin, always pale,

looked nearly translucent. I had the cast on my arm, of course, and dark purple circles smudged under my bloodshot eyes, but otherwise I did not look as if I had come into Germany in the trunk of a car. I also did not look like I could have killed a Gestapo man by the road-side. I remembered his face now, but I did not let myself speculate about his life outside of the night I had met him. I would not think about the wife and children he might have had. The mother who waited at home for him.

I pushed the thoughts down and busied my hands. I teased the gauze bandage from my hair. The wound was so small that it did not warrant a new bandage. I threw away the gauze, wondering how much damage had been done to my head where I could not see it.

I donned the green dress. Buttoning the front took time because I had only one hand. But when I was finished, I was satisfied with the results. The long sleeves hid most of the cast on my right arm and the bandages on my left wrist. I peeled back the bandages and checked. Lacerations and bruising, but nothing serious. I must have been handcuffed.

How had the Gestapo known to find me at the inn? They had called me Hannah Vogel. That left out Fräulein Ivona and the Polish soldiers, since they knew me as Adelheid Zinsli. So my message to Bella had tipped them off.

Unless someone had linked my Hannah Vogel identity with my Adelheid Zinsli one. Last time I left Germany, no one had known that I was both women, except Lars's old chief, Sturmbannführer Hahn. But it could not have been him. When last I saw him, he lay dead on a warehouse floor. By my hand.

I had since checked my sources to see if Hahn had left notes, and they had turned up nothing to link Hannah Vogel to Adelheid Zin-sli. Much could change in two years. Perhaps new evidence had been unearthed.

I found my satchel near the bed and walked more or less steadily to the front room. Anton and Lars stretched out on the floor playing backgammon.

"You're up!" Anton cried. "You look wonderful!"

He leaped to his feet and hugged me. When I kissed his forehead, he gave me an aggrieved look, but he did not step back.

Lars put away the game before standing. "Indeed you do."

"When can we leave?"

"Now," Lars said. "I could take you to a restaurant to wait and eat while I fetch the lorry and my passport."

"That sounds like a fine plan," I said.

"Are you certain that the trip won't overtax you?" He studied my face.

"Staying here would also be taxing." My legs wobbled as I walked toward the door.

Lars helped me into a woman's coat, his hands lingering longer than they should have. As much as I did not want to, I stepped away. I stroked my palm down the dark blue wool. The coat did not belong to me, and I did not wish to know its provenance. Another of his conquests, no doubt.

What had happened to my own coat? It hung in my hotel room in Zbąszyń. I felt proud that I had found the memory in my battered head. I now remembered arriving at the hotel. A little less time remained lost to me.

I drew on a pair of black leather gloves I found in the coat pocket.

Lars shrugged into a dark brown overcoat. He pulled his fedora low over his eyes, like a police detective hiding his expression from a suspect. An old habit from the days when it was true. Anton put on his own coat and took my satchel.

Anton bounced next to me down the hall and into the street. He studied shops and people with interest. He had not been back in the country of his birth in four years, an eternity in, now Nazi, Berlin.

The neighborhood felt decidedly working class, very different from Lars's previous apartment. Soot streaked dark brick buildings thrown together decades ago to house workers. Bare trees cowered in hard dirt squares in the sidewalk. The branches did not look as if they would leaf out even in summer. Holes left by missing cobblestones

gaped in a street with more horse-drawn wagons than cars. I was not certain where we were, but it looked like a bad patch of the district of Moabit.

"Mind your step." Lars led me around a broken beer bottle. I tried to avoid a squashy white object that I hoped was a sodden newspaper.

Anton stopped next to a battered wooden door. "What about this restaurant?"

It did not look promising. Grime caked dark windows, and dirty ocher paint outside did not speak to clean conditions indoors. Its battered sign read HAUS HUBERTUS.

Lars shook his head quickly. "That one is no good."

Although I agreed with him, something in his tone gave me pause. "Why not?"

He glanced at the windows. "The quality of the food is—"

A chubby blond woman in her early thirties bustled out the restaurant's door. She wore a waitress uniform, a black dress with a white apron and cap.

"Lars!" she screeched, grasping his arm. "It's been more than a week!"

He peeled her hand off his arm. I clenched my good hand in my pocket, but kept my face impassive and waited to see what would happen next.

Lars turned a pleading gaze on me. I gave him a stiff smile. I had no intention of helping him to resolve this. It was painful enough for me already.

His scowled. "Adelheid, may I present Fräulein Gretl? She works here. Gretl, this is my wife, Frau Lang."

Gretl's face fell. Anton's mouth dropped open. My headache returned full force.

"How do you do, Fräulein Gretl?" I thought of denying that I was Lars's wife, but that might lead to more complications. "Is this a favorite restaurant, Lars?"

Anton started. He knew that tone meant trouble. I took a deep breath.

"I have dined here from time to time." Lars's gaze fixed some-where beyond my left ear.

"I see that," I said.

"Should we ask Gretl to find us a table?" Lars asked me.

Gretl looked at me with sympathy. She would certainly be correct to pity Lars's wife. However, I was not.

"I think not," I said. "Although I enjoyed meeting you, Fräulein Gretl."

She blushed and curtseyed.

Lars reached for my arm, but I set off down the street without him, my hand on Anton's shoulder. Out of the corner of my eye, I watched Lars bow to Gretl and follow.

My head ached so much, I wanted to curl up in a ball in a dark room, but I would not give Lars the satisfaction of knowing how upset I was. To think that I had believed this situation could not become more intolerable. I cursed my paucity of imagination. Why did I care? Once I knew he had lied to me and betrayed me while I mourned in Switzerland, why should I care if he slept with one woman or one hundred? Yet, I cared.

I had to stop letting my emotions distract me. What did all this mean? It meant that Lars had relationships and loyalties I knew nothing about. Still, he had kept Anton away from the Gestapo in Poland, and risked his life to help rescue me.

"Lars," I said when he caught up. "Perhaps we could skip lunch and go straight to the lorry?"

"Spatz," he said. "I—"

"Please," I said. "Just get us to the lorry."

Lars turned on his heel and led us in the opposite direction. "As you wish."

Anton spoke up. "Are you really married?"

"No." I wished my head did not hurt so much. I might have been able to think of a way to explain it to him. "When I was in Berlin last—" I stopped when I saw the expression on Anton's face.

"1936?" Anton asked in a small voice.

"Yes," Lars said. "And—"

Anton drew back his fist and punched Lars full force in the groin. Lars folded to the ground. Anton ran.

I followed him, trying to suppress my feeling of immense satisfaction at Lars writhing on the cobblestones.

"Anton!" I ran out of breath. "Stop!"

I stumbled to a streetcar stop and held on to the streetlamp. Black paint peeled off the stem in curls. "Anton! Please!"

What if he kept running and disappeared in the streets of Berlin? He could get stuck in an orphanage or worse. Panic rose in my throat. Red and white lights blinked at the edges of my vision. I sagged against the lamppost.

I would not faint in the street in front of Lars. I would pull myself together and catch Anton.

Anton hurried back to me, shaking with rage.

"Need to catch—breath." I owed him an explanation, but I could not give it here, with Lars hobbling toward us, only meters away.

Anton waited, blue eyes turned from angry to anxious. I tried to think what to do. If I had a few hours' rest and a good meal, I would think of something.

Lars's limp was more pronounced than usual. Not surprisingly, he looked furious. He brushed off his coat. The ground rippled as if made of water. I knew the ground stood still, and that my perception was faulty, but the knowledge did me no good. Not for the first time.

Lars approached us both cautiously. "What was that for?"

Anton set his jaw and glared at Lars.

"Anton. Please apologize to Lars for your behavior," I said.

Anton looked at me hanging on to the streetlamp. He unclenched his jaw. "I apologize for what I did."

I recognized that he apologized only out of sympathy to me, and I doubted that any of us thought he meant it, but I suspected that it was the best we would get.

"I did not start a fight with you," Lars said to him. "And I do not want one."

I met Lars's dark eyes. "Our fight started two years ago. Anton is not to become part of it."

Lars held up both palms in a placating gesture. "Apologies all around."

I pushed off the lamppost.

"Are you all right?" Lars asked me.

"Are you?" I asked.

Lars grimaced. "I've taken worse." He looked over my shoulder. His eyes went cold.

"What is it?" I asked.

Lars took my arm and pulled me in the opposite direction. Under his breath, he said, "The lorry is gone."

"Stolen?" I whispered. Without the lorry, we were trapped.

"Or the Gestapo has a good idea what I was up to in the woods last night." Lars's face was expressionless, which meant real trouble.

The ground kept moving, but I tried not to stumble. "Should we separate?"

"Can you get yourself to safety?"

"Of course," I said, irritated. "I am not an invalid."

"For all that you have been conscious for less than an hour," he reminded.

"I will take care of her," Anton said.

"We will be fine," I said.

"I will check my apartment, and my sources," Lars said. "Where can we meet tomorrow?"

"Anhalter Bahnhof, track three. At noon," I said. The train station would be packed with people then. With luck, no one would notice us. "I have my own resources. If I am not there, you can assume that we are safely in Switzerland and you can get yourself out as well."

Lars smiled. "You cannot imagine how much I have missed you, Spatz."

"Perhaps," I said, "I can."

Lars looked surprised again, and I wondered what else he was not telling me.

Just then, a streetcar rattled up. Lars pushed a handful of German marks in my palm. I had only Swiss francs and Polish zloty. "Safe journeys," he said

"Likewise," I answered. He leaned forward as if to kiss me good-bye. I stepped back and herded Anton onto the streetcar.

9

The streetcar pulled off. Lars had already walked away.

We were now on our own, in Nazi Germany.

I sank onto the nearest empty bench. My legs shook. Doctor's orders: no stress. I stifled a bitter laugh.

Anton sat next to me on the wooden bench. His eyes were wide and frightened.

"Anton," I said, trying to tease him to lighten the mood. "Would Winnetou have hit his opponent there?"

His hero as a young boy had been Winnetou, the honorable Apache brave from the Karl May series. He relaxed a little. "If his opponent was that much bigger, he might have."

"Might have?" I had read every book aloud to him. Winnetou had never hit anyone in the groin.

"Winnetou's honor didn't help to save the Apache from the white man. Did it?" He stuck out his pointy chin.

As usual, his logic was irrefutable. "You know that it was inappropriate to hit Lars."

But I knew why he had. He had seen my grief when Lars did not return from Russia, as much as I had tried to hide it from him. And he blamed Lars. Well, so did I.

I gave him a stern lecture about being respectful to adults, but I knew he did not regret his action.

The streetcar jolted. I gritted my teeth and struggled to convince myself that my head did not hurt.

We traveled south. Eventually we would end up at a major station. I would find my way from there. It looked as if I was correct, and we traveled through Moabit. I felt better. This streetcar should end up at Alexanderplatz. We could walk from there.

I watched out the back window until reasonably certain that no one followed, then relaxed against the hard oak seat. The streetcar's rocking reassured me, and I closed my eyes.

"Were you two really married?" Anton asked.

I sat back up and examined the other passengers. A tired woman rested a string shopping bag between her shoes. A mother balanced a dirty two-year-old on her lap, a three-year-old fidgeted next to her. Two young girls chattered on the seat behind. No one seemed a threat, but caution was my watchword.

"This is not the place," I said.

"Where, then?"

Stung by his tone, I lowered my voice. "We will be going to the Jewish quarter. It is not a safe place, but I know of an empty apartment there."

"Miriam's?" He was a step ahead.

"Yes. I have her key. We can stay there until I sort things out."

"How?"

"I know someone who might help us." Herr Silbert could procure papers for Anton. "Then, we take a train home."

"What about our things in Poznań?"

"I will see if I can have them shipped to the newspaper," I said. "If not, we will do without them."

At the next stop, an SS man in full black and silver uniform boarded. We had no papers. If his suspicion should fall on us, I hated to think of the consequences. I hoped that our blue eyes and blond hair would shield us from notice.

Tension blew through the car like a cold wind. The chattering girls fell silent. As everyone else did, I watched the man in the black uni-

form until he chose a seat. He faced forward, seemingly unconcerned about those of us in the car with him. The girls resumed their conversation in subdued tones.

Anton said not another word until we arrived at our destination, and neither did I. My headache lessened. The rest did me good.

At Alexanderplatz, I steeled myself against glancing at the imposing police headquarters. In the late 1920s, I visited weekly to gather information for stories I wrote as crime reporter Peter Weill. In fact, I had met Lars in that building when he was still a police *kommissar*. I had not liked him on first meeting. I thought of Gretl. Clearly, I should have trusted my instincts.

Once, I had valuable sources in the building, but now it held only danger. Anyone who recognized me knew that I was wanted by the Gestapo for kidnapping and, perhaps now, murder.

The SS man from our streetcar approached the main entrance. He probably had offices there. Since the police and the Gestapo had merged, the only justice was Nazi justice.

Walkers jostled us as we crossed the busy intersection. I hurried into the deserted streets of the Jewish quarter. Thousands lived here, but they stayed indoors, probably to avoid attacks. Ada Warski had walked down these Berlin streets carrying her baby while German friends screamed slurs. We, too, had best get inside—and soon.

Although I had expected it, the anti-Semitic graffiti shocked me. *Der Stürmer* vented anti-Semitic hate from specially built display boxes. Black paint outlined a cartoon figure with a huge nose and yarmulke. JEWS OUT! was scrawled on one wall. I looked around. Every building had been defiled.

Anton stared at large white letters on a brick wall that read DEATH OF THE JEWS, WOULD BE THE BEST NEWS. I had seen anti-Semitic graffiti before, but it felt worse to read it on every wall in my home city. Once these buildings were covered with honest soot.

"Control your expression," I said. "If you truly lived in Berlin, you would be inured to this."

He looked down at the dirty sidewalk. "Let's get inside."

We walked down the once bustling street to the apartment that had belonged to my Jewish friend Sarah. After she and her son fled in 1931, she lent it to Paul and Miriam. The door to the apartment building had been freshly painted black. I shuddered to think of the foul graffiti the paint concealed.

I took Miriam's key out of my satchel and fitted it clumsily in the lock with my left hand. It took three tries, but I managed. When I tried to turn the key, it caught, and I wondered if she had given me a key to something else entirely. I rattled the key, and the door opened.

We stepped into the lobby. A single bare bulb illuminated the well-cared-for room. I spotted the mailbox where I had hidden Röhm's incriminating letters in 1931. Would revealing them have changed the course of Germany's catastrophe?

"Mother?" Anton was already halfway up the first flight of stairs. I walked quickly up to him. We had no time for thinking about things that might have been. We lived in what was.

The stairwell itself was clean, but the paint was dingy. It looked as if it had not been repainted in years. Presumably they used their available paint on the building's outside, covering insults.

"We came here when I was little," he said. "Once when you were looking for something and once after your apartment was destroyed. They were beating a man in the street."

He forgot nothing, poor child. "Yes. A good friend lived here, but she left before I met you."

"Is this where Miriam lived, too?" he asked.

"Until they deported her." *And killed her,* I added silently.

Someone had wrenched the mezuzah from Sarah's doorframe. It had taken with it several layers of paint. Before unlocking the door, I touched the splintered wood where the mezuzah had been.

Inside the hall smelled of stale cabbage, as it had on my last visit. I closed the door and turned on the light.

As Miriam had said, in the hall near the front door was a cupboard. It had two doors. Both had been torn from their hinges and thrown to the floor. The little girl was gone.

I motioned to Anton to stand quietly by the front door, then did a quick pass through the apartment to see that it was empty, and that Paul and Miriam had no telephone. The Gestapo often opened a line and listened to occupants' conversations. But as I suspected, Paul and Miriam could not afford such a luxury.

I returned to the hall. "You can talk now. There is no telephone to listen in on what we say."

In my mind, I drew a half circle around the cupboard. I dropped to my hands and knees and searched that half circle.

"What are you doing?" Anton asked.

"Looking," I said. "Please keep out of the light."

"She's not here."

"I know." I picked up a door. "Let's see what is. Perhaps something will give us a clue to her whereabouts."

The door had little dents hammered on the inside near the bottom. Had the little girl tried to kick herself free? I stared at the smooth depressions and admired her grit. It must have hurt to kick the wood that hard, but she had kept at it. The dents were in a nearly straight line across the back of the door, showing determination as much as desperation.

A scrap of white fabric dangled from a broken hinge. I carefully picked it free and held it in my open palm.

"What is that?" he asked.

"I would guess that it belonged to Ruth, or to the person who freed her from the cupboard." I studied the cloth. Thick cotton and expensive looking.

"A piece of a dress? Or a shirt?" he asked.

I rubbed the cloth between my fingertips. "It feels thicker than that. Perhaps a jacket?"

"Not a warm one," he said.

I opened my satchel, pulled out my notebook, and pressed the cloth between the pages.

He pointed to a dark mark in the middle of a door. "What made that mark?"

"Something small," I said. "Perhaps a pen."

"Or a screwdriver."

"Could be." I ran my fingertips over the mark. Whoever had opened these doors had no key and had not bothered to look for one. Surely that boded well for Ruth. She was with someone who cared more for her than for the furniture and worries about the noise of wrenching off the doors. I stacked the doors atop the cupboard, not sure what else to do with them.

Why had Miriam not left the key here? If she had a key, she would have given it to me at the stable, with her house key and locket. I checked atop the cupboard. The key rested there, in plain sight.

I searched the rest of my imaginary half circle. Shoes lined up near the door: a pair of old slippers that probably belonged to Miriam, worn patent leathers for Ruth, and brown slippers for Paul.

Who had ripped the doors off? It could have been Lars. I regretted not asking him for more details. Where he was concerned, I regretted much, I reminded myself, and cupboard keys were the least of it.

With any luck, she was with Paul. I told myself that, but I did not believe it. Miriam had not thought so.

The cupboard smelled of urine. The little girl had wet herself. No matter how brave she was, she was only two years old. The terror that she must have felt while sitting in the dark, listening to them take away her mother.

The last thing the cupboard held was a soft green blanket. I sniffed it—Miriam's perfume and urine. I folded it and set it on top of the ruined doors.

There was no sign that whoever had rescued the girl had brought her back inside the apartment.

We checked the bedroom that my friend Sarah had used for her son, Tobias. It probably belonged to Ruth now. The white-painted wardrobe held little girl's clothing, neatly hung or folded on the shelves. Most of the dresses had stains on the knees. I thought of the many pair of pants that I had mended for Anton. I was proud of

Miriam and Paul for letting their daughter get dirty. My own dresses had been pristine at that age. Even then I feared my father.

No evidence of hasty packing, so the person who took her away had taken their time and packed carefully, or they had taken nothing at all. I searched for a urine-soaked dress. That, too, was gone. Was she still wearing it?

I saw nothing that would explain who had taken Ruth, or why her mother had thought that she might be safer locked in a cupboard than on a train to Poland. Did she fear what the Nazis would do to her, or someone else?

I gave up, for now, and went to the kitchen where I found stale bread, butter, and honey. I heated water for tea and found eggs to boil.

I cut a piece of hard bread and handed it to Anton. He smeared it with butter and honey and devoured it. I sat at the table and ate a piece myself, more slowly.

"So," he said. "Are you and Lars married?"

"We are not married." I struggled to decide how much to tell him. He might as well know most of it. "When I was last in Berlin, Lars and I ran afoul of the Gestapo. We had fake identities made and the man who made them, for reasons of his own, decided it would be easiest to make us married."

He looked unconvinced. "Why would he do that?"

I sighed. There would be no peace until I had explained it to his satisfaction.

Stalling, I removed the eggs from the stove and poured water for tea. As on my last visit, they had only odious nettle tea. They must have gathered the leaves themselves because they could afford no other tea. "Lars and I had been pretending to be engaged."

"Why?"

"To make my visits to Berlin have a reason besides the obvious one: spying. And you may not tell anyone this."

He gave an exasperated sigh. "I am not a child."

I did not point out that he was, in fact, a child. "Do you have your pocketknife?"

He drew a bone-handled folding knife out of his coat pocket and dropped it in my palm. It smelled faintly of sawdust, probably from his pocket.

I set my satchel on the table and emptied its contents. I snapped open his knife and slit the satchel's lining.

"What's in there?" he asked.

I plucked my Hannah Schmidt passport out with a sigh of relief. At least now I had valid papers, even if they were not properly stamped.

I handed him the passport. He read it. "You're Hannah Schmidt?"

"You are Anton Schmidt," I said. "We shall get you proper papers tomorrow."

"Who is my father?"

I hesitated, but it was there on the passport. "My husband, Lars Schmidt."

"From Lars Lang?"

"Yes." I threaded a needle from my sewing kit and began to stitch up the satchel's thin lining.

He put the passport back on the table. "Do you love him?"

"I am certainly grateful that he rescued me from the Gestapo yesterday." I kept my eyes on my needlework, partially so I did not have to look at Anton, but also because I wanted to make the stitches as small as I could so that they would not be visible to a casual searcher.

"That is no answer," he said, as I had so often said to him.

I pulled the next stitch taut. I did not know the answer. I had loved Lars very much. I still did. But acting on that was another matter. "I did."

"Is that why you've been so sad since you came back from Berlin last time?"

"What do you think?" It was, but I did not wish to talk about it.

"I'm glad I punched him." Anton took a defiant gulp of tea.

"It was completely inappropriate to hit him," I said. "Whatever happened between Lars and me is my concern, not yours."

"But you would never hit him yourself." He put his teacup down on the table.

"No," I said. "Because it is an inappropriate way to solve problems."

"Isn't Gretl inappropriate?"

I tied off the last stitch and cut it with a little pair of folding scissors.

"Did Fräulein Ivona turn you in, back in Poland?" he asked.

"Did she seem surprised when the Gestapo came in and took me?"

"I wasn't paying attention." He leaned forward on his elbows and looked away guiltily. "I was trying to listen to you and Lars, and then I was trying to help you."

"You did the correct thing to listen to Lars."

I stood and took a hot egg from the pan. I placed it in an egg cup for him, then fished out one for myself.

"So, did she turn you in?"

"I think not," I said. "But only because the Gestapo arrested me for being Hannah Vogel, not Adelheid Zinsli, and I believe Fräulein Ivona did not know my real name."

We finished our eggs and bread in silence. Anton looked at my cast. He stood to do the washing up.

I went to the living room to see if Ruth's savior had left a note. I riffled through papers on Paul's desk. Handwritten letters in a language I did not know, but I guessed it was Polish. The other letters were official looking, and they came from the Reich. A letter stating that Paul must append the name Israel to his identity card, officially changing his name to Paul Israel Keller. A Jewish Asset Inventory Form where he and Miriam had been required to list their possessions. I skimmed it. It included even the locket I now wore around my neck.

Anton came into the living room wiping his hands on his pants. "Any clues in there?"

I shook my head. "Receipts, paperwork for various visas, and notifications from the Reich announcing further restrictions against Jews."

I opened the drawer and sorted through pens, pots of ink, and rubber bands. At the back, folded into a square, was a sheet of paper.

I unfolded it and smoothed it flat. The undated and unsigned typewritten note read:

> Enough. I will not continue paying. I cannot do what you ask.
> It ends now.

I turned on Sarah's old desk lamp and held the paper under it.
The watermark was the same as on the letters I had been receiving
from Berlin. The paper trembled in my hand.

"Mother?" Anton asked. "What does it say?"

I handed it to him.

He skimmed it and gave it back. I folded it up and returned it to
its place at the back of the desk. I did not mention that it matched
my other letters. Anton did not know about them. And he did not
need to.

"What does it mean?"

"I am not certain," I said slowly. "But I think it might be a reason
for Miriam to leave Ruth here instead of taking her along. Perhaps
she was being threatened."

My heart beat faster. It did not matter what I found in the desk. I
had to get Anton and myself out of Germany. Ruth was no longer in
the cupboard, and there was little I could do for her now.

Should I chance going to Herr Silbert's tonight? The sky outside
was already growing dark, which made it around four. His shop
would close before we got there. First thing tomorrow morning, I
would get Anton a Swiss passport and get mine stamped. We might
be on a train to Zürich by lunch. But what of Ruth? What if the person who typed the letter had taken her? What if she had not been
rescued at all?

10

The lock in the front door clicked.

I pushed Anton ahead of me into the kitchen, where we would not be visible from the front door, and took a carving knife from the drawer by the sink. I had a quick memory of the last time we had stayed here. Then, too, I had drawn this knife to defend myself against a mysterious late-night threat. I hoped this one would prove as harmless. I pushed Anton behind me, knowing he would hate it.

The front door closed quietly.

"Miriam's boots are gone," said a deep voice. Paul. I relaxed. He belonged here. "She must be at her mother's."

"Thank god for small mercies," said a woman. Maria? Paul and Maria had been lovers before he married Miriam and, perhaps, after. Had Maria broken the Nuremberg Laws forbidding sexual relations between Germans and Jews? She hated to risk herself, but I thought that she did love Paul as much as she could love anyone. So perhaps she had.

"I'd hate to run into her so soon after our two-week trip," Paul said. "It takes some time to adjust."

"Since she's not here . . . ," Maria said.

I put down the knife on the table so that the tablecloth would muffle the sound. "He is Miriam's husband," I whispered to Anton. "We are old friends, but stay here, just in case."

Paul and Maria stood next to the sofa with their arms wrapped around each other. A small suitcase rested on the floor next to Paul's stocking feet. I cleared my throat loudly and felt gratified when both jumped. They turned to look at me. Paul ran his elegant hand quickly through his thick dark hair, straightening it where Maria has mussed it.

"Hannah?" said Maria. "What the hell are you doing here?"

"I could ask you the same." My voice shook with anger. He had been off gallivanting with his mistress while his daughter crouched, terrified, in a cupboard and his pregnant wife died alone in a stable.

"Hannah," Paul broke in. "I don't understand."

"Have you any idea where your daughter is?" I had no time for social niceties.

"It's not your concern." Paul leaned against the arm of the sofa and angled his long legs to the side. He still carried shrapnel in his leg from the War, and it pained him to stand for long.

"Nor, obviously, are you concerned about the whereabouts of her mother," I said.

"I don't know what you are implying," he said, "but that is not your concern either."

"I saw Miriam," I said. "Yesterday."

Maria scrutinized me.

"In Poland," I said.

Paul's eyes dropped to the locket around my neck. He must have last seen it around his wife's neck. He could not know that I had taken it from the soldier who had removed it from her corpse, but he had to know that she never would have given it to me unless the situation were dire.

"Where were you?" I asked. "Where is your daughter?"

He dropped onto Sarah's old purple sofa. The wood groaned. Maria stayed put.

"Why was Miriam in Poland?" he said.

"Deported. With the other Polish Jews." Now that I saw his worry, I regretted my hostile tone. I would have to tell him his wife and

unborn child were dead. I should not do that from a place of anger. And if Ruth was not his, perhaps he had expected someone else to stand by her and Miriam.

"How was she?" He picked at his cuticles.

I stood next to the sofa. "She went into labor there. The refugees were quartered in a stable."

His burnt umber eyes stared into the distance. "How is she? Is the baby a boy or a girl?"

"I am so sorry, Paul." I hesitated, hating to finish the sentence. Maria watched avidly. "Miriam. She . . ."

A smile twitched on Maria's lips and was quickly hidden.

I took a deep breath. "Miriam did not survive the birth."

He gulped. "The baby?"

I shook my head.

Maria stood stock-still. I tilted my head to indicate that she should sit by Paul and comfort him. Not surprisingly, she did not.

"Ruth?" he said hoarsely.

"She left Ruth here," I said. "Locked in the cupboard by the front door."

He leaped to his feet. Maria and I jumped. He raced to the broken cupboard and threw himself on his knees in front of it.

"Where is she?" His voice rose in panic.

"I arrived here not long ago," I said. "I had hoped that you had come home and found her."

Someone else had taken Ruth.

"The neighbors, Maria," he said. "We must ask the neighbors."

She backed away from him. "You can't expect me to be seen with you. I can't traipse around announcing my presence to your neighbors."

He gaped at her as if he did not know her. But I did. She would not help him. She did not know how.

"I think it's best if I leave." She collected her hat and coat and fled without closing the door.

He slumped to the floor and stared at the empty cupboard.

I eased the front door closed.

Anton appeared in the hall and looked from the cupboard to Paul. Every day he witnessed more than I would ever want him to. I squeezed his hand and quickly let go.

"Paul." I knelt and put my hand on his shoulder. "We should ask the neighbors now. Perhaps one of them has Ruth. If so, she needs her father. She needs you."

He looked up. His eyes had gone blank. I had seen that look in his eyes long ago, when I was a nurse. He had been brought back from the trenches as the only survivor in his battalion, carried in, nearly comatose, with a badly wounded leg. It had taken a week before he spoke, months before he learned to walk again. He had to recover faster this time.

I left him on the floor and crossed back into the living room. I poured out a glass of schnapps and brought it to him. He had not moved. When I handed him the glass, he tossed the schnapps back in one swallow and dropped the glass onto the floor.

"Anton," I said. "Please finish washing up in the kitchen."

He shot me a worried look and backed out of the hall.

I knelt beside Paul again. "Paul?"

He clenched the stained green blanket in his fist. I sat next to him, keeping one hand on his arm. I waited.

An hour passed. Still he remained silent. I wondered if I should go to the kitchen for Anton, but he would be all right. He had seen much in the past days, but he was strong. Paul was not.

I touched Paul's shoulder and spoke his name once more. "Paul?"

Without looking at me, he stood and shambled to his bedroom. I followed a few paces behind. He threw himself on his marriage bed face-first. I covered him with a well-worn quilt.

"Should I stay?" I asked. When he did not respond, I closed the door. I could not leave him alone with the knowledge that his wife and baby were dead and that two-year-old Ruth was lost. We would spend the night here.

I went to the kitchen. Anton sat on the floor, whittling what re-sembled a duck from a stick he picked up on the way to Zbąszyń.

"A duck?" I asked.

"A duck-billed platypus." He held it up. I recognized the plump shape of the mammal now, with webbed flippers and a bill. A crea-ture caught between two worlds, like us.

"Very lifelike," I said. "Are you hungry? How was the tea?"

He made a gagging noise. "What kind of tea was that?"

"Nettle," I said. "I never liked it either."

"Should we go ask the neighbors about Ruth?"

I sat next to him. "I think not yet."

He leaned his head against me. "But shouldn't we find her?"

"Tomorrow." I had been thinking about this while waiting for Paul to speak. "If the neighbors were kind enough to rescue her, she is better off there tonight than with her father. And I doubt they would give her up to me if they had her. I am a stranger to them. And an Aryan German to boot. They will view me as the enemy."

"Will your friend be all right?"

He had lost his wife and baby, perhaps his daughter as well. He would never be all right again. "He will manage as best he can."

Anton blew shavings off the platypus bill.

"Let's see if we can find some nightclothes and a place to sleep," I said. "But first you must clean up the wood shavings."

I found an old straw broom in the corner where Sarah had always kept it and Anton swept the shavings into a pile. He deposited them in the stove in the living room. Although it was cold in the apart-ment, I hated to light it, worried about using up Paul's winter coal.

Anton followed me to Ruth's bedroom. The corner held old boxes. One contained clothes that once belonged to Sarah's son, Tobias. I pulled out a nightshirt and handed it to Anton. Last time he wore Tobias's undershirt, it hung to the floor. I bet now it would fit.

While he changed, I stripped to my slip and inspected the box. It contained a pair of trousers, a shirt a few sizes too big for Anton, and

a single Karl May book from Tobias's old collection, too dog-eared to sell. The book was *Deadly Dust,* and it featured Winnetou.

I bedded down on the sofa and spread blankets for Anton on the floor next to me. I tucked him in and read him stories about Winnetou, the Apache brave, written by a man who had never been to the American West. Anton had surely outgrown it, and probably knew it by heart, but he did not object. The familiar words soothed us both.

After he fell asleep, I stared at the photograph in my Hannah Schmidt passport, remembering the day that Herr Silbert took it. Not surprisingly, I looked exhausted. The day before, I had been struck by a car, then almost succumbed to Lars's charms. I should have stayed that course. I closed the passport. Tomorrow the inestimable Herr Silbert would make a new one for Anton, stamp them both, and we could leave. The neighbors must have Ruth, and soon she would be reunited with her father.

I rolled over on the sofa, trying to wriggle away from a sharp spring. In the days following my fiancé Walter's death in the War, I had slept here often, but nothing felt the same, except my sense of grief and worries for the future. I fell asleep with my hand dangling over the edge, centimeters above Anton's head, just to make certain that he could not move without my noticing.

Much later, bare feet scuffed across the floor. I opened my eyes, my heartbeat pounding in my head. Paul stumbled past into the kitchen, wearing only an undershirt and his pants from yesterday.

I slid off the sofa, careful not to wake Anton, and went to talk to Paul. The day felt early still, but a hint of gray in the sky told me that it was getting on toward morning.

Paul busied himself shaking leaves of undrinkable tea into Sarah's familiar blue and white teapot.

"Paul?" I asked from the doorway. My head ached, and I rubbed my temple.

He turned. Red rimmed his eyes. Sorrow rested there, but they were no longer blank. I let out my breath.

"Thank you, Hannah," he said. "For coming here to check on my daughter and for not leaving me alone last night."

"Of course," I said. "You would have done the same for me."

"I doubt that. I am not you, Hannah. I should not have let you go."

Hardly a comment to make mere hours after learning of his wife's death. "You did not let me go. I left against your advice, remember?"

His lips twitched in a reflexive smile that did not reach his eyes. "Quite." He turned to the sink with the kettle in his hand. His shoulders shook.

I went to him. Whatever he had been doing with Maria, he had lost his wife, his baby, and his daughter. He turned into my arms, and held on to me so tightly, it hurt. I had no words to comfort him. His life was irretrievably damaged.

Eventually, he loosened his arms, and I looked up into his familiar brown eyes. It had been a long time since we had stood so. He caressed my cheek. I closed my eyes.

Behind me someone coughed. We jumped apart as if caught by disapproving parents.

I turned to face the intruder. Lars. I realized that I wore only my slip. I crossed my arms across my chest.

"Who are you?" Paul asked with the fear of a Jewish man who had just been caught with an Aryan in arms.

"A friend of Hannah's." Lars looked ready to hit us both. A paper bag in his hand crackled. In spite of his half dozen interchangeable lovers, he was jealous of my standing here with Paul.

"I was making tea," Paul forced out. "Please join us."

Lars walked past me and sat at Paul's table. I backstepped away from him.

"Why did you come here?" I asked through gritted teeth. "We were to meet at noon. Elsewhere."

He looked embarrassed. "I—I came to see how you were. To explain a few things, but perhaps outside?" Paul looked from Lars to me.

I remembered my manners. "Paul, this is Lars." I did not say his

last name, not certain which to use. "Lars, this is Paul Keller. This is his apartment. His wife was Miriam."

Lars's expression softened. "I am sorry to hear of your loss."

Paul went very still. Lars was the first one who had offered him condolences, not counting me. I walked over, took the full kettle from him, and placed it on the stove.

"Paul?" I asked softly.

"I must go speak with the neighbors." He wiped his eyes with the back of his hand. "Enjoy your tea."

It was early to be calling on the neighbors, but I did not stop him.

He walked straight to the front door, still in his socks and under-shirt, Paul, the man who was always impeccably dressed. When he came back through it, Ruth would be with him. One of the neighbors must have heard her crying after Miriam's departure and come in to free her.

"Excuse me, Lars." I went to wash and dress.

As I walked through the living room, Anton sat up, looking sleepy. "What's going on?"

"Nothing," I said. "You can go back to sleep."

He slumped back down, and I tucked the blanket around his shoulders. He was probably asleep before I reached the bathroom. I felt a strong desire to be thirteen years old.

I completed my toilet hastily. When I returned to the kitchen, the kettle had begun to whistle. Lars poured steaming water into the teapot and brought it to the table, which he had set with items from his bag: rolls, butter, and jam. He had brought breakfast, either as an apology or a tactic to ensure that I spent time sitting at the table with him while he pumped me for information.

"Nettle tea?" he asked. "I thought you hated that."

I sat and folded my hands in my lap. "Why did you break into Paul's apartment to meet early?"

"Where was he when they took his wife and daughter?" he asked.

"With his mistress." I clenched my hands together. "A situation I am certain you have faced yourself."

Lars checked the tea. It probably needed more time to steep, but then again, I did not want it to have a stronger flavor. I poured myself a cup with my left hand without offering to pour for Lars.

I spooned in honey awkwardly, cradled the warm cup against my cast and my left hand, and waited, but he stayed silent, so I gave up and asked. "Why are you here now?"

He lowered his gaze to the table. "My lorry is definitely gone. My apartment is under surveillance by the Gestapo."

"I am sorry I landed you in this mess, Lars," I said. "If you had not come after me, you would be safe and happy in Poland."

"Safe, perhaps," he said.

I took a quick sip of too-hot tea. "I have a few questions about Fräulein Ivona."

"Have you?" He poured his own tea, looked at it as if it might be poisoned, then grimly took a sip. I hoped he would hate it as much as I did.

"I want to be certain that she did not turn me in to the Gestapo," I said. "I have enough enemies already."

"If she is your enemy, then she's my enemy as well, now." He held up his cup in a mock toast.

I did not lift mine. "Sun Tzu said to keep your friends close and your enemies closer."

"How fortunate when my enemies are attractive twenty-five-year-olds." He took a long sip of tea to punctuate his words.

That hurt. I dropped my gaze to my disgusting tea. His visit changed nothing. I must visit Herr Silbert at nine, the moment his store opened, so we could leave Germany. Still, I was curious. "Did you send her to drive for me, and to spy on me?"

"As I said earlier, no," he said. I wondered how true that might be. "But she is a very jealous woman, so I'm not surprised that she sought you out to make a scene after she saw you on the station platform."

I toyed with my spoon. I longed to ask him what he had been doing on the station platform watching me arrive in Poland after

abandoning me for two years, but I did not want to give him another chance to say something hurtful. "How do you know that she is not a danger to us?"

He pressed his lips together in irritation. "I investigated her, of course. A colleague in Berlin checked out her file. She worked as a secretary in some minor department having to do with road building and then came to Poland to study engineering. She is unmarried. She has never been under investigation for anything. None of her associates are suspicious either."

Lars had been, as usual, thorough. So Fräulein Ivona posed no official threat, although perhaps a personal one. "Do you think she turned me in to the Gestapo in Poland?"

"I checked with my contacts this morning before I came here. According to the file, you were arrested based on a phone call to a Bella Fromm, whose telephone was answered by an informant. I am under suspicion because I crossed the border so soon after you were arrested and taken across. The detectives investigating the disappearance of the Gestapo agents feel that, based on our previous engagement, I might have been tempted to help you."

So, we were both wanted, and all because of my indiscreet telephone call. I should have been more careful. "I am sorry that you are under investigation. I should have—"

He sipped his tea. "Do not concern yourself overly. It's not the first time."

"How did you find us here? Were you followed?" I itched to peer out the closed kitchen curtains and into the street. But then if someone was down there, they would know that I was looking for them.

"Don't insult my intelligence, Spatz. I knew you would not trust my assessment, that you would let no time elapse before coming to check on the girl yourself."

I hated being predictable, especially to him. My head throbbed. "Clever, Herr Kommissar."

"You looked pale when we parted, so I assumed that you might have to spend the night. Are you feeling better this morning?"

"Much," I lied. I took my gold pocket watch from my pocket. Still too early for Herr Silbert.

"Do you have an appointment?" he asked testily. "Or have I overstayed my already tenuous welcome?"

"Lars," I said. "I appreciate all you have done for us. I am certain it has been a burden—"

"Not at all." He set his cup on the table and sat up.

"How gallant of you to say."

"I did it for quite selfish reasons." He gave me a flirtatious smile. "I can assure you of that."

Looking at him, I lost my train of thought. I well remembered where that smile led. I forged on. "Be that as it may, it was very kind—"

He smiled with half his mouth. "I sense a *but* coming."

He had always known me too well. I twisted my hands in my lap. "But I think it might be best if you and I have no further contact."

"Where will you stay?" he asked. "I could—"

"I believe where I sleep is as much my affair as where you sleep is yours." My head spun, and I swallowed. I would not get upset and throw up on the table.

"I'm sorry about this, Spatz," he said. "I am not without resources, perhaps I—"

"You are too kind," I said. "But I believe we are safer without you, thank you."

"Will you stay here? With a Jewish man?" He stood. "You will be charged with race defilement. It's not safe." He paced around the kitchen, trying, I knew, to think of an argument to change my mind.

"Lars." In spite of myself, I spoke too loudly. "Even though you have apparently been thriving here for the past two years, Anton and I cannot call anywhere in Germany safe."

"As for the matter of the last two years. I hardly think that you—"

Anton appeared in the doorway, rubbing his eyes with his fists. "Mother?"

"Good morning, Anton," I said.

Anton pulled out a chair and sat. He looked greedily at the food, probably hungry after last night's pitiful dinner. "May I start breakfast?"

"Yes," I said. "I must pack."

Lars sat across from him and picked up a roll. He handed the basket of rolls to Anton. "Did you sleep well?"

I left them sitting at the kitchen table and walked to Paul's empty bedroom. I found a box in the corner with Sarah's things. They were out of fashion, but many women in Germany these days could not afford to keep up with the latest fashions. I packed dresses and underthings for me and Tobias's hand-me-downs for Anton into an oversized bag I found in the closet. Sarah would not care if we took them, and we would look less suspicious on the train if we had luggage.

When I returned to the kitchen, Lars and Anton chatted companionably. I made myself a roll while standing. "Has Paul returned?"

"No." Lars gestured to the satchel on my shoulder and the bag in my hand. "Where are you off to?"

I hesitated. "Shopping."

"I shall accompany you."

"No."

He gave me a long-suffering look. "I can walk with you, or tail you from a distance, but I am not letting you out of my protection until you are safe on Swiss soil."

I bit back a sarcastic comment about the value of his protection. I wanted nothing more to do with him, but it might not be a bad idea to keep him where I could see him. Just as Sun Tzu said, friends close, and enemies closer.

I finished my roll. We left the table set for Paul and, hopefully, Ruth.

I wrote a note for Paul, thanking him for the use of his house and saying that we most likely would not be returning. I gave him my number in Switzerland, although I suspected that he would not call

it. I would try to check in on him again before we left Germany, to make sure that he and Ruth were all right, but I could do little else.

I turned to Anton. "Let's go."

He rose and shrugged apologetically to Lars. Apparently they had moved past the groin-punching incident. As I had told Fräulein Ivona, I did not understand men.

Before we got to the door, Anton tapped my cast and reached for the bag. "It's my job to carry the heavy things."

I gave him the bag, and kept the heaviest burden for myself.

We rode to Kreuzberg in the same subway car. Lars sat at a bench opposite and did a credible job of pretending we did not exist by reading the *Völkischer Beobachter*. I tried my best to ignore him and his Nazi newspaper. Anton looked at the two of us as if we were insane, probably grasping the subtleties of the situation better than we did.

I had thought of trying to evade Lars, but Anton's presence complicated the situation. In any case, yesterday's chase after Anton had proved that I was not up to running. Lars probably already assumed that Herr Silbert's store was my first stop, and he had been there before, so I revealed nothing by taking him there.

Besides, he might need Herr Silbert's services to get out of Germany. No matter how angry I was at Lars, I owed him. He would not be stuck here if I had not been arrested, and he had not followed to help me.

The subway stopped, and we bustled up the stairs with a crowd of workers starting their day. The men wore suits and hats, but few women joined them on their way to work. The Nazis' efforts to force women back into the kitchen seemed to be working. I turned up my collar, wishing I did not stick out against this background of men, and wondering how I would have survived here had I stayed. How I might have to survive if we could not leave.

Outside, the streetlights' glow fought against the cold gray sky. Anton stayed close. I did not see Lars, but he was there. I did not have the luck for him to have lost interest.

My steps quickened when I spotted the familiar cobalt blue storefront. When I stopped in front of the door, I paused. GERMAN BOOKSTORE flowed in gold Gothic-style letters across the plate glass front window, not SILBERT AND SONS. Panic fluttered in my stomach. Perhaps he used such nationalistic language only to keep the Nazis at bay.

I glanced up as I stepped across the threshold. The brass bell that Herr Silbert usually hung over the door was gone. I took a step into the store, then turned to Anton.

"Could you please wait for me at the candy shop across the street?" I pressed coins into his palm. "I would like a packet of mints."

He wanted to come in with me, but he understood my tone and left for the candy store.

I walked past a giant exhibit of *Mein Kampf* topped by a black-and-white glamour photo of Hitler staring pensively out a window.

A stranger stood behind the counter. His white shirtsleeves gleamed, and his green eyes had a questioning look.

"Excuse me." I mustered a polite smile.

"Good morning, madam," he said. "How may I be of service to you on this fine German morning?"

So the Nazis now used their nationalistic terminology on even the weather.

I pulled my jade green fountain pen out of my satchel. "I bought this here years ago. Lately, it keeps getting clogged. Can you fix it?"

My brother had given me the pen as a gift. I had no idea where he had purchased it, but it seemed a safe way to start a conversation. In addition to his illegal activities, Herr Silbert had sold and repaired fountain pens.

The man took a pince-nez up out of his pocket and settled it on his round nose. He peered down at the pen in my hand.

Behind me, the door opened and closed. I hoped for Lars and not someone worse.

"We don't repair pens here anymore," he said. "We only sell books."

I stuck the pen back into my satchel. "Do you know where the previous owner has set up shop? He was so meticulous."

The man put his palms flat on the counter. "Prison."

"Oh, dear." I sounded like my grandmother.

He regarded me coldly.

"I suppose I shall have to find another place to repair my pen. Is there a shop nearby that does that sort of thing?"

"No," the man said.

Lars put a firm hand on my elbow. "There you are, my dear! I'm glad I found you. We are so very late."

I looked up at him. "Are we?"

He led me onto the sidewalk. As we passed the candy store across the street, Lars waved, and Anton came out. As if by some unspoken plan, Anton did not cross the street but kept pace with us on the other side. Lars and I did not speak.

Anton caught up with us at the station. Lars bought tickets; then we stepped into a crammed subway car. I held on to a leather strap and wondered what to do next. Herr Silbert had been my only hope.

Anton offered me a mint from a brown paper bag. I shook my head. Lars took one.

"Did you get what you needed?" Anton asked.

"No," I said without explaining. Anton sucked a mint and stared out the window. I looked at Lars. Perhaps he had a useful contact. "Do you have a source?"

He looked pained. "No."

I had not expected him to, but having it confirmed was still a blow. The car carried us forward through a dark tunnel. We stopped at a station, but I did not bother to read the name on the wall. They were all the same to me now. My shoulders sagged as the implications of Herr Silbert's absence came home to me. I tried to come up with a new strategy, but my head would not comply.

Anton rose at Alexanderplatz, and I followed, feeling dizzy and nauseated. Lars stuck close by my side, no longer pretending that he

was not with us. I felt grateful for his presence. Berlin felt different now that we were trapped here.

Anton led the way back to Paul's apartment. We had nowhere else to go. I tried not to notice the graffiti. A nearby shop window had been broken the night before, and our shoe soles crunched on shards of glass.

Again I had trouble working the key with my left hand. Lars held out his hand for it, but I gave it to Anton instead.

"You hold on to the key, Anton," I said when he tried to return it. He dropped it into his pocket.

We reached Paul's door without exchanging another word.

I walked straight to the kitchen and swallowed four bitter aspirin. I did not expect them to help my headache, but I had to try something. Lars watched from the doorway.

"How much does it hurt?" he asked.

"More than I want it to."

I walked past him into the living room. Paul sat on the sofa with his head in his hands, still wearing only his undershirt and rumpled pants.

I sat next to him. "News?"

"No one has her. No one knows where she is, or no one's telling." He sounded beaten. Stubble lined his cheeks. He had not bothered to shave or dress.

"Why not?" I supposed his desertion of his pregnant wife had earned him enemies.

"I imagine you know," he said. "But I truly think they do not know where she is."

I itched to question the neighbors myself, but they would reveal nothing to me. "Perhaps we could ask Bella to intervene?" And I needed to warn her that someone in her household was an informant.

"You are losing your touch, Hannah," he said.

"Pardon?"

"Bella left over a month ago. She's in New York now. Last I heard she was making gloves in a factory."

"Bella, working in a factory?" It saddened me to think of aristocratic Bella laboring in an American factory. She must have been forced to flee without her assets. She deserved better. "I left a message for her when I was in Poland."

"That was foolish," Paul said. "They've been rounding up her friends."

That confirmed what Lars had told me. My call to Bella had landed us here.

Anton peeked out the window. "May I go out? They are playing football down there."

I peered over his shoulder. A group of children around his age kicked a raggedy brown ball around the back courtyard. My every instinct screamed to keep Anton where I could touch him.

"Please," he begged. "I can't sit around all day."

"I could come and watch you," I began.

"You will cause me trouble." He crossed his arms. "I bet some of their parents know you. They know you're not Jewish."

"You are not Jewish either," I said.

"I've decided on a story to tell." Anton was full of stories. And the telling often ended with problems for me. "I'm a Jewish boy from Switzerland. I was sent here to visit my uncle Paul with my mother. I need a good Jewish boy name."

"Aaron," Paul said woodenly. "Aaron Baumgartner."

I glared at Paul. Lars stifled a smile, probably grateful to see someone else in disfavor.

"I have a cousin named Aaron," Paul said.

"Aaron," Anton said. "That will do. Please?"

His pleading blue eyes softened my heart, as he knew they would. What was the sense in keeping him inside worrying with me? If we were trapped here, who knew how long it would be before he got to play again?

"Be careful," I said. "Stick to your story. And stay in the courtyard. I will be watching from up here."

He was halfway to the front door before I finished my admonitions.

"Your coat!" I called.

He snagged it from the hook by the door and dashed out without a second glance.

"You cannot wrap him up in cotton wool," Lars said.

"Thank you for that bit of wisdom from your vast treasury of child-rearing experience," I snapped. Lars smiled, but I ignored him.

I fetched a chair from the kitchen. I sat it next to the window, where I waited with held breath until Anton appeared in the courtyard below. He ran to join the group and in less than a minute was part of the game. How would I safely get him out of here? I rested my forehead against the glass, hoping that the cool would soothe my head.

"Do you have a picture of your daughter?" Lars asked Paul.

I turned to see. Paul took down a picture of a blond girl with light-colored eyes and handed it to Lars. It was the same as the picture in the locket. "It's only a few months old. We had a devil of a time getting her to be still during the sitting. Ruth is a feisty girl. She knows her own mind."

Lars looked sidelong at me. "That can be a challenge."

Paul stared at the picture. "She's a tough one. Smart, too."

Lars drew the corner of his mouth down slightly. A small change of expression, but it usually meant that something did not make sense. "She does not resemble you. Does she favor her mother?"

I thought of Miriam's dark eyes and hair and the man in the locket. I glanced back out the window without saying anything. Anton ran with the ball across the courtyard.

Paul took the photograph from Lars. "She looks like my father's side of the family. The Aryans."

I winced at the pain and bitterness there. I stood and gestured to my chair. Lars sat in it and stared down at the courtyard while I took his place on the sofa, next to Paul.

Paul stroked the glass with one fingertip, eyes far away. I took his free hand and waited. Lars kept his head pointed toward the window, his back rapier straight. I wished for words to comfort Paul.

"We will find her," I said.

"There's not much point to anything otherwise," Paul said.

"Don't talk like that." I stroked the back of his hand. Lars twitched but did not turn his head. "We have uncovered many things over the years, Paul. We are reporters, remember?"

"I was a reporter," Paul said. "I was many things. But now . . ."

"What now?"

"I don't know." He stared at the floor. "I don't know if I can be anything now."

"You can. You will."

Paul was silent for a long time.

"Thank you for those years after the war," he said finally. "They were good years."

"I like to think I was at least better for you than Maria," I said. "I mean, honestly, whatever possessed you?"

His surprised brown eyes met mine. "The challenge."

"Like Russian roulette," I said.

Paul gave me a ghost of a smile. I viewed it as a victory. He could not slide into despair. I had to do something.

Lars coughed.

"Did Miriam have any enemies?" I asked.

"Not that I know of." Paul's left eyebrow raised a millimeter. He was lying.

"When I spoke to her in Poland, she seemed concerned that she was not safe, and I wondered if that is why she did not take Ruth with her when she left."

"Things happened to Miriam in Poland." Paul ran his hands along his face. "She was terrified about going back."

Lars spoke without turning his head. "And you just left her?"

Paul dropped his head into his hands.

"You are a fine one to talk," I said to Lars.

"I hardly think a privileged life in Switzerland can compare to a stable in Poland," Lars said.

I stood up from the sofa and went to the window. Anton ran back and forth as lightly as if we were in Switzerland and not in the Jewish

quarter of an anti-Semitic country with no identity papers. He seemed to fit in with the group, but I wished that he were with me instead.

"You have clearly not seen my life in Switzerland," I said quietly.

"Haven't I?"

I peeked at Lars out of the corner of my eye. He looked tired and surprisingly handsome. I quickly looked back into the courtyard so that he could not see my expression.

Paul came to stand behind me. "I think I'll fetch Anton."

Relief shot through me. "Thank you, Uncle Paul."

He touched my nose with one finger. "You're welcome."

Seconds later the front door closed.

"Did you pry open the cupboard doors?" I asked Lars.

He looked as if he were about to say something, but changed his mind. "They were like that when I arrived. Both cupboard doors were off their hinges and on the floor. The front door was locked. No sign of forced entry."

"So whoever took Ruth had a key to the front door?" I wondered who had a key. That might narrow it down.

"It seems that way. But it may have been left open. If I were Miriam, I would have left it open."

The boys below stopped playing and lay in a circle in the dirt. I could not tell, but it looked as if they played marbles. Anton's confident head turned from side to side, probably telling them Indian stories. Unlike me, he had always been accepted by his peers.

Lars leaned close to me. The scent of starch rose out of his warm shirt. Obviously the woman who washed them for him did exemplary work. "What will you do now, Spatz?"

I leaned away. "Same as before. Flee Germany as soon as we can." I had no idea how. "If Herr Silbert had been able to provide us papers, we would already be on a train to Switzerland."

"What about your friend?" He lingered over the last word.

"Why is Paul your concern?" I glared at him.

"Because," he said. "I suspect you will look for that little girl and try to fix her father's broken heart."

"And why is that your concern?" I clipped off each word.

He sighed. "We are linked. In the eyes of the Gestapo if nothing else. I intend to get you out of Germany without your implicating me."

"I have yet to betray you." I could not help where the emphasis fell on that sentence. "My decisions are my own. You have no claim on me."

He looked down at Anton's figure far below. "There are those who do."

"You will not tell me how to raise my son, either."

"Spatz, I—"

A woman called down into the courtyard. A boy stood and raced toward the building. Another woman called and another boy left. The others stood and moved as a pack toward the door.

Paul appeared below and beckoned to Anton. Anton waved at the window where he must know I sat vigil before trotting over to Paul.

"I have no intention of implicating you," I said to Lars. "As you well know, I have had many opportunities to do so in the past, and I have not succumbed to the temptation. Although perhaps it was not so great then as it is now."

His lips twitched. "I appreciate the restraint."

"You should." Once again, my tone was more bitter than I would have liked. I clamped my mouth shut.

We stared down at the empty courtyard in stony silence.

"Perhaps you should exercise the same restraint regarding your friend Paul?" Lars said.

"What, exactly, do you mean by that?" My uncasted hand clenched into a fist.

"Only to ask if you are free to make those kinds of decisions." Lars enunciated each word carefully, as he always did when he was pretending that he was not angry.

"My life and my freedom are my own," I said. "You forfeited any right to be involved in either when you chose not to come back from Russia."

"Did I choose that?" he asked.

"You tell me."

Anton saved him from answering by bursting through the front door. "Hello!"

His eyes shone, and his cheeks were flushed from exercise. He looked better than he had since we left Poland. I was glad that I had let him play.

"I have news!" Anton sang out.

He reminded me of my old mentor, Peter Weill. He, too, always had news and announced it just so. Anton had never met him, so he must have heard the expression from me. What else slipped out when I was not thinking?

I looked at Lars. I did not trust him, but he probably knew more about how to find a missing person in Berlin than anyone else. "What news do you have?"

Anton shifted on the balls of his feet. Paul walked into the living room and stood behind him, arms loose by his sides as if he did not know what else to do.

"I asked them about my uncle Paul and my cousin Ruth."

Color drained from Paul's face at the sound of Ruth's name. I ached for him.

"And?" Lars leaned forward like a Bavarian mountain hound on a scent. "What did they say?"

"You should not have done that, Anton," I said at the same time. "We are not here for you to play detective."

Anton smiled his pirate smile. "But I did, and now I know something you don't."

"This is no game." I scolded. "We must be careful here, Anton."

"Aaron," he corrected. "And I was."

"Hannah." Paul raised a hand as if I were a teacher. "Please, could you chastise him after we find out his news about my daughter?"

For Paul's sake, I turned back to Anton. "Well, then, out with it."

"Say *please*." His eyes crinkled at the corners.

I drew in a breath to admonish him. This was no time for games.

"Please," Lars said. "Tell us."

"Reuben said that an Aryan man always used to visit Miriam," Anton said.

"What did the man look like?" Lars asked. "How did they know that he was Aryan?"

Anton grimaced in self-reproach. "I didn't ask."

"Did the man take Ruth?" Paul asked.

"Nobody saw him on the day of the deportations," Anton said. "But still."

"Do you know who the man is?" I asked Paul.

He shook his head.

"Yet he came often." Lars had a challenge in his voice.

Pain lingered in Paul's eyes. He lowered his head.

"Not everyone compiles a dossier on their friends, Lars." I glared at him. "And I rather suspect this man's visits were timed to match Paul's absences."

"Is it really so easy for a woman to betray her husband?" Lars asked sharply.

Paul looked at me, clearly waiting for a response. I did not answer. I had never betrayed any man, including the ones in this room. Not that it had done me any good.

I frowned at Paul and Lars. Neither of them had any right to speak of betrayal.

Anton rocked back on his heels and raised an eyebrow questioningly at me. I forced out a smile.

"I'm hungry," Anton said.

"As am I." I was grateful for the change of subject.

"I would be honored to invite all of you to a meal," Lars put in quickly.

"Because it was such a delightful experience last time." I thought of Gretl. "I think perhaps—"

"We don't have much money," Anton pointed out helpfully. "There's practically no food in the house."

I said, "I will remedy—"

Lars slipped my new coat onto my arms, gently moving it up over my cast. "I think it might be good to leave the apartment for a while. To help us all think. Will you join us, Paul?"

"No, thank you," Paul said.

"Please," Anton wheedled. "Mother won't go without you, and we'll all starve."

Paul looked at me uncertainly.

"Do come," I said. "There is nothing you can do here right now."

Paul glanced around the apartment as if realizing that there was, in fact, little he could do. "Very well."

We waited for Paul to shave and dress. When he rejoined us, he looked more like his old self.

I gathered up my satchel. Paul locked the door and took my arm. We followed Lars and Anton down the stairs.

Anton prattled about horses to Lars, who listened with every appearance of interest. He knew a great deal about the topic. In a long-ago conversation, he had told me that he spent much of his childhood on horseback. Anton, too, was obsessed with riding. He had learned trick riding when we were in Argentina, much to the vexation of his current Swiss riding instructors. They endured his showy maneuvers because he was the top rider in his school, and they needed him to win competitions for them.

"What is he to you?" Paul watched Lars.

"We have a complicated history," I answered. "The present even more so."

"Do you trust him?" he asked quietly. We both knew the dangers of misplaced trust.

"I used to."

We turned at the landing. The doors were closed, and I wondered about those inside. Whom did they trust?

"What happened to the banker?" Paul asked. "I quite liked him."

"Boris married someone else," I said quietly. Unfortunately, Anton had stopped talking, and my words fell into a moment of utter silence.

Lars stopped so abruptly that I ran into him.

I stumbled on my stair. "Pardon me."

Paul steadied me.

Lars looked back, face stricken.

Anton, unheeding, tugged Lars down the stairs. "I'm hungry."

"What was that about?" Paul released my arm.

"I have no idea," I said. "Until a few days ago, I had not seen Lars since the Olympics."

"That does not sound as complicated as you describe," Paul said. "Perhaps you are omitting details?"

Perhaps Lars regretted his earlier assumption that I was betraying my husband with Paul. But why had he assumed that I married Boris?

We arrived at the bottom of the stairs. When Anton opened the front door, the brisk air felt good against my face. Afternoon sunlight fought through high gray clouds. People bustled by, heads down. Anton darted toward the sidewalk.

"Hannah," Paul said before we stepped outside. "You must take Lars's arm before we go onto the street."

Lars turned and stiffly extended me his arm. "Shall we?"

"We shall not," I said. "I am fine on my own, thank you."

"It would not do for you to be seen walking around with a Jew," Paul said.

"Paul!" I said. "You know full well that I do not—"

"Hannah," he said. "I have no desire to be arrested because someone suspects that we are having . . . relations."

I gulped.

"Certainly"—Paul guided my hand to Lars's arm—"not without having the fun of actually doing so."

Lars tucked my gloved hand in his elbow and pivoted toward the door like a machine.

Out on the sidewalk, Anton called, "Come on!"

Lars and I walked out together, Paul a few paces behind. Lars looked straight ahead as if I were not there. We certainly did not make a convincing portrait of a couple out for a stroll.

When Anton, waiting outside, saw that we were on the sidewalk, he raced ahead.

"Go left," Paul called to him.

Anton turned left, and we followed. Paul stepped up and walked on the other side of Lars. We walked past apartment blocks defaced with anti-Semitic graffiti. Here and there, glass glittered on cobblestones, probably knocked out by a Nazi with a rock. I thought of families inside, sleeping, eating, and going about their normal lives

when their windows shattered, reminding them that nowhere was safe.

"Do you have a place in mind?" I asked Paul.

"To the right are the Aryan-only restaurants. As a Jew, I'm no longer allowed to enter them, so we must go left." He spoke matter-of-factly, used to these circumstances.

I thought of the many years that we had spent in Berlin, researching stories and eating out. In those days, we could go anywhere we could afford. "I am sorry, Paul."

"You say that often," he said. "Yet, is it your fault?"

I wondered how much blame was mine to carry. I was a German, an Aryan, and I had not done all I could to stop the Nazis from coming to power. I carried more blame than most. As if he knew what I thought, Lars tightened his grip on my arm.

Anton stopped in front of a bright storefront with a large yellow star painted on the window. Inside stood four empty tables covered with dark green cloths, set for lunch. "How about this one?"

The waitress, in a black dress with a white apron and cap similar to Gretl's, wiped her hands on her apron and watched us suspiciously. Anton looked at Lars, probably thinking of our last restaurant incident.

I looked at him, too. "Does your collection of women extend this far?"

Paul tilted his head to the side. He clearly wanted to know the rest of that story.

"Paul." Lars spoke with an obvious effort. "Is this acceptable?"

"Certainly." Paul led us inside and procured a table near the back. I hung my coat over the back of my chair. When I tucked my gloves into the pocket, I realized that they did not match. Lars must have substituted one of his gloves for my right one so that it would fit over my cast. For someone who claimed to care about getting me out of the country only to save his own skin, he was surprisingly thoughtful.

Lars did not say a single word during the meal. Anton sat to my right and went on about his football game, reliving each play. Paul sat next to him and tried to put in a desultory word or two. My headache

grew as I watched them. I ate chicken soup with matzo balls, happy to have something familiar and well cooked in my stomach. Lars ate mechanically and paid the check without looking at it.

I reached for my coat. Paul rose quickly. "Thank you, Lars. Anton, let's go see if they have candy at the counter."

As Paul stepped by, he shot me a meaningful look before propelling Anton toward the front of the restaurant where a long glass counter displayed colorful candies in trays. I pursed my lips in exasperation. I understood his intent. Busybody.

"Lars," I said quietly. "What is wrong?"

When his dark eyes met mine, a wall had gone up behind them. Nothing came through—not anger, not worry—nothing at all. "Could I prevail upon you to remain at Paul's until tomorrow morning?"

I hesitated. "Why is it suddenly your concern where I sleep?"

"Promise me you won't disappear before then," he said. "Just that. Promise."

"This afternoon you told me I had to leave Paul's." And he had no right to dictate where I slept. I donned my gloves.

"Where would you go?" A muscle jumped under his eye.

"I do not see how it is any of your concern. We discussed this earlier." I picked up my coat.

"Promise." His voice broke. "Please."

"Lars." I put my hand on his arm. "Tell me why."

"Promise you won't disappear."

"Like you did?"

He closed his eyes.

"Lars?"

"Like I did," he whispered. "Yes."

Behind his head, I watched Paul and Anton heading toward us. When they got close enough for Paul to see Lars's face, he took Anton by the shoulder and led him away.

Pain knifed through my head. This was not the calm suggested by Doktor Anonymous. I massaged my temples. "Why do you care now?"

Lars opened his eyes. "Spatz, please. One night. I'll be back to-morrow morning. I will explain then."

"One night," I told him.

Instead of answering, he stood. I rose, and he helped me into my coat. His hand lingered on the small of my back. "Thank you."

Anton came over with a paper bag of candy. "Cat's tongue lico-rice! Would you like one?"

I took a strong black lozenge from his bag. When I glanced back, Lars and Paul were speaking by the door. By the time I reached them, Lars had limped down the street.

"Now what?" Anton asked. "There's an afternoon football game back at Herr Keller's."

"Lars suggested I try the Jewish orphanage," Paul said. "He thought that the neighbors might have taken her there."

"We will come, too," I said.

"I can go on my own," Paul said. "I am quite grown up."

"I would prefer to go with you," I said, remembering his expres-sion last night.

Paul and Anton looked at each other and shrugged. Both knew better than to argue.

Paul used his passport to change some of my Swiss francs for Ger-man marks, since my passport was still not properly stamped. I tucked the bills in my pocketbook and dropped it into my satchel. I felt better with my own money, although it would not last long.

We took the subway to Baruch Auerbach Orphanage, the most likely place for Ruth to have been taken if someone thought her an orphan. Paul carried her framed photograph, her birth certificate, and an expression of hope so fragile, it hurt to look at him.

The orphanage was only two stops on the subway, but the first one had been renamed to Horst-Wessel-Platz to celebrate a Nazi folk hero. I thought of Jewish orphans, many of whose parents had been killed or imprisoned by the Nazi regime, riding through that station every day. Bile rose in my throat. I stared down at my tightly locked hands to conceal my expression.

On the train I prepared a cover story about being a Swiss reporter interested in the deportations to Poland. I had my Adelheid Zinsli press credentials ready in my satchel. Unlike a German orphanage, a Jewish one would be unlikely to check my identity with the Gestapo, so I felt safe using my Adelheid Zinsli identity there.

We climbed out at Senenfelderplatz and walked up Schönhauser Allee to the orphanage. Gently arched windows welcomed light. It looked friendly, but the exposed bricks on the first floor were the same hue as those at the stable in Zbąszyń. A crudely painted yellow star on the front door ensured that no passersby could fail to treat the children with the expected contempt.

Gray trees rose on both sides of the stoop. Bare limbs rattled above our heads. In summer, these trees probably provided leafy green shade, but now their skeletal forms outlined the chill.

Paul took the broad steps to the front door three at a time.

A harried matron opened the door, wiping her square hands on a starched white apron. Her dark eyes skated over Paul and me and settled on Anton.

"We're not taking older boys." Her tightly coiled bun quivered with disapproval.

Anton seized my hand.

"We are not here to drop off a child," I said.

"I'm here to find my daughter." Paul showed her the picture of Ruth. "Her mother is Polish, and during the deportation they were . . . separated."

The matron stepped briskly out of the doorway and gestured for us to enter. "Follow me."

Her round form sped down the corridor, and I hastened to keep up. She stopped at a closed door. A rustling and squeaking sounded behind it. "A moment, please."

She flung the door open. I peered into the dark room. Shapes humped under blankets. They looked asleep, but judging from the sounds of a second before, most of them had just jumped into their squeaky beds.

"There will be no more horseplay," she said sternly. "It is nap time."

"Yes, Frau Goldberg," chorused several young voices.

She closed the door softly and herded us to an office at the end of the hall. We followed, as obedient as the children. She ushered us inside and sat us down.

Not a speck of dust had dared to settle on her gleaming desk. "Tell me about this child."

Paul handed her the picture again. "My wife was deported to Poland a few days ago. She and our daughter were separated, and I thought someone might have brought Ruth here."

"She has been missing for that long?" The matron scowled. "Yet you just now come?"

"I thought that she was with my wife." Paul wrung his hands. "I found out only last night that they were not together."

"How did you find out?" The matron straightened the blotter and lined an old-fashioned inkwell next to it.

He looked at me helplessly, too worried to come up with a good lie.

I held out my hand for the matron to shake. "I am Adelheid Zinsli, a reporter for the *Neue Zürcher Zeitung*. I was recently in Zbąszyń reporting on the plight of the refugees."

"I read your piece." The matron softened and shook my hand. She had a strong, confident grip. "On the young mother in the stable."

"And her curly-haired daughter." I gave her my official Swiss press pass, glad that she had broken the law and read foreign papers. "While I was interviewing refugees, I came across Herr Keller's wife, Miriam. She told me that her husband had been away during the deportations and that their daughter was left behind. So I traveled to Berlin to see for myself."

The matron held my press credentials at arm's length and scanned them. "You came all the way to Berlin for that?"

"Not just for that," I said. "I also intend to write a story on the situation here, about children left behind, the effect of the deportations on those who remained here, and so on." I stopped and looked

at Paul's worried face. "But first I would very much like to see Herr Keller reunited with his daughter."

"How do I know that you are this girl's father and not someone intent on stealing a beautiful little girl?" She looked down her nose at us as if we were kidnappers or worse.

Paul handed her the documentation that he had brought. "She's mine."

I wondered if that was true. And did he know?

"She is just over two years old. She loves to play on the swings and her favorite food is turnips, because I once told her that children didn't like them. She's contrary. And she loves butterflies." He listed the facts desperately, as if their simple accrual would convince the matron.

She pulled a pair of reading glasses from a drawer and read each document thoroughly before handing them back.

"Very well. Let's go see." She unlocked the center desk drawer and took out a giant ring of metal keys. "While the little ones are down for their nap."

We bustled along behind her.

"I can't say that we have your daughter. We have had several children brought in, I'm sorry to say. Between parents being taken to the concentration camps, the deportations, and the suicides, we have more children here than ever before. It's becoming difficult to keep track of them."

Anton clung to my hand. I remembered his fear after I took him in that I would abandon him at an orphanage. "No need to worry," I whispered. "You leave with me."

His grip did not loosen. I stepped close to him.

The matron stopped in front of a light blue door. "This is the ward for girls under five. Please keep your voices down."

We followed her into a darkened room. Two dozen cribs lined the walls on either side. We walked between them, close enough to touch the cribs' slats. To the side of each crib stood a simple oaken wardrobe.

Anton and I stood in the center of the room while Paul and the

matron checked each sleeping girl's face. No Ruth. Paul's shoulders slumped.

When the matron closed the door behind us, she turned to him.

"Are there any more?" he asked. "Any more wards?"

She shook her head. "Not for girls that age."

"Where else might she have been brought?" I asked.

The matron's eyes fixed on Paul. "Nowhere."

He crumpled back against the wall.

"Could you make inquiries?" I asked.

The matron hesitated. "Of course. Do you have a telephone?"

"No," Paul said.

"I will telephone you tomorrow evening," I said.

She patted Paul's back and led him to her office, where she gave him a shot of schnapps. I declined. I should not be drinking with so recent a head injury.

He stared at his shoes while the matron reeled off statistics about the number of children they had taken in because of the deportations. I took notes and asked questions. Paul drank. Anton sat so quietly, I worried for him.

The matron caught my shoulder as we stepped through the front door. Anton and Paul walked forward, but I stayed.

"You realize"—she leaned forward to speak into my ear—"that there are no inquiries I could make?"

I had suspected as much. "Where is the harm if it gives him another day of hope?"

"Eventually he must face the truth." She put her hands on her ample hips. "His daughter is gone."

"Or perhaps we will find her." Paul had to have that hope.

She gave me a pitying look and stepped backwards into the hall.

Paul and Anton stood at the foot of the stairs, illuminated by pale golden light from inside the orphanage. The matron closed the door. Darkness swallowed them.

"Mother?" Anton's voice quavered.

I hurried toward him.

13

I embraced Anton. He hugged me back hard before stepping away.

"I told you that you would leave with me," I said.

Anton lightly punched my shoulder. "I know."

"I need to find a telephone booth," I told Paul. "It will take only a moment."

Paul's haunted eyes glanced once more at the dark front of the orphanage. He did not answer.

I quickly found a telephone booth and left them outside while I called in a story about the Berlin orphans to my Swiss paper. Herr Marceau dutifully took notes.

I already wrote under a pen name, but I could not take even the slightest chance that someone had connected that name to Adelheid Zinsli.

"I need this to come out under a different name," I said. "Until I leave Berlin, it is too dangerous to let anyone reading the paper know I am here."

"You are in Berlin?" His voice rose in astonishment.

"Yes."

Icy silence poured down the line. Herr Marceau was having an affair with a German actress and longed for a posting in Berlin. I knew that he viewed my filing stories from here as a personal affront, but I would not hide the orphans' story to mollify his ego. He said, "I see."

"I have no intention of staying longer than I need to." I glanced through the glass at Paul. He stood with his hands in his pockets, weight on both legs, even though I knew it must hurt him.

"You got another letter today from Berlin," he said. "It was no love note."

"Same author as before?" Nearby, Anton had crossed his arms and leaned against the side of the booth, staying as close to me as he could. And eavesdropping.

"Same as before, except that the author said something about how 'he wrote her and said that he would meet with you that day.' Does that make any sense?"

"No." But I wished that it did.

"Should I fetch the letter?" Herr Marceau asked. "I'm sure you will want to hear it in its entirety. It is quite . . . colorful."

I bet. I had no desire to spend even a second on such foolishness. Paul and Anton needed to get home. "I have to get off the line soon. But tell Herr Knecht that I did not intend to come here."

"So someone coshed you on the head and dragged you across the border?" he sneered.

"After a fashion," I said, "yes. Please, see if Herr Knecht can get me back out."

Astonishment crackled down the line. "You are not joking."

"I wish that I were." I pulled my wool coat tight against the cold. "Get a lawyer on this."

"Why not take the next train home? The paper could send someone else to cover the story." He meant himself, of course, and I would have been happy to give him this one.

"It is not about the stories. I was forced into the country illegally," I said. "And I am not certain they would let me leave again."

He sucked in a long breath. "The Swiss embassy?"

"Find out if Herr Knecht can get assurances that they will help me leave," I said. "And I will be on their doorstep in an hour."

"That sounds very dangerous." He did not believe me.

"I know," I said. "Can you get Herr Knecht?"

He hesitated. "He is not here."

I wondered if he told the truth.

"Are you certain you do not wish to hear the letter?"

"I have to get off the line now," I said. "If it is tapped by the Gestapo, they might be on their way."

"You sound like a spy film."

"I have stumbled into one," I said. "Take care, Herr Marceau."

I broke the connection and herded Paul and Anton into the nearest subway station.

Dark and cold pressed against us as we rode back to the apartment.

I massaged my temples. My head still ached, and I felt more tired than I should. Still, I had managed to stay awake the entire day, which had to be an encouraging sign.

Anton rode next to me, subdued by the trip to the orphanage. He was deeply shaken by what he had seen, aware that might have been his fate had I not taken him in. I wrapped an arm around his shoulder, and he leaned against me.

Paul sat in silence on a different bench. I suspected that he had not expected to find Ruth in the orphanage, but now he had no hope and no idea where to turn. His best source would be the mysterious man whom Anton had discovered, but who might know more about him? Miriam must have had friends, surely. Hopefully friends who had not been deported. Tomorrow we would find them.

We arrived at the apartment building. Paul insisted that Anton and I go in a few minutes before he did, so that no one would think that we were together. He had not been that careful when he had come in with Maria yesterday. Or perhaps he had.

I got ready for bed. Paul had pressed me to use Ruth's bed instead of spending another night on the tired sofa. Anton had already lain down on the blankets I spread for him on the floor next to me. Before I settled in to bed, I donned Sarah's old nightgown and robe and padded out to the living room, where Paul sat on the sofa in darkness. "Paul?"

He raised his head slowly. "Yes?"

"We will start fresh tomorrow. Someone will know this man who visited Miriam. And he might well know where Ruth is."

"That's kind of you to say, Hannah."

Helpless, I stared at him.

"Good night," he said, and I understood his tone of dismissal.

I left him sitting in the dark and returned to Ruth's room, where I stepped carefully over a sleeping Anton, who lay on his back, arms flung out to both sides as if he had to cover as much of the floor as possible. He had kicked off the blanket. I covered him again.

I lay on my side on the little bed and watched his boyish chest rise and fall. I could not imagine life without him, as I suspected that Paul could not imagine life without Ruth. He would not have to. We would find her.

Tomorrow morning, Lars would return from his mysterious errand. He would have some idea of what to do. He had been an effective police detective. He would think of things that we could not. He would help Paul to find Ruth.

Stop that, I told myself. *Do not rely on him. You should know better.*

A knock on the door interrupted my thoughts. Murmurs came from the front hall. Two men, by the sound of it. Paul and Lars, or someone else?

I peered out my door and down the hall. A man in a white coat stood behind the sofa, talking to Paul. Was he the mystery man and was that a scrap of his coat on the cupboard hinge?

I waited until he left before venturing out in my robe. Paul sat alone on the sofa, hands resting on his knees.

"Was it someone with news of Ruth?" I stood next to him.

He stared at his knees. "Yes."

"Where is she?" I asked. "Is she well?"

"She is in a safe place." He sounded defeated rather than relieved. "And she is fine."

My heart lightened. Ruth was well. "Where is she?"

"Somewhere where she is better off than she ever could be with me."

"What nonsense! Who told you that? You are her father."

He turned his hands palm up. "Perhaps she needs to start a new life, with a new identity."

"Paul—"

"What can I provide for her?" His words were angry, but his eyes were sad. "The same misery and death that her mother suffered? That's all I have to offer, Hannah. To her or myself."

"She is your daughter and she loves you. You cannot take away her father so soon after she lost her mother. Whom did you just speak to?"

"She is better off without me." He sank deeper into the sofa. "I wish it weren't true. But it is."

"Who was here?" I put my hands on my hips.

"I will not tell you, Hannah," he said. "So, please, stop asking."

"Then tell me where she is, so we can make certain that she is well." I felt like Paul's mother. I took my hands off my hips and sat next to him instead. The sofa creaked.

"She is my daughter. Not yours." He shifted until his leg was straight out in front of him

"Are you certain that—?"

"Any decisions about her welfare are mine alone. And she is better off without a Jewish father weighing her down. Everyone is." It was rare for Paul to speak with such authority, and I knew I would not be able to dissuade him. Not tonight, anyway.

"I hate to ask this, Paul." I hesitated. "Is Ruth yours?"

His shoulders slumped.

I pulled out the gold locket and removed Ruth's picture to reveal the blond man behind. "Do you know this man? Might he be Miriam's brother? Or a friend?"

"He is not her brother," Paul said. "Or a friend."

"But—"

"Enough, Hannah," he said. "Just . . . enough. Please, let me be. This is difficult enough without your meddling."

I shifted away from him on the sofa. He was correct.

"Don't be angry." He took my casted hand. "It's just all so hopeless."

"Sleep on it, Paul. Things will feel different in the morning."

"What if—?" His voice quavered, but he steadied it. "What if they don't?"

"Then we will see." I sounded brave, but I had no idea what we could do either.

He gathered me into his arms and rested his chin on my head, as he used to twenty years ago. Back then it felt hopeful, but tonight it felt lonely. Eventually, he kissed the top of my head and said, "It's late, my dear."

He disentangled himself and stood, extending a hand down to help me up. "Is your complicated friend Lars coming by tomorrow?"

"He says he is." I took his hand and let him pull me to my feet. "But he is not always reliable."

"Really? He strikes me as a very reliable man indeed, where you are concerned."

"That is exactly what I used to think," I said, "until I was proved wrong."

We walked back to our separate bedrooms.

"Best of luck with him," he said. "Thank you for all you have done for me."

"Of course," I said.

He touched my nose lightly with his fingertip. "Good night."

It sounded more like good-bye than good night. He turned and went into his room, pulling the door closed behind him. I stood uncertainly in the hall, staring at his closed door. I would talk to him again tomorrow, and make him see reason. If he just checked on Ruth once and made sure that she was safely settled, I would let it go.

I crept past Anton and settled into my child's sized bed. My head ached for a long time before I drifted off to sleep.

I awoke to the sound of a clatter, as if something had dropped to the floor. My heart raced. I lay still, listening. Silence shrouded the apartment.

The sound might have come from upstairs or outside, but I could not shake a feeling of dread. I sat up and listened. Nothing. I got quickly out of bed, driven by a sense of urgency I did not understand.

The streetlamp's dim light provided enough illumination for me to see Anton, still sound asleep. I dropped a hand to his warm head, stepped around him, and padded to the door, wood cold under my bare feet.

I crept through the living room, the bathroom, the kitchen, and the hall, searching for an intruder. All cloaked in late-night darkness, but empty. I paused in front of Paul's door. I thought of knocking, but decided instead to glance in without waking him.

I eased the door open. Hinges squeaked, and I froze. Paul's curtains stood open to the streetlamps, his room brighter than ours. His form lay at an angle under the quilt, taking up more than half the mattress. Years before, I had chided him about using more than his fair share of the bed.

One pale hand dangled off the mattress almost to the floor. Nothing looked out of place, but a compulsion rose up my spine. I pushed the door open and stepped into the room.

The floor was empty except for a small thin shape, centimeters below Paul's fingers. It rested in a pool of liquid. Had he spilled water?

I stepped closer. The familiar smell of blood filled my nostrils. It dripped from the tips of his fingers, landing on the small object. A straight razor. Had that caused the clattering that woke me? I wished I had gotten right out of bed and come straight here, before he'd had time to lose so much blood. Now that I looked for it, blood was everywhere. It stained the bedspread and pooled on the floor. Sadness unfolded in me like a giant bird.

I brushed it away and dashed to the bed. When I rolled him over, his eyelashes fluttered against his white skin. I felt for his pulse. Weak and thready.

"Paul," I said softly so as not to wake Anton. He did not move. I dropped to my knees next to the bed. How could he leave Ruth? Leave me?

I fumbled for a wrist, but the cast made me clumsy. His right arm seemed uninjured, but blood slicked the left. I lifted his wounded arm high above his heart and pressed hard against his wrist with my left hand.

I was slow, and every second counted. I cursed the Gestapo man who broke my arm.

Paul moaned and tried to pull his arm back down.

"Don't you dare fight me." I sounded harsh and angry, but I did not care. I smashed his arm against the wall and pressed on his wrist. He had missed the artery, but opened a large vein. He struggled weakly.

I tucked my chin to see better. A slit ran from his elbow to his wrist. I winced at the determination that the cut revealed. *Oh, Paul,* I thought. *Paul.*

I stared at the wound, trying to think as a nurse. He did not need stitches, I thought or hoped. I had no idea how I could get them into him if he did. He twisted his wounded arm. I pressed it harder against the wall with my good hand.

"Stay still," I said through gritted teeth. He collapsed, either because he understood or because he was too weak to fight.

With my casted hand, I yanked the frayed pillowcase off Miriam's pillow. I bit down on the edge and tore off a strip, the ripping sound loud in the quiet room. Even though my casted arm seared each time, I tore off another and another, dropping them awkwardly on the quilt and cursing my cast. Through it all, he barely stirred.

When the pillowcase lay in shreds, I bound up his arm. I worked from elbow to wrist. I had only one strong hand, so I had to tie the knots with my left hand and my teeth. Frau Doktor Spiegel would have marked me down on neatness, but by the time I finished, the bandage was secure.

When his arm was covered and the bleeding stopped, I wiped my hands on my nightdress, leaving streaks down the front. Both my hands were still sticky with blood. It had soaked into my nightgown at the knees when I knelt next to him. How much blood had he lost?

I felt for his pulse in his good arm. His heart beat steady and stronger than before. I let out a breath of relief, suddenly aware of the room's temperature, and that I had left Sarah's robe hanging next to my bed. Just as well, since it, too, would have been soaked in blood now. My headache returned full force, and I slid down to the floor by the bed. The wood felt cold on the backs of my legs.

He clutched my hand. "Hannah?"

"Here, Paul." The room whirled. Nausea grew in my stomach. I took a deep shuddering breath. I had to hold it together, for him.

"Why stop me?" he whispered.

"I am a nurse." I swallowed bile. "I could not help myself."

"Damn," he said. "Damn. Damn. Damn."

"We should get you to a doctor." Although I did not know if either of us could stand.

"Please," he said. "Let me stay here. Just don't leave me alone."

"I won't." I took his good hand and leaned my back against the side of his bed. It felt better to have something propping me up.

He stirred.

"Hush," I said, as if he were Anton, newly wakened from a nightmare. "Tomorrow."

He quieted.

Soon I would get up and call Frau Doktor Spiegel. I closed my eyes for a moment to rest. Only a moment.

14

Light seared my sleeping eyelids. I tried to open them, but they were too heavy. Was my injury to blame? A flame of panic ignited at the back of my skull, too small to help me.

"My god." A familiar voice.

Hands lifted me. I struggled through the pain in my head. Someone said the word *no* over and over, a litany.

Arms tightened around me, and the sound stopped.

"Not now," he whispered. "Please not now."

Arms crushed me. I conquered the pain in my head and pushed through to wakefulness. "Let me go!"

The arms did not release. Whoever held me rocked us both from side to side. Where was I? Why was I so cold?

"Can't breathe," I choked out.

The arms loosened. A fingertip trailed down my cheek. I wrenched open my eyelids. Lars had arrived and turned on the overhead light. He held me tightly.

"Forgive me," he said. "Please."

I focused on his familiar dark eyes, but a stranger looked back. As one had during my last visit, in 1936. Blood had triggered an episode in him, then. My blood. "Lars?"

He stared as if he truly could not believe that I spoke. He still did

not recognize me. He was having another episode. I yanked my arms free and put my filthy hands on his warm cheeks. "Lars?"

Something stirred behind his eyes. Recognition? I held his face so that he could not look away. "Come back to me."

He blinked, but his expression did not change. I had not reached him. He fought his own demons, either the ones he had created as an interrogator for the SS or others I did not know.

"It's me, Hannah." I could barely move in his grip. I shivered, from cold and from fear.

Probably to warm me, he shifted me closer to his chest, hiking me into his lap. I felt him harden under my leg. Recognition dawned in his eyes. "Spatz?"

So that part remembered me best. Any other time, it would have been funny. I did not know whether to be offended or flattered. "Lars?"

His eyes cleared. He was back.

"Where?" He felt my head, my arms, my shoulders. "Where are you hurt?"

I put my hands over his, stopping his exploring. His eyes spoke a question. He was still there.

"I am not hurt." Or at least nothing new.

He pulled his hands free and went back to checking me. "But you're covered in blood. Where are you hurt, Spatz?"

"Not mine." I struggled to sit up. "Paul's."

Expressions chased across his face, ending with relief. He sagged against the side of Paul's bed. "Thank god." He kissed the top of my head, my forehead, my cheeks.

I leaned back before he could get to my lips.

He gently released his hold on me.

"What are you doing here?" I rested my palm on Paul's chest. He slept deeply. I took his pulse. Strong. He would make it through.

"I came back to . . ." Lars's gaze traveled around the room, noticing blood on the walls and dried in blotches on the floor. "What happened here?"

He noticed the razor. I had not bothered to move it. He picked it up. "I see."

"I need to clean up," I said.

He eased me off his lap and stood. Light-headed, I closed my eyes and leaned back against Paul's bed.

Lars put a hand down and helped me to my feet. I swayed.

"Your head?" he asked.

"Hurts. Dizzy." I read alarm in his eyes. "Not like right after."

His eyes said that he did not believe me, but at least his mouth stayed silent.

I took an unsteady step to the door. "I must wash up."

He walked next to me, opened the bathroom door, and watched while I sat on the vanity bench in front of the sink. When he clicked on the light, I stared into the mirror, shocked. Blood smeared my cheek. Blood crusted on my hands and cast. Blood streaked the front of my nightdress. No wonder he had thought me injured or worse.

He ran hot water into the sink and wet the washcloth. I watched him in the mirror as he stroked it gently across my face. His expression said he expected me to stop him. I touched his hand. "I can do the rest."

He bowed slightly, picked up another washcloth, and left the bathroom. I listened to his steps approaching Paul's room before I closed the bathroom door. I took another four headache tablets, hoping they might temper the pain.

I studied my bloodstained hands. Paul's blood. It was caked in my knuckles and under my nails. If I had gotten to him much later, he would not have survived. Paul, gone.

I savagely scrubbed my hands clean and pulled the nightdress over my head. I stared at the bloodstains. I shivered, but I had nothing else to put on.

As if on cue, Lars rapped on the door. "I have your robe."

I opened the door a slit, and he handed it through. "Thank you."

I closed Sarah's too-short robe tight around me. At least it was warm.

Although chilled through from sitting on the floor and from washing up, I lingered in the bathroom. I did not want to face Lars. He moved quietly around the living room, and I wondered what he was doing.

Eventually, Lars called softly. "Spatz?"

I stumbled out of the bathroom into the living room.

He led me to the white-tiled stove that Paul and Miriam used to heat the apartment. I touched the smooth tiles, warm under my icy fingertips, glad that he had built a fire in it. He helped me into one of the chairs drawn up close to the stove, wrapped a warmed blanket around me, and tucked it under my feet. I took a cup of hot tea from his hand, and he sat in the other chair, very close. "I made it while you were washing up."

I wrapped my cold hands around the warm cup. "Would I frighten Anton if he saw me now?"

Lars shook his head, eyes still worried. He handed me headache tablets, and I swallowed another two with a long sip of tea.

"I should sit with Paul, in case he wakes and tries to do himself harm again." Warmth soaked into me. I felt drowsy.

"I tied him to his bed," he said. "It seemed the best way for all of us to get some sleep."

"I thought you did not have the heart to tie someone down. Or so you told me."

He smiled with half his mouth. "I said I didn't have the heart to tie *you* down. I have no such qualms about Paul."

"Poor Paul," I said.

"And I would much rather climb into your bed than his."

I blushed and looked at the steaming tea. "I had better clean Paul's room before Anton sees it."

"I already did," Lars said. "As best as I could in the overhead light. You just sit."

I set down the tea and settled into my soft blankets, grateful that I had nothing else to do. "Thank you, Lars."

He took my hand. "How do you feel?"

"Tired," I said. "But my head feels much better."

He squeezed my hand. "I am relieved to hear that."

"Thank you," I said again.

Fingers lingering on my temple, he tucked a strand of hair behind my ear. "My pleasure. More than you know."

I grazed my fingertips down the line he had traced across my temple. I should get up and take myself to bed. I closed my eyes. I drifted off to sleep wondering what he was doing in Paul's apartment, in Paul's bedroom, in the middle of the night. Why had he not waited until morning to come around?

I awoke in Ruth's bed. Anton's blanket lay neatly folded on the floor. I touched my temple. For the first time since Poland, my head did not hurt. I lay there, savoring the absence of pain.

But I could not lie in bed forever. Judging by the light, it was late morning. I had slept long and deeply. I put on a dress, made my bed, and headed for the living room.

On the way, I peeked into Paul's empty room. Lars had cleaned away every trace of last night's disaster so thoroughly that I wondered if I had dreamed it. My glance fell on my cast. Blotches of blood stained its surface. No dream, then. Where was Paul? My heart beat faster.

In the living room, Lars and Anton sat on the sofa building a kite of brown paper and sticks. Lars had rolled up his shirtsleeves.

"Good morning!" called Anton. "Lars and I went shopping already. Your breakfast is laid out in the kitchen."

Lars looked up from the kite. He was tying a knot with his teeth, while he held the kite's ribs with both hands. He looked as carefree as Anton. My heart somersaulted in my chest. *No,* I told myself sternly, as if I spoke to a disobedient child. My feelings for Lars did not matter. Only my actions counted, and I had best mind them.

Lars finished the knot and handed the kite to Anton. "Good morning, Spatz. You look better than you have for days."

"As do you." He was shaved and showered and looked as if he'd

had a good night's sleep, although he had to have slept less than I. "Where is Paul?"

"Kitchen," Lars said. "I rebandaged his arm."

"You are a full-service man."

He gave me a wicked grin. "Not all my services have been fully utilized."

In spite of myself, I smiled.

"But," he said, "it's early yet."

I shook my head at him and walked into the kitchen. My smile faded when I saw Paul. He hunched over the table, deathly pale, clutching a teacup with his right hand. Lars had done a neat job with the bandages, but I itched to take them off and see if Paul needed stitches. I did not think so last night, but it had been dark, and I had been too concerned with stopping the blood flow to worry about long-term healing. "How are you?"

Paul raised sunken eyes to me and grimaced.

I helped myself to a roll, drizzled it with honey, and poured a cup of tea. Lars and Anton talked in the living room about the best ways and places to fly a kite.

"Do you intend to try that again?" I asked Paul.

His lips thinned. "I think I'll take your friend Lars up on his offer instead."

I choked on a crumb and coughed. "What offer?"

"He said that you were badly injured a few days ago, that he will not let me make you another one of my casualties, and if I had any more drama I needed to exorcise, he would happily put me out of my misery somewhere quiet so you wouldn't be disturbed."

I stared at him openmouthed. I would have a word with Lars. He had no right to speak so to Paul. I started to stand.

"He was correct to be angry." Paul put his hand on my arm. I stopped. "I did not know that you were so ill. Are you all right?"

"I am fine." I sat. "I am more worried about you. I apologize for Lars—"

"I don't know your complicated history with him," he said. "But I'm starting to like him."

I grimaced. "It is not his right to tell you what you can or cannot do in your own home. With your own life."

"But you had the right to stop me from doing what I wanted with my own life?" He took a sip of tea.

"That was—"

"Different?" he interrupted. "Because you did it?"

"I am not going to apologize for trying to save your life," I snapped.

"Perhaps you should not make Lars apologize for trying to save yours." He splashed more tea into his cup, as if this ended the discussion.

I swallowed my retort. I slept in for a few hours, and suddenly everyone had befriended Lars.

I had to admit that he had taken good care of me last night, that he must have spent a great deal of time cleaning up blood in Paul's room, that breakfast was lovely, and that he had entertained Anton so that I could sleep in. If I were not careful, I would end up friends with him as well. Fräulein Ivona's red mouth appeared in my mind, and I took a deep breath. I remembered too well where befriending Lars led. I would not let him betray me again.

I tasted my tea: orange pekoe, my favorite. Lars again.

"Paul," I said finally. "What will you do?"

He picked at his bandage. "I don't know."

"You cannot try to take your own life again." I moved his fingers off the bandage before he unraveled it. He let me.

"You won't allow it?" He dropped his injured hand in his lap.

My teacup clanked into its saucer. "Think about Ruth. She needs a father more than ever."

"Perhaps she has a better one." His brown eyes held so much pain, it hurt to look at him.

"What does that mean?" I asked. "Who?"

"Enough, Hannah. As I said last night, I'm not going to explain myself to you." He sat up straighter. "I am no good to her here."

"Then leave Germany," I said. "Take her out. I know a man who might get you false papers—"

"Where would I go?"

"New York," I said. "Sarah would take you in. Herr Klein has a spare room."

Herr Klein was an ancient Jewish jeweler who had fled Berlin in 1931. He and Paul had been friends. He would help Paul, and Ruth, too.

Paul put his bandaged hand gently over mine. "Always working to solve the world's problems, aren't you?"

"I did not spend years of my life dragging you back after the War to lose you now, Paul."

He smiled, not a real smile, but something. "So I owe it to you?"

"You owe it to Ruth. And yourself. And some of it, yes, to me."

He squeezed my hand. "We'll see."

"See what?"

"What's next." He studied our joined hands.

"You have to see that she is well settled," I said. Hopefully, when he saw her, he would change his mind. "At least that."

"Do I?"

"Who once told me that one cannot make a decision without all the facts?" I said. He had told me that.

He smiled reflexively. "Some fool or other, I imagine."

"No fool like an old fool." I put my hand on top of his. "Let's find out the facts, Paul. Then you can make your decision."

"I'll go see," he said. "Happy?"

He meant it. I smiled with relief. "Yes."

"But alone." He took his hand back and stroked his bandaged arm. "I don't want either of us to do anything that might endanger Ruth in her current situation."

"What could we—?"

"Leave it." He sounded worried. "Please, Hannah. Trust me?"

I wanted to ask how I could trust him after last night, but when I looked into his eyes, all I could do was nod. I could not add to his burden.

I put away the breakfast things, hoping that the familiar domestic tasks would bring me peace. But they did not. Paul seemed safe for today, but tomorrow, I could not see. Then again, were any of us safe? Could I find someone to create false papers for all of us, including Paul and Ruth?

Herr Silbert was in prison. Or was he? I had only the shopkeeper's word. I looked at the sun outside. In a few hours, a good friend and police officer would be having his lunchtime cigar. I could catch up with him and ask him to check on Herr Silbert's whereabouts. I only hoped that this meeting would go better than my last meeting with the police officer, when he and his wife had expressed their loyalty to the Nazi government and summarily dismissed me after I had choked down a piece of strudel.

I ran water in the sink. Paul stood next to me. He picked up a plate. I took it out of his hand. "You cannot wash with your wounded arm."

"But you can?" he asked tiredly.

"We have two arms between us," I said.

"Like a three-legged race." He stepped closer and wrapped his wounded arm around my shoulder. "I have a right, you have a left."

I held a plate while he washed it and rinsed it, then passed it to him to place on the drainboard.

Behind us, Lars cleared his throat. Paul lifted his arm off my shoulder. I turned to face Lars, who gave me an icy look. I glanced up at Paul. Lars, with his different young girlfriend every week, dared to be jealous of my friendship with Paul? I stayed close to Paul's side.

"May we go to the park to fly my new kite?" Anton popped out from behind Lars. Perhaps not such a bad idea. The best concealment was pretending to be a normal German family doing normal family activities. Hiding in an apartment, particularly in the Jewish quarter, was likely to invite questions from the neighbors. Playing in the park was not.

But everything in Nazi Germany had risks.

I sighed. I might as well let Anton have a fun afternoon. I had a few hours to spare before I hoped to meet my friend with his lunch-time cigar and find out more about Herr Silbert.

"It will do us all good to get out into the fresh air." Lars nodded toward Anton, but he meant Paul.

"That sounds delightful." I said with forced enthusiasm.

Lars looked at Paul and me, still standing close together. He raised his teacup toward me as if in a toast. So, he thought I was interested in Paul now. Let him. I tilted my head to show that I acknowledged Lars's gesture.

"The paste is dry on the kite," Anton said. "See?"

He turned to show me. The kite's wooden rib jostled Lars's arm. Tea spilled down the front of Lars's white shirt.

He pulled the shirt away from his undershirt, but both were already soaked through.

"I'm sorry," Anton said.

"It serves to reinforce my point that indoors is no place for a kite." Lars unbuttoned his shirt. He slipped it off and hung it over his arm. "I'll go wash up."

He had always looked good in an undershirt. I turned back to the breakfast things so that he would not catch me looking.

"I have something you can borrow," Paul said.

But before he could fetch it, someone knocked on the front door.

"I'll get the door," Paul said. "Into my room. All three of you."

15

Anton, Lars, and I slunk down the hall to Paul's bedroom. My heart sped up when I stepped across the threshold. The clean bedspread, the light through the curtains. Everything felt warm and friendly, as if last night had never happened.

Lars rested his palm on my lower back, as if to keep me in balance, and I found myself leaning against it. I stood up straight. What did he feel in this room? What had he been thinking as he held me on the floor last night, soaked in blood? To whom did he think he apologized? It had not been to me; of that I was certain.

A little boy's voice piped up from the front door.

"Reuben." Anton stepped toward Paul's door. "May I go talk to him?"

"But stay in the apartment," I said.

Lars pulled his undershirt over his head and wiped the back of the shirt across his chest, which looked every bit as muscular as I remembered. He dropped the soiled undershirt on Paul's bed. Last night I had rested against the side of that bed in Lars's arms. I tried hard not to think about how much I wanted to be there again.

Instead, I stepped to Paul's wardrobe and opened the door one-handed. Shirts and undershirts were stacked neatly on the top shelf, where he had always kept them. I took out a white shirt and an undershirt and turned to give them to Lars.

He stood by the window with his back to me, looking at the street below.

Walking over with the shirts, I noticed his back. In 1936, it had a few shrapnel scars, but a new story of pain was inscribed on his skin now. Angry pink lines of scar tissue crisscrossed his back.

He caught my expression reflected in the window. "Quite a mess, isn't it?"

I offered him Paul's undershirt. "How?"

"Russian prison." The undershirt muffled his words as it went over his head. "About a week after we parted. Not a hospitable lot, I'm afraid."

I gasped.

He gently tilted my chin up so I had to look into his eyes. "You didn't think I was avoiding you on purpose, did you?"

Shame burned in my cheeks. I had thought just that. "Why were you arrested?"

"A charge of espionage," he said. "Carelessness."

If I had not uncovered the evidence that had sent him to Russia, he would never have been there to be arrested. "Lars—"

"Don't take responsibility for that." He released my chin and put on Paul's shirt. "You have enough already."

"How did you get out?"

"The prison decided to withdraw its hospitality in January." He quickly buttoned the front of the shirt. Paul was taller than he, so the shirt hung on him as if he were a boy dressing in his father's clothing. It looked strangely endearing. I folded one of his cuffs back, conscious of how close my fingers were to the soft skin of his wrist. He drew my hand up toward his lips.

Anton spoke from the doorway. "January was ten months ago."

I took my hand off his shirt and stepped back from Lars. Ten months was a long time. What had he been doing?

"You certainly did not teach him to hold his tongue," Lars said.

"I do not excel at that myself, so I find it difficult to teach." I rubbed my fingers across the top of the hand that he had almost kissed.

Lars tucked in the shirt. "I can imagine."

I turned to Anton. "Do not be impertinent, Anton."

Anton crossed his arms.

"What, exactly, have I done to make you both so angry with me?" Lars asked.

He had left me waiting in Switzerland, thinking him dead, and he wondered why I might be angry? My head started throbbing, and I took a shaky breath.

"One of these days," Lars said, "perhaps we can have a conversation when you have no injury to hide behind."

"Doubtful." I thought back to conversations we had after I had been shot, had a broken rib, and had been poisoned by toxic gas. "I so often come to harm around you."

"Due to your efforts and in spite of mine." He swept past me into the hall.

"What did Reuben want?" I folded Lars's tea-stained things.

"To play marbles," Anton said. "May I?"

"We are just about to leave," I said. "How about you two play in the stairwell? I will fetch you on my way out."

Anton ran back toward the living room. Still thinking about Lars in prison, I followed more slowly.

Lars and Anton chattered in the living room about the kite.

"Where is Paul?" I asked.

"He left to borrow the neighbor's telephone," Lars said. "He said that he had an important call to make."

"We must wait for him," I said.

"But can I go play with Reuben right now?" Anton asked.

"Go," I said. "Do not leave the building."

I stood awkwardly next to Lars. I wanted to apologize for implying that he caused the trouble in my life, but the words stuck in my throat.

He watched me for a long moment. "Spatz—"

Paul opened the front door and strode into the living room, his face relaxed.

Lars's brow furrowed in exasperation. I knew how he felt. But I also felt afraid to hear what else he might say.

"How did your call go?" I asked Paul.

"Good news," he said. "I have an appointment in an hour."

"With whom?" I asked.

"Someone," he said. "That's all you're getting, Miss Journalist."

"Come with us to the park," I said. "If only for a little while."

"It is on my way," Paul said. "I think that is a capital idea."

From the top of the doorless cupboard that Ruth had been hiding in, Lars took a gray wool blanket. He slung it over his arm.

"We are ready to go now," Lars said. "Right, Spatz?"

Paul helped me into my coat. As he slipped it over my shoulders, he whispered in my ear. "What happened while I was gone? You look as if you've seen a ghost."

I shook my head. The question was, what had happened to Lars in prison? More important, what had happened since his release?

We trooped downstairs. Lars several steps ahead, Paul and I lagging behind.

"I'll go with you to the park." Paul said quietly, probably to keep Lars from overhearing. "Because I think you and Lars might need time with someone else minding Anton. But I can stay only a few minutes before I go see about Ruth."

I squeezed his arm. "You can leave now. Lars and I can sort things out."

He raised one eyebrow. "I have a little time."

Lars slowed, but he did not turn around.

"Please," Paul said. "Let me do this for you."

I looked up into his eyes, trying to decide whether he needed to gather his courage, or perhaps he was correct that Lars and I would not manage to sort things out with Anton around. Or both. "If you wish."

Anton and Reuben started guiltily when they saw us. What were they up to?

Lars took my arm before we stepped into the street. To have a

Jewish friend in Germany was shameful, but not illegal. An Aryan with a Jewish lover, however, was breaking the law, and both partners could be sent to a concentration camp. Any of Paul's neighbors might turn him in. Paul fell back to walk with Anton. Dark clouds glowered overhead.

We had gone only a few steps when Anton said, "I have more news."

I turned around in time to see Paul's shoulders raise. Anton looked at him worriedly. We all stopped walking. Luckily the sidewalks in the Jewish quarter were deserted.

"Out with it," I commanded.

"Reuben said that he did see the man who visited Miriam on the day of the deportations." Anton rushed through his words. "Reuben saw him come after everyone else left."

"Did he take her?" Lars asked. "Or any kind of bundle at all?"

I winced, not wanting to think about that.

"Reuben didn't see," Anton said. "But he might have."

"What else did you find out?" Lars asked. "Any new details?"

"This time I asked what he looked like," Anton said proudly. He was learning to be a detective. "He was tall and very thin. Reuben said he was a doctor. He had blond hair and round glasses and a long white coat." He looked at me meaningfully.

I thought of the scrap of white cloth that had been caught on the cupboard hinges. It could have belonged to a doctor's coat. And what of the mysterious visitor in the white coat the night before?

"Reuben also said—" Anton shifted his feet. He gulped and kept going. "—that the doctor asked to buy a baby once from his mother—"

"I know about the doctor," Paul interrupted. "He doesn't have her."

"Really?" I asked him. "Perhaps he and Miriam—"

"She is my daughter," Paul said, "not yours. And, yes, I am certain."

He brushed past us and trotted up the sidewalk.

Anton hurried to catch him. Paul's reaction was another mystery

to solve. But first I had some questions for Lars. He took my arm, and we followed the others.

A woman hurried out of a kosher butcher shop with a packet wrapped in white paper. Two small children hung on her skirt. She kept her eyes low and stepped into the street to pass us.

Lars gripped my arm.

"It is because you look like a policeman," I said.

"I do not." He pursed his lips in irritation.

I studied his straight posture and his low fedora. "I see."

We walked a few steps in silence.

"Why were you at Paul's apartment in the middle of the night?" I asked Lars.

He patted my hand. "I had an errand to run. I came back when I completed it."

I hated it when he patted my hand, and he knew it. "What errand?"

"The second we have privacy, Spatz, I shall reveal all." He raised his eyebrows dramatically.

"Reveal all?" I asked. "What about public decency laws?"

"I shall exercise what restraint I can." He leaned close to my ear. "Which isn't always much."

I held my tongue. We caught up with Paul and Anton. Paul gave me an apologetic smile for walking off. I smiled back.

Shop after shop sported the same sign in their front windows: JEWS ARE NOT WELCOME HERE. Crudely painted yellow stars adorned a few buildings. I could not accept that this was my Berlin. Even though I now lived in Switzerland, I considered Berlin my home, had always treasured a hope that the Nazis were wrong about their Thousand-Year Reich, and that I would return someday for good. But there seemed no way to undo this.

Paul caught my eye. "You can become accustomed to it."

"I hope not," I said.

"How can you get used to it?" asked Anton. "It's wrong."

"You do it because you have no choice," Paul said. "I've done

nothing but try to emigrate since 1935. I can't get out. They canceled all the passports of German Jews in October, so I can't even take a trip and fail to come back."

Anton looked at me, as if he knew that he should not be listening.

Paul kept talking. "I have no relatives outside of Germany to sponsor me. And my job skills are useless abroad. Newspaper writing? In German?"

"What will you do?" Anton asked. I wondered what we would do and how we would get out ourselves.

"Get to Palestine," Paul said. "However I can."

I took a step toward him, but he sidestepped away. "You don't want to be seen as having any kind of relationship with a Jewish man, Hannah. Anything sets tongues to wagging."

As if to agree with him, Lars kissed the top of my head. I glared at him. Out of the corner of my eye, I saw Paul smile.

"There's the park!" Anton pointed ahead of us at a long stretch of dead brown grass surrounded on all sides by tall apartment buildings. On the edges, bare trees lifted heavy limbs up to the steely sky as if they never expected spring to return. Wind blew my hair across my cheek. I shivered. If nothing else, it was enough wind to get the kite aloft.

Anton shifted the kite to his other hand and tugged on Paul. "Let's go! You, too, Lars!"

"I think I will stay here and keep an eye on your mother," Lars said.

Paul and Anton headed farther into the park.

Lars spread a gray woolen blanket on dead grass and patted it. I sat, but left a wide stripe of space between us, trying not to think about the gray wool blanket we had spent so much time under in 1936. This might be the same blanket. I blushed.

"How are you feeling today?" Lars asked. "Is your head better?"

"I am not interested in small talk." I tucked my hair behind my ears. "I believe this counts as privacy. Tell me why you came to Paul's apartment so late?"

"You do seem back to your old self." He lay on his back on the blanket and laced his fingers behind his head. He would feed me his story at his own pace. "It took me some time to complete my errand, and I came as soon as I finished it. I came in the middle of the night because I wasn't entirely certain that you would be at Paul's if I waited till morning."

I turned to face him so that I could watch his expression, careful to maintain space between us. "And? What were you doing?"

He studied my face long enough to make me uncomfortable before answering. "The *kommissar* acquired another lorry last night." He smiled impishly. "With a bit of skill."

"Herr Kommissar is a felon at heart."

"I have many things in my heart, Spatz." His eyes turned serious. "What about you?"

For years, my heart had caused me nothing but pain. Instead of answering, I watched Anton sprint across the brown grass with his kite.

"I built the compartment in the first lorry," Lars said finally. "I know a warehouse where I can work undisturbed by official questions to build a compartment in this one. When I'm done, I can smuggle you and Anton into Switzerland."

I let out a sigh of relief. "Thank you."

"I love that expression on your face," he said. "Relaxed. I haven't seen enough of it lately."

"How long will it take to build the compartment?"

"A few days," he said. "I can work only at night, when the shop is closed."

I studied him. "Why are you doing this?"

"Three reasons." He rolled onto his side, closing the space between us. I stiffened, but stayed put anyway.

He propped his head on one hand and lifted the thumb of his other hand up to tick off his first reason. I stifled a smile at the familiar gesture. "One, if you are caught, things would go badly for me."

"Self-interest?" I did not believe it. His Lars Lang identity was

already useless, and nothing I said would change that. His smartest course of action was to leave Germany himself as Lars Schmidt immediately, without waiting to build a compartment in the lorry.

"Something like it." He extended his index finger. "Two, I landed you in this mess by not turning straight around and driving to Poland after we killed the Gestapo men."

I winced at the bald words. But he spoke the truth. We had killed them. I had killed one myself. I swallowed. "Why did you press on to Berlin?"

"Because I thought you might not live through the trip back to Poland."

"That would have been an easy solution to problem one." I pointed to his thumb.

"Simple," he said. "Not easy."

I could not meet his eyes. Anton had the kite in the air now and ran with it. Paul limped a few steps, then stopped. His leg clearly pained him.

"Spatz?"

I did not know what to say to his last words. "I believe you said you had three reasons."

Lars drew in a shaky breath. I turned my full attention to him. This was the real reason. My heart sped up.

"And third, and probably most important . . ."

"Lars?" I prompted.

"I've spent the last six months trying to convince myself that I don't." He rolled and unrolled the edge of the blanket.

"Six months?" I asked.

Lars raised his head and met my eyes. "When I saw you in Poznań, I realized that I do. I . . ."

"Do what?"

"I love you."

I stopped breathing. I should have a reaction to his words, but I felt numb, as if I waited for my emotions to catch up. I had never stopped loving him, but that did not mean that I was ready to fall

into his arms and forgive him for everything he had done, or not done, in the ten months since his release from prison.

He looked terrified, which was how I felt. "Spatz? Do you still—?"

"What happened six months ago?"

Before he could answer, across the field, Anton cried out. I jumped to my feet. I sprinted across dusty grass and around an obstacle course of molehills. In the mostly empty park, no one else seemed to notice that Anton scuffled with three boys in a tangle of arms and legs. Two were his size, one larger. Halfway across the field, Paul gazed up at the kite now caught in a tree. He turned slowly.

Behind me I heard Lars and Paul running, too, but I outdistanced them easily.

I grabbed the tallest boy's bony arm as he drew back his fist to strike Anton and yanked him to his feet. His friends stood, too. Two were taller than I, one only slightly smaller. All three were flushed pink with exertion or anger. None lowered their fists. Anton scrambled up and held his fists up, too.

I gulped and raised both hands, palm out. "Stop this at once."

In the dirt at their feet, a fourth boy of six or seven curled in a sobbing ball.

Paul and Lars arrived and waded in, and the boys dropped their fists.

"I am a police *kommissar*," Lars said sternly. "You will tell me what this is about."

Blood ran out of Anton's nose and dripped onto his shirt. I fished a handkerchief from my pocket and handed it to him. I longed to sweep him up in my arms, but knew that he would not thank me for it.

"That boy didn't want to prove he was no Jew pig." The tallest boy pointed scornfully at the little boy, whom I now saw had no pants. The older boys must have removed them to see if he was circumcised. I looked at Paul. He held one of the larger boys by the collar and looked unsurprised by the revelation.

Lars snatched a pair of shorts from the second tallest boy's hand and dropped them on the little one.

I knelt beside him. "Are you all right?"

He unrolled and grabbed his shorts. He slid both legs in, yanked them up, and ran. No one tried to stop him.

"Was he Jewish?" Lars asked.

"No." The tallest boy kicked a dirt clod near where the little boy had cowered. "That would have been the end of it, if this kid hadn't stuck his long nose in."

Anton glared at him. A bruise darkened his cheekbone, but other than that and his nose, he seemed in fairly good shape, considering that there were three of them.

"Is that what it has come to?" I asked. "Big boys like you picking on a little boy still in short pants?"

"Don't matter what size he is. A Jew's a Jew."

"Yet he was not Jewish, correct?" Lars rebuked him. "So you beat up and humiliated another good German boy."

I winced at the easy way those words came out of his mouth. Good German boy, as opposed to a Jew. A former SS officer, he was adept at navigating Nazi speech.

"We didn't know." Chastened, the three boys shifted their feet.

"Be off home," Lars said. "Think better next time."

Muttering, the boys marched off.

"I believe I must take my leave as well," Paul said. "As we discussed earlier."

He was going to visit Ruth. "Do you want me to—?"

"No." He shook his head. "This will be painful enough without spectators."

Imagining the unpleasantness that lay ahead, I took a step toward him. Lars dropped his arm around my shoulder, establishing ownership for anyone who watched.

Paul stuck his hands in his pockets. "I am quite able to shift for myself, Hannah."

I thought about the night before.

"Stop by the apartment tonight," he said. "We can talk about the next step."

So, at least now, he thought that there was a next step. "See you then, Paul."

"Until then." He nodded to Lars and Anton and left.

As his tall form limped across the grass, I longed to follow, but I stayed put.

Anton wiped the back of his hand across his bloody nose. "Where is he going?"

"To visit Ruth. He knows where she is now." I reached for the handkerchief that Anton held.

"I can do it." He gingerly wiped his nose.

"Just your nose?" Lars asked.

"They didn't land a lot of punches," Anton said.

"Good man," Lars said. "Three against one, and all larger than you."

"Lars," I said. "I do not wish him to be encouraged in fighting."

"I didn't encourage him before," Lars said. "Merely congratulated him after."

Anton beamed.

"Anton," I said. "Learn to restrain yourself. Things are different here than at home. The consequences of your actions can be much more severe."

"Yes, Mother," Anton said in a singsong. "I shall."

He had no intention of following my advice.

Lars laughed heartily.

I rounded on him. "What, exactly, is humorous here?"

He stopped laughing, but still smiled. "Watching you beset by problems that usually face me."

"What does that mean?" Anton asked.

"Trying to get someone to change their nature because you worry about them," Lars said.

"I am not your child." I crossed my arms.

"That is not what I meant," he said. "Only that it is difficult watching the brave and sometimes foolish."

Anton looked from one of us to the other. "I'm going to get my kite."

He bounded across the grass.

I turned and searched the empty field for Paul. He was gone.

"He told you not to follow him," Lars reminded.

"His Jewishness is a liability," I muttered. "Something he, as a man, cannot hide."

"Of course it is," he said gently. "Have you forgotten where you are?"

But Ruth could hide. She looked Aryan. And, as a girl, she was not circumcised. As much as it pained me to think it, perhaps Paul was correct to let her go.

16

Lars and I came to the blanket. I took one end, Lars the other. We shook off the grass and folded it in half, then stepped close together. Our knuckles touched. I admired the way his eyes crinkled in a little arc in the corners when he smiled like that. It was his first real smile since before Poland. I smiled back.

"Spatz." His voice was low. "You never answered my question."

I glanced over his shoulder at Anton halfway up a tree.

I took the blanket from his hand and completed the final folds before giving it back. I did not know what to say, and I could not even begin to discuss it with Anton seconds away.

I cleared my throat. "I need someone who can make inquiries without being suspicious. A policeman."

"Despite what I just said," he said. "I am no longer a policeman."

"I know," I said.

He hung the blanket over his arm. "But I can make inquiries."

"Not you." I pulled my gold watch out of my satchel. "I need to run an errand, alone."

"Dare I ask what it is?" He straightened his hat again, a nervous habit.

"I want to talk to a friend and find out where Herr Silbert is. Can you mind Anton?"

"I have sources I could contact about Herr Silbert."

"As do I." I did not trust his sources, and I was still unsure if I trusted him, in spite of what he had said on the blanket. He had told me that he loved me before, but it had not been enough for him to meet me in Switzerland, or even to tell me that he was still alive.

I could see that he wanted to argue the point, but he merely said, "How long do you need?"

I watched Anton climb down the tree with the rescued kite. "A few hours?"

"Some days," Lars said, "I feel like an errand boy."

"But a reliable one?" I asked.

He smiled. "Full service. And don't forget it."

Anton jogged across the field, winding up the kite string. "Really?" I asked.

Lars touched my shoulder. "Oh, yes."

Anton reached us. "The rib cracked when it hit the ground."

"We can repair it later," Lars said. "I believe your mother has a mission."

"A mission?" Anton smiled conspiratorially. "What's my part?"

"Helping me take a stolen lorry to an illegal shop to have it painted," Lars said.

Anton looked delighted.

"Lars," I said, "could you not think of something more—?"

"You have errands to perform," he said. "As do I."

I put his Lars Lang and Lars Schmidt passports in my satchel. With luck, Herr Silbert could use the German entry stamp on the Lars Lang passport for both Schmidt passports, and Anton's. I had a goodly amount of Swiss francs. If I found Herr Silbert, it ought to be all he needed.

We arranged to meet at five o'clock at the Brandenburg Gate. I kissed Anton good-bye, and he let me. I did not kiss Lars, although I was tempted when he proffered his cheek.

Before I went down the stairs to the subway, I turned around to wave good-bye one last time.

When I got to Alexanderplatz, I checked my watch. I had ten min-

utes. Plenty of time. I took the steps up to the daylight, emerging a block from the police station. I sat on the bench at the bus stop, drew out my sketch pad, and sketched an old Alsatian dog resting under his master's table at a café across the street. White fur stippled the black on his muzzle. Careful to appear engrossed while watching the street, I took my time with the drawing. But because I could not control the pencil properly with my hand in a cast, the picture was terrible.

I had not sketched anything in a long time, and I missed it. When I worked in Berlin as Peter Weill, I drew courtroom sketches every day for the newspaper. All those criminals seemed small time, now that the real criminals were in charge.

If Fritz Waldheim followed his old patterns, he would come by soon, smoking his after-lunch cigar and taking his after-lunch walk. If he did not arrive, I would have to go to his home and leave a message with my friend, Bettina. I hoped it would not come to that, as on my last visit they had sung the praises of the Nazi regime, and I did not trust them not to turn me in. The memory still stung. The Nazis had robbed me of my oldest friend, and I would not forgive them for it.

But here he came. His rolling gait was unmistakable, even though he wore a long brown overcoat and a new fedora, pulled low like Lars's. My hand sketched a nervous line on the paper, ruining the shading. Out of the corner of my eye, I watched his approach. What came next had to be handled delicately.

"Excuse me," I said when he was only a few steps away. "Would you care to buy my drawing?"

"No, thank you." He touched his hat politely before he recognized me. He faltered, but covered for it by sitting next to me on the bench. "Perhaps I will have a look at it."

"It looks a bit like your dog, Caramel."

"He died." Fritz's gray eyes were hard.

I slid my palm across the paper. "How are Bettina and the children?"

"Better than you," he said. "Someone who knows that we were friends from before showed me your file. You are wanted for murder. Double murder."

"They threw me in the trunk of a car in Poland," I said. "They intended to kill me."

"I don't want to know any of that," he said. "Get the hell out of Germany."

"I cannot," I said. "My passport was not stamped when we crossed the border because I was, as I said, in the trunk."

He bit down on his cigar. "What do you need?"

"Information on the whereabouts of Herr Silbert, the forger I did that piece on in the twenties. Do you remember him?"

"I'll get a look at his file," he said. "Meet me two blocks farther south in half an hour."

"Thank you, Fritz," I said. "You might be saving my life."

"I might not be either." He took the cigar out of his mouth and pointed it at me. "Don't hold out too much hope. If he was arrested these days, he'd need a wily lawyer to get back out."

"How is it here?" I asked.

"It's bad. Loyalty to the Party is everything." A shadow passed across his eyes. "The children are part of the Nazi machine now. Soon enough, they'll send my boys off to war."

I ripped out the sketch. "Tell Bettina I said hello."

"I'd rather tell her you said good-bye." He took the sketch and handed me a ten-mark note before marching down the sidewalk toward Alexanderplatz.

I drew another sketch, this one of a young couple lingering late over coffee. The picture could have been drawn any time in the last twenty years. I liked that about it. If I had done a better job of it, I would have offered it to them.

Instead I closed the sketchbook and left for Fritz's suggested rendezvous point.

Once I arrived, I found little to draw to keep me occupied, but it would not do to be seen as loitering suspiciously, so I drew a section

of cobblestones with a cigarette butt lodged between stones. I sketched and shaded happily, glad to be doing something innocent and mundane. I was getting better at working with the cast, too.

A shadow fell over my picture. I looked up to see Fritz's back retreating down the sidewalk. I stood to follow and noticed a scrap of white paper on the ground. I dropped my pencil next to the paper and picked up both. The paper contained only an address. And that, I suspected, was all I would get out of Fritz.

I packed everything back into my satchel and took the subway to Kreuzberg, and the address Fritz had left for me.

Dark trees stood sentinel on the sidewalk. I stood between them in front of a brown brick building of four stories capped by a high copper roof. The building was well kept, stoop newly swept, curtains drawn to keep in the warmth.

I scanned the names on the bells, stopping at SILBERT. I rang his bell and waited. No answer. I rang again and again. Perhaps he was away at a job; it was the middle of the day. I smiled at the thought of Herr Silbert toiling behind a desk at a legitimate job.

I rang the landlady's bell.

A woman with a back bowed with age came to the door. She held the door with one gnarled hand and stood in the threshold. "We have no free apartments."

"I am here looking for someone. A Herr Silbert."

She angled her head to look at me. Milky cataracts covered one blue eye, but I suspected that she saw fine out of the other. "What for?"

"We are old acquaintances," I answered. "May I leave him a message?"

"He's not here," she said. I could not tell if she told the truth. "Perhaps he'll pick it up when he gets back."

I scribbled a quick note on a page torn from my notebook, telling him that I was in town and would love to meet him. I wrote the number of the paper in Switzerland and asked him to leave a message with a suggested meeting time. I suspected that Herr Silbert, being

rather an expert in the field, would recognize my handwriting, but I signed it only Weill. That, he would know for certain. He had saved the articles I wrote about him as Peter Weill in a scrapbook

I folded the note and handed it to the old woman. Her swollen fingers unfolded it. She settled a pair of wire-framed glasses on her nose and read it in front of me while I stared at her incredulously. I had assumed she would read it, but had expected at least a pretense of privacy.

"Like Peter Weill, from the newspaper?" she asked.

I stepped back in shock, glad that she looked at the paper and not my face. "Similar."

"Paper's garbage now," she said. "Used to enjoy his stuff."

I wished that Maria could have heard that. I had written under the Peter Weill byline before her, and she wrote under it now, but all I said was, "I believe it is a pseudonym that the newspaper owns, so the writer can be changed."

"A good alias." She dropped the note into the pocket of her faded yellow dress.

"When is Herr Silbert expected to return?"

"Don't know," she said. "Before you ask, I don't know where he's gone. Keeps his own hours and keeps his business to himself. Pays his rent promptly."

"Will you see that he gets my note?" I wondered if she even knew Herr Silbert.

She studied me with her good eye before answering. "I will."

I thanked her and returned to the sidewalk. I leaned against a cold streetlamp and waited, in case Herr Silbert was inside and would come out in response to my note or send me a note himself.

I could not stand too long without attracting suspicion and had decided to find a stoop and pull out my sketch pad when curtains on a window on the fourth floor twitched. Someone watched the street, and me. I returned to the door and rang the Silbert bell again. This time the door swung open, and I stepped through.

The landlady stood in the hall. She held up four fingers and pointed to the stairs. I plodded up. My tired legs asked why he had to live on the top floor instead of the bottom. When I arrived at the landing, I hurried to the single door that stood ajar.

Suddenly conscious that it might be a trap, I hesitated. But I had to have valid papers. I went in.

No one stood in the darkness in the hall. I waited, one hand on the cold door handle.

Someone whispered my name.

"Herr Silbert?" I whispered back. I let out my held breath when I recognized him. He wore an immaculate white shirt, as always, although he had lost a great deal of weight.

"How did you find me?" His usually perfectly coiffed hair was longer than I had ever seen it. He had not been taking care of himself as well as he usually did.

"The police." I stayed near the door in case I needed to leave quickly. "An old police friend gave me this address."

"Who?"

"You know I cannot tell you that."

"Put down the satchel," he said. "Face the wall."

Fear coursed through my limbs. "Herr Silbert—"

"Quickly," he said. "I am no longer the patient man that you remember."

I slowly bent my knees and lowered my satchel to the ground, then turned to face the dingy gray wall.

He stepped close and ran trembling hands over my coat. I submitted. I could do little else.

He stepped back and held out his hand. When I shook it, his handshake had none of its usual strength.

"What do you need?" he asked.

"Exactly what I needed the last time I visited."

He wiped his hand on his fine tweed pants. They, too, hung loosely on his gaunt frame.

"Have you been ill?" I asked.

"I've been in a concentration camp," he said. "So I've been more than ill. Come along and leave the satchel there."

He led me out of the hallway and into a bare living room. It contained two leather club chairs and a coffee table, but none of the books or tools of his trade that I had expected.

He sank into one chair and gestured to the other.

I sat, aware that my satchel was not close to hand. When I was in Germany, it never left my side.

He leaned back in his chair with his eyes closed. He looked frail and weak. "I do not have the . . . facilities that I once had."

"What can I do for you?" I asked. "Do you have medication?"

He shook his head once and pointed his finger to a door. "Water?"

I hurried through that door and into a kitchen. In the cabinet I found a single glass, a single plate, and a single cup. He must live quite alone here. With growing uneasiness, I opened a bottle of mineral water and filled the glass.

When I brought it out and handed it to him, he took a sip and leaned back in his chair again.

"You should see a doctor," I said. "I can call a taxi and take you there myself."

He shook his grizzled head.

I knelt next to his chair and took his pulse. Fast, but slowing. "Do you have a heart condition?"

He slid his arm back so that I held his hand instead of his wrist. "Such a surprising one you are."

"Herr Silbert, your heartbeat is dangerously erratic, you must—"

"I know what you think I must do." He squeezed my hand. "Your kind heart will be your undoing."

"Your heart may be your undoing as well."

"Tell me why you are here," he asked.

"I have need of your expertise." I moved my fingers up to his wrist again to take his pulse. "I require passports for—"

"I no longer have the equipment for that."

I lifted my chin. "Can you recommend someone else?"

"No."

I could think of no other way to procure passports for Anton, and perhaps for Paul and Ruth. Perhaps, if Paul wanted to leave, they would all fit in the compartment Lars had promised to build. If so, I needed only to get my and Lars's passports stamped to show that we had entered Germany legally so that we could present them at the border. "Can you put stamps in existing passports?"

"For that I need only ink," he said. "Show me what you require."

I took out the Hannah and Lars Schmidt passports and handed them to him. He opened them and smiled. "You are still together. When I saw your reaction to the marriage certificate, I thought perhaps I had made a mistake."

I had no desire to explain my complicated relationship with Lars. I took out his Lars Lang passport and flipped it open to the last stamp, showing that he had entered Germany legally on the night I was kidnapped. "This is what I need to have copied."

Herr Silbert drew a pair of horn-rimmed spectacles from his shirt pocket and studied the stamp. "Of course."

We haggled over the price, as we so often had in the past. I paid him with Swiss francs that I had not yet exchanged.

"You may wait here, if you wish." He stood, seemingly steady on his feet.

"I think my time would be better spent making soup," I said.

"*Ach*, Frau Schmidt," he said. "You should have told me that before we agreed on the price."

I returned to his kitchen and made a quick soup, using a withered carrot, one old onion, potatoes, and a yellowed stalk of celery, seasoned with a couple of beef Maggi cubes. It was the first meal that I had cooked in days, and I realized how much I missed the everyday feeling. Setting the pot to simmer, I made a list of groceries that I thought he might eat and presented it to him.

"I have finished the passports." He handed them to me. "Would you care to stay for dinner? It smells wonderful."

"I have an appointment soon." I thought of Anton and Lars waiting for me. "But I can spare a few minutes."

I had dished him out a large bowl of soup, me a small one.

I remembered one more thing in my satchel. "On the way over, I picked up your favorite cigarettes," I said. "Ravenklaus."

I had brought him those cigarettes when he was in prison for forgery and I had visited him as Peter Weill. Cigarettes for interviews.

He smiled, and new, deep wrinkles appeared around his eyes. "Bless you, Fräulein Vogel."

We ate our soup with little conversation and he saw me to the door. "I will be leaving Germany soon, and for good," he said.

"Good for you." I did not think he would live long enough to leave Germany. "I shall, too."

"Thank you for the soup," he said.

"Not my best meal," I said. "But I work with what is at hand."

We shook hands. I wondered if I would ever see the charming criminal again.

It was dark when I reached the Brandenburg Gate. I turned my side to the cold rain and paced anxiously next to the stone pillars. Punctual, Lars drove up in a black Opel Blitz lorry. The streetlights showed a tarp tied tightly over the contents of the lorry's bed. When I got close, I smelled a whiff of new paint.

Lars got out, and I slid in the driver's side to the middle of the seat. He piled in and slammed the door.

"Hello!" Anton said. "Isn't the lorry beautiful?"

"You are an Opel man," I said to Lars, remembering the Opel Olympia he drove during the 1936 Olympics.

"I had little time to shop," he said.

"Every busy man's curse." I imagined him searching the streets late last night, looking for a convenient Opel to steal.

"They're reliable." Lars pulled into traffic. The windshield wipers worked to keep up with the rain.

"What did you do while I was gone?" I asked Anton.

"We went shooting!" Anton's eyes shone in the light from the streetlamps. "At the Wannsee shooting range."

"Did you, now?" I said, staring at Lars.

"He's quite a good shot," Lars said. "We practiced with different pistols, and he was good with all of them."

"Lars gave me a gun." Anton drew out a Luger. I had carried one around myself in 1934, and Boris had killed a woman with it in self-defense. She had stabbed me, and we were being shot at as well, but I knew Boris still regretted his actions. It was not easy to take a life, especially not in the days and years after.

I took the pistol out of Anton's hand. It smelled of gun oil. "You cleaned it, too?"

"It's part of owning a gun," Anton explained.

I turned the heavy weapon over in my hands. At thirteen, Anton was too young for it. Did Lars seek to buy his affection, or did he truly think Anton needed to be armed?

"Lars," I said, "we shall discuss this later."

"Don't make him be in trouble," Anton said. "I think it's a very logical decision."

"I bet you do." I stuck the gun in my satchel.

"How was your meeting?" Lars kept his eyes on the road.

"The Schmidt passports are stamped, but I could not get any new ones." I knew I sounded defeated. Anton still had no papers, and how could I help Paul and Ruth?

Lars briefly touched my shoulder. "Once we get the compartment built, that won't be a problem."

"Can we go shooting again tomorrow?" Anton fidgeted on the seat. "I need all the practice I can get."

"I think we shall have to leave that up to your mother," Lars said. "For now, where are we going?"

"Take us to Paul's," I said.

"This is a mistake, Spatz." Lars stopped at a red traffic light. "Stay anywhere else, but not there."

"I need to check on him, Lars." The streets were completely empty. It felt eerie, like wartime.

"We should keep out of the Jewish quarter. We've been over this before. You cannot live with Paul there or you run the risk of being arrested for breaking the Nuremberg Laws." Lars's voice sounded like a lecture.

I bristled. "Paul and I are not—"

"You know better than to believe that the truth will save you. Or him."

I did. "I agreed to meet him tonight." To find out what he had decided about Ruth.

"I'll go with you," Lars said. "When you are done, we should spend the night elsewhere. I have a safe place where you and Anton can sleep. It's not luxurious by any means, but it will do."

"How irresistible you make it sound."

He dropped his hand off the steering wheel onto my knee. "I could be irresistible, if you were so inclined."

I moved his hand. Lars drove to Paul's apartment and parked out front. Anton jumped down first, still full of energy from his time at the shooting range.

I stepped out and looked up at Paul's dark bedroom window. Perhaps he was not home.

A white light flashed from Paul's kitchen. A gunshot broke the silence.

Anton took off at a run toward the front door.

"Stop!" I yelled, already knowing that he would not.

He was at the door first and streaked through before I made it to the stairs. I wished that I had not given him the key.

Anton pounded up the inside stairs, with me close on his heels. Far behind us, Lars uttered a muffled curse.

Paul's front door stood open. Anton burst through and ran for the kitchen. I raced after him. Anton stopped in the living room, staring through the doorway.

I stepped past him and into the kitchen. Paul sat on a dining room chair, head back. A splash of darkness marred the wall behind him.

"Wait here," I told Anton.

He nodded, eyes on Paul. I put my hand on Anton's head and turned it so that it faced away from Paul. He let me. His neck drooped forward. I held him in a hug. I should have protected him from this. I should have protected Paul.

Lars appeared in the doorframe, gun drawn and held in front of him. "Touch nothing. If you listen to only one thing I say, let it be that."

"Yes, sir," Anton said.

Lars quickly surveyed the kitchen. "Stay here. Both of you."

"Yes, sir," Anton repeated. Lars looked at me.

"I am going to examine Paul," I said. "I will not leave this room."

Lars nodded and walked down the hall, gun still out. Did he think someone else was in the apartment?

I walked Anton a few paces into the room, still facing away from Paul's body.

I left him there and stepped past the chair where Paul and I had sat and talked only this morning. My shoe crunched on broken crockery. Someone had torn the tablecloth from the table and knocked the dishes to the floor.

Unheeding, I walked through the mess to reach Paul. His elegant hands dangled over the chair's arms, his head leaned back, his familiar brown eyes frozen wide in death.

Far behind me, I heard Lars walk through the apartment, opening and closing doors, but it seemed as if he must be in another house. Here there was only Paul and me.

I reached out and closed his eyes. His eyelids felt soft and warm under my fingertips. I stroked his cheek with the back of my hand. A long day's-worth of stubble roughened it. I thought back to when I first met him, after the War. The hours we had spent as nurse and patient, the hours we had spent as young lovers planning a future together. Even after our affair ended, we had stayed friends for two decades. Grief clogged my throat. Tears blurred my eyes.

Footsteps came into the room.

"Steady, Anton," Lars said. "We'll be leaving soon."

Lars wrapped an arm around my shoulders, squeezed, and let go. I could not stop studying Paul's face. Paul. Gone.

Lars squatted and investigated the floor. Ever the clinical police officer. Or so I hoped. What if the scene triggered an episode in Lars? His right hand held his gun by his leg. I glanced back at Anton, still facing the wall.

"Lars?" I had to keep myself under control, particularly if Lars could not.

"Spatz." His voice was matter-of-fact. "There's no gun."

Paul's hand hung over the side of the chair. No gun rested below

it. He had not committed suicide. I took his left hand, running my fingertips along the bandage. His long legs angled off to the side as if he might stand up and walk away.

Lars examined the bullet hole in Paul's forehead and tilted his head forward to look at the back. He stepped to the broken kitchen window, careful to touch nothing. He nodded once, pulled a handkerchief out of his pocket, and opened my satchel.

"Lars?"

He touched one finger to his lips, put his hand into my satchel, and took out the Luger I had confiscated from Anton in the lorry. He opened the handkerchief and wiped the gun down thoroughly. He curled Paul's fingers around the stock. Then he dropped the Luger onto the floor. It landed with a clunk.

"Please, Spatz," Lars said quietly. "We must go."

"Good-bye," I whispered to Paul. Lars put one arm around my waist and guided me away. I dropped my head and let him lead me.

He stopped at the table and picked up the only thing on its surface—a sheet of paper. I stopped, too, head down. He folded the paper and slipped it into his pocket.

"Now," he said, with new urgency. "We must go at once."

He shoved us through the living room, gun drawn again.

"Back door or front?" Lars muttered.

"There's a cellar," Anton said. "Paul showed me. It has a door, too."

"Perfect," Lars said. "Lead the way. No talking."

We stepped out of Paul's apartment into the deserted hall. Lars wiped fingerprints off the handle and left the apartment door open, as we had found it.

Anton stealthily led the way down the stairs, past the lobby door to the cellar.

We walked between tall slatted compartments used by the apartment dwellers for extra storage. In the gloom, I recognized boxes, chairs, a tall lamp. One of these compartments stored Paul's medals from the Great War and the typewriter he had lent me to type my first stories as a reporter.

Anton scurried through the maze like a mouse, sure in his route. We kept close to him. Anton found the back door, and Miriam's key opened it. We stepped into the cold night. Far above, hung stars that Paul would never see again.

Lars herded us a few blocks before pushing us into a dark doorway.

Sirens grew louder.

He cursed. "Their response time is too quick. Something's wrong."

"We need to keep moving," I said.

"I have to go back and get the lorry." He fit his pistol into my palm. "This is a Vis. Polish. You have eight rounds."

I gripped the stock tightly, comforted by the heft of it, but worried about aiming it left-handed.

"If I'm not back in five minutes, you're on your own. Good luck." He brushed my lips with his and stepped away.

Anton and I huddled in the cold doorway behind a chained-up bicycle that leaned against the railing. Left there by someone who did not trust his neighbors. Probably right not to.

With my right arm, I hugged Anton close. He shuddered, but fought down his tears. A brave boy.

"Is it always like this?" he whispered.

"What?" I whispered back.

"When you come to Berlin?"

I thought of my last visit, when my friend Peter Weill had died in my arms, or when I had stumbled on a dying man in my search for Anton in 1934. Corpses and grief littered my trips to Berlin. "Sometimes."

"I see why Boris doesn't want you to go."

"Boris is a wise man." Wise enough to leave me when he realized that I would not change.

Sirens closed in. I longed to run, but I wanted to wait another minute for Lars.

"I know why you go anyway," Anton whispered.

"Why?"

"To see. To help. To do what's right."

The Opel Blitz stopped in front of us.

We ran to it and climbed through the passenger door. Lars held out his hand for the pistol. I gave it to him.

"No one on the street," Lars said. "I can't tell if anyone's in the other apartments, of course, but it's the best I can do."

"Were the police there yet?"

"Almost." He pulled into the street and set out at a sedate pace. "But I think we got away clean."

"What's next?" Anton asked.

"I know a warehouse." Lars sounded tired. "We can stay there nights, but we must be gone during the workday."

I hunched into my coat. Lars patted my knee.

Anton huddled close to my side.

I thought of the look of resignation on Paul's face. His killer had not surprised him. He had expected to die. I shivered.

Lars put his arm around me and drove one-handed. I remembered how difficult it had been for me to drive with only my left hand when I followed him in his car full of dead Gestapo agents. So much death.

"Thank you," I said.

"I haven't done much that's useful," he muttered through tight lips.

"Yes, you have!" Anton objected. "You saved my mother from the Gestapo. And you're helping us now."

"Thank you, Anton," Lars said. "It is kind of you to say."

We drove away from the Jewish quarter in silence, through the still-teeming streets around Alexanderplatz, and over to the warehouse district by the river.

"We're here." Lars stopped in front of a dark warehouse.

I glanced nervously around the lot, but I saw only the silhouettes of weeds.

"I'll open the door. Wait here." Lars left the lorry, and a blast of cold air entered.

"What are we going to do?" Anton asked.

"Lars is going to build a compartment into this lorry," I told him. "In a few days, we will be home."

"What about Paul?"

"He is dead," I said. "We can do nothing for him now."

"We could find out who killed him," he said.

"So can the police, better than we." I did not mention that Lars must have left his gun on the floor to make Paul's death look like a suicide. The police were unlikely to investigate it further. In fact, even if it were ruled a murder, I doubted that they would trouble themselves over the death of another Jew.

The door opened. Lars slid into the seat next to me. "Just a second now."

He drove into a mechanic's bay and turned off the engine. Darkness cloaked the room, but I got a sense of tall ceilings and faraway walls. When Lars opened the car door, smells of grease, metal, and turpentine filled the cab. He squeezed my hand once, then was gone. Anton moved to follow.

"Wait until he closes the door," I said.

Lars returned soon. "Door's closed. You can get out now."

Lars led the way across the darkened room. I barked my shins on a heavy angular object. Other mysterious shapes looked equally menacing.

Lars opened a door into an office, stretched his arm, lowered the blinds, and turned on the light. He looked pale but calm. Tears had left streaks on Anton's dirty face. I did not want to think about how I must look.

"Beds here." Lars gestured to two automobile seats that had been removed and set on the concrete floor. "Washroom in the back."

His gloved finger pointed to a half-open door. Then he left.

The office felt barely warmer than outside. I set Anton on the cleanest-looking car seat. "Tonight I think we skip washing up and tooth brushing and go straight to bed."

He craned his head to see a calendar with a girl in a red bathing suit hung on the wall. Even though it was November, the calendar

read July. I shook my head. Obviously the calendar's function was not to help them keep track of the date.

I dug through the bag I had packed at Paul's apartment days before. I had no blanket in there, but I drew out a nightshirt for Anton and folded it into a pillow so that his face would not come in contact with the seat's cracked leather. I counted out headache tablets and dry-swallowed them without any belief that they would help.

I opened the blinds a crack so that I could see the warehouse floor. No one there.

Lars returned with a dark brown blanket that stank of beer and the gray one we had used at the park. "We can get better blankets tomorrow."

Anton took off his shoes and lay down on his side. I covered him with the gray blanket, tucking it around his legs, and spread his coat over him as well. I slipped my hand under the blanket and found his.

He gripped mine tightly. "Aren't you going to take the other seat?"

"I think I may sit here until you fall asleep," I said.

Anton smiled. "That would be nice."

He closed his eyes, and I stroked his hair, as I used to when he was little.

Through the glass I watched Lars. He took off Paul's too-large shirt, folded it, and hung it over the steering wheel. I looked back to Paul's shirt. It would be cold now without Lars's warmth. Paul's body would never warm it again.

I closed my eyes. Memories of Paul in clean white shirts through the years streamed through my mind. Too painful to see. I opened my eyes and blinked away tears.

Lars reached into the lorry for his overcoat. After he put it on, he drew the Vis from the pocket, checked it, and stuck it in his waistband. What kind of trouble did he expect here? I surveyed the empty-seeming warehouse again. Still no one.

Anton's grip on my hand loosened. He kicked once. I knew by the sound of his breathing that he slept. I watched him sleep for a full minute before going out to talk to Lars.

He rummaged through a stack of metal scraps in the corner, holding an electric torch awkwardly in his left hand. Why did he not use his right?

"Lars," I called softly across the room. He did not act as if he heard me.

I walked gingerly toward him. When I reached him, I tapped his shoulder. His right hand drew the gun from his waistband as he turned. Now I knew why he held the torch in his left.

"Lars!" I lifted both hands to shoulder height. "Don't shoot!"

He lowered the barrel. "Apologies."

I put down my hands, shaking.

He tucked the gun back into his waistband. "You startled me."

"I am sorry." I pulled my coat close against the chill.

"It has been a difficult evening."

"Yes," I said, "it has."

He led me back to the lorry, set the gun on the dash, climbed in, and handed me up beside him. I glanced toward the office where Anton slept.

"You should be working on the compartment," I said.

Lars tightened his lips. "I don't have the materials I need here. I'll make a list for my friend in the morning."

I wished that he could start sooner. But where would we find sheet metal in the middle of the night? Even Lars had limits.

"I would have talked to him earlier today," he said. "But I didn't want to meet the other workers."

His caution was warranted. "So, you start tomorrow?"

"Tomorrow night," he said. "I can't work here during the day without raising questions. I don't trust the men here."

"But you trust your friend?"

"I do." He removed a flat glass bottle from the glove box. He took a swig and handed it to me. I shifted it from the hand with a cast to my left hand and drank. Korn schnapps burned my throat.

"Show me the paper," I said.

"What paper?" He took another drink.

"The one that you nicked off Paul's table."

He hesitated, then drew a sheet of paper from his overcoat pocket.

I turned on the lorry's overhead light. Block letters in familiar handwriting goose-stepped across the page.

TO ADELHEID ZINSLI,

   THE SUFFERING THAT JEW-FUCKERS LIKE YOU HAVE CAUSED THE GERMAN PEOPLE CAN NEVER BE UNDONE. JUST AS YOU STOLE A LIFE FROM ME, I STEAL ONE FROM YOU. THE JEWS ARE NOT DONE MURDERING THOUGH, ARE THEY? NOR AM I.

18

I gulped. The handwriting matched the threatening letters that had been mailed to the *Neue Zürcher Zeitung*. My head throbbed. Red and green lights flickered in my peripheral vision.

Lars pushed my head between my knees. "Breathe."

I breathed until the lights went away; then I sat up. "Paul's death was about me," I whispered. "It was my fault."

"You did not kill him."

"I brought him grief, then death," I said.

"You are missing the essential element in that note."

I stared at him.

"Someone wants to hurt you. It's why they killed Paul."

"It worked." Paul's life had ended because of something I had done. Or not done. I had never taken the letters seriously.

Lars put his arm around my shoulders to steady me. I leaned against him and closed my eyes. He stroked my hair. I stayed there, matching my breaths with his, calming down.

"Spatz?" He sounded sleepy.

I sat up. "I imagine they will not stop trying to hurt me either."

I looked again toward the office where Anton lay asleep.

"They know you are Adelheid Zinsli." Lars buttoned the top button on my coat. "When we leave, they'll know to look for you in Switzerland."

"Did anyone follow us here?" My heart raced as I scanned the dark warehouse, as if I could spot someone.

"No," he said with great finality. "I watched behind us, and we took a most circuitous route. I never saw anyone."

I struggled to pull myself together. He handed me the schnapps. I took a long swallow. I had to think. I had to get myself and Anton out of this. And I had to warn Lars that he might well be in danger, too. "I have received other letters."

"What?" He choked on the schnapps and coughed. "You didn't tell me."

"They came to the paper. In Switzerland. I get all kinds of crank letters. I have for years, even when I worked crime. Peter always used to say, 'If you're not getting letters, you're not writing pieces that move people.'" I shuddered. "Now I get political ones. I never take them seriously. But these were written in the same handwriting as—" I held up the letter that he had taken from Paul's table.

"How many letters? How long?" He rapped out questions.

"Ten or twelve, I think," I said. "They started coming a month ago, right after I wrote a piece criticizing the French and British governments for giving Hitler a giant swath of Czechoslovakia."

"You can't ever leave well enough alone?" His brow furrowed in irritation.

"I would not call that situation well enough." I took another drink of schnapps. It barely burned anymore. "What would you have me do, Lars, join the French throngs throwing roses?"

He pursed his lips. "Perhaps you could allow another journalist to draw attention to it."

"I will not sit by." I met his eyes calmly.

"My apologies, Spatz," he said. "You are correct, of course. Please tell me more about the letters."

I thought back to the last letter and the ones before, when I had been safe and warm in Switzerland. "When the first one came, a secretary opened it by mistake and took it to my editor. Since then,

he has been confiscating them and giving them to the police. For my safety, he sent me to Poland to write a nonpolitical feature."

Lars raked his fingers through his hair. "That turned out well."

"Quite."

"What do the letters say?"

"They say—I—they." I took a long shuddering breath. "The letters call me a traitor and a whore and a Jew-fucker."

He winced, unused to hearing me swear.

I forged on. "They say that I will be called to answer for my crimes against Germany. And they urge me to come back to Germany to face my punishment, which they hint is to be a slow death."

"Where are they postmarked?" His unfocused eyes stared out the windshield. I knew that expression. He was thinking.

I took another drink of schnapps. "Berlin."

He took the flask off me, but he did not drink. "How often?"

"At first weekly, but lately almost daily. One arrived yesterday in Switzerland." I watched dark shapes in the warehouse. I had not taken the letters seriously, and now Paul was dead.

As usual, Lars read my mind. "Don't blame yourself, Spatz."

"I have no one else to blame, Lars. I did not warn Paul. And I left him alone." I looked longingly at the schnapps flask, but did not reach for it. I would not numb myself to this.

Lars took another drink. "What happened to you a month ago, when the letters started?"

"I have been over that again and again on my own and with Herr Knecht. Nothing significant happened to me."

"If the letter writer is indeed the killer, he is targeting you." He took a deep breath. "Who would want to kill you? Whose life did you steal?"

"I killed one of the Gestapo men who kidnapped me in Poland."

"Too recent to have written the letters," he said.

"The Röhms," I said. "Frau Röhm blamed me for her son's death

back in 1934, and she was certainly willing to kill Anton and me to avenge him."

His eyes narrowed. "They are good candidates for something like this. They have no more political power, so they couldn't just have you arrested and shot. They'd have to do it themselves."

"Comforting." I shifted on the car seat. The smell of old leather wafted up.

"Who else?" Lars tapped his fingers on the steering wheel impatiently.

"Bauer's family. Or Hahn's. Or the other two," I said. A policeman named Bauer and Lars's former superior, Sturmbannführer Hahn, had died in a gun battle in 1936, along with two other men, moments before they would have killed us.

He sat quiet for a moment. "I don't know much about Bauer or the other two. Hahn was estranged from his wife for years before his death, I believe. They had a child, but I can't remember if it was a boy or a girl. I do know that Hahn often beat his wife so badly, she ended up in hospital."

I remembered how Hahn had broken Lars's nose and his ribs, and the plans he had stated that he had for me. I had killed him to stop him, and while I did not regret it, I still had nightmares about what I had done.

Lars kept talking. "I don't imagine his wife or child would search hard for his killer, except perhaps to give him a reward."

"Bauer?" He and Hahn were the only two whose names I knew.

"They are long shots," he said. "If it's Gestapo-related, they would have had you arrested at Paul's house and shot you, not him. Nor would they waste time with threatening letters."

"So, a civilian?" I held the letter up to the light in the lorry. "I found a letter in Paul's apartment typed on this same kind of paper."

Lars stared at the paper, thinking. "Do you think Paul could have written the letters? Or Miriam?"

"Paul?" I straightened up on the seat. "Never."

"Miriam, then?"

"Some of them arrived after she died," I said. "And the letter I found in their apartment seemed to have been sent to them, not from them."

"Was the handwriting the same?"

"The one in the apartment was typewritten." I repeated it back to him.

Lars touched the watermark. "This is government paper."

"Where does the paper come from?" I did not question that he was correct.

"You sign it out a hundred sheets at a time." He rubbed the paper between his thumb and forefinger. "The paper company has a contract with the government, so this paper is not available to civilians. That is why you need to sign for it."

"So whoever wrote the letters to me works for the government, or at least has access to the paper." That sounded promising. Whom did I know who worked for the government?

"That narrows the field of suspects down to thousands." Lars squelched my hope.

"Not counting the Gestapo men, who else in government thinks I took the life of someone they love?"

"It doesn't have to be someone whose life you took," Lars pointed out. "It could be someone who feels that you ruined his life."

"A much wider field," I said. "Are you on that list?"

He draped his arm across the seat behind me. "I am on the other end. You redeemed mine."

"Did I?" I picked at my glove. It felt as if every single thing I had done to try to help people had backfired. "Before you met me, you were a successful police *kommissar,* a Hauptsturmführer in the SS. Now you are sleeping in a garage."

"Spatz—"

"You were correct to stay away, Lars. I have never loved a man who did not come to grief."

"The banker seems to have ended up in quite satisfactory

circumstances," he said. "Perhaps I should have read the fine print at the bottom of the contract and applied for a position in Switzerland."

I appreciated his effort to lighten the situation and forced a smile.

He tucked a strand of hair behind my ear.

I looked into his questioning dark eyes. Dark like Paul's. I wanted Lars to explain his past before I made any decisions. I would regret this action later, but now was all I had. All anyone really had.

I leaned forward and kissed him hard. My teeth clacked against his, and I tasted blood, but I did not care. I wanted to forget everything else.

He curled his hands around my shoulders. "No, Spatz." He pulled back from me. "I won't. Not like that."

Face hot with shame, I fumbled at the door handle. I could not get out of the lorry fast enough.

He kept hold of my shoulders. "Stay. Please."

I dropped my hands into my lap, head down so he could not see my face.

He took my head between his hands and drew me close. "It's me, Lars. And you, Hannah. No one else is here."

He tried to banish Paul's ghost. I doubted that he could, but I nodded. I closed my eyes. I saw Paul's face.

"Look at me," Lars said softly.

I looked into his face and saw the expression that Fräulein Ivona had recognized from across the train station.

"Please?" He traced my lips with his fingertip.

I kissed him then, gently and for a long time, until I wanted to be filled, not emptied. When his lips finally peeled off mine, I had forgotten everything outside the lorry. Steam coated the windows, and he was half naked.

"I surrender," he whispered.

I kissed him. "Looks more like an advance than a retreat."

He kissed my throat. "One touch of your skin and every single resolution disappears."

I arched my neck back. "What resolutions?" I asked breathlessly.

His fingers undid the front of my dress. I had no idea what had happened to my coat, but I did not worry about it. I was far from cold.

"Tomorrow," he whispered. "Time for resolutions then."

I resolved only to enjoy this moment. I had waited years to be with him again.

I caressed his scarred back, and moved my hands lower.

Lars moaned. "Spatz."

I smiled into his shoulder.

He removed the last bit of clothing between us.

Much later, we fell asleep in a jumble of coats on the lorry's leather bench seat.

I woke with a start, seeing Paul's empty shirt in my dreams. Lars's arms were tight around me. I could scarcely believe that I lay next to him again, our bodies pressed close together on the small seat. I inhaled mingled scents of leather, cigarettes, oils, and metal tools. I moved my cheek off his chest to look at him. Golden light from the overhead lamp softened the years on his face and rendered the scar on his eyebrow invisible.

He opened his eyes and smiled lazily. "Hello, Frau Schmidt."

The last time he had said that was when I woke up in his arms for the first time. Back then, I had not called him Herr Schmidt, not ready for the intimacy of a marriage in real life instead of on counterfeit papers. Things were much more complicated now, yet I surprised myself. "Hello yourself, Herr Schmidt."

He tightened his arms. I held him close. For a long time neither of us spoke.

He caressed one palm down the length of my back and I shivered. "How did you sleep?"

In answer, I only smiled.

He rolled over onto his side and faced me. Our legs intertwined on the narrow lorry seat. "Where does that leave us now?"

The warm feelings evaporated as I thought about our future. "Tell me about Russia."

"It's not a happy story," he said. "Shouldn't we tell only happy stories in bed?"

"I want us to tell only true stories," I said. "And those are not always happy."

He propped himself up on his elbow. "I've told no one. That has worked so far. Why do you want to know?"

"Why do you not want to tell me?"

He studied my face for a long time before speaking. "I will tell you once. But only once."

"I will take notes."

"I'd rather you didn't," he said. "I'd rather you forget it, as soon as I tell you."

I waited, not certain what to say.

He reached up and switched off the lorry's light. I felt him turn onto his back. I stayed on my side pressed tight against him. "I was arrested almost immediately. At first I thought that your SS friend had missed my name on some list, and that I was arrested for being Lars Lang and my work with the British."

Perhaps my SS friend, Wilhelm, had been wrong. "That was not the reason? Are you certain?"

"Fairly, yes." Irritation sounded in his voice. "I was quite good at my former job, you may recall. I know how interrogations work. The first interrogators were not particularly skilled and made their intentions perfectly clear."

I covered him with his coat. The lorry felt colder now.

"They started with simple physical violence, the kind that can kill the suspect before you get any real information. Careless work." He glided his hand along the coat, making sure that I was covered, too. "Of course, I was barely healed from our encounter with Hahn when I arrived."

I winced. That, too, had been my fault.

"Spatz," he said gently. "It was my own fault I was caught."

He put one arm around me and kept the other behind his head. I suddenly wanted him to stop talking. I did not want to send him

back into the Russian prison, but if I stopped him, I might never hear what had happened, and despite what he said, he needed to tell someone, and I needed to know. "Go on."

"They would not have started with that kind of violence if they thought I had anything valuable to tell them, so I decided that the best way to stay alive was to wait out the first round. I stuck to my story of being a German businessman investigating the industry in Saratova."

"How long?"

He settled my head against his chest. I suspected that he did not want me to see his face, even in the darkness. "It's tough to say precisely. I'd say no more than a week."

In the Gestapo warehouse, the interrogators had broken his nose and two ribs in less than a minute. "A week?"

"There's a cycle to it," he explained. "They didn't expect to get information of value out of me, so they were more perfunctory."

Perfunctory? I thought of the scars on his back and flattened my palm over his heart.

"Once they finished, they dumped me in the general prison population. I figured they would either let me rot there, or things would get more interesting."

He did not speak for several seconds, and I kept my head on his chest, listening to his heartbeat. When it had slowed, I said, "Did they get more interesting?"

"Oh yes." He took a shuddering breath. "They did."

"How?"

"First, they sent in a physician to stitch me up and set my various broken bones."

Which bones? I wanted to ask, but I stayed quiet. As lightly as he talked, his heart raced under my ear. I slid my leg across his and held him.

"That showed that they suddenly thought I was of value. You never want your interrogator to believe that you have any value, unless it's so much value that they will release you immediately. Clearly that was not the case."

I stayed silent. He lay still. Together we waited until he got his breathing under control. "After that, as expected, they sent in a team more skilled in extracting information."

I hated to ask the question. "What did they do?"

"Let's just say that I quickly came to miss the simple beatings."

All the time that I had been mourning his death, he had been being tortured. "I am so sorry, Lars."

"It was over a year ago," he said. "I am quite recovered."

His entire body was taut next to mine, and his breaths came rapid and shallow. I stroked my hand in a circle on his chest and, slowly, his breathing eased.

"Once they started using more . . . finesse, I realized that I was in the second stage of the cycle. I had hoped that would never happen, of course."

"What did you do?" I asked.

"I prepared a second cover story. I decided that enough time had passed for me to have reached a breaking point, and I told them that I had been sent by Hahn to do an undercover investigation of Project Zephyr."

"But he did not send you. Hahn was already dead."

He laughed mirthlessly. "Yes, Spatz. I knew that, even though I was not sure of many things by that point. But since I had arrived in Russia little more than a week after his death, the assumption might be that he had given me the order, I had prepared myself, and left. Hahn, of course, could not gainsay it."

"What happened?"

"My story within a story impressed them enough for them to talk to their German allies, and after another short stint in the general population, they released me to the SS."

"What did the SS do?"

"I had expected them to kill me or torture me for details about Hahn's death, which is why I did not try that story earlier." He sighed. "But, oddly enough, they believed that one. They got me a real doctor. I healed for a few months. When I was well enough to leave the

hospital, I first took a short leave of absence to take care of a small matter in Russia, then went to Switzerland to see you."

"What small matter?"

"Not today." He rolled onto his side, facing away from me.

"All right, Lars." After hearing him talk about being tortured, I wondered what could be worse. If he did not want to tell me, I could wait. I fit myself against his back and asked. "What happened in Switzerland?"

He slowly rolled to face me. His breath whispered against my cheek. "I was afraid that I was being monitored by the SS, of course, but for me to visit Adelheid Zinsli was a reasonable thing, even though I had told them that I had ended our engagement before I went to Russia."

"You did?" Although the engagement had been fictitious, I was surprisingly hurt.

"It was the only way I could explain why you did not contact me in Berlin when I was in Russia, Spatz."

I felt like a child, and a dull one at that. "Of course. Please go on."

He took in a long breath and let it out slowly.

"Lars?"

"I went to Switzerland to break it off with you."

I jerked my head back from him so hard that it smacked the glove box. "Break it off with me?"

He slipped his fingers through my hair. "Did you hurt your head?"

"W-why?" My head whirled. I had not expected this.

"I was . . . broken, not fit to be in a family. I saw that."

"I would have welcomed you," I said.

"Of course you would have. You would have taken care of me as best you could, without regard to the cost to you." He stroked my hair.

"But—"

"If you had known I was alive, you would have destroyed your life for me. As you risked death for your friend Paul, even though you have not been romantically involved with him for almost twenty years." His muscles bunched.

"I did Paul no favor." I pulled away from him. "And helping you would not have destroyed my life."

"I was a mess, Spatz," he said. "I could not sleep. I could barely eat. I was drunk more than I was sober. I was useless."

"I do not love you because you are 'of use' to me." I forced myself to touch him, to swallow my anger. For now.

He traced a fingertip down my cheek, and I turned to kiss it. "That's why I had to leave." He took his hand back. "Because I was damned if I would drag you and Anton down with me."

"Lars—"

"It's past the point of discussion now."

"It most certainly is not," I said. "But not now."

"Something to look forward to," he said. "The reporter forgets nothing."

I ignored that. "You did not break things off with me. We never spoke. I did not know that you came to Switzerland. What happened?"

He settled deeper into the seat. "I spent a few days seeing if I was followed. When I was confident that I was not, I staked out the newspaper offices, as I did not know where else to find you. I did not have the banker's address."

"I was not living with Boris," I put in.

"I know that now. Or at least I hope I do."

"Lars!"

I heard the smile. "I do."

"Did you find me at the newspaper?" I went there often now that Anton was in school, enjoying the collegial atmosphere. Or at least the collegial atmosphere before Herr Marceau started to resent my political pieces.

"I followed you to the park and saw you and the banker and the woman I assumed to be the nanny with a new baby." His words sped up. He must be anxious to get through this part. "Boris and Anton played football and were happy together. You seemed content playing with the baby. I assumed that it was yours, and that you had married him."

We visited Boris on weekends so that he and Anton could spend time together. I sometimes stayed to play with the little girl that Anton called his sister. "I did not marry him, and that baby is not mine."

"I know that now," he said. "But at the time it seemed logical. You had assumed me dead, perhaps mourned for a time, and moved on with your life. With the life you would have led had I never recruited you to courier for me. The life you should have led. I thought it would be easier if I did not reopen any old wounds you might have had and let you continue to think me dead."

"Those wounds never closed." I grazed my fingertip over the scar on his eyebrow. "I mourned you every day until I saw you in Poland."

He shifted, and the seat squeaked. "I could not provide for you as he could. I could not father Anton as he could. I still can't."

"How do you know what I want?"

"I know what you need," he said. "You didn't need me."

I swallowed another argument. "After you inadvisably left Switzerland—"

He chuckled. "Yes?"

"What did you do next?"

"I returned to Berlin and drank myself out of the SS, whored myself out of Berlin—" I flinched. He kissed the top of my head. "I'm sorry, Spatz."

I lay still. It hurt to hear him say it, but no more than the rest of it. The thing that hurt the most was that he had left me.

"I read your articles. When I heard that you were going to Poznań, I adjusted my route and went there to keep an eye on you, little knowing how much danger you would find. You know the rest."

"I think you may be leaving out as much as you are telling."

He sat up suddenly. Cold air blew across my bare skin. I sat next to him and pulled the coat over us. I wondered what our lives would have been like if I had fallen in love with him in my twenties. Could I have lived the domestic life of a policeman's wife, as my friend Bettina did? I tried to imagine us leaving for work in the

morning, coming home at night, and not worrying about being arrested or killed. I could not picture it, and I reminded myself, he had been a Nazi when I met him. I had hated and feared him at the time. Besides, for many years after I had left Paul and realized that I did not wish to be married, I had closed the door on the thought of falling in love, until I met Boris. Even if Lars and I had met in our twenties, we would not have fallen in love.

He adjusted my upside-down coat across my shoulders, fingertips lingering on my collarbone. A slight contact, but electric.

I had fallen in love with him two years ago, unexpectedly and against my better judgment. The feelings had not gone away when I thought him dead, or when I saw him again in Poland with Fräulein Ivona. Whether I liked it or not, I still loved him. A better question was what I intended to do about it.

"At Paul's last night," I said. "When I woke up and looked at you, you did not recognize me."

"What do you mean?" His heart beat faster. He must know I could feel it.

"What happened to you?"

He stared into the windshield as if the answer might be hidden in the dark garage. "I don't know."

"I have worked with shell-shocked soldiers—"

"Sometimes I'm somewhere else." I felt his hand outside the coats clench into a fist.

"Where?" I spoke as gently as I could.

"I don't know." His tone was anguished. "My body is still there, functioning, but my mind is in a fog. I . . ."

"Does it happen often?"

"Not like it used to. It's better, but I can't promise that . . ."

"That what?"

"That I won't end up back there in the fog." He pulled me close. "I've never hurt anyone, not during those moments. If I thought that I would hurt you, that I could hurt you, I would stay away. I promise you that."

"You already made good on that promise," I said bitterly.

He put one hand on the crown of my head. "It was the best I could do."

"What is the best you can do now?"

"I think I can stay. I'm better," he said. "I can sometimes sleep more than a few hours. I am mostly sober again. Sometimes I can see through the . . . episodes, and stop them."

"How do I know you won't leave—?"

"Because." He cleared his throat. "It would kill me to leave you again."

I heard truth in his words. "Can we build something where no one leaves? And no one dies?"

He swept me into a rough hug. "God help us, Spatz."

I held him.

Eventually, we lay back down on the lorry's seat. He rearranged the coats over us. I stroked my hands along his body, exploring the things that had changed in the last two years. He had so many scars now. I began to kiss them, one by one.

He arched under my lips and moaned softly. I smiled.

A weight fell against the outside of the lorry. Knuckles pounded the window glass.

20

Lars snatched his gun off the dashboard and pointed it at the lorry's window. With his other hand, he pushed my head down against the seat.

"Lang? Is that you?" called a male voice with a Russian accent. "What the hell are you doing here?"

Lars's shoulders relaxed, and he lowered the gun to his side. I ducked my head under my coat collar. Safe from danger, but not from embarrassment.

Lars sat abruptly. A gust of cold air shot into our nest. I drew my coat high around me. He slung his coat over his shoulders, put a finger to his lips, and rearranged my coat.

He cranked down the window. "Good morning, Herr Populov. I stopped by for a bit of sleep."

"Can't spring for a hotel anymore, Lang?" Herr Populov laughed. "Hope he paid you in advance, Fräulein."

I gritted my teeth and kept my face hidden, wanting him to simply go away.

"I paid her plenty in advance," Lars said. "She's my wife."

What a lovely introduction. I stifled a groan. I would have to meet Herr Populov now, and under the worst of circumstances. I sat up, careful to keep myself covered by my coat. My cheeks burned. What would my mother have said about me being caught naked on the

front seat of a lorry and being mistaken for a prostitute, even with a man who was allegedly my husband? My father would have beaten me so hard, I could not have sat down for days. Then again, he had done that often, and for less.

"Spatz, I'd like you to meet Herr Populov, the man who kindly extended us his hospitality last night. Herr Populov, my wife, Frau Lang."

I stretched my good hand across Lars. Herr Populov shook it with his calloused one. "I'm sorry, Frau Lang. I meant no offense. I'll go wait in the office."

"My son is sleeping in there," Lars said.

"Son?" Herr Populov looked as if the roof had caved right in on his head. I imagine I looked no better, but Lars seemed to be enjoying himself.

"If you could give me a few minutes," Lars said. "I will meet you by the front door, and we can all pretend that this didn't happen."

Herr Populov's face retreated. Footsteps echoed off the walls of the cavernous warehouse. The overhead light snapped on, and the front door closed with a bang.

"Sorry, Spatz," Lars said.

"You do not look particularly sorry." I felt around on the floor for my clothes.

He handed me my slip. "I am not particularly sorry to be here now. Perhaps it shows."

He kissed me gently on the lips, and I had to smile at him. "Embarrassed, yes. Sorry, no." I wriggled my cold slip over my head and finger-combed my hair.

"My god," he said. "You are beautiful."

"I probably look a sight!"

He gathered me into his arms. "A more beautiful sight I have never seen."

We stared at each other like love-struck teens.

He cleared his throat. "I'd better get shaved and go talk to Populov before he comes back."

"I want to be dressed the next time I meet him," I said. "So, go."
He climbed out of the lorry and shut the door.

I resumed my search on the lorry's floor. My clothes were scattered, and it took me some time to find them and get dressed. I lifted Paul's shirt off the steering wheel and hung it over my arm before stepping into my cold shoes and hurrying across the concrete floor to the office.

I stood next to Anton's makeshift bed and studied his face, relaxed in sleep. I folded Paul's shirt and added it to my bag. "Anton?"

"Here." He yawned loudly.

"We have to leave now, so that the shop can open for business."

Lars emerged from the washroom, wiping shaving cream off his face. "My apologies, Frau Lang." He kissed me on the nose and was gone, leaving behind the scent of his eucalyptus shaving cream.

Anton rubbed his eyes and sat. "Are you two pretending to be married again?"

"After a fashion." I handed him his shoes and pointed to the washroom. "And if it comes up outside, Lars is your father."

Shaking his head, he trudged over to the washroom.

I folded his blanket, then packed the nightshirt he had used as a pillow. We had unpacked nothing else.

Anton stumbled back out and leaned against the wall. "What time is it?"

"Almost seven." I stepped past him into the washroom. I looked at the filthy floor and wished for the luxury of waiting for better facilities. Instead, I splashed cold water on my face and hands, and smoothed my hair. I chanced a glance in the mirror. My relaxed face told the story of last night's events in the lorry. I hoped that it would be too dark outside for Herr Populov to notice.

Best to get it over with. I collected our things, and Anton and I walked to the front door.

Herr Populov and Lars stood next to the warehouse. The cherry of Herr Populov's cigarette shone red against the early morning gloom.

Lars took my bag. He ruffled Anton's hair. Anton gave him an

aggrieved look, me a warning one, lest I decide that hair ruffling was suddenly acceptable.

"My apologies for the . . . the inconvenience," I stammered to Herr Populov, blushing.

Herr Populov's hearty laugh rolled out. "Not a problem, Frau Lang. Your husband explained to me that you will be here for the next few nights."

"We appreciate the hospitality." I hoped that darkness hid my glowing face.

"Anton," Lars said. "How about you open the door so I can fetch the lorry out here before your mother faints on the grass?"

Anton stepped over to me. "Are you all right?"

"I am fine," I said. "Thank you. But, please, do get the door."

Lars and Anton walked back toward the warehouse door together.

"He's a fine man, your husband," Herr Populov said. "It's an honor to help him, and you and the boy."

"Thank you." I wondered what he knew about Lars. Had they met in Russian prison?

He opened a pack of Sobranies. Russian cigarettes, too. "May I?"

"Of course." I hated the smell, but could hardly tell him what to do at his own warehouse, especially considering my own actions here. "Have you known my husband long?"

"Long enough. He's helped me more than once, if that's what you're asking."

I itched to ask more, but Lars stopped the lorry and stepped down to open the door and help me in. He slid in beside me.

"Breakfast?" Lars asked.

"Places are open this early?" Anton rested his head against the window. "People eat in them?"

Lars chuckled. He waved to Herr Populov as we drove away.

Even at this early hour, lorries had begun to arrive at the warehouses around us. The workers wore mostly blue overalls and shouted greetings to one another. I sank down in the seat, wondering if they

were watching me as much as I watched them. Tomorrow, I would wake up earlier. "A tea would not come amiss."

I looked over at Anton. He had gone back to sleep.

"I envy him the sleep." Lars turned off onto a street that led out of the warehouse district. We passed battered brick apartment buildings.

"Me, too."

"I left Populov a list of supplies. He said he will have them by the end of the day, so tonight I can build the compartment."

"Wonderful." I covered my mouth and yawned.

"My apologies for the wake-up call," he said.

"The warehouse experience was not quite up to Hotel Adlon's standards."

"I don't know," he said. "Parts of it were sublime."

I leaned against him. "They were."

We drove in silence. The sky slowly turned dove gray. We stopped near a café as its inside light flickered on. The waitress took chairs off the tabletops. We would have a bit of a wait before she was ready to accept breakfasters.

Lars gestured at the sky. "So, in the cold gray light of morning, do you want me to slip quietly away from this noisy crowd?"

I recognized the Rilke quote. I also knew the last line. "Only if I come, too."

He dropped his arm around me and drew me in close. "Good, Spatz."

Together we watched the waitress bustle around. He rested his cheek against the top of my head. His breath stirred my hair. This moment, this sky, Lars warm by my side, and Anton asleep a meter away. That was what we had.

Paul had nothing. Grief choked out my feeling of peace. I had no right to it.

The waitress unlocked the front door. Lars stirred. I shook Anton. "Breakfast time."

Anton stretched like a cat. Looking at him made me yawn.

In the restaurant, Lars convinced the waitress to give us a large table at the back. All three of us were ravenous and ordered eggs, rolls, meat, and tea. She shook her head, clearly disbelieving that we would finish it all.

But we nearly did. Lars paid and slipped her an extra bill to give us longer use of the table.

He cleared his throat and sat up straight, suddenly looking like a headmaster. I crossed my hands in my lap and assumed my best attentive pupil posture. Anton followed suit.

"I think we need to talk about the implications of what happened to Paul last night," Lars said.

Anton sucked in a quick breath. I put a hand on his shoulder. He promptly shook it off, trying to act the part of a man in front of Lars.

Lars looked at me. "How much do we tell Anton?"

Anton crossed his arms.

"All of it," I said. "He runs the same risks that we do."

Anton raised his eyebrows in surprise.

"Very well." Lars drew a worn black notebook out of his inside coat pocket. "Do you have a pen, Spatz?"

I handed him my fountain pen.

"Let's start with what we know." Lars quickly wrote down the time and cause of death. Anton and I tried to decipher his handwriting upside down as the pen flew across the paper, filling in details of last night's events.

"How long were you a policeman?" Anton asked.

Lars smiled briefly. "I was a *kommissar* in the police for more years than I want to think about. In fact, I was a *kommissar* when I met your mother. I investigated murders in Berlin."

"You can find out who killed Paul?"

"I hope so." Lars tapped the pen's nib against the paper. "But I don't have the resources I'm used to. And I didn't solve every case when I did."

"Really?" Anton sounded surprised.

"I did have the highest solve rate in Berlin," Lars said. "So there is hope for me."

Anton nodded sagely.

"Spatz," Lars said. "This won't be easy for you, but . . ."

"Yes?" I said.

"Do you have a sketch pad, or a notebook?"

I took out my sketch pad, its leaves considerably larger than Lars's notebook.

"I wish I had a photograph," he said. "But we will make do. I would like you to draw me two sketches. One of the kitchen as we saw it when we entered last night. Everything but the body."

"Paul's body," I corrected.

"Apologies." He briefly touched my shoulder. "After you finish that sketch, I would like a sketch of Paul. Add nothing. If you are uncertain, leave it blank."

I dug in my satchel for a pencil and started work. Drawing the kitchen without Paul in it was easier than I had expected. I sketched in the table, bare except for the note that Lars had taken. I cross-hatched in shadows in the corner. One chair was pushed into the table. Another sat at an angle, the third pushed back against the wall, and the final chair held Paul. He had been eating and drinking with his killer. I drew his chair in quick strokes, then moved down to the floor. Broken dishes, an empty glass, and a rumpled pile of tablecloth.

I sketched in the window. The bullet had passed through Paul and pierced the glass. A round spiderweb of cracks radiated from the hole. Undisturbed curtains hung on each side.

Lars and Anton talked quietly next to me. Lars took a statement from Anton. The building door had been locked; Anton had un-locked it. Paul's front door had been left open. Anton thought he might have heard footsteps going up the stairs above him. No one passed him on his way up. I shuddered at the thought that Anton might have met the murderer.

I handed Lars my sketch and started drawing Paul's outline. They pored over the first sketch, discussing its accuracy. I blocked out

their voices and concentrated on Paul. He had slumped sideways in the chair, as if he had yanked off the tablecloth but had not had time to raise his arms again. I took a deep breath.

I started with his feet. He wore the old brown slippers he always donned inside. His shoes, I knew, were lined up by the front door. His pants had been darker near the bottom. Wet. He had been out in the rain. Had he walked in the rain with his killer, or let him in later? Whom would he let into his home so late? Not a stranger, surely.

I finished his rumpled shirt, the slump of his shoulder, his empty hands, until all that remained was his face.

I took a long drink of tea.

"If you can't finish it," Lars said. "I—"

"If Paul can die there, I can certainly stand to sketch it." The pencil trembled in my hand when I went back to work. I pretended to be a camera, taking a picture, that I had not loved Paul, that I did not care that he was gone.

I finished the sketch, turned it over, and slid it across the table.

Lars studied the sketch, and I studied him. His eyes darted around the picture, taking in every detail, lingering on some, skipping others.

"What do you think, Herr Kommissar? Give me your report."

He paused, thinking. "Paul had no defensive wounds on his hands or arms. I didn't have time to check elsewhere. Based on the door's condition, I would say that he let his killer in, so it may well have been someone whom he knew."

"Someone he thought he could trust," I said bitterly.

"Or at least someone from whom he did not fear harm," Lars said.

"What will the police think? Will they look for the killer?" Anton looked at my sketch. I turned it over, not wanting him to remember Paul that way.

"I am hopeful that they will write it off as a suicide. That's why I left my gun. If they do, no one will bother to dust the room for prints and find yours, mine, and your mother's."

"But the bullet that killed him will not match your gun," I said.

"We got lucky there," Lars said, and I grimaced. "Considering. The bullet went through his head and out the window. A diligent search may find it, but it just as well may not. I don't expect an investigation. A Jewish man is not one whose death greatly concerns the Nazi police. Even if it did, he had recently lost his wife and child to the deportation. There is evidence that he tried suicide the night before."

I thought of struggling with Paul yesterday, saving his life only so that someone else could take it. I felt his blood-slick wrist under my fingers and remembered closing his familiar eyes for the last time. Lars took my hand.

"Why would someone want to kill Paul?" Anton asked.

"I think that his killer was after me, not Paul," I said.

Anton gasped, and I felt a fool for saying it.

"Possibly," Lars said. "But we cannot be certain of that."

"The note?"

"What if the note was left in Paul's mailbox, or pushed under the door and he put it on the table? And what about the note in the desk?"

"What note?" Anton asked. "I don't remember a note on the table."

Lars took the folded-up note from his inside notebook and looked at me. After I nodded, he handed it to Anton.

"Whose life did you steal?" he asked.

"No one's, except in self-defense," Lars answered for me.

"That is true," I said. "But that does not change the fact that men have died by my hand."

"How many?" Anton asked.

I closed my eyes, but the truth did not go away. "Two."

I opened my eyes. "Put them on the list, Lars."

"I would prefer to start with Paul and Miriam," he said. "I have no idea who wrote the note. Neither do you. It is possible that the killer was trying to punish you, but it is also possible that the note arrived before the killer came for Paul."

I wondered if he believed it, or if he only tried to assuage my guilt.

"Since Paul and Miriam are the ones who are dead," Lars tapped his pen against the notebook. "Let's start with their enemies."

"I have no idea what enemies Paul or Miriam had." Paul had been living mostly in seclusion since the Nazis came to power, avoiding trouble until I came along. "Miriam's family? He was betraying her, and was gone when she was deported."

Lars wrote that down in his precise, cramped handwriting. "Anyone else?"

"Before this visit, I had not spoken to Paul in two years, and we barely spoke then." I clenched my hands in my lap. I had not helped him then or later.

"Who might know more about his enemies?" Lars prompted. I wondered if he cared, or if he sought only to distract me.

"Maria at the *Tageblatt*. Paul's mistress," I said promptly. She would know exactly which rocks to turn over to find Paul's secrets. But would she tell me?

"How does she feel about you?" Lars asked.

I fiddled with a leftover sausage on my plate. "She hates me."

Anton looked at me in shock. I felt flattered that he had thought no one hated me. I wished I felt the same.

"Did she know that you were Adelheid Zinsli? Did she hate you enough to write the letters in Switzerland?" Lars asked.

"She might have known that I was in Switzerland. Paul might have told her I covered the Games in '36. If so, she might have guessed that I was Adelheid Zinsli. Not many female reporters from Switzerland covered the Games."

Lars underlined her name.

"She might have written the letters, but I do not see why. I do not think she would have killed Paul. It seems as if she would have killed me first."

"Perhaps she intended to kill you, but something went awry," Lars said.

Anton's eyes widened.

I pulled a handful of coins out of my pocket and handed them to Anton.

"Could you please fetch us a newspaper?" I pointed to a wizened newspaper seller hunched in a stand outside the restaurant.

Anton knew what I was up to, but he took the coins and tore out the door.

"I think we are frightening Anton," I said.

"Good," Lars answered. "He should be frightened. This is a frightening situation. He would be a fool if he were not frightened. A fool in danger."

Like Paul.

"I want to protect him," I said.

"You can't protect every single person in the world, Spatz," Lars said.

"First, Anton," I said. "Then you."

He brushed the back of his hand along my cheek. "What about yourself?"

"I am on the list, too," I said.

Anton dumped the paper on my lap and sat next to me. "Did I miss anything?"

Lars slowly drew his hand back. "No."

Anton's pointy chin jutted, and I knew that he was trying to decide what we had been doing. "Are you two pretending to be married?"

"Lars and I are . . ." What were we?

I could not explain to Anton what we were to each other when I had no idea myself. I began anyway. "It is a complicated situation."

Lars moved to stand next to my chair. Was he leaving us alone so I could explain the situation to Anton?

Instead, Lars dropped to one knee next to me. "Hannah, would you—?"

"That is not how you do that," Anton interrupted. "She's my mother."

Lars took my hand and slipped off the ring he had placed there two years ago. My ring finger felt cold.

So far, no one in the restaurant had noticed. "Lars, you are making a spectacle of   "

"Do I have your permission to ask her hand in marriage?" Lars asked Anton.

I stared at them both, dumbfounded. The waitress eyed us suspiciously.

"Are your intentions honorable?" Anton's expression was as serious as Lars's.

"Nothing but," Lars said.

"Will you take care of her?" Anton asked. "And not abandon her again? Especially with other women."

"Anton—," I began.

"Please, Spatz." Lars held up his palm. He turned to Anton. "I promise."

"Will you keep her out of trouble?" Anton asked.

Lars took my hand again. "I would give my life to keep her safe. But I don't think anyone can keep her out of trouble."

"At least he's no liar," Anton said. "I give my blessing. The rest is up to you, Mother."

Both turned to look at me, Anton's blue eyes expectant, Lars's dark ones frightened. Did he fear that I would say no or that I would say yes?

"It is up to me," I said. "Anton, you are not—"

"Hannah Vogel," Lars interrupted, his voice pitched low so that it did not carry beyond our table. "Will you marry me?"

I took a deep breath. Lars looked ready to faint.

Logically, I should wait. In many ways, I barely knew him. In others, I knew him better than I had ever known anyone. There were a very great many reasons to say no or maybe.

"Yes," I said.

He slid the ring back onto my finger. It felt colder than my skin, but still felt right. He dropped a light kiss on my lips, and I shivered.

"Are you going to eat that?" Anton pointed his fork at my plate.

We laughed. I pushed my plate toward Anton.

He speared my last sausage and ate it in two quick bites.

"From this point on, at least in Germany, we are Hannah and Lars Schmidt," Lars said. "You are Anton Schmidt. Do you understand?"

Anton set down his fork. "Yes, sir."

Smiling gazes of the other customers followed us as we walked out together, Lars holding my arm and Anton on my other side. I was happy to have them close.

Workers in caps and short open jackets jostled by on their way to the warehouse district we had left behind earlier. They were different from the office workers in suits I had passed on my way to Herr Silbert's. They looked more carefree, but also more tired. I wondered how much the Nazis influenced the day-to-day workings in most factories. I imagined that the Nazis were a heavier burden for those in management.

Lars navigated us deftly across the sidewalk to the lorry. Water beaded on its surface from a shower that had passed over while we ate breakfast. Oyster gray clouds promised more of the same before the day was out.

Anton squeezed my hand before he let it go. I looked over at him. "How are you holding up?"

"I want to be a policeman." He bounced on the balls of his feet, excited at the prospect. "Last night Lars told me about some cases that he's worked and—"

"Appropriate conversation for a thirteen-year-old?" I asked Lars.

"Appropriate for this thirteen-year-old," Lars said. Anton smiled.

I swallowed my protest. Considering the alternatives he had recently seen, I could hardly fault Anton's decision to be an honest policeman.

Lars opened the door for me and helped me in. His hand lingered on my side, and I leaned against it. We both smiled.

"Where do we go next?" Anton slammed the door on his side of lorry. "To solve the case."

"I can't work on the lorry until tonight," Lars said. "Our best plan would be to keep our heads down until we get out of Germany."

"I agree," I said. "But I have a few things to do first."

Lars smiled. "Safe things? Like the zoo? Or a quick trip to the cinema?"

I ignored him and unfolded the newspaper Anton had fetched while we were still in the restaurant. The familiar smell of newsprint filled the air.

But that was the only good thing about the newspaper. The headline screamed: JEWISH SWINE SHOOTS GERMAN DIPLOMAT. With growing dread, I read the article. Leaving out the racial outrage, the facts seemed to be that a Jewish teenager named Herschel Grynszpan had shot a German diplomat named Ernst vom Rath in Paris to protest the treatment of his family at Zbąszyń.

I read excerpts aloud. Lars's face grew more serious with each word. I felt as if the world had just shifted. More restrictions on Jews in Germany. A ban on Jewish children attending German schools. A ban on Jewish newspapers. The suspension of all Jewish cultural activities.

A turning point.

"If vom Rath dies," I said, "there will be terrible reprisals against Jews in Germany."

"We had best get out before that diplomat dies," Lars said. "After those reprisals, they'll surely increase security at the borders."

I wished that the lorry were already complete.

"It might not be as bad as that," Lars said. "He might live."

A few straggling workers passed by the lorry, hurrying to get to work before it rained again.

"Even if that young man's gunshot does not kill him, someone else's will." I refolded the newspaper and dropped it on the lorry's floor. "It is the perfect opportunity for the Nazis to exact their revenge for the fictitious crimes of the Jews. They will not let a chance like that pass."

A flash of recognition flitted across Lars's face. He had just

thought of something, and I realized what. "Last night's note. Let me see it."

Reluctantly, he handed it to me.

I unfolded it and read it again. It said: *The Jews are not done murdering though, are they?*

I looked at Lars. "Do you suppose the letter writer meant this attack in Paris?"

"It seems paranoid," he said. "How could he know of a shooting in Paris? The newspapers did not report the attack on vom Rath until this morning."

I could tell that he argued only for argument's sake; he was worried, too. "When did the Nazi leadership know it? Or the Gestapo?"

"I don't know, Spatz."

"Let's find a telephone booth," I said, "and I will see."

Lars drove slowly down the wet street. Telephone booths were not so close together as in tonier neighborhoods, but we found one.

I dropped in coins and asked for the newspaper. Lars and Anton stood next to the booth. Anton was deep in some complicated story, pausing only to give Lars a chance to nod to show that he was still listening.

I called the newspaper for a quick rundown of the Grynszpan story. He had shot vom Rath at five thirty yesterday evening, only a few hours before Paul's murder. If the news had reached Germany by then, it probably reached only the highest levels of the Gestapo. So, either the person who killed Paul was very highly placed, or the note could not possibly refer to vom Rath's shooting. Someone highly placed would have waited and killed me last night, instead of bothering with letters.

Herr Knecht himself came on the line. "Frau Zinsli."

"Good morning. What did the embassy say?" I asked.

He sighed, a long windy exhalation that told me the news was bad. "They are not inclined to help you, but I am exerting pressure. It may take a few more days."

"Thank you," I said. "I am sorry to have dragged the paper into this."

"A daredevil reporter trapped in Nazi Germany will be a top story," he said. "Once you get back out. Keep a journal."

Ever the newsman. "I shall."

"In the meantime, try to stay out of trouble. Call immediately if your situation changes."

"I intend to."

"Good girl," he said. "Keep your chin up. We'll get you out of there, eventually."

I thanked him again and rang off. If something went awry with Lars's plan with the lorry, I hoped that Herr Knecht might help us escape, although it seemed less likely with each call.

I stood alone in the phone booth. I had two things that I needed to do for Paul. This was least important, but perhaps most dangerous. But I owed it to Paul. That and much more besides. I braced myself against the wooden side of the booth and dialed the *Berliner Zeitung*.

I asked the chirpy secretary for Maria, giving my name as Petra Weill, which would make Maria angry enough to take my call. She would hate the thought of anyone poaching on her Peter Weill pseudonym.

"Yes?" Maria asked peremptorily as soon as she got on the line. I relished the familiar sound of her irritation.

"Petra Weill here," I said. She would recognize my voice.

"How kind of you to telephone, Petra." Sarcasm overlaid her words. "To what do I owe the pleasure?"

"I have news for you."

When she paused, I knew she tried to decide whether I might have useful information. I forced a carefree tone. "It has been such a long time, but I remember the good times we had, you and I, and our good friend Paul?"

"Fine," she said flatly.

What else could she say? By bringing up Paul's name, I had re-

minded her that I knew enough to cause her trouble. "Where should we meet?"

"Let's have dinner tonight at the restaurant where I broke the strap on my shoe. What's it called?" she said.

She had once broken the strap on her shoe when we were at the Ufa-Palast am Zoo movie theater. We were standing in line to see Marlene Dietrich in *The Blue Angel*. Maria had been furious about the broken strap. She probably would have gone straight home if she had not been too jealous to leave us alone at the cinema. It had been an unpleasant night. She wanted me to meet her there. The restaurant was code so that no one overhearing the call would know where she was headed.

I played along. "I remember. The restaurant was called the Angel."

"Exactly!" she said. "I'll see you there at around seven."

So, we would meet in the theater at the Palast am Zoo during the showing closest to seven. I rang off.

Lars and Anton practiced boxing moves on the sidewalk. I did not like to see Anton fight. But he had good reach, and Lars appeared to be giving him solid tips about increasing his punching power.

I had one more thing to do for Paul. I had to explain his death to his father. I called, and Herr Keller asked that I meet him at Saint Hedwig's, the largest Catholic church in Berlin.

I stepped into the brisk fall air. The boxers had taken off their coats and sparred in rolled-up shirtsleeves. Their faces glowed from the exercise.

Anton gauged my reaction. "Bad news?"

"The newspaper confirms that vom Rath was shot last night, probably too late for our note writer."

"That's good news," Lars said.

"You made three calls." Anton crossed his arms. "I counted."

"You will make a fine detective one day," I said.

"The second call?" he persisted.

"Later," I said.

"The third call?" Lars shrugged his coat back on.

"To Paul's father. I must go meet him now."

Lars put his hand on the small of my back. I savored how it felt there.

"Why must you notify them yourself?" Lars said. "It might be dangerous, and the police will have informed his parents of his death."

"The police." I swallowed. "The police told them that their son committed suicide. His parents are practicing Catholics."

"I thought that Paul was Jewish," Anton said.

"Half Jewish, but he was raised Catholic," I said. "His mother was born Jewish, and that is enough for the regime, even though she converted to Catholicism when she married Paul's father. Catholics believe that you go to hell if you commit suicide. I cannot let his parents add that to their grief."

"Where are you meeting?" Lars asked.

"Saint Hedwig's."

He stared off into the distance. "It's a bad idea."

"Regardless," I said.

"You'll never win when she uses that voice." Anton pulled his coat back on. "Even if you are married."

A muscle twitched under Lars's eye. "Thank you for the tip, Anton."

"Would you care to come with me?" I patted Lars's arm.

"I would like to follow up on Paul's death." Lars donned his fedora again.

"What does that mean?" Anton asked. "How do you follow up?"

"If I were still in the police force, I would interview the suspects, see if they had alibis for the time of Paul's death, and check those alibis. Check their fingerprints against the scene. Check their weapons to see if they matched the bullet that killed Paul. Talk to the people in Paul's building. Look for eyewitnesses. Go over the scene again and see what else I could find."

"Can you do all that?" Anton asked.

A woman dressed all in blue walked by, carrying two shopping

bags from Wertheim, a formerly Jewish-owned department store. Like everything else, it had been Aryanized. She paid us no heed.

"No, but I can consult with someone who has."

"Who?" Anton clearly wanted to get going. I wished that he were not so enthusiastic about looking for a killer, but I said nothing. The alternative might be a child properly frightened out of his wits. Better for him to think that there were things that he could do.

"Whom can you consult with?" Anton repeated.

"An old friend," Lars said. "He works for the police."

"May I come, too?" Anton asked.

"I'm afraid not," Lars said. "I have to do this by myself."

We separated and agreed to meet back at Friedrichstadt subway station, not far from the church, in a few hours.

Anton and I took the subway to Saint Hedwig's. He told me all about his shooting trip with Lars and the boxing techniques he had just learned. I pretended to listen, my mind already with Paul's father.

Across the square stood the cathedral. It had been modeled after the Pantheon in Rome. My brother always called it "the Catholic breast." When we neared the curved cathedral, I interrupted Anton. "We will go in separately. You go in first and sit in a pew on the left-hand side. I will come in a few minutes later and, if I can, I will sit on the right-hand side a row behind you. I can see you, and you can see me without too much trouble. But do not look at me. Wait quietly until you see me get up to leave. Then follow. Do you understand?"

"Will you be long?" Anton's eyes darted around the square, suddenly looking for enemies.

"I do not know." I stopped. Cooing pigeons flew around us. Errant feathers floated to the ground.

"What if something bad happens?" Anton looked into the gray sky as if he expected a soldier to appear there.

"I doubt that anything will." I put a reassuring hand on his shoulder. "If it does, take the side door. Meet up with Lars as we planned. He will know what to do." By the time he met up with Lars, it would

most likely be too late to do anything, but Lars would get Anton out of Berlin safely.

Anton looked as if he knew that, too. "But—"

"This is the time to be a scout," I said. "And bring back reinforcements. Scouts do not enter the battle. That is not their mission."

He dropped his eyes, and I knew that he understood, and hated it.

He walked ahead of me and disappeared into the cathedral. I dreaded losing sight of him, even for a minute, but I counted to sixty and followed him through the arched doorway.

I walked slowly around the inside of the church, aware of Anton every second. My eyes were drawn to the curved ceiling, with its strong ribs and the circle of light at the top. I wished I could have told him that Lorenz Adlon, owner of a hotel where Anton had once stayed with his purported grandmother, was buried in the cemetery in the back. Herr Adlon died in a car accident. A devout monarchist, he refused to enter the Brandenburg Gate using the middle line, as that was once reserved for royalty. For his pains, he had suffered two car accidents at the Brandenburg Gate, the final one fatal. It was exactly the kind of story that Anton enjoyed.

I kept an eye on his blond head, which faced obediently forward, as I searched for Herr Keller. When I was certain that he was not there, I sat at a pew to wait. I curled my hands around the aged oak back of the pew in front and breathed in the smell of stone dust and the lingering traces of incense. My thoughts turned to Ruth, the child that Paul had loved, in spite of her parentage. She was too young to remember him long.

Where was she? Paul had told me that she was with someone who could provide more for her than he could. Was that true? I did not entirely trust his judgment, and I would rest easier if I could see her safe and sound for myself.

Would Herr Keller know? I prayed so. I said a prayer for Paul, too.

I hoped that he had found peace, and I promised him, as I had promised his wife, that I would help Ruth if I could.

A figure sat next to me. I unfolded my hands and sat back to look at him. Herr Keller looked so much like Paul that tears jumped into my eyes. He had aged much in the past ten years and looked as if he had not slept, but his familiar brown eyes studied me with curiosity and suspicion.

"Good evening, Fräulein Vogel." His deep voice was quiet.

"Hello, Herr Keller." I held out my hand, and he took it. He shook it once, then held on to it.

"Why are you here? Paul said that you escaped. Proud of you for it, he was."

"I am here only for a few days." I hoped. "I want to talk to you about your son."

"I suppose you heard that he's dead? Took the coward's way out, the police tell me."

"They are wrong." My words swelled in the empty space.

"You know better than the police? They said he'd tried the night before, too. I always knew they'd kill him before this ended."

"I—" I cleared my throat. "I was there the night before, and he did try. I bandaged his wrist. By the next morning, he knew that what he had done was wrong, that he had to take care of Ruth. He said he would make sure she was safe."

"Why would Ruth not be safe?" He let go of my hand and lowered his eyebrows.

I kept going. I would never get through it if I stopped. "The night that he died, I was the first one to come upon his body and—there was no gun in the room. He could not have shot himself without a gun."

Herr Keller raised his long elegant hands to his face and ran them down his cheeks. "You told this to the police, I imagine?"

"I cannot."

He put both hands on the back of the pew in front of us and gripped it tightly. "Don't suppose you'll tell me why not?"

I shook my head.

"You always were a closemouthed one." He leaned back. We sat together in silence. Anton bowed his head in front of us. From what I could tell, he read the Bible.

"Still, my son loved you. Should have married you. Hard to imagine now, but we worried that you weren't Catholic. I wasn't so happy when he dated that hard number from the newspaper. She turned out all right, in the end, I think."

I did not think that Maria had turned out all right, but I did not contradict him.

"In the end, when he married, it was a Polish girl. Turned him into a devout Jew. He would have been better off letting you turn him into a Protestant or an atheist, or whatever it is you are."

"Herr Keller—" I did not know how, or if, to defend Miriam or myself.

"Where's his wife got to? I visited the apartment to—to collect some things, but no sign of her."

I briefly told how she had been deported to Poland and died there.

"Little Ruth?" he asked. "Is she in Poland, too?"

"No. Paul said he knew where she was. Did you speak to him in the last few days? Did he tell you?"

He squeezed the pew so hard that his knuckles whitened. "Not in the last few weeks. Not since Ruth's second birthday. How did he lose track of her? Do you know where she is? Is she safe?"

"Paul thought she was safe." I wished I had a better answer.

Herr Keller's grip on the pew did not loosen. "Have you told the police?"

"I cannot."

"I will," he said. "Today."

That might open an investigation into Paul's death. But if there was a chance they might find Ruth, it had to be done.

"My wife and I adore that girl. Bundle of trouble she is. Parents always fighting over her. Her mother wanted her to be a little lady.

Paul wanted to let her run a little wilder, feel the mud between her toes."

I studied tall arched windows. They had beheld much grief since they were built, and they were likely to see much more. "Do you know where she might be? Perhaps with Miriam's family?"

"They're all dead, so far as I know," he said. "This whole Nazi business has gone too far. I've been trying to convince Paul to leave for years. He wouldn't budge. But we'll take Ruth out, Frau Keller and I, if you bring her to us."

They had been good parents to Paul. Ruth would be safer with them than hiding in a box being smuggled across the Swiss border, and I worried that Lars's shell shock was not something that a young girl should see. Anton probably should not either.

"If I find her," I said, "and I can, I will bring her to you."

"Bless you." He wrapped his arm around my shoulder and drew me close. He smelled like Paul. He felt like Paul. I closed my eyes and pretended that he was.

I sat back up before I started to cry. "What about Miriam's friends?"

"I don't know of any," he said. "She spoke only Polish, so we never had a proper conversation."

Miriam and I had had only one conversation, too, where I promised her to help Ruth. So far, I had failed at that.

"About Paul." He paused.

"Yes?"

He drew a packet of letters tied with a green ribbon out of his pocket. I recognized my handwriting on the envelopes. Love letters that I had written to Paul twenty years before. He had saved them all this time. Herr Keller handed me the packet. "I found these in the cupboard in the bedroom. I couldn't go into . . . the kitchen."

I turned the envelopes over in my hands, a lump in my throat. I had been so young, battered by my childhood and Walter's death, but still so much more hopeful than now.

"I didn't think you would want anyone to read them," he said. "So I took them. Paul would want you to have them."

I stroked my thumb down the stack. I had purchased the cream-colored paper and envelopes in Herr Silbert's shop, long before I was a reporter and before his first arrest for forgery. Memories and these pieces of paper were all that remained of Paul for me. That and his little girl, Ruth.

I turned into Herr Keller's arms and cried for Paul. For the years we had, for the years we had lost, and for all the years he would never see.

Eventually I wiped my eyes and sat back up. "I am sorry."

"Don't be," he said. "It's good to know he'll be missed."

"Thank you for the letters." I blew my nose on my handkerchief.

A priest in a cassock stopped at the end of our pew. He inclined his balding head toward us. "Herr Keller?"

"Everything is fine, Rector," Herr Keller said. "She is an old friend of Paul's."

"You have my condolences," the rector said. "Paul was a good man."

He turned and walked silently toward the altar. "Was that Rector Lichtenberg?"

"A friend to Christians and Jews," Herr Keller said. "He has spoken out against the mistreatment of the Jews since the beginning."

A brave stance, and one that not many Catholic or Protestant priests were prepared to take under Hitler. I hoped it would not get him killed.

"Who would want to kill Paul?" he asked. "He was a good boy. Doing the best he could."

I had hoped that he would have an answer to that question. Paul was not a man who accumulated enemies. Unlike me. "Do you know anyone who might have had a grudge against Paul, or against Miriam?"

He looked at me sharply. "I thought you said that she died in childbirth."

"I am taking nothing for granted," I said.

He ran his hands down his face again. "I don't know who would want to kill either one."

I had little idea either. But both of them were dead.

"If you find out who killed him," he said raggedly, "tell me. Please."

"I will." I gripped the letters tightly.

"And, please, find Ruth. She loves our house. My wife and Ruth have so many tea parties together." He swallowed heavily. "She has her own set of dishes with butterflies on them. For her birthday I bought her a matching set for her house."

An image out of the sketch I had drawn flashed in my mind. A plate on the floor with a butterfly on it. Had Ruth been at the table when Paul was killed? Or, perhaps, I was remembering it wrong. I had to go back and see. But I could not drag Anton back there. If it was a murder scene, I might be able to get past the policemen on my own, but not with Anton in tow. "But first you must do me a favor."

"Anything."

I pointed to the back of Anton's head. "Take him to the Friedrichstadt subway station in two hours. He will be met by a man named Lars."

"Why can't you do it yourself?" He tilted his head to the side, waiting for an explanation.

I could give him none. "It is an uncertain world, Herr Keller."

"If this Lars isn't there?"

"He will be."

He studied me for a good long time before nodding. "It's for Paul, isn't it?"

"And for Ruth."

"Let's get started," he said. "And thank you for coming to tell me that Paul did not commit suicide. It will be a comfort to his mother, as much as anything can be right now."

I stared into the older version of Paul's eyes. He turned away.

"Anton," I called softly.

He turned his head, surprised.

"Come here."

He walked back to us.

"Herr Keller," I said, "I would like you to meet Anton."

They shook hands and looked at me.

"I have an errand to run," I began.

"No." Anton shifted his feet wide apart, a fighting stance.

"Herr Keller will take you to the subway station. I will meet you and Lars there."

"I want to go with you." Anton's eyes widened. I knew he was afraid.

"It is nothing dangerous," I said. "Merely complicated."

"Are you at least taking Lars?" he pleaded.

"No. And try not to worry. It is not dangerous." No more so than anything else.

"When I'm older, I won't let you," he said.

"I have to." I hugged him hard and kissed him on the forehead. "Stay here for at least five minutes."

I watched him struggle with his desire to disobey me. In the end, I saw him relent. "All right."

"I love you," I said.

"I love you, too."

I dropped my hand to his shoulder and squeezed it before walking out the door.

I crossed the square and boarded the subway, trying not to cry. I hated to leave him, but I dared not take him with me. It felt good to be on my own again, running risks that affected only me.

23

I found an empty bench on the subway. The car held only a few passengers. Most people were at work for the day. I had only a few hours, so I had to plan this carefully.

A man sat too close to me on the bench. I raised my head to glare at him. Lars.

"Wouldn't it be more convincing if you pretended you knew me?" He leaned in close and kissed my cheek. Even such a trivial contact caused my heart to beat faster.

"Where did you come from?" I whispered, and gave him a faux welcoming smile. He must have followed me. How dare he?

"Where's Anton?" He dropped his arm along the back of the seat.

"Safe. Now, why did you follow me to the cathedral? That seems rather dishonest."

"Less so than ditching Anton and, presumably, me so you can strike out on your own?"

I had no good answer to that. "What did you find out?"

He looked around the empty car before answering in a hushed voice. "Paul's death is considered a suicide. No investigation."

Unfortunate for Paul, but lucky for us, as our fingerprints were everywhere and who knew how many people had seen us coming and going out of his apartment.

"If there is no investigation, it means that there is no police guard on his apartment," I said. That would make things easier.

"Dangerous ideas are running through your head." He shifted his arm on the back of the seat to cup my shoulder.

"I want to find evidence of where Ruth ended up." I sat very straight. "I promised her mother, and I would have promised her father, too."

He tipped his hat up. "I thought you said Paul thought she was better off where she was."

"That was only hours after he tried to commit suicide." I stared out at the concrete wall sliding along centimeters from our window. "I do not know how accurate his assessment was."

"And?" He drew out the word as if to indicate that there were many responses to inaccurate assessments.

"I will feel better if I know for certain that he was correct."

He let out a long breath and settled into the seat. He disagreed, but would not argue further. Fine with me.

"Why did you follow me?" I tapped his knee.

"I followed you because I wanted to see if anyone else followed you. I did not expect you to come out alone."

"Did anyone follow us?"

"Not so far as I could tell." He leaned back and crossed his legs. "So, where are we going? Alexanderplatz?"

"You are going to Friedrichstadt subway station to meet Anton, as scheduled."

"I have a bit of time yet." He tilted his hat forward over his eyes and pretended to sleep, but I knew better. As angry as I was at him for following me, I was glad to have him along.

We reached Alexanderplatz station and climbed the stairs holding hands. It was the first time we had held hands in years, and I quite liked it. I felt hopeful that we could sort things out in Switzerland.

As we walked around Paul's apartment building, hand in hand, I filled Lars in on my conversation with Herr Keller. "He wants Ruth, if we find her."

"You won't take her?" Lars doubled back. He seemed to be count-ing people on the street.

"She is not mine to take." I slowed to keep pace with him.

He raised his eyebrow.

"If she had no one else, I would take her," I admitted. "Who would not?"

Lars squeezed my hand. "I suppose I should be grateful that you take in strays."

"Are you a stray?" I leaned over and kissed his cheek.

He slid an arm around my waist. "More than you know."

We had completed our trip around Paul's building. Nothing seemed amiss.

"Windows in the building across the street can look into Paul's. Anyone could be in there, and we would not know. There is no safe way to do this," Lars said. "Let me go in alone."

"Or you let me do it." I put my hands on my hips.

He shook his head. "Which one of us has the most experience with crime scenes? Which one of us has the most training? Which one of us was a policeman and a soldier?"

He was correct, but I did not care. He read my expression, and his face softened. "Fine, Spatz. You win."

"If someone is watching the apartment," I said. "The most logi-cal place is the front, so we can take the back way in."

We used the entrance from the cellar. Once inside, he drew his gun and stuck it under his coat. He insisted on going up the stairs first, with me steps behind. We made it to Paul's apartment without incident.

He checked each room. I went straight to the kitchen, drew the curtains, and turned on the light. Paul's blood still stained the wall. I stared at it, transported to last night. If we had arrived only min-utes earlier, he might still be alive.

I turned my back on the chair where Paul had died and surveyed the room. Nothing had been cleaned up. Someone had kicked a path through the dishes, probably to remove Paul's body, but otherwise everything was untouched.

Back to the broken window and chair, I squatted on the kitchen floor and examined broken crockery. A broken plate, a glass. I sucked in a breath in surprise. "Lars!"

He came in at a run, gun held in front of him.

I picked two pieces off the floor and fitted them together. It was a child's plate with a butterfly on it. I held it up for Lars. "A child's place setting."

Lars picked up a tiny bowl, cup, and spoon. The bowl, too, had a butterfly on it.

"Ruth was here," I said. "Eating dinner with her father." I lifted a piece of broken glass in my gloved hand. "And a woman."

"A woman?" He took the piece from me.

"Lipstick stains." I pointed. "Near the top rim."

"He could have had dinner with Ruth and the woman, but they left before he was killed," Lars said.

"Or he had dinner with them, the woman shot him, and Ruth watched." My head throbbed. I struggled not to be sick.

"Or that." He checked his wristwatch. "We have fifteen more minutes before we need to leave to get Anton."

I sifted through the rest of the dishes, but found nothing else of note. In the living room, I could not find the picture of Ruth or her birth certificate. Had the killer taken them? Or had Herr Keller?

A cursory search of Ruth's bedroom revealed that her clothes were as they had been when I left, yesterday morning. Whoever took her had not packed any of her things. But if they had just shot Paul and saw us running for the building, they would have known that there was no time.

When I came out of the room, Lars stood in the living room reading a letter from a pile. I looked over his shoulder. It was in Polish.

"You can read Polish?" I asked, surprised

"Polish is similar enough to Russian that I can make out a bit of it. Nothing seems significant."

"How fluent is your Russian?"

"Fairly," he said. "I had a great deal of free time to practice it, although considering where I learned it, I doubt that it is drawing room Russian."

I touched his back.

He put the letters back on the desk. "Did you find anything?"

"None of Ruth's clothes are missing."

As we walked out into the hall to the door, I noticed that the green blanket was gone. I hoped that Ruth had it with her, and that she was still alive.

We crossed into the rear courtyard where Anton had played football and marbles and into the adjoining building, through it to the street behind. We walked a few blocks before circling back around to Alexanderplatz subway station. I bought the tickets, because Lars kept his gun drawn but hidden by his coat until we were on the train.

Once the subway doors closed, he stuck his gun into his waistband, put his hand on the small of my back, and directed me to a seat. The subway car was too full to talk, and I had nothing to say.

The killer had taken Ruth.

We had to find her. Lars slipped an arm across my shoulders. I dropped my head against him. He stroked my hair gently, over and over. He knew how worried and terrified I felt.

We arrived at the Friedrichstadt station early. He led us to an empty corner and leaned me up against the wall as if to kiss me.

"Spatz?" he asked. "Are you all right?"

"No," I said. "Some woman murdered Paul and took Ruth. Who knows where Ruth is, and what they have done to her."

He slid his arms around my waist and bent his head close to mine. "We'll find her, if we can."

"The only woman I can think that he might have let in so late is Maria," I said. "But I cannot see why she would kill Paul, or take Ruth."

"Are you going to meet her?" He asked the question, but his taut expression said that he knew the answer.

"At seven," I said. "At the Palast am Zoo."

He closed his eyes.

"If she killed him, I want to know," I said. "If she did not, she deserves to know that he did not commit suicide. That he did not choose to leave her."

"Impeccable at logic." He kissed the tip of my nose. "Terrible at risk assessment."

"Sometimes," I said, "that works to your advantage."

"Not so frequently as you may think."

I glanced once around the bustling station. Everyone seemed to be going about their business and ignoring us. "I am meeting her."

"I expected nothing less." He tucked my hair behind my ears. "If she plans to shoot you, her best chance is while you're still on the street, so she can run afterwards. If she plans to knife you, however, she's best going into the theater with you, so she can stab you in the dark and leave before the film is over."

"She would not have killed Paul," I said. "And she will not kill me. She is vicious but cowardly."

"Be that as it may," he said. "How about you get there early and go in? We will follow. I'll sit in the row behind you. A few seats in. I want you on my left side, in case I need to use my gun."

A shiver of fear ran through me. "All right."

He pulled me closer. I put my arms around his neck.

His lips almost touched mine when he spoke. "If I begged you not to go, would you change your mind?"

My heart hammered so erratically that I had trouble concentrating on his words. "No."

"I didn't think so." He kissed me gently on the lips. "I never thought we would spend our wedding night like this."

"It is not our wedding night." Propriety demanded that I move out of the circle of his arms before things became too heated in the subway station. I rested my head on his shoulder.

He threaded his fingers through my hair, and I nestled deeper in his shoulder.

"I put the ring on your finger this morning. Or have you forgotten?" he said.

"I do not think that is legally binding—"

"It's binding in every way that counts." He kissed me on the lips, and I forgot that I was frightened and sad and that we were in a public building. He pulled back and traced my lips with his fingertip. I smiled.

Behind him, Anton and Herr Keller strode through the door. I slipped out from under Lars's outstretched arm and hurried toward them.

Relief flashed across Anton's face, quickly replaced by a scowl. "Hello."

I thanked Herr Keller and promised to tell him what I found out about his granddaughter. I already lied, as I did not tell him what I had discovered at Paul's apartment and my worries that Ruth was with his murderer. I did ask if he had taken Ruth's birth certificate. He had not.

Lars led us aboveground. Rain drizzled, and Lars opened an umbrella. He and I crowded under it, but Anton stayed outside its circle, shoulders stiff with fury because I had left him with Herr Keller.

"The lorry is a few blocks up," Lars said. "On the way, Anton, please give me a report on your mission."

"Mission?" Anton's delicate eyebrows lowered suspiciously.

"Your mother sent you there to see if Herr and Frau Keller would make good parents for Ruth. What is your assessment?"

Anton's shoulders relaxed. I could see him thinking that he had not been sent away. He had been sent on a mission. Lars had defused the situation.

"I liked them." Anton moved under the umbrella. "They were very sad, but they were kind to me. Frau Keller made me a special dinner, and they had pictures of Ruth up on the walls."

"That sounds promising," Lars said. "Thank you for the report."

Anton smiled at Lars. "What's the next mission?"

"Protection." Lars explained how things would work at the theater. Anton listened earnestly. Watching them together, I understood why Lars was a good leader. Anton would follow him anywhere. Even with his ring on my finger, would I? I had never followed a man before.

I bade them farewell and took the stairs down to the Zoologischer Garten subway station. I threaded through the crowd, taking the exit near the movie theater. Dark came early to Berlin in November. Neon tubes outlining the theater's arches and roofline glowed eerily through the evening mist.

The clouds had finally released their store of rain, so I walked across shiny wet cobblestones to queue up. Lars and Anton arrived and queued up, too. Four people were in line between us.

I pretended that I did not notice them as I scanned the film start times to find the film starting closest to seven. *Thirteen Chairs* with Heinz Rühmann. How delightful. The film must be based on the similarly titled 1928 novel by the Russian writing team Ilf and Petrov. Apparently the Nazi regime had not noticed that Ilf was Jewish. That thought cheered me. I spoke a little loudly when I purchased my tickets, so that Lars would know what movie I saw.

I let the usher lead me to an end seat near the back. I did not see Maria, but I did not expect to. I expected her to arrive late and sit next to me as if by accident. Fortunately, the show had been out for weeks. The half-empty theater would make it easier for us to speak unobserved.

Lars and Anton arrived and sat behind and to my right, as Lars had said they would. They were so close that I could hear their conversation. I heard Anton list off the Heinz Rühmann films he had seen. Far more than I had taken him to. Did he go with Boris and Nanette, or was he sneaking out with schoolmates?

While I wondered about that, I studied other patrons. A young couple in the back looked eager for the lights to go down so that they could turn their attention properly to each other. I once sat back there myself with Walter and did not begrudge them. Other seats

held more sedate couples and solitary older women like me. Heinz Rühmann, with his cleft chin and ready smile, was a German cinema idol. I had met him in all his charismatic glory once, briefly, when my friend Sarah worked on hats for his film *Those Three from the Gas Station*. A Jew, she certainly would not be allowed to work on films at UFA today. I caressed the dress I wore, one of hers, and felt grateful that my borrowed papers had got her safely to New York.

A propaganda reel flickered to life. Preparations were in place for a fifteen-year celebration of Hitler's Beer Hall Putsch tomorrow, on November 9. Hitler had taken only fifteen years to go from Stadel-heim Prison to the Reichstag. I had certainly accomplished nothing so grand in the last fifteen years.

Finally the film started. I settled in to watch. Heinz Rühmann's expressive face filled with dismay when he learned that his rich aunt had left him only thirteen chairs in her will. *Be careful, Heinz,* I told him. *Everyone conceals something.* Heinz did not listen to me and sold those thirteen chairs anyway.

I smelled rain and cigarette smoke. Maria.

"Excuse me." She stepped on my feet and took the seat next to mine. She was now between Lars and me. Perfect.

"Hello," I whispered to Maria. I glanced at her small leather purse. Too little to hold anything but a small gun or a knife. I felt better.

She took off her hat and raincoat, showering me with cold raindrops. She still wore her dark hair in a bob, and it still did nothing for her severe schoolmistress's face.

"What do you want?" Maria could make even a whisper sound angry.

"Do you know where Ruth is?" I said.

"Paul knows." She fiddled with the hat in her lap. "We talked about it yesterday afternoon."

So, while I had been visiting Herr Silbert, Paul had been with Maria. Perhaps the glass with the lipstick on it was hers. "Where did you meet?"

She snorted and watched Heinz discover that one of those thirteen chairs he had sold contained 100,000 Reichsmarks, thus starting the frantic search that would propel the film forward.

"At a hotel," she said finally. "And that's all I'll say."

If true, then it was not her lipstick. But if she had shot Paul, she would lie. "Where is Ruth?"

"If Paul wants you to know," she whispered. "I imagine he'll tell you himself."

Once I told her that he was dead, I might get no more information from her. I shifted in my velvet chair. Out of the corner of my eye, I saw Lars reach into his coat. I forced myself to look more relaxed. "Did he also tell you that he tried suicide?"

Her mouth dropped open slightly. He had not told her.

I relayed a quick version of events, ending with bandaging his wrist, and omitting Lars entirely. I downplayed the seriousness of the wound, even as I remembered the blood everywhere.

"Always there to comfort him, aren't you?" she hissed.

"What do you mean by that?"

"You know exactly what I mean." She leaned so close that I felt her stale cigarette smoke breath on my cheek. "Even though you've moved to Switzerland and are living with some banker getting fat on chocolate, it's always you."

"Paul and I have been over for two decades." I moved away. "This is about his daughter."

"It is, is it?" Her sharp features contorted into a snarl. "When you told him that his wife was dead and his daughter was missing, whom did he turn to?"

"The sofa, as I recall." I struggled to keep my voice down. "You left as fast as you could make it out the door."

"You," she whispered. "He turned to you. He's barely seen you in seven years, but it was still you."

"Paul's like a brother to me."

"A brother that you used to sleep with?"

We had strayed far from my entreaties for Ruth. "Please, Maria, help find Ruth. I will be gone in a few days, and with any luck, you and I will never see each other again."

She pursed her too-thin lips. "That would be too much to hope for."

"This is more important than the enmity between you and me. This is about a lost little girl," I said. "Ruth. Did Paul give you a name?"

She scowled. "I don't have a name. Paul said he would meet with

the people who had Ruth after we parted, but he did not say who or where. Why don't you ask him yourself?"

If she did not know, how would I find out whom he had met with on the night of his death?

We sat together and watched the film. I struggled to figure out a way to break the news of Paul's death to her. I knew that I was stalling as I watched the audience laugh when Heinz found and destroyed all the chairs one by one, until he found the final chair in an orphanage. Maria glared at me as soon as Heinz entered the orphanage.

"You picked the film," I whispered.

She snorted again.

I watched Heinz, but spoke to Maria. The film was almost over. "One more thing—"

"Good god, isn't there always?"

I had to tell her. If I did not, it might be weeks before she learned of Paul's death. He would not have wanted that. "Maria—"

"Where's Paul?" she asked. "I went by his apartment this morning, but it was locked."

"Last night," I began. "Paul—"

"Did he take Ruth and leave?" She pinned me with her intense gaze.

"I do not know if he found Ruth." I turned in my seat to watch her face. "But—"

"He left without me, didn't he?" She sounded more hurt than angry.

How could I tell her that he was dead, here, in the middle of the theater? But the darkness was probably the best place to tell her. Would I tell her that he had been murdered, or stick with the police's suicide theory?

My mind raced. She could view a copy of the police report deeming his death a suicide. If I told her otherwise, she might start an investigation. She, too, was a crime reporter. She had her own sources.

She stopped pretending that she watched the screen. "Enough, Hannah. Tell me where he is."

"Last night I went to Paul's," I began. "And he—"

"Stop." She held up a palm like a traffic policeman. "I don't want to hear the rest."

"All right," I said.

She turned her hat around and around in her lap. "He's dead, isn't he?"

"I am sorry, Maria." I had no better words than that, as much as I wished for them.

It hurt to see how hard she tried not to cry. In her own way, she had loved him. And I was likely the only one who knew that. Because their relationship had been a secret, she would have to conceal her grief from everyone. I wished that I had picked a better place to tell her. It felt spiteful to have told her here.

"All that worry over a child that wasn't even his." She crushed her hat between her hands. I did not think it would be salvageable. "I never understood it."

"Not his? You are certain?" The man in the locket who looked so much like Ruth must be her father. Paul had said that he was no friend or relation.

"He never told you, did he?" Her tone held satisfaction, even in grief. If she had been in Poland, I could have seen her killing Miriam. But she was with Paul in Germany. "A few years ago we had a fight, and she seduced him away from me. When she told him she was pregnant, he married her."

"Who was the father?" Did he have Ruth? Did he kill Paul? And perhaps Miriam as well? Lars moved his hand toward the front of his coat again. I forced myself to sit back.

"Paul never knew. But he knew enough biology to know it wasn't his when Miriam gave birth to a beautiful blond baby six months after their wedding instead of eight." She spat the words out savagely. Poor Paul.

Paul had raised someone else's child with a faithless wife. I stopped blaming him for having an affair with Maria, even as I faulted his taste. "Why did he stay married to her?"

"Are you so naïve?" She jeered. "She asked him to stay married to her, for the baby's sake, and he did. He thought that his German passport might afford them some protection. That child that wasn't his was always more important to him than me. The second one probably wasn't his either, but he would have loved it more than he did me, too."

I saw the sorrow behind the anger. "Maria, I—"

"Save your pity, Hannah," she said, "and yourself. Get out while you still can."

She walked out of the theater, holding herself carefully erect, as if she expected, with every step, to fall. I let her go.

Hearing the movie nuns describe how they would use the money to help the orphans made Heinz and his partner in crime realize that they could not in good conscience recover the money. The film ended with Heinz becoming rich off a hair tonic he had invented. A random event, but at least virtue was rewarded, and we had a happy ending all around. I should be so lucky.

I waited for the lights to come up before leaving. Out of the corner of my eye, I saw Lars and Anton stand to follow me and kept my pace slow enough that they could keep me in sight. I walked through the lobby like a spinster who needed to get home to feed her cat— quick but not suspiciously so. I took the stairs down to the subway, meandered along the platform, and climbed out a different exit. I waited. I knew that Lars would find me. And he did.

He looked at my face and drew me into a long embrace. "I'm sorry, Spatz."

I took a deep shuddering breath, and another. I would not cry here. I stepped back and hugged Anton briefly.

"Does she know where Ruth is?" Lars asked.

"No. But she thinks Ruth might be with her real father."

Lars tightened his lips. "Do you have a name?"

I shook my head. It made no sense. If her father had killed Paul last night and taken her, why was there lipstick on the glass? If he had Ruth, why bring her to Paul's apartment only to kill him?

"Let's get to the warehouse," Lars said. "I want to start working on the compartment as soon as I can."

I had no better suggestion, so I nodded.

On our way to the warehouse, we drove through the Jewish quarter. Lars pulled over next to a man with a lorry heaped high with household goods. Chairs, boxes, bags, a bicycle, and more were tied in with rope. A FOR SALE sign was tacked to the side of the lorry. What could Lars possibly want to buy off him?

Lars turned off the engine and went to talk to the man. We followed.

"Is it all your stuff?" Anton pointed.

"It is." The man ran one hand down his curly white beard. "We're leaving as soon as I have enough money together to buy gas."

Crowded in the front seat of the lorry, a woman in a black dress who looked young enough to be his daughter and three children stared glumly at us. I was reminded of the refugees in Zbąszyń. "You are not going to Poland, are you?"

He folded his hands in front of him. "Holland."

Lars examined the man's bald tires. "You won't get far on those. Especially if it rains."

"So, buy something and pay me extra." The man chuckled, then grew serious. "We'll have to buy new tires when they blow out. We must be out of Germany before that diplomat in Paris dies."

"Do you expect reprisals?" I asked.

"I'm a Jewish man living in Hitler's Germany," he said. "How could I expect otherwise?"

Lars pointed to the back of the lorry. "How much for the mattress?"

I smiled tiredly. He had promised to make sleeping in the warehouse more comfortable.

The old man and Lars haggled about the price.

"Just pay him what he asked," I told Lars. He needed the money to get his family away.

Lars looked ashamed. He drew out his wallet.

I walked to the front of the car and peeked in at the woman and children. Anton stayed with Lars. The woman's dark eyes studied me curiously.

"Good evening," I said.

She answered in Dutch. I had a strong feeling that she also spoke German, but chose not to.

"Safe journeys." I hurried back to Lars and Anton.

Anton untied the tarp so they could load the mattress. He clambered into the back of our lorry and surveyed the mattress's position, tugging it back and forth as if it were a deadly serious job.

Lars whispered in my ear. "I'm sorry that I have nothing better to provide for our wedding night."

I slipped my arms around his waist. "What could be better than a magical carriage to spirit us out of Germany?"

"That it shall be. I promise that as soon as we get out of this god-forsaken mess, I will give you a proper wedding night."

"I only want a real husband."

He kissed me on the forehead. "Soon. Our simple life together will start soon."

I look skeptically into his dark eyes. "Do you think we will ever achieve simple?"

He chuckled. "Simpler?"

"Simpler would be wonderful."

He kissed me on the lips, and I suddenly did wish for a proper wedding night. Immediately.

Someone coughed. I reluctantly drew back. Lars held me a second longer, then turned to pay the man for the mattress. Together we refastened the tarp and drove to the warehouse.

The warehouse was dark and looked empty, but again Lars left us in the lorry while he scouted it out. This time he left me the Vis pistol.

"Clear." Lars opened the door and helped us out. Cold from the concrete floor seeped through my shoes. The warehouse felt colder than last night.

I sent Anton to brush his teeth while I crawled around the back of the lorry, making up the bed with the linens and blankets Lars had purchased when he bought the mattress. Lars climbed in next to me, expression impenetrable in the gloom.

"Are your supplies here?" I spread a blanket across the old mattress.

"They are. If all goes well, I can get the box built tonight. Tomorrow, I'll ask Herr Populov to stay late and help me attach it to the lorry."

"I can help."

"You can't," he said. "It's too heavy. I'll need at least two other men."

I folded the blanket back for Anton.

"Tell me what happened in the theater," Lars said.

I told him.

"If her father does have her, he has a better claim to her than Paul's parents." He tucked the blanket under the mattress at the bottom, cracking his knuckle on the metal bed of the lorry.

He held it up for me to kiss, and I did. His hand smelled like gun oil.

"He docs have a better claim on her, Spatz," he repeated.

I held his hand between mine. "Unless he murdered Paul."

"Unless that." He sat next to me in the dark. "How do you plan to find him, as I imagine you do?"

"Perhaps he is the doctor that Reuben told Anton about. Or that doctor knows who he is." I knew I sounded crazy. I had no proof. "Maybe he killed Paul to get to Ruth. After all, he took her before."

"How do you know that?" Lars kept his voice gentle, but I heard the skepticism that underlay his words.

"I will show you."

We crawled out from under the tarp that covered the back of the lorry. I took the scrap of white fabric from my satchel and gave it to Lars. "I found this on the hinge of the cupboard where Ruth was hiding. I think it is a piece of a lab coat."

He studied it. "Perhaps."

"If he wore a lab coat, he must have been an Aryan doctor," I said.

Anton walked up and perched on the tailgate. "Why?"

"Because Jewish doctors in Germany are forbidden from practicing medicine. Some probably still do, but I doubt that they walk around in lab coats."

"Sounds reasonable," Lars said.

"Probably very few Aryan doctors make house calls in the Jewish quarter." Excited, I spoke more quickly. "And I have a friend, a doctor, who might know their names."

"The woman who stitched you up last time?" Lars asked.

"Yes." Frau Doktor Spiegel. I thought about visiting her tonight, but knew that she liked to go to bed early and asking her for favors in the middle of the night was a mistake.

Anton and I bedded down in the lorry while Lars went to work building the compartment. Anton fell asleep easily, but sleep eluded me. I continued to worry about Ruth. Either she was with her father, or with the person who murdered Paul. Perhaps they were one and the same. And how to explain the lipstick on the glass?

Eventually I fell into a restless sleep. I awoke with my heart pound-

ing. I had dreamed of finding Paul dead. I heard men talking and quickly slipped into my dress and shoes. Not intending to be caught in a state of undress again, I had left them by the side of the mattress the night before. I crept to the end of the lorry and listened through the tarp.

The voices spoke Russian. Lars and Herr Populov. Lars seemed to be asking for something. Herr Populov seemed reluctant to give it. Was he asking for help to install the compartment when the shop closed again tonight? Whatever it was, Lars pressed him, and he agreed.

I roused Anton, and we went to breakfast at a different restaurant from the day before. Afterwards, we drove to the Jewish quarter. Lars decided to rest in the back of the lorry while Anton and I went to talk to Frau Doktor Spiegel. First I stopped by her favorite bakery to pick up rugelach. Their cinnamon scent filled the lorry's cab.

Anton fixed his best beseeching eyes on me.

"One," I said. "The rest are for Herr and Frau Doktor Spiegel."

He fished out a pastry and took a satisfied bite.

"You just had breakfast," I pointed out.

"I'm always hungry for treats." He spoke around the rugelach.

He was. I reparked the lorry just outside the Jewish quarter in a sunny spot. Hopefully that would warm up the back a bit for Lars. He had looked exhausted after breakfast, having traded last night's sleep for finishing the compartment. We would install it after Herr Populov's shop closed at six and be in Poland before bedtime. As much as I wanted to find Ruth, I dared not endanger Anton another moment.

That left me only one day for sleuthing.

I picked up the brown bag of rugelach. Together Anton and I walked into the Jewish quarter. Fresh graffiti jeered from the buildings. Boards covered more windows. I wondered if it was the result of everyday anti-Semitism or if it was in response to vom Rath's shooting. If he died, I feared much worse than rocks through windows.

We hurried through unnaturally quiet streets to Frau Doktor Spiegel's ground-floor apartment. It looked the same as always. The

lace curtains were perfectly aligned on either side of her front window. The building's smooth stone front had been cleaned during the Olympics, and its tan surface was cheery in the morning light.

Anton brushed crumbs off his shirt while I rang the bell. The blue and white sign near her door that advertised her services as a doctor was gone, but the brass door handle and bell were still brightly polished.

Frau Doktor Spiegel answered the door herself. Her hair was now more gray than black, and her dark eyes looked tired. She had aged ten years in the last two.

"Fräulein Vogel?" She scrutinized me. "You look better than last I saw you."

Last time I went to visit her, I had just been hit by a car and was bleeding from a head wound. "That is no great feat," I said. "You, too, look well."

She harrumphed. "What a charming liar you make. Who is this?"

I put my hand on Anton's shoulder. "Anton. We brought breakfast."

She stepped out of the doorway. "Come inside, then. I just made tea."

I followed her back to her kitchen and set the rugelach on her long mahogany table. She handed me an absinthe green translucent glass plate, and I arranged the pastries on it.

"Have one," she said. "You as well, Anton. Although it looks by the crumbs on the corners of your mouth that you started early."

He wiped his mouth. "My apologies. I didn't know how many people there would be to share it with."

She busied herself setting out teacups, a pot of cream, and a sugar bowl, all made of the same peculiar glass. "Just me."

"Where is Herr Spiegel?" I asked, surprised.

"Dead," she said. "They arrested him a year ago. He didn't last a month in the camps."

A memory of Herr Silbert's emaciated frame flashed in my mind. "You have my condolences."

"Thank you."

I poured tea for the three of us. She sat and put a rugelach on her plate. But, although I knew it was her favorite pastry, she did not take a bite.

"Does that glass glow?" Anton pointed to a collection of green glass plates lined up on a shelf above the sink, similar to those she had set on the table.

"In some lights, it does," she said. "It's called Vaseline glass. Uranium makes it glow under certain lights."

"I've heard of that!" He walked carefully over to the plates, as if afraid his mere presence might break them. "Isn't uranium poison?"

"In larger doses," she said. "These days, I think I will die of other causes long before uranium poison would do me in."

He studied the plates.

"My husband used to buy them for me. I kept them crated up because they're expensive, but after he was taken away, I found I wanted to see them every day."

"Do not touch," I said. He would not, but I could not help myself. Sometimes my mother's voice spoke from my mouth.

He swallowed a retort.

"Why are you here, Fräulein Vogel?" she asked. "Not for emergency medical care, I see."

"A social call?" I used the silver tongs to add a cube of sugar to my tea.

"Strange time to be sociable. Vom Rath lingering on the edge of death. Broken windows and new graffiti last night. If he dies, it'll be worse. You're here for something else. As always."

I thought of concocting a story, but decided to try the truth. "Do you remember Paul Keller?"

She patted my shoulder. "I heard about his suicide. You have my condolences. I know that you were close."

I blinked back surprise tears. "We were."

Anton turned from the plates, eyes sad. He sat next to me again and pushed away his plate of rugelach.

"So were you the mystery blond woman and child seen at his apartment when he died?"

My breath caught. We had been seen, too. It had been a close escape on many levels. "Unfortunately, too late. But I am here on his behalf." I explained about Ruth's disappearance and finished with, "Do you know the doctor who might have carried her away?"

She stared into her translucent teacup, as if reading the tea leaves on the bottom.

"Frau Doktor Spiegel?"

"Of course I know him," she said. "He took over my practice, didn't he?"

"Why did he do that?" Anton asked.

"Someone had to. As a Jew, I haven't been able to practice medicine since July twenty-fifth. Another Nazi law. They're trying to starve us out, and most of us would go eagerly if we had a place to land."

I drew back. "About this doctor—"

"I've nothing against him. I'm grateful that he treats Jews. Precious few Aryan doctors do anymore." She slugged her tea like whiskey.

"Could you give me his name?" I asked. "I wish to ask him about Ruth today."

"No." She set the teacup down with a clank. "I think I'll leave him out of this."

"But I heard that he has been offering to buy babies."

"Just one baby, I should think." She turned the cup around on the saucer. "And he has since sorted that out."

"So, one baby is acceptable to sell?"

"He wanted to adopt a baby." She picked up the empty teacup. "His wife is infertile."

"And he cannot formally adopt? Surely an Aryan doctor would have no trouble legally adopting a child."

"The Party wants all good German mothers to bear many children, so they can send them into the new *Lebensraum*." She splashed tea into her cup and onto the table. "He worried that if his wife's infertility were known, it could be used to disadvantage them. As it would if they started formal adoption procedures."

"So, he asks pregnant Jewish women if they will give up their child to him?" I asked. Horrified, Anton clamped his mouth closed.

"I know you think it sounds horrible, Fräulein Vogel, but be practical." She set down her full cup of tea and shook her finger at me to emphasize her points, as she used to when she taught. "If he can identify an adoptive mother before she delivers, he can send his own wife out of the country for the pregnancy and birth and she can come back with a baby, and no one the wiser. The baby will be much better off with a German physician than being raised as a Jew in Hitler's Germany. And that is where we all live. Hitler's Germany."

I sat back in my chair and studied the eerie green dishes. If I did not find out what had happened to Ruth today, I would never know. I tried to formulate a better argument, but once Frau Doktor Spiegel made up her mind, she was rarely swayed.

"I will help you," she said. "Don't fear."

I sat forward so suddenly, my chair legs clacked against the floor. "How?"

"I'll give you the name of the girl's father."

I gaped at her. Anton did, too.

"Don't look so surprised. Doctors talk, although we were both discreet about this, and not only for poor Paul's benefit."

Poor Paul, indeed.

"His name is Heinrich Stauffer." She scratched the address on her old prescription pad and handed it to me. "Here's his office address. He's married and in the Party, so don't expect a warm welcome."

I puzzled out the address. Her handwriting, never good, had not improved with age. "Wilhelmstrasse? He works—"

"At the Ministry of Propaganda and Enlightenment," she interrupted. "The irony is not lost on me."

Ruth's father worked, probably indirectly, for Joseph Goebbels. I could see how a relationship with a Polish Jew would be complicated. How could he care for Ruth? I folded the scrap of paper and handed it back to her. I could not take the paper with me; it had her name on it. "Do you think he has her?"

She shrugged. "With Miriam and Paul gone, the doctor would have taken her there. What happened after, I can't say."

I finished my tea in one gulp. "We must be—"

"Leaving now that you have what you needed?"

Half standing, I stopped.

She laughed heartily. "The expression on your face, Fräulein Vogel."

"I . . . that is we . . . this evening—"

"I quite understand." She handed Anton his half-eaten rugelach. "As always, you are on a tight schedule."

I sat down again. "What are your plans? Will you stay here?"

"Not a second longer than I must." She wiped her hands on her napkin. "Which appears to be many more seconds than I would like."

"You would leave everything behind?"

She gestured around the empty apartment. "What everything?"

Perhaps I could help her as I had not helped Paul. Lars's compartment was big enough for her and Anton. "Will you be here this evening? I can make no promises, but I might have a solution to your problems."

"Better than Paul's?" she asked.

So she believed the suicide story as well. "I hope so."

"I'll be here," she said. "I have nowhere else to go."

26

Back at the lorry, I checked to see that Lars was still there. Feeling ridiculous, I paused to make sure that he was breathing, taking nothing for granted since Paul's murder.

Anton and I piled into the front seat, and I eased into the busy street. It hurt to shift with the cast, but I hated to ask Anton to shift for me in this kind of traffic.

"Are we going to see Ruth's father now?" Anton asked.

I was not certain if he was coming. "I am."

"Did you love Paul?"

"Yes." I gripped the wheel. "We were close friends for many years."

We had left the Jewish quarter. The absence of graffiti made everything feel safer.

"Did you love him more than Lars?"

I halted to let a group of girls dressed in the brown uniforms of the League of German Girls cross the street. Every one of them was younger than Anton.

"Did you?" he asked again. Sometimes, he reminded me of myself.

"I loved him longer than Lars." The girls reached the cobblestone sidewalk. We lurched forward again. I gritted my teeth and shifted into first. "I almost married Paul twenty years ago."

"Why didn't you?"

None of the reasons I had listed twenty years ago made sense now, especially knowing that Paul would have been protected from the Nazi government if I had. He would have known the parentage of his children. I would have insisted that we emigrate years ago. And he would still be alive. "I do not know."

"How can't you know something like that? Do you know why you agreed to marry Lars this morning?"

I shifted into second and hoped I could stay there for a while. "I think I understand that less than why I did not marry Paul."

He groaned. "How am I supposed to ever understand?"

I shook my head. "I do not think you are supposed to. I cannot claim that I do."

He crossed his arms and stared moodily out the window. I resisted the urge to tousle his hair and instead drove straight to the government offices in Wilhelmstrasse. The buildings here were cleansed of graffiti and soot. They looked clean enough to eat off, despite the filth that they contained.

Not wanting Lars to be caught sleeping next to a government office, which might have more thorough police sweeps, I drove past the Ministry of Propaganda and parked several blocks away, in a residential district.

I left my old Hannah Vogel and Adelheid Zinsli passports, and the Vis, in the glove box. The only identification that my satchel contained was my, now properly stamped, Hannah Schmidt passport. Venturing into a Nazi edifice without proper papers was suicidal. But the passport would hold up. Herr Silbert's work had always been reliable.

I brushed my hair and applied a fresh layer of pink lipstick while trying to decide what to do with Anton. In the end, I decided to take him with me, so that I could watch him. He would probably tail me if I left him alone in the lorry.

"You are Anton Schmidt," I said. "If anyone asks, your passport is at your aunt's house. You are Swiss, and not Jewish."

"I am ready." He used the accent he had acquired in Switzerland and immediately lost when we returned to Berlin.

"It is no game," I said. "Do exactly as I say."

"Don't I always?"

"No. That is why I am making the point."

"I understand," he said.

Together we walked to the new Ministry of Propaganda. Its stark lines said that its purpose was serious, with no time for frills, and the sharp angles told of the importance of order to the new regime. The eagle topping the walls looked ready to drop his stone swastika on our heads.

I presented my papers to a stern-looking man in uniform whose bushy eyebrows looked weighted down with invisible rocks. Beetle-brown eyes sized me up and found me wanting.

"I am here to see Herr Stauffer." I stood as straight as I could, acutely aware that I was much shorter than he. "On personal business."

The man's eyes flicked from my breasts to Anton. "Upstairs, second office on your right."

He had a visitor log, but did not ask me to sign it, and I did not mention it. Instead, I hurried up the imposing stairs. Did Herr Stauffer entertain so many women in an average workday that they no longer bothered to keep track of them? That gave me something to work with.

Tall ceilings swallowed the sounds of our steps. I put a hand on Anton's sleeve. "When we get to his office, I will go in and sit down without being asked. If there is a second seat, you sit as well. Otherwise stand directly behind my seat with your hands on the back. Do not move from that position or say a word unless I tell you to. Understood?"

"Yes," he said. He looked serious, and grown up.

We turned right at the top of the stairs. I opened the second door without knocking and strode in as if someone expected me. The room contained a small metal desk, lines of gray filing cabinets, a typewriter, and a rooster of a man with a barrel chest and a cockscomb of red hair cut bristly short. The man from the locket. His fingers hung motionless above typewriter keys.

I dropped into the chair in front of his desk uninvited. Anton stood behind me, as it was the only free chair in the room.

The man swept his report into a drawer and stood. As I suspected, he was barely my height.

"What are you doing here?"

I said nothing and kept my face stony. Let his conscience tell him.

He studied my face, then Anton's. "He's not mine," he said. "I don't remember you."

I clenched my teeth, angry for Miriam, and for Ruth. They were only two in a long line of women and abandoned children. "Fortunately," I said icily, "that is true. I am here for a child who is."

"Preposterous!" His face reddened.

"A Jewish child."

He sat down. The flash of terror in his eyes told me that Frau Doktor Spiegel had named the correct man. Then he deserved everything he got.

"We can discuss this here." I spoke slowly so that he would feel the weight of each word. "Or we can discuss it at the courthouse. I believe that the Nuremberg Laws were fully in effect when you impregnated a young Jewish woman in early 1936."

He gulped. "That is—"

"A crime punishable by prison or hard labor, which might include a stint in a concentration camp." Let this Nazi think about the consequences of his own laws.

"You have no proof," he said weakly. "No proof at all."

"I do," I lied. "Eyewitnesses, diaries, papers, medical statements."

He dropped his face into his square hands. "How much do you want?"

"Knowledge," I said. "To start."

Anton's hand twitched on the back of the chair, but he said nothing.

Herr Stauffer raised his head to look at me. His freckled face had gone blank. I was glad that he had his hands where I could see them.

"Where is the child now?" I asked.

"An orphanage." He bit his chapped lips.

"Aryan or Jewish?" I spoke like an interrogator.

"I'll not tell you that." He glared at me.

If it was a Jewish orphanage, he would have told me the name. So he must have delivered her to an Aryan one. At least he had done something to make things easier for her. "Another law broken, I suspect." I did not keep the disdain from my voice. "But for the sake of a child." It had been for his own sake.

"What do you want?" He sounded calmer now. He had adjusted to the situation. I had to keep him off guard.

"Why did you take her to an Aryan orphanage?" I stressed the word *Aryan*, to remind him that I knew it, and if I turned him in, things would go even worse for him.

"There was nowhere else to take her." He worried his lower lip. "I couldn't find that Jew that Miriam married."

Paul.

"What about keeping her? You are her father." She was better off in an orphanage than with him, but someone should remind him of his responsibilities.

"Impossible! I tried to explain that to the damn doctor. I told him what I would have to do, where I would have to take her, but he didn't care."

Because there were no better options for Ruth than an Aryan orphanage, with her mother dead in a refugee camp, and Paul nowhere to be found. The doctor must have told Paul where Ruth was on the night that he tried to commit suicide. Paul, too, had thought an Aryan orphanage would offer her the protection that he could not.

In the end, Paul had changed his mind and fetched her home. And his killer had her now. The man in front of me had not killed Paul. Stauffer would have been thrilled to dump his illegitimate child on Paul. But what about Miriam?

Herr Stauffer fidgeted with a piece of blank paper on his desk. The watermark looked familiar. Government paper, the same as on my notes. And Miriam's.

"I have a letter typed on this stationery, threatening the mother of the child." I clipped out each word.

He scooted his chair back from me.

"Would a police investigation find that it came from that typewriter?" I knew it would, as did he.

His eyes shifted down to the typewriter and back up. "I have no idea what you are talking about."

"The letter threatens to end things," I said. "And now she is dead."

His freckles stood out in sharp relief in his suddenly pale face. "Miriam, dead?"

"In a refugee camp in Poland," I said.

Tears welled up in his eyes. "The baby?"

"Dead, too," I said. "A stable is no place to deliver a baby."

He lowered his head. He seemed genuinely upset over Miriam's death, in spite of his bold talk earlier.

"What did she want from you that you would not give her? Money?"

He shook his head.

"You are Aryan, are you not?"

He did not raise his head. "Completely."

"She wanted you to claim your daughter." I did the horrific Nazi calculation in my head. "If the child had two Aryan grandparents, then she would be classed as a Mischling, not a Jew."

Paul had only one Aryan parent, Miriam had zero. Not enough to save Ruth.

"She was born one month too late." He directed his words down at his desk. He still would not look at me. "If she had been born before the end of July in 1936, then she would have been a Mischling, but she was born in late August. I tried to tell Miriam. I could not help her. But she would not listen."

"And?"

"I paid her." He sounded numb now, as if he was past caring. "I gave her money to leave so that she could have the other baby somewhere free. But the only place that she could go was Poland, and she would never go there."

I remembered Paul's words. "What happened to Miriam in Poland?"

He spread his hands wide. "Horrible things. It's why she came here. And then I met her, and everything got so complicated."

"She died there," I said. "In Poland."

He gulped back a sob. "She always said that Poland would kill her quicker than the Nazis ever would."

"Did you have a hand in that?"

"Me?" He blew his nose on a crisp white handkerchief. "If I had wanted to kill her, I would have done it here. No one would investigate the death of another Jew in Germany."

I studied him. His words seemed true, but even if they were not, I would not come to the root of them here. If Miriam was murdered, I might never know. I thought back to the mysterious translator in the stable. What had become of her?

I stood so suddenly that Anton almost tipped my chair over. "I am done with you, for now. But I am watching you. If you do not change your behavior, I will turn you in. I have heard that Oranienburg is lovely this time of year." Just a quick reminder of the concentration camp near Berlin where he might be sent.

He flinched.

I swept out with my head held high, my shoulders square and angry. Anton was so close behind me that I worried he would tread on my heels. "Not a word," I told him.

We made it past the disapproving officer by the door and walked several blocks before I cut left and circled back toward the lorry.

"All right, Anton," I said. "You may speak again."

"I had no idea you could lie like that!" He looked at me with admiration. "He was terrified!"

I hated to hear his enthusiasm over my skills in deception. "Unfortunately, that is probably all the punishment he will ever receive for abandoning his daughter."

"You should have shaken some money out of him."

"Anton!" Shocked, I stopped walking.

"For Ruth," he said. "She probably needs it more than he does."

"Blackmail is . . ." I wound down. I had blackmailed him for information, if not for money. "For life and death, I will do it. But not for cash."

That was a fine distinction to make, and I was not certain that Anton agreed, but he held his peace.

We stopped at a telephone booth on the way to the lorry. I called the newspaper again. Herr Marceau answered on the first ring.

"It is I," I said. "No names."

"I have news for you." He paused uncertainly.

"Is it good?" I asked, although I could tell from his tone that it was not.

"No—"

"First answer a question for me." I glanced up and down the nearly empty street. I had assumed that the Gestapo monitored the telephones near the ministry, but I could not be certain about this one either. "Could you look at the envelopes of the letters I received and tell me where they were postmarked?"

"Berlin, but—"

"I know that, but do they have anything on them to indicate where in Berlin?"

"The police have them," he said. "Now, be quiet and listen."

"Go ahead." I paused at his tone, worried about the reasons behind it.

"A woman called today to leave a message for you. She claimed to be the one who has been sending you the letters. I spoke to her myself."

I sagged against the wood and glass side of the booth. The letter writer had escalated to calling. Anton looked at me worriedly. "A woman?"

"She said that if vom Rath dies, so will the little girl. She wants you to know that it's your fault, as it was the day before yesterday."

My throat was too dry to speak. It was her lipstick on the glass.

She had killed Paul. She had Ruth, and she planned to kill her, too. I cleared my throat. "Why?"

"I asked her that, too. She said that you know why. You murdered someone whom she loved."

Frau Röhm had once thought that I killed her son and had been willing to kill Anton in revenge, but what other woman could link me to Ruth, Paul, and Berlin? I discounted Maria. She might have killed me, but she would never have killed Paul. And as much as I hated her, I did not believe that she would kill Ruth either.

"What was she talking about?" He sounded more perplexed than accusatory. Even Herr Marceau did not think me a killer. Except, I was.

"I never murdered anyone," I said. Self-defense was not murder. A fine line, but all I had to cling to. "I have no idea what she meant."

"She certainly seemed angry at you," he said. "She felt wronged."

I gripped the black Bakelite receiver, trying to think. "Can you find Herr Knecht?"

"I will see." He put the phone on the desk with a clunk. While I waited, I thought about Paul. The woman he let in the night he was murdered was someone he trusted. Someone he did not think would ever harm him. Regardless, she had chosen him because of me. Guilt over having brought Paul into the line of fire welled up in me. No matter who had killed him, it was my fault.

Cold fury overrode the guilt. His murderer had killed an innocent, and threatened to kill another. I would stop her. Or die trying.

"I'm back," Herr Marceau said. "I could not find Herr Knecht."

"Could you please—?" I cleared my throat again. "Could you please stay by the phone for more messages? All day, even into tonight? I hate to ask—"

"I'll stay," he said. "Of course."

"I am going to try to find the little girl," I said. "As soon as I can, I am coming home."

"We miss you," he said. "Be careful."

I thanked him and broke the connection. Did Herr Marceau have a heart, or a deeper agenda? I left my hand atop the phone box.

A woman caller. Maria? Paul would certainly have let her in. But I could not picture her killing him, and certainly not taking Ruth. Did Paul entertain other women visitors late at night? Or had it been someone who looked like Maria? Or like me?

I took a deep breath. The person I could think of who looked the most like me was Fräulein Ivona. That seemed ridiculous. She was somewhere in Poland. But it was a lead to follow, and I had no others. She and Lars had been together less than a month, and I did not think that her feelings for him were deep enough to kill just to hurt him. But I could be wrong about that. I had been wrong about everything else. I turned toward the door, and Anton. I had to think. I had to set aside my anger and guilt to save Ruth.

The timing, I told myself. Start with the timing. The letters started a month ago, before Fräulein Ivona met Lars. So what had happened a month ago? Fräulein Ivona's mother died. Perhaps, then, she had started writing me letters and sought out Lars and their meeting had not been a chance encounter in a bar, as Lars thought.

But why? Did she blame us for her mother's death? I had never killed another woman. Had Lars? She had said that her mother had been ill. I did not see how we could be responsible for that. Perhaps her mother told her something before she died.

The other person who became agitated with me a month ago was Herr Marceau. I had only his word that there had been a woman caller. Was he trying to frighten me into leaving Berlin? But how could he know about Ruth's disappearance? Or perhaps this woman was related to his beloved actress in Berlin.

Anton knocked against the glass. I pushed the door open and stepped into the cold afternoon.

"What happened?" he asked. "You look like a horse rode over your grave."

"Truer than you think," I said. "We have to get back to the lorry."

27

I walked him there too quickly for either of us to speak. I was out of breath when we arrived. A rumpled and tired-looking Lars leaned against the back of the lorry.

I filled him in on my conversation with Herr Marceau. Lars did not believe that it was Fräulein Ivona. Logic, passion, or self-deception?

"Give me another name, Lars," I said. "One other woman who sought us both out?"

"I don't know," he said. "That does not mean that the name doesn't exist. Why would Ivona go to these lengths?"

"Why would anyone?" I put my hands on my hips. I could think of no other suspect, and neither could he.

"What about Ruth's father?" He ran his fingers through his mussed hair, and I felt sorry for him. He was exhausted, he had done nothing but work to get us all to safety, and he could not have known about Fräulein Ivona either.

I told him of my encounter with Stauffer, the only other lead we had.

"What is Fräulein Ivona's last name? Did you know?" She had presented herself to me as Fräulein Ivona, so I had assumed that was her surname, but now I knew it was her given one.

"Of course I know! It was Fischer," he snapped. "Ivona Fischer."

Fischer was one of the most common surnames in Germany. "Did you ever see her passport or identity papers?"

"I was sleeping with her," he barked. "Not interrogating her."

"More's the pity." I bristled at his tone. "So you have no proof that her name was, in fact, Fischer?"

"I did see a student identification card," he said. "There was no picture. But everything that she told me fit in with the file my colleague checked for me. Ivona Fischer is not your culprit, no matter how jealous you may be."

"This has nothing to do with your philandering." I stepped closer to him. "I am trying—"

"Arguing won't solve anything." Anton took my arm and pulled me back a step.

"How about," Lars said coldly, "I visit the Berlin address from her file? I have it in my notebook. Perhaps she is even there. If not, will childhood photographs convince you that she is who she says and that she has no connection to this affair?"

He opened his old notebook. I watched him flip past the list of suspects, remembering the names of those who had died because of me: Hahn, Bauer, and two unnamed Gestapo agents in the warehouse, plus the two by the side of the road. I wished that I had never met any of them.

We drove to the address without speaking. Anton pressed himself against the door and stared out the window, probably wishing he did not have to be in the cab of the lorry either.

Lars stopped the lorry and wrenched up the parking brake with such force that I worried he might yank it out entirely. He stomped up the drive of a well-kept house.

"Please stay here," I told Anton.

"I have no wish to follow you." He took out his platypus and began to shape it.

I hurried after Lars.

He rang the bell. A young woman with long dark hair tucked into a bun answered the door. A black cat twined around her ankles.

"Yes?" she said in a high-pitched, almost childish voice.

"We wish to speak to Ivona Fischer," Lars said.

"That's me," she said.

Lars took a quick step back.

"Do you work for the department of road building?" I asked.

"I do," she said. "Is something wrong? I only work part-time. I was told not to come in today."

Lars was unable to take his eyes off her.

"Nothing wrong," I told her. "I just wanted to confirm that you made your donation to the Winter Relief Fund."

"But I did!" She shifted nervously from foot to foot. "I can give again."

"Not necessary. Thank you." I took Lars's arm and walked him back down the path to the lorry.

I had seldom seen him so shaken.

"We need to find another telephone booth," I said. "I know someone who might be able to find out Fräulein Ivona's last name."

He nodded. He seemed to have lost the power of speech.

I found a telephone box on a busy shopping street. Anton insisted that I leave the door open so that he could hear. Lars crowded next to him.

While the operator worked on the connection, I wondered if the man I was trying to reach had changed his number. Much might have changed since he gave it to me in the Olympic Village two years ago. The phone rang through.

Now I could only hope that he was home for lunch.

"Lehmann," said a deep voice. I almost cried with relief.

I thought how to play it. He might not recognize my voice, so I used a variation of my brother's name. "This is Ernestine. I am in town for a few hours and—"

"Wondered if I had spare time over lunch? So you called me at my home?" Wilhelm asked. "Naughty girl."

I hoped that Anton could not hear what he had just said. "How about we meet outside the restaurant where I had lemonade last time and then . . ."

A short pause, then Wilhelm said, "The one with your favorite cowboy?"

He had guessed correctly. "You know how I feel about cowboys."

He chuckled. "Give me half an hour. I need to get a hat."

I rang off.

"I am meeting an old friend," I said to Lars. "He might help us."

"Who?" Anton asked.

"Wilhelm Lehmann," Lars said. He had met Wilhelm as part of my brother's murder investigation. And he had heard both sides of my conversation.

"I remember him!" Anton said. "He gave me a ride up the stairs and told me stories, and he was in that meeting. The one where . . ."

The one where I was shot. "Yes. Him."

I turned to Lars. "We need to drive to Haus Vaterland. I am meeting Wilhelm out front. You and Anton must stay out of sight."

"I don't like leaving you alone," Lars said.

"Wilhelm might get spooked if you are there." He certainly would not tell me much with Lars listening.

"I want to spook him a little," he said. "To keep you safer."

"If you cannot bear it, follow me. But out of sight. I would be interested to know if anyone follows Wilhelm. I will stoop down and pretend to fix my shoe when you should pick me back up."

"Spatz—"

"I would not have to do this if you could verify Fräulein Ivona's last name." A mean thing to say, and I regretted it. But it was true. "I am not going to let Ruth die without trying to save her."

He held his finger under his eye, on the muscle that twitched when he was angry. "As you wish."

He dropped me a block from Haus Vaterland. He pulled into traffic and disappeared. I trusted him to keep track of me unseen, in spite of our squabble.

I walked in a seemingly aimless fashion down the Kufürstendamm. I noticed how shops on this fashionable street took great pains to advertise their German-ness, probably to ingratiate themselves with the Nazis to protect their windows. I passed signs advertising German restaurants, a German candy store, and a German store that sold umbrellas and luggage.

I stepped into a German tobacconist's next to Haus Vaterland to wait for Wilhelm. The scent of pipe tobacco reminded me of my father. He had usually been happy while smoking his pipe in the evening. Before he got to his third or fourth drink.

I walked between glass cases of pipes, cigarettes, and tobacco. A mural of an exotic-looking tobacco plant covered the wall behind the counter. A dapper man puffed on his pipe, a perfect advertisement for his wares.

I stopped next to a life-size wooden carving of an Indian. Brick red paint covered his face and hands, the wooden feathers on his headdress were brown tipped with white. The costume was wrong, as Anton would have pointed out.

"How may I help you, Fräulein?" the clerk asked. "Cigarettes, perhaps?"

"I do not smoke," I said automatically.

"Filthy habit for a woman." He stroked his long mustache.

I suppressed a smile. It was an equally filthy habit for a man. "I am looking for a pipe for my father."

The shopkeeper lifted out a tray of expensive pipes and set them on the display case. The shelves behind him showcased brightly packaged cigarettes.

I angled my body so that I could see Haus Vaterland and, hopefully soon, Wilhelm. I picked up a smooth briar pipe. My father would not have liked it. He liked the feel of a meerschaum.

As if reading my mind, the salesman stroked his finger along the foam-white surface of a meerschaum pipe. "This one is popular with our older customers."

I pretended to study it. A horse was carved into it, and my father had liked horses. If he had been alive still, the meerschaum would have been his favorite. Clearly, the salesman knew his business.

I spotted Wilhelm's tall blond form half a block away and waited for him to draw closer.

"I must think on it a bit," I said. "But that horse pipe is lovely."

"You can't do better than that," the shopkeeper said. "Solid crafts-manship. It'll last a lifetime. If you have boys, perhaps one of them might use it later."

"Indeed." I intended to prevent Anton from smoking as long as I could. "Excuse me."

Wilhelm looked startled when I stepped out of the tobacco store into his path, but he swept me into a hug all the same. I had quite forgotten how tall he was. As tall as my brother had been. They had been a handsome couple.

"To what do I owe the pleasure?" he asked.

"Trouble," I said.

He slipped my hand into his arm. We strolled down the street as easily and companionably as if we had done it a thousand times. Women in fashionable clothes walked by us. Very few women wore makeup or trousers, as that was discouraged by the government. It was hard to believe that the Nazis were able to find time for fashion edicts. Yet, they did.

"How are Frieda and the baby?" I looked up at him. He was a man now, although still a young man in his mid-twenties, but I re-membered him as a teen, blue eyes uncertain and gawky limbs crash-ing into things, hoping that my brother would notice him and fall in love with him. And Ernst had, almost too late.

"Frieda is tiresome," he said. "By tonight she will be very jealous of you."

"The way you spoke to me on the telephone, I can hardly blame her."

"Stirring up a little jealousy in her for another woman will do her good," he said.

We passed the German luggage store. The shop window contained open red umbrellas with swastikas on them. I looked back at Wilhelm. "Your child?"

"It's a boy, as I hoped," he said. "I named him Ernst."

For my brother. My eyes teared. Wilhelm had loved my brother very much. "He would be proud of that, I think."

He barked out a laugh. "Proud of me married to a woman when I should have been with him? Not likely."

To that I had no ready answer. We strolled to the end of the block and turned to walk back. We stopped in front of the plate glass window of a fashionable dress shop. The dresses were boxy, utilitarian, and there were no trousers for women in the store at all. Nazi fashion, again. I studied Wilhelm's reflection in the mirror. He was grown up, to be sure, but still so young. I remembered how young I had once been, even when I thought myself grown, and all the boys I had nursed back to health after the men in charge had sent them to play and die at war. Would that be Wilhelm's fate, too?

"Tell me your troubles," he said. "Mine bore me."

"I need to know if there is anyone with a first name of Ivona who might be related to the men who died in the warehouse in 1936." Back then, he had checked their files for me, and mine and Lars's, to see if we were under investigation for those murders. He might be able to look at them again.

"I don't need to check for that," he said. "Which is just as well, since I can't."

"Why not?" I stopped, suddenly worried.

"My friend in Records has been reassigned." He pulled me closer to him to let group of young women enter the dress store. One of them eyed him appreciatively. He touched the brim of his uniform cap, and she giggled.

I made a *tsking* sound. "You are married to one woman, out with another, and making eyes at still a third."

We were well away from everyone else. "And for all that," he said, "I'm not interested in any."

I nodded ruefully. "You said you did not need to check for an Ivona. Why not?"

"I remember it. It's an unusual name. Dirk Hahn's daughter was named Ivona."

My heart raced. I was correct. Fräulein Ivona had targeted me because she thought I had killed her father. And I had.

I knew my enemy now. This was my first real lead. Now that I had named her, I would catch her. She would pay for what she had done, somehow. And Ruth would walk free. I hoped.

Wilhelm steered us down the sidewalk, but I no longer saw the bright shops. I was thinking about Ivona Hahn. How had she known to come after me? The letter. Herr Marceau had quoted it to me when I phoned in the orphanage story, but I had given it little thought after. What had he said? *He wrote her and said that he would meet with you that day.* Hahn must have written a letter, either to Fräulein Ivona or her mother, telling her of the meeting he was to have with me on the last day of his life. The meeting from which he had never returned.

Paul and Ruth had not earned her wrath, but I had.

"Before my friend left, I checked your files again, and Lang's. They noted you as residing in Switzerland and separated from your fiancé." He chuckled. "I rather thought it wouldn't last with Lang. Did it at least end well?"

I thought of Lars's activities over the past years and said nothing.

"According to the file, after he left you, he was arrested in Russia." Wilhelm walked faster than I, and I found myself taking extra steps to keep up. "He spent over a year in a Russian prison, before being traded to the SS for a Russian political prisoner."

I felt relieved that his story tallied with what Lars had told me and chastised myself for a lack of trust in Lars. "Oh."

"He was apparently quite badly tortured, and spent several months in an SS hospital near Munich." I sensed that even Wilhelm did not want to talk about Lars's experiences in prison.

"Did he?" So, it had taken him months to recover enough to make his mystery trip to Russia.

Wilhelm guided us around an old woman carrying a vase wrapped in brown paper before speaking again. "He left the SS and seemed to fall off the map. Are you still in touch?"

"I have no idea where he is now," I said. "But I am curious."

Accurate, if not entirely truthful.

"He had quite a time in Russia, did you know?" We stopped at a traffic light.

"I did not know." At least not until last night.

He hesitated. "Do you want to?"

"Not particularly." I longed to ask for details, but I could not snoop on Lars that way. I would have to wait until he was ready to tell me. If he ever was.

We crossed the street to circle the Kaiser Wilhelm Memorial Church, which sat like an island on the Kufürstendamm, across from Haus Vaterland. Wilhelm stopped to stare at the grand rose window. Last time I had stood here I had admired it myself, shortly before I entered the church, and Frau Röhm told me that Anton had been killed. A lie, but one powerful enough to almost destroy me.

Wilhelm pulled on his lip, as he had when he was thinking since he was just a boy. "I don't know, Hannah."

"About what?"

He leaned in close, and I wondered what Lars would think. "About it all."

He glanced around the square. I followed his gaze. No one close. Or at least no one who seemed to be watching. "Wilhelm?"

"I'm sick to death of the whole thing." He sounded sad, and a little angry.

He had a love of the dramatic, but this time the emotions felt true. I waited.

"You were correct. About the Nazis. I used to see just the strength and pageantry. Now—" He spread his strong fingers out as if casting a net and drawing it in. "Now I see behind it. I see the weakness. The meanness."

"You do?" He had always been a devout party member.

"When it was a revolution to sweep away corruption, to make Germany strong again, it made sense."

He felt nostalgia for the early days of Nazism. "Did it?"

"I know it never made sense to you. But it did to me. Now it doesn't."

I almost felt proud of him.

"I'm married to a woman I don't love to satisfy a party I don't believe in." He spoke more to the church than to me, as if confessing. "He'll know."

"Who?"

"Little Ernst." He seemed surprised that I could imagine him speaking of anyone else. "When he gets older. He'll know I don't love Frieda, and that she doesn't love me. That it's based on lies and rot. I can't bear the thought of him looking at me and knowing. I want to leave it behind and be authentic again. Divorce Frieda and start over."

We crossed the street and entered the park.

"What does Frieda think?" We walked among bare trees now, sometimes hidden from view. I wondered what Lars thought of that.

"I don't know what Frieda thinks. About anything. I sometimes think we've never exchanged a single honest word."

"What if you start?" I asked.

"If only it were so simple."

I had no answer for that. Nothing was simple anymore.

"Enough self-pity." He ran one hand through his thick blond hair. "Now, in case anyone is watching me, I'd like to establish a useful reason for this meeting."

He gave me what from a distance must have looked like a passionate kiss. I hated to think of Lars's reaction to that.

He moved his mouth away from mine. "The idea that I'm meeting an attractive blond piece over lunch is too good an opportunity to pass up."

"I am flattered," I said, rather breathless. "But I have always been far too old for you."

"Your most important quality is that you are a woman, and a mysterious one at that."

He positioned a tree between us and the street, and stayed close. I was concealed, but he was mostly visible. It must look like a quick tryst in the trees, barely discreet. I leaned back against the tree trunk, hoping my shoes would not get muddy. I imagined that Lars must be livid, but then again, he had slept with a raft of women since we parted, so he had no right to be jealous. On the other hand, I would have to explain it to Anton. We kept our heads close together.

"Do you have an address for Ivona Hahn?" I asked.

"I don't remember one. I think she lived with her mother."

"Can you get me her file?"

He moved closer. "As I said before, I don't have the access to the file room that I once did."

His tone told me that it would make no sense to argue. Besides, I suspected that Fräulein Ivona was too smart to take Ruth to her own home, in case Lars or I knew someone who could find it.

We talked about my brother and the old days. Eventually, he stepped back and adjusted his suit. I brushed off the back of my dress.

"Maybe next time we should rent a hotel room." He picked a piece of bark out of my hair.

"I am hopeful that there will not be a next time."

"Aren't you always?" He smiled. "If there is, we shall rent a room."

I had to smile back. "How extravagant!"

He kissed the top of my head. "I have to get back to work."

"Well, that was certainly quick."

He gave me a lazy smile. "I got what I needed, and so did you."

"I suppose that is the best one can expect of any rendezvous."

"Take care of yourself, Hannah."

We embraced. I held him for a long while, wondering if it would be the last time.

"Until we meet again." He gave me a mock salute.

As I watched his tall, strong form lope off, I wondered what would become of him. Germany marched toward war. Chamberlain would not keep handing Hitler territory forever, even if he had traded those bits of Czechoslovakia easily enough a little more than a month ago. The Sudetenland and Austria would not suffice for Germany's former corporal. Eventually someone would have to fight back. I hoped that Wilhelm would not be sacrificed on a battlefield for the Nazi cause, one he no longer believed in.

I walked slowly back to the street. Once I reached the sidewalk, I bent to fiddle with my shoe. Anton darted over.

Without Lars.

28

I stood and nodded to Anton.

Where was Lars? How jealous was he? Would it keep him from believing what I had uncovered about Fräulein Ivona?

"That was not what it looked like," I said to Anton.

"I understand." He fiddled with something in his pocket. "It's the most logical thing for a man and woman to do in the woods in the middle of the day."

Sometimes I forgot how much he must have learned in his years with his prostitute mother. "But we did not."

He laughed. "I know, but Lars doesn't. His head got very red. He looked as if he would explode. He said we are to meet him at the Wild West Bar. He will join us soon. He's going to follow Herr Lehmann first."

I imagined that he needed to calm himself, too, and was grateful for the reprieve. I was also impressed that he had thought to choose the Wild West Bar. Years ago, I had vowed to take Anton there if we ever returned to Berlin together. I suspected that this might be our only opportunity.

Rain drizzled down. I hurried across the square. We stopped at the traffic light. "That was the first traffic light installed in Europe," I said. "In 1924, a few years before you were born."

He studied it with interest. "How do you know?"

"I came to marvel at it," I said. "It was news."

"A stoplight?" He shook his head in disbelief.

"Technology marches on," I told him. "Someday your child will be amazed that you rode in something as old-fashioned as a zeppelin."

We crossed with the light and walked toward the curved front of Haus Vaterland. I had rarely come to this building of themed restaurants when I lived in Berlin. Since I left, it had practically become my home away from home. I had met Wilhelm at the Wild West Bar to exchange information in 1934 and Lars at the Türkische Café in 1936.

We paid our entrance fee, trotted up the ugly staircase, and marched through swinging saloon doors into the Wild West Bar. It had changed little since 1934. Anton gaped as a cowboy in a ten-gallon hat strode over. I smiled to see Anton happy.

"Howdy, ma'am," the cowboy said in English. He touched the brim of his felt hat with two fingers and a thumb. Anton was enchanted.

"A table for three," I said.

"Follow me." He stepped past a brass spittoon to a round table with poker chips and playing cards painted on it.

He pulled out my rough-hewn wooden chair, and I sat. Anton scooted his chair forward and studied his painted cards.

"I win," he said. "Full house. Three jacks and a pair of deuces."

"When did you learn to play poker?" I asked.

The cowboy handed me a menu full of American specialties and left.

"At riding school," Anton said. "Back of the stable."

"I am glad to hear that they are broadening your education."

"You don't sound glad." He counted his painted chips.

"You do not play for money, do you?"

He shook his head. "Not yet. No money."

"That is not so reassuring," I said.

The waiter returned. "Something to wet your whistle?"

Our waiter in 1934 had used just those terms.

Anton ordered a High Noon, lemonade with a shot of cola. It sounded terrible. I had a tea, straight up.

Lars slid in next to me and ordered a Schultheiss beer with no Western pretense.

The waiter sauntered off.

Lars picked up his menu without meeting my eyes. He barely glanced at the menu before dropping it on the table.

"Poker," Anton said, pointing to the cards.

Lars looked at his cards and moved to my other side.

"Why did you move?" Anton asked. "I already have the best hand."

Lars pointed to his first cards. "A pair of aces and a pair of eights. That's called the 'dead man's hand' because that's what Wild Bill Hickok was holding when he was shot."

"How do you know that?" Anton asked.

"I make it my business to know things." Lars gave me a meaningful look.

"Sometimes," I said. "Things slip through. Wilhelm said—"

The waiter returned and set down my thick mug of tea, Anton's tin one frothing over with a fizzy brown mixture, and Lars's familiar beer glass.

"Know what vittles you'll be needing?" The waiter hooked his thumbs in his braces and leaned back as if he had just jumped off his horse on the trail.

Lars and I each ordered a plate of beef stew. Anton asked for the pork and beans with sourdough biscuits.

I decided to ask Lars a few questions before revealing Fräulein Ivona's identity. I expected that to render him speechless, at least for a while. "Was Wilhelm followed?"

"Inexpertly. By his wife." Lars drank a long swallow of beer.

"He is married?" Anton asked.

"And he has a little boy," I told him. "Did anyone else follow him?"

"Not that I could see. I tailed him after you parted as well. His wife left when you started your performance in the woods."

I blushed and looked over his shoulder at a cactus. "That is all it was."

"What information did you extract from him?" Lars clipped off each word angrily.

"Ivona's last name is Hahn."

Lars rocked back in his chair. He looked as if he might be ill on the table.

I drank my strong tea and waited for him to collect himself. Anton stared at his painted poker chips.

The waiter clanked tin plates in front of us. The beef stew looked better than I had expected. I tasted it. Salty, but edible. I took a few bites, watching Lars.

Anton pretended to ignore both of us and swabbed his biscuit through the sauce on his pork and beans. I supposed that was standard manners in the Old West and said nothing.

"Lars?" I asked. Finally, he had outwaited me.

He pushed his plate away untouched. "I'm sorry, Spatz."

I pulled a handful of coins out of my pocket and handed them to Anton. "Please select a song on the player piano and stay next to it until the song ends."

Anton jumped to his feet, clearly eager to have a good excuse to get away from the argument he knew must be coming. He hurried across the room. Seconds later, a Western-style song plonked away.

"I should have checked further," Lars said. "I didn't, and that's landed us all here."

"Hopefully there will be time for self-recrimination later," I said. "Now we need to find Ruth. What do you know about Fräulein Ivona?"

"I knew her only three weeks," he said. "I did a quick check on her file and it seemed fine. We shared drinks, meals. I slept with her because she resembled you."

I winced.

"I'm sorry. I'm sorry. I'll say it a thousand times if you like."

"I do not like it." I spoke too loudly. I brought myself back under control. I had to stay calm. "Please, I want to focus on Ruth and only Ruth. Where would Fräulein Ivona take her?"

"I don't know," he said. "Hahn is dead. I don't know where her mother lived."

I kept my voice even. "Do you know where Hahn lived?"

"Yes." He tapped his spoon against his tin plate. "But his wife did not live with him. I went back to his apartment after I was released from the hospital, as part of my sanctioned but unofficial investigation into his death. His apartment had long been rented to someone else."

I stopped his spoon from tapping. "Did you find out much about his wife or daughter in your investigation?"

His lips thinned. "Obviously not. They were not suspects in his death."

Across the room, Anton fed another coin into the piano. He looked like he wanted to stay there all day. I wanted to join him.

"She said that her mother died recently. Do you know where?"

Lars looked at me in surprise. "Her mother is dead?"

"She told me her mother died a month ago." I thought back to her words in front of Doktor Volononki's fireplace. "It is no more reliable than anything else she said, but the letters started then, too. It did not seem like a lie at the time, but—"

"Many things didn't seem like a lie at the time," he muttered angrily. "Can we get her file? That should have some facts in it."

His faith in the accuracy of Nazi record keeping was disconcerting. "Wilhelm cannot. What about your sources?"

He studied the untouched stew congealing in front of him. "Doubtful."

"We have to assume that she will kill Ruth." My voice wavered. "As she killed Paul."

"If she favors her father, she is sadistic enough to want us to suffer as long as possible before she kills us," he said. "So Ruth is probably safe."

I did not point out that she could already have killed Ruth while still continuing to torture us. I did not want it to be true. "You know her better than I."

"I don't think I know her at all," he said. "But I know that she's a fervent anti-Semite. She worshipped her father, and he was a devoted Party man." He ticked off the point on his thumb.

I waited for him to keep counting. He knew more than he thought. I hoped.

He raised a finger. "And she's a clever strategist. Assuming someone else's identity because she thought I might check. Writing you the letters to lure you here. Those are all thought-out maneuvers. Whatever she's doing, she's doing it carefully."

The song ended, but Anton quickly dropped in another coin. The waiter watched us with interest. "What else do you know about her?"

Lars took a deep breath. "She's a crack shot. We went hunting together a few times."

"I wonder why she did not shoot you?"

"Why did she start with me?" Lars asked. "Why not you?"

"You were easier to find. Hahn's colleagues might have told his daughter where you were. You are probably listed as one of the last people to speak to him, so it would not be unreasonable for her to use that as a pretext to want to speak to you. Or perhaps she thought that you might be easier to control."

He grimaced. "As I was. I led her straight to you. The minute you arrived in Poland."

She was no fool, and clearly determined to get us both.

"That makes it my fault," he said. "All of it."

"You could not have known."

"Couldn't I?" he said savagely. "It's my job to know."

I touched his shoulder, but he shook off my hand. The third song ended. Quiet expanded through the room. Anton was out of coins. He looked to see if he should come back. I gestured him over, and we finished our lunch.

The day passed in a frenzy of useless activity. We visited Hahn's old apartment. Lars talked his way in again, but found nothing. I called the newspaper every hour, but they had no more messages.

Evening came with no answers. The sun set, and darkness rolled in. Still we drove around Berlin. We had no idea how to find Fräulein Ivona and Ruth, but when we were moving, it at least felt like we were doing something.

At eight thirty that night, the radio announced that Ernst vom Rath had died of wounds inflicted by a vicious Jew. They called for two minutes of radio silence. Once it was over, they announced that the Führer had said that no official actions would be taken against the Jews, but that citizens could use their own judgment. Everyone knew what that meant. Lars pulled the lorry to the side of the road.

I brought my hands together under my nose and rocked back and forth. We had lost Ruth. Fräulein Ivona might already have killed her.

"The newspaper," Anton said. "Let's call them again."

I called them again. Lars hovered outside like a nervous parent. Anton stayed in the lorry.

"Thank god," Herr Marceau said as soon as he heard me.

"She called?" I dreaded hearing what she might have said.

"She said that 'the Jew bastard in Paris chose Ruth's fate but—' "

I gripped the phone tightly. "But what?"

"She says that she'll trade you for the girl."

Lars studied my face. I pressed the receiver tight against my ear, hoping that he could not hear. But I knew he already had.

"Where?" I said.

Lars shook his head. I turned so that I could not see him.

"I don't think you should go, Frau Zinsli." I heard the crackle of Herr Marceau shuffling papers, his nervous habit. "It's probably a trap."

Of course it was a trap. A trap that she had baited with something that she suspected I could not resist. I could not let Ruth die without trying to prevent it. "Where?"

He gave me the address of the warehouse where Hahn had died. She intended to kill me there. It was the perfect place to do it. Dark, deserted, and the right site for an act of revenge.

"Do you know where that is?" Herr Marceau asked.

"Yes." I still had nightmares about it. I had watched Hahn die there a hundred times in my sleep. In some dreams, I died there myself. To think I once thought that dreams do not come true.

"Call the police," he said. "Send them there."

I almost laughed. The police would not listen to an anonymous tip. "Thank you, Herr Marceau. Is there anything else?"

"Good god, isn't that enough?"

I swallowed. "More than enough."

I broke the connection and turned to Lars.

"You can't go," he said quickly. "She intends to kill you."

So, he had overheard the entire conversation. "If I stay away, she kills Ruth."

"If you go, she'll kill you both," he said. "I won't allow that."

"You do not allow or forbid me to do things, Lars." I knew he was frightened for me. I was frightened for me, too. But that did not change what I intended to do.

Anton got out of the lorry and jogged over.

"I cannot live with myself if something happens to Ruth because of me," I said. "You know that."

"She knows it, too." Lars jammed his hands into his pockets.

Anton took my hand. "What's going on?"

"You explain it to him." Lars stalked off. Perhaps a walk would calm him down.

"Anton," I began. "Fräulein Ivona called the newspaper and left a message."

I had to think of someplace safe to stash him. Herr Keller's, perhaps?

"What message? Is Ruth all right?" He could tell how serious things were.

"She said—"

Before I could finish the sentence, the lorry roared into life.

Lars drove off and left us alone in the dark.

I ran a few steps before realizing the futility of trying to catch him on foot. I stood in the street cursing him until I remembered Anton.

He stared at me with his jaw hanging open, too surprised to speak. He was getting quite an education this trip.

As soon as I calmed down enough to think, I called a taxi. While we waited, I explained to Anton that Lars had gone to get Ruth from Fräulein Ivona, and we were following.

"How do you know?" Anton asked. "What if he just left?"

That had not occurred to me. I shook my head. "I just do."

In my heart, I knew that Lars had realized the futility of arguing and taken matters into his own hands. If someone had to walk into a trap, he chose himself. I viewed his action with equal parts of love and fury.

Anything that was going to happen would have happened before we arrived. And I did not think I could bear it if another man I loved died for me.

The taxi driver did not want to take us to a warehouse so late at night, but agreed after I said that I would double his fare, which took every pfennig I had. When we arrived, the taxi dropped us off and disappeared with the squealing of tires.

I pushed Anton behind me, drew the Vis from my satchel, and approached the warehouse.

Lars stepped out of the shadows. "Don't bother."

I holstered the Vis. If he did not need a gun drawn, I probably did not need one either.

"God damn you!" I yanked Lars into a tight embrace. He was alive. That was the most important thing.

Lars gave me a quick smile. He pulled us both back toward the lorry, practically shoved us in, and drove off. Only when the warehouse was well behind us did he speak.

"She never showed up," he said. "She left you a note on the front of the warehouse door. I've checked around. I don't think she went inside."

He handed me a folded sheet of white paper written in the blocky printing of the letters I had received at the paper. I turned on the overhead light and held the paper where Anton could not see it. The watermark matched the other letters that Fräulein Ivona had sent.

My dear little Frau Zinsli,

You have been a wilier prey than I expected. I can see why Lars and my father were attracted to you. Both underestimated you, but I won't make their mistake.

I learned much about you, my dear, in the scant time we were together. I once thought to turn you in to the Gestapo so you could face the justice of the Reich.

But now I know that it will be worse for you to hear of the little girl's death. I can only imagine how the death of your friend must haunt you.

That was an accident. I intended to wait for you there, but he wanted to protect you, so . . . I panicked afterwards and took the girl, but it turns out that was my best decision of all.

She looks so very Aryan, doesn't she? Aryan enough to support a charge of blood libel. It has been a long time since the Jews have paid for their crimes. After tonight, we will rain down misfortune on all the Jews in Berlin.

Don't worry. I'm not yet done with you. Or that annoying son of yours. Or Lars.

Until later,

I

I dropped the letter back in Lars's lap, wanting it as far away from Anton as possible. I turned off the overhead light and took Anton's hand. If she could, Fräulein Ivona would make good on her threats. She would kill Ruth, and she would kill Anton.

I stared into the blackness rushing toward us on the other side of the windshield. We would never be safe from her. She intended to torture me by killing my loved ones, then me. How could I find Ruth? How could I protect Anton?

"Where are we going?" Anton asked.

"To Populov's warehouse," Lars said. "In a few hours, I'll have the compartment installed. We can get out of Germany and decide what to do somewhere safe."

"What about Ruth?" Streetlamps slid by outside, but beyond that, there was little to see. He drove so fast, I worried that a policeman would stop him.

"I am so sorry, Spatz, but there is nothing that we can do. We've spent the whole day thinking and searching. We don't know where Ivona is."

"She mentioned blood libel." I kept my voice even with an effort. I did not want Anton to know how frightened I was.

"What's blood libel?" Anton asked.

"Blood libel is an accusation that Jews kill Christian children to use their blood in their Passover bread," I said.

"Is it true?" he asked, aghast.

"No," I said, "but thousands of Jews have been murdered because of it. Which means the results are real, even if the accusation is not."

"What does it mean for Ruth?" Anton pulled his knees up to his chin.

It meant that Fräulein Ivona intended to kill her, probably drain her blood into a bowl, and leave the body somewhere where the Jews would be blamed. But where?

"Well?" Anton hugged his knees and looked at me.

"A synagogue," I said. There was little I could do to shield him from the truth now. "She intends to kill Ruth in a synagogue and leave her body there to be discovered."

"Assuming that were true." Lars looked behind us again, probably checking to see if we were being followed. "There are nineteen synagogues in Berlin."

"How do you know that?" I asked.

"I was in the SS." He took a quick left turn and I grabbed the dash to keep from plowing into him. "You did not think we counted?"

"Which synagogue would she pick?" I asked Lars. It was a slender hope, but it was the only one that we had.

"I've no idea," he said. "It never came up in conversation."

"Bronislawa Hahn died a month ago," I mused.

"I doubt that they had a service in a synagogue for her," Lars said.

"Of course not," I snapped. "She was Catholic."

"How do you know that?" he asked, surprised. "Did Ivona tell you that she was Catholic?"

"Did she ever say that she was Catholic?" I asked Anton.

He shook his head. "Not to me."

I thought back to our conversations. Lars kept driving. Fräulein Ivona had never mentioned her religion. Most Berliners were Protestant, so why did I think she was Catholic? I ran over the things she had told me about herself, her father, and her mother. The nuns. "She said that the nuns were very kind to her mother before she died."

"Nuns?" Anton asked.

"Only Catholics have nuns." I had an idea. "Take us to Saint Hedwig's Hospital."

"Why?" Lars asked.

"There are two Catholic hospitals in Berlin with nuns in attendance. Saint Hedwig's is next to the Neue Synagogue. The largest synagogue in Berlin."

Lars turned right so abruptly that Anton slammed into the door.

"Are you all right?" I asked.

He sat up. "I am not made of glass."

"She might not be there," Lars said.

But we both knew that it made sense. "It is a place to start. And it is all we have."

"Have you ever been inside?" Lars asked.

"Of course. It is a Berlin landmark. You have not?"

"I've never been in a synagogue. Why would I go?"

His SS past rankled. "Because it is beautiful."

"Yes, Spatz," he said. "I'm certain it is. Could you describe it for me? Especially the entrances and exits."

I closed my eyes. "The front door is on Oranienburgerstrasse. After you enter, you come into a large hall. There are stairs on both sides to the women's section upstairs. If you stay downstairs and head for the back, there are a couple of smaller halls before you get to the main one. Stools on either side with an aisle up the middle. At the back is the Ark. The Ark is on a kind of stage. With her flair for the dramatic, I think that is where she would . . . take Ruth."

"Windows?"

"Yes. Windows line both sides of the main hall. I think there is a side entrance on the left halfway down, and a rear entrance that opens onto the back, near the Ark and the room where weddings are performed."

"I'll go in through the back," Lars said. "It's closest to the Ark. I won't have to go through the whole open hall."

"Fine," I said. "I will follow."

"This is not something for a civilian," Lars said. "She is armed. She has a hostage."

I did not pretend to mull that over. Logically, he was correct, but I had no intention of waiting in the lorry and hoping for the best. I took the Vis out of the glove box and awkwardly checked that it was loaded with my left hand, wishing again that I had the use of my right arm.

29

We sped down Oranienburgerstrasse. Shouting men thronged the sidewalks. They had heard Hitler's veiled call to arms, too.

Lars drove past them and on to the synagogue.

"Right there!" I pointed.

He mashed on the brakes, and the lorry stopped so suddenly, it stalled. He started it again and drove more decorously past the opulent Moorish-style synagogue.

A crowd had gathered there. A group of men, some in uniforms and some in civilian clothing, milled on the sidewalk. Many carried torches. Mounted police had joined them. A gray and a chestnut horse shifted in the crowd. A fire truck passed us and parked. We drove past the crowd before parking behind another Opel Blitz lorry.

I craned my neck around to study the mob. "They are going to burn the synagogue."

"Why do they have a fire truck?" Anton asked.

I looked at the buildings built flush against the synagogue. It was horrible, and it made perfect sense, if one thought like a Nazi. "Those buildings are not Jewish-owned, I suspect. They will let the synagogue burn, but they will try to save the buildings around it."

"This complicates matters." Lars tapped his fingers against the steering wheel.

I reached over Anton and opened his door. We climbed out into the cold night. If Ruth was in the building, Fräulein Ivona would be found soon. We had to go in now.

No one in the mob noticed us. They probably thought that we had come to enjoy their spectacle of hate.

"Anton," I said. "Stay with the lorry."

He did not look any more pleased about this news than I had when Lars told me the same thing. "But—"

"You must cover my retreat," Lars said. "When we come out, we might not have much time."

Anton nodded, and I was again struck by how easily Lars convinced him to follow orders. I wondered what Lars had tricked me into against my better judgment, but came up with nothing. I had known what I was doing all the time, for better or for worse. Lars handed Anton a gun.

"If you see Ivona," Lars said. "Shoot her."

Anton's eyes grew round. He hefted the gun in his hands, looking young. I wished again that I had left him in Switzerland.

"No." I took the gun away from him. "Just run."

I had formulated a plan for him in the lorry. I gave him quick directions to the Swiss embassy. "Stay out front. If I am not there in two hours, go in and tell them that you are a Swiss citizen named Anton Zinsli. You sneaked across the border on a dare. Tell them to call Boris. He will get you out."

Lars looked impressed with my plan for Anton, but in truth it was sheer desperation. On top of everything else, I was not certain that Boris could get Anton out, even with his expensive lawyers. Boris himself was wanted by the Gestapo, but I knew he would do everything that he could. If things went that badly, he was the best hope that Anton had.

"I'll steal one of those horses." Anton gestured to the police mounts now tethered a short distance away, riders gone to join the mob. I gave him a worried look. He had stolen horses once before, on a dare.

"Don't do anything fancy," Lars said. "Just run."

I gave Lars's gun back to him and stuck the Vis in my pocket. It pulled my dress out of shape, but I had no belt to tuck it into. I glanced once more at the shouting men brandishing torches.

"Spatz," Lars said. "Stay here. Please."

I was not a lady out of the Middle Ages, ready to send a knight into battle for me. I would run the risks he did, or I could never live with myself after. We both knew that I had no intention of staying. Two of us might be more successful than one. Our lives, and Ruth's and Anton's, might depend on that success.

"Stay on my left, and let me go in first," he said finally.

That I would do.

I hugged Anton hard. "We will be back soon."

He sucked in his lower lip as he always did when he tried not to cry, and held out a hand for Lars to shake.

Lars shook his hand. "Mind the retreat, Anton. I truly need you here."

I hoped that would be enough to keep Anton in place.

Lars started toward the synagogue. As I had been told, I stayed on his left side.

The crowd clearly readied itself to storm the synagogue, but they were more organized than I had expected. They behaved more like a unit of soldiers than like a mob. A man in front exhorted them for patience. Even though he wore no uniform, I sensed that he was their commanding officer.

We circled the outside of the crowd, slipped around the block and to the back of the synagogue. Through the back window, a light flickered. The eternal flame. Soon, I predicted, it would be extinguished.

I gripped Lars's tense arm. "She does not expect us. With the noise of the crowd, we may slip in undetected."

He drew a stag-handle knife with a dull nickel blade out of his boot. It was short, about twenty centimeters from handle to tip; half of that was blade. "It's a trench knife. I've had it since the War." He handed it to me handle first. "I keep it sharp."

I weighed it in my palm. I had no boot to stuff it into. Instead, I carefully slipped it blade first into my cast at the wrist. He winced. It slid in easily, stopping before my elbow. Uncomfortable, but reassuring, rather like my relationship with Lars.

"If you have to," I said, "could you kill her?"

He hesitated. "I will do what I have to do to keep Ruth safe. Or you."

I did not believe him. He had some kind of feelings for her, whether he admitted it or not. And those feelings might be enough to make him pause. I knew the cost of killing a human in cold blood. I still woke screaming from nightmares where I killed Hahn, and I would never again forget the face of the Gestapo man lying in the gravel next to the car, but if it came down to it, I would do what had to be done. Killing Hahn had saved my life and the lives of who knew how many others. Killing Fräulein Ivona to save Ruth came with a cost that I would pay. But hopefully, it would not come to that.

A shadow crossed in front of the eternal flame. Someone was inside the synagogue. Fräulein Ivona?

We crept to the imposing back door. Not so dramatic as the front, it was still twice as tall as I. I tried the handle. Unlocked. Lars shouldered past me and opened it. The shouting of the crowd was quieter here, but still loud enough to mask our approach.

I slipped off my shoes and left them by the back door. The hard stone, cold under my feet, rendered my footsteps soundless.

Lars was ahead of me, moving sideways through the oval-shaped room, his boots quiet, too. I followed close behind until we stood in the back corner of the main hall. Arched ceilings soared above us. Light from the eternal flame cast a dull glow. It burned around the corner.

I turned left toward the light. Ruth lay on her back atop the Ark, a few meters away. She wore a simple white dress and shiny patent leather shoes. Her long blond hair hung across her face. I hoped that she was still alive. Next to her sat a ceramic bowl with a razor next to it. Next to that a Luger. There was no sign of Fräulein Ivona.

"Ruth?" I whispered. She turned her head toward me, eyes shin-

ing in the candlelight. She was alive. I sighed with relief. I beckoned
for her to come to me. As quietly as I could, I crept closer.

Out of the corner of my eye I saw Lars motion for me to stop. I did.

Ruth sat up and looked behind her. Fräulein Ivona stood there
with the Luger pointed straight at me. She had been kneeling behind the Ark. With the other hand, she scooped up Ruth and held
her in front of her like a shield. She balanced Ruth in the crook of
her elbow. In her hand glittered the razor.

"Hello!" Fräulein Ivona cried cheerfully. "This could not go better!"

I could not shoot her without harming Ruth. I was no marks-
man. But Lars was.

She pressed her elbow harder against Ruth's throat. "I can crush
her trachea. I did it to a pig once."

A shot whistled past my head. Lars. He missed.

In almost the same instant, Fräulein Ivona swiveled the Luger
toward him and shot. He thudded to the floor. *Please,* I begged silently, *don't let Lars die.*

Before I had time to react, the Luger was aimed at me again.

"Drop the Vis," she said. "We don't want the girl to be hurt early."

I complied, eyes never leaving Ruth. She stared at me with wide
eyes, too frightened to speak. "Please, Fräulein Ivona. She is only
a child."

"She is only a Jew." She tightened her grip on Ruth. The child
gasped for air.

"She is just a little girl." I took one slow step toward them, then
another. Unless Lars was seriously wounded, he would try again.
But could he shoot her, in spite of his determined words earlier? I
did not believe that he had missed by accident, even if he did not
know it.

"Don't come any closer," she said. "I can crush her throat long
before you reach me."

Ruth whimpered and twisted. Fräulein Ivona was correct. Ruth
would be dead before I made it to her. I stopped.

"Be still," she said sharply. Ruth went limp. "I chloroformed her earlier. I'll do it again soon. She won't feel a thing. It will just be like going to sleep."

Tears trickled from Ruth's eyes, but she stayed very still.

"How about we work out a trade?" I said. "Let the girl go, and I will come up there unarmed and lie down on the Ark in her place."

Ruth gaped at me.

"I don't need you here," she said. "I need a child."

I swallowed. I had to save Ruth. Nothing else mattered.

"This isn't mere sport, like hunting." She shook Ruth. "When they find the child's body and the basin of blood next to her, it will start a pogrom like we haven't seen since the Middle Ages."

I feared that the world was poised to see that anyway.

Fräulein Ivona shook her head, hair still perfectly combed. "My father will see that I am strong. He will be proud of me. At last."

"Ivona," I said softly. "Your father is dead."

She glared at me. "By your hand. You'll be on this altar soon enough. My father was a great man, and his death won't go unavenged. Then he will forgive me for my weaknesses."

Two deaths on my conscience. "It was self-defense. There is nothing to avenge."

Fräulein Ivona tightened her grip on Ruth, and the little girl cried out. "It might have meant nothing to you, but not to me."

I calculated the distance between us again. I would not make it before she killed Ruth. "Fräulein Ivona, your father—"

Something smashed through the side window several meters away. Broken glass crashed to the floor. Ruth flinched. I smelled gasoline. I looked to see what had come through the window. A bottle, and stuffed in its neck was a flaming piece of fabric.

"It has begun." Fräulein Ivona smiled beatifically and reached for the razor. I tensed. If she moved that razor toward Ruth's throat, I would have to intervene, no matter the risk.

"The police know that Ruth is missing," I said desperately. "They have already started an investigation. They will identify her body and know that she is Jewish, not Aryan. Your plan is flawed."

A wooden chair ignited. Then another.

Fräulein Ivona laughed. "Such a clever tongue."

"It speaks the truth," I said. "Let her go. She and I will leave by the back door. No one need ever know that we were here."

Fräulein Ivona gestured around the room with the razor. "I think you put too much faith in the police. They won't investigate her disappearance. They don't care."

Fire crackled behind me. Fräulein Ivona looked past me at the flames, as transfixed as she had been in the doctor's office. This distraction was my only chance.

I charged her and grabbed the Luger. Its barrel was still hot from shooting Lars. With one twist, I yanked it out of her hands and threw it into the burning synagogue.

Fräulein Ivona rolled Ruth down toward the razor in her left hand.

I pushed my cast between Ruth's throat and the razor. With the other hand, I yanked Ruth out of Fräulein Ivona's grasp and dropped her to the floor. She ran into the smoke.

Before I could follow, the razor sliced through my cast and clanked against metal. The trench knife.

I ripped the knife out of my cast and slashed her upper arm, aiming for the brachial artery. The blow knocked her down to the side.

We grappled. She was younger and stronger than I, but the blood spurting out of her arm weakened her. As I had hoped, I had severed the artery.

"You will bleed out in under a minute," I told her. "Stop."

She lay still, probably because she had lost too much blood to struggle further. I thought of two nights ago when I had held Paul's blood in. I had saved him, only for her to kill him. I wanted to let go, but I pressed hard against her severed artery. I could still save her, as I had saved Paul.

Behind us, the wooden seats in the synagogue crackled with bright flames. Acrid smoke billowed toward us. I stifled a cough.

"Ruth?" I called. No answer.

"What now?" Fräulein Ivona asked.

"If I let go, you die," I said. "Stay still, and you might live."

She laughed. "I didn't think you had it in you to be a killer."

"I am no killer."

"But you are," she said. "You murdered my father."

My good hand began to go numb. "Self-defense."

Her lips curved into a pale smile. "Everyone's a killer."

Not far away, Ruth coughed weakly. I wished I knew how near the flames were, but I could not afford to look.

"He is hurt," Ruth's childish voice called. "Like my *Vati*."

She had watched her father die. Ruth would carry that memory for the rest of her life. I glanced back into the smoke, searching for Ruth.

The second I was distracted, Fräulein Ivona twisted out of my grip.

Blood pumped out of her shoulder, drenching her white shirt. I struggled to put pressure on her wound, but it was too late. She went limp under me.

I coughed. My eyes teared in the smoke.

"Ruth?" I called. "Lars? Where are you?"

"Here!" piped up Ruth.

I followed the sound of her voice. She stood next to a crumpled form. Lars.

I pulled Lars's coat back. Blood stained his chest. I grabbed the cloth covering the Ark with my casted hand. The ceramic bowl fell to the ground and shattered. Ruth yelped, but she kept hold of Lars's hand. I felt the edge of the cloth, sturdy and hemmed. It would not tear so easily as Paul's worn pillowcase had.

I held it in one hand and turned my attention to Lars. Flickering light from the eternal flame revealed a bullet hole below his left clavicle. Blood frothed out. I heard a sucking sound when he breathed. The bullet had punctured his lung.

His dark eyes watched me from a face gone pale as ashes. I kept my face impassive so he would not know how frightened I was. I slid one hand under his armpit and around to his back. No exit wound.

I reached behind me for the trench knife and used it to cut the edge of the cloth, then tore off a strip.

"Good girl, Ruth." While I talked, I made a quick bandage for Lars. "In just a minute, we can go and visit your *Opa*. Can you wait one more minute?"

She stuck the corner of her green blanket in her mouth and nodded. I folded the bandage quickly. Fräulein Ivona's slice through my cast had made it easier to move, if more painful.

"Ivona?" Lars coughed and blood stained his lips.

I glanced back to where she lay unmoving on the floor. Her chest no longer rose and fell.

"Departed." I hated to say *dead* in front of Ruth. She had already seen too much death in her short life.

Lars knew what I meant.

"Not your fault." I lay the bandage on his chest. "Mine."

"Sorry."

"Me, too." She was correct. I was a killer. She and her father had set up the circumstances, but I had killed. Three times. "Now, hush."

He nodded.

"Breathe out and hold your breath."

He complied. As soon as the air was out of the lung, I tied the bandage tight across his chest.

"Breathe," I whispered.

He did. The wound sounded mostly closed, for now. I kept both hands pressed against it. Smoke filled the synagogue. I could see barely a meter in front of me. If I did not get him to a doctor soon, he would die. Even if I did, he might die anyway.

Lars put his hands on top of mine and pressed on the bandage. He jerked his head toward Ruth. I took my hands away, and he kept applying pressure.

"Ruth?" I asked. "Are you hurt?"

She shook her head. I patted her all over quickly, just to be sure.

Blood streaked her once white dress, but it was Lars's. Physically, she was unharmed. That at least.

How could I get them out of the synagogue before it burned down? Flames filled the main hall. Something else crashed through the window. Glass rained onto the floor.

"Take Ruth," Lars coughed.

He knew how futile it would be to try to save him, too. But how could I leave him? I cradled her against my chest and stood. If I left him, he would die. If I did not, we might all die.

30

I set Ruth on her feet. I saw the reflection of the flames behind us in her eyes.

"Ruth?" I said. "Hold on to my dress and don't let go. Can you do that?"

She gripped a fistful of my skirt.

I bent my legs, draped Lars's arm over my shoulder, and hoisted him to his feet. I knew that if he'd had any breath, he would have argued. But he did not.

We stumbled to the back door of the synagogue. Ruth doggedly kept hold. The heat of the flames beat against my back. Smoke boiled around us.

Ruth coughed. She wiped her eyes with her green blanket. But she did not let go.

A few more steps and we reached the door.

"Ruth," I said. "Please push on it for me."

She opened the door. I dragged Lars through.

I gulped deep breaths of the fresh air. The grass felt cool on my bare feet.

Lars sagged against me. I had no time to catch my breath. I hauled him one step, then another. Anton waited with the lorry. All we had to do was get there.

My legs threatened to give out. Ruth hung on my dress, adding her little weight to Lars's. Just a few more steps.

I stopped and raised my head to look for the lorry. It was where we had left it. "Anton?" I called softly.

He did not answer.

I hauled Lars closer.

Smoke curled out of the cab of the lorry.

It was on fire.

I lowered Lars to the ground. Ruth clung to me like a monkey. I hefted her onto my hip and ran to the lorry.

A broken bottle rested on the floorboards. Flames licked the bottom of the dash. I smelled gasoline. Where was Anton?

The mob rushed the burning synagogue. No one paid us any heed.

"Anton!" I screamed.

"Here!" he called.

Shadows approached, too big to be Anton. "Where?"

"Mother?" Anton led a chestnut horse out of the darkness. Next to it was the dapple gray. He had stolen the police horses, just as he said he would. I wanted to kiss him. "When the lorry caught fire, I knew we would need something else."

"Good." For this, I would not lecture him later.

"Where's Lars?"

"Wounded." I handed him Ruth. "This is Ruth."

He held her on one hip. "Hello, Ruth," he said softly. "Do you like horses?"

She nodded.

I took the leather reins and led the gray to Lars. Well trained, the animal flared its nostrils at the smell of blood, but did not bolt.

When I hefted Lars upright, he groaned. Anton hurried to help. Together we hoisted Lars on my mount. Anton held him on the horse while I swung up behind. Lars slumped in front of me, but he had enough strength to keep his seat, at least for a while. He seemed to breathe better sitting up. Anton got Ruth on the other horse on his own.

Even though barely conscious, Lars settled into the rhythm of the horse. I hoped that the riding of his childhood might save his life now. We galloped through the grounds of Saint Hedwig's Hospital like something out of a Karl May book.

"No," Lars said weakly. "Questions."

He was correct. I could not ride up to the hospital on stolen police mounts with a gunshot victim and a child in a bloody dress. We would all be arrested. I turned my horse's head toward the Jewish quarter. I knew only one doctor who would help without asking questions.

Behind us, the synagogue blazed, but the fire truck already strove to put it out. I hoped that they would save it.

We galloped down cobblestone streets, turning heads. Anton rode close to my right flank, holding Ruth's waist with one hand and the reins with the other. As always, he was most agile and at ease on a horse.

"Frau Doktor Spiegel's!" I yelled above the wind. He nodded. He rode confidently, as if we were out for a quick canter in the woods.

Lars, on the other hand, barely managed to stay in the saddle. I dropped the reins from my left hand and held him against me, hoping I could stay balanced.

Anton watched the reins fall and moved his horse ahead of mine. Smart boy. Instead of swerving off, my horse followed his lead. I trusted that Anton could control both horses.

I wrapped both arms around Lars and threaded my fingers through the gray's mane. I felt Lars fighting to keep his balance, but I also felt his strength ebbing. We were close, but I did not know if we would make it.

We rode past crowds ranged on the edges of the Jewish quarter. They carried lit torches and baskets of rocks. Stones flew through shop windows. Looters were already inside others, throwing items into the street. The horses' hooves crunched in the broken glass.

I gripped the gray more tightly with my knees.

We galloped to Frau Doktor Spiegel's street, a few blocks from the edge of the Jewish quarter. The mob had not ventured so far in yet. A hurricane lamp burned in her front window, but otherwise the apartment looked deserted. Streets stretched dark as far as I could see. Someone must have cut the power to the entire Jewish quarter. Telephones, too, I imagined. But we had nowhere else to go.

Anton jumped off his horse before it stopped moving, and helped Ruth down. He grabbed my reins and steadied the gray with one hand and soft words. A wobbly Ruth clung to his shirt.

Frau Doktor Spiegel's door opened. "Fräulein Vogel?"

"I cannot get him down on my own."

They steadied Lars while I slid off. Together, she and I carried him toward the apartment.

"The horses," I called to Anton. "Send them off."

He slapped their rumps, and hooves rang against the street as they trotted away, probably heading home to their nice quiet stables. I envied them.

Anton took Ruth's hand and led her inside.

"The kitchen," Frau Doktor Spiegel said.

We got Lars up on the table. I stripped off his coat and stained shirt. Blood soaked my makeshift bandages. "He has a gunshot wound to the lung. The bullet is still in there."

"Get me a torch!" she ordered. "By the sink."

Anton found the electric torch and clicked it on. When he shone the beam on Lars, I feared that he was already dead. My heart stopped. After all this time, I had come to view him as indestructible. That, no matter what, he would endure. But he was just a man.

Outside, the mob grew louder. They were only a few streets away.

"He's not dead yet, Fräulein Vogel!" Frau Doktor Spiegel snapped. "Can you assist me here, or should I haul him back out to die in the street?"

I fumbled with his bandages. "I have never had problems assisting."

"You've also never looked at one of your patients the way you just looked at him, not even Paul."

Lars's lips moved into a faint smile. He was still conscious.

"Once he is well, he will be insufferable." I kissed his blue lips, hoping my words would be true.

She pulled a vial with three white pills out of her brassiere. I worked on preparing Lars for surgery. "What is that?"

"It's my opium," she said. "I keep it there. In case of emergency." She studied it, face ghostly in the glow of the electric torch.

"What emergency?" Anton asked.

The same emergency that Paul faced. She kept that opium so that when things became unbearable, she could commit suicide. "Frau Doktor?"

She removed a pill and stuck it in Lars's mouth. "I suppose this is an emergency as well."

His chest was fully exposed. She doused her instruments with carbolic acid, and we began work. Anton sat on the floor, holding Ruth. He told her a story of Winnetou and his sister Nscho-tschi in the Wild West. I had never been more proud of him.

I held the light with one hand and assisted with the other while she took out the bullet and stitched Lars up. Side by side, we both worked as quickly as we had under fire in the war. It was the same. If the mob outside found her practicing medicine on an Aryan, they might well kill us all.

But she finished before they arrived.

We moved Lars into the bedroom. I stayed with him while Frau Doktor Spiegel and Anton cleaned the kitchen. No one could see the bloody instruments and cloths, or they would know that she had broken the law to save his life.

Ruth sat on the floor next to me with both arms wrapped around my legs. I stroked her back with one hand, and held Lars's hand with the other. He was a fighter. He was still alive. He would not die now. But as I knew from many battlefield surgeries, he very well might later.

Frau Doktor Spiegel appeared in the doorway. "Clean yourself up, Hannah. I can't have you covered in blood when they get here. They're close."

She handed me a wet towel and a clean dress. I changed and wiped myself as clean as I could, then dropped the bloody items into a bag she held.

"Take this to the back courtyard. Dump it with the rest." She handed Anton the bag. He ran.

I sat next to Lars and adjusted the blankets, pulling them to his chin.

"I want to transfuse him," she said. "He's lost too much blood. Now that I don't need you standing . . ."

"Of course." My blood type was O. Because I was a universal donor, I had spent the last year of the War perpetually anemic from emergency blood donations.

"I'll fetch my—"

Something crashed through the front window. Ruth yelped. Anton rushed into the room.

"There is brandy in the front room," I said. "Bring it now."

He was back quickly, bottle in hand.

The front door splintered open. Did they have an ax? Frau Doktor Spiegel went toward the sound.

I sprinkled brandy on Lars, then hid the bottle under the bed.

In the living room, something hard smashed against the walls. Glass broke and crashed to the floor with each stroke.

"Get behind me," I told Anton. "And hold Ruth."

He scooped her up in his arms and stood near Lars's head. I stepped in front of them, although I could do little against an organized mob.

I pulled my Hannah Schmidt passport out of my satchel and took Lars's from his back pocket. It seemed dry. I wished I could check to see if it had bloodstains.

Two men in SA uniforms stormed into the room. Both were tall. I could only hope I would be able to convince them to let us go. They glared at me.

"What are you doing?" I trembled with fear, but they expected that. It would have been suspicious otherwise.

"We're teaching you filthy Jews a lesson." One spit on the floor.

"I am not Jewish," I said. "I am not even German. I am Swiss."

They both stopped. During the Games in 1936, the storm troopers had been issued orders not to harm foreigners. I could only hope that they had similar orders now. In the front room, a different soldier yelled at Frau Doktor Spiegel. Glass crashed to the floor.

I walked over and handed my passport to the soldier who had not spit on the floor. He turned on a torch and examined it, studying the last stamp, the false one from Zbąszyń. He pointed his light at my eyes. I squinted.

"I am sorry, Frau Schmidt," he said. "This is not a safe place to be tonight."

I silently thanked Herr Silbert.

The soldier shone his light on Lars and the children. Something thudded against the floor in the front room.

"Those are my children, and that is my husband." I hoped that Ruth would stay quiet.

"Does he have identification? If not, we must arrest him. All Jewish men between the ages of sixteen and sixty are being arrested tonight."

"He is Swiss." I handed him Lars's passport. My hands shook. He would not survive the trip to a concentration camp.

"How old is the boy?" The soldier jerked his thumb toward Anton.

"Thirteen." I grabbed Anton with one hand. He was tall for his age, and I had no identity papers for him at all. His Anton Zinsli passport was back in the hotel in Zbąszyń.

What if the soldier demanded proof? I would not let Anton go without a fight, even if I knew it was futile. I could not win a battle against the two soldiers, but it might buy Anton enough time to run out the back door. If he would go.

The soldier directed the torch at Anton's face. I held my breath. I loosened my grip on Anton's arm and steadied myself.

I turned my back to the soldier and mouthed, *Swiss embassy,* to Anton.

He understood what I said, but looked mulish. *Oh please,* I begged silently. *Just this once, son, do what I say. I would hate to throw my life away for nothing at all.*

The soldier gave a brief nod. "Tall one," he said, "but you're not sixteen."

Anton was spared.

The soldier studied Lars's false passport. My heart beat hard in my throat. Like everyone in the Jewish quarter tonight, I had no recourse but hope. Actually, I had more. I had hope and forged Swiss passports. Would that be enough?

Behind me, I heard Anton and Ruth's quick breathing, and Lars's slow breaths. I was grateful that Lars, at least, would sleep through whatever came next.

The sound of tearing fabric came from the front room. Were they ripping up the drapes?

The soldier passed the beam of the torch across Lars's pale face. "Why is he in bed?"

"I—" I dropped my gaze to the worn Persian rug. "He—overindulged and passed out."

The soldier took a step toward the bed and sniffed. The smell of brandy was strong there, as I had hoped it would be.

"My advice, miss," he said calmly, "is to get him and the children out of here as soon as you can."

"Yes, sir," I said. "When will it be safe to travel?"

"I think we will be at this all night," he said.

"I see."

"Stay near the bed," he said. "I'll let that alone, as a favor to the Swiss."

I stood between the children and the soldiers, my arms centimeters out from my sides, as if that could protect them.

He flicked his truncheon casually at the wall toward Frau Doktor Spiegel's wedding picture. So much younger than now, she stood proudly next to her husband, surrounded by family and friends. In the back right corner, Paul smiled out from a different time. The truncheon shattered the glass. The soldier flipped the picture out of its frame, tore it in half, and dropped it on the floor.

He swiped a pair of reading glasses off the dresser and ground them under his heel. Ruth whimpered. I covered her eyes, hoping to keep her from seeing as much as I could. Anton watched every movement. And I could do nothing about that. I drew him close to my other side.

The soldier dumped each drawer. I was grateful that Frau Doktor Spiegel was not here to see him stomp on her underthings, although by the crashing coming from the kitchen, things were no better there. He opened the closet door and began methodically removing everything, breaking what he could.

The thorough way he destroyed her possessions was more terrifying than mob violence would have been. He did it efficiently, like a familiar job. He had orders.

He spotted the electric torch in Anton's hand. Anton offered it up to him, but he shook his head. "I'll assume that it's Swiss."

Ruth stared at him, as nonplussed as the rest of us.

"My apologies for disturbing you, Frau Schmidt," he said.

I gaped. I had no response for his polite address in the midst of his destruction.

He touched his cap, turned on his heel and left, taking his companion with him. I let out a long breath. I left the children on the bed with Lars and went to check on Frau Doktor Spiegel.

The noise had not prepared me for the extent of the damage. Every picture had been removed from the wall and had its glass smashed. Her books had been ripped from the shelves. Torn pages littered the floor.

They had even sliced open the upholstery on her sofa and slashed the rug on the floor. My bare feet stepped carefully around the glass. I thought of my own shoes, lined up by the synagogue door.

In the kitchen, her precious Vaseline glass collection lay in shards. I shone the torch around. They had even broken the jars of jam and honey.

Through her broken front door, I watched them move on to the next house, remembering the soldier's words. They would be at this all night.

She knelt on the floor, one fist pressed tight against her heart.

"Frau Doktor?" I hurried to stand next to her.

She stood. She held a long black tube with large needle at one end, a smaller at the other. "They broke my transfusion glass, of course, but we can do a direct one. I'm old enough to remember how."

She gestured at the wrecked apartment. "This will wait, but I think my patient will not."

I followed her into the bedroom, awed by her matter-of-fact courage. She had watched everything she owned destroyed in front of her. If Lars's wounds had been discovered, she might have been executed on the spot, and still she kept moving.

I lay on the bed next to Lars. Anton held the torch while she stuck the large needle into my arm, the small one into Lars's. Ruth covered her eyes.

"Hold the light on my watch." Frau Doktor Spiegel took my pulse, trying to calculate how much of my blood had flowed into Lars. Without a glass to measure, it was the best that we could do.

Eventually, she pulled out both needles and taped a strip of gauze over my arm, then his. His color looked better. I took his pulse as soon as I could move my arm. Weak but steady.

"Yes," she said, reading my expression. "It looks promising for him."

"Now I need to get him out of Germany." The burnt-out lorry was back at the synagogue, and useless to us regardless. Yet none of us could stay here for long.

"Fräulein Ivona drove Lars's old lorry to the synagogue," Anton piped up. "I saw it by ours."

I remembered the Opel Blitz that was parked in front of us.

"Are you certain it is the same one?" I asked. That lorry had a finished compartment, because she had stolen it from Lars. Anton had ridden in it when he crossed the Polish border.

"Yes," he said. "It had an extra gas tank, the fake one. And it had a dent in the tailgate."

"Wait here," I said.

Over Frau Doktor Spiegel's protestations, I left them all in the apartment to fetch the lorry, borrowing Anton's shoes for the trip.

Light-headed from the blood donation, I stumbled down glittering streets.

All of Berlin seemed to be covered in broken glass. In every direction, columns of smoke marked where synagogues burned.

Weeping old men, women, and children lined the street. Lorries rolled by filled with Jewish men. Many bore the marks of SS fists. The men's next stop would be the concentration camps. Paul, at least, had been spared that.

I quickened my step, swerving around the remains of a grand piano. Boys just a few years older than Anton stood next to it, hacking at the ebony wood with hatchets. I looked up. Someone had pushed the piano out of a third-story window. The cloth that once covered it had caught on a shard of glass and fluttered like a flag of surrender.

Unnoticed in the confusion, I reached the synagogue without incident. The fire department had put out the blaze, and a policeman stood guard in front of the building, stopping further vandalism. Destruction raged around him, but he stood firm. He caught my eye and I bowed my head in thanks. Whoever he was, he had risked much to keep this one building safe.

I clomped to Lars's old lorry. I opened the driver's door and felt in my pocket.

I did not have a key.

I would have to sneak into the synagogue and see if I could find Fräulein Ivona's purse. I glanced back at the policeman, wondering how I could get past him.

I reached inside and felt the ignition, just in case Fräulein Ivona had left them there for a quick getaway. My fingers touched the key. I blew out my breath in relief.

I started the lorry, returned to Frau Doktor Spiegel's, and loaded everyone inside. Lars and Frau Doktor Spiegel rested in the back on a mattress; the children huddled together on the front seat. Lars was still completely unconscious. She had given him enough opium to knock out a horse.

We drove out of the Jewish quarter into well-ordered neighborhoods where nothing had been disturbed. Moonlight reflected off intact windowpanes. The night was quiet here, everyone sleeping, everyone safe. None of them knew what horrible crimes were being committed just a few miles from their soft pillows.

The Kellers owned their own house. I parked in front. "Say good-bye to Ruth, Anton."

He gave her a quick good-bye, and she ducked her head shyly.

"I will be back soon, Anton," I said. "After that it is straight on to Switzerland."

"I've heard that before." He chucked Ruth under the chin.

"This time," I said. "It is finally true."

I lifted her out of the front seat and paused near the bed of the lorry. "Is everything in order, Frau Doktor Spiegel?"

She chuckled. "In this neighborhood, it certainly is."

"Is Lars—?"

"He is as well as can be expected. As am I." She held up her wrist-watch. "Stopped. The men must have broken it. I didn't even notice. Remember how I said I would not stay a extra second?"

I nodded.

She shook her wrist. "My second's up. Stopped with the watch."

"After we get across—"

"Palestine," she said. "Even if I have to ride there in the back of another lorry. I expect they need doctors there, too."

Ruth rested her head against my shoulder.

"Get that little one into bed," Frau Doktor Spiegel said. "It's very late. We all need a rest."

"*Jawohl,* Frau Doktor."

She gave me a tired smile.

Relieved that she had a plan that did not involve the rest of the opium, I hurried up the walk with Ruth on my hip. She looked around excitedly, clearly recognizing the yard.

I rapped on Herr Keller's door until footsteps stomped down the hall. He flung open the door. "What is it that cannot wait until a decent hour?"

"Opa!" Ruth wriggled out of my arms and ran to him. He swept her into a hug and turned to me, disbelieving.

"Take good care of her," I said.

Tears spilled down his cheeks. "You are an angel."

"Leave Germany as soon as you can," I said. "Promise?"

"I promise," he said. "Of course, I promise."

I lifted Miriam's locket's delicate chain over my head. "Ruth?"

She stared at me, arms still locked tight around Herr Keller's neck. "Yes?"

I draped the chain over her head. She gripped the locket with tiny fingers.

"It is from your mother," I said. "She wanted me to give it to you."

I kissed her once on the top of her head. She smelled like smoke, blood, and horses. The smells of war.

"Good-bye," she said.

I turned and hurried back to the lorry.

The drive ahead promised to be long.

Glossary

Alexanderplatz. Central police station for Berlin through World War II. Also called "the Alex."

Bella Fromm. A German Jewish aristocrat who worked as a reporter in Berlin in the 1920s and 1930s. Her fascinating diaries have been published as *Blood and Banquets: A Berlin Social Diary*.

Bernhard Lichtenberg. Rector of Saint Hedwig's Church who spoke out against the treatment of the Jews during the Nazi regime. He was arrested for "abuse of the pulpit and insidious activity" for praying for the Jews. He died while waiting to be sent to Dachau concentration camp.

Blood libel. A false accusation that Jews use the blood of Christian children in religious rituals. There have been more than 150 recorded cases of blood libel accusations, which have resulted in the deaths of thousands of Jews. These accusations continue today.

Ernst Röhm. Early member of the National Socialist party and close friend to Adolf Hitler, often credited with being the man most responsible for bringing Hitler to power. Openly gay.

Ernst vom Rath. German diplomat in Paris shot on November 7, 1938, by Herschel Grynszpan. Grynszpan was protesting the deportation of his parents and sister to Zbąszyń. Vom Rath died on November 9, 1938. News of his death led to Kristallnacht.

Évian Conference. Conference held in July 1938 to determine how to respond to the burgeoning number of Jewish refugees from Germany and Austria. Although much sympathy was expressed, most countries refused to accept more refugees.

Gestapo. Abbreviation for Geheime Staatspolizei (Secret State Police). The official secret Nazi police force. It was formed in 1933, and investigated treason, espionage, and criminal attacks on the Nazi party and Germany. In July 1936, the Gestapo and the regular police force were merged. The Gestapo had various departments, including one dedicated to "the Jewish question."

Hauptsturmführer. Rank in the German Schutzstaffel (SS) equivalent to captain.

Herschel Grynszpan. Polish refugee in Paris, France, who, at age seventeen, shot German diplomat Ernst vom Rath to protest the deportation of his family from Germany and their treatment in Zbąszyń. He was held until the Nazis occupied Paris; then he was transferred to Germany. He allegedly died sometime in 1945, although the manner and date of his death are unknown.

"Horst Wessel Song." Anthem of the Nazi party. The lyrics were written by Horst Wessel, a Sturmabteilung (SA) commander in Berlin. He was killed by Communists in 1930, and the song later became the official anthem. Since the end of World War II, the music and lyrics have been illegal in Germany and Austria.

Hotel Adlon. Expensive hotel in Berlin, built in 1907. It quickly became known for its vast wine cellars and well-heeled clientele. On May 2, 1945, the main building was burned to the ground, either accidentally or deliberately, by Russian soldiers. The East German government opened a surviving wing as a hotel, but demolished it in 1961 to create the no-man's-land around the Berlin Wall. A new Hotel Adlon was rebuilt on the original location and opened on August 23, 1997.

Kommissar. Rank in the police department similar to a lieutenant.

Korn schnapps. Strong German alcoholic drink.

Kristallnacht. "Night of Crystal" or "Night of Broken Glass" refers to a series of state-sanctioned attacks on Jews in Germany and Austria on November 9, 1938, and November 10, 1938. According to the Holocaust Museum, 267 synagogues were destroyed, 7,500 Jewish businesses were destroyed, and at least 91 Jewish people were killed. An increased number of rapes and suicides were also recorded. Many view these actions as the beginning of the Holocaust.

League of German Girls (*Bund Deutscher Mädel*). The female branch of the Nazi youth movement. The male branch was called the Hitler Youth (*Hitler-Jugend*).

Mischling. A term created in the Nuremberg Laws to define which German citizens would be considered Jewish. If a Jewish person was not practicing Judaism and was not married to another Jewish citizen, he or she would be considered Jewish if they had at least three Jewish grandparents. A person with two Jewish grandparents (like Ruth in this novel) was considered Mischling of the first degree. A single Jewish grandparent made one Mischling of the second degree. These legal distinctions could, and often did, mean the difference between living through the war and being deported to a concentration camp.

National Socialist German Workers' Party (Nazi Party). Party led by Adolf Hitler that assumed control of Germany in 1933.

Nuremberg Laws. Anti-Semitic laws announced at the Nazi Party Rally in Nuremberg in 1935. These laws defined who was considered a Jew (someone with three or four Jewish grandparents). The laws then prohibited Jews from marrying or having sexual relations with "Germans of non-Jewish blood," forbade Jews to hire German domestic workers under the age of forty-five, forbade them to display the German or Reich flag or the national colors, and stripped German Jews of their citizenship. More anti-Semitic laws soon followed.

Obersturmbannführer. Rank in the SS equivalent to lieutenant colonel.

Paragraph 175. Paragraph of the German penal code that made homosexuality a crime. Paragraph 175 was in place from 1871 to 1994. Under the Nazis, people convicted of Paragraph 175 offenses, which did not need to include physical contact, were sent to concentration camps, where many died.

Pfennigs. Similar to pennies. There were one hundred pfennigs in a Reichsmark.

Reichsmark. Currency used by Germany from 1924 to 1948. The previous currency, the Papiermark, became worthless in 1923 due to hyperinflation. On January 1, 1923, one American dollar was worth nine thousand Papiermarks. By November 1923, one American dollar was worth 4.2 trillion Papiermarks. Fortunes were wiped out overnight. In 1924, the currency was revalued and remained fairly stable until the Wall Street crash in the United States in 1929. When the novel takes place, one American dollar was worth approximately 2.49 Reichsmarks.

Schutzstaffel (SS or Blackshirts). Nazi paramilitary organization founded as an elite force to be used as Hitler's personal bodyguards. Led by Heinrich Himmler.

Spatz. Sparrow. A German term of endearment.

Sturmabteilung (SA, Brownshirts, or storm troopers). Nazi paramilitary organization that helped intimidate Hitler's opponents. Led by Ernst Röhm.

Sturmbannführer. Rank in the SS equivalent to major.

Treaty of Versailles. A peace treaty that negotiated the end of World War I between Germany and the Allied powers.

UFA (Universum Film AG). Principal film studio in Germany during the Weimar Republic and World War II. UFA went out of business after World War II, but now produces movies and TV shows.

Winnetou. The Apache brave hero in a series of bestselling books written by German author Karl May. Originally published in the late 1800s, the novels are still very popular today.

Zbąszyń, Poland. Town on the border with Nazi Germany where Polish Jewish refugees were deported between October 27 and October 28, 1938. As in the novel, refugees were housed in stables, the flour mill, and other locations.

Author's Note

My books are often inspired by major historical events, so I feel an obligation to get the history right or to explain why I deviated from it. *A City of Broken Glass* sprang from the real-life events of the deportation of the Polish Jews from Germany and the ensuing Kristallnacht Pogrom of 1938. I stayed true to historical events whenever possible, but sometimes the emotional truth of the story required small changes.

The deportations of the Polish Jews from Germany to Zbąszyń, Poland, took place on October 27–28, 1938. To meet the refugees the morning after they arrived, Hannah would have had to have been there on October 29, 1938. Because I wanted her to bear witness to both the immediate aftereffects of the deportation and Kristallnacht on November 9–10, I changed the historical timeline in the story. I carefully avoided giving specific dates in the novel until she wakes up on the fifth of November so that my readers would not put wrong dates to the earlier events.

Just as Hannah reports, the refugees in Zbąszyń were housed in stables and a flour mill, among other places. The stories she hears of people walking back and forth across the border in the rain while being beaten and shot at are taken from actual survivor accounts.

I don't know how the Polish government numbered the refugees, or even if they did, but I wrote a prisoner number on Miriam's arm as a foreshadowing of what would come when such numbers would be tattooed into the arms of prisoners in concentration camps.

The Neuen Synagogue on Oranienburgerstrasse was not destroyed on Kristallnacht but, as Hannah witnesses, it was set afire and desecrated. A German police lieutenant named Wilhelm Krützfeld intervened after the synagogue was set alight, drawing his pistol and placing himself between the mob and the building. He also ordered the fire department to extinguish the fire, which they did, in spite of standing orders not to put out any burning synagogues. That's why Hannah sees them working to control the fire—because, in spite of the danger, one man stood up and made a difference.

Byzantine Art in the Making

Byzantine Art in the Making

Main lines of stylistic development
in Mediterranean Art

3rd – 7th Century

ERNST KITZINGER

Harvard University Press

Cambridge, Massachusetts

1977

709.02

Publication of this book

has been supported

through the generous provisions

of the

Maurice and Lula Bradley Smith

Memorial Fund

CONTENTS

to SUSAN

PREFACE

This book is based on a series of lectures I gave as Slade Professor of Fine Art at the University of Cambridge in the Michaelmas term of 1974. Some material has been added and rearrangements have been made at certain points. But the basic structure of the lecture series has been retained.

In this relatively restricted format I have tried to encompass five centuries in the history of Mediterranean art; centuries, moreover, with which modern scholarship has concerned itself extensively. Although an exhaustive bibliographical annotation was not feasible in the circumstances, sufficient references have been provided in the notes to direct the reader to specialized literature on the monuments and objects under discussion.

To convert the lectures into a book within a reasonable time would not have been possible without a grant from the National Endowment for the Humanities, which enabled me to spend the entire academic year 1974–5 on sabbatical leave. Much of the work was done at the Warburg Institute in London, for whose hospitality I am extremely grateful.

In preparing the book I have incurred numerous other debts of gratitude for help of many kinds. Sir Ernst Gombrich and Florentine Mütherich, two friends of long standing, were kind enough to read the lectures in manuscript. I trust that I can be allowed to acknowledge the benefit I have derived both from their encouragement and from their critiques without thereby implicating them in the book's short-comings. Colleagues and friends in many places have assisted me in the procurement of photographs for the illustrations. In this regard I owe special thanks to Janine Balty, Alice Banck, François Baratte, John Beckwith, Herbert Bloch, Beat Brenk, Alison Frantz, Danielle Gaborit, Theodor Kempf, Eugene Kleinbauer, Irving Lavin, Paul Lazaridis, Inabelle Levin, William Loerke, Arif Müfid Mansel, Per Jonas Nordhagen, Walter Schumacher, Maria Sotiriou, Marie Spiro, Lee Striker, Cornelius Vermeule, John Ward-Perkins, Kurt Weitzmann, William Wixom, Joanna Woods-Marsden and David Wright; as well as to the staff of Dumbarton Oaks in Washington, D.C., the Fototeca Unione in Rome and the photographic departments of the German Archaeological Institutes in Rome and Istanbul.

Two debts of a more general kind also call for acknowledgement. One is to the

Dumbarton Oaks Center for Byzantine Studies, where I spent the greater part of my professional life and where much of the work that has gone into the making of this book has matured. I owe a great deal both to the unique resources of that institution and to the manifold contacts it has afforded me over the years with scholars knowledgeable in a variety of germane fields. The other debt is to my students at Harvard University. Without the challenge of an organized course in which to present a complex and often not very approachable body of material, and without the students' reactions and critiques, I could not have attempted a synthesis such as the present. I am particularly grateful to William Tronzo, who helped me with a critical reading of the manuscript I had prepared for my lectures in the other Cambridge; and to Natasha Staller, who went through the final text with extraordinary care and discernment.

Finally, I must thank Mary Katherine Donaldson, my ever-faithful assistant whose tireless help, always cheerfully given, was indispensable at all stages of the work; my son Stephen Anthony, who has undertaken the task of design and production; and – last but not least – my wife, to whom I dedicate the book knowing that what it owes to her can never be adequately expressed.

Cambridge, Massachusetts   August, 1976

INTRODUCTION

Titles often either understate or overstate the contents of books. In the present instance the title does both. 'Byzantine Art in the Making' is an appropriate designation for the central process within the period of art history to which this study is devoted. My actual subject is both larger and narrower.

The book is concerned with art in the Mediterranean world from the third through the seventh century. Roman art was still in its fullness in the third century; Constantine's new capital on the site of ancient Byzantium had not yet been founded; and although the city of Constantinople ultimately assumed undisputed leadership in the arts, this was a slow and gradual process. Even in the fifth and sixth centuries we shall encounter many important monuments that cannot properly be called Byzantine.

In this sense the scope of the book is broader than its title implies. On the other hand my coverage will not be comprehensive. It will extend only to the pictorial arts and will not include architecture. I shall be dealing, as the subtitle indicates, with stylistic developments only. And finally, in illustrating these developments, my procedure will be selective. It will be my purpose to trace, on the basis of a representative series of monuments, the main lines in the evolution of artistic forms during a particularly critical and complex period in the history of Western art.

The period is often referred to as Early Christian. This term, however, has connotations of the catacombs, of hesitant, tentative, perhaps even furtive beginnings. I find it inappropriate for works such as the mosaics of S.Vitale in Ravenna or the great encaustic icons of Mount Sinai. Although architecture is outside the scope of this book, in that field the suitability of the term for our period as a whole is even more uncertain. A building such as Justinian's church of St Sophia is not Early Christian.

Nor can monuments such as these properly be termed late antique. There has been a tendency to extend the concept of *Spätantike* to include not only the last centuries of Roman art but also succeeding developments at least to the period of Justinian if not, indeed, to the seventh or eighth century.[1] Admittedly this usage has its advantages. It puts proper emphasis on the continued strength of the Graeco-Roman tradition. But it overemphasizes the past at the expense of the future. Again, S.Vitale and St Sophia are not late antique.

[1]

There is, in fact, no simple term which adequately covers the entire period with which we are concerned, and it is obvious that in this problem of nomenclature there lies concealed a problem of identity. The period does not have the same kind of clear profile as other major phases in the history of Western art.[2] We cannot readily associate with it – as we can, for example, with Gothic or Baroque art – a distinctive set of forms in a distinctive combination. It is true that under close scrutiny any period in art history tends to lose some of its unity and cohesion. But we can still name many works of art that are quintessentially Gothic or quintessentially Baroque. For our period this is far more difficult. Nor is there a readily intelligible evolutionary curve in its artistic development. However differentiated the history of Gothic or Baroque art may have become, we can still speak with justice of Early, High and Late phases, of a style in the making, fully matured and finally in a state of hypertrophy foreshadowing its demise. No such life cycle can be discerned in the art of our period. Instead we are confronted with a coexistence or an abrupt and seemingly erratic succession of diverse and contrasting styles. Notorious cases of wide disagreement among scholars as to the dating of major monuments highlight this situation.

The period can be defined quite readily in terms of its boundaries. Historically, its beginning is marked by the first unmistakable signs of disintegration, the appearance of the first serious cracks in the structure of the Roman empire as a universal power; its end by the emergence of two great new powers with which the successors of Augustus and Constantine henceforth had to share possession of what had been the ancient world. With the Arab domains established on its southern flank and a Germanic empire in process of formation to the North, by the eighth century the old empire was finally and irrevocably reduced to regional status. Our time span is similarly set off in terms of art history. The third century witnessed the first crisis, the first major step in the disintegration of the classical tradition; the eighth century, the emergence of Islamic and North European art as separate entities and, simultaneously, the outbreak of the Iconoclastic Controversy which produced a major hiatus, at any rate for religious art, within the Byzantine empire itself. By then, however, firm foundations had already been laid for medieval art both in the East and in the West. To a very great extent Byzantine art of the post-Iconoclastic period resumed and built upon the traditions established before that great crisis; and the nascent art of the medieval West, while dependent on the contribution of the northern countries and the aesthetics of their 'barbarian' past, likewise drew heavily on these traditions.

In a very real sense, therefore, our period is one of transition – a bridge between Antiquity and the Middle Ages – and therein, one might say, lies its true identity. 'Pre-medieval', in fact, might be a suitable term with which to encompass it.[3] Yet there is something intrinsically awkward about labelling five hundred years in the history of Western art simply as transitional. For the great monuments of the period – again I cite St Sophia and S.Vitale – it is hardly an adequate classification. And even if the term were applied to artistic achievements of such magnitude, what exactly is their place within this transition? There was, as I have indicated, no simple progression from a starting point to a goal.

In one sense – and it is an important one – the centuries which concern us do offer a rather clear picture of an organic development. I refer to the emergence and first full elaboration of art with a Christian content. An extraordinary process of growth lies between two definite, if negatively complexioned, landmarks – the taboo against religious images which obtained in the early Church until about A.D.200, and the new ban on such images in eighth-century Byzantium. From modest beginnings there arose a pictorial art of increasingly diverse content and scope and of ever more central and vital importance in public and private life. The very weightiness and centrality this imagery attained was what finally provoked the Iconoclastic reaction. Unquestionably this is a major aspect of Mediterranean art from the third to the eighth century. Indeed, in this sense the term Early Christian could well be applied to the period as a whole – provided that term were taken to denote not just a groping start but a fully rounded achievement. The process, though not our principal subject, will have a bearing on our discussion at many points.

But in matters of form and style, too, the period as a whole does have an internal development of its own. There is an intrinsic pattern, though it does not take the form either of a simple one-way progression from one style to another or of a life cycle of a single style through successive phases. To elucidate this pattern – a pursuit which is surely relevant to the problem of the period's unity and separate identity – will be the purpose of this book.

There was a time, earlier in this century, when scholars tried to establish an art-historical framework for our period in essentially geographic terms. The coexistence of different regional 'schools' with different artistic traditions and the interaction of these 'schools' were thought to go far in explaining the apparent lack of cohesion and unity in the overall picture. Charles Rufus Morey's antithesis of an 'Alexandrian' and an 'Asiatic' style is perhaps the best-known example of this approach.[4] Early in my own work, when sketching an art-historical synthesis of this period, I also made extensive use of the concept of regional styles as a means of correlating a mass of seemingly disjointed stylistic phenomena.[5] The regional factor is undoubtedly important, and I do not intend to ignore it. To have done so is one of several basic points to be held against the one scholar who in the last twenty or thirty years has made a serious attempt to give a coherent account in stylistic terms of the history of art from the fourth to the seventh century. In an exceedingly audacious essay Andreas Rumpf has forced upon the disparate material a highly schematic pattern that does not allow for the variety of factors involved.[6] I do not think it is possible to isolate stylistic features – in the rendering of the human figure, for instance – that characterize works of a given date regardless of where they originated and regardless also of their subject matter and of the purpose for which they were made. Style changes occur at particular times, in particular places or regions and often in particular contexts which can sometimes be fairly narrowly circumscribed. Many of these impulses do, however, fall into broader patterns so that, over a longer period, one can speak of dominant stylistic trends. Over the years I have come to recognize more and more the existence and importance of such trends which follow one another in time and whose sequence and interaction constitute an intelligible and meaningful process. It is this sequence of trends – something far looser and more flexible than Rumpf's *Stilphasen* – which I propose to illustrate.

The process as I see it is a dialectical one. At certain times and in certain places bold stabs were made in the direction of new, unclassical forms, only to be followed by reactions, retrospective movements and revivals. In some contexts such developments – in either direction – took place slowly, hesitantly and by steps so small as to be almost imperceptible. In addition there were extraordinary attempts at synthesis, at reconciling conflicting aesthetic ideals. Out of this complex dialectic, medieval form emerged. My purpose will be to define the dominant trends as they succeeded one another. And, up to a point, I shall try to make sense of them in broader historical terms.

In some future analysis of twentieth-century intellectual history a footnote might well be devoted to a minor paradox. Many of the most significant advances made in the middle decades of this century in art-historical research – and this applies to all of its fields, but to late antique, Early Christian and Byzantine art more particularly – have been through iconographic and iconological approaches. That is to say, scholars have focused intensively and most fruitfully on the subject content of works of art, on the rationale behind the choice and grouping of themes and on their use in a given context or in relation to a particular patron, purpose or function. Yet this development in scholarship has coincided with a period of the most radical formalism in art itself. Art historians were concentrating on content and messages at a time when painters and sculptors were eliminating subject matter altogether. I mention this rather odd disjunction merely to point out that no period more than our own has proclaimed in its art the meaningfulness of visual form as such. In our universities students flock to courses in which modern non-objective art is discussed and interpreted. Evidently they believe that it can tell them something about the period in which they live.

There is a general proposition involved here – namely, that the formal aspects of works of art hold important clues to an understanding of the period which produced them. This proposition I plan to take seriously. The concept of a stylistic trend with which I shall operate itself implies that a given set of forms becomes significant from a historical point of view. A form which 'catches on', as distinct from a purely ephemeral or accidental departure from an established norm, is liable to be meaningful to a group, a movement, an entire age. The difficulty lies in determining why.

There is, of course, an interrelationship between form and content. By stressing the importance of form *qua* form I do not imply any kind of dichotomy in this respect. In an attempt to interpret stylistic phenomena in historical terms, every aspect of a work of art must be taken into account: subject matter and the message it carries; the functional context; the patron's interest and intent; the use of established prototypes and formulae and their possible connotations. Sometimes there is a very definite and obvious relationship between one or another of these factors and the artistic form. At other times such interconnections are more indirect, subtle and elusive. But there are also instances where none of these approaches yields a satisfactory interpretation, and then one must have recourse to other kinds of data not provided by or gleaned from the work of art itself but from the social, intellectual or religious history of the period. And finally, there are cases where leads are lacking altogether and where the art historian can interpret style only intuitively or else must abandon the pursuit. No attempt will be made in this study to provide interpretations at all costs.

I have previously referred to the rise of Christian imagery and to the central role of that process within our period. The interpretative clues I have just mentioned will in many instances come from this sector. It is not feasible, however, to encompass the subject in all its fullness and complexity in the present framework. The early history of Christian imagery has its own dynamics.[7] We must be content to glimpse it at those points where it is clearly of significance for the process of stylistic development which is our concern. We shall see that in the first phase the Christian contribution was negligible. The history of the first great crisis in Roman art in the third century can be written practically without reference to Christian works. Thus in my first chapter Christian monuments will figure only briefly and mainly on account of their bearing on what was to come later. Early in the reign of Constantine, however, at the time when Christianity gained official recognition, we shall encounter Christian works of art with distinctive formal characteristics, unprecedented and unparalleled in pagan art and apparently bound up with their religious content and function. We shall see that the increase in Christian patronage and the expansion and diversification of Christian subject matter which began with Constantine certainly had a bearing on stylistic developments, although all through the fourth century much of the initiative in matters of style still came from other sectors. It was in the fifth century that art which was Christian both in content and in functional purpose assumed undisputed leadership. To a correspondingly larger degree this content and these purposes will thereafter prove to be relevant to our understanding and interpretation of specifically artistic achievements.

It will be clear from these introductory remarks that this study is not a hand-book or in any sense a work of reference. Even within the limits implicit in its particular approach no attempt will be made to cover uniformly the entire artistic patrimony of the centuries concerned – fragmentary as that patrimony is in any case. Certain places and certain media will receive more attention than others. Illuminated manuscripts, for instance, will figure very little. While reflecting the same basic trends as work in other media, they often pose special problems for the stylistically oriented art historian, problems which are rooted in the conditions of their manufacture and to which it would be difficult to do justice in a book covering a large time span in a restricted space. In general the text will be sparing both on descriptions and on the discussion of contro-versial questions of chronology, although the literature cited in the notes will enable the reader to inform himself on these matters. My aim is to trace a broad picture of stylistic developments with the help of selected monuments, and the selection will, I trust, prove to be sufficiently representative to give that picture validity and meaning.

Ancient Art in Crisis

The stylistic developments with which we are concerned were set in motion by the collapse of the classical Greek canon of forms during the late Roman period. To gain an understanding of this breakdown must be our first task. The process, which for obvious reasons has held great fascination for twentieth-century observers, was as complex as it was momentous. For our purposes it must suffice to view it globally, focusing on certain key questions.

No monument embodies the demise of classical art more dramatically than the great triumphal arch in Rome dedicated to the Emperor Constantine by the Roman Senate in A.D.315 and commemorating Constantine's victory over his rival Maxentius in A.D.312 (fig. 1).[1] The sumptuous sculptural decoration of this structure comprises a large number of reliefs taken from imperial buildings of the second century, specifically from monuments honouring the Emperors Trajan, Hadrian and Marcus Aurelius. These reliefs appear here cheek by jowl with others expressly made for the arch, notably the long frieze band which encircles all four of its sides and which depicts in a succession of episodes the story of Constantine's victorious campaigns, essentially in the same way as the *res gestae* of Trajan and Marcus Aurelius had been illustrated (albeit with a far greater wealth of descriptive detail) on the spiral bands of their respective triumphal columns.

The contrast in style between the second- and the fourth-century reliefs on the arch is violent (figs. 2–4). The sculptor of a roundel of the period of Hadrian, representing that emperor's exploits as a lion hunter, was still rooted firmly in the tradition of late Hellenistic art. He creates an illusion of open, airy space in which figures move freely and with relaxed self-assurance. By contrast, the figures of the Constantinian reliefs are pressed, trapped, as it were, between two imaginary planes and so tightly packed within the frame as to lack all freedom of movement in any direction. While in the earlier work actions and gestures are restrained but organically generated by the body as a whole, in the later one they are jerky, overemphatic and uncoordinated with the rest of the body. (Suffice it to compare the manner in which the two sculptors represent the raising of an arm or the upturn of a head.) Accordingly, what holds the group together is no longer a rhythmic interplay of stances and movements freely adopted by the individual figures, but an abstract geometric pattern imposed from outside and based on repetition of nearly identical units on either side of a central axis. Clearly, this pattern is designed with a view to a direct impact on the beholder. The earlier group is turned in onto itself. No one looks out towards us; the figures move and act in a self-contained, stable world. The scene of Constantine's distribution of largesse, on the other hand, which features as the grand finale of his triumphal progress, is spread out before us. Its unmistakable focus is the figure of the enthroned emperor who occupies the centre of the panel and who, though engaged in an action that involves the bystanders on either side, addresses himself first and foremost to the beholder and faces him in strict frontality. The group does not cohere intrinsically. The geometric pattern which holds it together makes sense only in relation to the spectator. Gone too is the classical canon of proportions. Heads are disproportionately large, trunks square, legs stubby. Nor is there consistency of scale. Differences in the physical size of figures drastically underline differences of rank and importance which the second-century artist had indicated by subtle compositional means within a seemingly casual grouping. Gone, finally, are elaboration of detail and differentiation of surface texture. Faces are cut rather than modelled, hair takes the form of a cap with some superficial stippling, drapery folds are summarily indicated by deeply drilled lines.

No doubt should arise concerning the legitimacy of the comparison between the two reliefs. They are fully commensurate in terms of their standing. We are not comparing a high-class work of art with a backwoods product. Both are official commissions honouring the ruler of the day. What is more, this is not a juxtaposition contrived by a twentieth-century art historian enjoying the freedom of Malraux's Museum Without Walls. These reliefs were placed side by side in the early fourth century under the eyes of the Roman Senate and the emperor himself.

This fact lends the Arch of Constantine special significance within the history of late Roman art. It compels us to face the question of awareness on the part of artists, patron and public vis-à-vis the radical reversal of aesthetic values reflected in its reliefs. The contrast between the contemporary work and the earlier pieces that were re-employed must have been obvious to all. Alas, no contemporary comment or explanation is on record. We are left to speculate, and I shall offer some thoughts on the subject in due course.

Attempts have been made at times to seek in accidental circumstances surrounding the creation of the arch the cause for the jarring juxtaposition of sculptures so utterly discrepant in style. There may have been a need to complete it in a hurry and this could explain the rifling of earlier imperial monuments to provide part of the decoration.[2] An exodus of skilled craftsmen from Rome during the troubled years preceding Constantine's victory may account for the crudity of the reliefs expressly made for the monument.[3] But whatever special factors may have played a part in this particular instance, the primitivism of the friezes on Constantine's arch was more than just a local phenomenon during the period in question. A well-known group portrait in porphyry of four emperors of the Tetrarchy now affixed to the exterior of the church of S.Marco in Venice exhibits essentially similar formal characteristics (fig. 5).[4] Here again we find stubby proportions, angular movements, an ordering of parts through symmetry and repetition and a rendering of features and drapery folds through incisions rather than modelling. Ten or fifteen years earlier than the Arch of Constantine, this too is obviously a work of official art. Porphyry was a material reserved for imperial use. The only quarry which produced the stone was in Egypt, and the S.Marco group, which came to Venice as crusader loot from Constantinople,[5] undoubtedly was made in the Eastern parts of the empire. The style, then, was not confined to Rome. It had, in fact, wide currency in official high-class art during the Tetrarchy and the early Constantinian period and may be found in a variety of media. A portrait of Maximinus Daza (A.D.305–13) on a gold coin minted at Antioch (fig. 9)[6] or a detail from one of the sumptuous floor mosaics of the same period in the great villa complex at Piazza Armerina in Sicily (fig. 6)[7] will serve to illustrate the point. The hallmark of the style wherever it appears consists of an emphatic hardness, heaviness and angularity – in short, an almost complete rejection of the classical tradition.

It is possible to consider this phenomenon essentially as a decline. This was the view taken, for instance, by Bernard Berenson.[8] To treat a figure as a single block is easier than to articulate it. To achieve compositional unity through repetition or axial symmetry is simpler than to do so through an interplay of postures and of movements. Less effort is needed to engrave features on a face or folds on a drapery than to model such elements. There was clearly a loss of craftsmanship. But the causes of this can be manifold (as Berenson recognized), and they can be aesthetic as well as material. Traditional forms might be abandoned not simply because they were difficult to execute but because they had ceased to be meaningful or – to use a favourite word of our time – relevant. They could be abandoned also because they carried mental associations that were no longer desirable.

Another approach to the problem – and this has played a large part in scholarship – is in terms of outside influences. At the beginning of this century Josef Strzygowski, having become convinced of the crucial importance of the countries of the Eastern Mediterranean littoral and their Asiatic and African hinterlands in the process of transition from ancient to medieval art, coined the phrase 'Hellas suffocating in the embrace of the Orient'.[9] The anti-classical tendencies, the taste for the abstract and the two-dimensional, for hieratic rigidity and geometric order, were thought of as re-emerging traditions of the ancient Near East which gained ascendancy as the classical world went into decline. Actually, in all the regions primarily concerned – the Anatolian highlands, the Syrian desert, Parthian Mesopotamia and Iran, Arabia and the valley of the Nile – art had been quite thoroughly permeated with Greek forms. What is important is not so much a survival and subsequent revival of ancient regional traditions in contrast or opposition to the Graeco-Roman *koine* – although such cases are known, for instance in Egypt – as the fact that, in the hands of local craftsmen in these fringe areas of the classical world, the Graeco-Roman *koine* itself had assumed a different accent. We may take as a characteristic example a tomb relief from Palmyra (fig. 11)[10] which displays the vocabulary of Roman statuary – the pose, the drapery, the facial type – but lacks the overall quality of a living, self-governing organism which this vocabulary is meant to convey. Instead, what mattered to the artist were a clear, simplified pattern, a timeless existence, a hieratic solemnity. There is, as a matter of fact, no great difference in principle between such hybrid art from the Eastern borderlands and some of the art produced in the Western and Northern border regions of the Roman world, regions such as the Rhineland (fig. 12)[11] or Britain or the banks of the Danube. In those areas, too, the Graeco-Roman repertory of forms was handled by artists who lacked comprehension of or interest in the basic concepts and urges from which these forms had arisen. A reassessment of classical values, then, had already taken place in the fringe areas of the Roman world, West as well as East, and influences or stimuli from these regions could well have become important for the late antique development in Rome itself.

Nor is this all. During the centuries when classical taste ruled supreme in imperial art, there was even in Italy a substratum of what has been variously called popular or plebeian art.[12] Indeed, it can be – and has been – argued that in imperial Rome Greek standards and values were never more than a veneer overlying an indigenous Italic aesthetic which was wholly different and which continued to assert itself in various ways throughout the centuries. Accordingly, the late antique development in Rome can be – and has been – viewed essentially as a massive re-emergence of this local plebeian tradition to the virtual exclusion of all external influences. For example, in the first half of the second century A.D., which was one of the most strongly classicizing periods in Roman art, it was possible for a Roman worthy and his wife to have themselves commemorated in a funerary relief (fig. 10)[13] replete with features that one normally thinks of as late antique: irrational spatial relationships; scale and proportions determined by symbolic importance rather than laws of nature; frontality; jerky and abrupt movements; hard, sharp-edged forms brought out by deep undercutting. From this it certainly becomes clear that there were forerunners in Rome itself of the stylistic revolution which we are considering.

The term 'sub-antique' may serve as a generic heading under which to bring together the various artistic manifestations both at the fringe of the ancient world and within the Roman empire, which these examples illustrate.[14] Although each regional style has distinctive characteristics of its own, they all have a great deal in common, not so much as a result of actual contacts or connections – indeed, in many cases there clearly was no contact whatever – but because they all arose in similar circumstances. In relation to the genesis of late antique art particularly, it is important to be aware of these sub-antique styles in their totality. I do not think that any one of them, to the exclusion of all others, can be claimed as a chief source of the radically new elements introduced into the mainstream of Roman art between the late second and the early fourth century. At any rate, we are not as yet in a position to make sufficiently fine distinctions. For instance, a tendency to present figures in an *en face* view directly confronting the beholder – one of the characteristic and important late antique innovations – was common in all areas of sub-antique art. It is useful and illuminating here to draw a parallel between late antique art and that of our own time by reminding ourselves of the wide range of exotic and primitive styles which exerted an influence on the nascent art of the twentieth century. At that critical point artists drew inspiration from a variety of sources outside their own culture – from the art of Japan, Africa, Polynesia and pre-Columbian America – as well as from primitive works immediately around them (*images d'Epinal*, Rousseau le Douanier, children's drawings); and some of the formal devices and principles in which they were interested they could find in more than one of these sources.

A question, however, arises as to the nature of the influence in the period which concerns us. Did Hellas in fact die embraced by the Orient, overwhelmed by an influx of artists from the provinces, engulfed in an upsurge of plebeians, as the case may be? In other words, was there some physical movement of peoples or classes which more or less automatically brought to the fore a style or styles that had previously been peripheral? Or can we make further use of the late nineteenth-/early twentieth-century analogy by saying that at the core of the development was an internal reorientation of Roman art itself? Were leading or pioneering artists attracted by provincial or primitive styles? Did they become aware of new possibilities of expression, new aesthetic stimuli thus offered? And did they, therefore, absorb these elements on their own terms?

Here we find ourselves face to face with a crucial problem in the interpretation of the entire late antique development. To me it seems quite impossible to account for this development simply through a physical dislocation of people. Influence from the sphere of sub-antique art on the massive scale on which it occurred implies a free and willing adoption of sub-antique forms. But adoption by whom and for what reasons and purposes?

Let us return once more to the porphyry group of the Tetrarchs (fig. 5), of which another version, smaller in scale and even more primitivistic in style, exists, adorning the tops of two column shafts in the Vatican (fig. 8).[15] As a rendering of human presences – to say nothing of imperial presences – these figures are ludicrous. With their block-like, repetitive forms riveted together by outsized arms they express one thing only, namely, the solidity of the compact between the persons portrayed, their absolute unity and inseparability, their unshakable amity and equilibrium. This, of course, was the theoretical premise on which the Tetrarchic system of government rested. It is proclaimed here with a brutal visual directness which a rendering of the four emperors in classical style could not possibly have achieved. Indeed, the classical apparatus of form with its varied rhythms and its elaboration of detail would have distracted from the basic point. In sub-antique art, on the other hand, one finds stripped down to essentials the imaging of relationships such as these groups were meant to proclaim. A small terracotta group representing a couple in loving embrace – one of a series of such objects which were deposited as votive gifts in a Gallo-Roman temple at Trier – bears witness to this (fig. 7).[16] It was a message of overriding urgency which in the portrayal of the four emperors led to the total rejection of the classical canon. Perhaps we can go further and say that the very radicality of the rejection implies that this canon was presumed to be still in the beholder's mind. In other words, the rendering of these figures may have a polemical aspect as well, which, given the context, would have been politically motivated. The idea may have been to link the rejected form to an era, an ideology, a social class that is itself implicitly being rejected. And there would be the further implication that the powers of the day have adopted the artistic language of another class hitherto submerged or peripheral and wish to proclaim their sympathy and solidarity with that class.

Twentieth-century experience has made us familiar with this kind of manipulation of artistic styles for political ends. An element of this nature may well be present in this instance. It is fully in keeping with the character and purposes of a ruler such as Diocletian, whose concept and method of government were totalitarian in the sense that he claimed control over every department of life; whose background and power base were military and thus placed him in opposition to the senatorial class and the tradition of aristocratic refinement and phil-Hellenism associated with that class; and who consciously and explicitly espoused and proclaimed the sturdy values and ideals of the Roman past.[17]

It follows that sculptures such as the porphyry Tetrarchs are not the work of third-century forerunners of a Picasso or a Klee who on their own discovered the aesthetic potential of certain exotic or primitive art forms. These sculptures must have been executed by artists who actually came from the sub-antique sphere and were deliberately chosen because of their ability to communicate a particular message in a language that was extremely forceful and direct and which common men all over the empire could recognize as their own. Thus the patron emerges as an important factor – not, to be sure, in creating an artistic form, but in promoting it, in setting it up as a norm and charging it with new content. By making a choice of one style over another and using it for his own ends, the patron in effect influences the stylistic development. Such development, therefore, is not always solely of the artist's own making. As I have put it in an earlier essay, borrowing David Riesman's terms, it can at a given stage be 'other-directed' as well as 'inner-directed'; that is to say, it can be affected by persons outside the realm of art and in that case certainly must be fully conscious and deliberate.[18]

I have already touched on the question of consciousness in connection with the Arch of Constantine, pointing out that people at the time must have been aware of the stylistic contrast between the contemporary and the earlier reliefs. In this case we cannot assume that the employment of artists practising an emphatically popular style of sub-antique origin involved a protest against aristocratic, phil-Hellenic traditions, since so many works embodying precisely these traditions were also incorporated in the monument. It is conceivable, on the other hand, that an excessively primitivistic workshop was purposely selected in a spirit of compromise, or at least that such reasoning served to justify a choice that may, after all, have been dictated by circumstances. One thing is certain: here, too, the sub-antique style became the vehicle of a message which the traditional classical vocabulary could not have conveyed with anything like the same directness and palpability. Once more I refer to the ceremonial scenes with which the Constantinian frieze closes and in which the primitive devices of axial symmetry, repetition, frontality and variable scale produce a simple, readily intelligible formula proclaiming with great force the concept of absolute rule and timeless superhuman authority (figs. 2, 4). Henceforth and throughout the Middle Ages this same basic formula was to be used many times not only in secular but also, and above all, in religious contexts to express this same idea.[19]

No doubt, then, the success of sub-antique forms in official art at the end of the third and the beginning of the fourth century was due in part to the fact that these forms provided a suitable means of expression for messages which important and influential patrons wished to communicate. To return to portraiture on coins, the hardness and simplified angularity characteristic of the imperial profile in many issues of this period minted in different parts of the empire cannot mean that artists capable of making dies in a 'better' style could no longer be found anywhere. It can only signify an official preference for the sub-antique manner with its ability to project an image of indomitable strength and toughness (fig. 9).

Important as the role of patrons and their conscious choices may be, however, this factor obviously cannot provide more than a partial explanation of a very complex phenomenon. The subversion of the classical canon was not a matter of a sudden assault by some powerful individuals during the Tetrarchy. It was a slow and gradual process which had begun more than a century earlier. The seeds of the late antique development were, in fact, sown in the late second century, in the era of the Antonines. The spiral band of the triumphal column of Marcus Aurelius, carved between A.D.180 and 193 in obvious emulation of the Column of Trajan made two generations earlier, affords excellent opportunities to observe this development in its incipient state.[20] For instance, the recurrent and more or less stereotyped motif of the emperor addressing his troops (figs. 13, 14) is here subtly transformed in such a way that the imperial person, rather than turning to his listeners, is in effect presented ceremonially to us, the beholders, anticipating in this sense the compositions on the Arch of Constantine. Raised to an upper register and entirely clear of the crowd gathered around him, Marcus Aurelius appears in an *en face* view and is flanked in near symmetry by two dignitaries and two groups of standards. Soldiers on the march, another recurrent motif in these war 'documentaries', are no longer shown in a variety of natural poses, but fall into a lockstep with postures, shields and spears creating a schematic, repetitive pattern.[21] We are faced here with relatively subtle and inconspicuous changes within what is clearly a continuous tradition, and it would seem unlikely that these changes were dictated by those who commissioned the work. On the contrary, we may presume that these modifications were introduced by the artist himself in an act of freely copying the model imposed on him. There is, indeed, a good chance that they were arrived at intuitively and perhaps not altogether consciously. In other words, here, at a point much closer to the beginnings of the decisive and fateful style change that spelled the end of classical art, we must reckon with an artist's 'inner-directed' action, whatever the deeper motivation of that action may have been.

Certainly, in the instances I have cited, the sculptors of Marcus Aurelius' Column seem to promote, or at least to be groping towards, a new exaltation of the emperor on the one hand and a new standard of regimentation of his subjects on the other. But it is with the benefit of hindsight (namely in the perspective of subsequent official art and especially that of the Tetrarchy and of Constantine) that the significance of these early steps becomes apparent. It would be difficult to prove a programmatic intent here. In any case, the changes and innovations in Roman art during the last decades of the second century involved much more than a shift in political concepts. What took place was an assault on tradition on a much broader front.

A comparison of two sculptured sarcophagi of this period may help us to enlarge our view of the process under discussion (figs. 15, 16).[22] Both reliefs represent battles against barbarians. One was carved about A.D.160–70, the other twenty or thirty years later. Crowded as the earlier relief is, it is still essentially a Hellenistic frieze in the tradition of the Pergamon Altar. Individual bodies are fully developed as organic entities; they strike dramatic poses which find an organic response in the pose of some adjoining figure. What looks like a melée consists, in fact, of a series of intricately interwoven duels. Deep shadows plough up the surface, but they coincide with the outlines of individual bodies and set off each one as an element in a fugue-like composition. In the later relief these contrasts of light and shadow no longer serve to define corporeal entities. They are so ubiquitous as to cut across all natural boundaries and themselves become a principal means of conveying a sense of chaotic, rapidly changing action. The whole surface consists of fragments of human figures, horses, weapons and other paraphernalia. Here, in principle, the Greek concept of a man-centred humanistic art is abandoned. The contrast of light and shadow, an element separate from and imposed upon the actors in the drama, becomes a major means of expression (as, incidentally, it does also on the Column of Marcus Aurelius). It has long been recognized that with the introduction of this 'optical' effect classical art is already at an end.[23] An element which is not generated by natural forms in their natural interplay but is abstracted from them and essentially independent of them becomes a vehicle of an intense aesthetic and emotional appeal. Thus the way is open to the more radical abstraction that was to follow.

A certain disinterest in the sculptural elaboration of individual forms is a logical corollary. The rendering of anatomy, of drapery, of a face or a horse's mane is relatively summary, and much use is made of the drill to produce deep shadows that indicate rather than define such detail. No doubt this involves a loss of careful craftsmanship. But here, if anywhere, this appears as a jettisoning of ballast, a breaking through of new concerns. A close-up view of one of the vanquished barbarians is enough to bear this out (fig. 17). The simplified outline uniting throat, chin and jaw in a single curve powerfully dramatizes the last desperate upward thrust of the doomed man's face, just as the few bold shadow lines that mark his drooping hair and the fold of his tunic spell the impending death-fall. Indisputably, simplification here serves to enhance expression.

Thus we are led to discern something of the inner forces behind the formal innovations of this period. This is a generation that revels in the representation of suffering. In the war scenes it is the defeated, the prisoners, the dying who seem most to engage the artist's attention – not in a spirit of compassion but because of the opportunity to represent great emotional stress. As the decades went by, these expressions became ever more extreme, as witness the heads of dying barbarians on the great mid-third-century battle sarcophagus in the Ludovisi collection (fig. 18).[24]

Scholars have spoken of an 'age of anxiety'.[25] The danger of an anachronistic diagnosis in terms of purely modern problems and experiences clearly lurks here. But one need only look at a representative series of third-century portraits to agree that we are indeed dealing with deeply troubled people. Or perhaps it would be more correct to say that it came to be considered appropriate in this period for the portrayal of any personage, however prominent or official, to convey a sense of anguish, though the expression may vary from worried concern to total absorption in a far-off vision, from defiant toughness to stoic resignation (figs. 19–22).[26]

The reasons, of course, are not far to seek. The Roman world was undergoing a profound material and spiritual crisis. I need mention only the rapid succession and violent overthrow of rulers; the military catastrophes; the mounting taxation and inflation; the abandonment of traditional religion in favour of Oriental cults with their emphasis on the mysterious, the ecstatic and the irrational; and the emergence of new trends in philosophy that offered an escape from the realities of this world. To decide which of these factors are primary and which secondary – what is cause and what is effect – cannot be our task. Their cumulative significance is not in doubt and, with contemporary portraits to guide us, we have no difficulty in recognizing in the massive assault on traditional aesthetic norms, in the mounting emotionalism and abstraction, a visual corollary to what was happening in other spheres of life.

Thus, in tracing the anti-classical development in late Roman art back to its earlier stages, we have arrived at a much broader, if less sharply focused, view of its scope and meaning. The messages are not as specific as those of the Tetrarchic and early Constantinian works with which we started; nor is there the same obvious correlation between messages and the visual devices conveying them. Also, in these earlier stages references to sub-antique style forms are less evident and tangible, and it would be hard to maintain that mental associations with the sub-antique sphere were being evoked deliberately. By the same token, it would be difficult to attribute an active role to the patron. Indeed, we cannot pinpoint with any accuracy the patronage behind many of the works in which the break with the classical past first becomes apparent.

But what we have lost in precision we have gained in depth. Going back in time, as we have done, we can no longer operate with the simple notion of a ruler manipulating artistic form to suit his purposes. The stylistic innovations that began in the late second century are rather in the nature of a broad irresistible stream engulfing everybody and everything and – so we have seen – springing from the whole human situation of the period, the hopes and fears, the preoccupations and sufferings of an entire society. We have penetrated to a far deeper level of contemporary life.

What emerges here is a dilemma which confronts the stylistically oriented art historian whenever he tries to go beyond the description, classification and interrelating of forms and undertakes to interpret their meaning in cultural terms. He can be specific in certain cases, particularly when the patron, his wishes and his programmes are tangibly involved. But such cases are like the tips of icebergs. They rest on a mass of widely diffused phenomena that can only be interpreted intuitively by invoking the mood of the age or, in other words, a Zeitgeist. The use of the term, it seems to me, is legitimate so long as we bear in mind that a Zeitgeist, in turn, is compounded of many elements, material and spiritual. In the present instance we are fortunate in knowing a great deal about the concerns which dominated people's lives, and the correlation between these concerns and the new stylistic forms which emerge is compelling. (At subsequent stages of our story the evidence will be far more meagre.) What is not susceptible to analysis in this remote and anonymous age is the actual linkage between the experiences of society as a whole and the workings of the aesthetic imagination. I have spoken of the innovations

introduced by artists at the end of the second century as essentially intuitive
and 'inner-directed'. By this I obviously do not mean that artists were not
affected by events, movements and ideas in the society around them. What I
do mean is that the translation of social experience into visual terms was their
own creative act.

I said at the outset that I would take a global view of the great stylistic upheaval
in late Roman art. The broad outlines of this process have, I hope, emerged,
but much of the detail has perforce been omitted. No account has been taken
of the ebb and flow of stylistic change from decade to decade. The assault on
the classical canon took different forms at different times, and there were
reactions, countermoves and retarding moments such as the 'Renaissance'
under the Emperor Gallienus (A.D.253–68).[27] Nor, in the present framework,
have I been able to do justice to regional differences. While the sculptors of
sarcophagi in Rome experimented with new formal devices that would heighten
the emotional impact of figures and scenes, their counterparts in Greece and
Asia Minor worked in a more conservative vein, producing reliefs that continued
to be based on the concept of the primacy, integrity and autonomy of the
individual human form (figs. 24, 25).[28] Finally – and this is of great importance
– a conservative and a progressive manner may appear side by side in the same
area, in the same workshop or even on the same monument. Certain subject
categories invited and encouraged the quest for the expressive or the abstract,
while others were felt to call for a more traditional treatment. The somewhat studied classicism I have just mentioned as being characteristic of Greek
and Asiatic sarcophagus reliefs is associated on these reliefs with mythological
figures and scenes. Now in Rome, too, a sculptor of the early third century
might persist in the loving elaboration of figures and, indeed, go out of his way
to achieve extremes of grace and surface polish when presenting a subject not
pertaining to the here and now. Thus on a Roman sarcophagus of this period
in New York (fig. 23)[29] the god Dionysus, his entourage of satyrs, maenads and
cupids and the four genii on either side personifying the four seasons are
rendered with an extraordinary if somewhat vacuous refinement and smooth-
ness. The delicate *sfumato* effect which envelops these figures seems to remove
them from our world altogether into a kind of never-never land.

Form, then, may be modulated depending on content. In a different way this
is illustrated by the Attic sarcophagus in the Capitoline Museum in Rome,
also of the first half of the third century, which bears on its front the story of
Achilles (fig. 25). The cool academic classicism which informs the mythological
scene (fig. 26) does not extend to the portrayal of the deceased who, with his

wife, is represented reclining on the lid of the tomb (fig. 27).[30] His is one of those mask-like, frozen, hard-edged faces which we found typical of third-century portraiture generally. Thus two different styles appear side by side on one and the same monument, one for contemporary mortal men, the other for figures from mythology. This is the phenomenon of the so-called 'modes' – the conventional use of different stylistic manners to denote different kinds of subject matter or different levels of existence. It is an extremely important factor which cuts across and to some extent negates the temporal succession of stylistic phases in Roman art. And, as we shall see, some of these conventions continue into subsequent centuries when such stylistic differentiation according to content will tend to be carried even further. This phenomenon, more than any other, adds to the complexity of the process we are studying.

But when all is said and done – and after making allowance for retarding elements, regional factors and the coexistence of different styles depending on subject content – the history of art in the period we have surveyed is still dominated by one central and crucial process, namely, the disintegration of the classical canon and the emergence of radically conceptual forms either abstracted from that canon or imposed upon it. It was the first and most decisive step on the road from classical to medieval art.

Finally, a few remarks must be added about Christian art, whose role in the third century was as yet marginal. Classical art transformed itself; it was not transformed by Christianity. There is only an indirect connection in the sense that the same material and spiritual crisis which underlies the aesthetic revolution of the period also caused a rapid expansion of the Christian religion, a development which in turn led to the rise of Christian art. But Christian art did not from the outset spearhead new forms.

There is no evidence of any art with a Christian content earlier than the year A.D.200.[31] In all likelihood this is not merely due to accidental losses. The surviving monuments of Christian pictorial art which can be attributed to the first half of the third century bear the marks of a true beginning.[32] Moreover, one can find in Christian literature of the period reflections of a changing attitude towards images and their role in religious life.[33]

That attitude was undoubtedly negative prior to this period. The root cause was not, as is often claimed, the Old Testament commandment against graven images but rather a state of mind which equated image-making with pagan cult practices and the entire pagan way of life. By the same token, the emergence in the third century of religiously meaningful images in Christian contexts was part of a process of coming to terms with that way of life. Naturally

Christians adopted artistic forms that were current in the society in which they lived.

Nowhere is this more apparent than in the early fresco decorations in the Roman catacombs. Wall painting, a medium we have not so far considered, had undergone a striking development in Rome during the late second and early third centuries. Simulated architecture, traditionally a favourite theme in painted mural decorations, had become increasingly attenuated and dematerialized until only a network of thin lines remained, covering ceilings as well as walls. Within this ethereal web isolated figures float on large expanses of plain white ground. Roman domestic interiors of the first half of the third century were painted in this characteristic style which in its own way bears witness to the anti-classical tendencies of the period (fig. 28), and the same system of decoration appears in the earliest of the painted chambers in the Christian catacombs (fig. 29).[34]

Yet there is a difference. There are, of course, new subjects expressive of Christian concerns and based mainly on the Old and New Testaments.[35] But there is also a difference in the way these images were intended to function. This no doubt has to do with the fact that they constituted in effect an infringement of a taboo. They point beyond themselves to a quite extraordinary degree. Biblical themes are represented for the most part in drastically abridged form, usually reduced to the minimum of figures and props necessary to call to mind a given text. It is not intended that the beholder should linger in contemplation of physical appearances. He is only meant to receive a signal. Furthermore, the texts to which the images refer are not invoked for their own sakes. There is no factual thread linking the various subjects together. What unites them is a common message which is of urgent concern to the beholder, a message of deliverance and security through divine intervention. Images are thus twice removed from an actual portrayal of sacred subject matter. They are ciphers conveying an idea. This method, which has been aptly described as 'signitive',[36] was not entirely new. It had previously been used in certain pagan contexts.[37] What was new was the intensity with which it was often applied in Christian contexts, the accumulation of 'signs' in a given space. The wall paintings in the catacombs are apt to be overcharged with content, for in this content lay the justification of the visual image.

Even this difference, however, tended to recede in the second half of the third century. There are Christian images of this period which were clearly meant to function more normally as representations in the classical sense and not merely as ciphers or pictographs. A remarkable group of small-scale marble sculptures of Eastern Mediterranean origin, acquired some years ago by the

Cleveland Museum of Art, is a particularly striking example (fig. 30).[38] Four of the pieces represent in sequence the sea adventure of Jonah, a 'deliverance' story familiar from the Roman catacombs. It is one subject which even in the earliest of the Roman paintings already appears elaborated to the extent of being shown as a story in successive stages. But here it is in the round – in the medium most closely identified with the idolatrous world of the pagans. The sculptor, steeped in the tradition of Hellenistic baroque, has dramatized the episode with a boldness and directness which almost foreshadow the art of Bernini; and to do this he has used the smooth, soft manner, the *sfumato* effects which, we have seen, were still favoured nostalgically in third-century pagan art for mythological and idyllic subjects. The Cleveland statuettes must have been intended for a well-to-do Christian who wanted an equivalent of a special kind of pretty decorative fountain sculpture fashionable among pagans at the time and featuring such subjects as Orpheus taming the animals with his music (fig. 31). The process of Christian assimilation to pagan usage has gone far here; and clearly it has not made for stylistic innovation – quite the contrary. Let us note incidentally that the same workshop in which the Jonah statuettes were carved also produced portraits of contemporary individuals which, while unmistakably related, show a more precise definition of forms (fig. 32). It is a good example of a style being modulated and attuned to different kinds of subjects.

The interest in representation for its own sake which the Cleveland marbles so clearly bespeak is evident also in certain Christian monuments of roughly the same period in Rome. Again the best examples are sculptures representing Jonah's ordeal and rescue, although the monuments in question bear no direct relationship, either iconographic or stylistic, to those Eastern statuettes. On the fronts of a number of sarcophagi made for affluent Christians in the late third century the story of the biblical prophet was spread out in sequence in much the same way as themes from mythology had been displayed on pagan tombs (fig. 33).[39] Indeed, stereotyped motifs that had served in the depiction of classical myths, pastoral idylls or the marine dream world inhabited by Nereids and Tritons, were drawn upon to pictorialize the Jonah story in loving detail. The most remarkable of these borrowings was the figure used to depict the prophet's rest under the gourd tree at the end of his ordeal. It is no other than Endymion, the beauteous shepherd boy whose awakening by Selene, the goddess of the moon, had long been a favourite subject of pagan sarcophagus reliefs (fig. 34). Christian interest and taste in this period clearly inclined to tradition rather than to the radical innovations which the third century had produced.

CHAPTER TWO

Regeneration

We ended our discussion of the great crisis in Roman art of the third century with a glimpse at Christian art of the period. It is with a category of Christian monuments that our survey of stylistic developments in the ensuing century can usefully begin.

There exists a class of marble sarcophagi preserved in numerous examples primarily in Rome, which in a purely visual sense strike a familiar note (figs. 35, 36). At first sight they might almost be taken for sections from one of the friezes of the Arch of Constantine (cf. fig. 4). Indeed, some of them seem to have been carved by the same workshop which produced those friezes. Others must have been made in closely related ateliers.[1] We recognize many of the most telling characteristics of the Constantinian work: the tight, isocephalous line-up of figures, the stubby proportions and angular movements, the crudely drilled lines denoting drapery folds. In some instances the similarity extends to minute detail such as the rendering of eyes or of beards (figs. 37, 38).

It is, however, a stylistic relationship only. Our sarcophagus reliefs turn out to be in a class of their own once their subject matter is taken into account. The tightly aligned figures of which these friezes are composed do not stand for anonymous crowds as do their equivalents on the arch. Nearly every one of them is a separate unit depicting a distinct event. At the most two or three together make up a scene. And these scenes, juxtaposed without separation and often in seemingly helter-skelter fashion, pertain to episodes in the Gospels and in the Old Testament and to apocryphal stories from the life of St Peter. For instance, on the sarcophagus illustrated in fig. 35 the five full-length figures on the right represent three different miracles performed by Christ. At the right end of the frieze he is shown raising Lazarus. Next he appears flanked by two apostles as he multiplies the loaves and fishes. Immediately to the left he appears again healing a blind man of diminutive size, while the bearded man in the background holding a finger to his mouth may stand – in drastically abridged form – for the scene in which an embarrassed St Peter is foretold that he will thrice deny Christ. There follows once more, to the left of a central orant figure flanked by apostles and intended to bear the portrait features of the deceased, the figure of Christ as he turns water into wine at Cana. Directly

[22]

adjoining him is one of the soldiers who take St Peter prisoner, while at the extreme left is the apocryphal scene of the apostle striking water from the wall of his prison for his thirsting guards. Two Old Testament scenes – the Fall and the Three Youths in the Fiery Furnace – are added on the short sides of the trough.

Such a way of representing a multiplicity of distinct events has no real precedent in ancient funerary sculpture. Normally when the subject matter of a Roman sarcophagus was narrative, the whole front of the trough was given over to a single myth recounted in epic breadth; and we have seen that in the late third century some Christians had begun to adopt this manner for their own tombs (fig. 33). One might find depicted on a pagan sarcophagus the Labours of Hercules or, in a rare instance, a series of scenes in the life of an official lined up in close formation.[2] But although this does mean an accumulation of many distinct events, the whole nevertheless forms a single sequence with an obvious narrative unity. In the case of our Christian 'frieze sarcophagi' there is no such obvious unity. What ties the scenes together is their implications. Most of them carry a single message – still, broadly speaking, the message of deliverance through divine intervention familiar from third-century catacomb art. Clearly the idea is to reiterate the point by exemplifying it with as many different episodes as possible. More than ever these images point beyond themselves. It is the 'signitive' method at its most extreme.[3]

The isocephalous frieze was an ideal vehicle for the purpose. It was like a line of writing which required the beholder's most active mental participation to enable him to decipher its content.[4] The monotonously erect figures of which it was basically composed allowed for only a minimum of visual enactment of the events concerned. To make the stories intelligible secondary figures and props were added on a much smaller scale; they provided the accents, so to speak. But, to continue the metaphor, there was no separation of words. It was left to the beholder to disentangle the scenes. At the same time space was saved for additional episodes. Never in the history of the sculptured sarcophagus had there been an attempt to say so much in so little space. It was the combination of isocephalous frieze and signitive method of narration which made this possible.

The frieze sarcophagus, despite its visual resemblance to the relief bands of the Arch of Constantine, is the first Christian artifact that is truly original and different in basic conception from anything that had ever been done in Graeco-Roman art. Produced serially, these tombs served for the burial of, presumably, middle-class Christians who died just before and in the first decades after their religion won official recognition. It can hardly be pure coincidence that the almost frenetic piling up of content and messages which is their distinctive characteristic occurred just at the time when Christianity was at last being set free in the Roman world. The problem of the graven image must have asserted itself with particular urgency at that moment. A way was found to justify visual representation by more than ever charging it with messages.

I have focused on these sarcophagi at the outset of this chapter not so much for their intrinsic interest – great as that interest is – but because, as already indicated, they offer an excellent point of departure for our investigation of ensuing developments. The frieze sarcophagus of the early Constantinian period had a rich progeny. By following the production of Christian tombs in Roman marble ateliers through the next several decades we can isolate and demonstrate within a single geographically, technically and thematically coherent series of artifacts a marked stylistic shift which will prove to be symptomatic of much larger trends dominating fourth-century art as a whole. In the aggregate, as we shall see, these trends amount to a massive reversal of the anti-classical tide that had reached a high mark in the decades around A.D.300.

Three well-known sarcophagi will serve to illustrate a step-by-step trans-formation within this particular category over a time span of about forty years. Common to these three examples is a basic feature which again is without precedent in the vast output of funerary reliefs in pagan Rome, namely, an arrangement of the figure friezes on the trough in two superposed registers of equal height. This device, which made it possible to pack the front of the tomb with even more content, seems to have been invented specifically for Christian purposes.[5] The so-called 'Dogmatic' sarcophagus, now in the Vatican and carved perhaps in the third decade of the fourth century, is one of the earliest to show this doubling of the frieze (fig. 41).[6] Within each register, scenes are juxtaposed with the same unconcern for separating historically disparate events that we noted earlier on the single friezes; for instance, in the lower zone, Daniel in the Lions' Den is flanked by the Healing of the Blind Man and by the scene in which Peter is foretold of his denial of Christ. At the same time there is a marked stylistic change here. The actors in the various episodes do not jostle one another quite so much. Each is separated from its neighbours by deep shadows. And, what is particularly important, the crudely drilled lines which on the earlier tombs had ploughed up all the sculpted surfaces and thus had spun a web of shadows over the entire relief have disappeared. As a result the figures stand out as so many solid blocks from which the sculptor has con-structed a firm and tight composition marked by strong accents in the centre of both registers, prominent framing bands and suitable props to close off each frieze at either end. To the left are high-backed chairs serving as seats for God the Father creating Adam and for the Virgin receiving the Magi. To the right are Lazarus' tomb and the wall from which St Peter produces drinking water. It is the assertion of each figure as a solid three-dimensional entity within this compactly organized framework which is of particular significance. We seem to be able to put our fingers around each one of them – so deeply are they undercut.

This is the direction in which the stylistic development will proceed, as shown by our second example – the sarcophagus of the 'Two Brothers' from S.Paolo fuori le mura (fig. 42).[7] If the two zones of the 'Dogmatic' sarcophagus seemed like shelves of a cupboard packed with solids, here spatial effects have become so strong that there is no longer a single coherent front plane. The medallion with the portraits of the deceased – now a decidedly concave form providing the busts with ample breathing space of their own – seems to float in front of the 'shelves'. The 'shelves' themselves have become so deep that they can accommodate figures and props that are fully in the round; and the figures use these 'shelves' as though they were miniature stages. For instance, in the Healing of the Blind (lower right) Christ turns on his own axis as he performs the miracle; and in the scene of Pilate Washing his Hands (upper right) the figures are arranged in a semicircle around a fully three-dimensional table that once supported the wash-basin.

Implied in this striking transformation is a fundamental change in the function and purpose of visual images on these tombs. If the figures on the early frieze sarcophagi were so many ciphers – shorthand pictographs intended to be read rapidly and to produce their effect cumulatively by recalling to the beholder's mind a multitude of meaningful stories and events – now the beholder is invited once more, as he was in the case of the more developed among third-century Christian images, to linger over each scene. Events are being re-enacted before his eyes. To do this, the artist again falls back on the enormously rich and immensely adaptable repertory of figure motifs that had been evolved in the Mediterranean world since classical times and more particularly in the Hellenistic period. The nude figure of Daniel in the Lions' Den had already been elaborated with some care on the 'Dogmatic' sarcophagus, whose sculptor in carving this figure must have had in mind Greek statues of ephebes; now it becomes a study in *contrapposto* in an almost Praxitelean sense. Similarly, the sister of Lazarus – in the earlier relief a mere accessory, a subsidiary sign spelling 'gratitude' – is now a full participant in the action (fig. 39). She is modelled (somewhat incongruously) after a figure from the repertory of pagan mythological sarcophagi, namely, Phaedra's nurse who sidles up to Hippolytus to bring him the fatal message from her enamoured mistress (fig. 40).[8]

One might interpret differently the stylistic change so clearly manifested in these reliefs. Rather than say that the sculptor uses the classical vocabulary to 'humanize' events and make them seem physically present, one could consider this effect a mere by-product of a renewed effort to create a Christian equivalent of the mythological imagery of pagan sepulchral art. In other words, the associative intent might be claimed to be paramount, just as it may have been previously in the case of those Christian paintings and sculptures of the third century in which biblical events had already appeared in decidedly Hellenistic garb. We lack the evidence to define with precision the artist's motivating force. What we can say is that the sarcophagi here under review truly reflect a stylistic development. We see a change taking place before our eyes over a period of a few decades. Nor is this only a matter of form. Hand in hand with the stylistic change goes a marked thematic expansion, a dilution of the single-minded message of personal salvation to which nearly all the subjects of Christian funerary art had hitherto been keyed. Cyclical narration spread during this period. A scene like Pilate Washing his Hands – here presented in elaborate detail – had had no place in the traditional repertory of themes. Now it serves as an epitome of events relating to the death of Christ, while on another, probably slightly earlier, sarcophagus it forms part of an incipient Passion cycle (fig. 44).[9] Sacred history is being factually re-enacted before the beholder's eyes rather than being merely recalled to his mind for the purpose of conveying an urgent personal message.

The third example in my series is the famous sarcophagus of Junius Bassus, city prefect of Rome, who died in A.D.359 (figs. 43, 46, 47).[10] In this, the best-known of all Early Christian sarcophagi, the frieze form is abandoned. Each episode is given its own niche (or, in the case of the Pilate scene, two niches) within an elaborate and ornate columnar framework. The result is a multitude of miniature stages, and the amount of space and depth in each varies according to the demands imposed by the setting and the disposition of the figures. Certainly the sarcophagus is rooted in the workshop tradition of the preceding decades. The arrangement in two registers alone testifies to this, and so does much of the iconography. There is here, however, a far more definite reattachment to aesthetic ideals of the Graeco-Roman past than we encountered in our earlier examples. In reintroducing a columnar framework – a feature familiar from some types of pagan sarcophagi of earlier centuries – our sculptor was anticipated by the carvers of other Christian tomb reliefs a decade or two before, witness the sarcophagus with Passion scenes already referred to (fig. 44). But we need only compare close-up views of the heads of Pilate from the two sarcophagi to become aware of quite distinctive new elements in the style of the Junius Bassus reliefs (figs. 45, 46). Forms have become extremely soft. There is a smooth transition from feature to feature and an alabaster-like finish to the whole surface. At the same time the face has become more animated. It has a gentle, lyrical quality, while the other still shows much of the hardness and angularity of early fourth-century reliefs. This lyrical, slightly sweet manner is characteristic of all the figures on the Bassus tomb — even of the Roman soldiers who lead St Peter to his martyrdom (fig. 47). There can be no doubt that the master who introduced this new element to the Roman atelier in which the sarcophagus was carved must have come from the Greek East. To be specific, there are close stylistic analogies between figures on these reliefs and the Cleveland portrait busts which were found together with the series of statuettes depicting the Jonah story. Making allowance for the difference in scale and subject matter, one may compare the head of St Peter with the male heads in Cleveland, and these same busts also show a rendering of draperies analogous to that of the soldier on the right (figs. 32, 47, 48).

This is not the first instance in which a classicizing manner in the art of Rome can be traced to the Greek world. Certainly the Eastern Mediterranean had reserves of Hellenism which the West lacked. We shall come upon this phenomenon again and again. But in the present context two points should be borne in mind. In the first place, the Eastern sculptures which I am citing for comparison are about three generations older than the Bassus tomb. There is no evidence to suggest – and some reason to doubt – that even in Eastern marble ateliers the same polished and soft manner was practised at this level of refinement through the Tetrarchic and Constantinian periods. Thus our hypothetical immigrant master from the East might well himself have been the product of a revival movement, a movement parallel to that which we have seen taking place in Rome. In the second place, the introduction of a soft, lyrical style in the Bassus sarcophagus merely reinforces this latter movement in Rome itself, a movement which had been building up within a single clearly definable workshop tradition for the preceding thirty or forty years. Foreign influence alone cannot account for this entire stylistic development, which we have indeed found to be a corollary to major changes in the function and content of images on these sarcophagi.

The process of regeneration which we have traced on Christian tomb reliefs was, as we shall see, the keynote, the common denominator of fourth-century style developments in general. By going into a certain amount of detail in regard to this one group I hope, on the one hand, to have demonstrated that organic, step-by-step style developments can and do occur, and, on the other hand, to have avoided the danger of describing such developments in too broad

and general terms. Our series of sarcophagi bears witness to a specific evolutionary process in the realm of form which calls for specific explanations. As I
have indicated, in this instance explanations are as yet only partially forthcoming. However, one additional factor may be cited. At the beginning of our
series of sarcophagi we were faced with a phenomenon of mass production,
presumably for a middle-class clientele. At the end stands an individual and
extremely elaborate tomb commissioned by or for a high official who was a
member of a prominent and wealthy family.[11] This is surely significant. The
aesthetic ideals embodied in the Bassus sarcophagus are those of the highest
stratum of Roman society. Taking a cue from this observation, one might
describe the entire development which I have outlined as a gradual appropriation of a popular type of Christian tomb by upper-class patrons whose
standards asserted themselves increasingly both in the content and in the style
of these monuments. The development could be seen as parallel to and con-
tingent upon the increasing rate of conversion of upper-class people to Christianity in the late and post-Constantinian period. But I find it hard to believe
that so gradual a transformation could have been initiated and guided solely
by patrons. To use again a term which served us in our description of style
developments in the third century, the progressive changes evident in so many
aspects of the imagery of these sarcophagi cannot have been wholly 'other-
directed'.[12] Let us also remember that in the early years of Constantine's
reign the 'aristocratic' form ideals had not been able to prevail even in work
commissioned by the conservative Roman Senate, as the friezes on the triumphal
arch of A.D.315 palpably demonstrate.

There is, then, a rising curve, a regenerative process powered, at least to
some extent, by forces within the artists' own sphere and gathering momentum
as the century progresses. We shall see this confirmed when we turn to other
categories of artistic production of the period after A.D.350. But before doing so,
we must return very briefly to the early decades of the century. For the overall
picture of stylistic currents and cross-currents in those decades is more complex
than I have made it appear so far. In laying stress on the anti-classical tendencies
in the art of the Tetrarchy and in the early Constantinian period, I have failed
to do justice to a number of initiatives in different media and different places
which foreshadow the regeneration to come and which it has become customary
to subsume under the heading of Constantinian classicism.[13] Each one of these
initiatives needs to be explained on its own merits before any conclusions can
be reached regarding their roots, their possible interrelationships or their
bearing on subsequent developments. The subject is too large to be dealt with
in detail here, and I shall have to limit myself to citing a few examples.

Even the work on the Arch of Constantine, an enterprise so largely dominated by craftsmen who were untouched by or unsympathetic to classical standards of form, entailed the activity of at least one sculptor of a different outlook. I refer to the master who recarved the imperial heads on the reused Hadrianic medallions in line with their new destination (fig. 49).[14] His soft, delicate rendering of the face of Constantine with its sensitive mouth and its boyish, carefully groomed haircut reminiscent of Augustus' is a far cry from the dominant style of the workshop. There is a related phenomenon in imperial portraiture on coins. Early portraits of Constantine on coins issued in the West (fig. 50) are remarkably classical in form and spirit, and subsequently this style spread to Eastern mints also.[15] Finally, to cite an example from the realm of painting, the magnificent fragments of frescoed ceilings which have been recovered in the excavation of the imperial palace at Trier and which can be attributed to the period *c.* A.D.315–25 also betray a decidedly classicizing spirit (figs. 51, 52).[16] Whatever their antecedents may have been, they are certainly in striking contrast to the ethereal type of wall decoration which had been current in Rome in the preceding century (fig. 28). An elaborate system of simulated coffers here serves as a frame for full-bodied figures of bejewelled ladies and nude cupids. Constantinian court art, then, is not without its 'Renaissance' phenomena; and undoubtedly these prepared the ground for the broad regenerative development which followed.

Turning now to the further progress of that development in the second half of the fourth century, I shall first draw attention to a category of objects which, like the Trier paintings, reflect the secular tastes of the wealthy upper class, namely, silver vessels with repoussé or engraved reliefs, of which an extraordinarily large number have survived from that period. Several hoards of such objects, such as the Treasure from the Esquiline in the British Museum and that from Traprain Law in the National Museum in Edinburgh, were unearthed a long time ago.[17] Others, like those from Mildenhall (also in the British Museum) and Kaiseraugst (the ancient Rauracum) not far from Basle, have only come to light in recent decades.[18] Rich in representations of subjects from Greek mythology and especially in those pertaining to Dionysus and his retinue of land- or sea-borne revellers, these silver objects were natural vehicles of classical form. Indeed, in this type of object a more or less pure classical style might be assumed to have been perpetuated almost automatically through the generations. There is, however, no evidence of a strong continuity in the manufacture of such silver work during the late third and the early decades of the fourth century. It is true that the strikingly great incidence of finds dating from the second half of the fourth century may not reflect increased production so much as more frequent burial (and hence preservation into modern times) due to the greatly increased threats of barbarian incursions in all parts of the Roman world. It is also true that a hoard buried at that time may well contain objects that are considerably older. But so far as research has elucidated this problem – and it should be emphasized that a great deal remains to be done in this area – it has not identified either for the period of the Tetrarchs or for that of Constantine full equivalents of works such as the Mildenhall Maenad Plate or the Achilles Plate from Kaiseraugst (figs. 53–5). The point is worth emphasizing. It does seem that the demand for such work increased after the middle of the century. And this demand was not purely frivolous. The attempt to relate the Kaiseraugst find to Julian the Apostate, who we know made repeated use of the Castellum of Rauracum during his Gaulish campaign (A.D.359–60), has aroused grave objections on chronological and other grounds.[19] But the increased production of such works in this general period may well be significant and connected with that reassertion of the pagan religion and the pagan way of life of which Julian was the most famous and most conspicuous exponent. For instance, the relief on a silver tray (or *lanx*) from Corbridge (fig. 56), which features Apollo and Artemis, has been plausibly connected with the cult of these divinities on the island of Delos, and it has been suggested that the object commemorates Julian's visit there in A.D.363.[20]

It is true that, retrospective as these silver reliefs are in both content and style, the third-century breakdown of classical form has nevertheless left its mark on them. None of the figures on the Corbridge *lanx* – man, woman or beast – bears close scrutiny by the standards of the classical canon of proportions or simply of anatomical verisimilitude, to say nothing of background features (the aedicula, the tree) or the spindly and highly schematic vine rinceau on the border. The whole representation is strangely anaemic. The figures on the Kaiseraugst Achilles Plate are more spirited, but they too have their flaws – what, for instance, happens to Deidameia's right arm as she tries to hold back Achilles in the group on the left in the central medallion (fig. 54)? – and both in their positioning and in their movements they lack a convincing three-dimensional development. In analysing works such as these, one becomes aware of how all-pervasive the third-century crisis had been and how basically irreversible were the trends which it had set in motion. But there can be no doubt that those who executed these silver reliefs – and those who commissioned them – were trying to hold fast to ancient tradition if not, indeed, to turn back the clock. Here, then, is an artistic vogue which, thanks to its subject matter as well as to the prodigal use of expensive material, can fairly confidently be attributed to a known element in the social and cultural history of the fourth century, namely, a wealthy and conservative elite which for a time resisted the onrush of Christianity.[21] It was especially in the Western part of the empire during this period that land-owning families were able to accumulate extraordinary wealth and power, and the great hoards of fourth-century silver plate have, in fact, all been found in the West. But the manufacture of these easily transportable objects was empire-wide the Kaiseraugst Achilles Plate, for instance, bears an inscription showing that it was made in Thessaloniki – and art historians have so far been unable to distinguish regional workshops or schools. Thus, definable as this particular impulse towards regeneration is in historical terms, we are not as yet in a position to measure its overall importance for the history of art in the second half of the fourth century. More specifically, we cannot yet gauge its precise bearing on two more broadly based movements belonging to the last decades of the century, to which I shall now turn. Centred in the Greek East and in the Latin West respectively both of these movements are sometimes subsumed under the heading of a 'Theodosian Renaissance'.[22]

Theodosius the Great, after Constantine the ablest and strongest of the emperors of the fourth century, ascended the throne in A.D.379 with the Eastern half of the empire as his domain. It is in works associated with his reign (which lasted until A.D.395) that we can first define a distinctive style centred at the new capital of Constantinople. Objects characteristically 'Theodosian' have come down to us in a variety of media and they display a considerable range of subject matter. One senses that some strong artistic personality or personalities who set the tone and aesthetic standards were active at the centre of political power, stamping the monuments of this era with an unmistakable imprint.

A good example is provided by a famous silver plate in Madrid, an object of imperial largesse commemorating the tenth anniversary of Theodosius' accession and undoubtedly made in an Eastern Mediterranean atelier (figs. 57–9).[23] Delicately wrought in low relief, it represents the emperor solemnly enthroned before a ceremonial palace architecture (a *fastigium*) as he hands a diploma of appointment to a high official depicted in much smaller size. Theodosius is flanked by his two co-emperors and bodyguards, while from the lower segment of the plate a recumbent female figure personifying the earth gazes up, recognizing in the enthroned monarch her lord and master. The gifts of her abundance are being offered to him playfully by three little nude putti surrounding her.

Since, as we have seen, silversmithing was a particularly flourishing craft from the middle of the fourth century on, the Madrid Plate gives us a good chance to define the Theodosian style in relation to immediately antecedent forms. It is best for this purpose to focus on the figure of *Terra* (fig. 59), since it belongs to the genus of idealized mythological images so prominent on fourth-century silver vessels generally. A kinship with figures such as those on the Corbridge *lanx* (fig. 56) is easily recognizable. Nude bodies have the same soft, rubbery quality; limbs are similarly unarticulated and, again, the anatomical construction does not bear close scrutiny. *Terra*'s left shoulder and arm, for instance, seem dislocated, and one wonders whether her bent near leg is her left or her right. But there is no direct continuity with the *lanx* or with any other known work of the preceding decades. The Madrid *Terra* is a far more pretentious representation, a figure in a contrived, artificial pose put on display self-consciously and theatrically. Each drapery fold is carefully modelled to suggest the part of the anatomy it conceals, and the hem lines, though rather artificially curled, evoke memories of Attic art of the fifth century B.C. There is an element of studied classicism here which indeed justifies the use of the term 'Renaissance'. But this is only one aspect of the style. There is at the same time an insistence on clear, continuous and simplified outline, on neatness and regularity. Flat as the relief is, the figure's silhouette stands out in long, straight or gently curving lines. The facial features merge into a smooth, elongated oval, and the line of the forehead with its surrounding wreath is echoed in the cornucopia to the left, just as the outline of the figure's intervening arm and hand is rhythmically correlated with that of the leaping putto immediately to the right. Classicist form is oddly paired with linear abstract order.

In the main part of the relief, the geometric element is much more in evidence. It may seem paradoxical to find schematism and abstraction carried farthest in the representation of the reality of Theodosius' court, while mythical *Terra* and her surrounding putti, whose presence clearly is meant to impart to the scene cosmic and timeless significance, have an air – however contrived – of playful casualness. The answer, of course, is that it was precisely in regard to the reality of the imperial person and its exercise of authority – as exemplified by the ceremony depicted – that timelessness and absolute stability most needed to be emphasized. The devices employed to this end – strict symmetry of composition, clarity and simplicity of line, repetition of wholly or nearly identical forms with circular and oval shapes predominating – leap to the eye.

Despite the difference of scale and material, it is not difficult to recognize the same essential qualities in the reliefs on the four sides of the cubic stone base which supports the Egyptian obelisk erected by Theodosius in the midst of the hippodrome of Constantinople and which stands in its original location to this day (fig. 60).[24] Executed a few years after the Madrid Plate and placed within a stone's throw of the imperial palace, the reliefs are proof that the Theodosian style was indeed practised – and very possibly created – in the capital. Like the silver relief, they depict solemn ceremonial appearances of the emperor and his entourage, and there is in them the same stylistic dualism (fig. 61): symmetry and geometric order are paired with careful, delicate modelling and loving elaboration of detail. Drapery folds form soft, flowing curves which enliven the surfaces of figures subtly modelled in very low relief. But nothing is allowed to interfere with the neatness of outlines repeated with monotonous regularity. The beholder is confronted with row after row of emphatically oval heads placed on drooping, rounded shoulders to form a continuous array of smooth, sinuous contours. Physiognomies too, while individualized to some extent, are not allowed to disturb the regularity of the ensemble. The artist operates with a limited number of facial types, all distinctive of this period. The most characteristic is a smooth, boyish face, already familiar to us from the Madrid Plate, with a single neat curve outlining cheek and chin, and a low forehead sharply delineated against a closely fitting cap of hair (figs. 58, 74). Combining a measure of 'Hellenic' idealization with a strange kind of blandness, these faces betray both the aspirations and the limitations of the 'Theodosian Renaissance'. The most perfect embodiment of that era's aesthetic and human ideal is a life-size portrait in the round from Aphrodisias (fig. 62).[25] It is a face of the same type and in all probability represents Valentinian II, Theodosius' co-emperor in the West (A.D. 375–92).

The court style of Theodosius I should be clearly recognized for what it was, namely, a new departure rather than the outcome of a gradual step-by-step development. The Madrid Plate – so we have seen – is not simply a sequel to earlier fourth-century silver work. Similarly, the reliefs of the obelisk base or the Aphrodisias portrait have no evident antecedents in their own century;[26] although it would be difficult to name one specific model from earlier times which the artist could have had in mind, his ideal of the human countenance – calm, serene and formally perfect – is clearly inspired by and suggestive of classical precedent. The most palpable proof that there was indeed under Theodosius a conscious revival of forms associated with distant 'golden ages' is provided by the great triumphal column which was erected on the emperor's new forum in the capital and of which only pathetic fragments now remain.[27] Adorned with a spiralling relief band which depicted in great detail Theodosius' military campaigns, this monument was obviously modelled on, and meant to rival, the Columns of Trajan and Marcus Aurelius in Old Rome. No such work had been created in the intervening two hundred years. Perhaps one can go a step further and suggest that this entire artistic effort with its classicizing overtones has to do with the fact that Theodosius was a 'new' man unrelated to the Constantinian house, determined to establish his own dynasty and hence a traditionalist in matters of style.[28]

This can only be a suggestion. Too little is known about the circumstances in which these works were created. We reach much safer ground when we turn to a Western development concurrent with the 'Theodosian Renaissance' in the East.

Among all the initiatives towards regeneration in the art of the fourth century, it is this Western development which is most clearly related to specific historical circumstances. Its primary exponents are objects commissioned during the final decades of the century by members of the old senatorial families in Rome, who in those years were making their last heroic effort at a pagan revival.[29] A famous ivory diptych (fig. 63)[30] with two officiating priestesses – the left half in the Musée de Cluny in Paris, the right half in the Victoria and Albert Museum – is the most eloquent artistic witness to this amply documented *Kulturkampf*[31] which was carried out on many fronts – political, religious and intellectual. Inscribed with the names of the Nicomachi and the Symmachi, two of the families most prominently involved in this struggle, these panels proclaim their patronage *expressis verbis*. They depict in solemn and accurate detail rites, attributes and settings appropriate respectively to Ceres and Cybele and to Bacchus and Jupiter, and are clearly intended as professions of unswerving devotion to the ancient gods. But what is most important in our context is the fact that the past is here being resuscitated also by purely formal means. The carver of these ivories must have studied classical Greek sculptures and their Roman replicas. Indeed, he must have deliberately set out to create an equivalent of such works. The setting, the composition and the figure and drapery motifs can be matched to a remarkable degree on the so-called 'Amalthea' relief formerly in the Lateran, one of several replicas of what must have been a well-known Greek original depicting an as yet not satisfactorily identified mythological scene (fig. 64).[32] Already the earlier work, which is a typical product of the Greek revival under Hadrian, has a chilly, academic quality. In our ivory this quality is enhanced. What distinguishes these carvings from a work such as the Corbridge *lanx* is that their classicism is so studied and conscious. They are exercises in nostalgia undertaken in the service of a very specific cause.

More than one atelier of ivory carvers must have worked for this powerful and enormously wealthy clientele. For instance, a diptych in Liverpool (fig.

65)[33] portraying figures – or, to put it more correctly, statues – of Asclepius and his daughter Hygieia (health personified) is clearly a work of the same period and the same retrospective spirit, but shows stylistic nuances different from those of the two priestesses. The modelling is softer, the figures are more ponderous, and as they stand on projecting pedestals they produce a more decidedly three-dimensional effect with space all around them.[34] Yet another variant of the style is exemplified by a silver plate from Parabiago in Milan (fig. 66), representing the triumph of Cybele and Attis, a work which must also owe its existence to the same group of last-ditch defenders of the old faith. So strikingly retrospective is its manner that the first study devoted to it attributed it to the second century A.D.[35]

In the history of late antique and medieval art there are few instances of a stylistic vogue so patently associated with an identifiable cause. The classicism of these works is insistent, not to say aggressive. It is not merely a by-product resulting more or less automatically from the depiction of pagan mythological themes. On the contrary, it is consciously elaborated and emphasized, so as to lend greater force – add another dimension, so to speak – to the message which these themes were intended to convey. The persons or groups responsible for the subject matter can be identified. May we not assume that these same patrons also instigated and promoted its formal corollary? Our earlier antithesis of 'inner directed' and 'other-directed' stylistic developments is clearly relevant here. The academic classicism of these late fourth-century Italian works is as good an example as one can find of a largely 'other-directed' style.[36]

This revival was to have a profound impact on the whole development in the West, as I hope to show. For the moment I shall confine myself to one of the most immediate ramifications of the movement, namely, its influence in the sphere of official art. The period which witnessed the manufacture of those nostalgically retrospective ivory reliefs was also the period when the annually appointed consuls and other high dignitaries adopted the practice of distributing among their friends and peers ivory diptychs to commemorate their assumption of office. It is another instance of the ostentatious consumption and display of expensive materials which we found became rampant among the wealthy and powerful during the latter half of the fourth century. Given this patronage, it is not surprising to find that some of these official diptychs were made in the same (or closely related) ateliers that produced those with pagan religious themes, and there can be no doubt that the aesthetic ideals which informed the latter also helped to shape the style of the former.

The diptych of Probianus, *vicarius* of the city of Rome, is a case in point (fig. 67).[37] At first sight it appears to have little in common with the pagan group. Its two halves present nearly identical compositions showing the principal figure immobilized in a strictly *en face* view on the central axis, with attendants of smaller scale flanking him, and acclaiming officials of yet another scale in a separate zone below. Once again abstract principles of symmetry, frontality, and differentiation by scale and registers serve to express power and authority. But the scene is enframed by a delicately wrought palmette ornament virtually identical with that on the borders of the diptych of the two priestesses (fig. 63). This is a tell-tale detail indicating a close relationship between the two works as regards both place and time of manufacture. It is true that the carver of Probianus' diptych, while taking over the classical ornament of the Nicomachi relief, did not similarly emulate the latter's 'wet drapery' style. The heavy official costumes worn by all his figures did not favour this particular revival element. It is true also that his figures are squatter in proportion and lack the harmoniously balanced poses of the priestesses. But their organic and well-articulated build, their strong bodily presences, their easy, natural movements and the soft, sinuous flow of their garments betray the hand of an artist determined to apply to the official imagery of the period traditional Graeco-Roman standards for the rendering of the human form.

What is significant above all is the artist's evident concern to place his figures in a plausible spatial ambient. To do this within the elongated format of the diptych he has even jeopardized its compositional unity by closing off the lower zone in a complete frame of its own. While thus incongruously dividing the acclaiming figures from the object of their acclamation, he has gained for the principal group a naturally proportioned panel which an architectural setting, designed in perspective, turns into a plausible view of an interior. Though far too small in scale for the figures inhabiting it, it is a remarkably life-like, even intimate, setting foreshadowing the box-like chambers of fifteenth-century painting. No exact antecedent for such a use of architectural perspective has yet been found in ancient art, but the elements are clearly those developed in Roman painting in the first century A.D.[38] Not to compete with this effect in the lower zone and yet to provide a spatial setting for the figures in that zone also, the artist has given them – again somewhat incongruously – a strip of outdoor terrain to stand on. The incongruity of this locale is enhanced by the ornate table he has placed between the figures, though in its foreshortened view the table also gives the composition a further spatial accent.

Other official ivories created during this period do not show the kind of tangible link with a workshop involved in the pagan revival that we find in

Probianus' diptych, but are nevertheless imbued with the spirit of that revival. Probus, a member of the great family of the Anicii, became consul in A.D.406, more than a decade after the pagan reaction had collapsed as a political movement. His diptych at Aosta (fig. 70)[39] portrays on both its leaves his sovereign, the West Roman emperor Honorius, in the classical guise of the cuirassed *imperator* familiar from Roman statuary. Indeed, one wonders whether the diptych was meant to represent not the actual person of the emperor but his statue, paralleling in this respect the Asclepius diptych in Liverpool (fig. 65), which it recalls also in its composition. But there is at the same time a definite suggestion of a locale as the massive, powerfully modelled figure moves forward from the plane of the relief.

The tall, narrow format of these diptychs lent itself well to this kind of statuesque presentation. The panel here assumed the role of a niche or a gateway with strongly spatial implications. Multifigured reliefs, on the other hand, posed a more difficult problem, witness the diptych of Probianus. Two other official diptychs (or rather, single surviving leaves of diptychs) of this period – one in Brescia, the other in Liverpool – are interesting in their attempt to inject into complex figure compositions a modicum of spatial illusion (figs. 68, 69).[40] They introduce a subject that was to be represented many times throughout the period during which these diptychs were in vogue, namely, a consul or other high dignitary presiding over circus or amphitheatre games of which he was the donor. The Brescia leaf is inscribed with the name of the Lampadii and its lost companion leaf bore that of the Rufii.[41] Once again we are in the sphere of the Roman senatorial nobility. With his smooth, carefully rounded face and his regular features, the dignitary, here shown seated in his loge between two lesser officials, recalls the portrayals both of Probianus on the Berlin diptych and of Honorius on that in Aosta, although a certain hardening of line may indicate yet another atelier or possibly a slightly later date. But what is especially noteworthy is the artist's success in suggesting actual physical relationships in space within the awkward format of the panel and despite his evident concern to make the donor of the games the centre and focus of the whole composition. He has not made use of a perspective architectural setting in the manner of the Probianus relief, but he has also avoided splitting the scene into two separate halves. Although he has combined an eye-level view of the official party sitting in its box behind an ornate parapet with a bird's-eye view of the chariot race in progress below, visually the two parts form a unit. There is, indeed, a suggestion that the box overhangs the arena.

The panel in Liverpool is clearly related. Here the event in the arena is a stag hunt whose episodes are arranged in a frankly abstract manner in five superposed registers. There are, in fact, other ivory reliefs of the same general period composed entirely in terms of such abstract two-dimensional designs. In particular, the composition of the circus scene in the Liverpool panel closely recalls that of a diptych with *venatio* scenes in Leningrad, which cannot with certainty be identified as an official diptych (since it lacks a representation of a presiding dignitary) and which displays on both its halves identical groups of men and animals neatly laid out in a vertical pattern (fig. 71).[42] The carver of the Liverpool panel must have been familiar with this type of composition. But he transmuted it, 'bent' it, as it were, to inject it with a measure of spatial plausibility. Half-open doors at the edges of the arena, with attendants emerging from them, are strongly suggestive of depth. As for the official spectators, who here, as in the diptych of the Lampadii, occupy the top part of the panel, they recede into what may be realistically considered as background. They are much smaller in scale than their counterparts on the Brescia relief; credibility is not strained by making the principal figure larger than the two companions; and, especially noteworthy, the lower edge of their box is slightly but effectively overlapped by the curved rim of the arena. This interest in natural spatial relationships goes together with a particularly soft and delicate manner of modelling and, once again, the use of a classical *kymation* as a frame ornament. Clearly the aesthetic ideals propagated by the patrons of the pagan revival have helped to shape such works.

That movement thus stands revealed in some of its wider repercussions. As I have said, scholars have at times lumped together the art to which it gave rise with the products of Constantinopolitan court art of the same period, including both under the heading 'Theodosian Renaissance'. From an ideological point of view this is misleading since the Western development is bound up with an active and militant opposition to Theodosius' anti-pagan policies. Nor is there much evidence of actual contacts between the Eastern and Western workshops concerned. Occasionally – in the facial type of the emperor on the diptych of Probus or in the extraordinary softness and delicacy of carving of the *venatio* relief in Liverpool – one may suspect a direct influence of East Roman court art. But on the whole the Western works we have discussed do not exhibit the specific style features we found to be characteristic of that art. At their core lies a separate initiative, distinct in patronage and intent, in subject and form.

There is, however, another factor common to the two movements, and it is an important one. Both carried over into the production of Christian imagery as well.

We have encountered the typical physiognomies of persons and dignitaries at Theodosius' court. Artists at Constantinople in the 380s and 390s A.D., when called upon to depict scenes from the Gospels, cast their image of Christ in the same mould. On a fragmentary marble relief at Dumbarton Oaks representing the Healing of the Blind Man (fig. 72), Christ unmistakably bears the same characteristic facial features (cf. figs. 73, 74). Nor is the influence of court art upon this work confined to the countenance of the Saviour. The entire event assumes the character of a court ceremony, with the afflicted man appearing in the role of a suppliant, the apostle accompanying Christ in that of a standard-bearer (the cross being the insignia of Christ's power), and Christ himself as the ruler performing his act of grace with sovereign ease.[43]

Infiltration of elements from imperial art into Christian contexts was a process which had been going on continuously throughout the fourth century. A major factor, particularly in the iconographic development of Christian art during that period, it reflects powerful and important ideological trends intimately connected with the Christianization of the state.[44] The process reached a climax in the Theodosian period. What we find in this period – and the Dumbarton Oaks relief exemplifies this very well – is a complete recasting of Christian subjects in terms of contemporary court art, undoubtedly at the hands of artists who actually worked for the court. As a result – and this is the aspect which specifically concerns us – Christian art in and around Constantinople became deeply imbued with the spirit and the forms of the 'Theodosian Renaissance'. Suffice it to cite one other monument which quintessentially embodies traditional values of formal purity and perfection thus powerfully injected into Christian imagery, namely, a small marble sarcophagus found in Constantinople some fifty years ago and generally thought to have been made for a prince of the Theodosian house (fig. 75).[45]

To observe the Western counterpart of this Christian classicism, we turn once more to small reliefs in ivory. A famous panel in the Bavarian National Museum in Munich depicts in similarly pure, clean forms and carefully elaborated detail the Marys' Visit to the Tomb and Christ's Ascension (fig. 76).[46] This remarkable work is not, however, simply an offshoot of Constantinopolitan court art. The direct antecedents of the figures of the Holy Women who here approach with measured step and restrained pathos the Lord's sepulchre are figures such as the priestesses on the ivory diptych of the Nicomachi and Symmachi (fig. 63). The whole elegiac atmosphere of this relief, with the hushed action taking place around an artfully wrought tempietto in some sacred grove, is inspired by those products of nostalgic paganism. The approximation would be closer still had not the innate Christian urge to pack the image with content resulted in a second and more dramatic scene being put into what should ideally have remained open and clear background space. This insertion negates the unity of scale and prevents the mood of idyllic calm which the setting engenders from being developed fully. But the ancestry of the work is unmistakable. The Holy Women's Visit to the Tomb is imbued with a spirit reminiscent of a Greek tomb relief. Once again we are led to ask what role this associative element played in the mind of the artist and in that of his patron. Was it the subject which prompted (or, at any rate, facilitated) the use of such emphatically pagan forms? Or was it, on the contrary, a desire to create a Christian equivalent to classical imagery in an elegiac mood which determined the choice of subject? This we cannot know. But there is, indeed, a second ivory relief of similar date and origin which depicts the same event (fig. 77),[47] and this panel bears evidence of having actually been carved in the same atelier which produced the diptych with the priestesses. Surrounding the door of Christ's tomb there appears once more the characteristic palmette ornament which we found on the frame of that diptych and also on that of the diptych of Probianus, the Roman official; as in the case of the latter work, the scene has been bisected quite irrationally so as to create two approximately square panel pictures, each with its own separate setting. It is evident that one and the same workshop served impartially the causes of pagan reaction, image-conscious officialdom and, we may now add, Christian devotion; in all three contexts it was apt to use the same formal and ornamental devices.

There is rich irony in the thought that it was the Nicomachi, Symmachi and other like-minded patrons who thus helped to bring about a massive transfer of pure classical forms into Christian art. They had fostered these forms – and the values underlying them – as part of their defence of the pagan religion and the old way of life. In effect they helped to set a new course for the art of their adversaries. The obvious explanation is that there was a large and important element on the Christian side eager to take up the challenge. By the late fourth century much of the Christian patronage of art in Rome and other Italian centres came from persons belonging to the same social stratum and nurturing the same aesthetic values as the die-hard defenders of the old faith. The great silver casket from the Esquiline Treasure in the British Museum may serve to illustrate the point. A bridal gift for Projecta – a member of another prominent and wealthy Roman family – it displays on its lid a very classical Venus on a seashell surrounded by Tritons and Nereids, while the accompanying inscription expresses a pious Christian sentiment (fig. 79).[48] When persons of such background and social rank commissioned work that was Christian not only in verbal expression but in subject matter as well, they naturally saw to it that the same artistic standards were maintained. The best way to ensure this was to employ the very same artists who were working for their peers in the opposite camp.

What we see happening here in the realm of the visual arts has an exact parallel in literature. It is sufficient to cite the name of St Ambrose, the great Bishop of Milan, who was also a scion of a prominent family. Although in theory he rejected artfulness in writing, the stylistic quality of his own literary production was of great concern to him. His models were classical writers such as Cicero, Livy, Tacitus, Sallust and Virgil, a roster which includes some of the very same authors whose texts his pagan opponents strove to keep alive and incorrupt by a systematic enterprise of editing and commenting.[49] It is exactly the same relationship as that between the pagan and Christian ivory diptychs of the period.

However, the parallel between art and literature goes further. It is a well-known fact that the literary and philological activities sponsored by the last defenders of paganism proved enormously important not only for contemporary Christian writing but also for passing on good texts of the classics to the Western Middle Ages.[50] In the same way, the pagan revival in art fostered by the Symmachi and their like-minded friends not only rubbed off on Christian work of the same age but also set standards and models of a classically oriented Christian art for centuries to come. In particular the Carolingian and to some extent also the Ottonian Renaissance were to draw on works of this period for inspiration and emulation. For instance, a Carolingian ivory in Liverpool reproduces with remarkable fidelity the scene of the Holy Women's Visit to the Tomb from the Munich ivory (figs. 76, 78).[51] A rich element of humanism was thus injected into the mainstream of medieval art. There are few examples in history that illustrate so dramatically what far-reaching effects a struggle for a lost cause may have. Foredoomed though it was, the last-ditch stand of the defenders of paganism in Italy probably had an even greater overall impact on medieval civilization than the 'Renaissance' sponsored by the court of Theodosius in the East.

To conclude this discussion of how Christian art in the West reflects the retrospective attitude of the late fourth century, I shall turn finally to a work of monumental art, namely, the mosaic in the Church of S.Pudenziana in Rome (fig. 80), probably of the period of Pope Innocent I (A.D.402–17). The earliest of the great Christian apse compositions to have survived (albeit as a ruin only), the mosaic can serve well both to substantiate and to broaden our view of the dominant stylistic trends of the period, formed so far on the basis of works of the minor arts.[52]

Mosaic is a medium which by this time had risen to special prominence and which was to play a key role for many centuries to come. To rehearse its earlier history even in outline would take us too far afield. It is enough to say that the emergence of glass mosaic as a principal form of decoration for walls and vaults was an outcome of an aesthetic revolution in architecture which was essentially a counterpart to the great upheaval in the pictorial arts discussed in the previous chapter, although it had begun as far back as the early imperial period. By the fourth century it had long since become the wall's primary role to delimit and define a hollow interior space rather than to function as an articulated bodily entity in its own right.[53] Thus three-dimensional membering and modelling of surfaces gave way increasingly to sheathing with polychrome and highly polished materials. The third and fourth centuries were a period of experimentation with different kinds of pictorial decoration that would leave the envelope of the interior space smooth and inviolate; be completely at one with it physically and aesthetically; and at the same time enhance its effect by the glitter and the richness of the materials employed. From these experiments mosaic emerged victorious being much the most supple and flexible of incrustation media.

In S.Pudenziana it was used in an illusionistic spirit reminiscent of Roman wall decorations of a much earlier period. A magnificent architectural vista, now sadly curtailed at either side, opens out before the beholder and serves as a dramatic setting for Christ enthroned in imperial splendour amidst his apostles. The two groups of disciples, truncated below and drastically restored (particularly on the right), can no longer be fully visualized in their compositional relationship either to the central figure or to the setting. What is clear is that although the apostles overlap one another – thus implying some recession into depth – they actually form (or formed) a solid front, with the ascending lines of their heads leading up to the majestic figure of Christ in the central axis.[54] But while the protagonists are (or were) thus displayed in an essentially two-dimensional triangular pattern, there is – an effect which can still be fully perceived today – a succession of receding planes behind them. Two female figures – generally interpreted as personifications of the Church of the Jews and the Church of the Gentiles – stand behind the seated apostles and by their position create a suggestion of an interval of open space separating the solemn assembly from the semicircular portico enclosing them. The portico in turn serves as a screen behind which we see the roofs and upper parts of distant buildings against a magnificent evening sky, from whose multi-coloured clouds the four winged beings of the Apocalypse emerge. The hill of Golgotha with its huge jewelled cross rising immediately behind the portico forms yet another, intermediate, plane.

One must not overstate the amount of realism that has been achieved in the depiction of space. There is no 'aerial perspective', no suggestion of haze enveloping the more distant figures and objects. Nor is there consistency of scale. The distant cross and the even more distant apparitions in heaven, being enormously large, dwarf the foreground group and seem to tower above it rather than recede behind it. The whole surface is cluttered and crowded. Nevertheless, the fact remains that the artist has provided his figures with a coherent spatial setting and that he has produced a highly dramatic effect by a succession of planes staged in depth. Spatial illusion gains further from the fact that the conch in which the mosaic is placed is not the usual quarter-sphere but a largely vertical expanse of wall curving forward only near the top.[55] As a result, the main group of figures is physically in an upright position and there is a smooth transition from the beholder's space to the space they inhabit, a space which with its curved architectural scenery echoes and underscores the real curvature of the apse. The sanctuary seems to be opening out, affording a vision of Christ's heavenly court.

The devices used by the artist are those developed in late Hellenistic and early imperial art. Vistas of the tops of distant buildings, their lower halves concealed by screen walls, are familiar background scenery in reliefs of that period and a key element in the so-called Second Pompeian Style of wall painting.[56] Elaborate architectural backdrops of various kinds were frequently used in official art of the first and second centuries A.D. to enhance the solemnity of imperial appearances.[57] Often these settings denote specific locales; and the same may be true of the scenery of the mosaic of S.Pudenziana, whose designer may have incorporated features of contemporary Jerusalem in the view of the heavenly city in which Christ holds council.[58] But in the art of the third and fourth centuries such topographic references had become more and more sparse and incoherent, and so far as assemblies of Christ and his apostles are concerned – a theme frequently depicted in catacomb paintings of the fourth century – there is no previous example which shows this scene placed against so elaborate a backdrop. Clearly our designer was harking back to the art of a much earlier age. Even in Hellenistic and early imperial art, however, his creation has no precise antecedent.[59] Like the designer of the exactly contemporary diptych of Probianus, but on a far more grandiose scale, he has operated freely with the spatial devices of that earlier period to create for a figure of authority a setting that makes the triumphant presence highly dramatic and palpably real.

The diptych of Probianus, so we have seen, has a tangible connection with the pagan revival in Rome. It was carved in a workshop which served that cause.

For our mosaic there is no such concrete link, and it would be rash to claim that it was made under the direct influence of that movement. Its Roman affiliation is not in doubt.[60] But we must remember that in Rome, as elsewhere, there had been other revival efforts in the course of the fourth century. The art of the pagan reaction is merely the culmination, the quintessential expression of much broader trends; while it had clear and demonstrable repercussions also in Christian art, in the case of a work such as the S.Pudenziana mosaic one can speak only in general terms of a response to the challenge that had been posed, a taking up of stimuli that had been received.[61]

In our survey of the art of the fourth century we have found a number of distinct impulses and initiatives in different places and at different times. Many were linked to some particular clientele and often they were concentrated in particular crafts. Undoubtedly, however, these impulses influenced one another and to some extent were sparked by or gained momentum from each other. It is surely remarkable that in different ways they all involve a return to classical formal standards. A more thorough investigation of fourth-century art would not substantially change this picture. There is a chain reaction, a snowballing effect. To unravel at this distance the precise interplay of forces which produced this effect is impossible, but its reality is undeniable. The whole is larger than the sum of its parts. If abstraction and anticlassicism were the keynote of the art of the third century, regeneration was the keynote of the art of the fourth. It was, let it be recalled once more, a period in which the classical heritage reasserted itself with equal force in the world of thought and letters, not only in the writings of professional pagans like Libanius and Julian, Symmachus and Macrobius, but also in those of Gregory, Bishop of Nyssa, and Ambrose, Bishop of Milan.

CHAPTER THREE

Fifth-Century Conflicts – 1

The fourth century confronted us with a variety of distinct artistic initiatives and impulses in different places and different media. This is even more true of the fifth. One of the striking characteristics of Mediterranean art of this century is a greatly intensified regional diversification. It was a natural corollary of strongly centrifugal processes in the political, cultural and religious spheres. With the empire divided between the two sons of Theodosius I, its Eastern and Western halves had been set irrevocably on separate courses. The West sustained the shocks of successive Germanic invasions and its entire political fabric was disrupted in the process. The East, while maintaining its essential political unity, developed deep religious cleavages over the question of the divine and the human nature in Christ, cleavages which brought to the fore particularist tendencies in countries such as Egypt and Syria.

The artistic heritage of the period, fragmentary as it is, concretely reflects this diversity. In Italy, for instance, distinct developments can be traced in Ravenna – successively the refuge of the Western imperial court and the seat of the Germanic kings of Italy – and in Rome, where the military and political upheavals left only the papacy intact as an effective power. In the East a number of countries evolved during this period regional idioms of their own, the most characteristic being the so-called Coptic style in Egypt. Diversity is accentuated further by the fact that many of the developments seem to be once again conditioned by particular crafts or associated with particular categories of objects.

At first sight the variety is indeed bewildering, and in attempting to give a unified account of the fifth century as a whole the art historian runs an exceptionally grave risk of oversimplifying matters. The very fact of fragmentation must be counted among the primary characteristics of the period. Yet as one surveys the different regions and the different crafts, common traits, or at any rate common symptoms, do emerge. Everywhere in one way or another the classical tradition which had so strongly reasserted itself in the course of the fourth century was subjected to new challenges. It was confronted with opposing tendencies of various kinds that brought about subtle and slow modifications in some instances, drastic and radical changes in others. This element

[45]

of conflict runs through all the new artistic departures of the century. In the aggregate they amount to a second major step in the transformation of the Graeco-Roman heritage, comparable to and perhaps to some extent inspired by that which had taken place in the third.[1] The very diversity of fifth-century developments makes this common basic tendency strikingly real and apparent. But it also raises in singularly acute form the problem of how such period trends should be explained and interpreted.

Our approach must of necessity be particularly selective when dealing with this period. Let us turn first to ivory reliefs which lend themselves well for an initial glimpse of the new stylistic departures of the fifth century.

The practice of celebrating the assumption of high office with the distribution of elaborately carved diptychs continued throughout this period and, indeed, well into the sixth century. Among surviving examples a fair number relate to known personages and thus provide us with secure chronological guideposts. It is instructive to compare the diptych of Boethius (fig. 81),[2] consul in A.D.487 (and father of a famous son, the author of *De Consolatione Philosophiae*), with examples of the period around the year A.D.400 which we have seen previously. Once again we are in the sphere of the high Roman aristocracy, and in having himself represented as a statuesque figure against an architectural frame Boethius adhered to an old-established type (cf. fig. 70). But the contrast in rendering is startling. On one leaf the consul is shown standing, on the other seated as a donor of games. Neither figure functions in space. Rather, it appears to be affixed to its architectural foil with the head oddly pressed into the entablature. The figure's bulk shuts off any glimpse of a third dimension behind it, and it hardly acts as an autonomous organism. The standing consul's arms and legs hang limply; the seated consul's right hand juts out jerkily and awkwardly – the upper arm seems missing altogether – as he gives the signal for the games with his *mappa*. There is no consistency of proportions just as there is no harmony or rhythm of movement or posture. An enormously large head rests on an underdeveloped bust. Classical standards are firmly rejected also in the manner of carving, which is almost aggressively hard and angular, especially in the rendering of folds reminiscent of the so-called chip carving techniques in sub-antique and Germanic art. With its square jaw, heavy bulk and big staring eyes, the portrait of Boethius seems to take us back to the days of the Tetrarchy. Like those earlier portraits it gives the appearance of having been designed deliberately to project an image of brutal strength.

It should not be inferred, however, that members of the Roman nobility were now – in the years following the final collapse of the Western empire in A.D.476 – suddenly and purposefully turning against the ideal of a refined academic classicism propagated by their forefathers three generations earlier. The loss of that ideal was a gradual process which can be followed in a series of diptychs made for high officials in the West in the intervening period. One can observe how figures lose their firm stance on a plausible base so that increasingly it is the background which provides them with material support. Suggestions of space around and behind them are correspondingly diminished or eliminated entirely. Proportions become ponderous, attitudes stiff and wooden, faces mask-like with big lifeless eyes staring into the void. Rounded relief gives way more and more to sharp incisions and hard schematic lines. While not every official diptych of the period between *c.* A.D.420 and 480 bears witness to every aspect of this development, there is unmistakably an overall progression in the sense indicated (fig. 82).[3]

A corresponding stylistic change can be observed in ivories depicting Christian subjects. The artist who carved a series of scenes from Christ's Passion on four small panels now in the British Museum (fig. 83)[4] – originally in all probability parts of a casket – clearly was rooted in the tradition which in the years around A.D.400 had produced those Christian reliefs of markedly classicizing character discussed in the preceding chapter. Indeed, the time lag vis-à-vis the Munich plaque with the Holy Women and the Ascension (fig. 76) may not be great, and the London pieces must have been made in much the same geographic ambient. Facial types, drapery style, attitudes and gestures are similar, and something of the gentle lyrical mood so characteristic of the Munich ivory also persists. But the figures have become much heavier and as their bulk has increased they have, as it were, consumed and gathered into themselves the space that had enveloped their counterparts in the earlier work. As a result, compositions have become extremely tight and, despite the very high relief, essentially two-dimensional. I would attribute to a slightly later date a group of small reliefs with Gospel scenes divided between the museums of West Berlin and the Louvre (fig. 84).[5] While less crowded, these carvings show a loss of feeling for or interest in the human figure as a smoothly functioning, three-dimensional entity. Not only is the relief here much flatter, but actions and movements tend to be projected on the background plane against which the figures are quite sharply silhouetted. Concern with narrative expressiveness had already operated to the detriment of grace and elegance in the case of some figures in the British Museum panels. On the panels in Berlin and Paris movements are generally jerky and rather mechanical; all action is plain and direct and nothing of lyricism remains. A course was set for a radical stylistic transformation that becomes fully apparent later in the century in the Gospel scenes carved on a pair of book covers in Milan Cathedral (fig. 85).[6]

These scenes combine the crowding of figures in the London panels with the drastic and lively depiction of action on the panels in Berlin and Paris, but now in a generally flat relief. Cursorily drawn, the figures do not project with any force even though many of them overlap their frames. Indeed, it is the framing system of squares, circles and oblongs which predominates. The carvings make a pattern, a foil for the cloisonné metalwork of the Lamb and the cross mounted as principal features in the central panels of the two covers.

All the ivories cited so far were made in the West and presumably in Italy. We cannot with certainty identify the centre or centres that produced them – Rome, Milan and Ravenna all have their claims and their advocates in specific instances[7] – but there is a strong coherence and consistency in the stylistic development to which they bear witness.

Turning to the Eastern Mediterranean, we do not find a similarly coherent sequence of ivory carvings of the fifth century, either official or Christian. Yet a corresponding, though quite distinct, development must have taken place there also. For such a development is presupposed by a remarkable group of diptychs made for Constantinopolitan dignitaries just after the end of the century.

At first sight it is hard to realize that the diptychs of Areobindus,[8] consul in A.D.506, and of Anastasius (figs. 86, 113),[9] consul in A.D.517, perpetuate the old theme of the circus games presided over by the official who has donated them (cf. figs. 68, 69). The curved edge of the arena is still shown, the proceedings within are lively enough, and we even see groups of spectators crowded behind the barrier. But the relationship between this scene and the donor, now an enormously enlarged, full-length figure majestically enthroned in splendid isolation on an elaborate seat, is conceptual only. The beholder is not given the slightest hint as to how the two parts of the composition might relate to one another in real space. The scene in the arena is relegated to a kind of predella. There are, it is true, much earlier precedents for this device. Thus on the base of Theodosius' obelisk (fig. 60) the events of the hippodrome are depicted in small scale in the bottom zone, with a correspondingly lopsided emphasis on the august person (or persons) presiding in the kathisma above. One may cite the precedent of Theodosian court art also for the strictly en face, full-length image of the enthroned potentate (see fig. 57). But granted that such antecedents played their part in shaping the composition of these diptychs, the difference is still enormous. Overloaded with paraphernalia and symbols of triumph and majesty – elaborately carved thrones supported by heraldic lions and adorned with victories and imperial portraits; heavily emblematic sceptres; garland-bearing putti – the relief forms a tight pattern closing off the third dimension entirely. The principal figure with its spherical face, its staring, circular eyes and its stiff and richly ornamented official costume which sheaths the body like armour, itself becomes an emblem and an integral part of this pattern. Compared with the gentle modulations of Theodosian art, the carving, particularly in Anastasius' diptychs, has a harder, more metallic quality.

Clearly the style of these reliefs presupposes a development corresponding to that which we have observed in the West. One finds in the East a similar hardening of forms, elimination of space and depth, creation of a surface pattern coextensive with and supported by the material surface of the panel, and a stiffening and schematization of figures and faces. Compared with their Italian contemporaries the Eastern diptychs display much greater precision, discipline and polish. The consul's physique is presented without undue distortion or imbalance of proportion, devices that helped to make the figure of Boethius the forceful portrayal that it is. But there is in the Eastern diptychs the same – or, indeed, an even greater – concern with a direct and palpable display of power, witness the almost obsessive accumulation of emblems and symbols around the consul's person. By locking his figure and his action firmly into an overall pattern the majesty of his office is given a precise visual expression. The image is made timeless and immutable. The consul's hand is not just raised momentarily to signal the opening of the games but seems to be frozen in this action permanently in token of an absolute and unremitting authority. Content and form appear to be tangibly and specifically correlated.

Might this not be a clue of larger relevance to the drastic stylistic innovations we have observed, a lead that could help us to interpret these innovations in terms of the motivating forces and pressures behind them? It will be best to leave this question in abeyance until we have seen more of the art of the fifth century.

To broaden our view of stylistic developments in this period, I shall turn to mosaics, now the major pictorial medium. It is on the lavishly encrusted walls and vaults of the churches of Ravenna and Rome, Milan and Thessaloniki that the greatest examples of fifth-century image-making survive. But before entering on a discussion of these celebrated monuments (or, at any rate, a selection of them), I want briefly to call attention to their more lowly cousins on pavements. I have said that wall mosaic did not fully come into its own until the fourth century. Floor mosaic, on the other hand, was a much more traditional medium; it was practised extensively in Hellenistic times and had become a ubiquitous form of decoration throughout the Roman world by as early as the first century A.D.[10] Since, in the nature of things, it has had a much better chance of survival (and retrieval through excavation), it permits – within the confines of what is admittedly often a craft rather than an art – a close study of formal developments on a regional basis. Focusing on the Eastern Mediterranean in the fifth century, I want to single out one episode in the history of floor decoration – the emergence of what may be called figure carpets. For in certain respects this phenomenon is not unrelated to developments we have seen in ivory carvings, and it will prove illuminating for the study of wall mosaics to which I shall turn subsequently.

The process in question can be observed most clearly at Antioch on the Orontes thanks to the large number of mosaics which came to light in the extensive excavations carried out on the site of that great Syrian metropolis in the 1930s.[11] The excavation of the nearby city of Apamea, also undertaken in the 1930s and resumed in recent years, promises to provide a welcome supplement to the Antiochene corpus once the pavements, which here too have been found in sizeable numbers, have been fully published and studied.[12] At both sites, and in many places elsewhere in the Near East, a new kind of floor decoration came into vogue in the fifth century. Figure compositions were taken apart, so to speak, and each element was set singly and with even spacing on neutral ground to form a pattern potentially extensible *ad infinitum*. The individual form may – and usually does – retain its three-dimensionality, and both man and beast may be shown in lively action. But their setting is disjointed. Instead of a landscape background, one finds isolated shrubs, trees and parts of terrain interspersed between the figures, and all motifs, regardless of their natural relationship, are more or less equidistant from one another. A splendid floor with hunting scenes, now in the Art Museum at Worcester, Massachusetts, is an outstanding example (fig. 90).[13]

Within the history of Antiochene floor decoration these figure carpets, showing a unified theme spread over large surfaces of varied shape, were an innovation. Traditionally, the normal way of depicting figure subjects – and complex scenes especially – on floors was in the form of *emblemata*, that is to say, simulated panel paintings with figures and objects shown in their natural relationship in settings that suggest depth. Such panels when placed on the floor evidently were meant to make one forget the solidity of the surface they occupied, much in the same way as a simulated vista painted on the wall of a Pompeian house may suggest an open window. But since the surface which is being dissolved is the very ground on which the beholder stands, the effect on him can be startling. Indeed, a deliberate attempt to tease him often seems to be involved. For example, on the floor of a third-century dining-room at

Antioch (figs. 87, 88)[14] an *emblema* is placed in the recess of a simulated niche which further reinforces the *trompe-l'oeil* effect. While the rest of the surface is covered with a geometric repeat pattern that is essentially two-dimensional and congruous with the floor *qua* floor, the *emblema* drastically interrupts this comfortable view. By contrast, on our fifth-century floor the figure composition is coextensive with the entire surface, and that surface, far from being dissembled, has itself become the matrix and carrier of everything that is depicted. The result is a unified design functionally appropriate also in the sense that it offers upright views of figures to the beholder regardless of where he stands or from which side he approaches. When Antiochene designers of earlier periods had composed floors that were meant to be viewed from more than one direction, they had normally done so by placing on them several *emblemata* with different orientations. A mosaic from a villa of the early fourth century (fig. 89)[15] is particularly instructive. While anticipating our fifth-century example in subject matter (through its hunting theme) and also to some extent compositionally (both artists used diagonal dividers, which they borrowed from ceiling decorations, to organize their designs), the earlier floor in effect offers the viewer four separate panel pictures or *emblemata*, each facing in a different direction. Within the Antioch mosaic corpus the figure carpet with its flowing continuity and its extraordinary adaptability to areas of any shape or size stands out as an innovation of the fifth century.

Nor was the phenomenon confined to Antioch. It was, as I have said, a characteristic development in floor decoration of this period all over the Near East. I shall illustrate one other example, roughly contemporary with the hunting floor in Worcester but situated in another region and different in its subject content as well as in its context, which is religious rather than secular. The wings of the transept of a basilica at Tabgha on the shore of the Sea of Galilee, which marks the site of the miracle of the Loaves and Fishes, are adorned with a pair of floor mosaics (fig. 92) depicting – it is not clear with what motivation in reference to the church – the scenery of the Nile.[16] But there is no coherent view or panorama. The component elements – aquatic birds and plants and various buildings, including a nilometer – are taken completely apart and scattered over the pavement. Although they all face in one direction – there are no diagonal dividers introducing different angles as in the Worcester floor – they form an even spread which potentially could be continued endlessly in every direction.

The sources of this new development have been much debated in recent years.[17] The problem can be mentioned here only in passing. A key fact is that the principles of floor design which are embodied in these fifth-century mosaics

have a long history in the Western Mediterranean world. Not that the custom
of adorning the floor with compositions in the form of panel pictures was not
popular also in the West. *Emblemata* abound in pavement mosaics in Italy, in
North Africa, in Gaul, in Spain and in Britain. But the tradition was not as
deeply rooted as it was in the Greek East.[18] In Italy the figure carpet emerged
as an alternative compositional device as early as the second century in the so-
called silhouette mosaics, which show black figures loosely distributed over
expanses – often very large expanses – of white ground. In the third and fourth
centuries similar principles can be seen coming to the fore in the polychrome
pavement decorations of North Africa, products of a prolific and extremely
inventive regional school whose influence abroad is evidenced by the spectacular
mosaics of the great villa complex at Piazza Armerina in Sicily (fig. 6). In this
context it is also interesting to recall certain ivory diptychs of the fourth and
early fifth centuries, now mostly considered Western, which present figures
distributed evenly over a neutral ground (fig. 71).[19] As well as being in some
instances thematically related to the Antioch figure carpets, the diptychs in
question are based on essentially the same compositional principles; they, too,
involve an acceptance of the material surface as a matrix for an even spread of
figure motifs. A case can therefore be made for the proposition that influence
from the West played some role in introducing these principles of composition
to floor mosaics in the East.

It is in pavements of purely ornamental design that one can see the idea of
radical surface acceptance first clearly asserting itself at Antioch. As early as
A.D.387, in the north arm of the great martyrium church of Kaoussie, we find
a very large floor area, which traditionally would be broken up into a sequence
of panels, treated as a unit with a single pattern extending over the entire
surface (fig. 91).[20] In effect, what happened at Antioch (and elsewhere in the
Greek East) in the fifth century was that this carpet concept was applied to
figure compositions and ousted the *emblema*. While the latter had deep roots in
the region's Hellenistic past, the former was essentially foreign to the Greek
tradition. A dramatic conflict between hardy conservatism and radical innovation is being played out before our eyes within a single medium and in a single
important centre in the Eastern Mediterranean world.

This glimpse at the art of the floor mosaicist will stand us in good stead as we
turn to mural mosaic, a medium which from here on, and in all subsequent
chapters, must receive much of our attention. By far the greater number of
decorations in that medium surviving from our period are in the Latin West.
But in discussing these Western works I hope to throw some light on mural

I. Mausoleum of Galla Placidia, Ravenna
North arm with Good Shepherd lunette

A.D.424-50
page 54

II. Church of St George, Thessaloniki
Detail of dome mosaic with Sts Onesiphorus and Porphyrius

Fifth century
page 57

mosaic in the Greek East as well, and I shall introduce extant Eastern monuments at appropriate points.

Leaving for the next chapter the one major ensemble of the fifth century that has survived in Rome, I propose to concentrate primarily on Ravenna. It is at Ravenna only that a consecutive series of fifth- and early sixth-century buildings with mosaic decorations can still be seen today. But these decorations, far from being products of a closed regional school, reflect much broader developments. Ravenna was a city without an important cultural or artistic tradition which suddenly, at the beginning of the fifth century, had thrust upon it the role of a capital. We know nothing about the origin and schooling of the generations of mosaicists who worked there for a succession of powerful patrons both lay and ecclesiastic. It is one of the basic uncertainties in the history of fifth- and sixth-century art. The mosaics themselves, however, suggest a variety of foreign affiliations and relationships, as we shall have occasion to see. On the other hand, continuity is by no means lacking in the Ravenna production. There are some quite obvious links between successive works. Thus by focusing on Ravenna I shall be able to trace an inner development of some consistency and at the same time sketch out a broader picture of which that development is a part.

We enter first the so-called Mausoleum of Galla Placidia (figs. 93ff.),[21] built as an annex chapel of the Basilica of the Holy Cross, which no longer exists in its original form. The basilica is said to have been erected by Galla Placidia, a daughter of Theodosius I and empress in the West from A.D.424 to 450; and although the chapel was almost certainly not her burial chamber, there is good reason to believe that it was built and decorated during her reign.[22] It is the earliest interior anywhere to have preserved its mural mosaics intact.

In approaching this exquisite ensemble our observations on floor mosaics will at once prove helpful and relevant. For basic to the entire design is a clear distinction and interplay between the two-dimensional and the three-dimensional, between surface acceptance and surface denial such as we found was characteristic of pavement decorations adhering to the *emblema* tradition.

There is indeed one element in the Ravenna interior which can only be described as a true *emblema*. I refer to the famous representation of the Good Shepherd in the lunette over the entrance door (fig. 94). Despite its heavily symbolic message – the figure's royal garb, halo and cross sceptre make it evident at first glance that this is no ordinary guardian of sheep – the picture preserves much of the character of a bucolic scene in the Hellenistic tradition. The rocky landscape, it is true, is made up of conventional motifs. But it is not just a backdrop. The shepherd really appears to be seated *in* it and responds to the spaciousness of the setting with a complicated torsion of arms and legs. Although in the placing of the six sheep heraldic symmetry is only barely avoided, the mosaic as a whole, with its rather low horizon and its trees and rocks outlined against a light blue 'sky', convincingly suggests an airy space receding into indefinite distance. The impression is powerfully reinforced by the threshold or step of cleft rocks in the foreground, an old device of late Hellenistic and Roman panel painters[23] which emphatically places the scene beyond the frame and at the same time strengthens the illusion of a horizontal floor beneath the figure.

In its successful simulation of a plausible locale, the picture calls to mind the apse mosaic of S.Pudenziana (fig. 80) and other works of the turn of the century (cf. fig. 67). Made about a generation later, the Ravenna mosaic still bespeaks a strong interest in creating an illusion of space receding into depth, and once again the artist achieves his purpose with the help of devices borrowed from a much earlier age. Undeniably this is a work still in the 'Renaissance' spirit of the late fourth century. But there is no tangible relationship with S.Pudenziana. The stylistic rendering of our shepherd has nothing in common with that of the few figures in the Roman mosaic which have preserved their original appearance; and it is a far cry from the grandiose vista opening out in that earlier apse to the intimacy of this pastoral idyll, so clearly suggestive of an easel painting. As in the pavements with *emblemata* (figs. 87, 88), the illusion of being afforded a view well beyond the solid surface is reinforced by the fact that in the area surrounding the panel the surface is vigorously affirmed. What is admittedly a trick photograph showing the mosaic in its setting brings out the point (pl.I). Taken with a wide angle lens, it allows a full view both of the Shepherd lunette and of the lovely star pattern on blue ground that covers the adjoining barrel vault over the entrance arm of the cruciform chapel. The pattern is purely two-dimensional – it is, in fact, borrowed from textiles and more specifically from woven silks of exotic origin[24] – and the effect is that of a sumptuous tent cover with a view into open space at the end. By the very contrast of its rendering the vault helps to dissolve for the viewer's eye the materiality of the lunette.

The interplay of surface-denying and surface-accepting elements pervades the entire ensemble, and it does so with a degree of sophistication that goes well beyond anything known in pavements. Correlated throughout with the component parts of the architecture, it systematically and rhythmically sets off these parts against one another and powerfully underlines the structural organization of the interior. In particular, the contrast between two-dimensional and three-dimensional forms is used to set off covers or roofings of individual compartments against their vertical enclosure walls. To a greater or lesser degree the former are affirmed in their reality while the latter are dissembled. The openness of the vista effected by the Good Shepherd mosaic is not matched by the composition in the lunette of the opposite cross arm depicting St Lawrence (figs. 93, 95). A window in the centre of the panel interferes with a unified illusion of depth. Nevertheless, the two objects with which St Lawrence shares the space – an open bookcase with the four Gospels displayed on its shelves and the grate of his martyrdom, both shown in strong foreshortening – create decidedly three-dimensional accents. These objects (which together with the saint himself make up a sort of rebus spelling out his role of martyr both in the sense of witness and of victim) give the impression of being displayed on some open stage. St Lawrence, book in hand and shouldering a cross, is hurriedly entering from the right to fulfil his mission. His image, like that of the Shepherd, is situational and perceived as lying beyond the frame, while overhead the same star pattern is spread out as in the barrel vault opposite.

The lunettes in the other two cross arms (fig. 97) are not opened up in the same way. Occupied by identical compositions of two stags on either side of a pool of water – recitations, as it were, from the famous verses of Psalm 42 – they are clearly subordinate to the Good Shepherd and St Lawrence mosaics, which they help to set off by their more heraldic design. Depth here is screened out by the tracery of the rinceau patterns in which the stags are entwined. While thus leading the eye on to the decorations of the adjoining barrel vaults, the stag lunettes are, however, still in decided contrast to the mosaics in these vaults. The animals, placed on green strips of terrain against blue ground, are fully modelled, and so is the foliage surrounding them. By contrast the equally rich rinceau patterns which adorn the barrel vaults – and even the four figures of apostles or prophets worked into these patterns – are rendered entirely as gold silhouettes, fully at one with the surfaces which bear them.

Once more, and most effectively, three-dimensional form is played off against an essentially two-dimensional design on the walls and ceiling of the upper zone (fig. 98). Here, in the central square, pairs of apostles stand in the four lunettes acclaiming the cross which appears in the centre of the star-spangled vault above them. Visually these figures correspond to those in the lunettes of the lower zone rather than to the silhouette figures in the barrel vaults just mentioned (even though iconographically they may relate to the latter). And, like the Good Shepherd and St Lawrence, they have a real stage on which to move and act (fig. 97). From a dark blue ground there mysteriously emerge strange pedestals for each pair to stand on. Rendered in shades of green, these platforms suggest meadows; but at the same time they are emphatic block shapes receding into depth, while above the apostles' heads shell motifs in strong foreshortening similarly help to define for the figures a plausible stage. By contrast the celestial vision in the vault above them – cross, stars, and, in the corners, apocalyptic symbols – is once again rendered as a mono-chrome gold pattern on blue ground.

There is thus a remarkable consistency in this decoration. Walls are dis-sembled to a greater or lesser degree while ceilings are aesthetically accepted as ceilings, even when they signify the starry sky. If we extended our analysis to the decoration of the framing arches that constitute the armature for both these elements, we would find that here the same rationality does not prevail. Some of the seemingly or actually load-bearing members are decorated with strongly three-dimensional motifs which in effect dissolve their physical substance. The twisted ribbon ornament on the arches supporting the central vault is particularly interesting in this respect. Here classical rules of structural logic seem to be deliberately perverted. But the rhythm of the basic design is classical (or, more precisely, Hellenistic) and, one may suspect, specifically indebted to a tradition that belonged to the Eastern Mediterranean world. It is in the painted decoration of a second-century tomb chamber at Palmyra that we find a lunette similarly set off against the adjoining barrel vault in terms of surface denial versus surface acceptance (fig. 96).[25] In this context let us also recall once more our observations on floor mosaics, for we found that the *emblema* concept – so crucial to the design of the Ravenna decoration – had been adhered to in that medium far longer and far more tenaciously in the Greek East than in the Latin West. In any case, whatever its precise geographic roots, the art of the chapel of Galla Placidia harks back to the Hellenistic past.

At this point, before continuing with the Ravenna series, it is well to turn to the Eastern Mediterranean region itself and consider the one major mosaic decoration of the fifth century which has survived, if only in a fragmentary condition, in that area. I refer to the mosaics that were placed in the dome of the great rotunda of the imperial palace at Thessaloniki when that structure, later dedicated to St George, was first converted into a church, probably in the decades just before A.D.450 (pl.II; figs. 99–101).[26] Although the Thessalonikan work has no direct relationship at all to that in the chapel of Galla Placidia, it exhibits a similarly conservative spirit, as will be seen presently. It will also provide a perspective for some of the other Ravenna interiors yet to be dis-cussed.

The scale here is vast – the clear diameter of the dome is approximately 24 m. – and, judging by what remains, the quality of the mosaic work was superb. To visualize the composition in its entirety requires an effort of the imagination, but it was clearly of a sumptuousness unequalled in mosaic decorations of the period and unsurpassed at any time. The basic theme was not entirely dissimilar to that which forms the core of Galla Placidia's decoration. Again a heavenly apparition at the summit was being received by a group of acclaiming figures in the zone below. But it was Christ himself who appeared in the centre of the Thessalonikan dome, and he was standing in an elaborately framed medallion carried by four flying angels (fig. 100). Of the figures receiving him, only some of the feet and the lower hems of some white garments remain. It was a large chorus – there must have been at least twenty-four figures standing in varying poses on light green ground – but we do not know who they were. What chiefly remains is the third and lowest zone – a magnificent golden band almost 8 m. wide, framed by a simulated entablature above and a simulated console frieze below and divided into eight panels of which seven are more or less preserved. Each of these panels is occupied by fanciful architectural scenery reminiscent of stage sets with either two or three figures of saints standing in front of it in an orant pose (pl.II). Because the identity of the figures in the second zone is lost, the overall theme of the composition remains in doubt. It has been persuasively argued, however, that the subject was Christ's Second Coming.[27]

There are precedents going back as far as the Hellenistic period for the decoration of a dome or dome-like vault or ceiling being devised as a sequence of concentric rings or bands; it is particularly noteworthy that the interpretation of the outer or lowest band as a kind of wainscoting or dado supported and crowned by simulated friezes and cornices is likewise of Hellenistic origin.[28] It is quite clear – and extremely important – that in the Thessalonikan dome the lowest band was indeed meant to suggest such a wainscoting. The architectural backdrops in each panel, for all their perspective renderings, do not really negate this effect. To depict these dream buildings so largely in gold on a golden background was a stroke of genius. They thus appear diaphanous, insubstantial and of a truly otherworldly richness appropriate to their role as 'the celestial palaces of Christ's athletes'.[29] At the same time they leave the surface they adorn basically intact and still able plausibly to support and be supported by the structural members that frame them. The saints themselves, all shown *en face* and with their bodies concealed behind large, solid expanses of plain cloaks, add to, rather than detract from, the wall-like effect of the entire zone.

Above the entablature, however, there was a change of scene and pace. A continuous ground, whose light green colour implies natural open terrain,

provided a stage for figures which, judging by the position of their feet, displayed a certain amount of movement. At least some of them must have been
turning in space; and, unlike the static and frontally placed martyrs below,
they must as a group have been in active contact with the great apparition of
the triumphant Christ being borne aloft in the summit of the dome. What
remains of the background in the area immediately surrounding the central
medallion is gold once more, and we do not know at what level and by what
means the change from the natural terrain colour to the golden ground was
effected.[30] But the zone as a whole was clearly in some contrast to the lower one.
While the latter had connotations of an enclosure wall, the former must have
suggested open space, affording a view of heaven itself. To be sure, this was not
illusionism in the sense of later European art. It is a far cry from here to
Mantegna's painted 'dome' at Mantua or the *trompe l'oeil* effects of baroque
ceilings in which 'real' sky is seen opening above a simulated architecture that
literally continues the actual architecture of the wall below. But unquestionably
the design of this dome decoration was rooted in a tradition going back to the
first century B.C., whereby the upper zone of a wall was made to suggest open
space above a closed zone of simulated wainscoting.[31] To the extent to which
this concept was realized here, the dome was made to appear as something
other than itself. The integrity of its material surface was visually dissembled
as, in their own different ways, the apse of S.Pudenziana and the lunettes of
the chapel of Galla Placidia had had their material solidity dissembled. In the
rendering of the heads of some of the saints (fig. 101) the forces of geometric
abstraction which throughout the Mediterranean area became increasingly
dominant in the course of the fifth century clearly assert themselves. But in its
basic concept the decoration of the Thessalonikan dome is still on the side of
Hellenistic make-believe.

Returning to Ravenna, we enter next the so-called Baptistery of the Orthodox
(pl.III; figs. 102, 103), an octagonal structure built as a baptistery for the
Cathedral towards the end of the fourth century and adorned with mosaics by
Bishop Neon not long after the middle of the fifth.[32] Neon's decoration was part
of a thorough remodelling of the baptistery whereby its original wooden roof
was replaced by a dome. The scale here is very much smaller than that of the
Thessalonikan dome; but to view Neon's lavish decoration with the latter in
mind is highly instructive.

No doubt the design of the Ravennate dome mosaic is also based on the
concept of two wide concentric bands around a central medallion in the apex,
with the outer or lower band presenting a relatively solid 'façade' and the
inner or upper band opening out into a distant airy space. Here, too, floral

candelabra divide the outer band into eight compartments, and here, too, these compartments are filled with fanciful architectural scenery, although the buildings are single-storeyed and do not serve as backdrops for human figures. The inner band shows dark blue 'sky' above a continuous strip of terrain comparable to that which appears in a corresponding position in the Thessalonikan dome; and here again, this open landscape serves as a stage for figures in lively movement – in this instance crown-bearing apostles in two files led by Peter and Paul respectively. But unlike the wreath of active figures in Thessaloniki, which may be presumed to have been in physical and emotional rapport with the heavenly apparition in the centre, this circular procession of apostles, for all its dynamic effect, is self-contained and without an evident goal or objective. The scene of Christ's Baptism in the central medallion, while appropriate enough for the location, is quite separate.

Thus the composition lacks the dramatic unity which the Thessalonikan dome mosaic undoubtedly possessed. By the same token, the visual effect of a vista opening out above a closed architectural band, while definitely present also at Ravenna, is far from being clear and unambiguous. Although the eight architectural views which make up the outer band of the baptistery dome suggest unearthly and celestial mansions as do their counterparts in Thessaloniki, compared with those gold-on-gold fantasies they give an impression of much greater solidity. On the diagonal axes the interiors of four sanctuaries are depicted, each with an altar-table displaying one of the four Gospels. The buildings on the principal axes, on the other hand, which serve as settings for jewelled thrones bearing the imperial insignia of Christ's universal rule, take the form of open garden pavilions and behind these we glimpse dark blue sky. Thus in these latter compartments at least the contrast with the inner zone is in effect negated. It is negated further by the fact that the partitioning with floral candelabra here extends to the inner zone as well. Since the procession of apostles necessitated twelve of these floral devices, their axes could not be made to coincide with those of the candelabra in the lower zone, axes which in turn were determined by the octagonal shape of the building. But despite this disjunction, it is evident that a totally different scheme of dome decoration has intervened here, a scheme based on radial partitions rather than concentric bands. This scheme has its own (predominantly Western) tradition, represented, for instance, by the lost mosaic decoration of the mid-fourth century in the dome of S.Costanza in Rome.[33] The influence of this radial design also accounts for the fact that the floral candelabra which divide the eight architectural views of the outer band here extend below that band. They rise from the spandrels beneath and thus connect with the system of vertical supports which articulates the walls of the building. In effect, then, the dome mosaic of the Orthodox Baptistery is the result of a conflation of two quite distinct schemes. [34]

Either scheme was capable of producing an effect of spatial illusion. We have seen how the outer or lower one of two concentric bands, especially when rendered architecturally, could serve as a kind of *repoussoir* for a spatially more open composition in the inner or upper band. Similarly, the spaces between the spokes of a radial composition could be treated in such a way as to provide an illusion of depth. The floral rendering of the spokes could, in fact, make it appear that the dome was a kind of open bower or pergola with the representations in the interstices receding into the distance. Such, indeed, must have been the effect in the dome of S.Costanza. But in the dome of the Orthodox Baptistery, where the two schemes are combined, the spatial implications of both are severely impaired. There is no unified pergola effect because a concentric circle intervenes and the floral supports are discontinuous. On the other hand, the contrast between the outer and the inner band is neutralized to some extent because solid three-dimensional forms and dark blue sky create unduly strong spatial effects in the lower zone, while the golden framework of foliate supports (with a canopy of white draperies conspicuously suspended between them) accentuate foreground rather than depth in the upper zone. Elements of the specific spatial illusions implicit in both basic schemes are clearly present. But they are in conflict, and what finally predominates is the complicated surface pattern resulting from their superposition. The pattern receives strong reinforcement from the rendering of the apostles in the 'free' zone. It is true that they move and turn, but each figure is fitted neatly into a compartment of uniform size and shape (pl.III). Heads are kept relatively small and lower contours expand to conform to these wedgeshaped frames. And, significantly, the apostles introduce no colour accents different from those of their framework, their tunics and mantles being gold and white in an alternating rhythm.

Thus it is a two–dimensional effect, a rich and agitated pattern which prevails over the elements that imply depth and spatial illusion. The equilibrium which had existed in the chapel of Galla Placidia is gone. There is tension and conflict here between the forces of surface denial and surface acceptance, a conflict no less significant for being traceable to the simultaneous employment of two essentially incompatible concepts of dome decoration.

Some fifty years later, in the dome mosaic of Ravenna's Arian Baptistery (fig. 104), [35] the conflict appears resolved. Built by King Theoderic for his Arian Goths, this second baptistery is clearly modelled on the earlier one. But in its mosaics the principle of surface acceptance has carried the day. The iconographic programme is reduced to the scene of Christ's Baptism in the central medallion and the encircling ring of apostles, which now has a focus of its own in a jewelled throne surmounted by a jewelled cross. The third zone has been omitted. But there is a basic stylistic change quite aside from this reduction. The designer has made a clear decision in favour of the concentric scheme of dome decoration. By replacing the floral candelabra between the apostles with free-standing palm trees he has done away with the suggestion of a radiating pergola, and by substituting gold for the dark blue sky in the zone of the apostles he has largely eliminated the spatial implications of the earlier design. It is true that he has retained a strip of green terrain for the apostles and the palm trees to stand on, just as he has retained the river scenery in Christ's Baptism. The feature that dominates overall, however, is the gold ground which both zones share. In effect the entire hemisphere of the dome is seen as a single surface subdivided only by a flat ornamental band which separates the outer ring from the central medallion.

Against this neutral foil the apostles stand almost motionless. The lively rhythm of the earlier procession – generated by the figures themselves and powerfully reinforced by the alternation in the colour scheme of tunics and mantles and, above all, by the strong undulating pattern of the draperies overhead – is gone. What remains is twelve staccato accents in white. The rendering of the figures is not uniform. Peter and Paul, flanking the throne, and the apostle standing next to Paul are distinguished from the rest by the bolder modelling, warmer colouring and more alert expressions of their faces. There evidently was a break in the work after the central medallion, the throne and the first three apostles had been completed. Another team took over to complete the ring. But by comparison with their counterparts in the Orthodox Baptistery, all the apostles are much harder and stiffer. The folds of their draperies are schematic and angular and all forms seem frozen.

The profound stylistic change which this decoration manifests vis-à-vis its model is symptomatic of a broad development in the second half of the fifth century. Leaving Ravenna for a moment, we find at Milan a small mosaic dome of this period whose designer went even further in accepting and accentuating the hemispheric surface as a basis and carrier of his composition, allowing it to make its effect as pure abstract form. Known, interestingly enough, as St Victor in the Golden Sky, the building in question is a memorial chapel for a local saint adjoining the Basilica of St Ambrose.[36] Its dome (fig. 105) is an expanse of gold unrelieved and unarticulated except for the central medallion containing the martyr's bust portrait. Gold here has fully come into its own as the ideal background medium, a role it was to maintain throughout the Middle Ages. While emphatically proclaiming the unity and integrity of the architectural shell, it at the same time dematerializes that shell, suffusing it with light. The saint, Christ's witness, dwells in solitary glory in the midst of a luminous sphere which is not of this world. To a remarkable degree, and on a miniature scale, the composition foreshadows the great dome mosaics of medieval Byzantine churches, in which a bust of Christ himself, the Pantokrator, will similarly appear, gazing down upon us from the summit of a golden heaven.

At Ravenna one of the major artistic efforts of the reign of Theoderic was the adornment with mosaics of his palace church, later rechristened S.Apollinare Nuovo (pl.IV; figs. 106–8).[37] The decoration bears witness to the same basic development that is so clearly manifest in the two domes just discussed. The entire wall surfaces of the basilican nave, above the cornices that crown the supporting colonnades, are evenly covered with mosaic, there is no articulation through profiles or mouldings, and gold dominates throughout. A flat ribbon bearing a meander ornament runs the entire length of each wall beneath the sills of the clerestory windows, setting off the lower zone of the decoration as a single, plain broad band. The stately processions of male and female martyrs which now fill the greater part of these bands on the right and left wall respectively, and which are so marvellously in tune with the even flow of the surfaces they occupy, are not part of the original design. They were put there by Archbishop Agnellus (appointed A.D.556) some twenty years after the Ostrogothic regime had given way to that of Byzantium, and took the place of long and solemn corteges of Theoderic's court, which must have been in this position. The views of the king's palace (fig. 107) and of the port city of Classe (pl.IV) from which the two court processions set out, as well as the representations of Christ (fig. 106) and the Virgin (each enthroned and flanked by angels) which were their respective goals, have survived, since they were retained in the Byzantine remodelling. Thus the original processions must be visualized as having been contained within the same monumental and static framing motifs as the present ones. Altogether, the aesthetic effect of Theoderic's corteges may not have been very different from that of the defiles of saints which have replaced them. Theoderic's figures, too, had a continuous gold background; and their movement may have been as restrained as that of the procession of apostles in his baptistery (fig. 104).

The upper zone, above the meander ribbon, is dominated by thirty-two tall, statuesque figures of haloed men in white placed singly against a gold background in the spaces between the windows and, three in a row, in the large windowless surfaces at either end of each wall which again provide a strong framing element. The figures carry books or scrolls and are thought to represent prophets and heralds of Christ both from the Old and from the New Testament. To create a setting for them, Theoderic's designer has harked back once again to an earlier decoration at Ravenna. Each figure has a green shaded pedestal to stand on and a shell-shaped canopy overhead as do the apostles in the Mausoleum of Galla Placidia (fig. 97). But the motif has been so drastically transformed that at first sight the relationship is not at all apparent. The pedestals lack substance and hover uncertainly on the gold background. As for the shells, they do not curve back with any force and thus fail to scoop out any overhead space. Indeed, the designer has gone out of his way to sever any connection between them and the figures for which they were meant to provide canopies. He has inserted a slender horizontal band, bearing a simple ornament and accentuated by a thin white line, which firmly relegates the shell motif to a separate and narrow sub-zone at the top of the wall. Nothing could be more characteristic of this artist's aesthetic preferences. He introduces a potentially space-creating element only to cancel its effect. The horizontal band is intersected by vertical bands of the same design so that a tall oblong panel is marked out as a frame for each of the statuesque figures beneath, as well as a much smaller frame for each shell motif above. Thus, in effect, it is a slender grid or lattice, lacking structural force and substance, which in conjunction with the plain contours of the profileless windows organizes the vast wall surfaces of the clerestory zone.

Alone among all the representations on these walls the shell 'canopies' are not placed against a background of gold. Rendered in gold themselves, they stand out from a dark blue foil reminiscent of the night sky of the Galla Placidia mosaics. But this blue ground has become part of a surface pattern. For it alternates with the gold background of the intervening panels which are given over to a sequence of scenes from the Gospels.

These scenes, of which those on the left relate to Christ's ministry and those on the right to his Passion and Resurrection, are justly famous. Not only are they the earliest extant examples of a cyclical representation of Gospel events on the walls of a church, but the manner of representation – stark and spare in its concentration on essentials of figures and settings – is powerful indeed. The fact that the scenes are relegated to those small inconspicuous panels at the top of the two walls, where they appear dwarfed by the shell motifs separating them, is all the more remarkable. The normal and obvious location for a sequential depiction of stories in a basilican nave was in the large expanses of wall spaces between colonnades and windows (compare, for instance, the fifth-century cycle of Old Testament scenes in S.Maria Maggiore in Rome, to be discussed in the next chapter). At S.Apollinare Nuovo, as we have seen, that prime space was given over to a display of court ceremonial ending up before solemn representations of Christ and the Virgin with their angelic guards. Presumably the fact that this was a palace church is not irrelevant here. But it is not only by its peripheral placing that the narrative element is played down. The rendering of the Gospel scenes (fig. 108) is such that there is little induce-ment to 'read' them as a continuous story. Action is reduced to a minimum; figures face the beholder; and scenes are individually centred, the actors being arranged in such a way as to form closed, self-contained compositions. Quite frequently outright symmetry is achieved, and when buildings or landscape settings appear they also help to create a static pattern within the panel. Im-mobility, then, and solemn display are all-pervasive characteristics of this decoration.

Turning finally to the third mosaic-adorned interior of Theoderic's period to have survived in Ravenna – a small chapel in the Archbishop's Palace (figs. 109–11)[38] – we find it to be an exponent of the same basic trend. The imagery here consists exclusively of single figures. The decoration is no longer quite complete, but there can be no question that it ever comprised any narrative elements. Medallions with busts of Christ, the twelve apostles and male and female saints are placed against a gold background on the soffits of four arches supporting the vault over the square central space. A medallion with the monogram of Christ in the apex of the vault is carried by four caryatid angels placed on the diagonal axes, while in the spandrels between the angels the four beings of the Apocalypse appear, again on a plain gold ground.

Simple, timeless portrayal and frozen action are as characteristic of all these ensembles as is the silhouetting of figures against large expanses of neutral foil.[39] It is tempting to connect the two phenomena and to see in the latter an aesthetic expression of the former. Indeed, might there not be some clue here to the whole trend towards acceptance (as against dissembling) of the given surface which we have found to be basic to fifth-century style developments in general? Could one not see in this entire development a quest, a steady groping for an image freed from all earthly contexts, immutably fixed and eternally valid? I shall return to this question in the course of our further exploration of fifth-century monuments in the next chapter.

Meanwhile the Ravennate series of mosaic decorations which we have passed in review certainly can be said to possess both inner cohesion and wider affiliations. I have previously remarked on the lack of evidence concerning the origin and background of the successive generations of artists who worked on these decorations. In the various enterprises of the period of Theoderic different ateliers undoubtedly must have been active side by side. But it is also evident that artists took note of each other's work, witness the instances of citations and borrowings of themes and motifs from antecedent monuments which we have encountered. We are not dealing with a succession of totally independent initiatives. Indeed, one might almost speak of a kind of dialogue, a sequence of action and reaction in the Ravenna series.

At the same time, however, this dialectical process, while to some extent locally conditioned, is in line with developments we have previously observed elsewhere and in the Greek East in particular. Contacts with the Greek world are, in fact, evident throughout the series, beginning with the mosaics of Galla Placidia and continuing with those of the Orthodox Baptistery (whose partial affinity with the decoration of the Thessalonikan rotunda indicates a Greek connection) and the works of the period of Theoderic. Regarding this latter group, I shall single out the atelier which produced the medallions with busts of apostles and saints in the Archbishop's Chapel, and which perhaps was also active in the lower zones at S.Apollinare Nuovo. The busts of apostles (fig. 110) may be compared with a similar series which has survived from a mosaic decoration of roughly the same date in the apse of the small Church of Panagia Kanakaria at Lythrankomi in Cyprus (fig. 112).[40] It is true that the Cypriot heads are softer and somewhat more summary in manner of execution as well as more relaxed in expression. They have neither the linear precision nor the spiritual intensity of their Ravenna counterparts. More of a Hellenistic tradition survives in this Eastern work.[41] But the Cypriot mosaic, whose central feature – now sadly fragmentary – was an enthroned Virgin rigidly enframed in a mandorla and flanked by two angels in an *en face* view, was certainly a work of the same general character as the Ravenna mosaics of Theoderic's time. Nor are the geometric precision and hypnotic power of these Ravennate images altogether without equivalents in the East. In this respect the heads of some of the saints in the Archbishop's Chapel make an interesting comparison with that of the Consul Anastasius on his ivory diptych (figs. 111, 113). There can be no doubt that the Ravenna series reflects fifth-century developments in the Byzantine world.

We shall continue our discussion of the momentously important stylistic innovations of that century in the next chapter.

CHAPTER FOUR

Fifth-Century Conflicts – 2

The city of Rome has a famous counterpart to Ravenna's great series of fifth-century mosaics – the decoration devised and executed during the 430s for the Basilica of S.Maria Maggiore.[1] Based on quite different premises – historically, ideologically and also stylistically – these Roman mosaics will help us to add both breadth and depth to the picture drawn so far of artistic movements in the fifth century.

What has survived of this extensive programme is only a torso. The original apse was destroyed in the thirteenth century when a transept was added to the nave. The fifth-century apse directly adjoined the triumphal arch, which therefore is really an apsidal arch (fig. 115). Its tiers of mosaics with scenes from Christ's infancy must be visualized as framing what was undoubtedly an important and sumptuous composition in the conch itself.[2] The mosaics of the entrance wall, which comprised a long inscription of Pope Sixtus III (A.D.432–40) dedicating the church to the Mother of God, had largely disappeared by the time of the remodelling of the church in the late sixteenth and early seventeenth centuries. That remodelling, which gave the interior more or less its present appearance (fig. 114), also brought changes to the longitudinal walls of the nave but spared the greater part of the mosaic panels with scenes from the Old Testament which occupy the spaces beneath the windows. Drawings made of the nave walls before they were transformed show, however, that the changes introduced by the architects of the late Renaissance were not as drastic as might have been supposed. The rich articulation of those walls was not a sixteenth-century innovation. There always were pilasters between the windows which gave relief to the large surfaces and provided them with a firm architectural framework (fig. 116). Within its allotted bay, each mosaic panel had its own pedimented aedicula. A strongly classicizing element has rightly been discerned in the design of these walls,[3] witness also the fact that they are placed on entablatures and not on arcades such as one commonly finds by this time in the naves of basilicas. The architectural membering does not, however, extend to the apsidal arch (figs. 115, 127, 128) whose huge surface – devoid of all framing and articulation – is displayed as a single, two-dimensional expanse, subdivided only in a geometric sense by the horizontal bands of its mosaic decoration. The design here involves an acceptance of the basic planimetry of the wall in its entirety, while in the nave the plain surface is dissembled. Classicism, then, does not reign unchallenged, and this is borne out by a study of the mosaics themselves.

The nave panels (figs. 117, 119, 129, 131, 132) depict, often in great detail, a series of episodes mainly from the Books of Genesis, Exodus, and Joshua. On the left-hand wall, beginning at the point next to the apse, are scenes pertaining to Abraham, Isaac and Jacob, on the right-hand wall, again beginning at the sanctuary, the stories of Moses and Joshua. Altogether, twenty-seven panels have survived more or less intact (out of an original forty-two), and most of them show two episodes superimposed. It is much the fullest example of cyclical narration in monumental art to have come down to us from the centuries with which we are concerned.

Any evaluation of the style of these mosaics must take as its point of departure their relationship to book illustration. This in turn makes it necessary to revert once more to the activities of artists who served Rome's reactionary pagan aristocracy at the end of the fourth century. The philological and editorial enterprises fostered by these aristocrats in their concern for the preservation of classical literature must have entailed also the production of illustrated *de luxe* editions. At least one illuminated codex has been plausibly related to this Roman milieu, namely, the famous Vatican Codex of Virgil's *Georgics* and *Aeneid* (figs. 118, 120).[4] And, as has long been recognized, there is a close stylistic relationship between some of the miniatures in this manuscript and certain mosaics in the nave of S.Maria Maggiore.

The illustrations in the Vatican Virgil manuscript are framed panel pictures. Many offer views of landscapes and some even of interiors. Although figures, buildings and other stage requisites all tend to be placed in the foreground or superposed in registers, and although there is often a lack of consistency in the scale of different parts of the pictures, the actors nevertheless appear enveloped in their settings and to perform within them. Many of the outdoor scenes in particular are remarkable for their success in creating an illusion of open space. Grey ground imperceptibly shades over into zones of pink, purple or blue, suggesting a view of hazy distances. In terms of the criterion of denial as against acceptance of the material surface, it is clearly the former principle which prevails. The illuminator opens up a 'window' on the parchment page, just as we have previously seen 'windows' opened up by mosaicists on floors and walls and by ivory carvers on the leaves of diptychs. It is the *emblema* concept once again. Indeed, we see here applied to the illustration of a codex compositional and pictorial devices that had been current in monumental painting during the early imperial period (fig. 121).[5] Whatever the sources and models were on which the painter of the Virgil manuscript drew – and this is at present very much an open question[6] – there is no doubt that these miniatures have a strongly retrospective cast, in keeping with the entire revival and preservation movement of which they are a product.

A connection between these illustrations of ancient Rome's greatest epic and the Old Testament cycle of S.Maria Maggiore may be assumed with all the more confidence because there is evidence of biblical manuscripts illustrated in the same style, if not, indeed, in the same atelier, as the Vatican Virgil. Such an extension of, or response to, the pagan revival effort of the period around A.D.400 in the realm of Christian imagery is not surprising in view of what we have previously seen in other media, especially ivory carving. The evidence for the illustration of biblical texts by artists related in training and outlook to those who worked on the Vatican Virgil comes from a few precious leaves with scenes from the Book of Kings discovered at Quedlinburg in the last century and now in the State Library of Berlin (fig. 122).[7] They testify to the existence of a biblical codex in the Old Latin version (the so-called *Itala*), richly adorned with 'panel pictures' similar to those in the Vatican codex. Evidently this book was commissioned by a patron who belonged to the same social stratum as the sponsors of *de luxe* editions of the classics and who shared many of the same cultural values. The Quedlinburg miniatures have in common with those of the Vatican manuscript the delicately shaded atmospheric backgrounds, the disposition of the figures within these settings, and even some of the figure types and motifs.

Clearly, the Old Testament cycle of S.Maria Maggiore owes much to the stylistic tradition which produced these two manuscripts. In a number of panels, particularly in the Moses and Joshua sequence, similar compositional schemes, similar atmospheric settings and some of the same figure types reappear (figs. 117, 119). If the miniatures of the Virgil and *Itala* codices were composed in a manner originally associated with mural paintings, many of the mosaic panels in turn seem like enlarged miniatures. It is true that the arrangement of distinct scenes in two coequal registers which most of the panels show has no full counterpart in either of the two manuscripts, but this device is used quite frequently in another illustrated *de luxe* edition of a classical text (though one that is slightly later in date and presumably of Eastern Mediterranean rather than Roman origin), namely, the *Iliad* Codex in the Ambrosian Library at Milan (fig. 123).[8] One feature entirely peculiar to the mosaics is the use made of gold. The illuminators of the Vatican Virgil and of the *Itala* employed fine lines of gold as highlights. In many of the Old Testament scenes

III. Orthodox Baptistery, Ravenna
Detail of dome mosaic with Sts James and Matthew

IV. S.Apollinare Nuovo, Ravenna
North wall

c. A.D.500 (procession of saints *c.* A.D.560)
page 62

in S.Maria Maggiore, on the other hand, fairly large expanses of gold appear as an intermediate background zone. The injection of this totally 'unreal' element into those vague and hazy settings is, of course, highly significant in view of the enormous role gold was shortly to assume as the foil *par excellence* for sacred persons and scenes on the walls of churches. But in many of the scenes at S.Maria Maggiore it is still very much part of an airy space – a luminous zone in the middle distance which takes over from the ground on which the figures stand and often merges on the far side into hills or clouds.[9] The figures themselves, agile in pose, summary in rendering and indefinite in contour, live and breathe in these spaces as do those in the Virgil and *Itala* miniatures.

It is interesting here to recall for a moment the mosaics of the chapel of Galla Placidia in Ravenna and to note that those of S.Maria Maggiore are their exact contemporaries. In the Ravennate decoration, too, wall surfaces dissolve as the mosaicist opens up views of distant spaces. But in S.Maria Maggiore the effect is achieved by entirely different means, and there can be no doubt that many of the devices which were used here came from the retrospectively oriented book illuminations of the period. As for the architectural organization of the walls, it provides a suitably classicizing framework for such pictures.

Quite different characteristics come to the fore in the scenes from Christ's infancy on the arch (figs. 127, 128). Figures are larger in relation to the total surface of a given scene. They are much more ponderous and block-like and they tend to face the beholder squarely. The whole pace of the narrative is much slower and more solemn. Figures also tend to close ranks, shutting off views into the distance. No longer do they inhabit a spacious setting. The background has become a backdrop in which gold predominates and often takes on the nature of a solid band with a sharply defined upper edge.

It used to be thought that these differences betoken a time interval. While the arch mosaics are of the period of Sixtus III, whose name is monumentally recorded in the dedicatory inscription in the centre of the top zone, the Old Testament panels were thought to have been made for an earlier building and to have been re-employed.[10] But this view is untenable. Not only is it hard to reconcile with the unity of concept which underlies the entire iconographic programme (this is a point to which I shall return), it is untenable also on stylistic grounds. If, instead of the broad categories of spatial concepts, settings and compositional arrangements with which we have operated so far, we use finer – more 'Morellian' – criteria relating to technique and craftsmanship we find many close ties between nave and arch mosaics.[11] For instance, the same characteristic device for depicting facial features occurs in both. Eyes are apt to be rendered by a juxtaposition of a single dark cube, denoting the pupil, with one or more white cubes, while a straight, dark horizontal placed directly above indicates the brow (figs. 124, 125). Mosaicists who worked on the arch no less than those who worked in the nave used this bold impressionist device which produces the effect of a piercing glance and is a major factor in endowing faces and even entire figures with intense animation.

Such close-up scrutiny of workmanship discloses at the same time strong variations *within* each of the two groups; witness, for instance, the mothers in the Massacre of the Innocents (fig. 126) in the third register of the left side of the arch as against the elders in front of the temple in the first register on the right (fig. 125). The obvious conclusion is that a considerable number of different hands must have been employed, as would naturally have been the case in so large and complex an enterprise. But there are too many technical and stylistic bonds between mosaics in the nave and on the arch not to consider these different hands as members of a single team working simultaneously.[12]

If, then, the discrepancy in basic conception which nevertheless exists between nave and arch mosaics cannot be explained by attributing the two parts of the decoration to different periods or different teams, one may be tempted to account for it by assuming that models of very different appearance were used for the Old Testament and New Testament scenes respectively. Here the relationship of the nave mosaics to book illumination would seem to provide helpful evidence. Have we not seen that many of the Old Testament panels look like enlargements of miniatures such as those in the Vatican Virgil or the Quedlinburg *Itala*? Does not this latter book provide tangible evidence that Bible manuscripts illustrated with pictures in the style of our mosaics did in fact exist at the time? And does not the history of art know other instances of biblical cycles on church walls being copied quite literally from illuminated codices, the best-known case being that of the Genesis scenes in S.Marco in Venice, which reproduce with remarkable fidelity miniatures in a famous Bible codex of the fifth or sixth century that once belonged to Sir Robert Cotton?[13] Assuming that similar use was made of illustrations of an Old Testament manuscript in devising the nave mosaics of S.Maria Maggiore, the specific characteristics which differentiate these mosaics from those on the arch might well be accounted for.

This is, in fact, the unspoken – and at times explicit – assumption underlying much of the discussion of the S.Maria Maggiore Old Testament cycle in scholarly literature. But the assumption is untenable. It has long been observed that a number of the Old Testament scenes bear a close relationship to the arch mosaics not only in details of workmanship but in their overall appearance as well.[14] The Separation of Abraham and Lot is an example (fig. 129; cf. fig. 130). The two protagonists are block-like figures squarely facing the beholder, filling a large part of the surface and in effect shutting off the view into the distance. The other elements of the composition – secondary figures and buildings – are joined to the two principal figures to form with them an extraordinarily expressive but essentially abstract pattern which, with its two more or less coequal halves and its central cleft, conveys unforgettably the substance of the event depicted. Now it is a striking fact that both on the left and on the right side of the nave – that is to say, both in the Genesis and in the Exodus scenes – it is in the mosaics closest to the sanctuary that this monumental style comes to the fore. It follows that the scenes cannot be outright copies of a cycle of book illustrations, for they were clearly designed with a view to their location in the building.[15] As one approaches the sanctuary, the pace of the narrative slows. There is a *ritardando*, as it were, or, to use another musical term, a change of key. A more solemn, more ceremonial note is introduced, and this note is then sustained throughout the cycle of Christological scenes on the arch.

Once again we encounter here the phenomenon of 'modes', a conscious choice made by artists between different manners in the light of the content, meaning or purpose of a given representation or group of representations.[16] There can be no doubt that this factor played a major role in the design of the mosaics of S.Maria Maggiore. To some extent form is correlated here with location, and, as we shall see, location in turn has to do with function and meaning.

How, then, are we to visualize the creation of these mosaics? Designed with a view to their place in the building, they cannot have been copied mechanically from a codex such as the Quedlinburg *Itala*. That manuscript does, however, provide us with an important clue. Beneath the badly eroded pigments of its miniatures, verbal instructions to the painter, or – in some instances – very rough disposition sketches, have come to light.[17] This can only mean that the miniatures themselves were not copied from another codex but were designed *ad hoc*. Evidently a painter of the period could be expected to be able to translate such verbal instructions into images with the help of a standard vocabulary. Similarly, our mosaicists must have operated with stock formulae. Their Joshua (fig. 119), for instance, is the same figure of an officer which in the manuscripts did duty for Saul or Aeneas.[18] The mosaicists may also have worked on the basis of verbal instructions and disposition sketches only. *Sinopie* or outline drawings have been found on the wall itself beneath some of the scenes on the arch, and it is interesting to note that they do not always correspond exactly to what was executed.[19] If small-scale preparatory paintings were used at all they must have been made *ad hoc*.

The undeniable resemblance of so many of the scenes to illustrations in the manuscripts of Virgil and the *Itala* (and, to a lesser extent, the *Iliad*) was not, therefore, an automatic inheritance from book illumination. I would go further and say that it too was a matter of deliberate choice. It too was a 'mode' purposefully cultivated. The biblical picture stories on the wall were meant to evoke the pages of a lavishly illustrated epic. In terms of legibility it was hardly an ideal format. At the great height at which they are placed, the mosaics which most resemble miniatures are difficult to read. One is led to conclude that the mental associations with the pages of a manuscript of Virgil or Homer which these scenes in their cyclical sequence could be expected to evoke in a fifth-century beholder were considered more important than his ability to follow each event in detail.

That the epic mode was introduced here with an associational intent seems all the more likely because it is in line with other references to the pagan past which have long been recognized in the S.Maria Maggiore mosaics.[20] One of the most interesting of these references occurs in the scene on the arch of the Presentation of the Christ Child in the Temple (fig. 128). Unmistakably the façade in front of which the event takes place is that of Rome's own Temple of the goddess *Roma*, so that Jerusalem merges with Rome and Simeon appears to be receiving the Child on behalf of the world's ancient capital.[21] But 'Roman' and 'imperial' connotations are strongly in evidence also in the nave, where they merge or overlap with those elements which evoke the great epics. Thus, while a number of the battle scenes in the Exodus and Joshua cycles are composed on lines familiar from the Milan *Iliad*, Joshua's defeat of the Amorite kings clearly recalls the composition of the great Roman battle sarcophagi of the third century.[22] The Marriage of Moses (fig. 131) takes the form of a Roman couple's *dextrarum iunctio* (with Moses wearing the costume of a high Roman official). Abraham's encounter with Melchizedek is modelled after an imperial *adventus* (figs. 132, 133).

There is, then, in this entire decoration an emphatic, demonstrative and surely deliberate appropriation or assimilation of the pagan past. The evocation of an illustrated epic in the nave mosaics is part of this. The forces which motivated this appropriation cannot be in doubt. While the major fourth-century basilicas in Rome were imperial foundations, S.Maria Maggiore is the first great church erected by the popes. Its founding reflects a situation in the fifth century when – with the seat of empire long removed, the pagan aristocracy finally defeated, and the venerable city sacked by Alaric – the bishop of Rome, the only effective authority left in the city, asserted his claim as the true and rightful heir of the Caesars.[23] Rome, the see of St Peter, was to be the centre of a new universal realm, the Church of Christ, ruled on his behalf by the occupants of the Apostle's Chair. The greatest and most eloquent proponent of this doctrine of papal power was Leo I, the immediate successor of Sixtus III. But Sixtus had already put forward the Roman bishop's claim to universality when he placed in huge letters at the focal point of his magnificent basilica the terse dedication: 'Xystus episcopus plebi dei'. 'God's people', in the new dispensation, is all of Christendom.

The insistent use both in the architecture and in the mosaics of forms and motifs associated with the pagan past must be seen in this light. It is not simply a carry-over from the late fourth-century 'Renaissance'. It is a counter-move, a conscious and programmatic appropriation of the past. It is as though the Church were addressing the defeated resisters – and perhaps, in a way, smoothing the path for them – by saying: Your temple has become the Lord's Temple, and the heroic deeds of bygone days in which you may glory and which will sustain you in the present are those performed at the Lord's command and with the Lord's help. These are the true epics, the true *res gestae*.

Yet the narrative does not proceed straight – certainly not on the arch, and not even in the nave. Epic story-telling is fitted into and subordinated to an overall programme of great complexity. As the nave is an anteroom to the sanctuary, so the Old Testament scenes in the former are preparatory to the Lord's actual epiphany portrayed in the latter. Progressing from the entrance to the altar, the faithful experience in space God's providential plan for the salvation of mankind as it has unfolded in time. But the story is pointed. It does not begin with Creation, as it will do in the Old Testament cycle painted only a decade or so later in the nave of S.Paolo fuori le mura;[24] it concentrates on a few great figures who under the Old Law were the recipients of God's promise to his Chosen People and the instruments of the fulfilment of that promise. And while much of the narration takes the form of a blow-by-blow account involving a great deal of circumstantial detail, there are also some interesting departures from 'historical' chronology.[25] The Melchizedek scene (fig. 132), showing the priest king of Salem offering bread and wine, is taken out of the correct sequence (I see no reason to assume that this is a mistake made in the sixteenth-century restoration) and placed monumentally as the very first panel immediately next to the sanctuary and the altar, in obvious reference to the Eucharist. And the Separation of Abraham and Lot (fig. 129) – the third scene in the same sequence – includes as a pendant to Lot's young daughters the boy Isaac (not yet born at the time) to

lend dramatic emphasis to God's promise to his people. For as he was to say to
Abraham: 'In Isaac shall thy seed be called' (Genesis 21:12).

It is hardly coincidental that these departures from 'history' occur in the area
where the narrative slows up, its tenor becomes solemn and ceremonial and its
formal representation more stylized and patterned. On the arch, where these
characteristics prevail throughout, the rearrangements of history are correspondingly more numerous and more drastic. I shall not enter into the old controversy
as to whether or not the iconography of the arch mosaics was inspired by (or at
least reflects) the decisions of the Council of Ephesus in A.D.431, which, in re-
futing the teachings of Nestorius, proclaimed the Virgin to be the Mother of
God.[26] Given the coincidence of dates and the princely splendour with which
Mary is presented in the mosaics (fig. 127), I find it hard to believe that there is
no connection with the Council of Ephesus at all. But it is only one theme among
others. The imagery of the arch is replete with unconventional renderings of
established subjects, enigmatic – and from the point of view of simple narration
clearly superfluous – figures and details, and strange transpositions in the
chronological order of events. As a result, it invites endless speculation by
iconographers and iconologists. Even the subject matter of some of the scenes
depicted is controversial. The key theme is without doubt the triumphal advent
of Christ as universal ruler. So much is clear from the choice and arrangement of
episodes on the arch as well as from the context created for them by the mosaics
in the nave.[27] But there are subsidiary themes in this intricately coded and
richly orchestrated ensemble. The Marian theme is one of them (after all, the
church was dedicated to the Virgin), the 'Roman' theme another. With a
multiplicity of dogmas, messages and allusions woven into the narrative, the
formal language becomes correspondingly weighty, pointed and emphatic. As
eternal, immutable verities are directly proclaimed, action freezes, the real world
recedes, and an abstract, static pattern is imposed on figures and compositions.

I have discussed the mosaics of S.Maria Maggiore at some length because we
see here being played out within a single monument some of the major stylistic
conflicts we have previously observed in fifth-century art. We see these conflicts
coming to the fore in the confines of what is undoubtedly a single unified project
accomplished within a limited time span – probably no more than a decade. And
more clearly than elsewhere can the differences in formal language be related to
different and competing ideological concerns and purposes. Both the classicizing,
retrospective style and the abstract – or, as it has also been called, 'transcendental' – style[28] correspond to ideas and intents that are at least broadly identifiable.

We do not know where the team of mosaicists came from. The question is as moot here as we previously found it to be in the case of the great fifth-century enterprises at Ravenna. There is little connection with what we know of earlier wall mosaics in Rome.[29] It is possible, therefore, that the team employed by Sixtus III included a sizeable foreign element; and, although the S.Maria Maggiore mosaics are in no way related to those commissioned during the same period by Galla Placidia in Ravenna, it is arguable that in the Roman enterprise too artists from the Greek East were at work. There appear to be some interesting parallels both for the poses and for the rendering of certain figures in floor mosaics at Antioch and Apamea (compare figs. 134 and 136 with figs. 135 and 137 respectively).[30] But wherever the artists hailed from and whatever their training may have been, they were not entirely free agents. Although we have encountered stylistic nuances which are due to different hands working side by side, we have also found a basic stylistic dichotomy which cuts across such groupings. This dichotomy, so we have seen, has to do with the content and location of different parts of the programme and must therefore flow from a master plan generated locally. It was imposed on the executant artists by a guiding mind which saw the imagery as a whole, in relation to the building and its functions and to the ideas that had created it.[31] Who this individual was we shall never know. But to the extent that formats, motifs and modes of presentation were here chosen deliberately as visual equivalents and expressions of what was ultimately an ideological programme, they confront us once again with the possibility of an 'other-directed' element in the shaping of stylistic forms.

It was to the abstract manner of the arch and of the nave panels nearest the arch that the future belonged. To realize this we need only recall the Ravennate mosaics of the period of Theoderic discussed in the previous chapter. No actual contact between the mosaic workshops of Ravenna and those of Rome has ever been conclusively demonstrated. But S.Maria Maggiore does show the abstract mode of the Ravenna mosaics of the period around A.D.500 *in statu nascendi*, and here already the striving after this mode is bound up with subjects that have to do with ceremony, with power, and with the proclamation of eternal verities. A true 'language of authority' does indeed emerge as a great and central concern of fifth-century pictorial art. The official ivories of the late fifth and early sixth centuries which combine a fully perfected, abstract, hard and static style with a vastly increased quantitative emphasis on the ruler figure are another manifestation of this (fig. 86). To a preponderant interest in the timeless and ceremonial in subject matter corresponds a full triumph of formal abstraction.

We have reached a point where we seem to be in a position to grasp some of the root causes and motivating forces that produced stylistic change in the fifth

century, and it might be best to leave it at that. We have discussed major monuments commissioned by, and reflecting the ideas and aspirations of, leading
powers of the day – imperial officialdom, the papacy, the Ostrogothic kingdom
in Italy. But in thus giving focus to our period portrait we have also narrowed our
field of vision. We must not lose sight of artistic impulses and initiatives which
came to the fore during the fifth century in less exalted spheres and less programmatic contexts and which similarly entailed new assaults on classical
traditions and new explorations in the realm of abstract form. The emergence
of the figure carpet in the floor mosaics of Antioch is a case in point.[32] Certainly
acceptance – as opposed to dissembling – of the physical matrix as carrier and
integrating element of a composition was a fundamental trend in the art of this
period; and with this went a loss of natural and organic relationships – or, to put
it another way, an assertion of purely conceptual relationships – on a very
broad front.

To assure a balanced picture of stylistic developments in the fifth century and
to guard against a one-sided interpretation of these developments I shall, in
conclusion, turn to a branch of artistic activity which we have not previously
taken into consideration – ornamental sculpture in stone. The category will
serve my purpose well. In the field of decorative sculpture for buildings the
period was exceptionally creative and innovative; and since little or no subject
content is involved, these innovations reveal with great purity basic aesthetic
interests and attitudes. There is the additional fact that much of the most interesting material comes from the Aegean region, so that we are able to focus
more definitely than in our discussion of other branches of fifth-century art on
the Byzantine heartland and on Constantinople itself.

In order to make the material manageable for the present discourse, I propose
to limit myself to one kind of ornamental sculpture only, namely, capitals. They
offer the best means to illustrate succinctly both the variety of new forms in this
branch of art and certain unifying style trends. They are also the best-explored
category, thanks largely to the pioneering work of Rudolf Kautzsch.[33]

Some of the innovations in the design of fifth-century capitals, such as the so-
called 'Theodosian' type, the type with animal protomes, and that with wind-
swept foliage, entailed revivals – on the basis of more or less tenuous survivals –
of earlier Roman forms.[34] Others are entirely new. I shall concentrate primarily
on what happened during this period to the traditional and conventional
Corinthian capital, a process which Kautzsch analysed with great thoroughness.
Through the fourth century the Corinthian capital maintained essentially its
classical shape and appearance, as a comparison of a Cypriot capital of that
period (fig. 139) with a second-century example from Pergamon (fig. 138) shows;

that is to say, the transition from circle at bottom to square at top is effected by means of the abacus, the square member placed on top of a cup-shaped core, the so-called bell.[35] The essence of the Corinthian capital is that it invests the purely static relationship between these two core members with a semblance of organic growth. It almost conceals the bell, making it disappear behind wreaths of acanthus foliage staged in depth and thus turning it into a foliate calyx. From behind the innermost row of these leaves, volutes grow as if pushed up by an innate live force, and the abacus, swerving out in response to their movement, appears to rest lightly on these springy supports. It is true that in our fourth-century example these elements and relationships no longer seem quite so natural. The acanthus leaves are more schematic, they lack true modelling, and the tips of their lateral lobes, which are deeply undercut, touch those of the adjoining leaves so that the interstices between them recede into deep shadows and form patterns of their own. On top, at the corners, the volutes which converge from adjoining sides coalesce into a single undefined mass, and the flowers that had adorned the centre of each side of the abacus (having grown on thin elegant stalks from behind the acanthus foliage) have become amorphous protuberances of the abacus itself.

These changes, however, though significant in view of what was to come, are minor compared with those wrought in the course of the fifth century. The capitals of S. Apollinare Nuovo, which take us to the very end of the century or, more probably, to the first decades of the sixth, and which on the evidence of their masons' marks were carved in or near Constantinople, can serve well to exemplify these changes (fig. 141).[36] The acanthus leaves are reduced in number and simplified in outline. The abstract pattern of diamonds, trapezoids and ovals formed by their interstices has become almost their coequal as a design element. What is most significant is the transformation of the upper zone. The volutes have atrophied. Instead of rising from the foliage, their stems are joined together on each side in a catenary curve, a form suggesting suspension and thus the very opposite of their former supportive function. In any case, the volutes are only superficially indicated on the rather amorphous plastic mass that fills the entire space enclosed by the foliate wreaths. No longer bell-shaped, this core mass itself emerges as the true load-bearing element; and it is within this core that the transition from circle to square is effected. Thus the function of the capital is no longer translated into organic terms. Indeed, the overall shape has ceased to be that of an expanding calyx. It has contracted, become a block. The boss on the abacus has also been enormously enlarged as though it were an outgrowth of a yet denser mass pushing out from inside this block. On the other hand, the almost *à jour* treatment of the leaves, suggesting as it does a shadow zone of indefinite depth behind the foliage, rather irrationally calls into question the solidity of the core, otherwise so emphatically asserted.

This radical transformation of the Corinthian capital, turning it from an organic and rational design element into an abstract and irrational one, was a slow but relentless process which took place with remarkable consistency in many different areas during the fifth century. Exemplified here by a single comparison, it was studied and analysed by Kautzsch in a variety of regional manifestations.[37] But it was the Aegean region that during this period led in inventive and innovative designs. The transformation of the foliate capital into an abstract block shape here received a powerful impetus from the concurrent development of another closely associated member, namely, the impost. First introduced in the late fourth century, the impost was by origin a structural device.[38] Its purpose was to help effect the transition from the top of the capital to the footing of the arch above, and it still appears as a frankly technical and auxiliary element in many instances of columnar architecture as late as A.D.500 or even later. S.Apollinare Nuovo itself provides an example (fig. 141). The imposts here are plain, truncated and inverted pyramids, adorned only with a cross on the side facing the nave. Elsewhere, however, the impost had long since begun to sprout a foliate ornamentation of its own, at first only on its front and in a subsidiary role as a frame for the cross (fig. 142), but soon spreading and at the same time eating into the substance of the block through the kind of undercutting and resultant deep shadows which we have encountered on capitals (fig. 143). By the second half of the fifth century one finds imposts whose entire surface is covered with a lacelike pattern of finely serrated acanthus foliage against a background of deep shadows, a decoration conceived entirely in terms of the plain solid of the block yet radically calling into question its very solidity (fig. 144).[39] Here the goal to which we saw the designs of Corinthian capitals progress slowly and gropingly was in effect already realized. And the impost carried the capital with it in its triumphant evolution. This is most clearly in evidence in its relation to the Ionic capital, on which at first one finds it perched rather stiffly and demurely (fig. 145), while subsequently it overpowered the Ionic element and invested it with its own increasingly luxuriant ornament. The so-called Ionic impost capital which resulted from this merger was one of the many original creations of the fifth century and became a vehicle for a great deal of imaginative play (figs. 146, 147).[40] But in due course imposts were to triumph over – and, in a sense, absorb – capitals of other types as well, including the Corinthian. The result was an entirely new form, the so-called impost capital, which streamlined completely the transition from circle to square, bringing this transition fully out into the open and effecting it smoothly within the block-shaped body itself. The impost capital was the climax of the entire development here under review.[41] Outstanding among early examples are the capitals in the lower storey of the Church of Sts Sergius and Bacchus, Justinian's first ecclesiastical foundation in Constantinople (fig. 148).[42] They are particularly interesting because they represent a variant clearly indebted to Corinthian antecedents, witness the curvatures of the abacus by which the shape of the entire body is here determined (cf., for example, fig. 139). In other instances – including examples that are certainly pre-Justinianic – the 'squaring of the circle' was accomplished in terms of the purest and most abstract stereometry.[43] Aesthetically, then, the capitals of S.Apollinare Nuovo (fig. 141), which come close to a pure block shape but still carry separate plain imposts, were already outdated in their time.

The development in ornamental sculpture which I have illustrated with these few examples shows extraordinary consistency. Resulting in momentous change and entirely new forms, it has an almost irresistible inner logic. It thus raises profound and disturbing questions of historical determinism. Consider a run-of-the-mill Corinthian capital in Jerusalem (fig. 140) which was certainly made before A.D.400,[44] but which, by comparison with our Cypriot example of that period (fig. 139), is less expansive in outline and shows the volutes losing some of their springiness and the core mass emerging above and below them. Was the carver of this capital already groping towards the block shape of the pure impost capital? If so, what was it that impelled him to make this as yet almost imperceptible change? And what, if any, connection is there between his innovation and the style changes we have previously observed in other media?

We must certainly accept a change such as this as wholly 'inner-directed', a pure manifestation of the sculptor's own aesthetic preference and intent. There is no content here, no point to be made, no message to be conveyed. No patron can have demanded, let alone generated this innovation. Indeed, I would maintain that the whole evolution of sculptural ornament which I have outlined was essentially autonomous and took place entirely within the aesthetic sphere. It was a kind of chain reaction among artists with each successive step being predicated on the preceding one. And whatever the motivation was in a specific instance, there is no doubt that the process as a whole has meaning. It has as much 'meaning' as the dissolution of organic and natural relationships in a cubist painting and has comparably profound implications, implications which have to do with man's perception of and attitude towards the physical world and the forces governing it.

At the same time, however, it also presents parallels with what we have seen happening in other media. The progressive rejection of classical forms; the increased abstraction; the bringing out (as against the dissembling) of basic forms and structural matrices; and the simultaneous dematerialization of these matrices – all these emerge as fundamental style trends common to fifth-century art as a whole. In this sense our impost block with its lacelike skin (fig. 144) is, in fact, an exact stylistic equivalent of the little golden dome of S.Vittore in Milan (fig. 105).[45] We must, I think, conclude that these broad trends, at different stages of their evolution, also played a part in shaping works as diverse as the mosaic decorations of S.Maria Maggiore and of S.Apollinare Nuovo. To a greater or lesser degree their style too was willed by the artist and was therefore 'inner-directed'. But the artist's intent and outlook was in turn shaped by forces in the spiritual and intellectual, social and political realm of which these highly articulate works can give us at least an inkling.

Perhaps it will be best, at the close of our inquiry into this complex period, to look once again at the face of an individual. We found the concerns and predicaments of the third century reflected in the countenances of men of the period. A justly famous portrait head from Ephesus (fig. 149)[46] – surely one of the most eloquent visual statements about a particular human being in all post-classical art – will render this same service for the fifth century. Its forms are rooted in the art of the Theodosian period. But these forms have been radically made over and redefined to convey with great power the consuming intensity of one man's awareness of the supernatural world.

CHAPTER FIVE

The Justinianic Synthesis

Some of the discussions in the last two chapters have already taken us well past the year A.D.500. We have considered ivory diptychs made for consuls in the early years of the sixth century. We have surveyed the mosaic decorations created at Ravenna in the time of Theoderic, whose rule lasted until A.D.526. In architectural sculpture we have traced a development which carried through to the time of Justinian. Obviously the historical process was continuous. The turn of the century does not constitute a landmark.

A new era, often acclaimed as the First Golden Age of Byzantine art, did, however, begin with the advent of Justinian in A.D.527. The great monuments of the ensuing quarter-century bear a character all their own. Yet the bold new departures of this period depended heavily on accumulated experiences of the past. In this sense the art of the early Justinianic age, to which this chapter will be devoted, constituted not so much an innovation as a fulfilment and a consummation. For a brief time seemingly conflicting forces and traditions were balanced out in a state of controlled tension. Like other such climactic efforts in the history of art, the synthesis was not sustained for long.

A change of style in this period is borne in sharply on the visitor to Ravenna, who, coming from S.Apollinare Nuovo or any of the other mosaic-adorned interiors of the period of Theoderic, enters the Church of S.Vitale. The famous mosaics in the chancel of this church embody the golden moment of Justinianic art as does no other extant work in a pictorial medium. They will be given pride of place in our discussion. Although they should and will be viewed in the light of their local antecedents, they will prove to be highly representative of the art of their time.

The Church of S.Vitale[1] was founded by Ecclesius, Catholic bishop of Ravenna under Theoderic, probably shortly after the Arian king's death. Construction, however, may not have got under way until after the conquest of the city by the Byzantines in A.D.540. As for the mosaics, they are entirely a work of the decade following that event. In the famous imperial panels, Bishop Maximian, who was appointed to the see in A.D.546 and who consecrated the church in A.D.547 or 548, is prominently portrayed. On the other hand, the Empress Theodora, who died in A.D.548, seems to be depicted as still living.

The iconographic programme of these mosaics is intricate. But there is a central theme clearly relating to the eucharistic rite for which they provided the setting. The Agnus Dei – the sacrificial Lamb – placed in the centre of the vault and directly over the altar is literally the keystone of the entire composition (fig. 153); biblical prototypes of offering and sacrifice are prominently displayed on the two side walls (pl.V; figs. 154, 155); and in the apse Justinian and Theodora appear with their retinue offering precious liturgical vessels as donations for the church (figs. 151, 152, 158). The liturgical reference, therefore, is central to the entire ensemble. But we are also shown a kind of conspectus, assembled in a unified space, of God's plan for the redemption of man. It is a conspectus to be experienced in a single view rather than in progressive motion as in S.Maria Maggiore, and it does not take the form of an epic narrative as it did in the Roman basilica, but rather of a selective portrayal of those who have succeeded one another in time as principal heralds and agents of the divine plan: prophets, apostles, evangelists and saints. Moses is depicted three times in different actions in the spaces adjoining the sacrifice scenes, and these spaces are shared by Isaiah and Jeremiah (pl.V; fig. 154); the four evangelists are fitted in the zone above (pl.V; figs. 154, 157); medallion busts of apostles and saints appear in the soffit of the entrance arch (fig. 153) ;and the celestial vision of the Apocalyptic Lamb overhead carries the unfolding of God's redemptive action to the end of time. The whole is presided over by the majestic figure of Christ seated in a paradisical landscape in the conch of the apse. Flanked by angels, he receives a model of the church from Bishop Ecclesius while handing a martyr's crown to its titular saint (fig. 156).

Thus images that are thematically static – single figures and slow ritual actions – predominate here as they did in the mosaics of Theoderic's court church. Yet the visual effect could hardly be more different. Severe geometry is replaced by luxuriant life. Even figures in isolation tend to be in action, gesticulating and turning. Many have outdoor settings. Whatever spaces remain are filled with rich vegetation. And the dominant colour is not gold but a verdant bluish green.

The S.Vitale decoration seems to take us back to a period much earlier than the age of Theoderic. Nor is this only a matter of more natural and lively motifs. With these elements the artist composes real pictures, self-contained compositional units strongly reminiscent of the traditional *emblema*. We see figures and groups of figures in a clearly delimited environment and in communication with that environment. A return to the past seems to be involved also in the overall structuring of the surfaces. That structure is firm and consistent, and it is carried through on the basis of a clear distinction of framing and framed parts. It is true that on the lateral walls of the chancel such a distinction was pre-established by the architect. Both in the lower and in the upper storey he provided the mosaicist with recessed surfaces (open arcades surmounted by lunettes) set in a wide frame (pl.V; fig. 154). But one wonders whether in creating this articulation the architect did not already have the mosaic decoration in mind. Be this as it may, the designer of the mosaics takes up the cue and follows it consistently even in the apse and the vault where, with but little aid from the architecture, he still makes heavy and emphatic frames the basic organizing element (figs. 150, 153).

Real and palpable as this return to the concept of picture and frame is, however, we do not find at S.Vitale what had been a corollary of this concept a century earlier in the decoration of the Mausoleum of Galla Placidia, namely, a rhythmic interplay of three-dimensional and two-dimensional surfaces (pl.I; figs. 93, 98). At S.Vitale the frames too are vehicles of *emblemata*, most conspicuously on the two lateral walls. The distinction so clearly established with one hand is taken away with the other. In part this might be said to be dictated by iconography. Not only the sacrifice scenes in the lunettes of the lower storey but also the Moses scenes in the broad framing spaces adjoining them called for an indication of locale. It was natural to provide a landscape setting for Moses pasturing Jethro's flock, loosening his sandals before the Burning Bush and receiving the law on Mount Sinai, as well as for Abel and Melchizedek making their offerings and for Abraham feasting the three angels and preparing to sacrifice Isaac. But the portrayals of the four evangelists with their symbols in the upper zones of what we have found to be framing surfaces likewise take the form of scenic *emblemata*, and in this case the iconographic motivation for such a device is far less evident and certainly less compelling. Here the desire to counteract the distinction between framing and framed parts of the wall system seems to be a primary factor.

The panels with the evangelists (fig. 157) are particularly interesting. As *emblemata* showing their subjects seated in rocky landscapes in the company of symbolic animals, they invite comparison with the classic instance of an *emblema* among the Ravenna mosaics, the Good Shepherd lunette in the Mausoleum of Galla Placidia (fig. 94). One might go further and suggest that the artist who designed these panels drew his inspiration from that earlier work. But what is chiefly illuminating in this comparison is the difference it reveals. No longer are the landscapes spacious settings receding into a distance. They are more in the nature of backdrops or curtains placed behind the figures. If in the earlier composition the horizon was remarkably low, here it is extraordinarily high. The rocky threshold with its cliffs, which in the earlier mosaic so effectively helped to make the space within the picture recede from the frame, is still present. But it is surmounted by tier upon tier of similar formations, all more or less equidistant from the beholder. Thus the rocky scenery is more like a wall mysteriously disappearing into nowhere below the lower frame and rising almost vertically. The symbolic animals at the very top are at no greater distance from us than the figures beneath and really play the role of headpieces or pictorial titles as they will often do subsequently on the pages of early medieval manuscripts depicting the authors of the Gospels. The evangelists themselves seem to be affixed to rather than supported by their settings. Shadows, reminiscent of an *en creux* relief, accompany some of their outlines and provide the figures with a kind of shallow niche, thus anchoring them more securely to the precipitous mountain sides on which they are placed. Actually, on closer inspection, one begins to have doubts as to the solidity and cohesiveness of these rocky walls. The cliffs and outcrops are interspersed with what might be considered hillocks, and some of these formations are so soft and fuzzy in outline as also to suggest clouds. Indeed, in two of the panels there appear at the top, behind the symbols, narrow sections of cloudy sky with which some of these 'hillocks' seem to merge. Such fusion of ground and sky is an old device of late antique impressionism which we have previously encountered in the mosaics of S.Maria Maggiore (figs. 117, 119). At S.Vitale it serves to call into question the material identity, the rational build-up of the landscapes and makes them appear even more like semi-abstract backdrops.

One might suppose that in designing the mosaics for these particular sections of the chancel walls the artist was conscious that he was dealing with what was structurally a frame and was therefore anxious to avoid the impression of a truly receding space such as the Galla Placidia mosaic offers. But when we turn to the pictures within the frames, that is, the lunettes with the sacrifice scenes, we find that the principles on which they are composed are not essentially different. In particular the landscape setting for the two Abraham scenes when examined closely turns out likewise to be semi-abstract (fig. 155). It is, in fact, a quite remarkable mélange, part meadow, part mountain, and part sky. Mounds and cliffs briefly appear and disappear again. How solid really are the outcroppings on the right, bending as they do with the curvature of the frame and the crouching figure of Isaac, for which they form the background? Is the striking form just to the right of the seated angels earth or sky? As for the scattered plants and trees, they do not really grow from the ground and scarcely add to its plausibility. This is true even of the great oak of Mamre near the centre of the panel, a pivotal element both iconographically and compositionally. The angels at their table are oddly interlaced with the trunk of the tree so that doubts arise in the

V. S.Vitale, Ravenna
South wall of chancel

VI. Two saints
Mosaic on apse wall of Chapel of S. Venanzio, Lateran Baptistery, Rome

A.D. 642–9
page 106

beholder's mind as to how much bodily substance any part of this entire con-
figuration really has. Seated on an orange-coloured bench, the angels overlap
the oak's trunk; yet they seem to be not in front of but behind it, since the legs
of the table that is placed before them appear to rest on the ground behind the
tree. None of this, then, bears rational analysis. Existence of real persons and
objects in real space is only approximated: in effect, like the evangelists, they
are attached to a backdrop.

What the artist has created here may appropriately be termed a pseudo-
emblema. It is a framed panel picture with seemingly unified and space-creating
scenery and with figures in seemingly natural relationships inhabiting this
scenery. In actual fact there is no recession into depth. The *emblema* is not a
'window' as it had been in the past. As for the frame within which it is set, it
in turn has become a vehicle of similarly pseudo-real views. In both cases the
surface remains basically intact. We found that the acceptance of the surface in
its totality, the frank display of the abstract matrix, was an essential formal
principle which came to the fore in the course of the preceding century. The
step is not reversed here. Nowhere is the surface really broken through. Its
integrity is merely disguised by the introduction of two other – more traditional –
factors: one is a structuring in terms of framing and framed parts; the other,
an abundance of 'nature' elements. The latter, however, are spread over *all* the
surfaces, thus making for uniformity. The overriding impression these walls
create is indeed that of a *horror vacui*. There is movement and luxuriant growth
everywhere. But it is only a veneer. Beneath it the wall is solid and intact.

The Justinianic pictorial style can thus be seen to be indeed a kind of balanc-
ing act which attempts to reconcile the irreconcilable. It involves a reattachment to past ideals of natural and organic relationships without abandoning the
new abstractness firmly established in the course of the preceding one hundred
years. In passing it may be noted that similar principles also govern Justinianic
architecture. *Mutatis mutandis* one finds the same paradoxes as in our mosaics
embodied in the design of St Sophia.[2]

In the apse of S.Vitale it is the composition in the conch which functions as
an *emblema*, while the rest of the decoration constitutes an elaborate framework
(figs. 150, 156).[3] The view of the paradisical garden in which Christ holds court
is set back from a heavy ornamental band, filled with a pattern of cornucopiae,
which arches around the opening of the conch; and although the arrangement
of the figures is formal and symmetric, the landscape in which they are placed
makes a plausible spatial setting. Yet once again this impression does not remain
unchallenged. The blue sphere signifying heaven on which Christ is seated is
fitted into a segment cut out, as it were, from the green ground, and thus the

materiality of the terrain is radically called into question. At a crucial point the landscape setting turns out to have a consistency no greater than paper.

Still, in relation to the whole, the scene does have the character of an *emblema* surmounting two tiers of wainscoting.[4] The lowest zone is an actual skirting of *opus sectile* articulated by a pilaster architecture which carries an entablature. The mosaic decoration begins above the latter's projecting cornice. But the first mosaic zone, on the level of the windows, is in effect another wainscoting. Simulated pilasters are placed between the windows. They stand on the axes of those in the *opus sectile* zone and on them rests the narrow band that is the actual border of the scene in the conch. On the sides this border rests on the two panels with the imperial processions which, extending as they do to the very front edge of the apse, are an integral part of this second support zone (figs. 151, 152). Indeed, the cornucopia band that enframes the paradise picture from the front, though contained within the latter's ornamental border, in effect also rests on these panels, and their supporting function is made explicit by the fact that the system of simulated pilasters carries through into their domain. Although, with characteristic ambiguity, the lateral pilasters are half-absorbed into the architectural scenery of the processions, they clearly relate to those in the centre, and they again stand on the axes of the *opus sectile* pilasters below. Justinian in his purple robe might himself be said to take the place of a missing pilaster (fig. 151).[5]

The picture-frame concept, then, is very definitely present in the apse as well. In fact, here too it constitutes the organizing principle. But again the frame has its own 'pictures'. The two imperial scenes are self-contained tableaux, each with its own setting, though only Theodora's is elaborated in some detail. With their tightly packed compositions, their severe lines and their precise delineation of every detail, the two panels differ so strikingly from all the other mosaics in the chancel that they have at times been thought to be of a different date, afterthoughts added by Maximian to a decoration already largely completed when he assumed office. But to consider this difference of styles as a matter of dates (or even of 'hands') is to disregard quite fundamental aspects of this art. It is a case not unlike that of the mosaics of S.Maria Maggiore in Rome discussed in the preceding chapter.[6] There can be no doubt that at S.Vitale too the difference was introduced intentionally and purposefully, although here it was done with an eye on the compositional context which I have just analysed, as well as for thematic reasons. With little space given to settings, the imperial processions in their tight alignment present a solid front – a wall, almost. This befits the function of these panels as part of a 'wainscoting' zone while at the same time expressing the fact that the figures here belong to a different world, distinct both from the heavenly paradise above and from the biblical ambient of the scenes on the adjoining lateral walls. In this sense it is once again a matter of 'modes', a deliberate change of key, with the most pronounced geometry, order and abstractness reserved for the world of the earthly ruler.

Thus the formal rendering of the imperial scenes ingeniously serves the needs both of their subject content and of their role in the compositional structure. Their differentiation vis-à-vis the *emblema* in the conch is, however, only a relative one. On closer examination, the imperial panels turn out to be not quite so static and rigid as they seem at first. Theodora's procession moves decidedly towards the centre of the apse, and Justinian and his suite too are in motion. In fact, the seeming simplicity of this panel with its isocephalic array of rigidly erect figures is wholly deceptive (fig. 158).[7] One need only attempt to plot on a 'ground plan' the position of all the figures in relation to each other and to the frame to become aware of two factors which, while mutually incompatible from a realistic point of view, are both in conflict with the impression of a simple line-up parallel to the picture plane.

For one thing, the entire retinue is staggered in depth behind the emperor. His figure in effect is at the head of a V-shaped column which, in terms of its three-dimensional implications, projects far out from the wall and well into the 'real' space of the sanctuary; at the same time the formation is placed diagonally in relation to the frame. At the left end the imperial bodyguard is overlapped by the frame, while at the right end hand and foot of the censer-bearing cleric cut across the framing pilaster. Both these devices entail a modicum of spatial illusion, and this is reinforced by the fact, noted earlier, that the pilasters themselves are in a sense part of the real architecture of the apse. Thus Justinian and his suite become a real presence in a way no other element in the entire S. Vitale ensemble does. Their diagonal alignment helps to underscore the impression that they are indeed a moving procession – an impression created primarily by the sideways action of arms proffering gifts or utensils and subtly aided by the fact that Justinian's position is slightly off centre. But the placing of the emperor at the apex of a 'V' reinforces the contrary effect of a static and symmetric composition of which he is the axis.

This latter effect is clearly meant to dominate, but it is cunningly challenged by those factors which imply movement in space. It is challenged in another way as well. Maximian, standing next to the emperor, is overlapped by the latter in the area of his right arm and must therefore be assumed to be in a second plane behind his sovereign. Yet he is taller than Justinian and actually appears to be standing in front of him. (He is also the only person singled out by a name inscription.) The emperor is made to share his prominence with the bishop.

Together the two figures in their dark robes form, as it were, the central part of a triptych whose wings are constituted by two pairs of courtiers and clerics clad in white. It is a picture within the picture, set off from the bodyguard on the left which has its own quite distinct colour accents; and it makes an unmistakable point, a point decidedly at variance with the idea of Justinian's sole and absolute power which is conveyed by the composition as a whole.

This panel, therefore, for all its apparent simplicity, is as intricately constructed and as highly charged as a Bach fugue. Nowhere is the 'reconciliation of the irreconcilable' carried through with such consummate artistry as here. Nowhere are the resulting tensions as effective and dramatic. But at the same time they are carefully controlled and calibrated so as not to impair the function assigned to the panel in the overall design. The picture very definitely remains part of the framing and supporting zone for the great celestial vision above.

Clearly the designer of the S.Vitale mosaics was a great master, one of the great artists of the first Christian millennium. We do not know where he came from. Undoubtedly he must have studied the earlier Ravennate decorations. But the roots of the stylistic innovations he introduced lie elsewhere. In its most essential aspects, the art of S.Vitale is not explicable in local terms. It becomes historically intelligible only in the light of certain antecedent developments in the Greek East. The master designer must have hailed from that area or at any rate have been in close touch with what was happening there.

To demonstrate this, it is best to turn once more to floor mosaics. They alone among works in the pictorial media are preserved in sufficient density in all parts of the Mediterranean world to permit comparative judgements as to trends and developments in different regions. Obviously it means a descent to a lower level – literally and artistically. But the descent will prove as illuminating as it did earlier in our study of fifth-century art.

A very few examples must suffice to bring out the key points.[8] We saw how in the pavement mosaics at Antioch the principle of surface acceptance had gained ground since the late fourth century, first in the form of unified geometric carpets (fig. 91) and then in the form of what I have called figure carpets (fig. 90). Now in the realm of purely ornamental floors a further striking change gradually took place both at Antioch and elsewhere in the Greek East as the fifth century progressed. Although carpets composed entirely of geometric motifs continued to be made, there was an increasing tendency to inject organic elements – animal and vegetable – into the designs. If a typical nave mosaic in a church of about A.D.400 offered a seemingly infinite expanse of repetitive geometric motifs, by the year A.D.500 a typical nave floor anywhere in the Greek world shows a variety of birds, animals and plants incorporated into

such patterns. These motifs in turn tend to be quite repetitive, so that the
overall character remains that of an endlessly expansible carpet. A floor in the
narthex of a basilica excavated at Delphi, probably of the period c. A.D.500,
provides a good example of this style (fig. 161).[9] By this time, however, many
designers of floor decorations all over the Near East had substituted floral for
geometric motifs in constructing the framework itself (fig. 162).[10] These floral
motifs are severely stylized, but they do carry suggestions of organic growth
which the geometric carpets had excluded entirely; and when, as presently
happened, these floral grids were also enriched with organic filler motifs, a
totally new kind of carpet was in effect created – still geometric in its basic
structure, but teeming with life. The 'Striding Lion' floor from Antioch, a
work of the advanced fifth or, more probably, the early sixth century, is a
good example (fig. 163).[11] The next logical step is the replacement of the floral
grid by an actual growing organism, a rinceau issuing either from stems in the
four corners or from a single stem at the base. A floor found outside the Damascus Gate in Jerusalem is a splendid example (fig. 164).[12] The involutions of the
rinceau are kept so uniform as to create what is still an abstract pattern to be
filled at will with animals, birds and other motifs. Yet it is an organism, coherent, unified and continuous, with a single live force flowing through it; and
it provides a natural habitat for the creatures it encloses.

It should be emphasized that 'inhabited' rinceaux as field patterns for floors
had existed at a much earlier period in Italy, North Africa and elsewhere in the
West.[13] But in the East, and particularly in Syria and Palestine where such
floors became commonplace in the sixth century,[14] they constituted at that time
a new vogue, a vogue prepared by and growing out of the process of floraliza-
tion of carpet designs which I have outlined. Although I have perforce simplified
and schematized this development its existence is undeniable and, as will be
seen readily, it has a bearing on the revolutionary change that we have observed
at S.Vitale.

The 'Striding Lion' floor at Antioch (fig. 163) is interesting also in another
respect. The handsome beast after which it is named is superimposed on the
grid pattern and provides it with an emphatic focus and centre. The birds and
quadrupeds which fill the grid face in four different directions; from whichever
side a beholder approaches he will see a group of them in an upright position. In
this sense the mosaic is multidirectional and endlessly expansible in true carpet
fashion. But the lion creates a principal viewpoint, and there is a heavy outer
frame to enclose him and to keep the flowing pattern within bounds. Increasingly
during the late fifth and early sixth centuries such focal motifs were placed at or
near the centre of repeat patterns, and increasingly also framing bands were

broadened, elaborated and multiplied.[15] There is thus a clear tendency in these floor designs to counteract the even spread and potential endlessness of carpet-type compositions; to make them finite and centralized; and to structure them in terms of primary and secondary components. In fact, the grid pattern of this mosaic is in a sense a foil for an image of a lion in an ample frame. There is here, in other words, a latent tendency to return to the *emblema* concept. But this change is accomplished within what remains very definitely a carpet-type design.

It is not surprising in the light of this development to find that certain mosaic floors made in Greek lands in the first half of the sixth century present once more real 'pictures', that is, panels of limited size offering views of natural objects in more or less natural relationships. A floor of *c.* A.D.525–50 in the Church of St Demetrius in Nikopolis in Epirus may serve as an example (fig. 165).[16] It shows a landscape with trees standing on (or, to be quite precise, hovering slightly above) a strip of ground, along with plants and some pecking birds, while other birds are in the air. Though obviously stylized and highly formalized, this is a view of a piece of the 'real' world in the tradition of the famous garden prospects painted in the Augustan age on the walls of the Villa at Prima Porta.[17] The picture is enclosed within no less than five framing bands beginning with a bead-and-reel border and a running spiral, which are classical framing motifs for *emblemata*. The principal frame is a broad strip of simulated water inhabited by fish and fishermen and in turn enclosed between two narrow ornamental bands. The mosaic, which covers the floor of one wing of the transept of the church, is intended to be far more than a mere ornament. It has a lengthy inscription in Homeric hexameters which invests it with an extremely interesting cosmographic symbolism: the tree landscape, so we are told, stands for the earth, the aquatic band around it for the encircling ocean. The injection of explicitly cosmological themes into the decoration of church floors was a characteristic and significant development in the Justinianic age.[18] Our concern here, how-ever, is the composition of the Nikopolis floor, which it is interesting to compare with that of an earlier landscape mosaic in a corresponding location in the Church of the Multiplying of the Loaves and Fishes at Tabgha (fig. 92).[19] The artist at Nikopolis regrouped the elements which in the earlier work had been taken apart, re-established their real relationships and firmly enclosed the re-sulting view in a multiple frame. But the view has no depth. The panel picture, unlike the true *emblema* of Roman times, respects the integrity of the floor. The matrix remains basically intact as it does in the Palestinian example. What the sixth-century artist has created is a pseudo-*emblema*.

In using this term again I am not implying any direct connection between the atelier of S.Vitale and the Greek workshops which created floor mosaics such as the one at Nikopolis. What I do suggest is that basically similar formal principles and ideals are involved in both cases. There is in both a desire to re-establish a natural view of things, to show their organic interrelationships and confine them within clear and reasonable limits; to tame infinity as it were, but without abandoning the premise of a potentially limitless foil that cannot be fully assimilated and mastered in terms of earthly experience. The special importance of the pavement mosaics lies in the fact that in them we can discern an evolutionary process leading up to this extraordinary reconciliation of opposites. Moreover, they show this process to be very definitely concentrated in the Greek sphere. There are occasional offshoots of the pseudo-organic style of pavement decoration in the Latin world.[20] But the West did not participate actively and consistently in creating it. The emergence of the style must be interpreted as a reassertion in the Greek East of traditions deeply rooted in that area's Hellenistic past. There is in these Eastern floor mosaics of the pre-Justinianic and early Justinianic period much groping towards forms compatible with that past. The latent (and finally not so latent) reassertion of the *emblema* concept is especially interesting in this respect. The end result is a floor such as that at Nikopolis, which can hardly be explained without assuming an actual revival, a conscious going-back to much earlier forms. This entire process is undoubtedly relevant to the art of S.Vitale. Without detracting from the achievement of the great master who created that magnificent decoration, the Eastern pavements help to put that achievement in context.

Before leaving S.Vitale a few words should be added about the mosaic of the ceiling with its celestial vision of the Agnus Dei (fig. 167). Four diagonal bands, richly adorned with flowers, fruit and birds support a central wreath in which the Lamb appears against a starry sky. The bands reflect and emphasize the shape and structural function of the groin vault which bears the mosaic. The wreath is supported additionally by four caryatid angels standing on blue spheres. The motif of the angels had appeared at Ravenna a few decades earlier on the ceiling of the small chapel in the Archbishop's Palace (fig. 109), and it is very evident that the S.Vitale master studied the local work that had preceded his own. Indeed, in this case he might be said to be quoting from it. But he has completely transformed the motif by reducing its relative size and embedding it in a sumptuous floral decor. In doing this he drew on other sources. Systems of bands, florally interpreted, as a support for a central element of a vault decoration are traditional, and by the fifth century had reached a degree of stylization such as we find here. In the vault mosaic of the Chapel of St John the Evangelist built by Pope Hilarus (A.D.461–8) as an annex to the Lateran Baptistery a scheme of this kind serves as a framework for a central Agnus Dei (fig. 166).[21] Rinceaux as an all-over design in vaults also have a long history; intended to suggest a bower or pergola, they too had become formalized. In a small fifth-century chapel at Capua (fig. 168) we find them fitted into each of the four spandrels of a groin vault as they are in S.Vitale.[22] It was by combining the firm structure of the garland bands with the spandrel rinceaux and by making of both a setting for the caryatid angels that the S.Vitale master achieved his extraordinarily rich effect. Once again there is a clear distinction between framing and framed parts. Structural differentiation is carried further by confining the gold background to the two spandrels in the longitudinal axis, while in the two transversal spandrels the colour scheme is reversed (the background being green and the rinceaux gold). But having thus differentiated the component elements, the designer unites them all by the ubiquity and luxuriance of the floral theme. Each element in itself is traditional. The combination is wholly new. More clearly than elsewhere we can see the master's achievement as a synthesis – not only in the sense that he unites what had previously been separate, but also in the remarkable balance he achieves between abstract order and organic life.

At the same time, the convergence with the evolution we have observed in Eastern floor mosaics becomes very evident here. We need not necessarily assume that the designer looked at floors. But there was an inherent relationship of long standing between floor and ceiling designs.[23] Hence at S.Vitale it is to the ceiling that the development we have observed in floor mosaics is more particularly relevant. But the whole decoration is a unit informed throughout by the same stylistic principles. The evidence of the pavement mosaics enables us to postulate a seedbed in the Greek East which generated these principles and brought them to maturity. This evidence is all the more valuable because in the East no wall mosaic has survived which fully embodies the essential characteristics of the early Justinianic style.

There is one major work in Rome which exhibits a variant of the style. A monumental apse mosaic (fig. 169) survives in fairly good condition in the Church of SS. Cosma e Damiano on the Via Sacra, a foundation of Pope Felix IV (A.D.526–30).[24] The central figure is Christ, as in the apse of S.Vitale, and again there is a ceremonial presentation scene in a landscape setting. But the action is far more dramatic. Christ – a majestic bearded figure in golden robes, reminiscent of the great ruler and teacher presiding over the assembled apostles in the apse of S.Pudenziana (fig. 80) – stands aloft in a magnificent expanse of dark blue sky on which his path is marked by multicoloured clouds. He strikes a pose long associated with the monarch's triumphant *adventus*,[25] and he is being acclaimed by the princes of the apostles who, standing beneath on the flowery bank of a paradisical River Jordan (thus inscribed), present to him the two titular saints. The latter step forward offering their crowns of martyrdom, and their action is echoed by the figures of St Theodore on the far right, also offering his crown, and the papal founder on the far left (a seventeenth-century restoration entirely), offering a model of the church. The whole is placed in a framework of apocalyptic motifs.[26]

Although many elements in this composition derive from a specifically Roman tradition of apse decoration,[27] there is no doubt that in its formal aspects the mosaic reflects broad trends of its period. Since most of the Roman antecedents are lost, it is hazardous to assert either that a strong element of drama has been newly injected into what in the prototypal works had been a solemn, static array of holy figures or, on the contrary, that dramatic action has been firmly contained within a static system. But certainly we see here – in an important monument created at the very beginning of the Justinianic era – a remarkable balance being achieved between these opposing factors. They are held in a state of tension which is the key to the mosaic's powerful effect. Christ's *parousia* is sudden and overwhelming. Yet he is also the apex of a solid and rigidly symmetric triangular construction. The scene takes place on a plausible, if shallow, stage, with grassy ground, water, cloud-bank and sky forming so many planes one behind the other; and the figures, which are voluminous, indeed ponderous, are organic entities using this space freely and expansively (fig. 170). Yet the beholder cannot for a moment lose sight of the geometric and purely two-dimensional pattern of which every element in the composition is a part.

These principles pervade every detail, above all the extraordinarily impressive heads (fig. 160). A firm linear framework, an inheritance from the preceding decades, underlies their construction (cf. figs. 110–13). But each component part of a face – forehead, nose, cheeks, beard, hair crown – is now strongly modelled; and they all seem to press forward against the framework without ever rupturing it at any point. A great force, concentrated most irresistibly in the huge, wide-open eyes, pushes from within, and subtle asymmetries enhance the effect of intense animation. But the glance remains immutably fixed in timeless authority.

Precisely these terms apply also to a head such as that of Justinian in the imperial mosaic at S.Vitale (fig. 159). Here, too, all features are contained within a clear geometric frame – in this case a parabolic shape of which the flattened band of the jewelled crown forms an integral part – but they are strongly modelled and again there are subtle asymmetries to offset the regularity of the design. Here, too, the result is a portrayal of overwhelming power, imperturbably timeless yet entirely real, individual and alive. The kinship between the Roman and the Ravennate work becomes most readily apparent in this comparison. The mosaic of SS.Cosma e Damiano, executed some twenty years before the mosaics of S.Vitale, shows that the essential principles of the Justinianic synthesis were then already operative.

It is, however, in the minor arts and more particularly in ivory carvings that the salient characteristics of the S.Vitale mosaics have, among extant works, their closest equivalents. Since the ivories in question are undoubtedly from the Greek East, they help to confirm the key role which that region played in generating and promoting these characteristics. A discussion of two of these objects will round out our exploration of the art of the early Justinianic era. Viewed in the context of their own craft, they will highlight further the vitality and creative power of that era as well as the remarkable consistency of its aesthetic aims.

By far the most sumptuous product of the ivory carver's art to have survived from the entire period with which this book is concerned is the decoration of Bishop Maximian's episcopal chair (figs. 171–5).[28] This, of course, takes us back to Ravenna once more and, indeed, to a man prominently associated with the S.Vitale mosaics. Together, the mosaics and the Chair, which bears on the front the Bishop's monogram artfully worked into its ornamentation, might, in fact, be taken as exponents of a local variant of Justinianic art, reflecting the taste of a particular patron or group of patrons. Most scholars, however, are agreed that the Chair is not of local Ravennate manufacture. Numerous other ivory reliefs are known which, on the evidence of their stylistic character, must have been carved in the same atelier as those adorning the Chair, or at any rate in closely related shops. There is a continuing debate as to whether this 'school' was located in Egypt or, as I believe, in Constantinople.[29] But it was certainly in the Greek East, and while the Chair may have been made to Maximian's specifications it also exemplifies that school's much larger production.

Front, sides and both faces of the back are covered with figure representations. On the front are standing figures of the four evangelists and, in the centre, John the Baptist holding the Lamb of God; on the two sides is a series of scenes depicting the story of Joseph; the back showed in twenty-four oblong fields events from the life of Christ, but a number of these panels are now missing. On all sides are framing bands richly carved with vine rinceaux.

The framework particularly calls for comment. Four upright posts, square in section and adorned with vines, form the principal supports on which the Chair rests. (There was, however, originally, concealed beneath the seat, a system of reinforcements in wood which has not survived.) Both on the front and on the sides the four posts are interconnected by broad horizontal bands which form with them a kind of armature within which other panels are contained. This distinction between framing and framed elements is basic to the whole composition. It rests on the fact that the broad bands with vine rinceaux on the front and three of the five Joseph panels on each side are entirely flush with the corner posts and are conceived by the eye as continuous with them, while the panels within this framework have their own heavy mouldings and, thanks to the shadows these mouldings create, appear quite deeply recessed. On the sides (figs. 171, 173), this alternation of framing and framed panels is readily perceptible, and the rhythm is accentuated by the fact that the latter are much wider than the former. But the series of vertical figure panels on the front (fig. 172) also shows the same differentiation. Here, too, broader panels recessed within mouldings alternate with narrow ones that are flush with the rinceau bands, with the result that two of the five panels with standing figures really belong with the armature and, aesthetically speaking, constitute additional upright supports firming up the structural framework of the Chair.

However, like the master who created the S.Vitale mosaics, the designer of the Chair also seems bent on negating the compositional structure he himself has so clearly created. The cycle of Joseph scenes is a single narrative covering all five of the tiered panels on each side, framing as well as framed ones.[30] Similarly, the holy figures in front – clearly a unit, a sort of *sacra conversazione* – cover all five of the vertical panels. And since, with the sole exception of Maximian's monogram, there is also a superabundance of organic motifs in the superbly carved ornamental bands above and below these panels, the overall impression of luxuriant life – of a *horror vacui* that seeks to cover all parts of the available surface with vibrant living forms – is even stronger here than in S.Vitale. Thus, both iconographically and aesthetically, the artist has to a considerable extent levelled the distinction between picture and frame. But in another sense again he has not. He has re-emphasized it perversely by a paradoxical treatment of the relief. It is in the framing parts – which provide the armature and which we would therefore expect to be the most solid – that figures and ornaments are most deeply undercut. As a result, these framing members – the three narrow Joseph panels, the two narrow evangelist panels, and the vine rinceaux above and below – have deeper shadows, less substance and more of an *à jour* effect than the reliefs within the frames. Irrationality is carried even further here than at S.Vitale.

Much else would have to be taken into account in a full stylistic analysis of the Chair. There are stylistic differences between individual parts that are due

not to the differentiation of structural roles but to different hands and the
use of different 'modes' for the different kinds of subjects. Yet the unity of the
design and of the overall character is undeniable. I shall draw attention to only
one other unifying feature, namely, a preference for *contrapposto* stances which
all the figure reliefs share, though this characteristic stands out most clearly in
the Joseph scenes (figs. 173, 175). Many figures in these scenes show an emphatic differentiation between free leg and engaged leg. Heads and shoulders
tend to bend in rhythmic correlation to the movement of the free leg, so that
entire bodies become swaying 'S' curves. Often the action portrayed provides
little or no motivation for these *contrapposto* rhythms which are, of course, an
inheritance from Graeco-Roman art, but which here become a kind of man-
nerism. The swaying motion they engender tends to be echoed throughout an
entire panel and repeated in adjoining panels. As a result, not only individual
scenes but also sequences of reliefs are knit together by an undulating movement.
This movement affects the Christological scenes as well (fig. 174) and even – by
dint of an alternating rhythm – two of the five great statuesque figures in front
(fig. 172). At S. Vitale, too, we found the movements and actions of figures to be
one of the factors contributing to the unity of the whole. But in the mosaics
movements are not so spe ifically correlated as they are here, and the *contrapposto* device does not occur there at all. In a sense, therefore, the ivories are
more classicizing and at the same time even more strongly and organically
integrated than the mosaics.

   The other ivory to be discussed is the so-called Barberini Diptych in the
Louvre (fig. 176).[31] Second only to Maximian's Chair in fame and interest, it
leads us into the sphere of secular imperial art and shows imagery in that sphere
shaped by the characteristic aesthetic preferences of the early Justinianic period.

   The diptych is of the 'five-part' type, a type which came into vogue in the
fifth century and was used for exceptionally sumptuous book bindings (cf.
fig. 85) as well as for exceptionally sumptuous objects of official largesse. In the
latter capacity the type may have been reserved exclusively for imperial
patrons.[32] One of the five panels of the Louvre piece is missing and the second
half of the diptych is entirely lost. The central panel of the extant leaf depicts
the emperor mounted on a richly caparisoned horse and attended by an acclaiming barbarian, a flying Victory and a recumbent *Terra*. A high-ranking military
officer approaches from the left, offering 'Victory' in the form of a small statue,
and no doubt there was originally a corresponding figure on the right. Homage
is also being paid by representatives of various exotic nations depicted in small
scale in the lower horizontal strip. Led by yet another Victory they bring
appropriate gifts and tributes, including wild animals. But the ruler triumphs

by the grace of God and on God's behalf, as witness the bust of Christ, borne by flying angels, in the top panel.

Scholars are not universally agreed on the dating of this work. There is, however, a specific stylistic relationship to the reliefs of Maximian's Chair. Indeed, the tribute-bearing barbarians are closely related to figures in the latter's Joseph scenes (fig. 175). Faces (particularly eyes) are cut in similar fashion and bodies move in the same characteristic swaying action. The Barberini Diptych must have been made in the same period and perhaps even in the same atelier as the Chair. It follows that the emperor whose success it extols must be Justinian.[33]

Five-part diptychs are framed pictures by definition. The central panel – here, as often, rendered in very high relief – dominates; the other four form its frame. What is remarkable in this instance is the amount of lively activity with which the central relief is packed. Most often in such diptychs that panel is occupied by a completely static image – a motionless figure of a ruler in rigid *en face* view or, in the case of religious pieces, an appropriate emblem (fig. 85) or an enthroned Christ or Virgin. A portrayal of the emperor in solemn repose would have been a natural subject in this case. He would have appeared simply as the ever-imperturbable recipient of the acts of homage and tribute by which he is surrounded, the immovable centre upon which all movement converges. Instead the scene here is crowded with momentary action so swift and intense that the panel can barely contain it. The emperor has arrived on his charger this instant, his mantle still flying in the wind. It almost appears as though he had just passed through a low city gate which had caused him to tilt his head. He pulls in the reins and makes a rapid half-turn as he rams his spear into the ground to use it as a support in dismounting. Earth herself renders a groom's service and puts a helping hand under his foot, while the cheering barbarian obsequiously brings up the rear and Victory flies in to crown him. In all Roman imperial art there is no more spirited portrayal of an imperial *adventus*.[34] It is not on a sedentary presence that the figures in the framing panels converge. Action is met by action, and all parts are knit together in indissoluble unity. Movements of figures in different panels respond to each other as they do on Maximian's Chair. The result is again a swaying rhythm pervading the whole and counteracting the distinction between picture and frame, a distinction which is none the less unmistakable. The only figure in repose is Christ in his celestial *clipeus* in the top panel. But taken in its entirety that panel, too, represents action – note how the angel on the left bearing the *clipeus* takes up the movement of the emperor's head – and this action must surely be understood as being closely parallel to that in the centre. The celestial vision cannot be meant to be stationary. Christ makes his appearance in heaven at the moment in which the emperor stages his triumphal *adventus* on earth. It is a graphic depiction of the harmony between heavenly and earthly rule, a concept basic to Byzantine political thought from the outset but proclaimed by Justinian's artist with unprecedented clarity and vigour.

The Barberini Diptych makes a fitting conclusion to our exploration of the art of the early Justinianic era. Particularly when viewed against the background of the official diptychs of the preceding generation (fig. 86), it palpably epitomizes the aesthetic achievement of this period. Once again there arises the question as to what the achievement means and whether it can be related in some way to a broader historical and cultural context.

There is no ready answer to this question, and I shall confine myself to two suggestions. One concerns the revival of forms and motifs associated with the Graeco-Roman past.[35] This was certainly an important factor in the stylistic make-up of the works we have studied; and it has quite tangible parallels in other areas, more particularly in Justinian's legislative work. His goal was, after all, a *renovatio* of the Roman empire.[36] Given the consciousness of this effort, a retrospective or even an antiquarian bent in the realm of art is readily understandable. In many instances the trend might indeed be promoted by the wishes and purposes of patrons and donors and therefore be 'other-directed'.

My second point is more elusive. It has to do with the quest for wholeness, for indissoluble unity – and a kind of structured and organic unity – which emerged as a fundamental trait of the art of the period. This is a more instinctive trend, implicit to some extent in antecedent developments and, I submit, largely 'inner-directed'. It has, however, an equivalent in the subject matter of works such as the Barberini Diptych or the chancel decoration of S. Vitale. The latter with its unified conspectus of divine *oikonomia* and its harnessing of that conspectus to the liturgy foreshadows the great systems of Byzantine church decoration in the centuries after Iconoclasm.[37] At S. Vitale we are as yet far from the uncluttered clarity, calm and simplicity of Daphni. The artists of Justinian's time conceived of wholeness and unity in terms of physical continuity and physical interconnections. They presented divine order in the guise of natural order. But it was a world order which they were building, an all-embracing view embodying past, present and future; earth and heaven; the visible and also the invisible. This was a concept which their stylistic devices helped to make concrete and with which these devices were fully in tune.

CHAPTER SIX

Polarization and Another Synthesis – 1

The aesthetic ideal of the early Justinianic period was short-lived. By its very nature it hardly could have been maintained for long. Aiming as it did at a total reconciliation of abstract forms and relationships with natural and organic ones, it presented challenges which only the most brilliant and sophisticated artists of the period were able to meet fully. By the year A.D.550 the impetus that had produced the great works of synthesis of the period – St Sophia, S.Vitale, Maximian's Chair – seems to have spent itself.

The ensuing period until the outbreak of Iconoclasm in Byzantium – a time span of close to two centuries – has a far less clearly defined profile than any of the preceding ones. It is a period of convulsive change, marked by the break-up of Justinian's empire, the intrusion of Slavs – and, above all, of Arabs – into the Mediterranean world, and the slow transformation of Byzantium into a regional power based on Asia Minor. In art history, too, the period constitutes a major turning point. But its specific achievements and its peculiar importance are only beginning to be fully recognized.

A marked stylistic shift in the later years of Justinian's reign is manifested by the sanctuary mosaics in the church of the fortress monastery at Mount Sinai, built by that emperor between A.D.548 and 565.[1] The principal subject, in the conch of the apse, is the Transfiguration, set in a frame of medallions containing portraits of apostles, prophets and two donors (fig. 177). There can be little doubt that the mosaics are contemporary with the building.[2]

The Transfiguration has a special relevance to the site, involving as it does Moses, the 'cult hero' of Mount Sinai, and showing him in dramatic association with Christ. The subject lends itself for display in an apse since the scene has a somewhat ceremonial character. Indeed, the Sinai mosaic invites comparison with the ceremonial representations in the apses of SS.Cosma e Damiano in Rome and S.Vitale in Ravenna. But the contrast is striking. Both in the Roman and in the Ravennate mosaics figures form a plausible group on a plausible landscape stage. At Sinai they are placed singly and without overlaps against the plain gold ground. The terrain at their feet is very much reduced and gold is insistently displayed as an abstract foil, much as it had been in the mosaic decorations of the pre-Justinianic era. To be sure, at S.Vitale the illusion of solid terrain supporting the figures is tenuous and, as we have seen, it breaks down in the central area.[3] But in the Sinai mosaic the indication of locale is altogether confined to a sequence of narrow bands – dark green, light green and yellow. Interestingly varied in width but sharply delineated throughout, these bands convey only the vaguest and most general suggestion of a sunlit meadow. Of the two conflicting elements in the S.Vitale landscape, it is the notion of a dematerialized 'baseboard' which prevails. The figures are not really supported by the terrain. One might just barely conceive of the two prophets as standing on it. The recumbent Peter is in front of it, while the two kneeling apostles, though strongly three-dimensional in themselves, are oddly poised on its razor-thin upper edge (fig. 179).

The utter reduction of the landscape elements in this mosaic is doubly re-markable when one considers that the subject called for the depiction of a mountain. It has been suggested that the mountain scenery – which is hardly ever absent in subsequent Byzantine representations of the Transfiguration – was omitted in order to transpose the event into heaven and equate it with Christ's Second Coming.[4] But the scenes at SS.Cosma e Damiano and S.Vitale are also celestial, and that locale is indicated by multicoloured clouds. In the Sinai mosaic the neutrality of the ground and the starkness with which the actors – including Christ in his magnificent blue mandorla – are set off against it must be seen as a stylistic trait. As such, it is of a piece with other features of the design: its essential symmetry; the simplified rendering of forms; the absence of strong colour accents within the figure group; the huge lettering of the name inscriptions. All these make for an abstract and unified pattern, for which the neutral ground is an appropriate foil. It is true that the figures retain much of the corporeality characteristic of those of the preceding period. Indeed, in the kneeling apostles bulk is emphasized almost to excess. Also, to the right of the head of Elijah (fig. 180) there remains, in an oddly residual form, one of those deep shadows which in S.Vitale were used to hollow out a niche or cavity for a figure from its landscape backdrop (fig. 157). In the absence of such a backdrop, the device hardly makes sense. But such features only confirm that a genuine stylistic change is here in the making.

The Sinai designer still surrounds his scene with a strong and heavy frame. But with the suggestion of a view into an open landscape so greatly reduced, the contrast of picture and frame, which at S.Vitale was basic to the entire composi-tion, is largely lost. The frame with its serried rows of medallions is set off against the scene within only by presenting an even denser and tighter pattern; between frame and 'picture' the designer has inserted another band bearing the dedicatory inscription, and he has made this band more nearly part of the

VII. The Maccabees
Fresco in S.Maria Antiqua, Rome

First half of seventh century
page 113

VIII. St Peter
Icon in Monastery
of St Catherine,
Mount Sinai

Here attributed
to *c.* A.D.700
page 120

'picture' than part of the frame. Evidently there is no longer a desire to create a clear distinction and a true functional tension between the two components.

It should perhaps be emphasized that the differences between the Sinai mosaic on the one hand, and the mosaics of SS.Cosma e Damiano and S.Vitale on the other, are not primarily a matter of quality. To be sure, in execution the Sinai mosaic is uneven. Although in the best passages the quality is very high, there are particularly among the busts of prophets and apostles – and also among the figures on the wall above the conch – some whose rendering must be described as provincial. Yet an increased abstraction is evident even in passages of indisputably high artistic merit; witness, for instance, the predominance of straight lines in the system of highlights and shadows on Christ's white raiment (fig. 178).

The Sinai mosaic has been attributed to an atelier from Constantinople.[5] Obviously artists must have been brought to this remote outpost from elsewhere, and the fact that the monastery was an imperial foundation makes it historically plausible that they came from the capital. The principal elements of the style of the S.Vitale mosaics likewise were Greek, as we have seen,[6] and it is entirely possible that they, too, derived from metropolitan Byzantium specifically. If both theses are correct, the difference between the two mosaic decorations cannot be explained in regional terms any more adequately than in terms of quality. When details from the two ensembles are put side by side, it can be seen readily that they are, in fact, fruits from the same tree (figs. 180–3).

We must reckon, then, with a rather fundamental change in Byzantine art itself around the year A.D.550. The exuberance, the crowding of organic forms, the emphasis on things growing, living and moving are gone. A chill has descended and has left the scene bare and figures frozen in their positions.

At Ravenna the change is reflected in the apse decoration of S.Apollinare in Classe, a church consecrated by Bishop Maximian in A.D.549, only two years after the dedication of S.Vitale (figs. 184–6).[7] Like the earlier Ravennate decoration – and like that on Sinai – the Classe mosaic is highly complex in subject matter. In this respect it is perhaps the most intricately constructed of all Justinianic programmes. An apotheosis of St Apollinaris – a confessor (if not, indeed, a martyr) who was thought to have been Ravenna's first bishop and whose tomb was enshrined in the church – is combined with the Transfiguration theme, but a Transfiguration strangely represented in a semi-allegorical, semi-symbolic manner, and here clearly to be perceived as an eschatological, or, at any rate, a timeless event.[8] There certainly is no falling off either in ideological intensity or intellectual subtlety on the part of those who commissioned this decoration and devised its iconography. Similarly, the standard of artistic quality is not in doubt; indeed, it is sustained more consistently than in the Sinai decoration. The magnificent mosaics of S.Vitale, only recently completed and only a few miles away, were bound to exert an impact on the work and they obviously did. In particular the S.Vitale master's treatment of the window zone and the idea of making the mosaics of that zone a 'wainscoting', a semi-architectural framework for a landscape view in the conch, influenced the designer at Classe. But this is neither a case of the same workshop trying to repeat its own triumph nor of some local followers trying to imitate it. In either of those cases one would be likely to find a far more literal, more slavish adherence to S.Vitale in details. What this decoration bespeaks is a turning away – surely on the part of a new team – from an ideal that has had its day. The comparison may seem a little far-fetched, but it is helpful here to think of the first mannerists in the Italian Cinquecento – Pontormo, Bronzino, Rosso – following upon the climactic period of the High Renaissance. Though unthinkable without that climax, they decisively veered away from its goals; and here again, quality is not the issue.

An analysis of the compositional principles underlying the design of the Classe apse mosaic is complicated by the fact that changes were made in the window zone in later times.[9] It is evident, however, that this register, when compared with the corresponding one at S.Vitale, is conceived far more as a figure zone in its own right. Its structural and supportive function is far less clear. Rather than being subordinated to the composition in the conch, it is more nearly its coequal. As for the conch mosaic, the landscape here has not been reduced to a mere strip at the bottom as on the Sinai mosaic, but, on the contrary, has greatly expanded in area and importance. It is a paradisical garden, appropriate as a setting both for the glorified saint standing in its midst and for the Transfiguration immediately above; the latter, as I have said, being presented here as an eschatological theophany. What concerns us particularly is the rendering of this garden landscape as a decidedly vertical backdrop. There is no longer any pretence, as there was in S.Vitale (figs. 155–7), that things cohere organically; that trees and plants grow at random in grassy meadows; that rocks are outcroppings of these meadows; and that in the distance the rocks may blend into clouds and clouds into sky. All these elements are there, but each one is isolated and sharply delineated, and they are tidily lined up in rows, tapestry-fashion (fig. 184). It is a method reminiscent of the one we have encountered previously in floor mosaics of the fifth century. There, too, landscapes were taken apart and their component elements spread out with a complete avoidance of overlaps (fig. 92). The appearance here of a comparable method is significant. Clearly in this apse composition, with its green and gold zones balanced and sharply set off against one another and with no indication of depth in either of them, the two-dimensional surface is strongly reasserted. The huge blue disc in the centre, bearing amidst its ninety nine stars a jewel-studded cross, has, it is true, suggestions of an *opeion*, a view of the night sky opening out in the apex of a dome. But placed as it is on the boundary between the two zones and forming a single vertical axis with the figure of the saint just below it, it, too, is very much part – indeed, the dominant part – of a surface pattern.

In sum, it is my contention that the Sinai and Classe mosaics are evidence of a major stylistic shift around the year A.D.550 and not simply chance survivals of the work of some undefined regional 'schools' that had practised their respective manners all along. Obviously the two decorations are very different one from the other. But they have in common a rejection of basic principles underlying the style of S.Vitale – this is particularly evident at Classe – and a bold reassertion of abstract principles of design that had been in vogue around A.D.500. The S.Vitale phase in this perspective seems like an interlude. The synthesis soon came apart. Its abstract component alone triumphed.

I feel the more confident in this interpretation because, moving forward to works of the ensuing period, one finds that the trend which these mosaics of the last ten or fifteen years of Justinian's reign indicate did indeed become increasingly accentuated as time went on. This can be seen in many places: in Ravenna itself, in Rome, in Thessaloniki.[10] Without tarrying at these intermediate stages, we proceed to the Church of S.Agnese fuori le mura in Rome, whose apse (fig. 187) was adorned with mosaics under Pope Honorius I (A.D.625–38).[11] Here abstraction has reached a new peak. Three single figures rise like so many vertical pillars on a vast expanse of gold ground, which they serve to divide with strict symmetry. Each is quite self-contained, even though the two lateral ones are donors subordinated to the saint in the centre in what is still a ceremonial presentation scene. All three are dressed in purple, so that colouristically, too, they create a unified pattern. The rest of the surface is likewise organized entirely on geometric principles. The dedicatory inscription, here definitely included within the principal scene (if 'scene' is the word), forms a bottom zone and is surmounted by a green band in two tones indicating terrain but, as in Sinai, devoid of all suggestion of depth. Above the main zone the sky is similarly composed of concentric bands. As for the figures, not only are they totally subordinated to the surface pattern in their positions and their attitudes; there is little in their rendering to suggest tangible and autonomous bodily presences. This is particularly true of the central figure of St Agnes.[12] In outline, proportion and rendering of features, she presents a degree of abstraction and dematerialization exceeding anything we have yet seen in the course of our journey through the late and post-antique centuries. With her elongated body, diminutive head and chalk-white face, she appears like a phantom. If the third and the fifth centuries saw drastic departures from the classical ideal of the human form, here we are confronted with a third major step. The two-dimensional, the linear and the geometric are consistently proclaimed as positive principles of design.

S.Agnese is a memorial church for a highly venerated martyr. It enshrines her tomb, as the basilica in Classe enshrines the tomb of the saint who was revered as Ravenna's first bishop. The practice of placing commemorative portraits on tombs – and on shrines of martyrs particularly – had been adopted by Christians long before this time.[13] It was an exceedingly important step. More than any other category of images the portrait involves representation for representation's sake. It is the very opposite of 'signitive' art.[14] To conjure up a physical presence is its chief *raison d'être*. In the apse mosaics of Classe and of S.Agnese we see such portraits assume a new and central importance. In both churches a great statuesque figure of the titular saint is prominently placed and not only dominates the pictorial decoration of which it is a part but is made a focal point for the entire sanctuary. At Classe the saint raises his hands in prayer, his role as intercessor with the deity being one of the many layers of meaning of this composition. St Agnes stands in complete repose in the centre of the apse of her church. The only 'narrative' elements are the two flames by her feet alluding to her martyrdom.

One associates such still and lonely figures – gaunt and remote, timeless and supremely authoritative – with Byzantine art in its mature state in the centuries after Iconoclasm.[15] But it was in the age before Iconoclasm, during the long stretch of time between Justinian and the outbreak of the conflict in A.D.726, that this important artistic concept was first fully realized. Nor was it confined to the portrayals of martyrs in the apses of their shrines. The image of the Virgin, too, was thus offered to the spectator's gaze – and to his worship – in a focal position and in solemn isolation as it was to be so often in later times. In this connection the apse mosaic of the Church of the Dormition at Nicaea, destroyed in 1922 but fortunately recorded in good photographs before World War I (fig. 188), is a document of great significance.[16] Unquestionably the figure of the Virgin which was to be seen in the apse was a work of the period *after* Iconoclasm. It was executed in the second half of the ninth century to take the place of a large cross – discernible in outline within the sutures in the gold background – that evidently had been the sole decoration of the apse during the period when the cross was the only 'image' permitted in a church. However, we owe to the late Paul Underwood's careful scrutiny of the photographs of the mosaic the irrefutable proof that the cross in turn was preceded by an earlier representation and that this earlier representation can only have been an image of the Virgin.[17] In other words, what was done in the ninth century was to restore the status quo that had existed before A.D.726. While in the details of its rendering the Nicaea Virgin displayed ninth-century characteristics, in terms of its position and its thematic context it was a document of pre-Iconoclastic art. That context, incidentally, and the whole programme of the pre-Iconoclastic decoration were once again multilayered and saturated with dogmatic and liturgical meanings. Though not datable with precision, in a broad sense this decoration was a contemporary of the mosaic of S.Agnese and testifies to the fact that during the period in question the lonely statuesque apse figure did not remain confined to martyria. Here it is in a normal church in the very heartland of Byzantium.

Such representations do indeed mark a great forward leap. They should be seen in the light of a changing functional role of the religious image in the period after Justinian.[18] The late sixth and seventh centuries saw the rise of a new kind of piety expressing itself in a vastly increased use of images in worship and in devotional practices; and the Byzantine government – in a period of unprecedented stresses and catastrophes – took a lead in fostering such practices. In order to proclaim the authority of Christ, the Virgin and the saints over human affairs it increasingly introduced their images into a variety of contexts. (Eighth-century Iconoclasm, in turn, was an official reaction in Byzantium to a development which the imperial government had done much to bring about.) It was in this situation that the holy figure in statuesque isolation assumed a central position in the church. The ground had been prepared in the preceding centuries by the use of commemorative portraits on the one hand, and by ceremonial representations with their majestic central figures of the Deity on the other (figs. 80, 156, 169, 177). Now these central figures were put before the worshipper in stark isolation as a statue of a god or goddess had been in a Greek temple.

Another characteristic manifestation of the new religious atmosphere was the votive panel. Whether painted on wood as a portable icon, or permanently installed on a church wall, such panels are not part of a systematic overall decoration embodying fundamental doctrine, but spring from the devotional needs of an individual or of a group. They tended to be placed in relatively low and readily accessible locations and thus responded to a desire for personal rapport with the saint. The *ex voto* mosaics in the Church of St Demetrius in

Thessaloniki exemplify this practice. They were sadly decimated in the fire of 1917, and the dating of a number of them is conjectural. But one major group, on the piers flanking the entrance to the chancel, certainly was put up about the middle of the seventh century (figs. 189, 190).[19] It shows the city's patron saint in the company of various dignitaries, on whose shoulders he places a protective arm, and two companion saints, one of them similarly protecting two children. Here again, as in the Roman mosaic of S.Agnese, we see the triumph of geometry and abstraction. The style is not identical, but there are the same gaunt proportions, the small heads on elongated bodies, the emphatic verticals, the firm subordination of the figures to an overall planimetry (which here takes the form of an actual architectural frame). In Rome, these Thessalonikan figures have their nearest equivalent in the mosaics of the Chapel of S.Venanzio in the Lateran, more particularly in the saints flanking the apse (pl.VI).[20] Even more phantom-like than St Agnes, these figures were commissioned some ten or fifteen years later by Pope Theodore (A.D.642–9), one of the many Greek popes of the period.

About twenty years ago I put forward the suggestion that there is an inner connection between this striving after abstraction which, steadily on the rise since the mid-sixth century, reaches a peak in these works of the mid-seventh, and the changing function of the religious image which these same monuments bespeak.[21] In other words, not only location and context, but the very rendering of these images may have to do with their increasingly central role in Christian worship. The case does not rest solely on circumstantial evidence. The Iconoclastic controversy which ensued in the eighth and ninth centuries produced a large amount of literature on the subject of holy images. From it we learn a great deal not only about the actual role of such images and about the uses (and abuses) to which they were put during the period in question, but also what they stood for in people's minds. A key element in the defence of holy images as it was evolved in the course of the seventh century, and more systematically during Iconoclasm, was the claim that the image stood in a transcendental relationship to the holy person it represents.[22] No longer was it merely an educational tool, a means of instruction for the illiterate or edification for the simple-minded, as earlier writers had claimed. It was a reflection of its prototype, a link with the invisible and the supernatural, a vehicle of transmission for divine forces. In a seventh-century account of miracles worked by an image of St Simeon the Younger we read that 'the Holy Ghost which dwelt in the saint overshadowed his image.'[23] Bearing this in mind while looking at actual representations of saints of that period, one is indeed tempted to see some connection. Are not the thinness and transparency of these figures fully in keeping with their being conceived as receptacles for the Holy Ghost and as channels of communication with the Deity?

General psychological considerations also support this interpretation of the abstract style. The hobby horse of Sir Ernst Gombrich's *Meditations* is relevant here. 'The greater the wish to ride' – so we have been shown – 'the fewer may be the features that will do for a horse.'[24] By the same token, when the desire to pray, the urgency to communicate with Christ and his saints are great enough, there is no need to elaborate the physical features of the holy persons. In fact, too much realism can be an impediment. In Gibbon's *Decline and Fall* there is a story of a Greek priest who rejected some pictures by Titian because the 'figures stand quite out from the canvas'. He found them 'as bad as a group of statues'.[25]

So there is a good deal of evidence to support my interpretation; and I continue to believe that in order to understand the extremes of abstraction and dematerialization reached in seventh-century art, the changing role and function of the religious image need to be taken into account. However, I have never considered the correlation to be a simple and straightforward one. It needs to be qualified in a number of ways, particularly in the light of certain other examples of iconic and devotional art yet to be discussed. But first let us broaden our view of the period by turning to some rather remarkable works produced in other spheres totally outside the realm of devotional art.

One of the major break-throughs in the study of Byzantine art was the discovery made by Russian scholars early in this century of the true chronological position of a series of silver vessels with classical mythological reliefs in repoussé, many of which have been found on Russian soil.[26] A number of the vessels in question bear hallmarks indicating that they were assayed, and their silver content guaranteed, by Byzantine imperial officials in the sixth and seventh centuries. It used to be assumed that the vessels themselves – with their representations of gods and heroes, of cupids and Nereids, of satyrs and maenads – were centuries old at the time. But careful examination revealed that the hallmarks were punched in when the vessels were in a semi-finished state, and that the reliefs were not fully worked out until after these stamps of approval had been applied. Art historians were thus confronted with the indisputable fact that from the period of the Emperor Anastasius (A.D.491–518) to that of Constans II (A.D.641–68) Byzantine craftsmen produced work sufficiently classical to have passed for being of the time of Hadrian or Marcus Aurelius. The two plates illustrated in figs. 191 and 192 – one showing Meleager and Atalante as hunters, the other Silenus and a maenad dancing – are characteristic examples.[27] Both bear hallmarks of the earlier part of the reign of Heraclius (A.D.610–41). Their reliefs, therefore, are nearly contemporary with the mosaics of St Demetrius and S.Venanzio – a useful reminder of how problematic the notion of 'one period, one style' can be.

We saw silver reliefs of the same kind in our review of the fourth century. The Silenus plate, for instance, calls to mind a plate with a similar representation in the Mildenhall Treasure (fig. 53). Indeed, the earlier relief seems to provide a historical perspective in which our seventh-century piece becomes intelligible. Evidently what we are dealing with is a branch of private and decidedly secular luxury art quite distinct from the church art that we have considered so far. While the latter developed towards ever greater solemnity and abstraction, there was still a market for imagings of the joyous, sensuous life that had always been associated with Dionysus and others of the ancient gods. Byzantium had never disowned the myths of antiquity. They were part of its cultural heritage. Literature as well as art is full of references to them. So it would not be difficult to imagine a group of workshops in the metalworkers' quarter at Constantinople where generation after generation through the fifth, the sixth and into the seventh century the traditional representations of whirling maenads and chubby Silenuses were turned out in the traditional style, while elsewhere in the city painters and mosaicists came ever closer to finding fully adequate forms for representing Christ and his saints as the transcendent and eternal powers that truly govern the lives of men.

Our seventh-century dish could well be a product of just the kind of workshop tradition that I have suggested. When compared with its fourth-century antecedent, it shows symptoms of a certain fatigue. Forms seem to be worn out by routine repetition. There is much slurring and simplifying, for instance, in the folds of the maenad's costume. Its flying ends stand out stiffly as though they were starched. The proportions of her trunk in relation to her legs do not bear close scrutiny. Her hair is oddly bunched on the side rather than on the back of her head. When Leonid Matsulevich, in an epoch-making book, first put before a larger scholarly public the case for the late date of these vessels, he systematically analysed the tell-tale signs in the style of their reliefs which, quite aside from the evidence of the hallmarks, show that they are not products of true Classical Antiquity. They are works of what he called *Byzantine* Antiquity.[28]

A correct understanding and a just evaluation of this phenomenon are important in relation to the whole congeries of stylistic developments with which we are concerned in this book. On the one hand there is the notion just expounded, namely, that a style involving – despite all the losses – a wealth of classical and organic forms was perpetuated more or less automatically by generation after generation of specialized craftsmen who met a continuing demand for silverware with mythological subjects. The style survived because the subjects called for this kind of treatment; and while in relation to the overall picture of stylistic developments this craft tradition may be only a side-line, the survival of Hellenism which it entailed could have wide ramifications. On the other hand, however, there is also the possibility that an object such as our Silenus plate constitutes a revival. A seventh-century craftsman may have gone back to much earlier work of the kind represented by the Mildenhall plate and tried to imitate it.

The question of revival as against survival presented itself even in relation to the mythological silver reliefs of the fourth century.[29] We found these silver objects to be natural vehicles of Hellenistic forms that were even then in grave jeopardy in other branches of artistic activity. The objects seemed to cluster in the latter half of the century, and there was reason to believe that this may not be just an accident of preservation. It was not readily apparent that the production had continued in a steady flow through the Tetrarchic and Constantinian periods. When we pursue this line of investigation through the fifth, sixth and seventh centuries, we find that the same pattern persists. There are clusters of mythological silver concentrated in certain periods with quite large gaps in between. The fifth century is an almost total void. Probably a statistical survey would show that altogether the amount of extant silver vessels from that century is smaller than that from the second half of the fourth. Accidental circumstances may well play a part here. Still, we do have fifth-century silver work that is either unadorned or bears other kinds of decoration (Christian, 'official', or purely ornamental), and the fact that mythological silver has not survived in a corresponding ratio is striking.[30] From the end of the fifth century on, when the system of regular hallmarking begins, we are on safer ground in establishing chronological distinctions. Two clusters can be identified for this period. One, not surprisingly, belongs to the reign of Justinian, an era notable for its interest in the Graeco-Roman past.[31] This Justinianic group comprises pieces such as the well-known plate with a shepherd in the Hermitage (fig. 193) or the fragment of a huge, heavy dish at Dumbarton Oaks (fig. 194).[32] The latter had as its principal figure a very corpulent Silenus who, despite his somnolence, was clearly a predecessor of the jolly dancer on the seventh-century dish in Leningrad. The second cluster is precisely in the period of Heraclius and his successor Constans II.[33] There is no lack of silver from the half-century intervening between Justinian and Heraclius. But most of these pieces are liturgical or neutral.[34] Obviously, further finds might change the picture. But it does begin to look as though the production of silver with classical subjects classically executed was not steady through the centuries which concern us. It seems to be governed by a pattern of ebb and flow.

I am using the metaphor of advancing and receding tides advisedly. My contention is that the flow never stopped entirely between the fourth and the seventh century even though at times it was apparently much reduced. An enlarged close-up view of the figure of Meleager on the Hermitage plate bears out the point (fig. 196). It does not suggest a hand setting out to copy self-consciously and deliberately a model from a remote past. On the contrary, it suggests a hand practising an accustomed technique with complete ease and assurance. It testifies to a current – or, at any rate, an undercurrent – of what I like to call 'perennial Hellenism' in Byzantine art,[35] although the statistics do seem to show that the current had been receding in the decades before this plate was made and had only recently begun to rise again.

This, however, is still not the complete picture to be gained from the silver work of the period. It is instructive to compare with the close-up view of Meleager a likewise enlarged view of the head of another young hero from another exactly contemporary relief. Fig. 195 reproduces the head of David from a great dish now in New York depicting David's combat with Goliath, the centrepiece in a famous set of nine plates with the story of David that was discovered in the early years of this century in Cyprus.[36] This set, so its hallmarks show, also belongs to the first half of the reign of Heraclius. In spirit the two youths – one pagan, the other biblical – are not too far apart. There is in both an afterglow of Hellenic radiance and grace. But clearly the workmanship in the case of the David is quite different – far more elaborate and less free and easy. Curls of hair are individually modelled and engraved. Facial features, too – eyes, eyebrows, lips – are far more precisely defined, as is the head as a whole. This precision and elaboration of detail pervades all the work on the David plates (figs. 197, 198). Limbs, armour and draperies are carefully modelled within insistently drawn outlines. Not since the fourth century – the days of the Mildenhall Treasure and the great missorium in Madrid – have hems been so minutely and artfully curled (fig. 59). While the mythological plates of the time of Heraclius can be understood as products of a tradition never completely broken through the centuries, here we are faced with an effort to leap back across the centuries and recapture forms from a distant past. The David plates are full of references to works of the fourth and fifth centuries, and more particularly to works of the Theodosian period. The similarity between the scene of the young David appearing before King Saul (fig. 198) and that of Theodosius holding court (fig. 57) is only the most immediately obvious of these relationships.

It is not likely that even if chance discoveries should add to our present knowledge of late antique and early Byzantine silver, these two reliefs will ever prove to have been linked by a steady production of similar pieces. The art historian, faced with this evidence, is compelled to make room for yet another classical revival. As yet this Heraclian revival has barely found its way into the textbooks. But specialized scholarship has for some time recognized the phenomenon, which has a counterpart also in literature, more particularly in the epics of George the Pisidian, Heraclius' court poet.[37] The whole classicizing episode is intimately tied to the imperial court. The Cyprus plates bear this out both through the context in which they were found and through their iconography. The set must have belonged to a high official who had close connections with the court in Constantinople[38] – and there are reasons to believe that concealed in this cyclical celebration of the career of the young Hebrew king is a celebration of the career of Heraclius himself, the youthful warrior who had come to power by overthrowing the terrible Phocas.[39] In effect, Heraclius was a usurper, and the elaborate and academic classicism in his court art should be seen in the light of this fact. The taste of upstart rulers often gravitates in this direction. Theodosius himself, on whom Heraclius fastened as a model, may provide an example, as I mentioned earlier.[40] The David plates again confront us with the phenomenon of a revival based on surviving classical trends, a revival so explicit and so contrived that it must have been conscious and purposeful. Inspired by persons at Heraclius' imperial court, as there is every reason to believe it was, it is yet another example of an 'other-directed' stylistic innovation.

We seem to have gone some way towards explaining the glaring dichotomy which has revealed itself as our view of late sixth- and seventh-century art has unfolded. The art of these silver plates, at any rate, is a hothouse plant artificially nurtured and consciously forced. As such it could well have coexisted with those gaunt and disembodied figures of saints we saw earlier in the apses and on the walls of churches of the same period. The latter were products of a broad and relentless development which we were able to trace from the late Justinianic period on. It was a development which seemed to be essentially of the artists' own making, even though it can be linked to profound spiritual and religious processes taking place during this period. Here, on the other hand, we have a group of objects brought into being by imperial command and purposely emulating the style of another age. It is true that the Cyprus plates are religious in subject matter. The extolling of the monarch in biblical guise rather than in the direct manner of the Madrid Plate is in itself an interesting sign of the times.[41] But functionally this is secular art. Altogether, then, the classical and the abstract style trends belong to different spheres, and one can well see how they could have existed side by side within metropolitan Byzantine art.

Another monument patently associated with the imperial court in Constantinople seems to be part of the same picture. The magnificent floor mosaic discovered in the 1930s during the excavation of a huge peristyle in the heart of the imperial palace is very much a work of secular art, displaying as it does a vast array of hunting, pastoral and other rustic motifs (figs. 199, 200).[42] In terms of its composition the pavement is an outstanding example of a figure carpet, a type of floor design we saw evolve at Antioch and elsewhere in the fifth century (fig. 90). But in execution the figures are much more lifelike and three-dimensional, much more strongly permeated with Hellenic traditions than those on the comparable pavements in the Syrian metropolis. At the time of its discovery, and for some time after, the palace mosaic was thought to be contemporary with the Antiochian figure carpets, its qualitative superiority and its insistent Hellenism being accounted for by the imperial milieu. But subsequent investigations produced solid evidence that this pavement cannot be earlier than the Justinianic period; and it may well be of the seventh century or even as late as A.D.700.[43] Once again, as in the case of the mythological silver reliefs, one is tempted to speak of perennial Hellenism, of a tradition never entirely broken within a specialized craft, although on the other hand here, too, an element of revival may well be involved. The work is too isolated to permit us to differentiate with any clarity between these two factors. But the mosaic is certainly a counterpart to the silver work we have seen, and as such it further encourages us to interpret the dichotomy which has emerged between abstraction on the one hand and Hellenism on the other as having to do with subject content and functional purposes.

It would be convenient if we could halt our inquiry into late sixth- and seventh-century art at this point. But there is yet another aspect to this complex picture. The period produced works which are clearly religious and devotional in function but decidedly Hellenistic in style. Polarization goes further than I have yet indicated. It not only pits imperial and profane silverware and floor mosaics against cult images and icons, but also manifests itself within iconic art itself. I shall turn to this phenomenon, its implications and its consequences, in the next and final chapter.

CHAPTER SEVEN

Polarization and Another Synthesis – 2

It was the discovery in the year 1900 of the Church of S.Maria Antiqua on the Roman Forum which first revealed the existence of a strongly Hellenistic current in religious painting of the seventh and early eighth centuries.[1] The church was installed, probably in the first half of the sixth century, in a building of the early imperial period and was abandoned in the ninth. It harbours a wealth of murals of various dates (some on superposed layers of plaster), including a large number of panels put up individually or in groups to serve special devotional needs such as the cult of particular saints. A bold impressionist style reminiscent of Pompeian frescoes is conspicuous in many of these paintings and appears at its most pronounced in certain works of the first half of the seventh century; that is to say, of precisely the period in which the abstract style reached a peak in the pier mosaics of St Demetrius in Thessaloniki and in the apse mosaics of S.Agnese and S.Venanzio in Rome, as discussed in the preceding chapter. By focusing on this phenomenon we shall be led to an enlarged and more balanced view of stylistic developments in the seventh century as a whole. Indeed, the Hellenistic current in religious painting will prove to be of crucial importance for a correct evaluation of the art of that century and a key element in making the period the critical turning point it was.

Among the frescoes of S.Maria Antiqua none exhibits a more accomplished impressionist manner than a panel on one of the nave piers depicting Solomone, the Mother of the Maccabees, with her seven sons and Eleazar, their tutor, who in the early Middle Ages enjoyed veneration as martyrs (pl.VII; figs.204, 205).[2] The picture, which in all probability was painted in the decades just prior to A.D.650, is not without firm linear coordinates. While Eleazar and the seven sons are loosely grouped in relaxed poses, the mother, standing erect and purely *en face*, forms a strong vertical axis (somewhat to right of centre). The blue sky in the background is schematically divided into two zones whose boundary forms a sharp horizontal accent and exactly bisects Solomone's halo. But the main background area, below the sky, is hazily rendered in shades of grey and brown, and since it also forms the ground on which the figures stand, it could be seen as a vast plain stretching behind them to a far horizon. In any case, the figures appear to be enveloped in air and atmosphere which dissolve their outlines. Bodies, draperies and particularly faces are indicated solely by means of contrasting hues. Deep shadows and sharp highlights suggest rather than delineate forms. The brushwork is executed with a verve and an ease which one associates with Graeco-Roman painting in its most developed phase in the first century A.D. Who were the masters who in the seventh century were capable of employing such a technique?

That they came from the Greek East there can be no doubt. Rome had not produced such painting for centuries. A break within the Roman development is brought home most dramatically at S.Maria Antiqua itself on the so-called Palimpsest Wall, an area to the right of the apse where remains of figures from several superposed decorations are preserved in a seemingly chaotic medley (fig. 201).[3] Among these fragments are two isolated remnants of an Annunciation scene – part of the face of the Virgin and much of the upper half of the angel (fig. 202) – which are among the most outstanding exponents of the Hellenistic style in the church. Yet this painting, which in due course was covered over by the decoration of Pope John VII (A.D.705–7), superseded an earlier one of the sixth century – a Virgin in Byzantine court costume flanked by angels – which shows hardness and abstraction carried to an advanced stage. Very clearly the Hellenistic style appears here as a new and intrusive element datable to the seventh century.[4] However, granted that during this period S.Maria Antiqua (and many other Roman churches) were in effect Greek enclaves, the impressionism of paintings such as the Maccabees and the Annunciation fragments just mentioned requires explanation in Greek terms, too. We can no longer operate, as Charles Rufus Morey and his disciples did in the 1920s and 1930s, with the concept of an Alexandrian school.[5] Alexandria and Egypt generally have produced no evidence of a survival of an impressionist style at so late a date. We have seen better indications of strong Hellenistic trends – at least in the secular sphere – in Constantinople itself.

The silver plates in particular, whose study revealed a pattern of development compounded of survival and a revival of ancient forms, can provide important guidance. A painting such as the Maccabees suggests, even more strongly than some of the mythological figures on the plates, a hand practising an accustomed style with complete ease. These boldly sketched figures imply a living tradition, not a self-conscious effort to emulate models from a remote past. A comparison between heads in the fresco and the head of Meleager in the Leningrad plate is suggestive in this sense (figs. 196, 205). May we infer that in painting, too, the continuity was never entirely broken through the centuries, though it may have been almost submerged at times and then come to the fore again? The example of the silver shows that there need not have been a broad stream through successive generations. And perhaps we can go further and say that in painting, too, it was the secular category – idyllic genre, mythology and other subjects in which the Hellenistic style was, so to speak, endemic – that was the principal vehicle of this perennial Hellenism; and that, particularly in periods when the tide was rising, impulses and stimuli were transmitted from it to the religious sphere. A somewhat analogous process had taken place once before in the fourth and early fifth centuries, and there were to be other such transfers from the secular into the religious category in later stages of Byzantine art, especially the period of the 'Macedonian Renaissance'.[6] The coincidence in time between the cluster of mythological silver reliefs under Heraclius and the most Hellenistic of the frescoes in S.Maria Antiqua is certainly suggestive.

A recent find in Istanbul, as yet published only in preliminary form, provides welcome corroborative evidence. In the course of a systematic investigation of the church of unknown name which later became the Mosque of Kalenderhane, a fragmentary mosaic panel has come to light, depicting in an ornate frame the Virgin as she presents the Christ Child to the aged Simeon (fig. 206).[7] The mosaic belongs to an early stage in the history of the building, but the context for which it was created is still unclear. What is certain is that it was an isolated panel in a low position – in this respect it is comparable to the votive images in S.Maria Antiqua and in Thessaloniki – and that it is a work of the pre-Icono-clastic period. It escaped destruction during Iconoclasm because a wall had been built in front of it, apparently by the time the conflict erupted. Thus it constitutes our first and so far only example of a mosaic with a Christian figure subject of pre-Iconoclastic date in the Byzantine capital, and stylistically it is not without relationship to the paintings of Hellenistic character in S.Maria Antiqua. Simeon the priest in particular, a powerful, strongly three-dimensional figure rendered entirely in terms of light and dark passages sharply and abruptly juxtaposed, invites comparison with some of the Maccabees in the Roman fresco. The Constantinopolitan mosaic may be attributed with confidence to the seventh century and proves beyond doubt that in this period religious art in the capital was deeply affected by the Hellenistic current.

We may assume, then, a kind of contagion. In the early decades of the seventh century a resurgence of Hellenism took place in Byzantine secular art on the basis of a surviving tradition, and as a result there was a burgeoning of this tradition also in some of the iconic art of the period. It is certainly re-markable that this resurgence and this contagion should have taken place during the very decades in which abstraction reached its peak and that both movements should be traceable to metropolitan Byzantium. But perhaps the resultant stylistic dichotomy in religious art is not as fundamental as it may appear at first

sight. Simeon, in the Constantinopolitan mosaic, for all his apparent corporeality and his lively, expressive movement, is yet strangely immaterial and
weightless. His feet are not placed on the ground but overlap the frame so that
he appears to be levitating in space in front of the panel. In their own way the
Maccabees in the Roman fresco are similarly insubstantial. Solomone – with
her diminutive head, elongated body and sketchily adumbrated features – is as
evanescent and transparent as any saint in the abstract style. Her sons are more
sturdily proportioned, but their forms, too, dissolve, suffused as they are by
light and air. Impressionism is a two-edged tool. It creates the illusion of bodily
presences, but it also transfigures these presences. If the aim is an image 'overshadowed by the Holy Ghost',[8] impressionism no less than linearism and
abstraction can serve that end.

Another panel at S.Maria Antiqua which bears this out is, like the mosaic in
Istanbul, a depiction of an event from the Gospels. In a position corresponding
to the 'icon' of the Maccabees, on the opposite side of the nave, is a fragmentary
scene of the Annunciation (fig. 208).[9] Later superseded by a fresco of the same
subject, it is undoubtedly of much the same date as its pendant. The angel in
this painting is slim and graceful, and although the brushwork is crude compared to that of the Maccabees, the figure is as bold an example of impressionism as the early Middle Ages have left us. It should be noted that the
depiction of angels gave artists particular scope for displaying virtuosity in this
style. Throughout the early medieval period, in fact – and our fresco is a good
example – angels tend to be relatively airy and insubstantial even when other
figures are firmly and solidly delineated. They are, after all, *asomatoi*, beings
without bodies; and the fact that they were frequently singled out for impressionist treatment supports my contention that this style can be a means of
emphasizing a spiritual order of being. At the same time this special treatment
of angels exemplifies the phenomenon of the 'modes', namely, the almost conventional use of a particular stylistic manner in connection with a particular
subject or type of representation.[10]

Hellenistic illusionism, then, is not incompatible with spirituality and other-
worldliness. But, I repeat, it is a two-edged tool, and for an understanding of
the role the style played in religious art of the seventh century it is important to
be aware of this ambivalence.

Nowhere are its shifting potentialities more apparent than in the frescoes of
S.Maria Antiqua. An 'icon' of St Anne with the Child Mary in her arms was
painted there about the same time as the panel with the Maccabees (figs. 203,
207).[11] The picture, which is on eye-level, must have enjoyed special veneration
because it was spared subsequently when the entire chancel was repainted

under Pope John VII early in the eighth century. Indeed, it was incorporated into that decoration. The figure, a close relative of the Mother of the Maccabees in stance, attire and facial type, is, like the latter, the work of a painter who had full command of the impressionist technique. The system of long, deeply grooved shadows and thin, sharp highlights in the mantle is identical and here as there suggests a garment of glossy and rather stiff silk densely creased. But if in the case of Solomone the overall effect was one of transparence and evanescence, here the same pictorial devices produce firm, tangible surfaces. This saint is a solid bodily presence. The head has not only increased in relative size but has also acquired weight and substance. Whereas Solomone's facial features were only hazily sketched on an indeterminate darkish ground, here they are firmly drawn and the flesh is carefully and naturalistically modelled by means of slow and gradual transitions from red-brown to light pink.

Much the same devices were used by the outstanding master who painted the Annunciation scene on the Palimpsest Wall (figs. 201, 202). The scanty remains of the angel and the Virgin exhibit characteristics similar to those of St Anne, though in a particularly subtle rendering. By contrast, the 'icon' of St Barbara (fig. 214),[12] which directly adjoins the panel of the Maccabees on the same nave pier, is the work of a less accomplished artist who somewhat slavishly imitated the adjacent figure of Solomone. But here again the head has been made larger and more solid and the face is fleshy and fully rounded.

The inherent ambivalence of the impressionist style is well brought home by these murals. To illustrate the point further I shall turn to an important painting from a different area and in a different medium. One of the rare wooden panel pictures of early date which the systematic exploration of the treasures of the Sinai Monastery has brought to light is an image of the Virgin and Child flanked by two saints in court costume and, in the background, two angels (figs. 210–12, 215).[13] Here is a true icon in the narrow sense of the word, a portable votive image, and it was done by a master skilled in the use of impressionist techniques. But what is remarkable is the variety of effects he was able to achieve by this means. The heads of the two angels are boldly foreshortened as they gaze upward to the Hand of God which appears at the top of the panel and to the ray of light descending from it upon the Virgin. Dressed in white, these angels are truly creatures of light and air, fleeting, transitory apparitions. They are examples of an extraordinarily pure survival of a Hellenistic tradition – the head of Achilles in a fresco from Herculaneum (fig. 213)[14] makes an interesting comparison – and confirm once again that the representation of angels afforded special scope to that tradition. The Virgin and the Child, however, though evidently painted by the same hand, have far more substance and weight. The chubby Child, dressed in a rich golden robe and shown comfortably seated on his mother's lap with his legs strongly foreshortened, is an outstanding piece of painting. The head of the Virgin in its fleshy fullness has some similarities with that of St Barbara in S.Maria Antiqua (figs. 211, 214). Admittedly, the latter is a cruder piece of work, but the affinity does suggest that the Sinai icon is of much the same date. Some scholars, it is true, have attributed it to the sixth century, but no concrete evidence has been produced to support so early a date.[15] Finally, in the two saints and more especially in the marvellous figure of the bearded St Theodore on the left (fig. 215), matter is entirely subordinated to spirit. The slim, ascetic face glows as if consumed by an inner fire. With his huge dark eyes firmly fixed upon us, the saint exerts an almost hypnotic power. His tall, thin body sheathed in a mantle that has the quality of glass but suggests little of the anatomy, also seems drained of substance. It neither requires nor creates space around itself. I know of no such figure in sixth-century art. Disembodied and columnar, the two saints recall figures such as those in the *ex voto* mosaics on the piers of the Church of St Demetrius in Thessaloniki (figs. 189, 190), a comparison which reinforces my contention that the Sinai icon is, indeed, a work of the first half of the seventh century.

We thus end up comparing figures from a painting clearly rooted in Hellenistic impressionism with figures from a monument previously cited among the exponents of abstraction during this period. It is the phenomenon of the 'modes' which explains the apparent paradox. The Sinai icon provides an outstanding example of an artist modulating his style within one and the same context to suit different subjects, to set off from one another different orders of being and to express different functions. His angels are airy and weightless. His Virgin, and especially the Child, are incarnate in the literal sense of that word. In his depiction of saints – those hallowed persons who are the faithful's conduits to the Deity – he has employed many of the devices of the abstract style.

It was the emphasis on the incarnate body which in the long run was to prevail. In the murals of S.Maria Antiqua, where in the first half of the seventh century Hellenistic impressionism had appeared in such purity and strength, we can observe that style's continued hold on religious painting during the latter half of the century and beyond; and we can see that increasingly its practitioners put emphasis on volume and fleshly reality as the painters of the St Anne and St Barbara panels had done earlier. For reasons unknown, the Annunciation scene in the nave (fig. 208) was covered over after about two generations with another fresco of the same subject, a painting quite similar in iconography but very different in style (fig. 209).[16] The impressionist technique, so boldly used in the earlier work, is still clearly in evidence, but it has become a means of modelling solid, massive forms. It is particularly interesting to find the figure of an angel made a vehicle of what might almost be taken for an artist's silent critique of a predecessor's work. This is one angelic figure which is anything but incorporeal. The modal convention for angels has had its character and meaning completely transformed by an overriding interest in monumentality and weight.

I have already referred to the comprehensive redecoration of the chancel of S.Maria Antiqua, which took place in the years A.D.705–7 under Pope John VII.[17] Probably it was then that the earlier Annunciation scene was replaced.[18] In any case, the same taste for large, massive figures as in the later version is very much in evidence in John VII's decoration. A series of well-preserved busts of apostles in medallions on the side walls of the chancel best exemplifies this (figs. 216, 217). Impressionist verve is not lost in these paintings, as witness the sharp, broken highlights juxtaposed with dark shadows on the mantle of Andrew or the equally bold rendering of the dishevelled hair that had long since become an established feature of that apostle's physiognomy. But the painterly detail is clearly contained and circumscribed by heavy lines that provide a firm and ample structure for the entire head. Far from making for evanescence and transparency, the strong highlights, shadows and colour accents serve to bring out the solidity of each component part of that structure. Thus the figures become commanding bodily presences. Though comfortably placed in natural three-quarter views within their circular frames, they still have their huge, dark eyes firmly and squarely fixed on the beholder.

There is an affinity here with the art of the early Justinianic age. Nowhere in the intervening period had natural and organic forms been fused so completely with firm geometric construction; and nowhere had there been, as a result, figures of such authority, weight and power. The head of St Peter, from the apse mosaic of the Church of SS.Cosma e Damiano – previously illustrated as an example of the great 'Justinianic synthesis' in Rome itself (fig. 160) – makes a suggestive comparison with the head of St Andrew in S.Maria Antiqua. In the nearly two centuries that separate these two works there had been much hieratic solemnity; there had also been a good deal of Hellenism, sometimes in exuberant forms. But there had not been any real fusion combining essential elements of both in a single unified conception.

It is not likely that this fusion took place without actual inspiration from Justinianic art. I believed at one time that this was a local Roman phenomenon. But subsequently evidence began to accumulate which suggests that the work commissioned by John VII (who was the son of a high Byzantine official in Rome) reflects a development within the mainstream of Byzantine art. The proposition has engendered a certain amount of controversy. But it is becoming increasingly apparent that in the Greek East as well as in Rome the decades around A.D.700 do indeed constitute a distinctive phase.[19]

In part the debate on this question has hinged on another of the early icons preserved on Mount Sinai, a portrait of St Peter (pl.VIII).[20] It is a work of exceptionally high quality which invites comparison with the portrayal of the same apostle in the mosaic of SS.Cosma e Damiano (fig. 160). In my opinion, however, the icon is not actually of the period of Justinian but rather, like the busts of the apostles in S.Maria Antiqua, an instance of an artist of the period *c.* A.D.700 reverting to a Justinianic ideal of lifelike monumentality. To be sure, in a comparison with the Roman busts the Sinai portrayal stands out both by the intense, if aristocratically restrained, humanity of the saint's countenance and by the extraordinary refinement of its pictorial technique. But it is precisely the technique which seems to me incompatible with a sixth-century date. I do not know in that period any parallel for the devices here used to represent drapery. Heavy, dark shadow strokes are accompanied by thin, sharp highlights, producing the same effect of a stiff, silky material with deep notch-like folds that we encountered in the work of Greek painters in S.Maria Antiqua (pl.VII; figs. 203, 207). The delicate hatching with fine highlights that appears both in Peter's mantle and in his hair is also familiar from the Roman murals. Unless or until evidence is produced that this specific brand of impressionism existed in the sixth century it is necessary to remain sceptical vis-à-vis so early a dating. Nor, on the other hand, is there a close relationship with the Virgin icon from Sinai which we considered before. The use made here of impressionist devices to create a figure of great volume, power and solemnity can be most plausibly explained in terms of a Justinianic revival subsequent to the period in which that icon was made.

Fairly recently another icon from Sinai has been introduced into this discussion. By a careful removal of later overpaint, a bust portrait of Christ, similar in dimensions and composition to the panel with St Peter, has been revealed as a work of much the same style (fig. 221).[21] Certainly, the technical detail in the painting of the two faces is similar,[22] and it seems likely that the two panels are roughly contemporary. In other words, I believe that the Christ portrait must also be of the period around A.D.700. Both reflect a new solidity, tangibility and monumentality achieved at that time on the basis – and to a considerable extent with the means – of Hellenistic impressionism. As we have seen, that style had developed in this direction for some time. Here the trend is brought to full fruition, with the art of the Justinianic era serving as a model and a catalyst. Paintings such as these were, in my opinion, the last great achievements of

Byzantine religious art before Iconoclasm. This is quintessentially what an icon was at the time the crisis erupted.

There is one class of precisely dated monuments which helps to reinforce and flesh out this view of late seventh-century developments, namely, coins. The design of coin dies was, of course, an activity very definitely concentrated in Constantinople itself. The late seventh and early eighth centuries were a period of intense and varied activity in this field, resulting in what has been called 'one of the culminating points in Byzantine numismatic art'.[23] The movement began with a reform under Constantine IV (A.D.668–85) which involved a return to types and designs not used since the reign of Justinian. Indeed, in coinage a conscious Justinianic revival is indisputable. Thus Constantine, who named his son after Justinian, reintroduced a martial portrait bust with helmet, cuirass, spear and shield that clearly harks back to issues of his great sixth-century predecessor (figs. 219, 220). At first the imitation is iconographic only. In its rendering the bust retains the schematic linearism that had increasingly characterized coin portraits over the preceding one hundred years.[24] But in the coins from the early 680s one observes a stylistic regeneration as well. Faces and features are carefully modelled (note the eyes) and the three-quarter view of the Justinianic prototype is successfully reproduced. This regeneration continues under Justinian II and comes to the fore particularly in that monarch's most momentous innovation, namely, the bust of Christ which he was the first to put on the obverse of coins in lieu of the emperor's own portrait (fig. 218). That image as it appears on issues of Justinian II's first reign (A.D.685–95)[25] is a highly competent small-scale replica of a fully modelled figure in painting or relief. Indeed, it is quite obviously based on the same prototype as the Sinai icon (fig. 221); and while this relationship does not conclusively settle the question of the latter's date, it certainly adds plausibility to the contention that the icon is a work of this same period. In any case, the entire development in late seventh-century Byzantine coinage is very much in line with the major trend we have traced in painting.

In trying to understand this trend and evaluate its significance, some further consideration of these images of Christ can be of help. Their ultimate source of inspiration has been sought in Pheidias' Olympian Zeus, of which a head in the Boston Museum of Fine Arts is generally agreed to be a good replica (fig. 222).[26] Whether or not one accepts this specific derivation, in a broader sense it is undeniably correct: the type is that of a Greek father god. A presence both authoritative and benign, Christ is here visualized, as were the gods of classical Greece, in terms of an idealized humanity. This provides us with an important clue to the entire phenomenon of the resurgence of Hellenism and the direction that style took in religious art of the seventh century. Fundamentally, what is involved is more than stylistic devices and pictorial techniques. Artists adopted and grappled with them to fashion with their help a new image of the celestial world. The holy figures they conjured up are tangible and human enough to be real, yet so generalized as to be beyond day-to-day experience.

This achievement of the seventh century proved to be a lasting one. The 'Jovian' image of Christ, so powerfully and authoritatively proclaimed and propagated on the coins of Justinian II, became the Byzantine image of the All-ruler *par excellence*. After the end of Iconoclasm it was reintroduced by the imperial mint, in direct and conscious imitation of the coinage of Justinian II.[27] It was in this same guise that Christ was to appear at that time, majestically enthroned, in the mosaic over the main door of St Sophia (fig. 223).[28] Thereafter the type was to be repeated again and again throughout the Byzantine Middle Ages.

The true significance of seventh-century Hellenism can best be perceived in this larger perspective. The period that began with the last decade or so of the reign of Justinian I had brought, in the first instance, a thrust towards abstraction more radical and extreme than any that had occurred earlier. At no previous time had the alienation from classical form and classical ideals been so great as in the late sixth and first half of the seventh century. But at this critical stage – and it is this which makes it a major turning point in the history of art – the classical tradition strongly reasserted itself in Byzantium. It did so not merely in marginal branches of artistic activity but in the central sphere of religious art, to result in the end in an image of the Deity in which the divine and the human, the solemn and the personal are superbly and lastingly blended. Both Byzantium after Iconoclasm and the Northern European countries just then beginning to move to centre stage were the heirs and beneficiaries of the tempered humanism which the seventh century ultimately achieved.

EPILOGUE

It is well to conclude this journey through five hundred years of Mediterranean art history with some reflections of a general kind.

I take my cue from the manner in which the Hellenistic tradition reasserted itself – and was developed further – in the seventh century. Undoubtedly in that reassertion conscious and deliberate revival efforts were involved. We need only recall the clear references to Theodosian court art in the Cypriot David plates or the Justinianic revival in the last part of the century so particularly manifest in coins. In these cases one has good reason to assume deliberate policy moves undertaken with a programmatic intent by persons in authority. They are, in other words, examples of essentially 'other-directed' stylistic changes. But these changes are based on movements that are far broader and far deeper. We saw in the mythological silver plates of the early seventh century a seedbed for the style of the David plates; and long before the end of the century we saw Hellenistic impressionism in painting developing in a direction that prepared the way for a Justinianic revival. Most clearly observable at S.Maria Antiqua, this latter development has every appearance of a gradual 'inner-directed' change.

Modal conventions were a factor of great importance in this entire complex interplay of currents and traditions. It was primarily the habitual and natural use of a Hellenistic style for secular subjects and contexts which kept that style alive at a critical stage. Within the religious sphere there were certain subjects which provided particular scope for this style and encouraged its use. Modal differentiations leap to the eye in a survey of the art of this period. This may well in itself be a symptom of crisis, of conflicts and indecision in the aesthetic field and of a search for form adequate to the expression of new concerns. But the wide adoption of the Hellenistic style for religious images and the transformation we saw this style undergo in the course of the seventh century cannot be explained adequately in terms of conventions. This was a slow and broadly based process of formal evolution with a powerful impetus of its own.

We have encountered such processes frequently in earlier periods. Suffice it to recall the gradual decomposition of classical form in Roman sculpture of the Antonine and Severan periods, the regenerative development in fourth-century sarcophagi, the new abstraction (springing from the principle of

[123]

affirming rather than dissembling basic surfaces and shapes) in fifth-century floor mosaics and capitals, or the dematerialization and reductionism in paintings and mosaics of the late and post-Justinianic period. All these are morphological changes traceable within a given medium and often within definable geographic areas. The transformation in seventh-century paintings rooted in the Hellenistic tradition is just such a process.

On the other hand, we have also encountered throughout our entire period innovative moves comparable to the Theodosian revival under Heraclius and the Justinianic revival in the late seventh century – moves that appeared to be deliberate, purposeful and inspired from above. The clearest earlier examples of such 'other-direction' were in Constantinople at the court of Theodosius and in Rome during the same period when the pagan senatorial aristocracy made its last stand. Other instances where this factor seemed at least to have played a part were the strongly 'sub-antique' art of the Tetrarchy, papal art in Rome in the fifth century, and the great artistic effort of the early Justinianic period. In all these cases a programmatic intent originating with a particular patron or a particular 'interest group' is more or less clearly in evidence, and always this programme is expressed visually by an open and insistent reference to a pre-existent style that is being quoted, so to speak, for the sake of its mental associations. The aggressively classicist style of the ivory carvings commissioned by the die-hard Roman aristocrats in the late fourth century is the most obvious example. But – and this is one of the principal conclusions we may draw in retrospect – these wholly or partially 'other-directed' efforts are in the nature of catalysts. They do not revolutionize but rather accentuate, reinforce and bring into focus existing trends by introducing a clear reference to an earlier style.

'Inner-direction' and 'other-direction', therefore, are inextricably interlocked. Indeed, the terms must not be understood in any rigid or absolute sense. Both factors may be involved in shaping the style of a given work of art, and often it is not possible to distinguish between features attributable respectively to the one and to the other. The antithesis certainly can help us to gain a better understanding of the historical process and the forces which shaped it. But it must not lead to a schematic or mechanical bisection of what actually happened.

In order to see the historical process in its wholeness and indivisibility I have in this book taken a macroscopic view. The third, fourth and fifth centuries – and, needless to say, these chronological terms are to be understood loosely – each proved to possess a distinct overall physiognomy. In each of these periods we found a convergence or congruence of major initiatives, trends and movements. Again, the art of the Justinianic era has pronounced characteristics of its own. The period which follows, down to the beginning of Iconoclasm, is stylistically less coherent. But here, too, an evolutionary pattern emerges from the multiplicity of currents and cross-currents, a pattern which in effect continues a dialectical process that had begun with the breakdown of classical art in the late second century.

The existence of these interlocking and interweaving trends is hardly open to question. The art historian's most difficult task is to identify the forces that set these developments in motion, the intent behind changes in form. He can do so with relative assurance in the case of those movements that are essentially 'other-directed'. In these cases the style is part of a programme, and the patron who in effect imposes the style represents in his person the social, political, intellectual or religious interests of which the style is an expression. The problem is far more intractable and elusive in the case of those broad, gradual and largely anonymous developments generated and brought to fruition within the artist's own sphere. There can be no doubt that these 'inner-directed' movements, too, are intimately related to and expressive of social and spiritual concerns and aspirations. But in most cases we lack reliable clues which would enable us to identify these motivating forces, and, quite naturally, the darkness deepens as general historical documentation becomes increasingly scanty with the progressing centuries. We can with some confidence interpret the breakdown of classical forms in the late second and third century in terms of an 'age of anxiety'. My attempts to interpret historically the renewed assaults on the classical tradition in the fifth century and in the late and post-Justinianic age were far more problematic; to say nothing of the new Hellenism in religious art of the seventh century, which so far can be explained only in an essentially intuitive way.

It must suffice to have drawn attention to these difficulties, which to a greater or lesser degree beset the path of any scholar who would view the history of art – and of artistic form in particular – as a history of the human mind. For the student of style there is always the temptation simply to relate forms to antecedent forms and leave it at that. The pursuit is wholly legitimate and indeed necessary. Form in art is never a direct transcript of extra-artistic concerns – political, religious or whatever. It is always a reaction to antecedent forms, either in the sense of building up on them – taking up a cue and pursuing it further – or in the sense of a (conscious or subconscious) differentiation, opposition or even protest. But the manner of this reaction and the direction it takes are determined by the forces that have shaped the artist's mind. Hence in these reactions and relationships important clues lie buried for the historian of culture.

In these terms our understanding of the five centuries of Mediterranean art surveyed in this book is still very incomplete. What we can perhaps say in a final look backward is that their greatest achievement lies not in their innovations – important as these are – but in having preserved, in the face of vast and cataclysmic changes, basic and essential elements of the Graeco-Roman heritage. Tempered in crisis after crisis and progressively adapted to new needs and concerns, much of that heritage still proved important and meaningful in a totally changed world.

The Monochrome Plates

1. Arch of Constantine, Rome
View from north

A.D. 315
page 7

2. Arch of Constantine, Rome
Medallions and frieze on north side

3. Imperial lion hunt
Medallion (from a
monument of Hadrian)
on north side of Arch of
Constantine, Rome

Second century
page 7

Constantine distributing largesse (detail)
Frieze on north side of Arch of Constantine, Rome

A.D.315
page 7

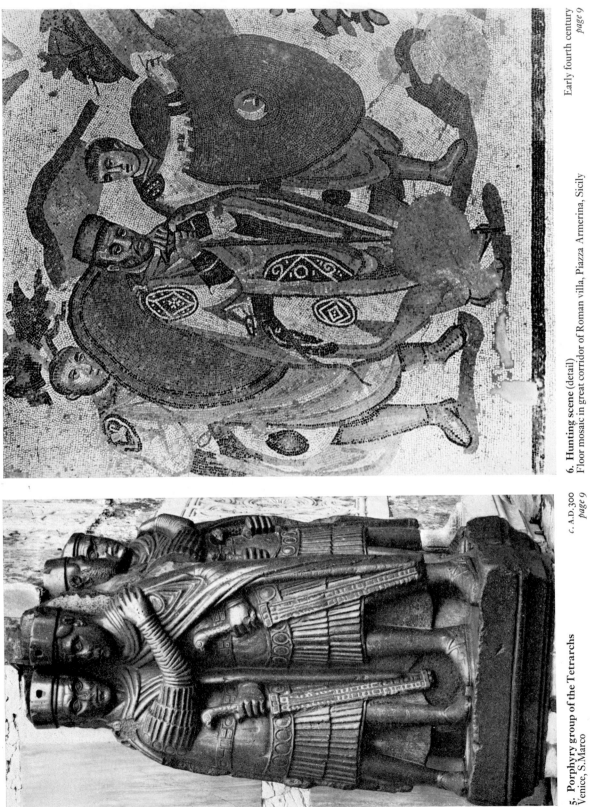

6. Hunting scene (detail)
Floor mosaic in great corridor of Roman villa, Piazza Armerina, Sicily

5. Porphyry group of the Tetrarchs
Venice, S.Marco

7. Couple embracing
Terracotta from the Altbachtal
Trier, Landesmuseum

Third to fourth century
page 12

8. Porphyry sculpture of two Tetrarchs
Vatican Library

c. A.D. 300
page 12

9. Gold coin of Maximinus Daza (A.D.305-13)
(enlarged 8·7 times)

c. A.D.310, Antioch
pages 9, 14

10. Tomb relief with circus scene
Vatican Museum (formerly Lateran)

First half of second century
page 11

11. Tomb relief from Palmyra   Second century
Malkou, son of Zabdibol, and his daughter   *page 10*
Copenhagen, Ny Carlsberg Glyptotek

12. Tomb relief of a couple, from Weisenau   First century
Mainz, Mittelrheinisches Landesmuseum   *page 10*

**13. Trajan addressing
his troops**
Detail from Column of
Trajan, Rome

A.D. 113
page 14

15. Sarcophagus with battle scene
Rome, Capitoline Museum

c. A.D. 160–70
page 15

14. Marcus Aurelius addressing his troops
Detail from Column of Marcus Aurelius, Rome

A.D. 180–93
page 14

16. Sarcophagus with battle scene
Rome, National Museum

c. A.D. 180–90
page 15

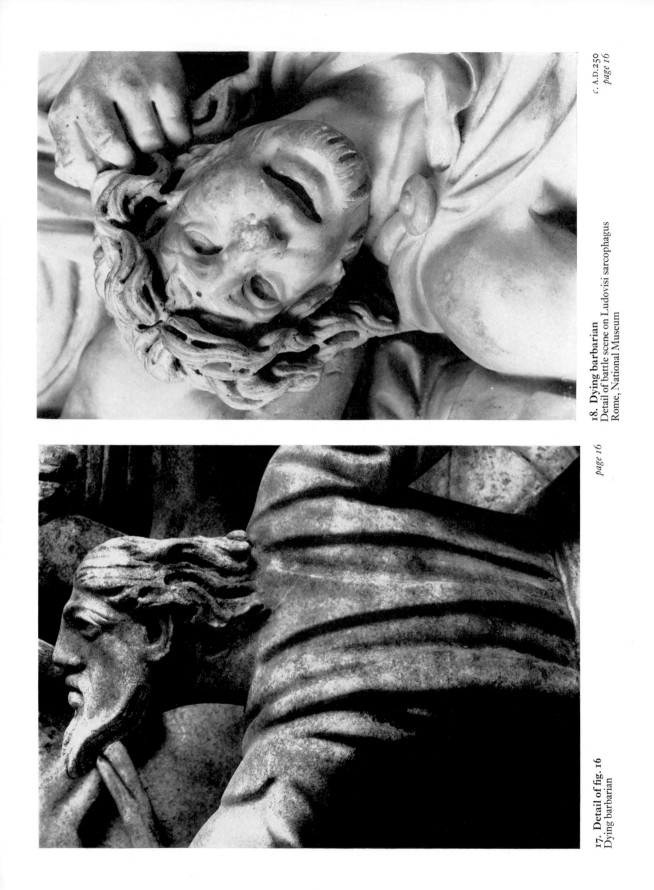

page 16

18. Dying barbarian
Detail of battle scene on Ludovisi sarcophagus
Rome, National Museum

c. A.D.250
page 16

17. Detail of fig. 16
Dying barbarian

A.D.249–51
page 16

19. **Portrait of the Emperor Decius**
Rome, Capitoline Museum

A.D.251–3
page 16

20. **The Emperor Trebonianus Gallus**
Head of portrait statue
New York, Metropolitan Museum

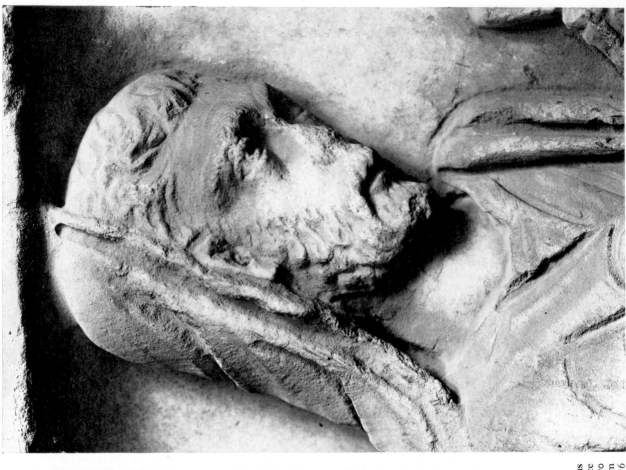

21. Portrait, so-called Plotinus
Ostia, Museum

c. A.D. 260–70
page 16

22. The Emperor Claudius II Gothicus
Detail of scene of sacrifice
A.D. 268–70
Rome, National Museum
page 16

23. Sarcophagus
Dionysiac procession
and Seasons
Early third century
New York,
Metropolitan Museum
page 18

24. Asiatic
sarcophagus from
Sidamara
c. A.D.250
Istanbul,
Archaeological
Museum
page 18

25. Attic sarcophagus with scene of Achilles on Skyros
Rome, Capitoline Museum

26. Detail of fig. 25
Agamemnon and Ulysses

27. Male portrait
From lid of sarcophagus, fig. 25

28. Painted interior
House beneath
S.Sebastiano, Rome

First half of third
century
page 20

**29. So-called
Chapel of the
Sacraments ('A3')**
Catacomb of
S.Callisto, Rome

First half of third
century
page 20

30. Jonah cast up
Marble group
Cleveland, Ohio, The Cleveland Museum of Art

Second half of third century
page 20

31. Orpheus taming the animals
Marble group
Sabratha, Archaeological Museum

Third century
page 21

32. Male portrait bust
Cleveland, Ohio, The Cleveland Museum of Art

Second half of third century
pages 21, 27

33. Sarcophagus with Jonah story
Copenhagen, Ny Carlsberg Glyptotek

Late third century
page 21

34. Sarcophagus with myth of Endymion
New York, Metropolitan Museum

Second century
page 21

35. Sarcophagus with miracles of Christ and scenes from life of St Peter
Vatican, Museo Pio Cristiano

Early fourth century
page 22

36. Sarcophagus with miracles of Christ and scenes from life of St Peter
Rome, National Museum

Early fourth century
page 22

38. **Roman soldier**
Detail of frieze on west side of
Arch of Constantine, Rome

A.D. 315
page 22

37. **Detail of fig. 35**
St Peter and soldiers

page 22

40. **Hippolytus with Phaedra's Nurse**
Detail of sarcophagus
Rome, Villa Albani

Early fourth century
page 25

35. **Detail of fig. 42**
Raising of Lazarus

page 25

41. 'Dogmatic' sarcophagus
Scenes from the Old Testament, the Gospels and the life of St Peter
Vatican, Museo Pio Cristiano

c. A.D. 320–30
page 24

42. **Sarcophagus of the 'Two Brothers'**
Scenes from the Old Testament, the Gospels and the life of St Peter
Vatican, Museo Pio Cristiano

c. A.D. 330–50
page 25

43. Sarcophagus of Junius Bassus
Vatican, Grottoes of St Peter

A.D.359
page 26

44. Sarcophagus with scenes of Christ's Passion
Vatican, Museo Pio Cristiano

c. A.D.340
page 26

45. Detail of fig. 44. Pilate   *page 26*

46. Detail of fig. 43. Pilate   *page 26*

47. Detail of fig. 43. Arrest of St Peter   *page 27*

48. Male portrait   Second half of third century
From same series of busts as fig. 32   *page 27*
Cleveland, Ohio, The Cleveland Museum of Art

49. Head of Constantine
Detail of medallion on north side
of Arch of Constantine, Rome

A.D.315
page 29

**50. Gold coin of
Constantine**
(enlarged 6·1 times)

A.D.309-13, Trier
page 29

51. Detail of fig. 52

page 29

52. Lady with jewel box, flanked by cupids
Section of ceiling fresco from imperial palace, Trier
Trier, Bischöfliches Museum

c A D 315-25
page 24

page 30

**54. Detail of fig. 55
Achilles on Skyros**

**55. Silver plate with
scenes of Achilles
From Kaiseraugst Treasure**
c. A.D.350
Augst, Museum
page 29

Second half of fourth century
pages 30, 108

**53. Silver plate with satyr and maenad
From Mildenhall Treasure
London, British Museum**

56. Silver tray with pagan divinities (Corbridge *lanx*)
Alnwick Castle, Collection of the Duke of Northumberland

57. Silver Missorium of the Emperor Theodosius
Madrid, Academia de la Historia

58. **Detail of fig. 57.** The Emperor Theodosius *page 31*

59. **Detail of fig. 57.** *Terra* *page 32*

60. Base of obelisk with hippodrome scenes
Istanbul, Atmeydani

61. Detail of fig. 60
The Emperor Theodosius
with entourage, musicians
and dancers

page 32

**62. The Emperor
Valentinian II**
(A.D. 375-92)
Head of portrait statue
from Aphrodisias
Archaeological Museum,
Istanbul

c. A.D. 390
page 33

64. 'Amalthea' relief
Vatican Museum (formerly Lateran)
Second century   *page 34*

63. Ivory diptych
Priestesses performing pagan rites
Late fourth century
Paris, Musée Cluny (*left*)
London, Victoria and Albert Museum (*right*)
page 34

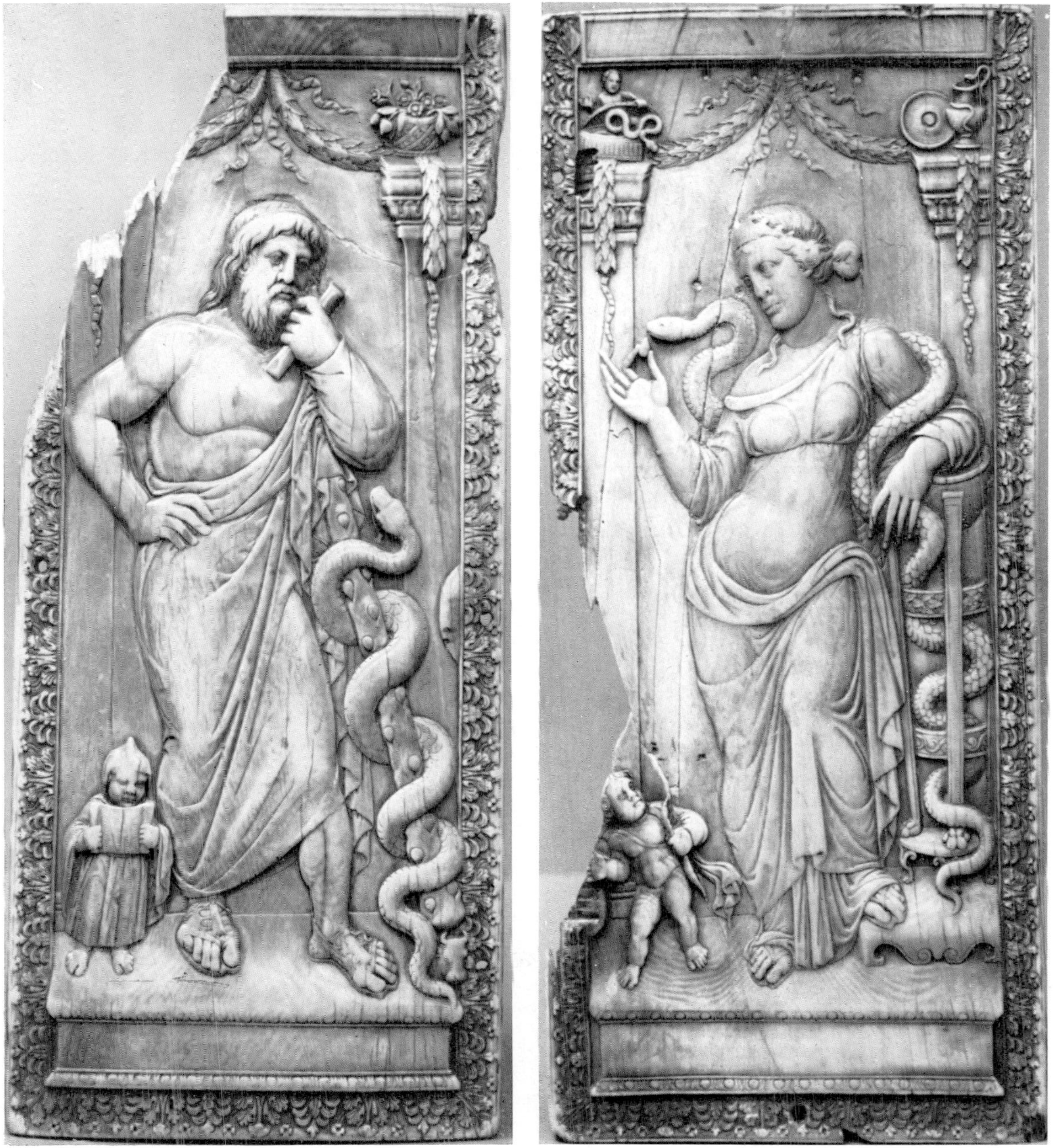

65. Ivory diptych
Asclepius and Hygieia
Liverpool,
County Museum

Late fourth century
page 34

66. Silver plate with procession of Cybele and Attis
From Parabiago
Milan, Pinacoteca di Brera

Late fourth century
page 35

67. Ivory diptych of Probianus
Berlin, Staatsbibliothek, Stiftung Preussischer Kulturbesitz

68. Leaf of ivory diptych of Lampadii
Circus scene
Brescia, Museo Civico Cristiano

c. A.D.400
page 37

69. Leaf of ivory diptych
Stag hunt in amphitheatre
Liverpool, County Museum

c. A.D.400
page 37

**70. Ivory diptych
of Probus**
Aosta, Cathedral
Treasury

A.D.406
page 37

71. Ivory diptych
Animal combats in amphitheatre
Leningrad, Hermitage Museum

c. A.D.400
page 38

72. Christ
healing the
blind man
Washington, D.C.
Dumbarton Oaks
Collection

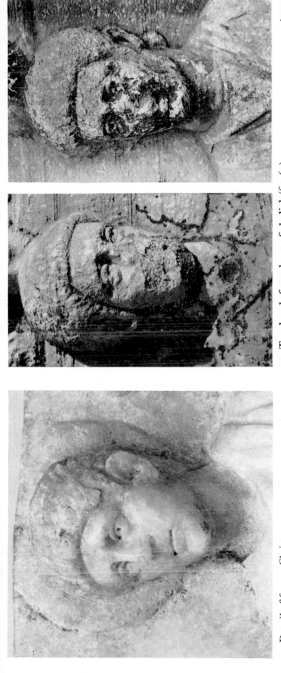

73. Detail of fig. 72. Christ   page 39

74. Two heads from base of obelisk (fig. 60)   page 39

75. Child's sarcophagus   Late fourth century
Istanbul, Archaeological Museum   page 39

76. Ivory panel
Holy Women at
the Tomb and
Ascension
Munich,
Bayerisches
Nationalmuseum

c. A.D.
400
page 39

78. Carolingian ivory panel   Ninth century
Crucifixion and Holy Women at the Tomb   *page 41*
Liverpool, County Museum

77. Ivory panel
Holy Women at the Tomb
c. A.D.400
Milan, Civico Museo d'Arte, Castello Sforzesco
page 40

79. Silver bridal casket of Projecta
London, British Museum

34 Apse mosaic of S. Pudenziana, Rome

A.D.402-17
page 41

81. Ivory diptych of Boethius
Brescia, Museo Civico Cristiano

82. Ivory diptych of high official
Novara, Cathedral Treasury

Mid-fifth century
page 47

83. Panel of ivory casket with scenes of Christ's Passion
Pilate, Christ carrying cross, Denial of St Peter
London, British Museum

First half of fifth century
page 47

84. Ivory panels with scenes from Christ's life and miracles
Paris, Louvre (*left*); Berlin-Dahlem, Staatliche Museen, Preussischer Kulturbesitz (*right*)

First half of fifth century
page 47

85. Ivory book cover
Scenes from life of Christ and portraits and symbols of evangelists
Milan, Cathedral Treasury

Late fifth century
page 47

86. Ivory diptych of the Consul Anastasius
Paris, Bibliothèque Nationale

87. Detail of fig. 88. Drinking contest between Hercules and Dionysus
Princeton University, Art Museum

page 50

88. Floor mosaic
House of the
Drinking Contest,
Antioch (*in situ*)

Third
century
page 50

89. **Seasons and hunting scenes**
Floor mosaic from Antioch
Paris, Louvre

90. Hunting scenes
Floor mosaic from Antioch
Worcester, Massachusetts, Art Museum

Fifth century
page 50

**91. Floor mosaic of
geometric design**
North arm of Church
of Kaoussie, Antioch

A.D. 387
page 52

**92. Floor mosaic with
Nilotic landscape**
Church of the Multiplying
of the Loaves and Fishes,
Tabgha, Sea of Galilee

Fifth
century
page 51

93. Mausoleum of Galla Placidia, Ravenna
Interior, view to south

94. The Good Shepherd
Lunette in north arm of Mausoleum of
Galla Placidia, Ravenna

A.D.424-50
page 53

96. Painted tomb chamber
Palmyra, Tomb of Three Brothers

Second century
page 56

95. St Lawrence
Lunette in south arm of
Mausoleum of Galla
Placidia, Ravenna

A.D.424-50
page 55

**97. Mausoleum of
Galla Placidia,
Ravenna**
West arm and lunette
with apostles

A.D.424-50
page 55

98. Mausoleum of Galla Placidia, Ravenna
View into vault

99. Church of St George, Thessaloniki
View into dome showing fifth-century mosaics

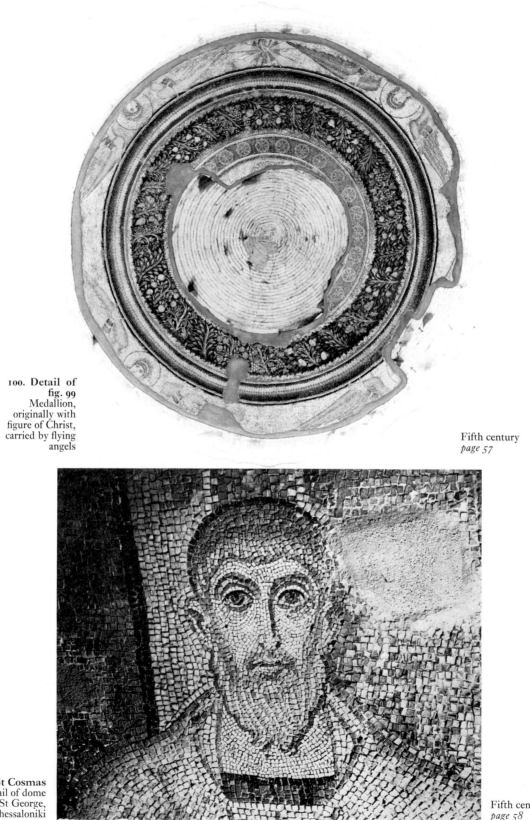

100. Detail of fig. 99
Medallion, originally with figure of Christ, carried by flying angels

Fifth century
page 57

101. St Cosmas
Detail of dome mosaic, St George, Thessaloniki

Fifth century
page 58

102. **Orthodox Baptistery, Ravenna**
Interior, view to north-east

Remodelled *c.* A.D.458
page 58

103. Orthodox Baptistery, Ravenna
View into dome

104. Arian Baptistery, Ravenna
View into dome

c. A.D. 500
page 60

105. Chapel of S. Vittore in Ciel d'Oro, S. Ambrogio, Milan
View into dome

107 **S. Apollinare Nuovo, Raverna**
East end of south wall with mosaics of Christ enthroned, biblical figures and Gospel scenes

c. A.D. 500 (procession of saints *c.* A.D. 560)

page 62

107. S.Apollinare Nuovo, Ravenna West end of south wall with mosaics of Theoderic's Palace, biblical figures and Gospel scenes

c. A.D.500
page 62

108. Detail of fig. 106 The Kiss of Judas

page 64

109. Archbishop's Chapel, Ravenna
View into vault

110. Detail of fig. 109   *page 65*
St Philip

111. Detail of fig. 109   *page 6*
St Cecilia

112. St Mark   First quarter of sixth century
Detail of apse mosaic,   *page 65*
Panagia Kanakaria, Lythrankomi, Cyprus

113. Detail of fig. 86   *page 6*
Head of the Consul Anastasius

114. S.Maria Maggiore, Rome
Interior, view towards apse

A.D.432-40
page 66

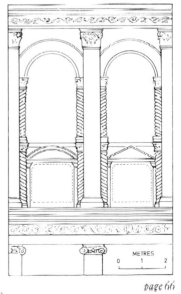

115, 116. S.Maria Maggiore, Rome
Reconstruction of original appearance of nave, apse, and system of clerestory walls (after Krautheimer)

page 66

117. Israelites threatening revolt; Stoning of Moses
Mosaic in nave of S.Maria Maggiore, Rome

DIDO

PRINCIPIODELUBRAADIUNTPACEMQUEPERARAS
EXQUIRUNTMACIANTLICIASDEMOREBIDENTES
IUCIFERAICERAIEPHOEBOQPATRIQASILVAEO
IUNONIANTEOMNISCUIUINCLAIUGALIACURAE
LESXTINENSDEXTRAPATERAAIPULCHRAIMADIDO
CANDENTISVACCAEMEDIAINTERCOANVAFVNDIT

118. Dido sacrificing
Illustration to Virgil's *Aeneid*, IV, 76ff.
Vatican Library, Ms. lat. 3225, f.33v

Early fifth century
page 67

119. Joshua and the Angel; Return of the Spies
Mosaic in nave of S.Maria Maggiore, Rome

120. The Trojans blockaded by Messapus Illustration to Virgil's *Aeneid,* IX, 211ff. Vatican Library, Ms. lat. 3225, f.72v

Early fifth century *page 67*

121. Farewell of Hector and Andromache Wall painting in Golden House of Nero, Rome

First century *page 67*

**122. Illustrations
to First Book of
Samuel, ch. 10**
Berlin,
Staatsbibliothek
Ms. theol. lat. fol.
485 (Quedlinburg
Itala)

Early fifth century
page 68

**123. Battle scene
of the Trojan
War**
Milan, Biblioteca
Ambrosiana
Ms. F. 205 P. Inf.
(*Iliad*) f.44v

Fifth century
page 68

124. Heads of Israelites (detail of Crossing of Red Sea) Mosaic in nave of S.Maria Maggiore, Rome

A.D.432–40
page 70

125. Heads of elders (detail of Presentation scene, fig. 128)

page 70

126. Heads from Massacre of the Innocents (detail of fig. 127)

page 70

127. Annunciation; Adoration of Magi; Massacre of Innocents
Mosaics on arch of S.Maria Maggiore, Rome

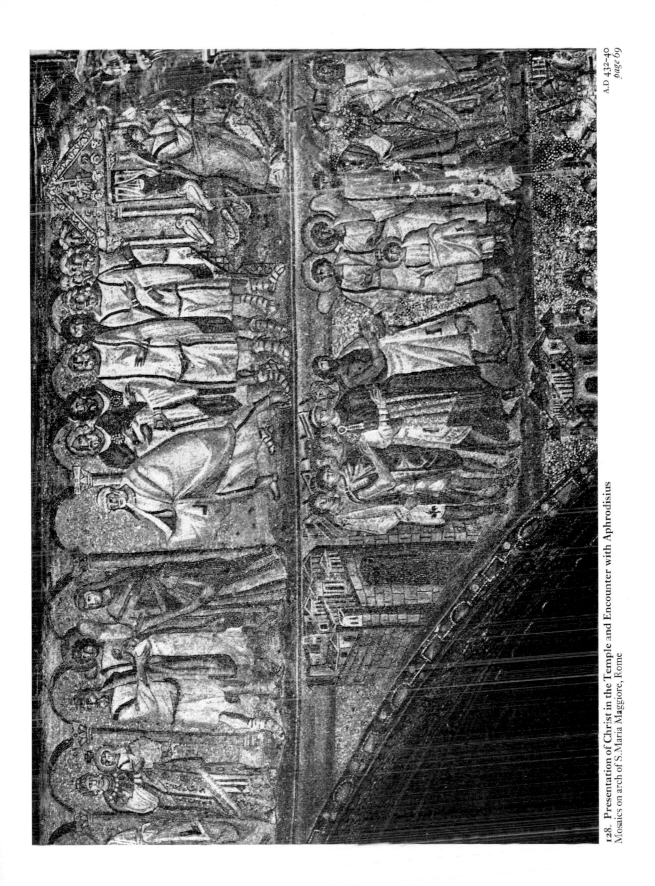

128. Presentation of Christ in the Temple and Encounter with Aphrodisius
Mosaics on arch of S.Maria Maggiore, Rome

129. Separation
of Abraham
and Lot
Mosaic in nave
of S.Maria
Maggiore, Rome

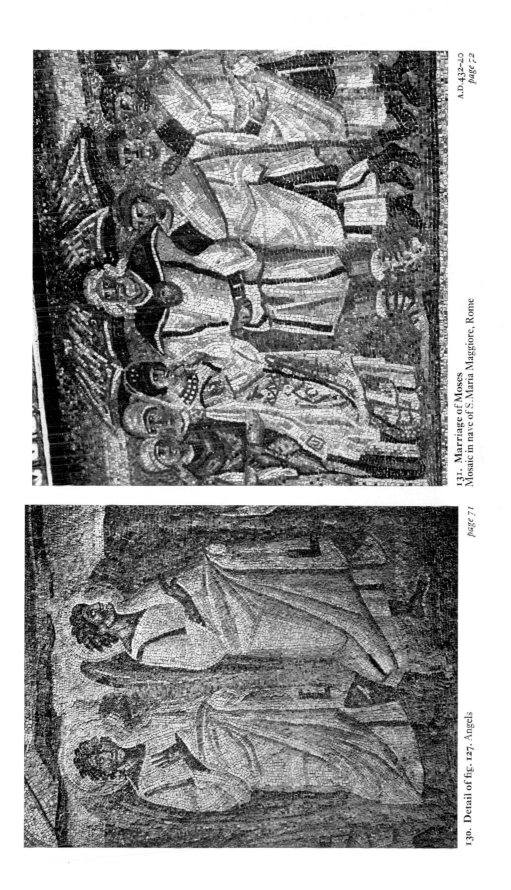

130. Detail of fig. 127. Angels   *page 71*

131. Marriage of Moses
Mosaic in nave of S. Maria Maggiore, Rome

A.D. 432–40
page 72

132. **Abraham and Melchizedek**
Mosaic in nave of S.Maria Maggiore, Rome

A.D.432–40
page 72

133. **'Adventus' of the Emperor Marcus Aurelius**
Rome, Capitoline Museum

c. A.D.176
page 72

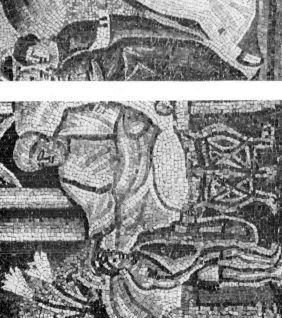

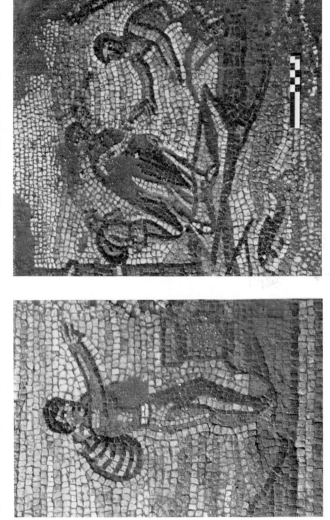

134. Jacob being blessed by
Isaac
Detail of mosaic in nave of
S.Maria Maggiore, Rome
A.D.432-40
page 75

136. Men of Shechem before
Jacob
Detail of mosaic in nave of
S.Maria Maggiore, Rome
A.D.432-40
page 75

135. Detail of floor
mosaic with port
scene
Apamea, 'Trichros' Villa
Fourth century (?)
page 75

137. Detail of floor
mosaic with port scene
Apamea, 'Triclinos' Villa
Fourth century (?)
page 75

**138. Corinthian
capital**
From Pergamon

Second century
page 76

139. Corinthian capital
Salamis, Cyprus
Fourth century
page 76

140. Corinthian capital
Jerusalem, Islamic Museum
Fourth century
page 79

141. Capital and impost
S.Apollinare Nuovo, Ravenna

c. A.D.500
pages 77, 79

142. Impost
Delphi

Fifth century
page 78

143. Impost
Perge

Fifth century
page 78

144. Impost
Nea Anchialos

Second half of fifth century
pages 78, 80

145. Ionic impost capital
Vravron (Brauron), Attica

Fifth century
page 78

148. Impost capital
Sts Sergius and Bacchus, Istanbul

c. A.D. 530
page 79

146. Ionic impost capital
St Demetrius, Thessaloniki

Late fifth century
page 78

147. Ionic impost capital
Sardis

Late fifth century
page 78

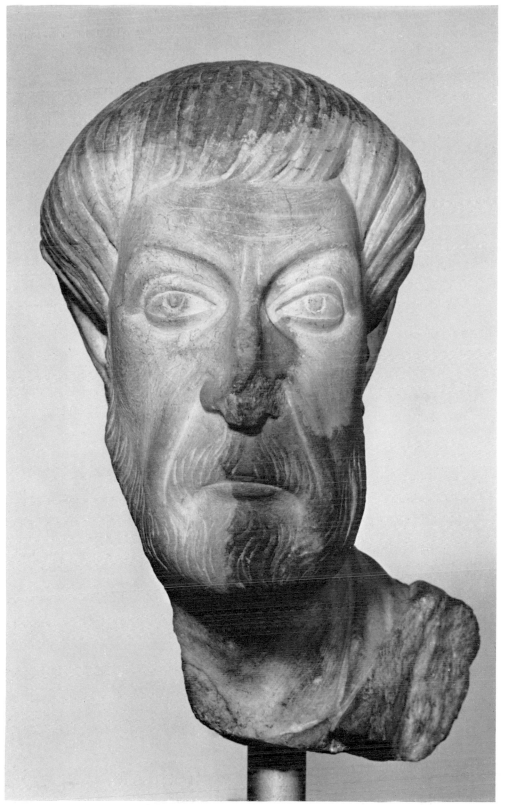

149. Male
portrait from
Ephesus
Vienna,
Kunsthistorisches
Museum

Fifth
century
page 80

150. S. Vitale, Ravenna. View into chancel with mosaics of c. A.D. 540-7

151. S.Vitale, Ravenna
North side of apse with imperial procession mosaic

c. A.D. 547
page 81

152. S.Vitale, Ravenna
South side of apse with imperial procession mosaic

c. A.D. 547
page 81

153. S.Vitale, Ravenna
View into chancel vault

c. A.D. 540–7
page 81

154. S Vitale, Ravenna
North wall of chancel

155. Detail of fig. 154. Hospitality of Abraham and Sacrifice of Isaac

page 84

156. Christ with St Vitalis, Bishop Ecclesius and angels
Mosaic in apse of S. Vitale, Ravenna

c. A.D. 540–7
page 85

157. Detail of
fig. 154
St Luke

158. Justinian and his retinue
Mosaic in apse of S. Vitale, Ravenna

160. Detail of fig. 169
Head of S. Peter

159. Detail of fig. 158
Head of Justinian

161. Floor mosaic from narthex of a church
Delphi, Museum

c. A.D.500
page 89

162. Floor mosaic from Antioch ('Green Carpet')
Washington, D.C., Dumbarton Oaks Collection

Fifth century
page 89

163. Floor mosaic from Antioch ('Striding Lion')
Baltimore, Maryland, Baltimore Museum of Art

c. A.D.500
page 89

164. Floor mosaic with birds in vine rinceau
Jerusalem, outside Damascus Gate

Sixth century
page 89

165. Floor mosaic ('Earth and Ocean') Church of St Demetrius, Nikopolis, Epirus

c. A.D. 525-50 *page 90*

166. Mosaic in vault Chapel of St John the Evangelist, Lateran Baptistery, Rome

A.D. 461-8 *page 91*

167. S.Vitale, Ravenna
Mosaic in chancel vault

c. A.D.540–7
page 91

168. Mosaic in vault
Matrona Chapel, S.Prisco, Capua Vetere

Fifth century
page 92

169. SS.Cosma e Damiano, Rome
Apse mosaic

170. Detail of fig. 169
St Peter with titular saint and St Theodore

71. Ivory chair
of Maximian
Ravenna,
Archiepiscopal
Museum

c. A.D. 547
page 94

172. Detail of fig. 171. The four evangelists and St John the Baptist

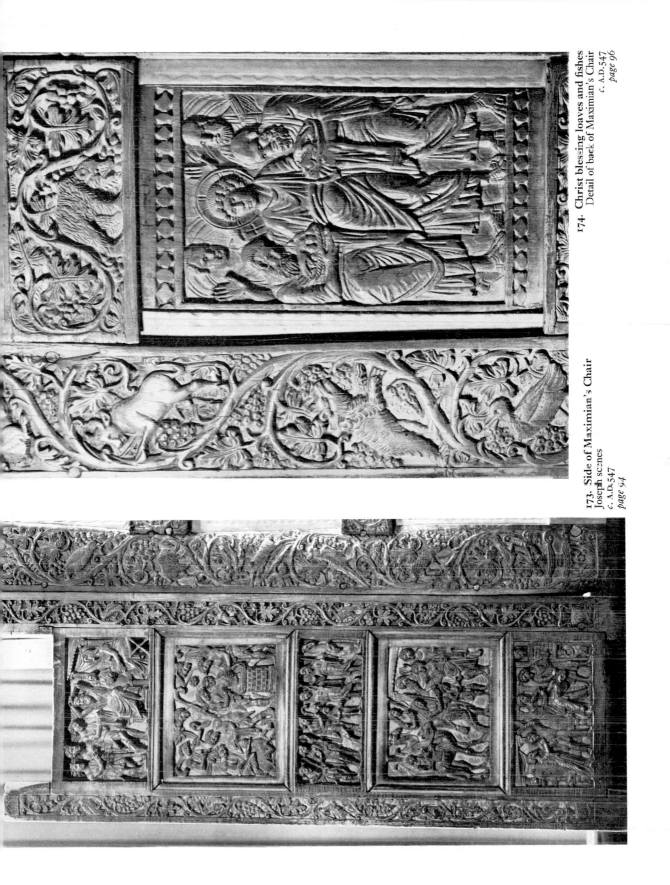

174. Christ blessing loaves and fishes
Detail of back of Maximian's Chair
c. A.D. 547
page 96

173. Side of Maximian's Chair
Joseph scenes
c. A.D. 547
page 94

175. Detail of fig. 171
Joseph scenes: His brothers before Joseph; Filling the sacks

176. Leaf of imperial ivory diptych ('Barberini Diptych')
Paris, Louvre

c. A.D. 540
page 96

177. **The Transfiguration**
Apse mosaic in Church of Monastery of St Catherine, Mount Sinai

179. Detail of fig. 177. Apostle James

178. Detail of fig. 177. Christ

180. Detail of fig. 177 *page 100*
Head of Elijah

181. Head of St John. Detail of mosaic on north *c. A.D.540-7*
wall of chancel, S. Vitale, Ravenna (see fig. 154) *page 101*

182. Head of angel *c. A.D.550-65*
Detail of mosaic on apse wall, *page 101*
Church of Monastery of St Catherine, Mount Sinai

183. Head of Angel of St Matthew *c. A.D.540-7*
Detail of mosaic on south wall of chancel, *page 101*
S. Vitale, Ravenna (see pl. V)

184. Detail of fig. 186

185. S. Apollinare
in Classe, Ravenna
View towards apse

186. S. Apollinare in Classe, Ravenna
Apse mosaic

187. S. Agnese fuori le mura, Rome
Apse mosaic

188. Virgin and Child
Ninth-century restoration of seventh-century
mosaic in apse of Church of the Dormition, Nicaea

page 104

189. St Demetrius and conors
Mosaic on chancel pier, Church of St Demetrius, Thessaloniki

c. A.D. 650
page 105

190. Saint and children
Mosaic on chancel pier,
Church of St Demetrius, Thessaloniki

c. A.D. 650
page 105

191. Silver plate with Meleager and Atalante
Leningrad, Hermitage Museum

A.D. 613-29
page 107

**192. Silver plate
with Silenus and
maenad dancing**
Leningrad,
Hermitage Museum

A.D. 613-29
page 107

193. Silver plate with seated shepherd
Leningrad, Hermitage Museum

A.D. 527-65
page 100

194. Fragmentary silver plate with Silenus
Washington, D.C., Dumbarton Oaks Collection

A.D 527-65
page 109

195. Detail of fig. 197
David

page 110

196. Detail of fig. 191
Meleager

pages 110, 114

197. Combat of David and Goliath
Silver plate from Cyprus
New York, Metropolitan Museum

A.D.613-29
page 110

198. David before Saul
Silver plate from Cyprus
New York, Metropolitan Museum

A.D.613-29
page 110

199. Floor mosaic with pastoral scenes
From peristyle of imperial palace, Istanbul

Seventh century (?)
page 112

200. Detail of fig. 199
Boy with donkey

page 112

201. S.Maria Antiqua, Rome
Superposed frescoes to right of apse ('Palimpsest Wall')

Sixth to early eighth century
page 114

202. Detail of fig. 291 First half of seventh century
Angel of the Annunciation *pages 114, 117*

203. Detail of fig. 207 *page 116*

204. Detail of pl. VII *page 113*
Head of the Mother of the Maccabees

205. Detail of pl. VII *page 113*
One of the Maccabees

206. **Presentation of Christ in the Temple**
Mosaic in Kalenderhane Djami, Istanbul

Seventh century
page 115

207. **St Anne**
Fresco in S.Maria Antiqua, Rome

First half of seventh century
page 116

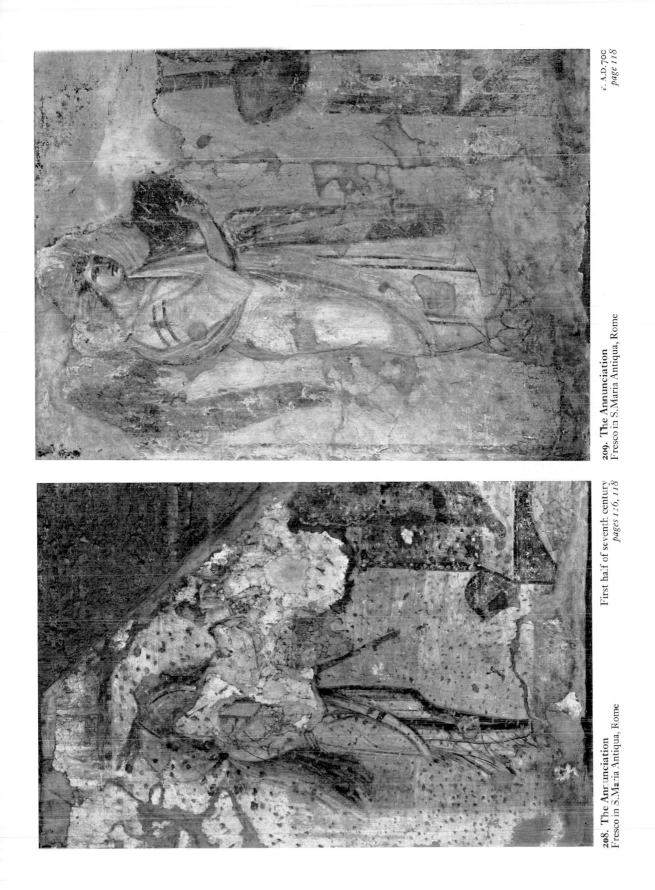

208. The Annunciation
Fresco in S. Maria Antiqua, Rome

First half of seventh century
pages 116, 118

209. The Annunciation
Fresco in S. Maria Antiqua, Rome

c. A.D. 700
page 118

210. Virgin and Child with angels and saints
Icon in Monastery of St Catherine, Mount Sinai

First half of seventh century
page 117

212. Detail of fig. 210
Angel

page 117

213. Achilles being taught by Chiron (detail)
Fresco from Herculaneum
Naples, National Museum

First century A.D.
page 117

211. Detail of fig. 210
Head of Virgin

page 117

214. St Barbara (detail) First half of seventh century
Fresco in S.Maria Antiqua, Rome *page 117*

215. Detail of fig. 210 *page 118*
St Theodore

216. St Andrew
Fresco in S.Maria Antiqua, Rome

217. St Paul
Fresco in S.Maria Antiqua, Rome

218. **Gold coin of Justinian II**
Obverse, with head of Christ
A.D.692–5, Constantinople
(enlarged 6·3 times)
page 121

219. **Gold coin of Justinian I**
A.D.527–38, Constantinople
(enlarged 3·7 times)
page 121

220. **Gold coin of Constantine IV**
A.D.681–5, Constantinople
(enlarged 4·2 times)
page 121

222. Zeus
Marble head from Mylasa
Boston, Massachusetts, Museum of Fine Arts

Fourth century B.C.
page 121

221. Christ
Icon in Monastery of St Catherine, Mount Sinai
Here attributed to *c.* A.D. 700
page 120

223. Christ
Detail of mosaic in narthex of St Sophia, Istanbul

NOTES

INTRODUCTION

1. G. Rodenwaldt, 'Zur Begrenzung und Gliederung der Spätantike', *Jahrbuch des Deutschen Archäologischen Instituts*, 59/60, 1944/5, pp.81ff.; A. Rumpf, *Stilphasen der spätantiken Kunst*, Arbeitsgemeinschaft für Forschung des Landes Nordrhein-Westfalen, Abhandlung, Heft 44, Cologne and Opladen, 1957; and, in the general sphere of social and cultural history, P. Brown, *The World of Late Antiquity: A.D. 150 750*, London, 1971.

2. K. M. Swoboda, 'Über die Stilkontinuität vom 4. zum 11. Jahrhundert', *Forschungen zur Kunstgeschichte und christlichen Archäologie*, I, 1: *Spätantike und Byzanz*, Baden-Baden, 1952, pp.21ff.

3. This term, or rather its German equivalent, was used by R. Kömstedt in the title of his book *Vormittelalterliche Malerei* (Augsburg, 1929), which deals essentially with the same period as the present study.

4. C. R. Morey, *Early Christian Art*, Princeton, New Jersey, 1942, *passim*; cf. *infra*, VII, n.5.

5. E. Kitzinger, *Early Medieval Art in the British Museum*, London, 1940, pp.17ff.

6. Rumpf, *Stilphasen* (*supra*, n.1).

7. For a comprehensive study scc A. Grabar, *Christian Iconography*, Princeton, New Jersey, 1968.

CHAPTER ONE

1. H. P. L'Orange and A. von Gerkan, *Der spätantike Bildschmuck des Konstantinsbogens*, Berlin, 1939.

2. *Ibid.*, p.28. It has been argued by J. Ruysschaert that the arch, erected to celebrate Constantine's decennalia in 315, may not have been planned until A.D. 314 ('Essai d'interprétation synthétique de l'arc de Constantin', *Atti della Pontificia Accademia Romana di Archeologia, Rendiconti*, 35, 1962–3, pp.79ff., especially p.82.)

3. B. Berenson, *The Arch of Constantine or the Decline of Form*, London, 1954, pp.31f.; cf., more generally, L'Orange and von Gerkan, *op.cit.*, pp.218f.

4. R. Delbrueck, *Antike Porphyrwerke*, Berlin and Leipzig, 1932, pp.84ff. and pls. 31–4. For a review of more recent literature see R. Calza, *Iconografia romana imperiale*

da Carausio a Giuliano (*287–363 d.C.*), Rome, 1972, pp.98ff. I find the various attempts to attribute the Venice group – or the related group in the Vatican (fig.8; cf. *supra*, p.12) – to a period later than the Tetrarchy unconvincing.

5. R. Naumann, 'Der antike Rundbau beim Myrelaion und der Palast Romanos I. Lekapenos', *Istanbuler Mitteilungen*, 16, 1966, pp.199ff., especially pp.209ff.

6. A. R. Bellinger, P. Bruun, J. P. C. Kent, C. H. V. Sutherland, 'Late Roman Gold and Silver Coins at Dumbarton Oaks: Diocletian to Eugenius', *Dumbarton Oaks Papers*, 18, 1964, pp.161ff., especially pp.173f., no.29.

7. G. V. Gentili, *La Villa Erculia di Piazza Armerina: I mosaici figurati*, Milan, 1959; for the mosaic of the Great Hunt, of which our fig. 6 shows a detail, see pp.21ff., with fig.5 and pls.24–35. For the chronology cf. C. Ampolo, A. Carandini, G. Pucci, P. Pensabene, 'La Villa del Casale a Piazza Armerina', *Mélanges de l'École française de Rome*, 83, 1971, 1, pp.141ff., especially p.179; J. Polzer, 'The Villa at Piazza Armerina and the Numismatic Evidence', *American Journal of Archaeology*, 77, 1973, pp.139ff.

8. Berenson, *The Arch of Constantine* (*supra*, n.3).

9. J. Strzygowski, 'Die Schicksale des Hellenismus in der bildenden Kunst', *Neue Jahrbücher für das klassische Altertum, Geschichte und deutsche Literatur*, 8, 1905, pp.19ff., especially p.23.

10. D. Simonsen, *Sculptures et inscriptions de Palmyre à la Glyptothèque de Ny Carlsberg*, Copenhagen, 1889, pp.12f. and pl.4. For Palmyrene sculpture in general see H. Ingholt, *Studier over Palmyrensk Skulptur*, Copenhagen, 1928.

11. Tomb relief, attributed to the first century A.D.; cf. R. Bianchi Bandinelli, *Rome: The Late Empire*, New York, 1971, p.156, fig.145, and p. 431.

12. G. Rodenwaldt, 'Römische Reliefs Vorstufen zur Spätantike', *Jahrbuch des Deutschen Archäologischen Instituts*, 55, 1940, pp.12ff.; R. Bianchi Bandinelli, *Rome: The Center of Power*, New York, 1970, pp.58ff. with figs.58ff.

13. Rodenwaldt, 'Römische Reliefs', *passim*.

14. Kitzinger, *Early Medieval Art* (*supra*, Introduction, n.5), pp.7ff.; cf. *idem*, 'Notes on Early Coptic Sculpture', *Archaeologia*, 87, 1938, pp.181ff., especially pp.202ff.

15. Delbrueck, *Antike Porphyrwerke*, pp.91ff. with fig.34; pls.35–7; Calza, *Iconografia romana imperiale*, pp.104f.; cf. *supra*, n.4.

16. E. Gose, *Der gallo-römische Tempelbezirk im Altbachtal zu Trier*, Mainz, 1972, fig.387, nos.2–8, 25–31; text, p.203; cf. N. Kyll, 'Heidnische Weihe-und Votivgaben aus der Römerzeit des Trierer Landes', *Trierer Zeitschrift*, 29, 1966, pp.5ff., especially pp.53f. and n.554.

17. H. P. L'Orange, *Art Forms and Civic Life in the Late Roman Empire*, Princeton, New Jersey, 1965, pp.62ff.

18. E. Kitzinger, 'On the Interpretation of Stylistic Changes in Late Antique Art', *Bucknell Review*, 15, 3, December 1967, pp.1ff.; reprinted in E. Kitzinger, *The Art of Byzantium and the Medieval West*, Bloomington, Indiana, 1976, pp.32ff.

19. L'Orange, *Art Forms and Civic Life*, pp.103f. and figs.50f.

20. M. Wegner, 'Die kunstgeschichtliche Stellung der Marcussäule', *Jahrbuch des Deutschen Archäologischen Instituts*, 46, 1931, pp.61ff.; P. G. Hamberg, *Studies in Roman Imperial Art with Special Reference to the State Reliefs of the Second Century*, Copenhagen, 1945, pp.135ff.

21. Wegner, *op.cit.*, pp.116f., 120, 135f.; cf. Kitzinger, 'On the Interpretation of Stylistic Changes' (*supra*, n.18), p.9 and figs.8f.

22. Hamberg, *Studies in Roman Imperial Art* (*supra*, n.20), pp.173ff. with pl.38 and pp.176ff. with pl.40; cf. also G. M. A. Hanfmann, *Roman Art*, Greenwich, Connecticut, n.d., pp.114, 205, no.121.

23. A Riegl, *Spätrömische Kunstindustrie*, Vienna, 1927 (reprint), p.35 *et passim*; for sculpture see pp.85ff.

24. Hamberg, *Studies in Roman Imperial Art*, pp.181ff. with pl.44; cf. Hanfmann, *Roman Art*, pp.120f., 214f., nos.134f.

25. E. R. Dodds, *Pagan and Christian in an Age of Anxiety: Some Aspects of Religious Experience from Marcus Aurelius to Constantine*, Cambridge, 1968; cf. Bianchi Bandinelli, *Rome: The Late Empire* (*supra*, n. 11), pp.1ff.

26. For figs. 19, 20, 22 see B. M. Felletti Maj, *Iconografia romana imperiale da Severo Alessandro a M. Aurelio Carino (222–285 d.C.)*, Rome, 1958, p.189, no.235, with pl.29, fig.95; p.203, no.260, with pl.36, fig.113; p.261, no.350, with pl.50, fig.170. For the portrait interpreted as that of the philosopher Plotinus (our fig. 21) see H. P. L'Orange, 'I ritratti di Plotino ed il tipo di San Paolo nell'arte tardo-antica', *Atti del Settimo Congresso Internazionale di Archeologia Classica*, II, Rome, 1961, pp.475ff. For third-century portraiture in general see L'Orange, *Art Forms and Civic Life* (*supra*, n.17), pp.105ff.

27. G. Rodenwaldt, 'Zur Kunstgeschichte der Jahre 220 bis 270', *Jahrbuch des Deutschen Archäologischen Instituts*, 51, 1936, pp.82ff., especially pp.99ff.

28. For the Attic sarcophagus, fig. 25, see H. Stuart Jones, *A Catalogue of the Ancient Sculptures preserved in the Municipal Collections of Rome: The Sculptures of the Museo Capitolino*, Oxford, 1912, pp.77ff. and pl.16; for Attic sarcophagi generally, A. Giuliano, *Il commercio dei sarcofagi attici*, Rome, 1962. For the Asiatic sarcophagus, fig. 24, see G. Mendel, *Musées impériaux ottomans. Catalogue des sculptures grecques, romaines et byzantines*, I, Constantinople, 1912, pp.288ff. For this type of sarcophagus generally, H. Wiegartz, *Kleinasiatische Säulensarkophage*, Berlin, 1965.

29. F. Matz, *Ein römisches Meisterwerk: Der Jahreszeitensarkophag Badminton-New York*, Jahrbuch des Deutschen Archäologischen Instituts, Ergänzungsheft 19, Berlin, 1958.

30. For this portrait see H. P. L'Orange, *Studien zur Geschichte des spätantiken Porträts*, Oslo, 1933, pp.9ff., 107f. and figs.12, 14.

31. Th. Klauser, 'Studien zur Entstehungsgeschichte der christlichen Kunst I', *Jahrbuch für Antike und Christentum*, 1, 1958, pp.20f. H. Brandenburg, *Überlegungen zum Ursprung der frühchristlichen Bildkunst*, IX Congresso Internazionale di Archeologia Cristiana, Rome, 1975, pp.3f.

32. Brandenburg, *op.cit.*, *passim*, especially pp.8f.

33. The writings of Clement of Alexandria and Tertullian are the principal witnesses to this change. Although both authors were hostile to images, we learn from Tertullian about chalices with representations of the Good Shepherd being in use in his time, while Clement lists symbolic subjects which he considers suitable for representation on seal rings. What is perhaps most significant is the fact that both writers put the case against images on a broader basis than earlier apologists had done. This suggests that the issue was becoming urgent within the fold; cf. H. Koch, *Die altchristliche Bilderfrage nach den literarischen Quellen*, Göttingen, 1917, especially pp.3ff., 14ff.

34. F. Wirth, *Römische Wandmalerei vom Untergang Pompejis bis ans Ende des dritten Jahrhunderts*, Berlin, 1934, pp.165ff.; Bianchi Bandinelli, *Rome: The Late Empire* (*supra*, n.11), pp.86ff.

35. Klauser, 'Studien . . . IV', *Jahrbuch für Antike und Christentum*, 4, 1961, pp.128ff. Brandenburg, *Überlegungen*, pp.5ff.

36. W. Weidlé, *The Baptism of Art*, London, n.d., pp.10f.

37. The stucco decoration of the basilica under Porta Maggiore (first century A.D.) with its abridged representations of a variety of classical myths which seem to have been selected to convey an esoteric message, is an example; cf. Hanfmann, *Roman Art* (*supra*, n.22), pp.107, 195, no.107.

38. W. D. Wixom, 'Early Christian Sculptures at Cleveland', *The Bulletin of the Cleveland Museum of Art*, 54, no.3, March 1967, pp.67ff. A paper on these sculptures which I read at the Ninth International Congress of Christian Archaeology (Rome, 1975), is due to be published in the Acts of that congress.

39. For the Jonah sarcophagus in Copenhagen (our fig.33) and its relatives see F. Gerke, *Die christlichen Sarkophage der vorkonstantinischen Zeit*, Berlin, 1940, pp.38ff. For an additional example, acquired some years ago by the British Museum, see M. Lawrence, 'Three Pagan Themes in Christian Art', *De artibus opuscula XL: Essays in Honor of Erwin Panofsky*, New York, 1961, pp.323ff., especially pp.325f. and pls.10of., figs.4f.

CHAPTER TWO

1. For a list of the sarcophagi in question see Gerke, *Die christlichen Sarkophage*, pp.351f.; cf. also L'Orange and von Gerkan, *Der spätantike Bildschmuck* (*supra*, I, n.1), pp.225ff. For the sarcophagi illustrated in our figs. 35 and 36 see F. W. Deichmann (ed.), *Repertorium der christlich-antiken Sarkophage*, I, Wiesbaden, 1967, pp.6f., no.6; pp.316f., no.770; pls.2, 121.

2. For sarcophagi with the Labours of Hercules see C. Robert, *Die antiken Sarkophagreliefs*, III, 1, Berlin, 1897, pp.115ff. and pls.28ff. For a third-century sarcophagus relief in Naples with scenes from the life of an official represented by a series of stand-

ing figures in tight alignment see V. M. Strocka, 'Zum Neapler Konsulsarkophag', *Jahrbuch des Deutschen Archäologischen Instituts*, 83, 1968, pp.221ff. and figs.1–4; note the author's comments pp.232ff.

3. Cf. *supra*, p.20.

4. E. Stommel, *Beiträge zur Ikonographie der konstantinischen Sarkophagplastik* ('Theophaneia, 10), Bonn, 1954, pp.27f., 64ff. *et passim*.

5. For possible antecedents see Gerke, *Die christlichen Sarkophage*, p.8 and the references *ibid.*, n.3; cf. also his index, p.392, *s.v.* 'Zweizonigkeit'. A most unusual pagan sarcophagus of the second century discovered at Velletri some twenty years ago is relevant in this connection, as was pointed out by M. Lawrence, 'The Velletri Sarcophagus', *American Journal of Archaeology*, 69, 1965, pp.207ff., especially p.209.

6. Deichmann, *Repertorium* (*supra*, n.1), pp.39ff., no.43; pl.14.

7. *Ibid.*, pp.43ff., no.45; pl.15.

8. For this comparison see Gerke, *Die christlichen Sarkophage*, p.21.

9. Deichmann, *Repertorium*, pp.48f., no.49; pl.16.

10. *Ibid.*, pp.279ff., no.680; pls.104f.

11. A. H. M. Jones, J. R. Martindale, J. Morris, *The Prosopography of the Later Roman Empire*, I, Cambridge, 1971, p.155.

12. Cf. *supra*, p.13.

13. G. M. A. Hanfmann, *The Season Sarcophagus in Dumbarton Oaks*, Cambridge, Massachusetts, 1951, I, pp.66ff.; A. Rumpf, *Stilphasen* (*supra*, Introduction, n.1), pp.12ff.; I. Lavin, 'The Ceiling Frescoes in Trier and Illusionism in Constantinian Painting', *Dumbarton Oaks Papers*, 21, 1967, pp.97ff., especially pp.110ff. (see also *idem*, in *Art Bulletin*, 49, 1967, p.58).

14. L'Orange and von Gerkan, *Der spätantike Bildschmuck* (*supra*, I, n.1), pp.165ff. and pls.43–5.

15. E. B. Harrison, 'The Constantinian Portrait', *Dumbarton Oaks Papers*, 21, 1967, pp.79ff., especially pp.82f., 90; figs.6, 34–6.

16. T. K. Kempf in W. Reusch (ed.), *Frühchristliche Zeugnisse im Einzugsgebiet von Rhein und Mosel*, Trier, 1965, pp.235ff. Lavin, *op.cit.* (*supra*, n.13).

17. For the Esquiline Treasure see O. M. Dalton, *Catalogue of Early Christian Antiquities*, British Museum, London, 1901, pp.61ff. (cf. also *infra*, n.48); for the Traprain Law Treasure, A. O. Curle, *The Treasure of Traprain*, Glasgow, 1923.

18. *The Mildenhall Treasure: A Handbook*, British Museum, London, 1955; cf. T. Dohrn, 'Spätantikes Silber aus Britannien', *Mitteilungen des Deutschen Archäologischen Instituts*, 2, 1949, pp.67ff. For the Kaiseraugst Treasure see the report by R. Steiger and H. Cahn in *Jahrbuch der Schweizerischen Gesellschaft für Urgeschichte*, 51, 1964, pp.112ff. and pls.23–35; also H. U. Instinsky, *Der spätrömische Silberschatzfund von Kaiseraugst*, Akademie der Wissenschaften und der Literatur, Mainz, Abhandlungen der geistes- und sozialwissenschaftlichen Klasse, 1971, no.5.

19. Instinsky, *op.cit.*, p.13.

20. O. Brendel, 'The Corbridge Lanx', *Journal of Roman Studies*, 31, 1941, pp.100ff.; cf. J. M. C. Toynbee, *Art in Britain under the Romans*, Oxford, 1964, pp.306ff.

21. A. Momigliano (ed.), *The Conflict between Paganism and Christianity in the Fourth Century*, Oxford, 1963; see especially pp.17ff. (A. H. M. Jones); pp.193ff. (H. Bloch).

22. Cf., e.g., Dohrn, 'Spätantikes Silber' (*supra*, n.18), pp.126f.

23. R. Delbrueck, *Die Consulardiptychen und verwandte Denkmäler*, Berlin and Leipzig, 1929, pp.235ff., no.62.

24. G. Bruns, *Der Obelisk und seine Basis auf dem Hippodrom zu Konstantinopel*, Istanbul, 1935; J. Kollwitz, *Oströmische Plastik der theodosianischen Zeit*, Berlin, 1941, pp.115ff. *et passim*; H. Wrede, 'Zur Errichtung des Theodosiusobelisken in Istanbul', *Istanbuler Mitteilungen*, 16, 1966, pp.178ff.; H. Kähler, 'Der Sockel des Theodosiusobelisken in Konstantinopel als Denkmal der Spätantike', *Institutum Romanum Norvegiae: Acta ad archaeologiam et artium historiam pertinentia*, 6, 1975, pp.45ff.

25. Kollwitz, *Oströmische Plastik*, pp.81ff. with pls.16, 34 and Beilage 13; H.-G. Severin, *Zur Portraitplastik des 5. Jahrhunderts n. Chr.*, Miscellanea Byzantina Monacensia, 13, Munich, 1972, pp.11ff., 152ff.

26. On this problem see B. Brenk, 'Zwei Reliefs des späten 4. Jahrhunderts', *Institutum Romanum Norvegiae: Acta ad archaeologiam et artium historiam pertinentia*, 4, 1969, pp.51ff., especially pp.54ff.; H.-G. Severin, 'Oströmische Plastik unter Valens und Theodosius I.', *Jahrbuch der Berliner Museen*, 12, 1970, pp.211ff., especially pp.226ff.

27. Kollwitz, *Oströmische Plastik*, pp.3ff., with pls.1–9 and Beilagen 1, 3–10; G. Becatti, *La colonna coclide istoriata*, Rome, 1960.

28. Severin, 'Oströmische Plastik' (*supra*, n.26), pp.230f.

29. H. Bloch, 'The Pagan Revival in the West at the End of the Fourth Century', in Momigliano, *The Conflict* (*supra*, n.21), pp.193ff. See now J. Matthews, *Western Aristocracies and Imperial Court A.D. 364–425*, Oxford, 1975; especially pp.203ff., 238ff.

30. W. F. Volbach, *Elfenbeinarbeiten der Spätantike und des frühen Mittelalters*, 3rd edn., Mainz, 1976, p.51, no.55; pl.29.

31. The term was aptly used by A. Alföldi, 'Die Spätantike in der Ausstellung "Kunstschätze der Lombardei" in Zürich', *Atlantis*, 21, 1949, pp.61ff. (see p.68).

32. W. Helbig, *Führer durch die öffentlichen Sammlungen klassischer Altertümer in Rom*, I, *Die Päpstlichen Sammlungen im Vatikan und Lateran*, Tübingen, 1963, pp.726f., no.1012; cf. H. Graeven, 'Heidnische Diptychen', *Römische Mitteilungen*, 28, 1913, pp.198ff., especially p.270.

33. Volbach, *Elfenbeinarbeiten*, pp.52f., no.57; pl.30.

34. For statuary models see Graeven, 'Heidnische Diptychen' (*supra*, n.32), pp.227ff.

35. A. Levi, *La patera d'argento di Parabiago*, R. Istituto d'Archeologia e Storia dell'Arte, Opere d'arte, V, Rome, 1935. The attribution to the late fourth century is due to A. Alföldi, 'Die Spätantike' (*supra*, n.31), pp.68ff.

36. Kitzinger, 'On the Interpretation of Stylistic Changes' (*supra*, I, n.18), pp.2f. See *supra*, p.13.

37. Volbach, *Elfenbeinarbeiten*, pp.54f., no.62; pl.34.

38. For this problem see E. Garger, 'Zur spätantiken Renaissance', *Jahrbuch der kunsthistorischen Sammlungen in Wien*, n.s., 8, 1934, pp.1ff., especially pp.23ff. (à propos of the related interior views in the Virgil Ms., Vat. lat. 3225).

39. Volbach, *Elfenbeinarbeiten*, pp.29f., no.1; pl.1.

40. *Ibid.*, pp.50f., 53, nos.54, 59; pls.28, 32. For the Western – and very probably Roman – origin of these diptychs see the important observations by J. W. Salomonson, 'Kunstgeschichtliche und ikonographische Untersuchungen zu einem Tonfragment der Sammlung Benaki in Athen', *Bulletin Antieke Beschaving*, 48, 1973, pp.3ff., especially pp.14ff.

41. C. Formis, 'Il dittico eburneo della cattedrale di Novara', *Pubblicazioni dell'Università Cattolica del Sacro Cuore, Milan, Contributi dell'Istituto di Archeologia*, 1, 1967, pp.171ff., especially pp.187ff. For the Lampadii see Jones, Martindale, Morris, *The Prosopography*, I (*supra*, n.11), pp.493f.; for the Rufii, *ibid.*, Stemma 13 on p.1138. At least two members of the latter family also bore the name Lampadius; cf. *ibid.*, pp.978ff.; Bloch, 'The Pagan Revival' (*supra*, n.29), pp.204ff.; A. Chastagnol, *Le sénat romain sous le règne d'Odoacre*, Bonn, 1966, p.6.

42. Volbach, *Elfenbeinarbeiten*, pp.53f., no.60; pl.32. The Leningrad diptych bears a stylistic relationship to a panel in the British Museum representing the apotheosis of an emperor (Volbach, *Elfenbeinarbeiten*, p.52, no.56; pl.28). The two reliefs may well come from the same atelier. On the evidence both of its subject matter and of the monogram inscribed in its frame, which has been plausibly read as 'Symmachorum', the British Museum ivory appears to have been made for a member of the pagan aristocracy. But its style, while distinctive, does not come under the heading of refined, retrospective classicism. One must conclude that patronage by the Symmachi and their class did not automatically lead to the adoption of a classicist manner. For the type of composition exemplified by these reliefs see *infra*, pp.50ff.

43. E. Kitzinger, 'A Marble Relief of the Theodosian Period', *Dumbarton Oaks Papers*, 14, 1960, pp.17ff.; reprinted in Kitzinger, *The Art of Byzantium* (*supra*, I, n.18), pp.1ff.; cf. Severin, 'Oströmische Plastik' (*supra*, n.26), pp.232ff. and fig.14.

44. Grabar, *Christian Iconography* (*supra*, Introduction, n.7), pp.37ff.

45. Kollwitz, *Oströmische Plastik* (*supra*, n.24), pp.132ff. and pls.45ff.

46. Volbach, *Elfenbeinarbeiten*, pp.79f., no.110; pl.59.

47. *Ibid.*, p.80, no.111; pl.60.

48. Dalton, *Catalogue* (*supra*, n.17), pp.61ff., no.304, and pls.13ff. For Projecta see Jones, Martindale, Morris, *The Prosopography*, I (*supra*, n.11), p.750. In a Columbia University thesis currently being prepared by Kathleen J. Shelton an attempt will be made to attribute Projecta's Casket, and with it the Esquiline Treasure as a whole, to a somewhat earlier date (middle of the fourth century).

49. R. Klein, *Der Streit um den Victoriaaltar*, Darmstadt, 1972, pp.55ff. For the literary activities of the pagan aristocrats see Bloch, 'The Pagan Revival' (*supra*, n.29), pp.213ff.; also *infra*, IV, n.4.

50. *Ibid.*, pp.216f.; L. D. Reynolds and N. G. Wilson, *Scribes and Scholars*, Oxford, 1974, pp.33ff.

51. A. Goldschmidt, *Die Elfenbeinskulpturen*, I, 1914, pp.68f., no.139; pl.59. For Ottonian art I cite the miniatures by the Gregory Master in the Codex Egberti (Trier, Stadtbibliothek, Ms. 24), which are heavily indebted to the art of our period; cf. C. R. Dodwell, *Painting in Europe 800–1200*, The Pelican History of Art, 1971, pp.58f.

52. J. Wilpert, *Die römischen Mosaiken und Malereien der kirchlichen Bauten vom IV. bis XIII. Jahrhundert*, III, Freiburg i. Br., 1917, pls.42–6. G. Matthiae, *Mosaici medioevali delle chiese di Roma*, Rome, 1967, pp.55ff. with pls.12f. and figs.36, 38ff.; for the date see pp.68f.; for the condition, the diagram on an unnumbered page at the end of the plate volume.

53. A. Boëthius and J. B. Ward-Perkins, *Etruscan and Roman Architecture*, The Pelican History of Art, 1970, pp.245ff., 512ff.

54. W. Köhler, 'Das Apsismosaik von Sta. Pudenziana in Rom als Stildokument', *Forschungen zur Kirchengeschichte und zur christlichen Kunst* (Festschrift J. Ficker), Leipzig, 1931, pp.167ff., especially pp.173f.

55. On this feature see R. Krautheimer, S. Corbett, W. Frankl, *Corpus basilicarum christianarum Romae*, III, Vatican City, 1967, pp.293, 297.

56. Reliefs: M. Bieber, *The Sculpture of the Hellenistic Age*, New York, 1961, figs. 656–8; cf. pp.153ff. Second Pompeian Style: see, for instance, the well-known paintings in the Metropolitan Museum in New York from a Villa at Boscoreale (Ph. W. Lehmann, *Roman Wall Paintings from Boscoreale in the Metropolitan Museum of Art*, Cambridge, Massachusetts, 1953, pls.10ff.; J. Engemann, *Architekturdarstellungen des frühen zweiten Stils*, Heidelberg, 1967, pp.102ff. and pls.36ff.).

57. See, e.g., I. Scott Ryberg, *Panel Reliefs of Marcus Aurelius*, New York, 1967, pls.9, 14f., 17, 22f., 26, 32f., 48.

58. For this much debated question see Matthiae, *Mosaici medioevali*, pp.58f.; also E. Dassmann, 'Das Apsismosaik von S. Pudentiana in Rom', *Römische Quartalschrift*, 65, 1970, pp.67ff., especially p.74. A special problem is posed by the jewelled cross which it is tempting to relate to the cross erected on Golgotha by Theodosius II in A.D.420 (Ph. Grierson, *Catalogue of the Byzantine Coins in the Dumbarton Oaks Collection and in the Whittemore Collection*, II, Washington, D.C., 1968, pp.95f.). Implicit in this identification is a *terminus post quem* for the mosaic that would be incompatible with a date in the period of Innocent I. But there was a cross on Golgotha already in the fourth century (Chr. Ihm, *Die Programme der christlichen Apsismalerei vom vierten Jahrhundert bis zur Mitte des achten Jahrhunderts*, Wiesbaden, 1960, p.14, n.8; Ch. Coüasnon, *The Church of the Holy Sepulchre in Jerusalem*, London, 1974, pp.50f.).

59. For early representations of 'councils' see Chr. Walter, *L'iconographie des conciles dans la tradition byzantine*, Paris, 1970, pp.165ff.; *ibid.*, pp.190f. for assemblies of Christ and the apostles in fourth-century art.

60. Köhler, 'Das Apsismosaik' (*supra*, n.54), p.179.

61. There must have been other works of painting or mosaic of similar character, some of them slightly earlier. They in turn found a reflection in relief sculpture of the late fourth century, of which the sarcophagus of S.Ambrogio in Milan provides the most outstanding example; see F. Gerke, 'Das Verhältnis von Malerei und Plastik in der theodosianisch-honorianischen Zeit', *Rivista di Archeologia Cristiana*, 12, 1935, pp.119ff., especially pp.146f. and fig.8.

CHAPTER THREE

1. Swoboda, 'Über die Stilkontinuität' (*supra*, Introduction, n.2), p.26.

2. Volbach, *Elfenbeinarbeiten* (*supra*, II, n. 30), p.32, no.6; pl.3.

3. Successive stages in this development are exemplified, within the category of diptychs with single standing figures, by the diptych of the consul Felix of A.D.428 (*ibid.*, p.30, no.2; pl.2); the diptych of a high official in Novara (*ibid.*, p.56, no.64; pl.36; our fig.82); the diptych in Vienna – not necessarily official – with personifications of Rome and Constantinople (*ibid.*, pp.43f., no.38; pl.21); and the diptych of the consul Basilius of A.D.480 (*ibid.*, p.31, no.5; pl.3). Although the Novara diptych appears to be substantially later than that of Felix, the date proposed by C. Formis (second half of fifth or early sixth century) is probably too late ('Il dittico eburneo' [*supra*, II, n.41], p.177). The style of the Vienna figures has Eastern affinities, but I agree with Volbach and others that the diptych is a Western work. Finally, the diptych of Basilius bears a close stylistic resemblance to that of Boethius (our fig. 81).

4. Volbach, *Elfenbeinarbeiten*, pp.82f., no.116; pl.61.

5. *Ibid.*, pp.80f., nos.112f.; pl.60. H. Schnitzler has reiterated and refined the argument that these panels once formed part of a 'five-part' diptych similar to, but substantially earlier than, that in Milan Cathedral to be cited presently and, like the latter, destined for a book cover ('Kästchen oder fünfteiliges Buchdeckelpaar?', *Festschrift für Gert von der Osten*, Cologne, 1970, pp.24ff.); see also *infra*, p.96.

6 Volbach, *Elfenbeinarbeiten*, pp.84f., no.119, pl.63.

7. See the literature cited by Volbach, *ibid.*, under the individual entries.

8. *Ibid.*, pp.32ff., nos.8–11; pls.4f.

9. *Ibid.*, pp.35ff., nos.17–21; pls.8f.

10. *Enciclopedia dell'arte antica, classica e orientale*, V, 1963, s.v. 'Mosaico' (D. Levi); H. Stern, 'La funzione del mosaico nella casa antica', *Antichità Altoadriatiche*, 8, 1975, pp.39ff.

11. D. Levi, *Antioch Mosaic Pavements*, Princeton, London and The Hague, 1947.

12. See the series *Fouilles d'Apamée de Syrie* and *Fouilles d'Apamée de Syrie Miscellanea*, in progress of publication by the Centre Belge de Recherches Archéologiques à Apamée de Syrie since 1969 and 1968 respectively; see also *infra*, IV, n.30.

13. Levi, *Antioch Mosaic Pavements*, pp.363ff. and pls.86b, 90, 170ff., 176f. For the rinceau border, not exhibited at Worcester, see *ibid.*, p.363, fig. 150; pl.144b,c.

14. *Ibid.*, pp.156ff. and pl.30.

15. *Ibid.*, pp.226ff. and pls.52ff.

16. A. M. Schneider, *The Church of the Multiplying of the Loaves and Fishes*, London, 1937, pls.A, B, 2–17.

17. For what follows see I. Lavin, 'The Hunting Mosaics of Antioch and their Sources', *Dumbarton Oaks Papers*, 17, 1963, pp.179ff.; E. Kitzinger, 'Stylistic Developments in Pavement Mosaics in the Greek East from the Age of Constantine to the Age of Justinian', *La mosaïque gréco-romaine*, I, Paris, 1965, pp.341ff. (reprinted in Kitzinger, *The Art of Byzantium* [*supra*, I, n.18], pp.64ff.). For critical observations see A. Carandini, 'La villa di Piazza Armerina, la circolazione della cultura figurativa africana nel tardo impero ed altre precisazioni', *Dialoghi di Archeologia*, 1, 1967, pp.93ff., especially pp.108ff.; Salomonson, 'Kunstgeschichtliche und ikonographische Untersuchungen' (*supra*, II, n.40), pp.38ff.

18. More often than in the East, *emblemata* in these Western countries are panels separately set on marble or ceramic trays and subsequently inserted into the pavement. The *emblema* thus tends to be quite literally more of a foreign body in relation to the overall design of the floor than it is in the East. For a recent survey of such 'true' *emblemata* see A. Balil, 'Emblemata', *Universidad de Valladolid, Boletin del Seminario de Estudios de Arte y Arqueologia*, 60–1, 1975, pp.67ff.

19. Volbach, *Elfenbeinarbeiten*, nos. 56, 60, 61, 108; cf. *supra*, p.38 with n.42.

20. Levi, *Antioch Mosaic Pavements* (*supra*, n.11), pp.283ff. and pls.113ff.

21. F. W. Deichmann, *Ravenna, Hauptstadt des spätantiken Abendlandes*, I, *Geschichte und Monumente*, Wiesbaden, 1969, pp.158ff.; II, 1, *Kommentar*, Wiesbaden, 1974, pp.61ff.; III, *Frühchristliche Bauten und Mosaiken von Ravenna*, 2nd edn., Wiesbaden, n.d., pls.I, 1–31.

22. *Ibid.*, I, p.158; II, 1, pp.51f., 63ff.

23. *Ibid.*, II, 1, p.75. An *emblema* with a pastoral scene on the floor of one of the rooms of a Roman villa at Corinth provides a particularly good example; see T. L. Shear, *The Roman Villa, Corinth*, Cambridge, Massachusetts, 1930, pls.3ff. and pp.21f.

24. Deichmann, *Ravenna*, II, 1, p.88. It is true that no precisely similar examples have survived, but the affiliation with textiles can hardly be doubted; see now also the fabrics (admittedly of somewhat later date) recovered in Chinese excavations in Central Asia (M. W. Meister, 'The Pearl Roundel in Chinese Textile Design', *Ars Orientalis*, 8, 1970, pp.255ff.; especially fig.41 with p.260, n.16).

25. J. Strzygowski, *Orient oder Rom*, Leipzig, 1901, pp.11ff. C. H. Kraeling, 'Color Photographs of the Paintings in the Tomb of the Three Brothers at Palmyra', *Les Annales Archéologiques de Syrie*, 11–12, 1961–2, pp.13ff., especially p.16 and pls.2f.,

13. The subject of the painting in the lunette was identified by Strzygowski as Achilles on Skyros (*op.cit.*, pp.13f., 24f.). For this scene cf. the central medallion of the Augst plate (our fig.54). The Mausoleum of Galla Placidia was cited by Strzygowski à propos of the architecture of the Palmyra tomb (*op.cit.*, p.19). His dating of the paintings was revised by Kraeling (*op.cit.*, pp.14ff.).

26. Full publication by H. Torp is being awaited; meanwhile see his preliminary article cited *infra*, n.29, and his monograph *Mosaikkene i St Georg-Rotunden i Thessaloniki*, Oslo, 1963; also the colour photographs by M. Hirmer in W. F. Volbach, *Early Christian Art*, New York, n.d., pls.123–7. Since the mosaics were cleaned – and fragmentary remains of those above the lowest zone of the dome discovered – in 1952–3, discussion of their date has focused mainly on two alternatives, namely, the period of Theodosius I (*c.* A.D.380–90) and the decades around A.D.450. The weight of the evidence is very much against the first of these alternatives; see W. E. Kleinbauer, 'The Iconography and the Date of the Mosaics of the Rotunda of Hagios Georgios, Thessaloniki', *Viator*, 3, 1972, pp.27ff., especially pp.68ff. On the basis of evidence derived from brick stamps M. Vickers has proposed a precise dating in the 440s, but his argument relies heavily on the still hypothetical identification of Hormisdas, the builder of the city walls of Thessaloniki, with an official of that period ('Fifth Century Brick Stamps from Thessaloniki', *The Annual of the British School at Athens*, 68, 1973, pp.285ff., with references to his earlier articles on the subject). Even so, I think it is most likely that the mosaics were made in the decade or decades just before the middle of the fifth century. The arguments recently advanced by B. Brenk in favour of the sixth-century date originally proposed by E. Weigand in 1939 do not appear to me strong enough to make it necessary to revert to that opinion (see p.154, n.168 of the monograph on the mosaics of S.Maria Maggiore cited *infra*, IV, n.1).

27. A. Grabar, 'À propos des mosaïques de la coupole de Saint-Georges à Salonique', *Cahiers Archéologiques*, 17, 1967, pp.59ff., especially pp.64ff.; Kleinbauer, 'The Iconography and the Date', pp.29ff.

28. Cf. especially the painted decoration of the 'dome' of a small circular tomb chamber of the early Hellenistic period discovered in 1944 at Kazanlak in Bulgaria (L. Zhivkova, *Kazanlushkata grobnitsa*, Sofia, 1974, pls.1, 12, 20, 26; *Enciclopedia dell'arte antica, classica e orientale*, IV, 1961, s.v. Kazanlăk).

29. H. Torp, 'Quelques remarques sur les mosaïques de l'église Saint-Georges à Thessalonique', *Acts of the Ninth International Congress of Byzantine Studies, Thessaloniki, 12–19 August 1953* (title in Greek), I, Athens, 1955, pp.489ff., especially p.498: 'le palais céleste des athlètes du Christ'.

30. Reconstruction drawings by M. Corres, published by Maria G. Sotiriou ('Sur quelques problèmes de l'iconographie de la coupole de Saint-Georges de Thessalonique', *In Memoriam Panayotis A. Michelis*, Athens, 1971, pp.218ff., especially pls.10f., figs.1f.), show a – purely hypothetical – ring of terrain inserted between the chorus of acclaiming figures and the angels carrying the central medallion, thus confining the former to a disproportionately narrow band and severing their connection with the latter.

31. The late Hellenistic and Roman antecedents that are specifically relevant here are not the views of upper parts of distant buildings behind screen walls, which I cited à propos of the architectural scenery of the mosaic of S.Pudenziana (*supra*, II, n.56), but rather instances in which a pictorial representation *complete in itself* and with a greater or lesser amount of spatial implications is placed above a zone of simulated wainscoting. The room to which the famous Odyssey landscapes in the Vatican belonged provided an outstanding example of a painted decoration of this latter kind. Although this decoration, which can be reconstructed at least in its broad outlines, entailed a framework of simulated full-length pilasters, within this framework the upper parts of the walls were played off against the lower parts in the manner indicated (see P. H. von Blanckenhagen, 'The Odyssey Frieze', *Römische Mitteilungen*, 70, 1963, pp.100ff., especially pp.102f., with further references; also Engemann, *Architekturdarstellungen* [*supra*, II, n.56], pp.141ff., especially p.143). In a more restrained and not always consistent form the concept is present in certain interiors of the Roman period in Eastern Mediterranean lands; for instance, in the painted decorations of some of the tomb chambers of the second century A.D. in the Crimea (M. I. Rostovtsev, *Ancient Decorative Painting in South Russia* [in Russian], St Petersburg, 1913–14, pp.283ff. and pls.73–5; pp.293ff., figs. 59f. and pls.76–81) and in the third-century decoration of the Christian Baptistery at Dura-Europos (C. H. Kraeling, *The Christian Building*, The Excavations at Dura-Europos, Final Report, VIII, Part II, New Haven, 1967, pp.160ff. and pls.24, 33, 44, 46). In these Eastern interiors the decoration is organized in terms of horizontal zones entirely as it is in the dome of St George.

32. Deichmann, *Ravenna* (*supra*, n.21), I, pp.130ff.; II, 1, pp.15ff.; III, pls.IIf., 37–95. S. K. Kostof, *The Orthodox Baptistery of Ravenna*, New Haven and London, 1965.

33. H. Stern, 'Les mosaïques de l'église de Sainte-Constance à Rome', *Dumbarton Oaks Papers*, 12, 1958, pp.157ff., especially pp.166ff. and figs.1ff., 22, 23. The mosaic in the dome of the Baptistery of S.Giovanni in Fonte in Naples is another example; see Wilpert, *Die römischen Mosaiken und Malereien* (*supra*, II, n.52), I, p.216, fig.68; III, pls.29ff.

34. Kostof's analysis of the compositional system of the dome fails to bring out this duality of sources (*The Orthodox Baptistery*, pp.112ff.). Deichmann clearly recognizes it but he places the phenomenon of conflation in an art-historical perspective somewhat different from the one offered here (*Ravenna*, I, pp.138ff.; cf. also II, 1, pp.31f.).

35. *Ibid.*, I, pp.209ff.; II, 1, pp.251ff.; III, pls.249–73.

36. G. Bovini, 'I mosaici di S.Vittore "in ciel d'oro" di Milano', *Corsi di cultura sull'arte ravennate e bizantina*, 1969, pp.71ff.

37. Deichmann, *Ravenna*, I, pp.171ff.; II, 1, pp.125ff.; III, pls.IV–VII, 98–213.

38. *Ibid.*, I, pp.201ff.; II, 1, pp.191ff.; III, pls.216–45.

39. One might also recall here once more the little chapel in Milan whose decoration comprises, in addition to the bust of St Victor in the dome, six single standing figures of local bishops on the lateral walls; see *supra*, n.36 and fig. 105.

40. M. Sacopoulo, *La Theotokos à la mandorle de Lythrankomi*, Paris, 1975. An exhaustive monograph by A. H. S. Megaw is in the press. Miss Sacopoulo attributes the mosaic to the second quarter of the sixth century (*op.cit.*, p.107), Mr Megaw to a date in or about the third decade of the century.

41. This is true also of some mosaics in Thessaloniki whose dates have been much debated and in which the relatively loose technique characteristic of the Lythrankomi mosaic is accentuated, at times to the point of fuzziness. The most important is the apse mosaic of the little church of Hosios David, which has been attributed to dates ranging from the fifth to the seventh century. For reproductions see Volbach, *Early Christian Art* (*supra*, n.26), pls.133 5; for the earlier literature, V. Lazarev, *Storia della pittura bizantina*, Turin, 1967, p.61, n.61. The debate concerning the date continues. R. S. Cormack advocates the late fifth century ("The Mosaic Decoration of S.Demetrios, Thessaloniki', *The Annual of the British School at Athens*, 64, 1969, pp.17ff., especially p.49); W. E. Kleinbauer a date later than that of the mosaics of St George but prior to Justinian (*op. cit.* [*supra*, n.26], p.85, n.215). There is similar uncertainty about the chronology of the first group of *ex voto* mosaics in the Church of St Demetrius, only a few of which have survived the fire of 1917. These mosaics are not stylistically uniform and need not all be of one date. But a panel still to be seen on the west wall of the south aisle exhibits characteristics which seem to have been shared also by many of the lost mosaics; and for work such as this the late fifth-century date advocated by Cormack (*op.cit.*, pp.49f.) seems to me too early (see *infra*, VI, n.10). I still believe that the curiously elusive style of these Thessalonikan mosaics should be understood in terms of a local tradition continued over a fairly long stretch of time in the wake of the great example set by the mosaics of St George; cf. E. Kitzinger, *Byzantine Art in the Period between Justinian and Iconoclasm*, Berichte zum XI. Internationalen Byzantinisten-Kongress, IV, 1, Munich, 1958 (reprinted in Kitzinger, *The Art of Byzantium* [*supra*, I, n.18], pp.157ff.), pp.20ff.

CHAPTER FOUR

1. H. Karpp (ed.), *Die frühchristlichen und mittelalterlichen Mosaiken in Santa Maria Maggiore zu Rom*, Baden-Baden, 1966. See now the comprehensive study (intended as a companion volume to Karpp's plates) by B. Brenk, *Die frühchristlichen Mosaiken in S.Maria Maggiore zu Rom*, Wiesbaden, 1975. The pages which follow recapitulate in large part observations I put forward in a recently published paper read at a Princeton symposium in 1973 ('The Role of Miniature Painting in Mural Decoration', *The Place of Book Illumination in Byzantine Art*, Princeton, New Jersey, 1975, pp.99ff., especially pp.121ff.). On most questions I find myself in substantial agreement with Brenk, and in my notes specific references to his text will be limited to major points.

2. On this question see Brenk, *Die frühchristlichen Mosaiken*, pp.3f.

3. R. Krautheimer, 'The Architecture of Sixtus III: A Fifth Century Renascence?', *De artibus opuscula XL: Essays in Honor of Erwin Panofsky*, New York, 1961, pp.291ff.; reprinted, with a *Postscript*, in R. Krautheimer, *Studies in Early Christian, Medieval, and Renaissance Art*, New York and London, 1969, pp.181ff.

4. J. de Wit, *Die Miniaturen des Vergilius Vaticanus*, Amsterdam, 1959; see especially pp.207f.

5. Compare the mythological scenes incorporated in the decoration of a ceiling in Nero's Golden House (our fig. 121; colour reproductions in *Enciclopedia dell'arte antica, classica e orientale*, VI, 1965, facing p.960; cf. Bianchi Bandinelli, *Rome: The Center of Power* [*supra*, I, n.12], pp.132ff.).

6. H. Buchthal, 'A Note on the Miniatures of the Vatican Virgil Manuscript', *Mélanges Eugène Tisserant*, VI (Studi e Testi, 236), Vatican City, 1964, pp.167ff. Brenk, *Die frühchristlichen Mosaiken*, p.128.

7. H. Degering and A. Boeckler, *Die Quedlinburger Italafragmente*, Berlin, 1932.

8. *Ilias Ambrosiana*, Fontes Ambrosiani, 28, Bern and Olten, 1953; R. Bianchi Bandinelli, *Hellenistic-Byzantine Miniatures of the Iliad*, Olten, 1955; cf. Kitzinger, 'The Role of Miniature Painting' (*supra*, n.1), pp.123, 134.

9. Brenk, *Die frühchristlichen Mosaiken*, pp.135f.

10. For the inscription of Sixtus III see *infra*, p.73. I agree with Brenk and others that the inscription is an integral part of the decoration of the arch (*Die frühchristlichen Mosaiken*, pp.15, 52, n.16). For the view that the nave mosaics are of substantially earlier date see the references *ibid.*, p.151, n.163.

11. *Ibid.*, pp.134ff.

12. *Ibid.*, pp.151ff.

13. J. J. Tikkanen, *Die Genesismosaiken von S.Marco in Venedig und ihr Verhältniss zu den Miniaturen der Cottonbibel*, Acta Societatis Scientiarum Fennicae, 17, 1889; cf. Kitzinger, 'The Role of Miniature Painting', pp.99ff.

14. Kömstedt, *Vormittelalterliche Malerei* (*supra*, Introduction, n.3), pp.14ff.; M. Schapiro, in *The Review of Religion*, 8, 1943–4, pp.165ff. (review of Morey, *Early Christian Art*), especially p.182; F. W. Deichmann, *Frühchristliche Kirchen in Rom*, Basle, 1948, p.65; Brenk, *Die frühchristlichen Mosaiken*, pp.62, 108, 110, 152.

15. It was P. Künzle who first drew this important conclusion ('Per una visione organica dei mosaici antichi di S.Maria Maggiore', *Atti della Pontificia Accademia Romana di Archeologia, Rendiconti*, 34, 1961–2, pp.153ff., especially p.162); cf. also Kitzinger, 'The Role of Miniature Painting', pp.128ff.; Brenk, *Die frühchristlichen Mosaiken*, pp.128, 180.

16. *Supra*, pp.18f.; cf. Brenk, *Die frühchristlichen Mosaiken*, p.152.

17. Degering and Boeckler, *Die Quedlinburger Italafragmente* (*supra*, n.7), pp.65ff.; for disposition sketches, *ibid.*, pp.72, 154 and pl.8; cf. Kitzinger, 'The Role of Miniature Painting', p.135 with n.76.

18. See our fig. 122, lower right hand panel (Saul); cf., in general, Brenk, *Die frühchristlichen Mosaiken*, pp.147ff. and figs.42ff.

19. *Ibid.*, p.8 and figs.2–4.

20. A. Grabar, *L'empéreur dans l'art byzantin*, Paris, 1936, pp.209ff.; *idem*, *Christian Iconography* (*supra*, Introduction, n.7), pp.46ff.; E. H. Kantorowicz, 'Puer exoriens', *Perennitas* (Festschrift Thomas Michels), Münster, 1963, pp.118ff.; Brenk, *Die frühchristlichen Mosaiken*, pp.178ff. *et passim*.

21. Grabar, *L'empéreur*, pp.216ff.; Kantorowicz, 'Puer exoriens', pp.118ff.; cf. also U. Schubert, 'Der politische Primatanspruch des Papstes dargestellt am Triumph-bogen von Santa Maria Maggiore in Rom', *Kairos*, n.s. 13, 1971, pp.194ff., especially pp.205ff. Brenk, *Die frühchristlichen Mosaiken*, pp.21f., rejects this interpretation, which, however, receives important support from representations on fourth-century contorniates; cf. Kantorowicz, *op.cit.*, p.121 with n.13; Schubert, *op.cit.*, p.205 with n.46 and fig.12.

22. Kitzinger, 'The Role of Miniature Painting', p.134 and figs. 25, 27; cf. Brenk, *Die frühchristlichen Mosaiken*, p.151.

23. Grabar, *L'empéreur*, pp.221ff.; Krautheimer, 'The Architecture of Sixtus III' (*supra*, n.3), pp.301f.; Kantorowicz, 'Puer exoriens', pp.121f.; Schubert, 'Der politische Primatanspruch', pp.222ff.

24. S. Waetzoldt, *Die Kopien des 17. Jahrhunderts nach Mosaiken und Wandmalereien in Rom*, Vienna and Munich, 1964, pp.56ff.

25. Cf. Brenk, *Die frühchristlichen Mosaiken*, pp.56, 108f.

26. *Ibid.*, pp.47ff. Brenk sees a possible reference to the Council of Ephesus primarily in the scenes in the second zone of the arch.

27. An important clue to the understanding of the iconography of the mosaics of the arch lies in the transposition of biblical chronology in the three zones depicting scenes from Christ's infancy; cf. Grabar's classical interpretation in *L'empéreur* (*supra*, n.20), pp.209ff.; also Brenk, *Die frühchristlichen Mosaiken*, pp.39ff.

28. Kömstedt (see *supra*, n.14).

29. Köhler, 'Das Apsismosaik' (*supra*, II, n.54), p.179. Brenk takes a less negative view of the relationship of the mosaics of S.Maria Maggiore to earlier Roman mosaics and believes that in all probability the artists were Roman (*Die frühchristlichen Mosaiken*, pp.154ff.).

30. At Antioch see especially the Topographical Border in the Yakto complex, a work of about the middle of the fifth century (Levi, *Antioch Mosaic Pavements* [*supra*, III, n.11], pp.323ff. and pls.79f.; see *ibid.*, p.582 for comparisons with figures in Old Testament scenes in S.Maria Maggiore). For the Apamea mosaic illustrated in our figs. 135 and 137, which is known to me only in black and white photographs, see J. Balty, 'Une nouvelle mosaïque du IVe s. dans l'édifice dit "au triclinos" à Apamée', *Annales Archéologiques Arabes Syriennes*, 1970, pp.1ff., especially pp.4ff., and figs. 5–10. The fourth-century date proposed for this mosaic by Mme Balty is based on comparisons with mosaics at Antioch. Brenk, it should be noted, finds in certain

heads at S.Maria Maggiore an influence of Theodosian portraiture, but sees no reason for assuming a collaboration of artists from the East (*Die frühchristlichen Mosaiken*, pp.139f.).

31. *Ibid.*, p.153.

32. *Supra*, pp.50ff.

33. R. Kautzsch, *Kapitellstudien*, Berlin and Leipzig, 1936. There has been extensive research in this field during the forty years since Kautzsch's book was published. Much new material has come to light and some of his datings have been – or may yet have to be – revised. But in its main lines his concept of stylistic developments is still valid.

34. *Ibid.*, pp.115ff., 140ff., 152ff. For the 'Theodosian' type see also F. W. Deichmann, *Studien zur Architektur Konstantinopels*, Baden-Baden, 1956, pp.59ff.; for capitals with animal protomes, E. Kitzinger, 'The Horse and Lion Tapestry at Dumbarton Oaks', *Dumbarton Oaks Papers*, 3, 1946, pp.1ff., especially pp.17ff. The existence in Asia Minor of a continuous tradition for capitals of the latter type throughout late antiquity is hypothetical (F. W. Deichmann, 'Zur Entstehung der spätantiken Zweizonen-Tierkapitelle', *Charisterion eis Anastasion K. Orlandon*, I, Athens, 1965, pp.136ff., especially p.142).

35. For the capital from Pergamon (fig.138) see Boëthius and Ward-Perkins, *Etruscan and Roman Architecture* (*supra*, II, n.53), pl.215. The capital from Cyprus (fig.139) may be compared with examples such as Kautzsch, *Kapitellstudien*, pl.5, no.69 (*ibid.*, pp.28, 39: 'second quarter of fourth century').

36. Deichmann, *Ravenna* (*supra*, III, n.21), I, pp.64f. and fig.30; II, 1, p.128 and figs.85ff.

37. Kautzsch, *Kapitellstudien*, pp.5–115 with pls.1–23.

38. Deichmann, *Studien zur Architektur Konstantinopels* (*supra*, n.34), pp.41ff.

39. For this development see *ibid.*, p.45. I am indebted to Dr Alison Frantz and the late Professor Arif Müfid Mansel for photographs of the examples illustrated in figs. 142 and 143 respectively. For the splendid example from Basilica A in Nea Anchialos (fig.144) see G. A. Sotiriou, 'Hai christianikai Thebai tes Thessalias', *Archaiologike Ephemeris*, 1929, pp.1ff., especially p.62 with fig.65.

40. For the capital from the basilica at Vravron in Attica, illustrated in our fig. 145, see the excavation report by E. Stikas in the *Praktika* of the Athens Archaeological Society for the year 1951, pp.53ff., especially pp.65ff. and figs.21f. (for this church cf. R. Krautheimer, *Early Christian and Byzantine Architecture*, The Pelican History of Art, revised edition, 1975, pp.127f.). For the capital from the Church of St Demetrius in Thessaloniki (our fig. 146) see Kautzsch, *Kapitellstudien*, pp.169f., no.548; pl.34. Its probable date is towards the end of the fifth century (*ibid.*, p.172; Krautheimer, *op.cit.*, pp.132ff. with n.49). For the capital from Sardis (our fig. 147), probably of much the same date, see F. K. Yegul, 'Early Byzantine Capitals from Sardis', *Dumbarton Oaks Papers*, 28, 1974, pp.265ff., especially p.272 and figs.8f.; *ibid.*, pp.267ff. (with figs.16ff.), a general survey of the development of the Ionic impost capital, with references to earlier literature.

41. See in general Kautzsch, *Kapitellstudien*, pp.182ff.

42. *Ibid.*, p.188, no.591; pl.37.

43. *Ibid.*, pp.184ff., and pls.37ff. Kautzsch's attribution of examples in the Church of St Sophia in Thessaloniki (*ibid.*, pp.184ff., no.586; pl.37) to a date before the accession of Justinian has been confirmed by the discovery of the architectural decoration of the Church of St Polyeuktos in Constantinople, a building erected by Juliana Anicia probably between A.D.524 and 527. The Thessalonikan capitals, which are in secondary use, bear ornament closely related to the work at St Polyeuktos (cf. M. Kambouri, 'Two Capitals of Hagia Sophia in Thessaloniki' [Greek, with English summary], *Aristoteleion Panepistemion Thessalonikes, Epistomenike Epeteris tes Polytechnikes Scholes*, 6, 1973, pp.67ff.). There were true impost capitals also at St Polyeuktos itself (R. M. Harrison and N. Firatli, 'Excavations at Sarachane in Istanbul: Fourth Preliminary Report', *Dumbarton Oaks Papers*, 21, 1967, pp.273ff., especially p.276 and fig.14; R. M. Harrison, 'A Constantinopolitan Capital at Barcelona', *ibid.*, 27, 1973, pp.297ff.; for the building cf. Krautheimer, *Early Christian and Byzantine Architecture*, pp.230ff.).

44. Kautzsch, *Kapitellstudien*, p.100, no.290; pl.19. For the date see *ibid.*, p.104.

45. *Supra*, pp.61f.

46. J. Inan and E. Rosenbaum, *Roman and Early Byzantine Portrait Sculpture in Asia Minor*, London, 1966, pp.151ff., no.194; pl.181. Severin, *Zur Portraitplastik des 5. Jahrhunderts n. Chr. (supra*, II, n.25), pp.108ff., 177ff.

CHAPTER FIVE

1. Deichmann, *Ravenna (supra*, III, n.21), I, pp.226ff.; III, pls.285–375. Publication of Part 2 of the *Kommentar* (vol. II), which will cover S.Vitale and also S.Apollinare in Classe (cf. *ibid.*, II, 1, p.ix), was announced for 1976 but was not available to me at the time this book went to press.

2. Cf. R. Krautheimer's analysis of the interior of the church: *Early Christian and Byzantine Architecture (supra*, IV, n.40), pp.219ff.

3. For a detailed analysis of this framework see G. Rodenwaldt, 'Bemerkungen zu den Kaisermosaiken in San Vitale', *Jahrbuch des Deutschen Archäologischen Instituts*, 59–60, 1944–5, pp.88ff.

4. See *supra*, pp.57f., and III, n.31 for the antecedents of this design concept.

5. See the colour reproduction in Volbach, *Early Christian Art (supra*, III, n.26), pl.164.

6. *Supra*, pp.69ff.

7. Cf. Rodenwaldt, 'Bemerkungen zu den Kaisermosaiken' (*supra*, n.3), pp.101ff.

8. For what follows see Kitzinger, 'Stylistic Developments in Pavement Mosaics in the Greek East' (*supra*, III, n.17), pp.346ff.

9. For references see J.-P. Sodini, 'Mosaïques paléochrétiennes de Grèce', *Bulletin de Correspondance Hellénique*, 94, 1970, II, pp.710f.

10. For the example illustrated in our fig. 162 see Levi, *Antioch Mosaic Pavements* (*supra*, III, n.11), pp.315f. and pl.128b. Attributed by Levi to a date after the middle of the fifth century, this floor is of special interest because of its colour scheme. Both the stylized buds making up the diaper grid and the rosettes filling it are pink, while the ground is green. Such extensive use of green is unusual in the floor mosaics of Antioch. Although the design remains severely abstract, evidently the artist went out of his way to convey a suggestion of a flowering meadow. The floor thus exemplifies particularly well the tendency in this period to reinterpret geometric patterns in organic terms.

11. *Ibid.*, pp.321ff. and pl.74a. For the date see Lavin, 'The Hunting Mosaics of Antioch' (*supra*, III, n.17), p.195 with n.46.

12. M. Avi-Yonah, 'Mosaic Pavements in Palestine', *Quarterly of the Department of Antiquities in Palestine*, 2, 1933, pp.136ff., especially pp.171f., no.132; *idem*, 'Une école de mosaïque à Gaza au sixième siècle', *La mosaïque gréco-romaine*, II, Paris, 1975, pp.377ff.; especially p.379 and pl.180, 1 (with wrong caption).

13. Lavin, 'The Hunting Mosaics of Antioch', pp.217f. and figs. 47–50. The early dating of the floor at Djemila (*ibid.*, fig. 50) has been questioned; see most recently M. Blanchard-Lemée, *Maisons à mosaïques du quartier central de Djemila (Cuicul)*, Aix-en-Provence, 1975, pp.88ff.

14. Avi-Yonah, 'Une école de mosaïque à Gaza' (*supra*, n.12).

15. See, e.g., Levi, *Antioch Mosaic Pavements*, pls.83a, 91.

16. E. Kitzinger, 'Studies in Late Antique and Early Byzantine Floor Mosaics, I: Mosaics at Nikopolis', *Dumbarton Oaks Papers*, 6, 1951, pp.81ff., especially pp.93ff. and figs.18f. For the pendant of this floor – a hunting mosaic whose composition bears witness to the same characteristic development – see *ibid.*, pp.108ff. and figs. 20ff.

17. Bianchi Bandinelli, *Rome: The Center of Power* (*supra*, I, n.12), pp.125f. and figs. 130f., 133.

18. E. Kitzinger, 'Mosaic Pavements in the Greek East and the Question of a "Renaissance" under Justinian', *Actes du VIe congrès international d'études byzantines*, II, Paris, 1951, pp.209ff.; reprinted in Kitzinger, *The Art of Byzantium* (*supra*, I, n.18), pp.49ff.

19. *Supra*, p.51.

20. See, for instance, the splendid floor in the nave of the Justinianic basilica at Sabratha (S. Aurigemma, *I mosaici*, L'Italia in Africa: Tripolitania, I, 1, Rome, 1960, pp.27ff. and pls.19ff.).

21. Matthiae, *Mosaici medioevali* (*supra*, II, n.52), p.85 and fig.77.

22. R. O. Farioli, 'La decorazione musiva della capella di S.Matrona nella chiesa di S.Prisco presso Capua', *Corsi di cultura sull'arte ravennate e bizantina*, 1967, pp.267ff.; cf. also the mosaic decoration of the year A.D.512 in the barrel vault of the chancel of the monastic church near Kartmin (Tur Abdin); the decoration consists of a vine trellis issuing from vases in the four corners and surrounding a central medallion with a cross (E. J. W. Hawkins and M. Mundell, 'The Mosaics of the Monastery of Mār Samuel, Mār Simeon, and Mār Gabriel near Kartmin', *Dumbarton Oaks Papers*, 27, 1973, pp.279ff.).

23. K. Lehmann, 'The Dome of Heaven', *Art Bulletin*, 27, 1945, pp.1ff., especially p.5. Stern, 'La funzione del mosaico nella casa antica' (*supra*, III, n.10), pp.47f., 51ff. See also *supra*, p.51.

24. Matthiae, *Mosaici medioevali*, pp.135ff., with pls.16–18 and figs.78, 80–5; for restorations see the diagram on an unnumbered plate at end of volume.

25. R. Brilliant, *Gesture and Rank in Roman Art*, Memoirs of the Connecticut Academy of Arts and Sciences, 14, New Haven, 1963, pp.173ff. *et passim*.

26. For the mutilated mosaic on the wall surrounding the apse, which represented the adoration of the Lamb by the twenty-four elders (Rev. 4 and 5), see Waetzoldt, *Die Kopien des 17. Jahrhunderts* (*supra*, IV, n.24), p.32 and fig.39. This mosaic has been attributed to the period of Pope Sergius I (A.D.687–701) by Matthiae (*Mosaici medioevali*, pp.203ff. with pl.26 and figs.126–31).

27. C. Davis-Weyer, 'Das Traditio-Legis-Bild und seine Nachfolge', *Münchner Jahrbuch der bildenden Kunst*, 3rd series, 12, 1961, pp.7ff., especially pp.17f.

28. Volbach, *Elfenbeinarbeiten* (*supra*, II, n.30), pp.93f., no.140; pls.72ff. Add to the bibliography S. Bettini's discussion in the introduction to the exhibition catalogue *Venezia e Bisanzio*, Venice, 1974 (pp.18ff.).

29. Kitzinger, 'Notes on Early Coptic Sculpture' (*supra*, I, n.14), pp.210ff.; *idem*, 'A Marble Relief of the Theodosian Period' (*supra*, II, n.43), pp.38, 42.

30. Oddly enough, the sequence is not strictly chronological in terms of the biblical text (cf. C. Cecchelli, *La Cattedra di Massimiano ed altri avori romano-orientali*, Rome, 1936, p.46 with n.14). The most striking anomalies occur on the right-hand side, in the second part of the cycle (figs.171, 175). They could be explained by assuming that on this side the scenes on the framing panels and those on the framed ones were thought of as distinct sequences, the latter to be read from top to bottom, the former from bottom to top.

31. Volbach, *Elfenbeinarbeiten*, pp.47f., no.48; pl.26.

32. Delbrueck, *Die Consulardiptychen* (*supra*, II, n.23), pp.12ff.

33. The case for the attribution of the diptych to the period of Justinian has been stated most cogently by K. Wessel, 'Das Diptychon Barberini', *Akten des XI. Internationalen Byzantinistenkongresses*, Munich, 1960, pp.665ff.

34. For Roman *adventus* iconography see the study by Brilliant cited *supra*, n.25 (with further references).

35. See *supra*, especially p.90 with nn.16f.; also *infra*, p.109 with n.31.

29. *Supra*, pp.29f.

30. A plate at Dumbarton Oaks with a hunting scene of mythological character is considered to be of fifth-century date but is not likely to have been made long after A.D.400 (M. C. Ross, *Catalogue of the Byzantine and Early Mediaeval Antiquities in the Dumbarton Oaks Collection*, I, Washington, D.C., 1962, pp.3f., no.4; pls.2f.); while a fragmentary bowl with a Dionysiac procession in the same collection probably is not much (if at all) earlier than A.D.500 (*ibid.*, pp.5ff., no.6; pls.6f.). For other categories of fifth-century silver objects see, e.g., *ibid.*, pp.5f., no.5 and pl.4; Volbach, *Early Christian Art* (*supra*, III, n.26), pls.120f.; Delbrueck, *Die Consulardiptychen* (*supra*, II, n.23), pp.154ff., no.35; J. Heurgon, *Le trésor de Ténès*, Paris, 1958, pp.51ff. and pl.6. At least some of the objects in the treasures from Canoscio and Canicattini Bagni, which are composed solely of pieces of Christian or neutral character, also appear to be of the fifth century, though these treasures in their entirety have been attributed to the sixth century (W. F. Volbach, 'Il tesoro di Canoscio', *Ricerche sull' Umbria Tardo-antica e Preromanica. Atti del II Convegno di Studi Umbri*, Gubbio, 1965, pp.303ff.).

31. *Supra*, p.98.

32. Dodd, *Byzantine Silver Stamps* (*supra*, n.26), pp.70ff., nos.9 and 10; cf. also pp.80f., no.14; pp.84f., no.16; pp.256f., no.93.

33. *Ibid.*, pp.174ff., nos.56 and 57; pp.202f., no.70; pp.214f., no.75; pp.218f., no.77.

34. *Ibid.*, pp.94ff., nos.20–36; cf. also the same author's *Supplements* in *Dumbarton Oaks Papers*, 18, 1964, pp.237ff. (especially pp.240f., no.19.1), and 22, 1968, pp.141ff.; and her monograph *Byzantine Silver Treasures*, Abegg Stiftung, Bern, 1973, *passim*. The only 'mythological' subject in this entire group is the 'Euthenia' relief (Dodd, *Byzantine Silver Stamps*, pp.106f., no.26).

35. See my study cited *supra*, n.10, especially p.7.

36. Dodd, *Byzantine Silver Stamps*, pp.178ff., nos.58–66. For what follows see my study cited *supra*, n.10, pp.4ff.

37. See the introduction to A. Pertusi's critical edition: *Giorgio di Pisidia, Poemi*, Ettal, 1959, pp.11ff.

38. See my study cited *supra*, n.10, especially pp.6f.

39. The thesis that the cycle of David scenes on the Cyprus plates has direct reference to Heraclius is now widely accepted. See I. Shahid, 'The Iranian Factor in Byzantium during the Reign of Heraclius', *Dumbarton Oaks Papers*, 26, 1972, pp.293ff., especially p.303, n.35; M. van Grunsven-Eygenraam, 'Heraclius and the David Plates', *Bulletin Antieke Beschaving*, 48, 1973, pp.158ff., especially pp.170ff.; S. H. Wander, 'The Cyprus Plates: The Story of David and Goliath', *Metropolitan Museum Journal*, 8, 1973, pp.89ff., especially pp.103f. There is, however, disagreement as to whether the reference is to the early part of Heraclius' career (as I prefer to assume) or to events during and after his Persian victory (A.D.627–9). It is not suggested, of course, that every event depicted on the plates has a precise counterpart in the emperor's life.

40. *Supra*, pp.33f.

41. See, in general, E. Kitzinger, 'Byzantium in the Seventh Century', *Dumbarton Oaks Papers*, 13, 1959, pp.271ff.

42. *The Great Palace of the Byzantine Emperors* (Walker Trust, University of St Andrews): *First Report*, Oxford, 1947, pp.64ff. and pls.28ff.; *Second Report*, Edinburgh, 1958, pp.121ff., pls.44ff., and colour plates.

43. For a summary of the state of the question see D. Talbot Rice, 'On the Date of the Mosaic Floor of the Great Palace of the Byzantine Emperors at Constantinople', *Charisterion eis Anastasion K. Orlandon*, I, Athens, 1965, pp.1ff. For the evidence of the pottery finds, cited by Talbot Rice, see now J. W. Hayes, *Late Roman Pottery*, London, 1972, p.418.

CHAPTER SEVEN

1. P. Romanelli and P. J. Nordhagen, *S.Maria Antiqua*, Rome, 1964.

2. *Ibid.*, pl.II and p.53. For the chronology see *infra*, n.4.

3. *Ibid.*, pp.32ff., 56f., and pls.I, 14–17.

4. In attributing dates to the paintings of Hellenistic style in S.Maria Antiqua, I am adhering to the chronology I worked out in 1934 (*Römische Malerei vom Beginn des 7. bis zur Mitte des 8. Jahrhunderts*, diss., Munich). In recent years two revisions have been proposed which, however, would entail moving in opposite directions. P. J. Nordhagen has attributed a large number of paintings (including those illustrated in our pl.VII and figs. 203–5, 207, 208, 214) to a comprehensive decoration supposedly undertaken by Pope Martin I in A.D.650 ('The Earliest Decorations in Santa Maria Antiqua and their Date', *Institutum Romanum Norvegiae: Acta ad archaeologiam et artium historiam pertinentia*, 1, 1962, pp.53ff., especially pp.58ff.; cf. Romanelli and Nordhagen, *S.Maria Antiqua*, p.34). The arguments for crediting Martin I with such a decoration – additional to four figures of Church Fathers on the walls flanking the apse, which certainly were painted during his pontificate – do not seem cogent to me. I continue to believe that the paintings in question, while undoubtedly of the first half of the seventh century, were done earlier than A.D.650. A more drastic chronological revision is implicit in the thesis that the apse of S.Maria Antiqua was installed between A.D.565 and 578 (Krautheimer *et al.*, *Corpus basilicarum* [*supra*, II, n.55], II, 1959, pp.254f., 263f.; cf. C. Bertelli, 'Stato degli studi sulla miniatura fra il VII e il IX secolo in Italia', *Studi medioevali*, 3rd series, 9, 1968, pp.379ff., especially pp.415ff.). Since the Annunciation on the Palimpsest Wall (our figs. 201f.) must have been painted in conjunction with, or, at any rate, very shortly after that operation, a substantially earlier dating would result for the first appearance of the Hellenistic style in Roman painting. But the alleged discovery of coins of Justin II, on which the argument is based, is at present so poorly documented as to be in effect unusable as evidence; and even if it were corroborated it could not prove conclusively the date of the apse. From a stylistic point of view – and not only in Roman terms but in

Byzantine terms as well – the 570s are an unlikely period for a work such as the Annunciation angel (see *supra*, pp.108ff.). I continue to believe that the heyday of Hellenism in Roman religious painting was in the 630s.

5. Morey, *Early Christian Art* (*supra*, Introduction, n.4); cf. the critical review by Schapiro cited *supra*, IV, n.14.

6. For the fourth and early fifth centuries see *supra*, Chapter Two (especially pp.38ff.). For the Macedonian period see K. Weitzmann, *Studies in Classical and Byzantine Manuscript Illumination*, Chicago and London, 1971, pp.199ff.

7. C. L. Striker and Y. D. Kuban, 'Work at Kalenderhane Camii in Istanbul: Third and Fourth Preliminary Reports', *Dumbarton Oaks Papers*, 25, 1971, pp.251ff., especially pp.255f. and fig.11.

8. *Supra*, pp.106f.

9. Romanelli and Nordhagen, *S.Maria Antiqua* (*supra*, n.1), pl.20 and p.58.

10. Kitzinger, *Byzantine Art in the Period between Justinian and Iconoclasm* (*supra*, III, n.41), pp.47f.

11. Romanelli and Nordhagen, *S.Maria Antiqua*, pls.18f. and pp.57f.

12. *Ibid.*, p.34.

13. G. and M. Sotiriou, *Icones du Mont Sinai*, Athens, 1956–8, pp.21f. and pls.4–7. K. Weitzmann, M. Chatzidakis, K. Miatev, S. Radojčić, *Icons from South Eastern Europe and Sinai*, London, 1968, pp.ixf., lxxix; pls.1–3. K. Weitzmann's new publication of the early icons of the Sinai Monastery (1976) did not become available to me in time to be consulted before this book went to press.

14. K. Schefold, *Pompejanische Malerei*, Basle, 1952, pp.136ff., 199 and pl.46.

15. For this problem see my study cited *supra*, n.10; especially p.30 with nn.113f.

16. Romanelli and Nordhagen, *S.Maria Antiqua*, pl.21 and pp.36, 58.

17. *Ibid.*, pp.34ff., 58ff.; pls.III–V, 22–8, 29B. P. J. Nordhagen, *The Frescoes of John VII (A.D. 705–707) in S.Maria Antiqua in Rome*, Institutum Romanum Norvegiae, Acta ad archaeologiam et artium historiam pertinentia, 3, Rome, 1968.

18. *Ibid.*, pp.78f., 107.

19. See my study cited *supra*, n.10; especially pp.32f. For a discussion of the problem see C. Bertelli, *La Madonna di Santa Maria in Trastevere*, Rome, 1961, pp.86ff. Nordhagen in his most recent statement on the subject agrees that the frescoes of John VII in S.Maria Antiqua 'are the signs of the penetration of a completely new phase of the "Hellenistic style" into Italy'. He also speaks of a 'Renaissance-like movement' in Byzantium under Heraclius and his dynasty – and I agree with him about the special importance of that movement for Byzantine *religious* art in the first half of the seventh century (see *supra*, pp.114f.) –, but he does not recognize in the 'new phase' of the end of the century a specific reattachment to the art of Justinian I ('"Hellenism" and the Frescoes in Santa Maria Antiqua', *Konsthistorisk Tidskrift*, 41, 1972, pp.73ff., especially pp.76f., 79).

20. Sotiriou, *Icones du Mont Sinai* (*supra*, n.13), pp.19ff. and pls.1–3; also colour plate. Weitzmann *et al.*, *Icons from South Eastern Europe and Sinai* (*supra*, n.13), pp.x, lxxix; pl.5.

21. M. Chatzidakis, 'An Encaustic Icon of Christ at Sinai', *Art Bulletin*, 49, 1967, pp.197ff.

22. *Ibid.*, figs. 3–7.

23. Grierson, *Catalogue of the Byzantine Coins in the Dumbarton Oaks Collection* (*supra*, II, n.58), II, p.568. For what follows see *ibid.*, pp.514ff. and pl.32.

24. Cf. *supra*, VI, n.10.

25. Grierson, *Catalogue*, II, pp.568ff. and pl.37.

26. J. D. Breckenridge, *The Numismatic Iconography of Justinian II*, New York, 1959, pp.56ff.

27. Grierson, *Catalogue*, III, Washington, D.C., 1973, pp.146ff. with Table 16 (pp.152f.); pp.164f., 151f. and pl.28. Justinian II in his second reign (A.D.705–11) had introduced on his coins a totally different, far less 'Grecian' image of Christ (*ibid.*, II, pp.569, 648 and pl.43); and it is worth noting that this second type was never revived after Iconoclasm (*ibid.*, III, pp.153, 164f., 454). The die-sinkers of the ninth and subsequent centuries reverted to the image of the father god exclusively. I have commented on this phenomenon in an article entitled 'Some Reflections on Portraiture in Byzantine Art', *Recueil de travaux de l'Institut d'Études byzantines* (Belgrade), 8, 1963, pp.185ff., especially pp.190ff. (reprinted in *The Art of Byzantium* [*supra*, I, n.18], pp.256ff.).

28. E. J. W. Hawkins, 'Further Observations on the Narthex Mosaic in St Sophia at Istanbul', *Dumbarton Oaks Papers*, 22, 1968, pp.151ff.; see also a forthcoming article by N. Oikonomides, *ibid.*, 30, 1976.

LIST OF ILLUSTRATIONS

I. Mausoleum of Galla Placidia, Ravenna. North arm with Good Shepherd lunette. Photo: von Matt (*Facing p.52*)

II. Church of St George, Thessaloniki. Detail of dome mosaic with Sts Onesiphorus and Porphyrius. Photo: Lykides (*Facing p.53*)

III. Orthodox Baptistery, Ravenna. Detail of dome mosaic with Sts James and Matthew. Photo: von Matt (*Facing p.68*)

IV. S.Apollinare Nuovo, Ravenna. North wall. Photo: Scala (*Facing p.69*)

V. S.Vitale, Ravenna. South wall of chancel. Photo: von Matt (*Facing p.84*)

VI. Two saints. Mosaic on apse wall of Chapel of S.Venanzio, Lateran Baptistery, Rome. Photo: Scala (*Facing p.85*)

VII. The Maccabees. Fresco in S.Maria Antiqua, Rome. Photo: P. J. Nordhagen (*Facing p.100*)

VIII. St Peter. Icon in Monastery of St Catherine, Mount Sinai. Photo reproduced through the courtesy of the Michigan-Princeton-Alexandria Expedition to Mount Sinai (*Facing p. 101*)

1. Arch of Constantine, Rome. View from north. Photo: German Archaeological Institute, Rome

2. Arch of Constantine, Rome. Medallions and frieze on north side. Photo: Alinari

3. Imperial lion hunt. Medallion (from a monument of Hadrian) on north side of Arch of Constantine, Rome. Photo: Anderson

4. Constantine distributing largesse (detail). Frieze on north side of Arch of Constantine, Rome. Photo: German Archaeological Institute, Rome

5. Porphyry group of the Tetrarchs. Venice, S.Marco. Photo: Hirmer

6. Hunting scene (detail). Floor mosaic in great corridor of Roman villa, Piazza Armerina, Sicily. Photo: Alinari

7. Couple embracing. Terracotta from the Altbachtal. Trier, Landesmuseum. Photo: museum

8. Porphyry sculpture of two Tetrarchs. Vatican Library. Photo: German Archaeological Institute, Rome

9. Gold coin of Maximinus Daza. Photo: Dumbarton Oaks

10. Tomb relief with circus scene. Vatican Museum (formerly Lateran). Photo: Alinari

[155]

53. Silver plate with satyr and maenad, from Mildenhall Treasure. London, The British Museum. Photo reproduced by courtesy of the Trustees of The British Museum

54. Achilles on Skyros. Detail of fig. 55. Photo: E. Schulz, courtesy of museum

55. Silver plate with scenes of Achilles, from Kaiseraugst Treasure. Augst, Museum. Photo: E. Schulz, courtesy of museum

56. Silver tray with pagan divinities (Corbridge *lanx*). Alnwick Castle, Collection of the Duke of Northumberland. Photo: D. M. Smith, courtesy of the Duke of Northumberland

57. Silver Missorium of the Emperor Theodosius. Madrid, Academia de la Historia. Photo: Victoria and Albert Museum

58. The Emperor Theodosius. Detail of fig. 57. Photo: Victoria and Albert Museum

59. *Terra*. Detail of fig. 57. Photo: Victoria and Albert Museum

60. Base of obelisk with hippodrome scenes. Istanbul, Atmeydani. Photo: German Archaeological Institute, Istanbul

61. The Emperor Theodosius with entourage, musicians and dancers. Detail of fig. 60. Photo: Sender

62. The Emperor Valentinian II. Head of portrait statue from Aphrodisias. Istanbul, Archaeological Museum. Photo: Hirmer

63. Ivory diptych with priestesses performing pagan rites. *Left*, Paris, Musée de Cluny. Photo: Hirmer. *Right*, London, Victoria and Albert Museum. Photo: museum

64. 'Amalthea' relief. Vatican Museum (formerly Lateran). Photo: Alinari

65. Ivory diptych with Asclepius and Hygieia. Liverpool, County Museum. Photos: museum

66. Silver plate with procession of Cybele and Attis, from Parabiago. Milan, Pinacoteca di Brera. Photo: Hirmer

67. Ivory diptych of Probianus. Berlin, Staatsbibliothek, Stiftung Preussischer Kulturbesitz. Photo: Münchow

68. Leaf of ivory diptych of Lampadii. Brescia, Museo Civico Cristiano. Photo: museum

69. Leaf of ivory diptych with stag hunt in amphitheatre. Liverpool, County Museum. Photo: museum

70. Ivory diptych of Probus. Aosta, Cathedral Treasury. Photo: Münchow

71. Ivory diptych with animal combats in amphitheatre. Leningrad, Hermitage Museum. Photo: museum

72. Christ healing the blind man. Washington, D.C., Dumbarton Oaks Collection. Photo: museum

73. Christ. Detail of fig. 72. Photo: museum

74. Two heads from base of obelisk (fig. 60). Photo courtesy of W. Schumacher

INDEX OF MODERN AUTHORS CITED

*Here and throughout, reference to the notes (pp. 129–53)
is made in the form, e.g., III, n.36 (Chapter three, note 36)*

[167]

GENERAL INDEX